NOV 2009

The Collected Stories of Roger Zelazny

VOLUME 1: Threshold

VOLUME 2: Power & Light

VOLUME 3: This Mortal Mountain

VOLUME 4: Last Exit to Babylon

VOLUME 5: Nine Black Doves

VOLUME 6: The Road to Amber

BIBLIOGRAPHY: The Ides of Octember

THIS MORTAL MOUNTAIN

VOLUME 3:
THE COLLECTED STORIES OF
ROGER ZELAZNY

EDITED BY
David G. Grubbs
Christopher S. Kovacs
Ann Crimmins

NESFA
PRESS

Post Office Box 809, Framingham, MA 01701
www.nesfa.org/press
2009

© 2009 by Amber Ltd. LLC

"Of Meetings and Partings" © 2009 by Neil Gaiman

"On Roger Zelazny" © 2009 by David G. Hartwell

"'…And Call Me Roger': The Literary Life of Roger Zelazny, Part 3" and story notes © 2009 by Christopher S. Kovacs, MD

Frontispiece Portrait © 1972 by Jack Gaughan

Dust jacket illustration and photograph of Michael Whelan © 2009 by Michael Whelan (www.MichaelWhelan.com)

Dust jacket design © 2009 by Alice N. S. Lewis

Dust jacket photo of Roger Zelazny © 1977 by Charles N. Brown

"Come to Me Not in Winter's White" by Harlan Ellison® and Roger Zelazny © 1969 by Harlan Ellison and Roger Zelazny. Renewed, 1997 by The Kilimanjaro Corporation. Harlan Ellison is a registered trademark of the Kilimanjaro Corporation.

Introduction to "Come to Me Not in Winter's White" by Harlan Ellison® © 1971 by Harlan Ellison. Renewed, 1999 by the Kilimanjaro Corporation.

ALL RIGHTS RESERVED.
NO PART OF THIS BOOK MAY BE REPRODUCED IN ANY FORM OR BY ANY ELECTRONIC, MAGICAL OR MECHANICAL MEANS INCLUDING INFORMATION STORAGE AND RETRIEVAL WITHOUT PERMISSION IN WRITING FROM THE PUBLISHER, EXCEPT BY A REVIEWER, WHO MAY QUOTE BRIEF PASSAGES IN A REVIEW.

FIRST EDITION, July 2009

ISBN-10: 1-886778-78-7
ISBN-13: 978-1-886778-78-8

A Word from the Editors

This six volume collection includes all of Zelazny's known short fiction and poetry, three excerpts of important novels, a selection of non-fiction essays, and a few curiosities.

Many of the stories and poems are followed by "A Word from Zelazny" in which the author muses about the preceding work. Many of the works are also followed by a set of "Notes"[1] explaining names, literary allusions and less familiar words. Though you will certainly enjoy Zelazny's work without the notes, they may provide even a knowledgeable reader with some insight into the levels of meaning in Zelazny's writing.

> "My intent has long been to write stories that can be read in many ways from the simple to the complex. I feel that they must be enjoyable simply as stories…even for one who can't catch any of the allusions."
> —Roger Zelazny in *Roger Zelazny* by Jane M. Lindskold

The small print under each title displays original publication information (date and source) for published pieces and (sometimes a guess at) the date it was written for unpublished pieces. The small print may also contain a co-author's name, alternate titles for the work, and awards it received. Stories considered part of a series are noted by a § and a series or character name.

---

[1] The notes are a work in progress. Please let us know of any overlooked references or allusions, or definitions you may disagree with, for a possible future revision.

Contents

Of Meetings and Partings *by Neil Gaiman* 11
On Roger Zelazny *by David G. Hartwell* 15

Stories

This Mortal Mountain 21
The Man Who Loved the Faioli 61
Angel, Dark Angel 71
The Hounds of Sorrow 85
The Window Washer 93
Damnation Alley 105
The Last Inn on the Road *with Dannie Plachta* 189
A Hand Across the Galaxy 195
The Insider *as by Philip H. Sexart* 199
Heritage 205
He That Moves 209
Corrida 221
Dismal Light *(§ Francis Sandow)* 227
Song of the Blue Baboon 243
Stowaway 249
Here There Be Dragons 255
Way Up High 273
The Steel General 295
Come to Me Not in Winter's White
   by Harlan Ellison® and Roger Zelazny 341
The Year of the Good Seed *with Dannie Plachta* 355
The Man at the Corner of Now and Forever 361
My Lady of the Diodes 371
Alas! Alas! This Woeful Fate 397

Sun's Trophy Stirring 403
Add Infinite Item 409
The Game of Blood and Dust 411
The Force that Through the Circuit Drives the Current 417
No Award. 425
Is There a Demon Lover in the House? 439
The Engine at Heartspring's Center 445

Articles

Tomorrow Stuff 457
Science Fiction and How It Got That Way 463
Self-Interview 469
The Genre: A Geological Survey 473
A Burnt-Out Case? 477
Ideas, Digressions and Daydreams:
    The Amazing Science Fiction Machine 495
Musings on *Lord of Light* 499
"…And Call Me Roger": The Literary Life of Roger Zelazny, Part 3 . 503

Curiosities

Family Tree from *Creatures of Light and Darkness* 547
The Guns of Avalon: deleted sex scene *(§ Amber)* 549
Bridge of Ashes (Outline) 553
Doorways in the Sand (Summary) 561

Publication History 571
Acknowledgments 573

Poetry

Lover's Valediction: Forbidding Day's Sacrament	60
Song (The Leaves are Gone)	70
Fire, Snakes & the Moon	84
Lobachevsky's Eyes	102
Beyond the River of the Blessed	104
Chorus Mysticus	194
Permanent Mood	203
Maitreya	204
Tryptych	208
Avalanches	218
Somewhere a Piece of Colored Light	219
We Are the Legions of Hellwell	220
Awakening	224
Night Thoughts	226
Paintpot	242
Reflection from an Oriental Ashtray	248
T. S. Eliot	252
Wall	254
Morning with Music	270
I Walked Beyond the Mirror	272
Museum Moods	292
Sentiments with Numbers (second half of Museum Moods)	293
Storm and Sunrise	294
Oh, the Moon Comes on Like a Genie	328
Between You & I	336
Words	336
Augury	337
Pyramid	339
Thundershoon	354
What Is Left When the Soul is Sold	360
LP Me Thee	370
The Thing That Cries in the Night	389
Dim	406
Dark Horse Shadow	408
Missolonghi Hillside	410
Ducks	416
Lamentations of the Venusian Pensioner	423
reply	435
Testament	444
Sonnet, Anyone?	454
Philip K. Dick	492

THIS MORTAL MOUNTAIN

VOLUME 3:

THE COLLECTED STORIES OF

ROGER ZELAZNY

Of Meetings and Partings

by Neil Gaiman

Speaking as an author, I have begun to suspect that the meeting of authors is overrated.

People are so much bigger on the inside, after all. And we are not what we appear to be on the outside. We are what we are on the inside, and that is quite a different matter.

I can tell you that Roger Zelazny looked, when I met him, a lot like Sherlock Holmes does, in my head; that he was polite and funny and mild, and very, very wise; that I liked him. I could tell you what he wore or how he sounded, any of that, and that doesn't get you any closer to the person who wrote the books.

I can tell you about the words and the way he inspired, about the magic and the stories and the books and what they did, but that's just not who he was; that's just something Roger made, even though his words changed my world, even though they may well have made me into an author.

Still, those are the only two ways we have of meeting writers, and they are neither of them entirely satisfactory.

This is how I met Roger Zelazny:

The first time I noticed Roger Zelazny's name, I was eleven, and I had picked up *Lord of Light* in my local High Street bookshop. The cover said the book had won the Hugo Award, and that was enough for me.

I loved *Lord of Light*. I could tell you how much I loved it and why I loved it, forever, and never tire. I loved the characters; I loved the idea of gods as men and men as gods. I loved the reinterpretation of Buddhist and Hindu religions. I loved Great-Souled Sam. The humor. The adventure. The gods. I loved rereading it, spotting more story with each reading. I loved it and there was an end to it. If you want to point to my work and talk about it as a shadow of *Lord of Light*, I don't think I would ever argue with you.

Then I found *Jack of Shadows* and the magical prose-poetry of *Creatures of Light and Darkness*. In a second-hand bookshop in West Croydon I found an American paperback of *The Doors of His Face, the Lamps of His Mouth*, his second short story collection, and it smelled a little like rose petals and baby powder. The cover painting was by Jeff Jones. In my head, to this day, in a rare bout of synesthesia, all the short stories in that collection smell like rose-petals and look like they were painted by Jeff Jones.

Roger Zelazny's work excited me. It was intoxicating and delightful and unique. And it was smart. And it hooked me so well and so hard that I was prepared to pay for it. *Roadmarks* was the first new hardback I bought with my own money, from Dark They Were and Golden Eyed in London. Even buying the book was an adventure.

Of the authors who made me, who furnished the inside of my mind and set me to writing, and there are a legion—Michael Moorcock and Harlan Ellison, Samuel R. Delany and Angela Carter, R. A. Lafferty and Ursula K. Le Guin, and the rest—Roger Zelazny was probably the most important. All of them made storytelling look wonderful, but Roger Zelazny made me want to do it too, because he made it look, well, fun. Somehow the joy and the delight that come from putting exactly the right word down in the perfect place for it, the joy he was taking in telling the story in that exact way, that magical thing made it through the words, into the story, and out again from the page. Zelazny was poet enough that the words mattered and were memorable, and they sang; he was craftsman enough that every short story, every novel, explored a new route into the process of storytelling, so that even as a boy how he did it became almost as interesting to me as what he did: I could see the bones showing, and interesting, diamond-covered bones they were.

During Roger's memorial at Fred Saberhagen's house, we got up, Steve Brust and George R. R. Martin and Walter Jon Williams and the rest of us, and we said the same things over and over: there are writers who are clever to make you feel stupid…and then there are writers who are clever to make you feel smart, whose brilliance makes you feel brilliant in your turn. Roger was the second kind of writer, the kind that makes you smarter. And reading Roger, each of us said, he made us want to write. We could see how much joy he was taking in telling the story, so much so that, reading it, we wanted to have that kind of fun too.

I was just a kid when I read *Lord of Light* for the first time, but I can still remember the dark delight I took back then in realizing that between the first chapter and the second we had slipped back in time several decades; I remember the glee I took in unraveling the structure of *Doorways in the Sand*, where each chapter ends on a cliffhanger; then the next chapter would begin *in media res* after the cliffhanger had unhung, and then would flash back to the resolution, and then move forward to the end of the chapter, to end on a cliffhanger.

I felt back then, and I still feel, that every Zelazny story was an adventure, as much an adventure for the reader as for the author.

And that was how I met Zelazny, the wordsmith.

By the time I met Roger, the person, I was as familiar as I could be with the published work of Roger Zelazny, the author, and that attempt was more or less a failure. I was a guest at the Dallas Fantasy Fair and was thrilled to discover that Roger was also a guest and even more delighted to discover that we would be doing a signing together. I looked forward to sitting at the signing table and chatting…

…which did not happen because the line for Roger's signature was out of the building. My line was fairly short and easily dealt with, and I never was able to chat with Roger, but as I left I gave him a copy of the just-published *Sandman* collection, *The Doll's House*, and I stumblingly told him how important he was—how important *Lord of Light* had been to *Sandman*, how important he was to me.

The next time we met, in Tucson, in 1991, at the World Fantasy Convention, I was with Steve Brust. The three of us talked about short stories, I remember, or rather Steve complained that he was unable to write short stories, that they got away from him, that they wanted to be novels. I said nothing, while Roger puffed on his pipe, in memory, at least, like Sherlock Holmes, and said, "Most of my better short stories are the final chapters of novels I haven't written." Which gave me a fresh perspective on his short stories and novellas. I had always been aware that there was an iceberg-sized mass of untold story beneath the glittering tip that we read, that Zelazny's characters live before the stories start, and that when the stories do begin, the stories of his protagonists have now reached crisis-point, and soon we will tumble deliciously into the moment when each of them must change or learn or die or live forever. Stories are implied, hinted-at, never-told; worlds go on beyond the walls of story in all directions. Each story can be seen as the last chapter of a novel unread and unwritten.

That was the time that Steve asked Roger if perhaps he would consider a short story collection set in the Amber universe. Roger said no, that other things he had made could be played with by others, but that Amber was *his*. I understood how he felt.

The last time I saw Roger was at World Fantasy Con in Minneapolis in 1993. He was with Jane Lindskold. I gave him a copy of my collection *Angels and Visitations*, and, embarrassed at having nothing to give me in return, he ran back to the dealer's room, bought, signed and gave me a copy of *A Night in the Lonesome October*.

And then, almost a year later, when my daughter Maddy was born, Roger sent me a Dreamcatcher to hang above her bed. I called to thank him for it, and we talked, and we talked, and we talked. He invited me to come and see him soon, and I said I would. There would be plenty of time.

And then he was gone.

It was frustrating. I had felt, as a reader in the early eighties, that Roger had lost his inspiration, lost his joy. I felt like the glorious process of discovery that had begun when he began publishing stories, felt sometimes, terribly, as if he was going through the motions. But in the late eighties and early nineties he got his joy back. The short stories returned to glorious form. *A Night in the Lonesome October* was pure delight—a mad confection narrated by Snuff, Jack the Ripper's dog. Some years later I found the unabridged audiobook, narrated by Roger, and was once more amazed and delighted by the magic and loved listening to him telling me the story, was charmed and captured and carried away.

Meeting authors is overrated. Honest. I'm an author. I know.

But I met Roger Zelazny in his fiction and in the flesh. And he made me want to write. I just wish I'd said thank you better at the time.

—Neil Gaiman

ON ROGER ZELAZNY

by David G. Hartwell

I wrote an introduction more than a decade ago to the SF Book Club edition of Roger Zelazny's "Home Is the Hangman" in which I related my first encounter with Roger Zelazny's fiction. It was the novella, "A Rose for Ecclesiastes" (1963) in *F&SF*, the cover story of the issue, with a glorious and colorful wraparound cover that was the last major work of the great fantasy artist Hannes Bok. That story was immediately evident as a new classic in the sf tradition of Mars stories set on a Mars not of contemporary scientific accuracy but of the sf imagination: the Mars tradition of Burroughs and Bradbury, of Brackett and Ballard. I became at that instant an admirer. Roger once said in my hearing to Brian W. Aldiss that Aldiss's story about a man fleeing from loving his mother, "A Kind of Artistry" (1962), was the breakthrough piece that showed him the way to write ambitious sf. The intense dramatization in the external world of inner psychological states colorfully transformed in an sf setting was there. I could see it, but it also struck me that his early fiction might owe something to "The Blind Pilot," a story by Nathalie and Charles Henneberg translated from the French by Damon Knight that appeared in 1960 in *F&SF*, and that shared the fascination evident in Aldiss with doomed, myth-haunted, heroic characters and image laden prose, with projections of the psyche in sf settings.

I was in the same room with Roger Zelazny at a number of parties and conventions in the late 1960s, and as the years went by, some of my friends were his friends. But I didn't have more than an acquaintance until I got my first editorial job at Signet books in 1970. I went to Balticon, riding the bus with my friend Stu Schiff. I went up to Roger in the con suite and said now I could be his editor at Signet. He grinned and winced, and said he had just sold a package of novels to Berkley. But he still had two books owed to Signet, *Jack of Shadows* and *Today We Choose Faces*, and we did work on those. I recall that at my suggestion he moved the middle section (originally a flashback) of *Today We Choose Faces* to the start of the book. He thought it didn't make much difference, but I did. I wonder what I would think nearly forty years later.

Because publishing was a lot different in those days (everyone got paid a lot less, for one thing), writers and editors moved around a lot. Three years later I got a job at Berkley and went up to Roger first thing and said that now I could be his editor. This time he laughed, because we knew each other better, and said that Berkley had just rejected his latest manuscript and that he had sold a novel to Harper. After my next job change, to Simon & Schuster / Timescape in 1978, I contacted Roger and bought a new sf novel that he thought would be done in less than a year. But Ace Books made enticing advances for *Changeling* and then *Madwand*, and he didn't finish *Eye of Cat* for four years. And then Avon called, and he signed up more Amber novels for six figures, a huge advance in those days. He couldn't sell me another book at Timescape after he delivered *Eye of Cat* in 1982 because of the pending Avon deal. He was a commercial writer and went with the biggest money first.

By the time I got to Arbor House as an editor in 1984, Avon was about to publish the last Amber books, and I was able to buy the hardcover rights and publish them first for a few years. And also by that time Roger and I were comfortable with each other. I took him to dinner when he came to New York. In the 1990s, when Roger's marriage had come apart, a couple of years after mine did, we became sort of old friends, not really close but able to go off and spend a day in the Everglades or elsewhere when we were sometimes in Florida at the Conference on the Fantastic. We had a lot of meals together and were in the same place at the same time over the decades when interesting things happened. I recall one particular convention occasion in the 1980s when Brian Aldiss gave a three-hour-long, late night reminiscence on the sexual appetites and habits of the British sf community, with broad gestures, perhaps the most intensive gossip session of that decade, during which there were only five of us present and at the end of which Roger fell off his chair. I guess I would have to say that for most of that time it was a professional friendship, though. We didn't visit each other's homes.

But for all those years I read his work and most often liked it a lot. I'll return to that, but more about the person. Roger was not much of a speech-writer or giver, but he had a great voice and read magnificently. There exist full text recordings by Zelazny of about ten of his novels in audio, and of them, I think that *A Night in the Lonesome October* is a great performance, worth seeking out. The last time I saw him, again in Florida, he read a short story he had just written for an anthology of mine, "Prince of the Powers of This World," and it was beautifully done. He did "voices," by which I mean that he changed his voice when reading the dialog of different characters. His reading was lively and animated. Mostly, in public, he was fairly quiet, choosing his words when he spoke.

A lot of people in the sf community felt that Roger Zelazny's literary career began to decline at the end of the 1960s as his commercial reputation grew. *Nine Princes in Amber*, a hard-boiled adventure fantasy, sold well but was compared unfavorably to his best early work by most genre commentators. No one could have guessed the profound effect it would have within a few years on the development of Dungeons & Dragons in what became the gaming community, and most sf readers waited for another masterpiece like *Lord of Light*. These were the days when the sf novel was coming into its own and surpassing short fiction as the primary reading material of most fans. Yet it is obvious in hindsight that Zelazny achieved his mastery of short fiction early, but that it stayed with him in full force til the end of his life. In spite of all the profound impact of his sixties work, his body of short fiction contains more masterpieces from later decades than from that first flowering.

I am left with many images of the gentleman who wrote all this fascinating work. Roger was quite tall, thin, lantern-jawed, a bit hunched over, with a deep, powerful voice. He could make wonderful cat's cradles of string. He studied martial arts. He collected comics—he owned a first issue of Superman, I believe. I once heard him say in a speech at ICFA in Florida that he had as a student read Northrup Frye's *Anatomy of Criticism* and decided that he would write in the mythic heroic mode in part because it was so little used today by serious writers. Perhaps that was partly a joke on the academics present when he said it—probably comic books and old sf magazines influenced him as strongly toward the heroic. And maybe Jacobean drama, too—one tends to forget how extraordinarily heroic, as well as violent, horrific, and twisted that dramatic era was. In some ways he reminded me of a younger version of Fritz Leiber. And before he died, he worked as hard as he ever had at the challenge of completing the draft of a novel [*Psychoshop*, 1998] Alfred Bester had left unfinished. What he worked to attain was an honorable emulation of Bester's pyrotechnic style—which he did accomplish. In the end he was himself, in love with what he did so well, writing.

—David G. Hartwell

STORIES

This Mortal Mountain

If, March 1967.
Nebula nominee 1968 (novelette).

I

I looked down at it and I was sick! I wondered, where did it lead? Stars?

There were no words. I stared and I stared, and I cursed the fact that the thing existed and that someone had found it while I was still around.

"Well?" said Lanning, and he banked the flier so that I could look upward.

I shook my head and shaded my already shielded eyes.

"Make it go away," I finally told him.

"Can't. It's bigger than I am."

"It's bigger than anybody," I said.

"I can make *us* go away…"

"Never mind. I want to take some pictures."

He brought it around, and I started to shoot.

"Can you hover—or get any closer?"

"No, the winds are too strong."

"That figures."

So I shot—through telescopic lenses and scan attachment and all—as we circled it.

"I'd give a lot to see the top."

"We're at thirty thousand feet, and fifty's the ceiling on this baby. The Lady, unfortunately, stands taller than the atmosphere."

"Funny," I said, "from here she doesn't strike me as the sort to breathe ether and spend all her time looking at stars."

He chuckled and lit a cigarette, and I reached us another bulb of coffee.

"How *does* the Gray Sister strike you?"

And I lit one of my own and inhaled, as the flier was buffeted by sudden gusts of something from somewhere and then ignored, and I said, "Like Our Lady of the Abattoir—right between the eyes."

We drank some coffee, and then he asked, "She too big, Whitey?" and I gnashed my teeth through caffeine, for only my friends call me Whitey, my name being Jack Summers and my hair having always been this way, and at the moment I wasn't too certain of whether Henry Lanning qualified for that status—just because he'd known me for twenty years—after going out of his way to find this thing on a world with a thin atmosphere, a lot of rocks, a too-bright sky and a name like LSD pronounced backwards, after George Diesel, who had set foot in the dust and then gone away—smart fellow!

"A forty-mile-high mountain," I finally said, "is not a mountain. It is a world all by itself, which some dumb deity forgot to throw into orbit."

"I take it you're not interested?"

I looked back at the gray and lavender slopes and followed them upward once again, until all color drained away, until the silhouette was black and jagged and the top still nowhere in sight, until my eyes stung and burned behind their protective glasses; and I saw clouds bumping up against that invincible outline, like icebergs in the sky, and I heard the howling of the retreating winds which had essayed to measure its grandeur with swiftness and, of course, had failed.

"Oh, I'm interested," I said, "in an academic sort of way. Let's go back to town, where I can eat and drink and maybe break a leg if I'm lucky."

He headed the flier south, and I didn't look around as we went. I could sense her presence at my back, though, all the way: The Gray Sister, the highest mountain in the known universe. Unclimbed, of course.

❖   ❖   ❖

She remained at my back during the days that followed, casting her shadow over everything I looked upon. For the next two days I studied the pictures I had taken and I dug up some maps and I studied them, too; and I spoke with people who told me stories of the Gray Sister, strange stories…

During this time, I came across nothing really encouraging. I learned that there had been an attempt to colonize Diesel a couple centuries previously, back before faster-than-light ships were developed. A brand-new disease had colonized the first colonists, however, wiping them out to a man. The new colony was four years old, had better doctors, had beaten the plague, was on Diesel to stay and seemed proud of its poor taste when it came to worlds. Nobody, I learned, fooled around much with the Gray Sister. There had been a few abortive attempts to climb her, and some young legends that followed after.

During the day, the sky never shut up. It kept screaming into my eyes, until I took to wearing my climbing goggles whenever I went out. Mainly, though, I sat in the hotel lounge and ate and drank and studied the pictures and cross-examined anyone who happened to pass by and glance at them, spread out there on the table.

I continued to ignore all Henry's questions. I knew what he wanted, and he could damn well wait. Unfortunately, he did, and rather well, too, which irritated me. He felt I was almost hooked by the Sister, and he wanted to Be There When It Happened. He'd made a fortune on the Kasla story, and I could already see the opening sentences of this one in the smug lines around his eyes. Whenever he tried to make like a poker player, leaning on his fist and slowly turning a photo, I could see whole paragraphs. If I followed the direction of his gaze, I could probably even have seen the dust jacket.

At the end of the week, a ship came down out of the sky, and some nasty people got off and interrupted my train of thought. When they came into the lounge, I recognized them for what they were and removed my black lenses so that I could nail Henry with my basilisk gaze and turn him into stone. As it would happen, he had too much alcohol in him, and it didn't work.

"You tipped off the press," I said.

"Now, now," he said, growing smaller and stiffening as my gaze groped its way through the murk of his central nervous system and finally touched upon the edges of that tiny tumor, his forebrain. "You're well known, and…"

I replaced my glasses and hunched over my drink, looking far gone, as one of the three approached and said, "Pardon me, but are you Jack Summers?"

❖ ❖ ❖

To explain the silence which followed, Henry said, "Yes, this is Mad Jack, the man who climbed Everest at twenty-three and every other pile of rocks worth mentioning since that time. At thirty-one, he became the only man to conquer the highest mountain in the known universe—Mount Kasla on Litan—elevation, 89,941 feet. My book—"

"Yes," said the reporter. "My name is Cary, and I'm with GP. My friends represent two of the other syndicates. We've heard that you are going to climb the Gray Sister."

"You've heard incorrectly," I said.

"Oh?"

The other two came up and stood beside them.

"We thought that—" one of them began.

"—you were already organizing a climbing party," said the other.

"Then you're not going to climb the Sister?" asked Cary, while one of the two looked over my pictures and the other got ready to take some of his own.

"Stop that!" I said, raising a hand at the photographer. "Bright lights hurt my eyes!"

"Sorry. I'll use the infra," he said, and he started fooling with his camera.

Cary repeated the question.

"All I said was that you've heard incorrectly," I told him. "I didn't say I was and I didn't say I wasn't. I haven't made up my mind."

"If you decide to try it, have you any idea when it will be?"

"Sorry, I can't answer that."

Henry took the three of them over to the bar and started explaining something, with gestures. I heard the words "...out of retirement after four years," and when/if they looked to the booth again, I was gone.

I had retired, to the street which was full of dusk, and I walked along it thinking. I trod her shadow even then, Linda. And the Gray Sister beckoned and forbade with her single unmoving gesture. I watched her, so far away, yet still so large, a piece of midnight at eight o'clock. The hours that lay between died like the distance at her feet, and I knew that she would follow me wherever I went, even into sleep. Especially into sleep.

So I knew, at that moment. The days that followed were a game I enjoyed playing. Fake indecision is delicious when people want you to do something. I looked at her then, my last and my largest, my very own Koshtra Pivrarcha, and I felt that I was born to stand upon her summit. Then I could retire, probably remarry, cultivate my mind, not worry about getting out of shape, and do all the square things I didn't do before, the lack of which had cost me a wife and a home, back when I had gone to Kasla, elevation 89,941 feet, four and a half years ago, in the days of my glory. I regarded my Gray Sister across the eight o'clock world, and she was dark and noble and still and waiting, as she had always been.

II

The following morning I sent the messages. Out across the light-years like cosmic carrier pigeons they went. They winged their ways to some persons I hadn't seen in years and to others who had seen me off at Luna Station. Each said, in its own way, "If you want in on the biggest climb of them all, come to Diesel. The Gray Sister eats Kasla for breakfast. R.S.V.P. c/o. The Lodge, Georgetown. Whitey."

Backward, turn backward...

I didn't tell Henry. Nothing at all. What I had done and where I was going, for a time, were my business only, for that same time. I checked out well before sunrise and left him a message on the desk:

"Out of town on business. Back in a week. Hold the fort. Mad Jack."

I had to gauge the lower slopes, tug the hem of the lady's skirt, so to speak, before I introduced her to my friends. They say only a madman climbs alone, but they call me what they call me for a reason.

From my pix, the northern face had looked promising.

I set the rented flier down as near as I could, locked it up, shouldered my pack and started walking.

Mountains rising to my right and to my left, mountains at my back, all dark as sin now in the predawn light of a white, white day. Ahead of me, not a mountain, but an almost gentle slope which kept rising and rising and rising. Bright stars above me and cold wind past me as I walked. Straight up, though, no stars, just black. I wondered for the thousandth time what a mountain weighed. I always wonder that as I approach one. No clouds in sight. No noises but my boot sounds on the turf and the small gravel. My goggles flopped around my neck. My hands were moist within my gloves. On Diesel, the pack and I together probably weighed about the same as me alone on Earth—for which I was duly grateful. My breath burned as it came and steamed as it went. I counted a thousand steps and looked back, and I couldn't see the flier. I counted a thousand more and then looked up to watch some stars go out. About an hour after that, I had to put on my goggles. By then I could see where I was headed. And by then the wind seemed stronger.

She was so big that the eye couldn't take all of her in at once. I moved my head from side to side, leaning further and further backward. Wherever the top, it was too high. For an instant, I was seized by a crazy acrophobic notion that I was looking down rather than up, and the soles of my feet and the palms of my hands tingled, like an ape's must when, releasing one high branch to seize another, he discovers that there isn't another.

I went on for two more hours and stopped for a light meal. This was hiking, not climbing. As I ate, I wondered what could have caused a formation like the Gray Sister. There were some ten and twelve-mile peaks within sixty miles of the place and a fifteen-mile mountain called Burke's Peak on the adjacent continent, but nothing else like the Sister. The lesser gravitation? Her composition? I couldn't say. I wondered what Doc and Kelly and Mallardi would say when they saw her.

I don't define them, though. I only climb them.

I looked up again, and a few clouds were brushing against her now. From the photos I had taken, she might be an easy ascent for a good ten or twelve miles. Like a big hill. There were certainly enough alternate routes. In fact, I thought she just might be a pushover. Feeling heartened, I repacked my utensils and proceeded. It was going to be a good day. I could tell.

And it was. I got off the slope and onto something like a trail by late afternoon. Daylight lasts about nine hours on Diesel, and I spent most of it moving. The trail was so good that I kept on for several hours after sundown and made considerable height. I was beginning to use my respiration equipment by then, and the heating unit in my suit was turned on.

The stars were big, brilliant flowers, the way was easy, the night was my friend. I came upon a broad, flat piece and made my camp under an overhang.

There I slept, and I dreamt of snowy women with breasts like the Alps, pinked by the morning sun; and they sang to me like the wind and laughed, had eyes of ice prismatic. They fled through a field of clouds.

The following day I made a lot more height. The "trail" began to narrow, and it ran out in places, but it was easy to reach for the sky until another one occurred. So far, it had all been good rock. It was still tapering as it heightened, and balance was no problem. I did a lot of plain old walking. I ran up one long zigzag and hit it up a wide chimney almost as fast as Santa Claus comes down one. The winds were strong, could be a problem if the going got difficult. I was on the respirator full time and feeling great.

I could see for an enormous distance now. There were mountains and mountains, all below me like desert dunes. The sun beat halos of heat about their peaks. In the east, I saw Lake Emerick, dark and shiny as the toe of a boot. I wound my way about a jutting crag and came upon a giant's staircase, going up for at least a thousand feet. I mounted it. At its top I hit my first real barrier: a fairly smooth, almost perpendicular face rising for about eight-five feet.

No way around it, so I went up. It took me a good hour, and there was a ridge at the top leading to more easy climbing. By then, though, the clouds attacked me. Even though the going was easy, I was slowed by the fog. I wanted to outclimb it and still have some daylight left, so I decided to postpone eating.

But the clouds kept coming. I made another thousand feet, and they were still about me. Somewhere below me, I heard thunder. The fog was easy on my eyes, though, so I kept pushing.

Then I tried a chimney, the top of which I could barely discern, because it looked a lot shorter than a jagged crescent to its left. This was a mistake.

The rate of condensation was greater than I'd guessed. The walls were slippery. I'm stubborn, though, and I fought with skidding boots and moist back until I was about a third of the way up, I thought, and winded.

I realized then what I had done. What I had thought was the top wasn't. I went another fifteen feet and wished I hadn't. The fog began to boil about me, and I suddenly felt drenched. I was afraid to go down and I was afraid to go up, and I couldn't stay where I was forever.

Whenever you hear a person say that he inched along, do not accuse him of a fuzzy choice of verbs. Give him the benefit of the doubt and your sympathy.

I inched my way, blind, up an unknown length of slippery chimney. If my hair hadn't already been white when I entered at the bottom…

Finally, I got above the fog. Finally, I saw a piece of that bright and nasty sky, which I decided to forgive for the moment. I aimed at it, arrived on target.

When I emerged, I saw a little ledge about ten feet above me. I climbed to it and stretched out. My muscles were a bit shaky, and I made them go liquid. I took a drink of water, ate a couple of chocolate bars, took another drink.

After perhaps ten minutes, I stood up. I could no longer see the ground. Just the soft, white, cottony top of a kindly old storm. I looked up.

It was amazing. She was still topless. And save for a couple spots, such as the last—which had been the fault of my own stupid overconfidence—it had almost been as easy as climbing stairs.

Now the going appeared to be somewhat rougher, however. This was what I had really come to test.

I swung my pick and continued.

❖ ❖ ❖

All the following day I climbed, steadily, taking no unnecessary risks, resting periodically, drawing maps, taking wide-angle photos. The ascent eased in two spots that afternoon, and I made a quick seven thousand feet. Higher now than Everest, and still going, I. Now, though, there were places where I crawled and places where I used my ropes, and there were places where I braced myself and used my pneumatic pistol to blast a toehold. (No, in case you're wondering: I could have broken my eardrums, some ribs, and arm and doubtless ultimately, my neck, if I'd tried using the gun in the chimney.)

Just near sunset, I came upon a high, easy winding way up and up and up. I debated with my more discreet self. I'd left the message that I'd be gone a week. This was the end of the third day. I wanted to make as much height as possible and start back down on the fifth day. If I followed the rocky route above me as far as it would take me I'd probably break forty thousand feet. Then, depending, I might have a halfway chance of hitting near the ten-mile mark before I had to turn back. Then I'd be able to get a much better picture of what lay above.

My more discreet self lost, three to nothing, and Mad Jack went on.

The stars were so big and blazing I was afraid they'd bite. The wind was no problem. There wasn't any at that height. I had to keep stepping up the temperature controls on my suit, and I had the feeling that if I could spit around my respirator, it would freeze before it hit the trail.

I went on even further than I'd intended, and I broke forty-two thousand that night.

I found a resting place, stretched out, killed my hand beacon.

It was an odd dream that came to me.

It was all cherry fires and stood like a man, only bigger, on the slope above me. It stood in an impossible position, so I knew I had to be dreaming. Something from the other end of my life stirred, however, and I was convinced for a bitter moment that it was the Angel of Judgment. Only, in its right hand it seemed to hold a sword of fires rather than a trumpet. It had been standing there forever, the tip of its blade pointed toward my breast. I could see the stars through it. It seemed to speak.

It said: *"Go back."*

I couldn't answer it, though, for my tongue clove to the roof of my mouth. And it said it again, and yet a third time, *"Go back."*

"Tomorrow," I thought, in my dream, and this seemed to satisfy it. For it died down and ceased, and the blackness rolled about me.

❖   ❖   ❖

The following day, I climbed as I hadn't climbed in years. By late lunchtime I'd hit forty-eight thousand feet. The cloud cover down below had broken. I could see what lay beneath me once more. The ground was a dark and light patchwork. Above, the stars didn't go away.

The going was rough, but I was feeling fine. I knew I couldn't make ten miles, because I could see that the way was pretty much the same for quite a distance, before it got even worse. My good spirits stayed, and they continued to rise as I did.

When it attacked, it came on with a speed and a fury that I was only barely able to match.

The voice from my dream rang in my head, *"Go back! Go back! Go back!"*

Then it came toward me from out of the sky. A bird the size of a condor.

Only it wasn't really a bird. It was a bird-shaped thing.

It was all fire and static, and as it flashed toward me I barely had time to brace my back against stone and heft my climbing pick in my right hand, ready.

III

I sat in the small, dark room and watched the spinning, colored lights. Ultrasonics were tickling my skull. I tried to relax and give the man some Alpha rhythms. Somewhere a receiver was receiving, a computer was computing and a recorder was recording.

It lasted perhaps twenty minutes.

When it was all over and they called me out, the doctor collared me. I beat him to the draw, though:

"Give me the tape and send the bill in care of Henry Lanning at the Lodge."

"I want to discuss the reading," he said.

"I have my own brain-wave expert coming. Just give me the tape."

"Have you undergone any sort of traumatic experience recently?"

"You tell me. Is it indicated?"

"Well, yes and no," he said.

"That's what I like, a straight answer."

"I don't know what is normal for you, in the first place," he replied.

"Is there any indication of brain damage?"

"I don't read it that way. If you'd tell me what happened, and why you're suddenly concerned about your brain-waves, perhaps I'd be in a better position to…"

"Cut," I said. "Just give me the tape and bill me."

"I'm concerned about you as a patient."

"But you don't think there were any pathological indications?"

"Not exactly. But tell me this, if you will: Have you had an epileptic seizure recently?"

"Not to my knowledge. Why?"

"You displayed a pattern similar to a residual subrhythm common in some forms of epilepsy for several days subsequent to a seizure."

"Could a bump on the head cause that pattern?"

"It's highly unlikely."

"What else *could* cause it?"

"Electrical shock, optical trauma—"

"Stop," I said, and I removed my glasses. "About the optical trauma. Look at my eyes."

"I'm not an ophtha—" he began, but I interrupted:

"Most normal light hurts my eyes. If I lost my glasses and was exposed to very bright light for three, four days, could that cause the pattern you spoke of?"

"Possibly…" he said. "Yes, I'd say so."

"But there's more?"

"I'm not sure. We have to take more readings, and if I know the story behind this it will help a lot."

"Sorry," I said. "I need the tape now."

He sighed and made a small gesture with his left hand as he turned away.

"All right, Mister Smith."

Cursing the genius of the mountain, I left the General Hospital, carrying my tape like a talisman. In my mind I searched, through forests of memory, for a ghost-sword in a stone of smoke, I think.

❖   ❖   ❖

Back in the Lodge, they were waiting. Lanning and the newsmen.

"What was it like?" asked one of the latter.

"What was what like?"

"The mountain. You were up on it, weren't you?"

"No comment."

"How high did you go?"

"No comment."

"How would you say it compares with Kasla?"

"No comment."

"Did you run into any complications?"

"Ditto. Excuse me, I want to take a shower."

Henry followed me into my room. The reporters tried to.

After I had shaved and washed up, mixed a drink and lit a cigarette, Lanning asked me his more general question:

"Well?" he said.

I nodded.

"Difficulties?"

I nodded again.

"Insurmountable?"

I hefted the tape and thought a moment.

"Maybe not."

He helped himself to the whiskey. The second time around, he asked:

"You going to try?"

I knew I was. I knew I'd try it all by myself if I had to.

"I really don't know," I said.

"Why not?"

"Because there's something up there," I said, "something that doesn't want us to do it."

"Something *lives* up there?"

"I'm not sure whether that's the right word."

He lowered the drink.

"What the hell happened?"

"I was threatened. I was attacked."

"Threatened? Verbally? In English?" He set his drink aside, which shows how serious his turn of mind had to be. "Attacked?" he added. "By what?"

"I've sent for Doc and Kelly and Stan and Mallardi and Vincent. I checked a little earlier. They've all replied. They're coming. Miguel and the Dutchman can't make it, and they send their regrets. When we're all together, I'll tell the story. But I want to talk to Doc first. So hold tight and worry and don't quote."

He finished his drink.

"When'll they be coming?"

"Four, five weeks," I said.

"That's a long wait."

"Under the circumstances," I said, "I can't think of any alternatives."

"What'll we do in the meantime?"

"Eat, drink, and contemplate the mountain."

He lowered his eyelids a moment, then nodded, reached for his glass.

"Shall we begin?"

❖   ❖   ❖

It was late, and I stood alone in the field with a bottle in one hand. Lanning had already turned in, and night's chimney was dark with cloud soot. Somewhere away from there, a storm was storming, and it was full of instant outlines. The wind came chill.

"Mountain," I said. "Mountain, you have told me to go away."

There was a rumble.

"But I cannot," I said, and I took a drink.

"I'm bringing you the best in the business," I said, "to go up on your slopes and to stand beneath the stars in your highest places. I must do this thing because you are there. No other reason. Nothing personal…"

After a time, I said, "That's not true.

"I am a man," I said, "and I need to break mountains to prove that I will not die even though I will die. I am less than I want to be, Sister, and you can make me more. So I guess it *is* personal.

"It's the only thing I know how to do, and you're the last one left—the last challenge to the skill I spent my life learning. Maybe it is that mortality is the closest to immortality when it accepts a challenge to itself, when it survives a threat. The moment of triumph is the moment of salvation. I have needed many such moments, and the final one must be the longest, for it must last me the rest of my life.

"So you are there, Sister, and I am here and very mortal, and you have told me to go away. I cannot. I'm coming up, and if you throw death at me I will face it. It must be so."

I finished what remained in the bottle.

There were more flashes, more rumbles behind the mountain, more flashes.

"It is the closest thing to divine drunkenness," I said to the thunder.

And then she winked at me. It was a red star, so high upon her. Angel's sword. Phoenix' wing. Soul on fire. And it blazed at me, across the miles. Then the wind that blows between the worlds swept down over me. It was filled with tears and with crystals of ice. I stood there and felt it, then, "Don't go away," I said, and I watched until all was darkness once more and I was wet as an embryo waiting to cry out and breathe.

❖ ❖ ❖

Most kids tell lies to their playmates—fictional autobiographies, if you like—which are either received with appropriate awe or countered with greater, more elaborate tellings. But little Jimmy, I've heard, always hearkened to his little buddies with wide, dark eyes, and near the endings of their stories the corners of his mouth would begin to twitch. By the time they were finished talking, his freckles would be mashed into a grin and his rusty head cocked to the side. His favorite expression, I understand, was "G'wan!" and his nose was broken twice before he was twelve. This was doubtless why he turned it toward books.

Thirty years and four formal degrees later, he sat across from me in my quarters in the lodge, and I called him Doc because everyone did, because he had a license to cut people up and look inside them, as well as doctoring to their philosophy, so to speak, and because he looked as if he should be called Doc when he grinned and cocked his head to the side and said, "G'wan!"

I wanted to punch him in the nose.

"Damn it! It's true!" I told him. "I fought with a bird of fire!"

"We all hallucinated on Kasla," he said, raising one finger, "because of fatigue," two fingers, "because the altitude affected our circulatory systems and consequently our brains," three, "because of the emotional stimulation," four, "and because we were partly oxygen-drunk."

"You just ran out of fingers, if you'll sit on your other hand for a minute. So listen," I said, "it flew at me, and I swung at it, and it knocked me out and broke my goggles. When I woke up, it was gone and I was lying on the ledge. I think it was some sort of energy creature. You saw my EEG, and it wasn't normal. I think it shocked my nervous system when it touched me."

"You were knocked out because you hit your head against a rock—"

"It *caused* me to fall back against the rock!"

"I agree with that part. The rock was real. But nowhere in the universe has anyone ever discovered an 'energy creature.'"

"So? You probably would have said that about America a thousand years ago."

"Maybe I would have. But that neurologist explained your EEG to my satisfaction. Optical trauma. Why go out of your way to dream up an exotic explanation for events? Easy ones generally turn out better. You hallucinated and you stumbled."

"Okay," I said, "whenever I argue with you I generally need ammunition. Hold on a minute."

I went to my closet and fetched it down from the top shelf. I placed it on my bed and began unwrapping the blanket I had around it.

"I told you I took a swing at it," I said. "Well, I connected—right before I went under. Here!"

I held up my climbing pick—brown, yellow, black and pitted—looking as though it had fallen from outer space.

He took it into his hands and stared at it for a long time, then he started to say something about ball lightning, changed his mind, shook his head and placed the thing back on the blanket.

"I don't know," he finally said, and this time his freckles remained unmashed, except for those at the edges of his hands which got caught as he clenched them, slowly.

IV

We planned. We mapped and charted and studied the photos. We plotted our ascent and we started a training program.

While Doc and Stan had kept themselves in good shape, neither had been climbing since Kasla. Kelly was in top condition. Henry was on his way to fat. Mallardi and Vince, as always, seemed capable of fantastic feats of endurance and virtuosity, had even climbed a couple times during the past year, but had recently been living pretty high on the tall hog, so to speak, and they wanted to get some practice. So we picked a comfortable, decent-sized mountain and gave it ten days to beat everyone back into shape. After that, we stuck to vitamins, calisthenics and square diets while we completed our preparations. During this time, Doc came up with seven shiny, alloy boxes, about six by four inches and thin as a first book of poems, for us to carry on our persons to broadcast a defense against the energy creatures which he refused to admit existed.

One fine, bitter-brisk morning we were ready. The newsmen liked me again. Much footage was taken of our gallant assemblage as we packed ourselves into the fliers, to be delivered at the foot of the lady mountain, there to contend for what was doubtless the final time as the team we had been for so many years, against the waiting gray and the lavender beneath the sunwhite flame.

We approached the mountain, and I wondered how much she weighed.

❖ ❖ ❖

You know the way, for the first nine miles. So I'll skip over that. It took us six days and part of a seventh. Nothing out of the ordinary occurred. Some fog there was, and nasty winds, but once below, forgotten.

Stan and Mallardi and I stood where the bird had occurred, waiting for Doc and the others.

"So far, it's been a picnic," said Mallardi.

"Yeah," Stan acknowledged.

"No birds either."

"No," I agreed.

"Do you think Doc was right—about it being an hallucination?" Mallardi asked. "I remember seeing things on Kasla…"

"As I recall," said Stan, "it was nymphs and an ocean of beer. Why would anyone want to see hot birds?"

"Damfino."

"Laugh, you hyenas," I said. "But just wait till a flock flies over."

Doc came up and looked around.

"This is the place?"

I nodded.

He tested the background radiation and half a dozen other things, found nothing untoward, grunted and looked upwards.

We all did. Then we went there.

It was very rough for three days, and we only made another five thousand feet during that time.

When we bedded down, we were bushed, and sleep came quickly. So did Nemesis.

He was there again, only not quite so near this time. He burned about twenty feet away, standing in the middle of the air, and the point of his blade indicated me.

"*Go away,*" he said, three times, without inflection.

"Go to hell," I tried to say.

He made as if he wished to draw nearer. He failed.

"Go away yourself," I said.

"*Climb back down. Depart. You may go no further.*"

"But I am going further. All the way to the top."

"*No. You may not.*"

"Stick around and watch," I said.

"*Go back.*"

"If you want to stand there and direct traffic, that's your business," I told him. "I'm going back to sleep."

I crawled over and shook Doc's shoulder, but when I looked back my flaming visitor had departed.

"What is it?"

"Too late," I said. "He's been here and gone."

Doc sat up.

"The bird?"

"No, the thing with the sword."

"Where was he?"

"Standing out there," I gestured.

Doc hauled out his instruments and did many things with them for ten minutes or so.

"Nothing," he finally said. "Maybe you were dreaming."

"Yeah, sure," I said. "Sleep tight," and I hit the sack again, and this time I made it through to daylight without further fire or ado.

❖   ❖   ❖

It took us four days to reach sixty thousand feet. Rocks fell like occasional cannonballs past us, and the sky was like a big pool, cool, where pale flowers floated. When we struck sixty-three thousand, the going got much better, and we made it up to seventy-five thousand in two and a half more days. No fiery things stopped by to tell me to turn back. Then came the unforeseeable, however, and we had enough in the way of natural troubles to keep us cursing.

We hit a big, level shelf.

It was perhaps four hundred feet wide. As we advanced across it, we realized that it did not strike the mountainside. It dropped off into an enormous gutter of a canyon. We would have to go down again, perhaps seven hundred feet, before we could proceed upward once more. Worse yet, it led to a featureless face which strove for and achieved perpendicularity for a deadly high distance: like miles. The top was still nowhere in sight.

"Where do we go now?" asked Kelly, moving to my side.

"Down," I decided, "and we split up. We'll follow the big ditch in both directions and see which way gives the better route up. We'll meet back at the midway point."

We descended. Then Doc and Kelly and I went left, and the others took the opposite way.

After an hour and a half, our trail came to an end. We stood looking at nothing over the edge of something. Nowhere, during the entire time, had we come upon a decent way up. I stretched out, my head and shoulders over the edge, Kelly holding onto my ankles, and I looked as far as I could to the right and up. There was nothing in sight that was worth a facing movement.

"Hope the others had better luck," I said, after they'd dragged me back.

"And if they haven't...?" asked Kelly.

"Let's wait."

They had.

It was risky, though.

There was no good way straight up out of the gap. The trail had ended at a forty-foot wall which, when mounted, gave a clear view all the way down. Leaning out as I had done and looking about two hundred feet to the left and eighty feet higher, however, Mallardi had rested his eyes on a rough way, but a way, nevertheless, leading up and west and vanishing.

We camped in the gap that night. In the morning, I anchored my line to a rock, Doc tending, and went out with the pneumatic pistol. I fell twice, and made forty feet of trail by lunchtime.

I rubbed my bruises then, and Henry took over. After ten feet, Kelly got out to anchor a couple of body-lengths behind him, and we tended Kelly.

Then Stan blasted and Mallardi anchored. Then there had to be three on the face. Then four. By sundown, we'd made a hundred-fifty feet and were covered with white powder. A bath would have been nice. We settled for ultrasonic shakedowns.

❖   ❖   ❖

By lunch the next day, we were all out there, roped together, hugging cold stone, moving slowly, painfully, slowly, not looking down much.

By day's end, we'd made it across, to the place where we could hold on and feel something—granted, not much—beneath our boots. It was inclined to be a trifle scant, however, to warrant less than a full daylight assault. So we returned once more to the gap.

In the morning, we crossed.

The way kept its winding angle. We headed west and up. We traveled a mile and made five hundred feet. We traveled another mile and made perhaps three hundred.

Then a ledge occurred, about forty feet overhead.

Stan went up the hard way, using the gun, to see what he could see.

He gestured, and we followed; and the view that broke upon us was good.

Down right, irregular but wide enough, was our new camp.

The way above it, ice cream and whiskey sours and morning coffee and a cigarette after dinner. It was beautiful and delicious: a seventy-degree slope full of ledges and projections and good clean stone.

"Hot damn!" said Kelly.

We all tended to agree.

We ate and we drank and we decided to rest our bruised selves that afternoon.

We were in the twilight world now, walking where no man had ever walked before, and we felt ourselves to be golden. It was good to stretch out and try to unache.

I slept away the day, and when I awakened the sky was a bed of glowing embers. I lay there too lazy to move, too full of sight to go back to sleep. A meteor burnt its way bluewhite across the heavens. After a time, there was another. I thought upon my position and decided that reaching it was worth the price. The cold, hard happiness of the heights filled me. I wiggled my toes.

After a few minutes, I stretched and sat up. I regarded the sleeping forms of my companions. I looked out across the night as far as I could see. Then I looked up at the mountain, then dropped my eyes slowly among tomorrow's trail.

There was movement within shadow.

Something was standing about fifty feet away and ten feet above.

I picked up my pick and stood.

I crossed the fifty and stared up.

She was smiling, not burning.

A woman, an impossible woman.

Absolutely impossible. For one thing, she would just have to freeze to death in a mini-skirt and a sleeveless shell-top. No alternative. For another, she had very little to breathe. Like, nothing.

But it didn't seem to bother her. She waved. Her hair was dark and long, and I couldn't see her eyes. The planes of her pale, high cheeks, wide forehead, small chin corresponded in an unsettling fashion with certain simple theorems which comprise the geometry of my heart. If all angles, planes, curves be correct, it skips a beat, then hurries to make up for it.

❖ ❖ ❖

I worked it out, felt it do so, said, "Hello."

"Hello, Whitey," she replied.

"Come down," I said.

"No, you come up."

I swung my pick. When I reached the ledge she wasn't there. I looked around, then I saw her.

She was seated on a rock twelve feet above me.

"How is it that you know my name?" I asked.

"Anyone can see what your name must be."

"All right," I agreed. "What's yours?"

"…" Her lips seemed to move, but I heard nothing.

"Come again?"

"I don't want a name," she said.

"Okay. I'll call you 'girl,' then."

She laughed, sort of.

"What are you doing here?" I asked.

"Watching you."

"Why?"

"To see whether you'll fall."

"I can save you the trouble," I said. "I won't."

"Perhaps," she said.

"Come down here."

"No, you come up here."

I climbed, but when I got there she was twenty feet higher.

"Girl, you climb well," I said, and she laughed and turned away.

I pursued her for five minutes and couldn't catch her. There was something unnatural about the way she moved.

I stopped climbing when she turned again. We were still about twenty feet apart.

"I take it you do not really wish me to join you," I said.

"Of course I do, but you must catch me first." And she turned once more, and I felt a certain fury within me.

It was written that no one could outclimb Mad Jack. I had written it.

I swung my pick and moved like a lizard.

I was near to her a couple of times, but never near enough.

The day's aches began again in my muscles, but I pulled my way up without slackening my pace. I realized, faintly, that the camp was far below me now, and that I was climbing alone through the dark up a strange slope. But I did not stop. Rather, I hurried, and my breath began to come hard in my lungs. I heard her laughter, and it was a goad. Then I came upon a two-inch ledge, and she was moving along it. I followed, around a big bulge of rock to where it ended. Then she was ninety feet above me, at the top of a smooth pinnacle. It was like a tapering, branchless tree. How she'd accomplished it, I didn't know. I was gasping by then, but I looped my line around it and began to climb. As I did this, she spoke:

"Don't you ever tire, Whitey? I thought you would have collapsed by now."

I hitched up the line and climbed further.

"You can't make it up here, you know."

"I don't know," I grunted.

"Why do you want so badly to climb here? There are other nice mountains."

"This is the biggest, girl. That's why."

"It can't be done."

"Then why all this bother to discourage me? Why not just let the mountain do it?"

As I neared her, she vanished. I made it to the top, where she had been standing, and I collapsed there.

Then I heard her voice again and turned my head. She was on a ledge, perhaps eighty feet away.

"I didn't think you'd make it this far," she said. "You are a fool. Good-bye, Whitey." She was gone.

I sat there on the pinnacle's tiny top—perhaps four square feet of top—and I know that I couldn't sleep there, because I'd fall. And I was tired.

I recalled my favorite curses and I said them all, but I didn't feel any better. I couldn't let myself go to sleep. I looked down. I knew the way was long. I knew she didn't think I could make it.

I began the descent.

❖   ❖   ❖

The following morning when they shook me, I was still tired. I told them the last night's tale, and they didn't believe me. Not until later in the day, that is, when I detoured us around the bulge and showed them the pinnacle, standing there like a tapering, branchless tree, ninety feet in the middle of the air.

V

We went steadily upward for the next two days. We made slightly under ten thousand feet. Then we spent a day hammering and hacking our way up a great flat face. Six hundred feet of it. Then our way was to the right and upward. Before long we were ascending the western side of the mountain. When we broke ninety thousand feet, we stopped to congratulate ourselves that we had just surpassed the Kasla climb and to remind ourselves that we had still not hit the halfway mark. It took us another two and a half days to do that, and by then the land lay like a map beneath us.

And then, that night, we all saw the creature with the sword.

He came and stood near our camp, and he raised his sword above his head, and it blazed with such a terrible intensity that I slipped on my goggles. His voice was all thunder and lightning this time:

"Get off this mountain!" he said. *"Now! Turn back! Go down! Depart!"*

And then a shower of stones came down from above and rattled about us. Doc tossed his slim, shiny case, causing it to skim along the ground toward the creature.

The light went out, and we were alone.

Doc retrieved his case, took tests, met with the same success as before—*i.e.,* none. But now at least he didn't think I was some kind of balmy, unless of course he thought we all were.

"Not a very effective guardian," Henry suggested.

"We've a long way to go yet," said Vince, shying a stone through the space the creature had occupied. "I don't like it if the thing can cause a slide."

"That was just a few pebbles," said Stan.

"Yeah, but what if he decided to start them fifty thousand feet higher?"

"Shut up!" said Kelly. "Don't give him any idea. He might be listening."

For some reason, we drew closer together. Doc made each of us describe what we had seen, and it appeared that we all had seen the same thing.

"All right," I said, after we'd finished. "Now you've all seen it, who wants to go back?"

There was silence.

After perhaps half a dozen heartbeats, Henry said, "I want the whole story. It looks like a good one. I'm willing to take my chances with angry energy creatures to get it."

"I don't know what the thing is," said Kelly. "Maybe it's no energy creature. Maybe it's something—supernatural—I know what you'll say, Doc. I'm just telling you how it struck me. If there are such things, this seems a good place for them. Point is—whatever it is, I don't care. I want this mountain. If it could have stopped us, I think it would've done it already. Maybe I'm wrong. Maybe it can. Maybe it's laid some trap for us higher up. But I want this mountain. Right now, it means more to me than anything. If I don't go up, I'll spend all my time wondering about it—and then I'll probably come back and try it again some day, when it gets so I can't stand thinking about it any more. Only then, maybe the rest of you won't be available. Let's face it, we're a good climbing team. Maybe the best in the business. Probably. If it can be done, I think we can do it."

"I'll second that," said Stan.

"What you said, Kelly," said Mallardi, "about it being supernatural—it's funny, because I felt the same thing for a minute when I was looking at it. It reminds me of something out of the *Divine Comedy.* If you recall, Purgatory was a mountain. And then I thought of the angel who guarded the eastern way to Eden. Eden had gotten moved to the top of Purgatory by Dante—and there was this angel… Anyhow, I felt almost like I was committing some sin I didn't know about by being here. But now that I think it over, a man can't be guilty of something he doesn't know is wrong, can he? And I didn't see that thing flashing any angel ID card. So I'm willing to go up and see what's on top, unless he comes back with the Tablets of the Law, with a new one written in at the bottom."

"In Hebrew or Italian?" asked Doc.

"To satisfy you, I suppose they'd have to be drawn up in the form of equations."

"No," he said. "Kidding aside, I felt something funny too, when I saw and heard it. And we didn't really hear it, you know. It skipped over the senses and got its message right into our brains. If you think back over our descriptions of what we experienced, we each 'heard' different words telling us to go away. If it can communicate a meaning as well as a psychtranslator, I wonder if it can communicate an emotion, also… You thought of an angel too, didn't you, Whitey?"

"Yes," I said.

"That makes it almost unanimous then, doesn't it?"

Then we all turned to Vince, because he had no Christian background at all, having been raised as a Buddhist on Ceylon.

"What were your feelings concerning the thing?" Doc asked him.

"It was a Deva," he said, "which is sort of like an angel, I guess. I had the impression that every step I took up this mountain gave me enough bad karma to fill a lifetime. Except I haven't believed in it that way since I was a kid. I want to go ahead, up. Even if that feeling was correct, I want to see the top of this mountain."

"So do I," said Doc.

"That makes it unanimous," I said.

"Well, everyone hang onto his angelsbane," said Stan, "and let's sack out."

"Good idea."

"Only let's spread out a bit," said Doc, "so that anything falling won't get all of us together."

We did that cheerful thing and slept untroubled by heaven.

❖ ❖ ❖

Our way kept winding right, until we were at a hundred forty-four thousand feet and were mounting the southern slopes. Then it jogged back, and by a hundred fifty we were mounting to the west once more.

Then, during a devilish, dark and tricky piece of scaling, up a smooth, concave bulge ending in an overhang, the bird came down once again.

If we hadn't been roped together, Stan would have died. As it was, we almost all died.

Stan was lead man, as its wings splashed sudden flames against the violet sky. It came down from the overhang as though someone had kicked a bonfire over its edge, headed straight toward him and faded out at a distance of about twelve feet. He fell then, almost taking the rest of us with him.

We tensed our muscles and took the shock.

He was battered a bit, but unbroken. We made it up to the overhang, but went no further that day.

Rocks did fall, but we found another overhang and made camp beneath it.

The bird did not return that day, but the snakes came.

Big, shimmering scarlet serpents coiled about the crags, wound in and out of jagged fields of ice and gray stone. Sparks shot along their sinuous lengths. They coiled and unwound, stretched and turned, spat fires at us. It seemed they were trying to drive us from beneath the sheltering place to where the rocks could come down upon us.

Doc advanced upon the nearest one, and it vanished as it came within the field of his projector. He studied the place where it had lain, then hurried back.

"The frost is still on the punkin," he said.

"Huh?" said I.

"Not a bit of ice was melted beneath it."

"Indicating?"

"Illusion," said Vince, and he threw a stone at another and it passed through the thing.

"But you saw what happened to my pick," I said to Doc, "when I took a cut at that bird. The thing had to have been carrying some sort of charge."

"Maybe whatever has been sending them has cut that part out, as a waste of energy," he replied, "since the things can't get through to us anyhow."

We sat around and watched the snakes and falling rocks, until Stan produced a deck of cards and suggested a better game.

❖   ❖   ❖

The snakes stayed on through the night and followed us the next day. Rocks still fell periodically, but the boss seemed to be running low on them. The bird appeared, circled us and swooped on four different occasions. But this time we ignored it, and finally it went home to roost.

We made three thousand feet, could have gone more, but didn't want to press it past a cozy little ledge with a cave big enough for the whole party. Everything let up on us then. Everything visible, that is.

A before-the-storm feeling, a still, electrical tension, seemed to occur around us then, and we waited for whatever was going to happen to happen.

The worst possible thing happened: nothing.

This keyed-up feeling, this expectancy, stayed with us, was unsatisfied. I think it would actually have been a relief if some invisible orchestra had begun playing Wagner, or if the heavens had rolled aside like curtains and revealed a movie screen, and from the backward lettering we knew we were on the other side, or if we saw a high-flying dragon eating low-flying weather satellites...

As it was, we just kept feeling that something was imminent, and it gave me insomnia.

During the night, she came again. The pinnacle girl.

She stood at the mouth of the cave, and when I advanced she retreated.

I stopped just inside and stood there myself, where she had been standing.

She said, "Hello, Whitey."

"No, I'm not going to follow you again," I said.

"I didn't ask you to."

"What's a girl like you doing in a place like this?"

"Watching," she said.

"I told you I won't fall."

"Your friend almost did."

"'Almost' isn't good enough."

"You are the leader, aren't you?"

"That's right."

"If you were to die, the others would go back?"

"No," I said, "they'd go on without me."

I hit my camera then.

"What did you just do?" she asked.

"I took your picture—if you're really there."

"Why?"

"To look at after you go away. I like to look at pretty things."

"..." She seemed to say something.

"What?"

"Nothing."

"Why not?"

"...die."

"Please speak up."

"She dies..." she said.

"Why? How?"

"...on mountain."

"I don't understand."

"...too."

"What's wrong?"

I took a step forward, and she retreated a step.

"Follow me?" she asked.

"No."

"Go back," she said.

"What's on the other side of that record?"

"You will continue to climb?"

"Yes."

Then, "Good!" she said suddenly. "I—," and her voice stopped again.

"Go back," she finally said, without emotion.

"Sorry."

And she was gone.

VI

Our trail took us slowly to the left once more. We crawled and sprawled and cut holes in the stone. Snakes sizzled in the distance. They were with us constantly now. The bird came again at crucial moments, to try to make us fall. A raging bull stood on a crag and bellowed down at us. Phantom archers loosed shafts of fire, which always faded right before they struck. Blazing blizzards swept at us, around us, were gone. We were back on the northern slopes and still heading west by the time we broke a hundred sixty thousand. The sky was deep and blue, and there were always stars. Why did the mountain hate us? I wondered. What was there about us to provoke this thing? I looked at the picture of the girl for the dozenth time and I wondered what she really was. Had she been picked from our minds and composed into girlform to lure us, to lead us, sirenlike, harpylike, to the place of the final fall? It was such a long way down…

I thought back over my life. How does a man come to climb mountains? Is he drawn by the heights because he is afraid of the level land? Is he such a misfit in the society of men that he must flee and try to place himself above it? The way up is long and difficult, but if he succeeds they must grant him a garland of sorts. And if he falls, this too is a kind of glory. To end, hurled from the heights to the depths in hideous ruin and combustion down, is a fitting climax for the loser—for it, too, shakes mountains and minds, stirs things like thoughts below both, is a kind of blasted garland of victory in defeat, and cold, so cold that final action, that the movement is somewhere frozen forever into a statuelike rigidity of ultimate intent and purpose thwarted only by the universal malevolence we all fear exists. An aspirant saint or hero who lacks some necessary virtue may still qualify as a martyr, for the only thing that people will really remember in the end is the end. I had known that I'd had to climb Kasla, as I had climbed all the others, and I had known what the price would me. It had cost me my only home. But Kasla was there, and my boots cried out for my feet. I knew as I did so that somewhere I set them upon her summit, and below me a world was ending. What's a world if the moment of victory is at hand? And if truth, beauty and goodness be one, why is there always this conflict among them?

The phantom archers fired upon me and the bright bird swooped. I set my teeth, and my boots scarred rocks beneath me.

❖ ❖ ❖

We saw the top.

At a hundred seventy-six thousand feet, making our way along a narrow ledge, clicking against rock, testing our way with our picks, we heard Vince say, "Look!"

We did.

Up and up, and again further, bluefrosted and sharp, deadly, and cold as Loki's dagger, slashing at the sky, it vibrated above us like electricity, hung like a piece of frozen thunder, and cut, cut, cut into the center of spirit that was desire, twisted, and became a fishhook to pull us on, to burn us with its barbs.

Vince was the first to look up and see the top, the first to die. It happened so quickly, and it was none of the terrors that achieved it.

He slipped.

That was all. It was a difficult piece of climbing. He was right behind me one second, was gone the next. There was no body to recover. He'd taken the long drop. The soundless blue was all around him and the great gray beneath. Then we were six. We shuddered, and I suppose we all prayed in our own ways.

—Gone Vince, may some good Deva lead you up the Path of Splendor. May you find whatever you wanted most at the other end, waiting there for you. If such a thing may be, remember those who say these words, oh strong intruder in the sky...

No one spoke much for the rest of the day.

The fiery sword bearer came and stood above our camp the entire night. It did not speak.

In the morning, Stan was gone, and there was a note beneath my pack.

> *Don't hate me*, it said, *for running out, but I think it really is an angel. I'm scared of this mountain. I'll climb any pile of rocks, but I won't fight Heaven. The way down is easier than the way up, so don't worry about me. Good luck. Try to understand.*
>
> S

So we were five—Doc and Kelly and Henry and Mallardi and me—and that day we hit a hundred eighty thousand and felt very alone.

The girl came again that night and spoke to me, black hair against black sky and eyes like points of blue fire, and she stood beside an icy pillar and said, "Two of you have gone."

"And the rest of us remain," I replied.

"For a time."

"We will climb to the top and then we will go away," I said. "How can that do you harm? Why do you hate us?"

"No hate, sir," she said.

"What, then?"

"I protect."

"What? What is it that you protect?"

"The dying, that she may live."

"What? Who is dying? How?"

But her words went away somewhere, and I did not hear them. Then she went away too, and there was nothing left but sleep for the rest of the night.

❖   ❖   ❖

One hundred eighty-two thousand and three, and four, and five. Then back down to four for the following night.

The creatures whined about us now, and the land pulsed beneath us, and the mountain seemed sometimes to sway as we climbed.

We carved a path to one eighty-six, and for three days we fought to gain another thousand feet. Everything we touched was cold and slick and slippery, sparkled, and had a bluish haze about it.

When we hit one ninety, Henry looked back and shuddered.

"I'm no longer worried about making it to the top," he said. "It's the return trip that's bothering me now. The clouds are like little wisps of cotton way down there."

"The sooner up, the sooner down," I said, and we began to climb once again.

It took us another week to cut our way to within a mile of the top. All the creatures of fire had withdrawn, but two ice avalanches showed us we were still unwanted. We survived the first without mishap, but Kelly sprained his right ankle during the second, and Doc thought he might have cracked a couple of ribs, too.

We made a camp. Doc stayed there with him; Henry and Mallardi and I pushed on up the last mile.

Now the going was beastly. It had become a mountain of glass. We had to hammer out a hold for every foot we made. We worked in shifts. We fought for everything we gained. Our packs became monstrous loads and our fingers grew numb. Our defense system—the projectors—seemed to be wearing down, or else something was increasing its efforts to get us, because the snakes kept slithering closer, burning brighter. They hurt my eyes, and I cursed them.

When we were within a thousand feet of the top, we dug in and made another camp. The next couple hundred feet looked easier, then a rotten spot, and I couldn't tell what it was like above that.

When we awakened, there was just Henry and myself. There was no indication of where Mallardi had gotten to. Henry switched his communicator to Doc's letter and called below. I tuned in in time to hear him say, "Haven't seen him."

"How's Kelly?" I asked.

"Better," he replied. "Those ribs might not be cracked at that."

Then Mallardi called us.

"I'm four hundred feet above you, fellows," his voice came in. "It was easy up to here, but the going's just gotten rough again."

"Why'd you cut out on your own?" I asked.

"Because I think something's going to try to kill me before too long," he said. "It's up ahead, waiting at the top. You can probably even see it from there. It's a snake."

Henry and I used the binoculars.

Snake? A better word might be dragon—or maybe even Midgard Serpent.

It was coiled around the peak, head upraised. It seemed to be several hundred feet in length, and it moved its head from side to side, and up and down, and it smoked solar coronas.

Then I spotted Mallardi climbing toward it.

"Don't go any further!" I called. "I don't know whether your unit will protect you against anything like that! Wait'll I call Doc—"

"Not a chance," he said. "This baby is mine."

"Listen! You can be first on the mountain, if that's what you want! But don't tackle that thing alone!"

A laugh was the only reply.

"All three units might hold it off," I said. "Wait for us."

There was no answer, and we began to climb.

I left Henry far below me. The creature was a moving light in the sky. I made two hundred feet in a hurry, and when I looked up again, I saw that the creature had grown two more heads. Lightnings flashed from its nostrils, and its tail whipped around the mountain. I made another hundred feet, and I could see Mallardi clearly by then, climbing steadily, outlined against the brilliance. I swung my pick, gasping, and I fought the mountain, following the trail he had cut. I began to gain on him, because he was still pounding out his way and I didn't have that problem. Then I heard him talking:

"Not yet, big fella, not yet," he was saying, from behind a wall of static. "Here's a ledge..."

I looked up, and he vanished.

Then that fiery tail came lashing down toward where I had last seen him, and I heard him curse and I felt the vibrations of his pneumatic gun. The tail snapped back again, and I heard another "Damn!"

I made haste, stretching and racking myself and grabbing at the holds he had cut, and then I heard him burst into song. Something from *Aida*, I think.

"Damn it! Wait up!" I said. "I'm only a few hundred feet behind."
He kept on singing.

I was beginning to get dizzy, but I couldn't let myself slow down. My right arm felt like a piece of wood, my left like a piece of ice. My feet were hooves, and my eyes burned in my head.

Then it happened.

Like a bomb, the snake and the swinging ended in a flash of brilliance that caused me to sway and almost lose my grip. I clung to the vibrating mountainside and squeezed my eyes against the light.

"Mallardi?" I called.

No answer. Nothing.

I looked down. Henry was still climbing. I continued to climb.

I reached the ledge Mallardi had mentioned, found him there.

His respirator was still working. His protective suit was blackened and scorched on the right side. Half of his pick had been melted away. I raised his shoulders.

I turned up the volume on the communicator and heard him breathing. His eyes opened, closed, opened.

"Okay…" he said.

"'Okay,' hell! Where do you hurt?"

"No place… I feel jus' fine… Listen! I think it's used up its juice for awhile… Go plant the flag. Prop me up here first, though. I wanna watch…"

I got him into a better position, squirted the water bulb, listened to him swallow. Then I waited for Henry to catch up. It took about six minutes.

"I'll stay here," said Henry, stooping beside him. "You go do it."

I started up the final slope.

VII

I swung and I cut and I blasted and I crawled. Some of the ice had been melted, the rocks scorched.

Nothing came to oppose me. The static had gone with the dragon. There was silence, and darkness between stars.

I climbed slowly, still tired from that last sprint, but determined not to stop.

All but sixty feet of the entire world lay beneath me, and heaven hung above me, and a rocket winked overhead. Perhaps it was the pressmen, with zoom cameras.

Fifty feet…

No bird, no archer, no angel, no girl.

Forty feet…

I started to shake. It was nervous tension. I steadied myself, went on.

Thirty feet…and the mountain seemed to be swaying now.

Twenty-five…and I grew dizzy, halted, took a drink.

Then click, click, my pick again.

Twenty…

Fifteen…

Ten…

I braced myself against the mountain's final assault, whatever it might be.

Five…

Nothing happened as I arrived.

I stood up. I could go no higher.

I looked at the sky, I looked back down. I waved at the blazing rocket exhaust.

I extruded the pole and attached the flag.

I planted it, there where no breezes would ever stir it. I cut in my communicator, said, "I'm here."

No other words.

❖   ❖   ❖

It was time to go back down and give Henry his chance, but I looked down the western slope before I turned to go.

The lady was winking again. Perhaps eight hundred feet below, the red light shone. Could that have been what I had seen from the town during the storm, on that night, so long ago?

I didn't know and I had to.

I spoke into the communicator.

"How's Mallardi doing?"

"I just stood up," he answered. "Give me another half hour, and I'm coming up myself."

"Henry," I said. "Should he?"

"Gotta take his word how he feels," said Lanning.

"Well," I said, "then take it easy. I'll be gone when you get here. I'm going a little way down the western side. Something I want to see."

"What?"

"I dunno. That's why I want to see."

"Take care."

"Check."

The western slope was an easy descent. As I went down it, I realized that the light was coming from an opening in the side of the mountain.

Half an hour later, I stood before it.

I stepped within and was dazzled.

❖ ❖ ❖

I walked toward it and stopped. It pulsed and quivered and sang.

A vibrating wall of flame leapt from the floor of the cave, towered to the roof of the cave.

It blocked my way, when I wanted to go beyond it.

She was there, and I wanted to reach her.

I took a step forward, so that I was only inches away from it. My communicator was full of static and my arms of cold needles.

It did not bend toward me, as to attack. It cast no heat.

I stared through the veil of fires to where she reclined, her eyes closed, her breast unmoving.

I stared at the bank of machinery beside the far wall.

"I'm here," I said, and I raised my pick.

When its point touched the wall of flame someone took the lid off hell, and I staggered back, blinded. When my vision cleared, the angel stood before me.

"*You may not pass here,*" he said.

"She is the reason you want me to go back?" I asked.

"*Yes. Go back.*"

"Has she no say in the matter?"

"*She sleeps. Go back.*"

"So I notice. Why?"

"*She must. Go back.*"

"Why did she herself appear to me and lead me strangely?"

"*I used up the fear-forms I knew. They did not work. I led you strangely because her sleeping mind touches upon my own workings. It did so especially when I borrowed her form, so that it interfered with the directive. Go back.*"

"What is the directive?"

"*She is to be guarded against all things coming up the mountain. Go back.*"

"Why? Why is she guarded?"

"*She sleeps. Go back.*"

The conversation having become somewhat circular at that point, I reached into my pack and drew out the projector. I swung it forward and the angel melted. The flames bent away from my outstretched hand. I sought to open a doorway in the circle of fire.

It worked, sort of.

I pushed the projector forward, and the flames bent and bent and bent and finally broke. When they broke, I leaped forward. I made it through, but my protective suit was as scorched as Mallardi's.

I moved to the coffinlike locker within which she slept.

I rested my hands on its edge and looked down.

She was as fragile as ice.

In fact, she was ice...

The machine came alive with lights then, and I felt her somber bedstead vibrate.

Then I saw the man.

He was half sprawled across a metal chair beside the machine.

He, too, was ice. Only his features were gray, were twisted. He wore black and he was dead and a statue, while she was sleeping and a statue.

She wore blue, and white...

There was an empty casket in the far corner...

But something was happening around me. There came a brightening of the air. Yes, it was air. It hissed upward from frosty juts in the floor, formed into great clouds. Then a feeling of heat occurred and the clouds began to fade and the brightening continued.

I returned to the casket and studied her features.

I wondered what her voice would sound like when/if she spoke. I wondered what lay within her mind. I wondered how her thinking worked, and what she liked and didn't like. I wondered what her eyes had looked upon, and when.

I wondered all these things, because I could see that whatever forces I had set into operation when I entered the circle of fire were causing her, slowly, to cease being a statue.

She was being awakened.

❖ ❖ ❖

I waited. Over an hour went by, and still I waited, watching her. She began to breathe. Her eyes opened at last, and for a long time she did not see.

Then her bluefire fell on me.

"Whitey," she said.

"Yes."

"Where am I...?"

"In the damnedest place I could possibly have found anyone."

She frowned. "I remember," she said and tried to sit up.

It didn't work. She fell back.

"What is your name?"

"Linda," she said. Then, "I dreamed of you, Whitey. Strange dreams... How could that be?"

"It's tricky," I said.

"I knew you were coming," she said. "I saw you fighting monsters on a mountain as high as the sky."

"Yes, we're there now."

"H-have you the cure?"

"Cure? What cure?"

"Dawson's Plague," she said.

I felt sick. I felt sick because I realized that she did not sleep as a prisoner, but to postpone her death. She was sick.

"Did you come to live on this world in a ship that moved faster than light?" I asked.

"No," she said. "It took centuries to get here. We slept the cold sleep during the journey. This is one of the bunkers." She gestured toward the casket with her eyes. I noticed her cheeks had become bright red.

"They all began dying—of the plague," she said. "There was no cure. My husband—Carl—is a doctor. When he saw that I had it, he said he would keep me in extreme hypothermia until a cure was found. Otherwise, you only live for two days, you know."

Then she stared up at me, and I realized that her last two words had been a question.

I moved into a position to block her view of the dead man, who I feared must be her Carl. I tried to follow her husband's thinking. He'd had to hurry, as he was obviously further along than she had been. He knew the colony would be wiped out. He must have loved her and been awfully clever, both—awfully resourceful. Mostly, though, he must have loved her. Knowing that the colony would die, he knew it would be centuries before another ship arrived. He had nothing that could power a cold bunker for that long. But up here, on the top of this mountain, almost as cold as outer space itself, power wouldn't be necessary. Somehow, he had got Linda and the stuff up here. His machine cast a force field around the cave. Working in heat and atmosphere, he had sent her deep into the cold sleep and then prepared his own bunker. When he dropped the wall of forces, no power would be necessary to guarantee the long, icy wait. They could sleep for centuries within the bosom of the Gray Sister, protected by a colony of defense-computer. This last had apparently been programmed quickly, for he was dying. He saw that it was too late to join her. He hurried to set the thing for basic defense, killed the force field, and then went his way into that Dark and Secret Place. Thus it hurled its birds and its angels and its snakes, it raised its walls of fire against me. He died, and it guarded her in near-death—against everything, including those who would help. My coming to the mountain had activated it. My passing of the defenses had caused her to be summoned back to life.

"*Go back!*" I heard the machine say through its projected angel, for Henry had entered the cave.

❖ ❖ ❖

"My God!" I heard him say. "Who's that?"

"Get Doc!" I said. "Hurry! I'll explain later. It's a matter of life! Climb back to where your communicator will work, and tell him it's Dawson's Plague—a bad local bug! Hurry!"

"I'm on my way," he said and was.

"There *is* a doctor?" she asked.

"Yes. Only about two hours away. Don't worry...I still don't see how anyone could have gotten you up here to the top of this mountain, let alone a load of machines."

"We're on the big mountain—the forty-miler?"

"Yes."

"How did *you* get up?" she asked.

"I climbed it."

"You really climbed Purgatorio? On the outside?"

"Purgatorio? That's what you call it? Yes, I climbed it, that way."

"We didn't think it could be done."

"How else might one arrive at its top?"

"It's hollow inside," she said. "There are great caves and massive passages. It's easy to fly up the inside on a pressurized jet car. In fact, it was an amusement ride. Two and a half dollars per person. An hour and a half each way. A dollar to rent a pressurized suit and take an hour's walk around the top. Nice way to spend an afternoon. Beautiful view...?" She gasped deeply.

"I don't feel so good," she said. "Have you any water?"

"Yes," I said, and I gave her all I had.

As she sipped it, I prayed that Doc had the necessary serum or else would be able to send her back to ice and sleep until it could be gotten. I prayed that he would make good time, for two hours seemed long when measured against her thirst and the red of her flesh.

"My fever is coming again," she said. "Talk to me, Whitey, please... Tell me things. Keep me with you till he comes. I don't want my mind to turn back upon what has happened..."

"What would you like me to tell you about, Linda?"

"Tell me why you did it. Tell me what it was like, to climb a mountain like this one. Why?"

I turned my mind back upon what had happened.

"There is a certain madness involved," I said, "a certain envy of great and powerful natural forces, that some men have. Each mountain is a deity, you know. Each is an immortal power. If you make sacrifices upon its slopes, a mountain may grant you a certain grace, and for a time you will share this power. Perhaps that is why they call me..."

Her hand rested in mine. I hoped that through it whatever power I might contain would hold all of her with me for as long as ever possible.

"I remember the first time that I saw Purgatory, Linda," I told her. "I looked at it and I was sick. I wondered, where did it lead...?"

(Stars.
Oh let there be.
This once to end with.
Please.)

"Stars?"

A Word from Zelazny

"This story appeared in the March 1967 issue of *Worlds of If*. The previous September, I had received my first Science Fiction Achievement Award (Hugo)—for my novel ...*And Call Me Conrad*—at Tricon, the World Science Fiction Convention which was held in Cleveland, Ohio. Fred Pohl had asked all of the award recipients that year to submit material for a special Hugo Winners issue of *If*.

"I forget now whether I had already begun work on this story and earmarked it for that purpose when he asked me, or whether I had only a rough idea and wrote it immediately thereafter. I feel it was the former, though.

"I recall that I hurried it somewhat, because of the deadline. If there had been no deadline, it would have been a longer and, possibly, different story. How, I couldn't say now, because I never go back and reread if I can help it. But I do not believe that I was unhappy with it as it turned out. I liked *Worlds of If*, and I was glad to be in that particular issue."[1]

Notes

Dante Alighieri's **Divine Comedy** describes his descent through *Inferno* (Hell); his climb through *Purgatorio* (Purgatory), and his ascension into *Paradisio* (Heaven). This story retells Dante's climb of Mount Purgatory by having Jack Summers climb **Purgatorio**; the novella's seven sections correspond to the seven terraces of Mount Purgatory. In *Purgatorio,* the angel inscribes seven letters on Dante's forehead; in "This Mortal Mountain," he receives a blinding shock. Dante's pagan companion Virgil may not enter heaven and vanishes; likewise **Vince**, the non-Christian in the group, vanishes suddenly ("right beside me one second, was gone the next"). *Purgatorio* ends with Dante gazing at the stars, anticipating his ascent to heaven; "This Mortal Mountain" ends with Summers begging for stars, praying that he'd saved the woman and his companions from Dawson's Plague.

There is no **Lady of the Abattoir** [slaughterhouse]; it may be a simple jest. A **basilisk** turned its victims into stone with a glance. **Koshtra Pivrarcha** is the forbidding high mountain climbed in E. R. Eddison's 1922 novel, *The Worm Ouroboros,* one source that J. R. R. Tolkien used to create Middle

---

1 *Worlds of If: A Retrospective Anthology,* eds. Pohl, Greenberg, Olander; Bluejay 1986.

Earth.[2] **Mallardi** was likely named after Bill Mallardi, the co-editor of the *Double:Bill* fanzine to which Zelazny contributed many pieces.

Alpha rhythms, as registered on an electroencephalogram (EEG), are caused by normal electrical activity of a conscious, relaxed brain. The **Phoenix** is a mythological bird that lives for five or six centuries, burns itself on a funeral pyre, and arises from the ashes with renewed life. **Nemesis** is the Greek goddess of vengeance. **Balmy** means eccentric or foolish.

Deva is deity in Buddhism. **Angelsbane** is a fictional poison (a pun on wolfsbane) that could kill angels. "When **the Frost Is on the Punkin**" is a poem by James Whitcomb Riley. A **harpy** had a woman's head and body with a bird's wings and claws, or was a bird of prey with a woman's face. **Loki** was the Norse god of trickery, foster brother of Odin, and father of three monstrous children who will be involved in the world's end. In Norse mythology, the **Midgard Serpent** (Jormangund) encircles the world, holding its tail in its mouth. *Aida* is an opera by Guiseppe Verdi.

---

2 *Letters of Tolkien*, ed. Humphrey Carpenter with Christopher Tolkien, George Allen & Unwin, 1981.

LOVER'S VALEDICTION: FORBIDDING DAY'S SACRAMENT

When Pussywillows Last in the Catyard Bloomed, Norstrilia Press 1980.
Written 1955–60 for *Chisel in the Sky*.

Phlox of the liberal phoenix,
breasting towers to day,
                                extensive
spirit ahead—
                repetitious Ananias,
forever forswearing azimuths at noon—
                                      sinking song
in centuries of idiom overflows thy habit,
as flocked thoroughfares spend sloped shadow.

                Where gnash thy left,
despairing doors,
                as cosmos-meeting crusts
cover a baked vacancy,
                I say,
out this emptied one,
                "Absence is not eaten".

Notes

This poem echoes John Donne's "A Valediction: Forbidding Mourning," which is a plea for an unemotional parting with a lover because physical absence should not cause despair when the spiritual connection continues.

    Valediction is parting, and saying goodbye. **Phlox** is a perennial that comes in a variety of colors. **Ananias** is a New Testament character who was struck dead for lying, and his name has become a term for a habitual liar. An **azimuth** is the arc of the horizon measured clockwise from the south pole (or from the north pole in navigation) to a point where a vertical circle through a celestial body intersects the horizon. The final line might be considered a pun on the phrase "absence is not forgotten."

The Man Who Loved the Faioli

Galaxy, June 1967.

It is the story of John Auden and the Faioli, and no one knows it better than I. Listen—

It happened on that evening, as he strolled (for there was no reason not to stroll) in his favorite places in the whole world, that he saw the Faioli near the Canyon of the Dead, seated on a rock, her wings of light flickering, flickering, flickering and then gone, until it appeared that a human girl was sitting there, dressed all in white and weeping, with long black tresses coiled about her waist.

He approached her through the terrible light from the dying, half-dead sun, in which human eyes could not distinguish distances nor grasp perspectives properly (though his could), and he lay his right hand upon her shoulder and spoke a word of greeting and of comfort.

It was as if he did not exist, however. She continued to weep, streaking with silver her cheeks the color of snow or a bone. Her almond eyes looked forward as though they saw through him, and her long fingernails dug into the flesh of her palms, though no blood was drawn.

Then he knew that it was true, the things that are said of the Faioli—that they see only the living and never the dead, and that they are formed into the loveliest women in the entire universe. Being dead himself, John Auden debated the consequences of becoming a living man once again, for a time.

The Faioli were known to come to a man the month before his death—those rare men who still died—and to live with such a man for that final month of his existence, rendering to him every pleasure that it is possible for a human being to know, so that on the day when the kiss of death is delivered, which sucks the remaining life from his body, that man accepts it—no, seeks it—with desire and with grace, for such is the power of the Faioli among all creatures that there is nothing more to be desired after such knowledge.

John Auden considered his life and his death, the conditions of the world upon which he stood, the nature of his stewardship and his curse and the Faioli—who was the loveliest creature he had seen in all of his four hundred thousand days of existence—and he touched the place beneath his left armpit which activated the necessary mechanism to make him live again.

The creature stiffened beneath his touch, for suddenly it was flesh, his touch, and flesh, warm and woman-filled, that he was touching, now that the sensations of life had returned to him. He knew that his touch had become the touch of a man once more.

"I said 'Hello, and don't cry,'" he said, and her voice was like the breezes he had forgotten through all the trees that he had forgotten, with their moisture and their odors and their colors all brought back to him thus, "From where do you come, man? You were not here a moment ago."

"From the Canyon of the Dead," he said.

"Let me touch your face," and he did, and she did.

"It is strange that I did not feel you approach."

"This is a strange world," he replied.

"That is true," she said. "You are the only living thing upon it."

And he said, "What is your name?"

She said, "Call me Sythia," and he did.

"My name is John," he told her, "John Auden."

"I have come to be with you, to give you comfort and pleasure," she said, and he knew that the ritual was beginning.

"Why were you weeping when I found you?" he asked.

"Because I thought there was nothing upon this world, and I was so tired from my travels," she told him. "Do you live near here?"

"Not far away," he answered. "Not far away at all."

"Will you take me there? To the place where you live?"

"Yes."

And she rose and followed him into the Canyon of the Dead, where he made his home.

They descended and they descended, and all about them were the remains of people who once had lived. She did not seem to see these things, however, but kept her eyes fixed upon John's face and her hand upon his arm.

"Why do you call this place the Canyon of the Dead?" she asked him.

"Because they are all about us here, the dead," he replied.

"I feel nothing."

"I know."

They crossed through the Valley of the Bones, where millions of the dead from many races and worlds lay stacked all about them, and she did not see these things. She had come to the graveyard of all the worlds, but she did not realize this thing. She had encountered its tender, its keeper, and she did not know what he was, he who staggered beside her like a man drunken.

John Auden took her to his home—not really the place where he lived, but it would be now—and there he activated ancient circuits within the building within the mountain. In response light leaped forth from the walls, light he had never needed before, but now required.

The door slid shut behind them, and the temperature built up to a normal warmth. Fresh air circulated. He took it into his lungs and expelled it, glorying in the forgotten sensation. His heart beat within his breast, a red warm thing that reminded him of the pain and of the pleasure. For the first time in ages, he prepared a meal and fetched a bottle of wine from one of the deep, sealed lockers. How many others could have borne what he had borne?

None, perhaps.

She dined with him, toying with the food, sampling a bit of everything, eating very little. He, on the other hand, glutted himself fantastically, and they drank of the wine and were happy.

"This place is so strange," she said. "Where do you sleep?"

"I used to sleep in there," he told her, indicating a room he had almost forgotten; and they entered and he showed it to her, and she beckoned him toward the bed and the pleasures of her body.

That night he loved her, many times, with a desperation that burnt away the alcohol and pushed all of his life forward with something like a hunger, but more.

The following day, when the dying sun had splashed the Valley of the Bones with its pale, moonlike light, he awakened and she drew his head to her breast, not having slept herself, and she asked him, "What is the thing that moves you, John Auden? You are not like one of the men who live and who die, but you take life almost like one of the Faioli, squeezing from it everything that you can and pacing it at a tempo that bespeaks a sense of time no man should know. What are you?"

"I am one who knows," he said. "I am one who knows that the days of a man are numbered and one who covets their dispositions as he feels them draw to a close."

"You are strange," said Sythia. "Have I pleased you?"

"More than anything else I have ever known," he said.

And she sighed, and he found her lips once again.

They breakfasted, and that day they walked in the Valley of the Bones. He could not distinguish distances nor grasp perspectives properly, and she could not see anything that had been living and now was dead. So, of course, as they sat there on a shelf of stone, his arm about her shoulders, he pointed out to her the rocket which had just come down from out of the sky, and she squinted after his gesture. He indicated the robots, which had begun unloading the remains of the dead of many worlds from the hold of the ship, and she cocked her head to one side and stared ahead, but she did not really see what he was talking about.

Even when one of the robots lumbered up to him and held out the board containing the receipt and the stylus, and as he signed the receipt for the bodies received, she did not see or understand what it was that was occurring.

In the days that followed, his life took upon it a dreamlike quality, filled with the pleasure of Sythia and shot through with certain inevitable streaks of pain. Often, she saw him wince, and she asked him concerning his expressions.

And always he would laugh and say, "Pleasure and pain are near to one another," or something such as that.

And as the days wore on, she came to prepare the meals, and to rub his shoulders and mix his drinks and to recite to him certain pieces of poetry he had somehow once come to love.

A month. A month, he knew, and it would come to an end. The Faioli, whatever they were, paid for the life that they took with the pleasures of the flesh. They always knew when a man's death was near at hand. And in this sense, they always gave more than they received. The life was fleeing anyway, and they enhanced it before they took it away with them, to nourish themselves most likely, price of the things that they'd given.

John Auden knew that no Faioli in the entire universe had ever met a man such as himself.

Sythia was mother-of-pearl, and her body was alternately cold and warm to his caresses, and her mouth was a tiny flame, igniting wherever it touched, with its teeth like needles and its tongue like the heart of a flower. And so he came to know the thing called love for the Faioli called Sythia.

Nothing must really happen beyond the loving. He knew that she wanted him, to use him ultimately, and he was perhaps the only man in the universe able to gull one of her kind. His was the perfect defense against life and against death. Now that he was human and alive, he often wept when he considered it.

He had more than a month to live.

He had maybe three or four.

This month, therefore, was a price he'd willingly pay for what it was that the Faioli offered.

Sythia racked his body and drained from it every drop of pleasure contained within his tired nerve cells. She turned him into a flame, an iceberg, a little boy, an old man. When they were together, his feelings were such that he considered the *consolamentum* as a thing he might really accept at the end of a month, which was drawing near. Why not? He knew she had filled his mind with her presence, on purpose. But what more did existence hold for him? This creature from beyond the stars had brought him every single thing a man could desire. She had baptized him with passion and confirmed him with the quietude which follows after. Perhaps the final oblivion of her final kiss was best after all.

He seized her and drew her to him. She did not understand him, but she responded.

He loved her for it, and this was almost his end.

There is a thing called disease that battens upon all living things, and he had known it beyond the scope of all living men. She could not understand, woman-thing who had known only life.

So he never tried to tell her, though with each day the taste of her kisses grew stronger and saltier, and each seemed to him a strengthening shadow, darker and darker, stronger and heavier, of that one thing which he now knew he desired most.

And the day would come. And come it did.

He held her and caressed her, and the calendars of all his days fell about them.

He knew, as he abandoned himself to her ploys and the glories of her mouth, her breasts, that he had been ensnared, as had all men who had known them, by the power of the Faioli. Their strength was their weakness. They were the ultimate in Woman. By their frailty they begat the desire to please. He wanted to merge himself with the pale landscape of her body, to pass within the circles of her eyes and never depart.

He had lost, he knew. For as the days had vanished about him, he had weakened. He was barely able to scrawl his name upon the receipts proffered him by the robot who had lumbered toward him, crushing ribcages and cracking skulls with each terrific step. Briefly, he envied the thing. Sexless, passionless, totally devoted to duty. Before he dismissed it, he asked it, "What would you do if you had desire and you met with a thing that gave you all the things you wished for in the world?"

"I would—try to—keep it," it said, red lights blinking about its dome, before it turned and lumbered off, across the Great Graveyard.

"Yes," said John Auden aloud, "but this thing cannot be done."

Sythia did not understand him, and on that thirty-first day they returned to that place where he had lived for a month, and he felt the fear of death, strong, so strong, come upon him.

She was more exquisite than ever before, but he feared this final encounter.

"I love you," he said finally, for it was a thing he had never said before, and she kissed him.

"I know," she told him, "and your time is almost at hand, to love me completely. Before the final act of love, my John Auden, tell me a thing: What is it that sets you apart? Why is it that you know so much more of things-that-are-not-life than mortal man should know? How was it that you approached me on that first night without my knowing it?"

"It is because I am already dead," he told her. "Can't you see it when you look into my eyes? Do you not feel it, as a certain special chill, whenever I touch you? I came here rather than sleep the cold sleep, which would have me to be in a thing like death anyhow, an oblivion wherein I would not even know I was waiting, waiting for the cure which might never happen, the cure for one of the very last fatal diseases remaining in the universe, the disease which now leaves me only small time of life."

"I do not understand," she said.

"Kiss me and forget it," he told her. "It is better this way. There will doubtless never be a cure, for some things remain always dark, and I have surely been forgotten. You must have sensed the death upon me, when I restored my humanity, for such is the nature of your kind. I did it to enjoy you, knowing you to be of the Faioli. So have your pleasure of me now, and know that I share it. I welcome thee. I have courted thee all the days of my life, unknowing."

But she was curious and asked him (using the familiar for the first time), "How then dost thou achieve this balance between life and that-which-is-not-life, this thing which keeps thee conscious yet unalive?"

"There are controls set within this body I happen, unfortunately, to occupy. To touch this place beneath my left armpit will cause my lungs to cease their breathing and my heart to stop its beating. It will set into effect an installed electrochemical system, like those my robots (invisible to you, I know) possess. This is my life within death. I asked for it because I feared oblivion. I volunteered to be gravekeeper to the universe, because in this place there are none to look upon me and be repelled by my deathlike appearance. This is why I am what I am. Kiss me and end it."

But having taken the form of a woman, or perhaps being woman all along, the Faioli who was called Sythia was curious, and she said, "This place?" and she touched the spot beneath his left armpit.

With this he vanished from her sight, and with this also, he knew once again the icy logic that stood apart from emotion. Because of this, he did not touch upon the critical spot once again.

Instead, he watched her as she sought for him about the place where he once had lived.

She checked into every closet and adytum, and when she could not discover a living man, she sobbed once, horribly, as she had on that night when first he had seen her. Then the wings flickered, flickered, weakly flickered, back into existence upon her back, and her face dissolved and her body slowly melted. The tower of sparks that stood before him then vanished, and later on that crazy night during which he could distinguish distances and grasp perspectives once again he began looking for her.

And that is the story of John Auden, the only man who ever loved a Faioli and lived (if you could call it that) to tell of it. No one knows it better than I.

No cure has ever been found. And I know that he walks the Canyon of the Dead and considers the bones, sometimes stops by the rock where he met her, blinks after the moist things that are not there, wonders at the judgment that he gave.

It is that way, and the moral may be that life (and perhaps love also) is stronger than that which it contains, but never that which contains it. But only a Faioli could tell you for sure, and they never come here any more.

A Word from Zelazny

This is another story Zelazny wrote to match a cover painting.[1] "This particular tale came into existence in a reverse-sequence sort of way, just the opposite from what the people who read it in its original magazine appearance probably thought had occurred. What happened was that Fred Pohl, who was then editing *Galaxy*, purchased a particular piece of artwork to use as a cover for the magazine: a bleak setting, a valley full of bones with multi-armed robots tromping through it like tired Sicilian grape-crushers, a prominent dark blue sun hanging in an eerie sky. He showed it to me and asked whether I might write him a story to go behind it. I agreed, although I had no idea at the time as to what I was going to do with it.

"I propped the painting on a table in my living room, where I could not fail to see it each time I passed through. A couple days went by and nothing recommended itself. It even accompanied me through a memorable New Year's celebration, where I tested whether a systematic derangement of the senses in its presence would serve to throw the switch on the story machine in my mind. The following day I thought a lot about graveyards.

"It was not until that evening while listening to the song, 'We'll Sing in the Sunshine,' that something clicked. It was the line '...But though I'll never love you, I'll stay with you one year' that did whatever was done. The graveyard world, the characters, the entire situation were suddenly all together—in short, the whole story. I sat down and wrote it in a matter of hours; Fred bought it and it subsequently appeared as planned.

"...Most writers will, I believe, agree that there is generally a gap between the way they see the goings-on in their tales and the way an illustrator does them up, the essence necessarily preceding the existence with an unavoidable slippage in between. It is often quite distressing. With the cover coming first for 'The Man Who Loved the Faioli,' however, it is one of the few instances where I felt things to be perfectly meshed.

---

[1] *Unicorn Variations*, 1983.

"...Thus it was brought home to me how an artist, given a story to read and illustrate, must feel when *he* has finished *his* work. For him, it would seem, the story and the artwork should always mesh more completely than they do for the writer. He draws and paints what he sees and feels in the story, just as I wrote what I came to see and feel in the first illustration.

"As for the story itself, now standing before you bereft of [the original cover painting], it doesn't really matter that it began in an unusual fashion, that I once sat regarding the Valley of Bones and muttering, 'Are those really Zoromes coming my way? Yes. No. Yes. Damn!' The story is itself, whole and entire, and I like it in, of, by and for itself...

"And unlike my cat and many other things that I have written, I know where this one came from. Sort of."[2] Zoromes are alien cyborgs featured in the Neil R. Jones's Professor Jameson stories, first appearing in 1931.

Editor Harry Harrison solicited the foreword quoted above for the anthology *SF: Authors Choice 4* and added, "I must admit that I have one small and personal complaint about the story! A rather exotic one. Faioli is pronounced almost exactly like "ailloli," the Greek garlic mayonnaise which I loathe and which instantly sprang to mind when I saw your word. All I can think of is cold white garlic sauce...! Sorry about that, my hangup."[3] Zelazny replied, "Cold, white garlic sauce... That does tend to detract from the dream-dust tone I was kind of hoping to spread around. There go the Greek sales."[4]

Notes

John Auden is named after the poet W. H. Auden, who declared "we must love one another or die" in the poem "September 1, 1939." **Consolamentum** is practiced by Cathars (a branch of Christianity) who conferred baptism, all spiritual gifts, power to bind and loose, absolution, and Ordination in a single ceremony. An **adytum** was the inner shrine or most sacred part of an ancient temple that the public was forbidden to enter.

---

2 *SF: Authors Choice 4*, ed. Harry Harrison, 1974.
3 Letter from Harry Harrison to Roger Zelazny, May 25, 1972.
4 Letter from Roger Zelazny to Harry Harrison, June 6, 1972.

Song

Written 1955–60 for *Chisel in the Sky*; previously unpublished.

I.

The leaves are gone
The trees are bare.

I am young.
You are fair.   II.

Love me.   The trees are full.
                        The leaves are blown.

                        I grow weary
                        Of you alone.   III.

                        Leave me.   The trees are spare.
                                                 The leaves are gold.

                                                 You are gone.
                                                 I am old.

                                                 Curse me.

Notes

Zelazny titled another poem "Song" in 1981's *To Spin Is Miracle Cat*; it appears in volume 5 of this collection.

Angel, Dark Angel

Galaxy, August 1967.

He entered the kiosk and escalated down to the deck that stood beside the rumbling strip. He was fifty-five years of age and he bore a briefcase in his right hand.

As he crossed toward the conveyor belt, a dozen heads turned in his direction because of the flash of light that occurred immediately before him.

For one bright instant, a dark figure stood in his path.

Then there came the *crack* of imploding air, as the figure vanished and the man fell to the deck.

Later that day, the death record read, "Natural causes."

Which was true. Quite, quite true.

❖ ❖ ❖

It slithered along the moist tunnel, heading toward the river.

It knew that its life had ended the moment that the blaze occurred; and the facets of its eyes held sixty-four images of the tall, leather-masked figure, garbed all in black, with its hard, dark hand upraised.

The hand extended toward it, offering that which it could not refuse.

The gift was thunder and pain, and the medical record prepared later that day said, "Natural causes."

❖ ❖ ❖

Putting down his champagne glass, he unfastened her negligee and pushed it back over her shoulders. His hands molded her, described her sex, drew her down onto the bed. She sighed as he raised himself onto an elbow and touched her lips.

She felt him stiffen, in the glare that came from the corner of the suite. She screamed within the thunderclap that followed, having glimpsed the Angel of Death for a single, dark moment as she felt her lover stop his loving, forever.

This, too, was the result of natural causes.

❖   ❖   ❖

The man called Stain was in his greenhouse, where he had spent some part of almost every day for the past two years, plucking dead leaves and taking cuttings.

He was slightly under six feet in height, and his eyes were iodine dark within his sharp-cornered, sunbaked face beneath black hair salted lightly at the temples.

His left shoulder brushed against an earthenware pot on the shelf at his back, and he felt its movement and departure.

Turning, he caught it at waist level and replaced it on the shelf.

He began repotting a geranium, and then the instrument strapped to his left wrist buzzed and he pressed a button on its side and said, "Yes?"

"Stain," said the voice, which could have been coming from the red flowers in his hand, "do you love the human races and all other living things within the universe?"

"Of course," he replied, recognizing the crackling sibilance that was the voice of Morgenguard.

"Then please prepare yourself for a journey of some duration and report to your old cubicle in Shadowhall."

"But I am retired, and there must be many others whose speed now exceeds my own."

"Your last medical report shows that your speed is undiminished. You are still one of the ten best. You were retired at the proper age because it is your right to enjoy the rest of your days as you see fit. You are not ordered to do the thing I now say. You are requested to do it. So you may refuse if you see fit. Should you accept, however, you will be compensated, and you will have served the things you profess to love."

"What would you have of me?"

"Come not in uniform, but in civil garb. Bring with you your gauntlets and your daily requirements in all things, save nourishment, for a period of approximately two weeks."

"Very well. I will attend directly."

The communication ended, and he finished potting the geranium and returned to his quarters.

To his knowledge, none such as himself had ever been recalled from retirement, nor was his knowledge inaccurate.

❖   ❖   ❖

Her name is Galatea, and she has red hair and stands to slightly over five and a half feet in height. Her eyes are green and her complexion pale, and men call her lovely but generally avoid her company. She lives in a big, old house which she has remodeled, on the outskirts of Cyborg, an ancient city on Ankus in the Ceti System. She keeps to herself and runs up large bills with the Cyborg Power Co.

She lives alone, save for mechanical servants. She favors dark colors in her garb and her surroundings. She occasionally plays tennis or else fences at the local sports center. She always wins. She orders large quantities of chemicals from local wholesalers. Men who have dated her say that she is stupid, brilliant, oversexed, a prude, fascinated with her deathwish, full of *joie de vivre*, an alcoholic, a teetotaler and a wonderful dancer. She has had many dates/few friends/no suitors, and her lovers be unknown. It is suggested that she maintains a laboratory and perhaps engages in unknown researches.

❖   ❖   ❖

"We do not know the answer," said Simule. "There is no defense against him, save here. I cannot remain here if I am to serve my function. Therefore, I must leave soon, and secretly."

"Wait," she said. "You are not yet ready to survive on your own. Another month, perhaps…"

"Too long, too long, we fear," Simule replied.

"Do you doubt my power to protect you?"

Simule paused, as if to consider, then, "No. You can save this body, but the question, 'Is it worth it?' comes forth. Is it worth it? Preserve yourself, lady. We love you. There remains yet more that you may do."

"We shall see," she said. "But for now, you remain."

She replaced him, upon the reading stand in her library, and she left him there with *Lear*.

❖   ❖   ❖

His name was Stain, and he came to her door one day and announced himself, saying, "Stain, of Iceborg."

After a time, the door let him in.

She appeared and asked, "Yes?"

"My name is Stain," he replied, "and I have heard that you play tennis, and are very good. I am looking for a partner in the Cyborg Open Mixed Doubles. I am good. Will you play with me?"

"How good?" she asked him.

"They don't come much better."

"Catch," she said, and picked up a marble figurine from off an inlaid table and hurled it toward him.

He caught it, fumbling, and set it on the ledge at his side.

"Your reflexes are good," she replied. "Very well, I'll play with you."

"Will you have dinner with me tonight?"

"Why?"

"Why not? I don't know anyone here."

"All right. Eight o'clock."

"I'll pick you up then."

"Till then."

"Till then."

He turned, and headed back toward the town and his hotel.

Of course, they took the tournament. They won hands down. And Stain and Galatea danced that night and drank champagne. And she asked him as he held her, both of them all in black, "What do you do, Stain?"

"Nothing but enjoy myself," he said. "I'm retired."

"In your thirties?"

"Thirty-two."

She sighed and softened within his arms.

"What do *you* do?" he asked.

"I, too, am retired. I enjoy my hobbies. I do as I would."

"What does that come to?"

"Whatever I please."

"I've brought you a Hylagian orchid to wear in your hair, or anywhere else you may choose. I'll give it to you when we return to the table."

"They're very expensive," she said.

"Not so if you raise them yourself."

"And you do?"

"*My* hobby," he replied.

At their table, they finished their champagne and smoked and she studied the flower and her companion. The club was done all in silver and black, and the music was soft—and as the dancers seated themselves it lost all semblance of a theme. Her smile was the candle of their table, and he ordered them a dessert and liqueurs to accompany it, and she said, "Your poise defies description."

"Thank you, but yours is superior."

"What did you do, before you retired?"

"I was a paymaster. What of yourself?"

"I dealt in accounts receivable, for a large concern."

"Then we have something else almost in common."

"So it would seem. What will you do now?"

"I'd like to continue seeing you, for so long as I am in town."

"How long might that be?"

"For so long as I might wish, or you desire."

"Then let us finish our sherbet; and since you wish me to have the trophy we will take it home."

He brushed the back of her hand, lightly, and for an instant their eyes met, and a spark that might have been electric leapt between them and they smiled at precisely the same instant.

After a time, he took her home.

❖ ❖ ❖

The bat-thing quivered and dipped, on the way to the council of its people.

As it passed by a mountaintop, there came a flash of light.

Though its speed was virtually inconceivable and its movement unpredictable, it knew that it would fall in an instant; and it did, as the thunder roared above it.

❖ ❖ ❖

He held her very closely and their lips met. They stood in the foyer of her big old remodeled house on the outskirts of Cyborg City on Ankus, of the Ceti System, and one of her mechanical servants had taken their cloaks and another the double-handled golden tennis trophy, and the front door had closed behind them and the night lights had come on dim as they had entered.

"You'll stay awhile," she said.

"Fine."

And she led him into a long, sunken living room filled with soft furniture, with a fresco upon one wall. They faced it as he seated himself on the green divan, and he stared at the wall as he lit two cigarettes and she handed him a final drink and joined him there.

"Lovely," he said.

"You like my fresco?"

"I hadn't noticed it."

"…And you haven't tasted your drink."

"I know."

Her hand came to rest upon his arm, and he put his drink aside and drew her to him once again, just as she put hers to rest.

"You are quite different from most men," she said.

"…And you from most women."

"Is it growing warm in here?"

"Very," he said.

❖   ❖   ❖

Somewhere it is raining. Controlled or artificial—somewhere it is always raining, any time you care to think about it. Always remember that, if you can.

❖   ❖   ❖

A dozen days had passed since the finale of the Cyborg City Mixed Open. Every day Stain and Galatea moved together somewhere. His hand upon her elbow or about her waist, she showed him Cyborg City. They laughed often, and the sky was pink and the winds were gentle and in the distance the cliffs of Ankus wore haloes of fog prismatic and crowns of snow and ice.

Then he asked her of the fresco as they sat in her living room.

"It represents the progress of human thought," she said. "That figure—far to the left, contemplating the birds in flight—is Leonardo da Vinci, deciding that man might do likewise. High at the top and somewhat to the left, the two figures ascending the ziggurat toward the rose are Dante and Virgil, the Classic and the Christian, joined together and departing the Middle Ages of Earth into a new freedom—the place where Leonardo might contemplate. That man off to the right is John Locke. That's the social contract in his hand. That man near the middle—the little man clutching the figure eight—is Albert Einstein."

"Who is the blinded man far to the left, with the burning city at his back?"

"That is Homer."

"And that one?"

"Job, on a heap of rubble."

"Why are they all here?"

"Because they represent that which must never be forgotten."

"I do not understand. I have not forgotten them."

"Yet the final five feet to the right are blank."

"Why?"

"There is nothing to put there. Not in a century has there been anything worth adding. Everything now is planned, prescribed, directed—"

"And no ill comes of it, and the worlds are managed well. Do not tell me how fine were the days of glorious discontent, days through which you never lived yourself. The work done then has not gone to waste. Everything is appreciated, used."

"But what new things have been added?"

"Size, and ease of operation within it. Do not preach to me of progress. Change is not desirable for its own sake, but only if it offers improvement. I could complete your fresco for you—"

"With a gigantic machine guarded by the Angel of Death! I know!"

"You are wrong. It would end with the Garden of Eden."

She laughed.

"Now you know the story of my fresco."

❖ ❖ ❖

He took her hand. "You may be right," he said. "I don't really know. I was only talking about how things seem to me."

"And *you* may be right," she said. "*I* don't really know... I just feel there should be something to counterbalance that wonderfully flexible mechanism which guides us so superbly that we are becoming the vegetables in that garden you would draw me."

"Have you any suggestions?"

"Have you read any of my papers?"

"I'm afraid not. I fool around with my own garden and I play tennis. That's about it."

"I have proposed the thesis that man's intelligence, extruded into the inanimate, has lost all that is human. Could you repair the machine that mixes our drinks, if it ceased to function?"

"Yes."

"Then you are very unusual. Most people would call in a robot which specializes in small-appliance repairs."

Stain shrugged.

"Not only have we given up this function of intelligent manipulation—but divorced from us and existing elsewhere, it turns and seeks to suppress what remains of it within ourselves."

"What do you mean?"

"Why has life become a horizontal line, rather than an upward curve? One reason is that men of genius die young."

"This I cannot believe."

"I purposely published my most important papers recently and I was visited by the Angel of Death. This proved it to me."

He smiled.

"You still live, so this could not be so."

She returned his smile, and he lit two cigarettes and said, "On what subjects were the papers?"

"The Preservation of Sensibility."

"An innocuous-seeming subject."

"Perhaps."

"What do you mean 'perhaps'? Perhaps I misunderstand you."

"It would seem that you do. Sensibility is a form of esthetic consciousness cultivated by intelligence. This is lacking today and I proposed a method whereby it might be preserved. The fruits of my work were then threatened."

"And what may these be?"

She tilted her head slightly, studied his face, then, "Come with me, and I will show you," she said, and she rose and led him into her library. As he followed her, he removed from an inner pocket his black gauntlets and drew them onto his hands. Then he jammed his hands into his side pockets to cover them and entered the room at her back.

"Simule," she called out, and the tiny creature that sat before a reading machine upon her desk leapt into her extended hand, ran up her right arm and sat upon her shoulder.

"What is it?" he questioned.

"The answer," she said. "Pure, mechanistic intelligence can be countered by an infinitely mobile and easily concealed organic preserver of sensibility. This is Simule. He and others like him came to life in my laboratory."

"Others?"

"There are many, upon many worlds already. They share a mass mind. They learn constantly. They have no personal ambition. They wish only to learn and to instruct any who wish to learn from them. They do not fear the death of their bodies, for they continue to exist thereafter as a part of the mind they all share. They—or it—are—or is—lacking in any other personal passion. The Simule could never represent a threat to the human races. I know this, for I am their mother. Take Simule into your hand, consider him, ask him anything. Simule, this is Stain; Stain, this is Simule."

Stain extended his right hand, and the Simule leaped into it. Stain studied the tiny, six-legged creature, with its disquietingly near-human face. Near. Yet not quite. It was unmarked by the physical conversions of those abstract passion-producers men call good and evil, which show in some form upon every human countenance. Its ears were large, doubtless for purposes of eavesdropping, and its two antennae quivered upon its hairless head and it raised a frail limb as if to shake hands. An eternal smile played upon its lips, and Stain smiled back. "Hello," he said, and the Simule replied in a soft, but surprisingly rich voice, "The pleasure is mine, sir."

Stain said, "What is so rare as a day in June?" and the Simule replied, "Why, the lady Galatea, of course, to whom I now return," and leaped and was upon her suddenly extended palm.

She clutched the Simule to her breast and said, "Those gauntlets—!"

"I put them on because I did not know what sort of creature the Simule might be. I feared it might bite. Please give him back that I might question him further—"

"You fool!" she said. "Point your hands in another direction, unless you wish to die! Do you not know who I am!"

Then Stain knew.

"I did not know…" he said.

❖   ❖   ❖

In Shadowhall in Morgenguard the Angel of Death stands within ten thousand transport cubicles. Morgenguard, who controls the destinies of all civilized worlds, briefs his agents for anything from ten seconds to a minute and a half—and then, with a clap of thunder, dispatches them. A second later—generally—there is a flash of light and a brief report, which is the word "Done," and there then follows another briefing and another mission.

The Angel of Death is, at any given moment, any one of ten thousand anonymous individuals whose bodies bear the mark of Morgenguard, after this fashion:

Selected before birth because of a genetic heritage that includes heightened perception and rapid reflexes, certain individuals of the *homo sapiens* variety are given a deadly powerful education under force-fed conditions. This compensates for its brevity. At age fourteen, they may or may not accept employment in the service of Morgenguard, the city-sized machine created by the mutual efforts of all civilized peoples over a period of fifteen years and empowered to manage their worlds for them. Should any decline, these individuals generally proceed to excel in their chosen professions. Should they accept, a two-year period of specialized training follows. At the end of this time, their bodies have built into them an arsenal of weapons and numerous protective devices and their reflexes have been surgically and chemically stimulated to a point of thoughtlike rapidity.

They work an eight-hour day, five days a week, with two daily coffee breaks and an hour for lunch. They receive two vacations a year and they work for fourteen years and are retired on full salary at age thirty, when their reflexes begin to slow. At any given moment, there are always at least ten thousand on duty.

On any given workday, they stand in the transport cubicles in Shadowhall in Morgenguard, receive instructions, are transported to the worlds and into the presence of the individuals who have become superfluous, dispatch these individuals and depart.

He is the Angel of Death. Life lasts long, save for him; populations would rise up like tidal waves and inundate worlds, save for him; criminals would require trials and sentencing, save for him; and of course history might reflect unnecessary twistings and turnings, save for the Angel of Death.

One dark form might walk the streets of a city and leave that city empty of life at its back. Coming in lightning and departing in thunder, no world is foreign, no face unfamiliar, and the wearer of the black gauntlets is legend, folklore and myth; for, to a hundred billion people, he is but one being with a single personality.

All of which is true. Quite, quite true.

And the Dark Angel cannot die.

Should the near-impossible occur, should some being with speed and intrepidity be standing accidentally armed at the moment his name on the roll yonder and up is being shouted, then the remains of the stricken Dark Angel vanish as, with a simultaneous lightning-and-thunder effect, another takes his place, rising, as it were, out of ashes.

The few times that this has occurred, the second has always finished the job.

But this time things were different; and what little remained of seven agents of Morgenguard had lain in cubicles, smoldered, bled, been dead.

❖   ❖   ❖

"You are the Dark Angel, the Sword of Morgenguard," she said. "I did not mean to love you."

"Nor I you, Galatea, and were you only a mortal woman, rather than a retired Angel yourself—the only being whose body would throw back the charge upon me and destroy me, as it did the others—please believe that I would not raise my hand against you."

"I would like to believe that, Stain."

"I am going now. You have nothing to fear of me."

He turned and headed toward the door.

"Where are you going?" she asked him.

"Back to my hotel. I will be returning soon, to give a report."

"What will it say?"

He shook his head and left.

But he knew.

❖   ❖   ❖

He stood in Shadowhall within the thing called Morgenguard. He was the Angel of Death, Emeritus, and when the old familiar voice crackled over the loudspeaker and said, "Report!" he did not say, "Done." He said, "Extremely confidential," for he knew what that meant.

There came a flash of lightning, and he stood in a larger hall before a ten-story console, and he advanced toward it and heard the order repeated once more.

"One question, Morgenguard," he said, as he hafted and folded his arms upon his breast. "Is it true that you were fifteen years in the building?"

"Fifteen years, three months, two weeks, four days, eight hours, fourteen minutes and eleven seconds," Morgenguard replied.

Then Stain unclasped his arms, and his hands came together upon his breast.

Morgenguard may have realized in that instant what he was doing; but then, an Angel's body has built into it an arsenal of weapons and numerous protective devices and his reflexes have been surgically and chemically stimulated to a point of thoughtlike rapidity; also, Stain had been recalled from retirement because he was one of the ten fastest who had ever served Morgenguard.

The effect was instantaneous. The clap of thunder was not Morgenguard's doing, for he did not remove Stain in time.

The Dark Angel might never strike itself. The seven who had approached the lady Galatea had suffered from a recoil-effect from her own defense system. Never before had the power of the Dark Angel been turned upon himself, and never in the person of one. Stain had worked it out, though.

Death and destruction meeting automatic defense meeting recoil meeting defense recoil defense recoil breakthrough, and a tremendous fireball blooming like an incandescent rose rose within the heart of the city-sized machine Morgenguard.

Right or wrong. Simule will have some years to grow, he knew, in that instant, and—

—And somewhere the sun is shining, and its heart is the möbius burn of the Phoenix Action/Reaction. Somewhere the sun is always shining, any time you care to think about it. Try to remember that, if you can. It is very important.

She remembers. Her name is Galatea. And we remember.

We always remember...

A Word from Zelazny

"Yet another variation on the way stories come into being... Back when Fred Pohl was editing *Galaxy, Worlds of Tomorrow* and *Worlds of If* magazines he used to encourage artists by buying pieces they'd painted to use as covers. These days, the contents of a magazine tend to come first, the cover subsequently commissioned to illustrate something within. But I can't complain about the old order of things, which paid a number of bills. Fred would send a reproduction of such a cover to a writer and request a story to go behind it. One of my better short stories—'The Man Who Loved the Faioli'—came about in such a fashion. (Also, my absolute worst [see afterword to 'Song of the Blue Baboon'], but never mind...) This one showed an extended, black-gloved hand, a strange little creature with a near-human face standing on the palm. All right..."[1]

---

1 *Unicorn Variations*, 1983.

Notes

Stain's name may mean "to bring reproach or dishonor upon" or may mean a "blemish" on the otherwise perfect society where, as Angel of Death, he destroys its controlling government. *Joie de vivre* is joy of living. **Galatea** was the statue made by Pygmalion that came to life when Aphrodite/Venus heard his plea; **Galatea** is also a sea nymph whose lover, Acis, was killed by the jealous Cyclops Polyphemus. Shakespeare's *King Lear* is an old king who unwisely gives his kingdom to two of his daughters; their actions reduce him to poverty and eventually to madness. His youngest daughter Cordelia remains faithful to him but is murdered, and Lear also dies at the end. **Orchids** have several meanings depending on context: purity or perfection; love, luxury and beauty; reproduction and fertility; aphrodisiac or sexual desire. An **ankus** is a spike used to goad an elephant; the name also evokes ankh, the Egyptian cross that symbolizes life. Several prominent thinkers and artists depicted in the fresco are mentioned in rapid succession: **Leonardo da Vinci** (painter and architect), **Dante** Alighieri (poet, *Divine Comedy*), **Virgil** (poet, *The Aeneid*), **John Locke** (philosopher who theorized that government is only legitimate if receives the consent of the people), **Albert Einstein** (Theory of Relativity), **Homer** (the *Iliad* and *Odyssey*), **Job** (who argues with God). "**What is so rare as a day in June?** || Then, if ever, come perfect days" is from the poem "The Vision of Sir Launfal" by James Russell Lowell.

Fire, Snakes & the Moon

Written 1965–68; previously unpublished.

> Fire, snakes & the moon,
> says Auden, somewhere, are sacred to poets
> & suchlike madmen. He may be right.
> Dogs warm themselves by one, kill another,
> howl at the third; & if anybody knows what's sacred,
> it's a dog. After all, we're their gods.

Notes

In a lecture at the University of Oxford on June 11, 1956, the poet W. H. **Auden** described the process of becoming a poet and the problem of remaining one. He said that a poem is "a rite of homage to sacred objects" and that "**Fire**, **Snakes**, Darkness, **the Moon**" are sacred objects and beings, to which the only possible poetic response is "awe and self-surrender."[1] Zelazny's response seems tongue-in-cheek.

---

1 *The Review of English Studies, New Series*, Vol. 9, No. 33, Feb., 1958.

The Hounds of Sorrow

Written in August 1967; previously unpublished.

When Mattie goes to sleep, I'm going to blow his goddamn head off. Or Jimmy. I'll shoot the first one that nods, if the other doesn't get him first. They're waiting to do the same to me, but it won't happen.

I've got insomnia. I've got it something fierce, and I've had it for the past two nights. So it won't be me.

Mattie's blinking his eyes. I think he'll be the first. The fire's getting low, and I'm still sweating like a pig. The only thing we need the fire for is the light, so we can watch each other. Tonight's as hot as hell's basement, so even the damn dogs can't sleep. They keep howling at that little piece of the moon that's come up in the east. I can see it through the opened door. Nice if the lights worked, but they don't.

Each of us is sitting with his back against the wall and his rifle across his lap, watching the kitchen table burn and watching each other. Mattie's nodding…

No. As soon as Jimmy moved his rifle barrel just a little, Mattie jerked and shook his head.

❖   ❖   ❖

It was just three days ago, I woke up with a funny feeling. I don't know how else to put it. I just woke up after a hot, sticky night like tonight, not really feeling rested after too much tossing and rolling around, the bedsheet all wet underneath me from my sweat, and I had this feeling, while I lay there and lit my first cigarette, sure that those damn dirty yellow curtains hadn't stirred or fluttered in a breeze the whole damn night long, I had this feeling that today was the day. For what, I didn't know. But something was going to happen. It had to.

I got up and into my T-shirt and jeans, and I pulled on my old Army boots. While I was futzing around in the john, the old lady must have heard me, because she started bitching from the kitchen. I could hear her even through the closed door.

"So, you're up! What're you going to do today?"

It was the usual question, and she repeated it three times and I didn't answer it until I walked out there.

"Get the hell out of here as soon as I can," I said. "What've we got to eat?"

"Feed yourself," she said. "It's on the stove."

There were beans and bread and coffee, so I filled a plate and a cup and started eating, standing up, there at the stove.

"I saw three mice since I've been up," she said, "and I've got a funny feeling today—"

"Sure they weren't snakes?" I asked, gesturing at the Gallo bottle on the countertop. There was less in it than there had been the day before.

"If you'd throw those old newspapers and magazines out in the alley, they wouldn't have so many places to hide."

"They live in the woodwork," I said. "You can't get rid of them. If you don't like the mess, do some housecleaning."

"My back—"

"—Hurts because you carry too much weight around," I finished. "Women always have their backs to fall back on when they feel like sitting on their asses."

Jenny was almost seven years older than I am, and once she looked pretty good. Now, though—Hell! She weighed around one-eighty, had three chins, wore house dresses that zipped down the front and looked like tents, and her dark eyes never seemed to focus—because she never wore her glasses and was half in the bag all the time. Also, she had hair on her chest, which she didn't use to. That was Jenny, and I'd have left her long before, except that we wouldn't have gotten as much out of the county then.

I finished eating and headed for the door.

"Hey! You going to wash those dishes?"

"Screw 'em!" I said, and slammed it behind me and headed down the steps. At my back, I heard the sounds of her footsteps crossing the kitchen. The other way. Towards the Gallo.

Out on the street, the morning sun was already coming up hard off the pavements. I still had the feeling that something was going to happen. I told Jake, the newsman, when I read the morning edition, "Something's going to happen."

"What?" he asked, hocking a gob of phlegm into the gutter.

"I don't know. But it will."

"I don't feel so good this morning." He coughed a couple times, to prove the point, then, "I've got a feeling like today is an important day," he said, shaking his head, "or a different kind of day—like a Sunday or a holiday. Like there's something special I'm supposed to do. It keeps nagging at me—like I'm forgetting something."

"What can it be?"

"I don't know."

I lit a cigarette. After awhile, a girl named Rose who called herself Jean and who was up too early for her line of work, strolled by.

"What's special about today?" I said to her.

"What do you mean?"

"Something special, about today," I said.

"I don't know. I got up early and I got all dressed. I don't know why."

The next one I asked was Mattie, and I'm going to blow his goddamn head off as soon as he closes his eyes.

Mattie agreed that there was something special in the air. Rose wandered away. Two fellows with whom we struck up a conversation felt the same way about the day. One of them was Jimmy and the other is dead. That was Bill.

We sat down on a bench and we heard sirens in the distance.

"Cop or ambulance?" Mattie said.

"Cop," I said.

But it was an ambulance that roared past and crashed the red light at the corner.

After a time, I got up and walked to a drug store up the block. I sat down at the soda fountain and ordered a cup of coffee. It was the girl behind the counter who asked if something special was going to happen today. I said, "Yes."

About two hours later it had built up into a terrible, steady pressure, both inside me and all around me. The streets, the storefronts with the faded paint on their glass, the bright shiny autos and the stripped hulks that lined the curb, the cotton and silk that hung dead and fading on backyard lines, the dark birds that watched from the telephone wires, and the faces of old women behind windows, and the dogs that wandered into the alleys, eating garbage and lifting their legs against the fences, and one somber cat I saw, black, atop a brick wall, still as a statue, with yellow eyes, and the empty bottles in doorways and the trashcan lid which had been run over in the street and the sun overhead like an orange hole in the side of a blue furnace and the brown grass and the green grass and a tree with a ridiculous high wire fence about it, all seemed to reach for, bend toward, expect—A clap of thunder? The Good Fairy? A bearded man in a white robe? The sound of a rock band?

I didn't know, but fifteen minutes later I was back in the apartment, cleaning the M-1 I kept in the back of the bedroom closet. Jenny was snoring, her head down on the kitchen table, so that she didn't even hear me.

Then I went up to the roof and waited.

I watched the people down below, moving slowly, stopping to talk. After a time, a fight broke out on the corner. It was over before too long, which I thought was too bad, because it would have been nice to watch it for a long time. On a building up the street, I caught sight of the glint of metal. Yes. It was going to happen soon.

The man who had been knocked down got up and jumped on the back of the man who had knocked him down, bearing him to the ground. They began to wrestle. Then a police car passed through the intersection, stopped, backed up, turned into the street. It drew up at the curb, and I waited until both patrolmen were out of the car before I fired.

They fell immediately. I had fired only one shot, but I'd heard dozens. Mine had been the first, though.

Then I knew, we knew. Today was the day that mankind would shed its City. Today was the day we stopped living together, honoring some damn deal that must have been made long before I was born that said we all had to stick together, to chop down trees and put up buildings so close together that we could all be neighbors and get on each others' nerves, to make each other do things, like digging holes in the ground so we could get all the oil and coal and minerals, in order to pollute the air and the water and fill the garbage trucks and the junkyards, in order to make other people be garbage collectors and factory hands and junkyard attendants, so that other people could be doctors, to take care of the silicosis and TB and hepatitis and industrial accidents, so that other people could be lawyers, to help us keep from paying the bills for the doctors' services, the cars, the buildings too close to one another, or to help the doctors, the banks and the landlords collect from us, and still others to drive the trucks and the trains and the buses back and forth, delivering things and people, delivering, always delivering, while others are made to go out selling, selling, selling things and people to be delivered to the places where more things are made and then delivered, so that everybody has to give the bulk of his time to the Big Rhythm, the eight or nine hours of the day to the City and not yourself or anybody else, but the City-Thing, the Thing that starts in working on you at age five or so, when it grabs you up to start teaching you how wonderful it is, releases you from school to work for it, lets you go when you can't any more, and invades more and more of the Earth's surface every year for purposes of burying you when you've stopped completely, and if you drop away from or are dropped by it before that time, it torments you and tugs at you, because you've got the Rhythm, man, and no place to put it, so you become a virus in its body and it begins to treat you like one. I knew, we knew. But the infection had now spread far. The old deal was off.

I stayed there for the better part of the afternoon, shooting anybody I felt like. And sometimes people shot at me.

That evening, I got me a bag of jewelry and a transistor radio. I got me more ammo and a better rifle, too. One with telescopic sights. All around me, I could hear gunfire and shattering glass, screams. Flames added to the night's heat and helicopters circled, spotlights licking the streets and buildings below them. I saw two of them shot down, bloom like orange roses, wither.

I holed up in a basement that had a lot of ways out. By then, I had a sack of food and a few bottles of whiskey. I drank and I listened to the radio.

It was the same all over the world. It had been the day, the special day, the last day. The last day of the City. Militias had been called up and there had been mass desertions. And money and politics and nationality had nothing to do with it. People were shooting and burning in all neighborhoods, all cities. It had been the day the Big Rhythm broke within us and we turned upon the City, its source, and each other, for we were all part of it.

I drank until I felt sleepy, then I decided against it and put it away. I smoked until I felt sober again, drank water, ate a peanut butter sandwich. The fighting was still going on and people were still looting like mad. It hit me then that I had to leave the City or be destroyed with it.

I waited in the alleyway, watching. I had a plan.

Three men passed, firing occasional shots behind them. I got the drop on them, and they happened to be Mattie, Jimmy, and Bill.

"I'm clearing out," I said. "If you're smart, you will, too. This place won't be worth a damn in another day or so. Why stay and get shot? Let's head for the hills."

"Why are you telling us this?" said Mattie.

"Because I'm going to take a car and head out of town. Somebody will sure as hell shoot me, too—or anybody who tries it alone. If we all go together, though, we can shoot back and maybe make it."

They thought about it awhile, and one by one they nodded or said, "Yes." None of our eyes met during this time. It was a strange combination of feelings we seemed to share: shame, fear and hatred, to and for one another.

But we found a big old Buick and piled in, Mattie driving, and he did a thing with a quarter and a piece of chewing gum under the dashboard and the engine started.

We were shot at as we fled, and once some juice from a Molotov cocktail singed the hood. We had two bullet holes in the rear window before we neared the city limits, and a third one before we passed them, which had taken care of Bill. We chuckled simultaneously as Jimmy pushed him out onto the road. Then we realized what it meant and were silent.

We began watching one another.

It's not that any of us had anything worth stealing. When we stopped at a small country house on the following day and cleaned it out except for the woman, Jimmy and I tried the color TV he'd brought along while Mattie had her in the other room. Nothing. Not even static. There was no power. I still picked up the news on my transistor, from stations that had their own generators, but that was it. Electrical appliances were worthless. The jewelry and cash I'd picked up meant nothing. No. They only had meaning in terms of the City, which was dying. None of these were the reasons we'd begun watching one another.

I found that I couldn't stand the sight of them. I felt, more strongly with each minute that passed, that I'd been too close to other people all my life, surrounded by them, rubbing up against them in crowds, on buses, in elevators, listening to them crunch popcorn at movies, having them kick sand on me at the beach, blow horns at me in traffic snarls, give me orders, take orders from me, be the subject of my conversation, be what I watched whenever my eyes fell upon a screen, a picture, read about in newspapers, magazines, books.

I knew Jimmy and Mattie wanted to kill me, too.

We drove in silence for the rest of that day. I couldn't sleep, like I said, and they were both awake last night, also. But with them, it seemed a matter of forcing themselves to keep awake. With me, it's this insomnia. We replenished our supplies earlier today and drove until we found this farm house. Now we're too tired to go any further, without sleep. Sooner or later it will come. Which means that only one of us will wake up, at most.

Last night, while I was sitting there awake, I thought about it some more. What happened, I mean, and what's going to happen now. That population problem everybody kept talking about has been solved now, I guess. Now there is plenty room for keeping to ourselves. I'll never go back to the City. What will happen to those big messes of stone and concrete and steel and glass, where we lived and worked and croaked? They'll burn out, rust out, fall down, be covered over, in time. And maybe we'll kill each other off, eventually. My transistor radio has been silent since yesterday morning. I keep thinking about what I saw, too, three days ago. We killed each other and we destroyed what we could of the objects which held us. But no one bothered with the dogs, who ate the garbage in the alleys and lifted their legs against the fences. It's almost as if they weren't a part of the thing, though they were. They wandered among those who shot and were shot at, scratched fleas, barked occasionally, sometimes howled. It didn't matter much to them. You know their philosophy—

The report filled the room.

I had been wrong.

Jimmy had nodded first, and Mattie got him before I could.

His chuckle is a weak and hollow thing. He looks like hell. I don't think he can keep awake much longer.

And I want to keep awake long enough to get him, because I just can't stand that sonofabitch.

You know, the only thing I really feel sorry about is those dogs. Soon there won't be any more garbage. But the hounds of sorrow will bay for a short time only, then the hot inherited pavements will crack like dreams do when your eyes come unglued on a summer morning, and they'll know what to do.

Mattie is nodding…

Notes

This uncharacteristically pessimistic piece was inspired by John B. Calhoun's 1962 *Scientific American* article, "Population Density and Social Pathology." Calhoun studied rats' behavior in crowded and uncrowded conditions and noted that when crowded, rats killed, maimed, sexually assaulted, and even cannibalized each other. Uncrowded rats did not. The paper was well publicized, and other researchers subsequently validated it, providing serious implications for humans in cities. More recent studies suggest that humans are not readily prone to such behavior.

This story also shares some themes with "The Window Washer", probably also inspired by the book that discussed the origins of cities (see afterword to that story).

Zelazny's agent acknowledged receipt of the "new story" in a letter dated August 15, 1967, and promised to read it and comment "by the end of the week."[1] His next letter expressed confusion about the characters' motivations, and he did not understand the references to Calhoun's work. "I've reread 'The Hounds of Sorrow,' and have a question: What is it that suddenly makes the narrator and his friends (and others, I suppose) leave the city? Is it a mystical force? Or that moment in history?"[2] His agent's puzzlement may have led Zelazny to shelve the story—not understanding the implications of Calhoun's research would make the story incomprehensible. It is unclear whether he ever submitted it for publication.

You know their philosophy refers to "it's a dog eat dog world."

---

1 Letter from Henry Morrison to Roger Zelazny dated August 15, 1967.
2 Letter from Henry Morrison to Roger Zelazny dated August 18, 1967.

The Window Washer

Written 1965–68 (but likely near "The Hounds of Sorrow"); previously unpublished.

I

It was when he noted that the window washer was not using a safety belt that he first became suspicious—especially when the man leaned far back to reach after the higher spots.

By then, however, it no longer mattered. It was time to clean up his desk, punch out, and head for *The Office*, a bar so named to assist the honesty of home-calling husbands replying to the standard question.

He did not require the assistance of nomenclature, since he had never obtained the necessary partner in inquiry. Still, his few friends frequented the establishment, with the periodicity of unstable elements, and so, when he flopped into the booth across from Good Old Charlie, first he sighed, then groped after the conversational ignition.

"Say, that window washer today didn't have on a safety belt. Pretty dangerous, eh?"

"What window washer?" asked Good Old Charlie.

He scratched a shaggy sideburn.

"You know, the one who washed the window across from me today."

"I didn't see no window washer," said Good Old Charlie.

"Well, he was there."

"Hmm."

"'Hmm' hell! Pretty dangerous, I say!"

"Okay, okay! He was there! I didn't notice."

"Always sleeping on the job. Good Old Charlie!"

"Yeah. Let's get stoned."
"Good idea."

❖   ❖   ❖

Because of the Good Old Hangover caused by staying late at *The Office*, he called in sick to the office the next day and, shutting out the bloodshot windows of his soul, rolled over and began to snore.

At two o'clock the telephone rang. He rolled back to his right side and knocked the receiver onto the pillow.

"What do you want, telephone?" he yawned.

"Charlie, here," it said. "Pretty terrible, huh?"

"Yeah. How do you feel?"

"No, I mean about the office."

"I forget what happened."

"The one where we work, I mean. Half an hour ago. Didn't you hear on the radio?"

He sat up and swallowed cobwebs.

"I don't know nothin'. Clue me."

"Gas leak. Thirty-one dead, five hundert thousand dollars damage."

"Lord!"

"Yeah, that's what I say. We're damlucky."

"Yeah," he breathed. "Look, I'll call you back when I'm a little more awake. I gotta take somethin' to stop the jitters. Thirty-one!"

"Sure, okay, see ya. Everybody in our department got it."

He reflected over the mahogany mirror in the coffee cup. He was dark and hazy, and something needed clearing inside his head. What was it? He gulped the mirror and it shattered in his stomach.

He washed the cup, but when he got to the bathroom he decided against shaving. He slipped on his loafers and went outside.

Walking, he recalled the evening before. Good Old Charlie was screaming:

"So he's a *genius loci*! So shut and drink your beer!"

He remembered the small, grinning man with the smooth, deft movements and no safety belt. He recalled the quizzical eyes and the odd ears.

He looked up and around, half-expecting to see him again, perched on some other ledge, drawing a squeegee, swirling his white rag.

He need a drink. No! He'd let things get him before, and had had to spend more than his vacation taking the cure.

It had to be nothing. The headshrinkers knew. When you have

paranoic tendencies and premonitions of doom, the spirits in the bottle don't chase the spirits in your head. They just get together and raise hell, that's what.

So he pushed through the crowd and stared at the five hundred thousand dollars worth of explosion. The whole face of the building was roped off, and traffic had been diverted a block west.

Windows were broken, all along the street. Powdered brick lay like red snow beneath his shoes. The barred mouth of the building was toothless, and half the face had caved in.

He backed away and, turning, fled into the park.

❖ ❖ ❖

Later, much later, when he was feeling better and very lucky, he called Good Old Charlie and they had dinner together.

"Has regional office called you?"

"I don't know," he answered. "haven't been home since I got up."

"Well, they called me and I'm on two weeks' leave. They'll find another office by then. So I guess you are, too. Looks like I'm being promoted."

"Great."

"I know you were kind of sweet on Dave's secretary…"

"Shut up! Don't talk about the dead!"

"I'm sorry, I just wanted to say…"

"Please."

"…Sorry."

❖ ❖ ❖

It was more than a month before he saw the window washer again. This time he couldn't be sure. He was standing on the corner waiting for his bus, when he happened to look up.

He spotted him just as the bus hissed to a halt before him.

High, high up over his head, on a ledge of the Board of Education Building, the half-familiar figure bent and wiped. He could not tell for certain, but it seemed that he was wearing no safety belt…

The next day the papers said that the blaze was the result of a short circuit, caused by lightning striking the building during the storm that had raged that night.

But he knew differently. He was sure now. It wasn't paranoia, he decided, or coincidence either. He did see supernatural phenomena. The window washer was not a washer of windows. He was a—something else. And whatever he did, it was like an undertaker cleaning up a messy cadaver for the funeral.

A shave, a haircut, a clean face, and into the dirt you go…

He took out a library card and signed for an extended leave of absence.

II

An encounter among portfolios…

Good Old Charlie was doing his homework for the night school course he was taking.

He took a left instead of a right turn in the stacks because it was the logical thing to do.

But libraries are never arranged logically. So, …

"Hey there!" He clapped him on the shoulder.

"Good Old Charlie!"

"Right. What have you been up to?"

He glanced at the books.

"Oh, nothing much…"

"The devil, you say? What's that you're reading?—*The City in History?* What's it about?"

"It's about the city," he answered, "in history."

"You don't say?"

"Yeah. You know how they started?"

"What?"

"Cities."

"Oh, no. How?"

"They grew up around the burying places. The city began as an extension of the graveyard."

A shrug. "So what?"

"So they took form at the hands of the living, but they were founded upon death. All the placid stone and the sleeping ores were cut, heated and tortured," he said. "Dragged from their eternal sleep and formed by the will of short-lived man into shapes from his fancy."

"They were heated, tortured, and made ugly… I don't dig this torture bit. What are you trying to say?" said Charlie, squinting. "Hold on, a cathedral is beautiful, so is a statue."

"Yes, but are they happy?"

"How should I know? Are they alive?"

"I think so, yes, but sleeping or half-aware."

"Bull!" said Good Old Charlie, who was taking a bio course. "No life functions!"

"Don't be so sure," he answered. "Perhaps they occur so slowly that we don't notice them. Supposing a may fly were hatched on a rainy day."

"Okay, suppose it. What then?"

"He only lives one day, is what. He'd spend his whole life thinking rain was the normal order of things."

"Is that all in that book?"

"No, it's an extrapolation from my observations. Mountains change shape, but no one around during the Ice Ages would have noticed anything unusual was occurring."

"Listen, don't take this wrong, but maybe you ought to see a doctor. They're starting to wonder about you at the office…"

He laughed. "So maybe I am a little abnormal. That's how I caught onto things in the first place."

"What things? What's all this relevant to?"

"The window washer I've seen. I recognized him when I got half-crocked and something inside me started to think."

"He was a figment."

"No," he tapped a book on mythology, "he is a Spirit of Place. This place. Don't you see what he's doing?"

"I'm afraid not."

"He's an Earth spirit, and this has been his domain since the beginning of Time. My human senses anthropomorphized him and what he was doing."

"Listen, why don't we go and get a good old drink or three, then you go home and get a good night's sleep, and then tomorrow you get a good checkup, and the next day you put in a good day's work?"

"Good Old Charlie," he sighed. "You still don't see. I didn't expect you would, but let me try to give you something to think about. Supposing a formless but living thing were given a form? Supposing over the eons, a dull awareness of this imposition entered its slow, non-human mind. Supposing, then, something happened, and it looked about and saw what uses the presumptuous vermin in its innards had put it to?"

"I'll have to ask you to leave or be quiet," said a fat little woman with white hair, appearing from behind a pillar.

"Spirit of Place," chuckled Charlie. "Okay, okay, we're going. But tell me," he turned again, "why a window washer?"

"He's opening the eyes we gave them," he replied.

"Then we should all return to the caves?"

"Once this thing gets started, it might not be a bad idea."

"Let's go get stoned out of our minds."

"Okay."

III

The next afternoon he saw the window washer again, on the third floor ledge of the Forum hotel. He asked the cop on the corner whether the man was wearing a safety belt.

The cop looked up.

"What window washer?"

He studied the unsmiling, unshaven face before him. His nostrils dilated as he appraised the atmosphere.

"Go get an Alka-Seltzer," he told him.

He entered the Forum instead.

The desk clerk was reading the morning paper.

"Everybody must leave this building at once," he told him.

The man lowered the paper enough so that his eyes appeared above the banner of baseball scores.

"Beat it, bud."

"This isn't a joke," he told him. "This building is going to be destroyed very soon."

The man lowered the paper all the way.

"Mice or termites?" he asked.

"Neither. Or maybe a mouse will gnaw through the wiring somewhere in the walls. I don't know how it will happen. But it will."

"Get out, or I'll have you run in."

He turned to the people in the lobby.

"This hotel is going to collapse tomorrow!" he cried. "Or possibly even today! Get out, all of you, while you still have the chance!"

The clerk rounded the counter and laid a hand on his shoulder.

"That does it," he said. "Leave now. Right now! Or I'll have you picked up and we will press charges."

"You don't understand."

"No, I don't. But I can't have you scaring the people away."

"Okay, I'll go."

He walked out onto the sidewalk, slowly, and he looked up.

The window washer was gone. Perhaps he could talk to him, and explain things. Maybe he would understand. Maybe he would stop...

A block up the street! Fourth floor! This was going to be a big one! He ran.

Uptown Medical Building, said the plaque. The directory listed three dentists and an optometrist on the fourth floor. He took the elevator.

He paced up the hall, looking for the right office. When he found it, he walked into the reception room.

"Do you have an appointment?"

"Uh, no, but is the dentist busy right now?"

"Yes, he is."

"Well, I'd like to speak with him. I'll wait."

"Perhaps I can help you."

"I'd rather wait and talk to him."

She shrugged her crinkly white and answered the telephone.

He rushed to the window.

"Listen," he said, "I know what you are and I know what you're doing! You must stop!"

Squish! Squish!

The window washer continued with his washing.

So he leaned forward and threw the window upward.

"You must not do that! You must let us live!" he screamed.

The window washer stared at him, his shaggy brows drawn together into a sharp frown, almost touching his dusky widow's peak. He vanished.

"What are you doing?" said the nurse, moving to his side.

"Nothing. I felt dizzy. I wanted some air."

"You weren't thinking of jumping, were you?"

"From the fourth floor?" he laughed. "If I were going to do it, I'd do it right."

She still looked unconvinced.

So he made an appointment for the following Tuesday, to have some nonexistent bridgework taken care of, confident that it could not be kept.

When he got home he wrote a letter to each newspaper, asking that they print a warning to the residents of the *Uptown Medical Building* and the *Forum Hotel*. Then he went to *The Office*.

IV

They were staggering through the park. He would call cadence, and Good Old Charlie would respond with verses from the endless marching song of their kind.

Which is why they were arrested for disturbing the peace. Or a part of why.

They might not have been booked, except that he began throwing stones through windows when he heard the patrol car coming, instead of running, as Good Old Charlie wisely proposed.

❖   ❖   ❖

"Okay, buster." The door clanged open. "You've got a lot of explaining to do."

He rose slowly.

"About the windows?" he asked. "I said I'd pay…"

"Windows, hell!"

He was escorted into the office and seated in a stiff-backed chair, so that the sunlight streamed over the Chief Inspector's shoulder and hit him in the face.

"You are the mad bomber," he said. "Aren't you?"

A man off to his left was writing on a notepad.

"I'm not mad, and I'm not a bomber," he told them.

"You wrote letters to the papers, warning them which buildings you'd blow up next. Didn't you?"

"Yes—I mean, no. I wrote letters warning them, but I didn't blow up any building."

"But you knew about them. Didn't you?"

"Yes, yes I did. I tried to warn them."

His eyes relaxed as the sun was obscured. He lowered his head and contorted his face. A hand pushed him gently.

"Sit up straight!"

"You knew about them," repeated the man at the desk. "If you didn't plant the bombs, who did?"

"There were no bombs!" he cried, trying to rise.

The hands gripped him firmly, and pushed him back into his seat.

"There were no bombs. There was no bomber."

"I suppose the buildings blew themselves up?"

"You might say that, yes. That's very nearly correct. They did it themselves."

The hand pushed him on the side of the head.

"Don't try to be funny! We're taking all of this down. It's serious."

"Who did it?" asked the Inspector.

"Everybody did it," he laughed. "We built them. The buildings did it themselves—they didn't like being built. And he did it!"

He pointed.

They all turned and stared outside.

"The window washer," he giggled. "He opened their eyes, he showed them how we had violated their substance! They," he choked as the hand shoved him back into the chair, "they rebelled!"

"They're all going to return to rock and dirt! They are being shown," he babbled, "and they do not like what they see! We are—"

The hand slapped him lightly before he grew hysterical. He collapsed and sat with his head in his lap, sobbing loudly.

"History of alcoholism," said the Inspector. "He's a nut, but he's always been harmless. —Finally went off the deep end."

He glanced at the window again, shaking his head.

"A real nut. Set up an appointment with the psychiatrist for tomorrow, before the hearing."

"Right."

"There won't be any hearing, or any appointments," he whispered through his fingers. "We won't be here tomorrow."

The window washer, slowly polishing, grinned at him through bars like teeth.

Notes

Zelazny retells the myth of the Spirit of Place (the Roman term for it was **Genius loci**). The Spirit of Place has been historically depicted as a guardian animal or minor supernatural being (puck, fairy, elf, ghost, etc.). In Zelazny's vision, the **genius loci** is something else.

The City in History: *Its Origins, Its Transformations, and Its Prospects* was a 1961 book by Lewis Mumford, an American theorist about society and technology. Reading that book inspired Zelazny to write this tale and likely also "The Hounds of Sorrow."

Lobachevsky's Eyes

Doorways in the Sand, Harper & Row 1976.
Separately: *To Spin Is Miracle Cat*, Underwood-Miller 1981.

Lobachevsky alone has looked on Beauty bare.
She curves in here, she curves in here. She curves out there.
Her parallel clefts come together to tease
In un-callipygianous-wise;
With fewer than one hundred eighty degrees
Her glorious triangle lies.
Her double-trumpet symmetry Riemann did not court—
His tastes to simpler-curvedness, the buxom Teuton sort!
An ellipse is fine for as far as it goes,
But modesty, away!
If I'm going to see Beauty without her clothes
Give me hyperbolas any old day.

The world is curves, I've heard it said,
And straightway in it nothing lies.
This then my wish, before I'm dead:
To look through Lobachevsky's eyes.

A Word from Zelazny

"In novels, [including poetry is] one thing I enjoy doing; not only can I sneak a poem in, put it in if it seems appropriate to the character, ['Lobachevsky's Eyes' in particular is] also a subtle clue to the concept of non-Euclidean geometry being important later in the story [of *Doorways in the Sand*]. I had so much fun with the character [of Fred Cassidy] and that novel, playing games with flashbacks and cliffhangers."[1]

Asked if the poet Gallinger in "A Rose for Ecclesiastes" is the author, Zelazny responded "A few people have said this or asked this. Personally, I think I put more of myself into Fred Cassidy."[1]

Notes

The title refers to two things: Russian mathematician **Nikolai Lobachevsky**, noted for contributions to non-Euclidean geometry, and a song that humorist Tom Lehrer wrote in the 1950s. Lehrer credited Lobachevsky with teaching him the secret of success as a mathematician: plagiarism. "I am never forget the day I first meet the great Lobachevsky — || In one word he told me secret of success in mathematics: plagiarize! || Plagiarize! Let no one else's work evade your eyes! || Remember why the Good Lord made your eyes, || So don't shade your eyes, || but plagiarize!" Lobachevsky was not a plagiarist, however.

Callipygianous (callipygous) refers to beautifully proportioned buttocks. **Bernhard Reimann** was a German mathematician who also made contributions to non-Euclidean geometry. **Teuton** originally referred to people of Jutland in the fourth century BC but can also mean someone who is German. An **ellipse** is an oval; a **hyperbola** is an open curve—thus a hyperbola better describes ideal buttocks and breasts than an ellipse.

---

1 *Critical Wave #33*, November 1993.

Beyond the River of the Blessed

The Guns of Avalon, Doubleday 1972.

Beyond the River of the Blessed,
there we sat down, yea, we wept,
when we remembered Avalon.

Our swords were shattered in our hands
and we hung our shields on the oak tree.

The silver towers were fallen, into a sea of blood.

How many miles to Avalon?
None, I say, and all.
The silver towers are fallen.

Notes

This poem is based in part on Psalm 137 ("By the rivers of Babylon, || there we sat down, yea we wept || when we remembered Zion.") and a nursery rhyme that begins "How many miles to Babylon? || Threescore miles and ten." In the novel, Corwin recites this to Ganelon.

Damnation Alley

Galaxy, October 1967.
Hugo nominee 1968 (novella).
Later expanded into a novel by the same name.

I

The gull swooped by, seemed to hover a moment on unmoving wings.

Hell Tanner flipped his cigar butt at it and scored a lucky hit. The bird uttered a hoarse cry and beat suddenly at the air. It climbed about fifty feet, and whether it shrieked a second time, he would never know.

It was gone.

A single gray feather rocked in the violet sky, drifted out over the edge of the cliff, and descended, swinging toward the ocean. Tanner chuckled through his beard, between the steady roar of the wind and the pounding of the surf. Then he took his feet down from the handlebars, kicked up the stand, and gunned his bike to life.

He took the slope slowly till he came to the trail, then picked up speed and was doing fifty when he hit the highway.

He leaned forward and gunned it. He had the road all to himself, and he laid on the gas pedal till there was no place left for it to go. He raised his goggles and looked at the world through crap-colored glasses, which was pretty much the way he looked at it without them, too.

All the old irons were gone from his jacket, and he missed the swastika, the hammer and sickle, and the upright finger, especially. He missed his old emblem, too. Maybe he could pick one up in Tijuana and have some broad sew it on and...No. It wouldn't do.

All that was dead and gone. It would be a giveaway, and he wouldn't last a day. What he *would* do was sell the Harley, work his way down the coast, clean and square, and see what he could find in the other America.

He coasted down one hill and roared up another. He tore through Laguna Beach, Capistrano Beach, San Clemente, and San Onofre. He made it down to Oceanside, where he refueled, and he passed on through Carlsbad and all those dead little beaches that fill the shore space before Solana Beach Del Mar. It was outside San Diego that they were waiting for him.

He saw the roadblock and turned. They were not sure how he had managed it that quickly, at that speed. But now he was heading away from them. He heard the gunshots and kept going. Then he heard the sirens.

He blew his horn twice in reply and leaned far forward. The Harley leaped ahead, and he wondered whether they were radioing to someone farther on up the line.

He ran for ten minutes and couldn't shake them. Then fifteen.

He topped another hill, and far ahead he saw the second block. He was bottled in.

He looked all around him for side roads, saw none.

Then he bore a straight course toward the second block. Might as well try to run it.

No good!

There were cars lined up across the entire road. They were even off the road on the shoulders.

He braked at the last possible minute, and when his speed was right he reared up on the back wheel, spun it, and headed toward his pursuers.

There were six of them coming toward him, and at his back new siren calls arose.

He braked again, pulled to the left, kicked the gas, and leaped out of the seat. The bike kept going, and he hit the ground rolling, got to his feet, and started running.

He heard the screeching of their tires. He heard a crash. Then there were more gunshots, and he kept going. They were aiming over his head, but he didn't know it. They wanted him alive.

After fifteen minutes he was backed against a wall of rock, and they were fanned out in front of him, and several had rifles, and they were all pointed in the wrong direction.

He dropped the tire iron he held and raised his hands. "You got it, citizens," he said. "Take it away."

And they did.

They handcuffed him and took him back to the cars. They pushed him into the rear seat of one, and an officer got in on either side of him. Another got into the front beside the driver, and this one held a sawed-off shotgun across his knees.

The driver started the engine and put the car into gear, heading back up 101.

The man with the shotgun turned and stared through bifocals that made his eyes look like hourglasses filled with green sand as he lowered his head. He stared for perhaps ten seconds, then said, "That was a stupid thing to do."

Hell Tanner stared back until the man said, "Very stupid, Tanner."

"Oh, I didn't know you were talking to me."

"I'm looking at you, son."

"And I'm looking at you. Hello there."

Then the driver said, without taking his eyes off the road, "You know it's too bad we've got to deliver him in good shape—after the way he smashed up the other car with that damn bike."

"He could still have an accident. Fall and crack a couple ribs, say," said the man to Tanner's left.

The man to the right didn't say anything, but the man with the shotgun shook his head slowly. "Not unless he tries to escape," he said. "L.A. wants him in good shape.

"Why'd you try to skip out, buddy? You might have known we'd pick you up."

Tanner shrugged.

"Why'd you pick me up? I didn't do anything."

The driver chuckled.

"That's why," he said. "You didn't do anything, and there's something you were supposed to do. Remember?"

"I don't owe anybody anything. They gave me a pardon and let me go."

"You got a lousy memory, kid. You made the nation of California a promise when they turned you loose yesterday. Now you've had more than the twenty-four hours you asked for to settle your affairs. You can tell them 'no' if you want and get your pardon revoked. Nobody's forcing you. Then you can spend the rest of your life making little rocks out of big ones. We couldn't care less. I heard they got somebody else lined up already."

"Give me a cigarette," Tanner said.

The man on his right lit one and passed it to him.

He raised both hands, accepted it. As he smoked, he flicked the ashes onto the floor.

They sped along the highway, and when they went through towns or encountered traffic, the driver would hit the siren, and overhead the red light would begin winking. When this occurred, the sirens of the two other patrol cars that followed behind them would also wail. The driver never touched the brake, all the way up to L.A., and he kept radioing ahead every few minutes.

There came a sound like a sonic boom, and a cloud of dust and gravel descended upon them like hail. A tiny crack appeared in the lower right-hand corner of the bullet-proof windshield, and stones the size of marbles bounced on the hood and the roof. The tires made a crunching noise as they passed over the gravel that now lay scattered upon the road surface. The dust hung like a heavy fog, but ten seconds later they had passed out of it.

The men in the car leaned forward and stared upward.

The sky had become purple, and black lines crossed it, moving from west to east. These swelled, narrowed, moved from side to side, sometimes merged. The driver had turned on his lights by then.

"Could be a bad one coming," said the man with the shotgun.

The driver nodded. "Looks worse farther north, too," he said.

A wailing began, high in the air above them, and the dark bands continued to widen. The sound increased in volume, lost its treble quality, became a steady roar.

The bands consolidated, and the sky grew dark as a starless, moonless night and the dust fell about them in heavy clouds. Occasionally there sounded a *ping* as a heavier fragment struck against the car.

The driver switched on his country lights, hit the siren again, and sped ahead. The roaring and the sound of the siren fought with one another above them, and far to the north a blue aurora began to spread, pulsing.

Tanner finished his cigarette, and the man gave him another. They were all smoking by then.

"You know, you're lucky we picked you up, boy," said the man to his left. "How'd you like to be pushing your bike through that stuff?"

"I'd like it," Tanner said.

"You're nuts."

"No. I'd make it. It wouldn't be the first time."

By the time they reached Los Angeles, the blue aurora filled half the sky, and it was tinged with pink and shot through with smoky, yellow streaks that reached like spider legs into the south. The roar was a deafening, physical thing that beat upon their eardrums and caused their skin to tingle. As they left the car and crossed the parking lot, heading toward the big, pillared building with the frieze across its forehead, they had to shout at one another in order to be heard.

"Lucky we got here when we did!" said the man with the shotgun. "Step it up!" Their pace increased as they moved toward the stairway. "It could break any minute now!" screamed the driver.

II

As they had pulled into the lot, the building had had the appearance of a piece of ice sculpture, with the shifting lights in the sky playing upon its surfaces and casting cold shadows. Now, though, it seemed as if it were a thing out of wax, ready to melt in an instant's flash of heat.

Their faces and the flesh of their hands took on a bloodless, corpselike appearance.

They hurried up the stairs, and a State Patrolman let them in through the small door to the right of the heavy metal double doors that were the main entrance to the building. He locked and chained the door behind them, after snapping open his holster when he saw Tanner.

"Which way?" asked the man with the shotgun.

"Second floor," said the trooper, nodding toward a stairway to their right. "Go straight back when you get to the top. It's the big office at the end of the hall."

"Thanks."

The roaring was considerably muffled, and objects achieved an appearance of natural existence once more in the artificial light of the building.

They climbed the curving stairway and moved along the corridor that led back into the building. When they reached the final office, the man with the shotgun nodded to his driver. "Knock," he said.

A woman opened the door, started to say something, then stopped and nodded when she saw Tanner. She stepped aside and held the door. "This way," she said, and they moved past her into the office, and she pressed a button on her desk and told the voice that said, "Yes, Mrs. Fiske?": "They're here, with that man, sir."

"Send them in."

She led them to the dark, paneled door in the back of the room and opened it before them.

They entered, and the husky man behind the glass-topped desk leaned backward in his chair and wove his short fingers together in front of his chins and peered over them through eyes just a shade darker than the gray of his hair. His voice was soft and rasped just slightly. "Have a seat," he said to Tanner, and to the others, "Wait outside."

"You know this guy's dangerous, Mister Denton," said the man with the shotgun as Tanner seated himself in a chair situated five feet in front of the desk.

Steel shutters covered the room's three windows, and though the men could not see outside, they could guess at the possible furies that stalked there as a sound like machine-gun fire suddenly rang through the room.

"I know."

"Well, he's handcuffed, anyway. Do you want a gun?"

"I've got one."

"Okay, then. We'll be outside."

They left the room.

The two men stared at one another until the door closed, then the man called Denton said, "Are all your affairs settled now?" and the other shrugged. Then, "What the hell *is* your first name, really? Even the records show—"

"Hell," said Tanner. "That's my name. I was the seventh kid in our family, and when I was born the nurse held me up and said to my old man, 'What name do you want on the birth certificate?' and Dad said, 'Hell!' and walked away. So she put it down like that. That's what my brother told me. I never saw my old man to ask if that's how it was. He copped out the same day. Sounds right, though."

"So your mother raised all seven of you?"

"No. She croaked a couple weeks later, and different relatives took us kids."

"I see," said Denton. "You've still got a choice, you know. Do you want to try it, or don't you?"

"What's your job, anyway?" asked Tanner.

"I'm the Secretary of Traffic for the nation of California."

"What's that got to do with it?"

"I'm coordinating this thing. It could as easily have been the Surgeon General or the Postmaster General, but more of it really falls into my area of responsibility. I know the hardware best, I know the odds—"

"What are the odds?" asked Tanner.

For the first time, Denton dropped his eyes.

"Well, it's risky…"

"Nobody's ever done it before, except for that nut who ran it to bring the news, and he's dead. How can you get odds out of that?"

"I know," said Denton slowly. "You're thinking it's a suicide job, and you're probably right. We're sending three cars, with two drivers in each. If any one just makes it close enough, its broadcast signals may serve to guide in a Boston driver. You don't have to go, though, you know."

"I know. I'm free to spend the rest of my life in prison."

"You killed three people. You could have gotten the death penalty."

"I didn't, so why talk about it? Look, mister, I don't want to die and I don't want the other bit either."

"Drive or don't drive. Take your choice. But remember, if you drive and you make it, all will be forgiven and you can go your own way. The nation of California will even pay for that motorcycle you appropriated and smashed up, not to mention the damage to that police car."

"Thanks a lot." And the winds boomed on the other side of the wall, and the steady staccato from the window shields filled the room.

"You're a very good driver," said Denton after a time. "You've driven just about every vehicle there is to drive. You've even raced. Back when you were smuggling, you used to make a monthly run to Salt Lake City. There are very few drivers who'll try that, even today."

Hell Tanner smiled, remembering something.

"…And in the only legitimate job you ever held, you were the only man who'd make the mail run to Albuquerque. There've only been a few others since you were fired."

"That wasn't my fault."

"You were the best man on the Seattle run, too," Denton continued. "Your supervisor said so. What I'm trying to say is that, of anybody we could pick, you've probably got the best chance of getting through. That's why we've been indulgent with you, but we can't afford to wait any longer. It's yes or no right now, and you'll leave within the hour if it's yes."

Tanner raised his cuffed hands and gestured toward the window. "In all this crap?" he asked.

"The cars can take this storm," said Denton.

"Man, you're crazy."

"People are dying even while we're talking," said Denton.

"So a few more ain't about to make that much difference. Can't we wait till tomorrow?"

"No! A man gave his life to bring us the news! And we've got to get across the continent as fast as possible now, or it won't matter! Storm or no storm, the cars leave now! Your feelings on the matter don't mean a good goddamn in the face of this! All I want out of you, Hell, is one word: Which one will it be?"

"I'd like something to eat. I haven't..."

"There's food in the car. What's your answer?"

Hell stared at the dark window.

"Okay," he said, "I'll run Damnation Alley for you. I won't leave without a piece of paper with some writing on it, though."

"I've got it here."

Denton opened a drawer and withdrew a heavy cardboard envelope, from which he extracted a piece of stationery bearing the Great Seal of the nation of California. He stood and rounded the desk and handed it to Hell Tanner.

Hell studied it for several minutes, then said, "This says that if I make it to Boston I receive a full pardon for every criminal action I've ever committed within the nation of California..."

"That's right."

"Does that include ones you might not know about now, if someone should come up with them later?"

"That's what it says, Hell—'every criminal action.'"

"Okay, you're on, fat boy. Get these bracelets off me and show me my car."

The man called Denton moved back to his seat on the other side of his desk.

"Let me tell you something else, Hell," he said. "If you try to cop out anywhere along the route, the other drivers have their orders, and they've agreed to follow them. They will open fire on you and burn you into little bitty ashes. Get the picture?"

"I get the picture," said Hell. "I take it I'm supposed to do them the same favor?"

"That is correct."

"Good enough. That might be fun."

"I thought you'd like it."

"Now, if you'll unhook me, I'll make the scene for you."

"Not till I've told you what I think of you," Denton said.

"Okay, if you want to waste time calling me names, while people are dying—"

"Shut up! You don't care about them, and you know it! I just want to tell you that I think you are the lowest, most reprehensible human being I have ever encountered. You have killed men and raped women. You once gouged out a man's eyes, just for fun. You've been indicted twice for pushing dope and three times as a pimp. You're a drunk and a degenerate, and I don't think you've had a bath since the day you were born. You and your hoodlums terrorized decent people when they were trying to pull their lives together after the war. You stole from them and you assaulted them, and you extorted money and the necessaries of life with the threat of physical violence. I wish you had died in the Big Raid that night, like all the rest of them. You are not a human being, except from a biological standpoint. You have a big dead spot somewhere inside you where other people have something that lets them live together in society and be neighbors. The only virtue that you possess—if you want to call it that—is that your reflexes may be a little faster, your muscles a little stronger, your eye a bit more wary than the rest of us, so that you can sit behind a wheel and drive through anything that has a way through it. It is for this that the nation of California is willing to pardon your inhumanity if you will use that one virtue to help rather than hurt. I don't approve. I don't want to depend on you, because you're not the type. I'd like to see you die in this thing, and while I hope that somebody makes it through, I hope that it will be somebody else. I hate your bloody guts. You've got your pardon now. The car's ready. Let's go."

Denton stood, at a height of about five feet, eight inches, and Tanner stood and looked down at him and chuckled.

"I'll make it," he said. "If that citizen from Boston made it through and died, I'll make it through and live. I've been as far as the Missus Hip."

"You're lying."

"No, I ain't, either, and if you ever find out that's straight, remember I got this piece of paper in my pocket—'every criminal action' and like that. It wasn't easy, and I was lucky, too. But I made it that far and, nobody else you know can say that. So I figure that's about halfway, and I can make the other half if I can get that far."

They moved toward the door.

"I don't like to say it and mean it," said Denton, "but good luck. Not for your sake, though."

"Yeah, I know."

Denton opened the door. "Turn him loose," he said. "He's driving."

The officer with the shotgun handed it to the man who had given Tanner the cigarettes, and he fished in his pockets for the key. When he found it, he unlocked the cuffs, stepped back, and hung them at his belt. "I'll come with you," said Denton. "The motor pool is downstairs."

They left the office, and Mrs. Fiske opened her purse and took a rosary into her hands and bowed her head. She prayed for Boston, and she prayed for the soul of its departed messenger. She even threw in a couple for Hell Tanner.

III

They descended to the basement, the sub-basement and the sub-sub-basement.

When they got there, Tanner saw three cars, ready to go; and he saw five men seated on benches along the wall. One of them he recognized.

"Denny," he said, "come here," and he moved forward, and a slim, blond youth who held a crash helmet in his right hand stood and walked toward him.

"What the hell are you doing?" he asked him.

"I'm second driver in car three."

"You've got your own garage, and you've kept your nose clean. What's the thought on this?"

"Denton offered me fifty grand," said Denny, and Hell turned away his face.

"Screw it! It's no good if you're dead!"

"I need the money."

"Why?"

"I want to get married, and I can use it."

"I thought you were making out okay."

"I am, but I'd like to buy a house."

"Does your girl know what you've got in mind?"

"No."

"I didn't think so. Listen, I've got to do it—it's the only way out for me. You don't have to—"

"That's for me to say."

"—so I'm going to tell you something: You drive out to Pasadena to that place where we used to play when we were kids—with the rocks and the three big trees—you know where I mean?"

"Yeah, I sure do remember."

"Go back of the big tree in the middle, on the side where I carved my initials. Step off seven steps and dig down around four feet. Got that?"

"Yeah. What's there?"

"That's my legacy, Denny. You'll find one of those old strongboxes, probably all rusted out by now. Bust it open. It'll be full of excelsior, and there'll be a six-inch joint of pipe inside. It's threaded, and there's caps on both ends. There's a little over five grand rolled up inside it, and all the bills are clean."

"Why you telling me this?"

"Because it's yours now," he said, and hit him in the jaw. When Denny fell, he kicked him in the ribs, three times, before the cops grabbed him and dragged him away.

"You fool!" said Denton as they held him. "You crazy, damned fool!"

"Uh-uh," said Tanner. "No brother of mine is going to run Damnation Alley while I'm around to stomp him and keep him out of the game. Better find another driver quick, because he's got cracked ribs. Or else let me drive alone."

"Then you'll drive alone," said Denton, "because we can't afford to wait around any longer. There's pills in the compartment to keep you awake, and you'd better use them, because if you fall back, they'll burn you up. Remember that."

"I won't forget you, mister, if I'm ever back in town. Don't fret about that."

"Then you'd better get into car number two and start heading up the ramp. The vehicles are all loaded. The cargo compartment is under the rear seat."

"Yeah, I know."

"...And if I ever see you again, it'll be too soon. Get out of my sight, scum!"

Tanner spat on the floor and turned his back on the Secretary of Traffic for the nation of California. Several cops were giving first aid to his brother, and one had dashed off in search of a doctor. Denton made two teams of the remaining four drivers and assigned them to cars one and three. Tanner climbed into the cab of his own, started the engine, and waited. He stared up the ramp and considered what lay ahead. He searched the compartments until he found cigarettes. He lit one and leaned back.

The other drivers moved forward and mounted their own heavily shielded vehicles. The radio crackled, crackled, hummed, crackled again, and then a voice came through as he heard the other engines come to life.

"Car one—ready!" came the voice.

There was a pause, then, "Car three—ready!" said a different voice.

Tanner lifted the microphone and mashed the button on its side.

"Car two ready," he said.

"Move out," came the order, and they headed up the ramp.

The door rolled upward before them, and they entered the storm.

IV

It was a nightmare, getting out of L.A. and onto Route 91. The waters came down in sheets, and rocks the size of baseballs banged against the armor plating of his car. Tanner smoked and turned on the special lights. He wore infrared goggles, and the night and the storm stalked him.

The radio crackled many times, and it seemed that he heard the murmur of a distant voice, but he could never quite make out what it was trying to say.

They followed the road for as far as it went, and as their big tires sighed over the rugged terrain that began where the road ended, Tanner took the lead, and the others were content to follow. He knew the way; they didn't.

He followed the old smugglers' route he'd used to run candy to the Mormons. It was possible that he was the only one left alive that knew it. Possible, but then there was always someone looking for a fast buck. So, in all of L.A., there might be somebody else.

The lightning began to fall, not in bolts, but sheets. The car was insulated, but after a time his hair stood on end. He might have seen a giant Gila Monster once, but he couldn't be sure. He kept his fingers away from the fire-control board. He'd save his teeth till menaces were imminent. From the rearview scanners it seemed that one of the cars behind him had discharged a rocket, but he couldn't be sure, since he had lost all radio contact with them immediately upon leaving the building.

Waters rushed toward him, splashed about his car. The sky sounded like an artillery range. A boulder the size of a tombstone fell in front of him, and he swerved about it. Red lights flashed across the sky from north to south. In their passing, he detected many black bands going from west to east. It was not an encouraging spectacle. The storm could go on for days.

He continued to move forward, skirting a pocket of radiation that had not died in the four years since last he had come this way.

They came upon a place where the sands were fused into a glassy sea, and he slowed as he began its passage, peering ahead after the craters and chasms it contained.

Three more rockfalls assailed him before the heavens split themselves open and revealed a bright blue light edged with violet. The dark curtains rolled back toward the Poles, and the roaring and the gunfire reports diminished. A lavender glow remained in the north, and a green sun dipped toward the horizon.

They had ridden it out. He killed the infras, pushed back his goggles, and switched on the normal night lamps.

The desert would be bad enough, all by itself.

Something big and bat-like swooped through the tunnel of his lights and was gone. He ignored its passage. Five minutes later it made a second pass, this time much closer, and he fired a magnesium flare. A black shape, perhaps forty feet across, was illuminated, and he gave it two five-second bursts from the fifty-calibers, and it fell to the ground and did not return again.

To the squares, this was Damnation Alley. To Hell Tanner, this was still the parking lot. He'd been this way thirty-two times, and so far as he was concerned, the Alley started in the place that was once called Colorado.

He led, and they followed, and the night wore on like an abrasive.

No airplane could make it. Not since the war. None could venture above a couple hundred feet, the place where the winds began. The winds. The mighty winds that circled the globe, tearing off the tops of mountains and sequoia trees, wrecked buildings, gathering up birds, bats, insects, and anything else that moved, up into the dead belt; the winds that swirled about the world, lacing the skies with dark lines of debris, occasionally meeting, merging, clashing, dropping tons of carnage wherever they came together and formed too great a mass. Air transportation was definitely out, to anywhere in the world. For these winds circled, and they never ceased. Not in all the twenty-five years of Tanner's memory had they let up.

Tanner pushed ahead, cutting a diagonal by the green sunset. Dust continued to fall about him, great clouds of it, and the sky was violet, then purple once more. Then the sun went down and the night came on, and the stars were very faint points of light somewhere above it all. After a time the moon rose, and the half-face that it showed that night was the color of a glass of Chianti wine held before a candle.

He lit another cigarette and began to curse, slowly, softly, and without emotion.

They threaded their way amid heaps of rubble: rock, metal, fragments of machinery, the prow of a boat. A snake, as big around as a garbage can and dark green in the cast light, slithered across Tanner's path, and he braked the vehicle as it continued and continued and continued. Perhaps a hundred-twenty feet of snake passed by before Tanner removed his foot from the brake and touched gently upon the gas pedal once again.

Glancing at the left-hand screen, which held an infrared version of the view to the left, it seemed that he saw two eyes glowing within the shadow of a heap of girders and masonry. Tanner kept one hand near the fire-control button and did not move it for a distance of several miles.

There were no windows in the vehicle, only screens which reflected views in every direction, including straight up and the ground beneath the car. Tanner sat within an illuminated box which shielded him against radiation. The "car" that he drove had eight heavily treaded tires and was thirty-two feet in length. It mounted eight fifty-caliber automatic guns and four grenade throwers. It carried thirty armor-piercing rockets which could be discharged straight ahead or at any elevation up to forty degrees from the plane. Each of the four sides, as well as the roof of the vehicle, housed a flame-thrower. Razor-sharp "wings" of tempered steel—eighteen inches wide at their bases and tapering to points, an inch and a quarter thick where they ridged—could be moved through a complete hundred-eighty-degree arc along the sides of the car and parallel to the ground, at a height of two feet and eight inches. When standing at a right angle to the body of the vehicle—eight feet to the rear of the front bumper—they extended out to a distance of six feet on either side of the car. They could be couched like lances for a charge. They could be held but slightly out from the sides for purposes of slashing whatever was sideswiped. The car was bullet-proof, air-conditioned, and had its own food locker and sanitation facilities. A long-barreled .357 Magnum was held by a clip on the door near the driver's left hand. A 30.06, a .45-caliber automatic, and six hand grenades occupied the rack immediately above the front seat.

But Tanner kept his own counsel, in the form of a long, slim SS dagger inside his right boot.

He removed his gloves and wiped his palms on the knees of his denims. The pierced heart that was tattooed on the back of his right hand was red in the light from the dashboard. The knife that went through it was dark blue, and his first name was tattooed in the same color beneath it, one letter on each knuckle, beginning with that at the base of his little finger.

He opened and explored the two near compartments but could find no cigars. So he crushed out his cigarette on the floor and lit another.

The forward screen showed vegetation, and he slowed. He tried using the radio but couldn't tell whether anyone heard him, receiving only static in reply.

He stared ahead and up. He halted once again.

He turned his forward lights up to full intensity and studied the situation.

A heavy wall of thorn bushes stood before him, reaching to a height of perhaps twelve feet. It swept on to his right and off to his left, vanishing out of sight in both directions. How dense, how deep it might be, he could not tell. It had not been there a few years before.

He moved forward slowly and activated the flamethrowers. In the rearview screen, he could see that the other vehicles had halted a hundred yards behind him and dimmed their lights.

He drove till he could go no farther, then pressed the button for the forward flame.

It shot forth, a tongue of fire, licking fifty feet into the bramble. He held it for five seconds and withdrew it. Then he extended it a second time and backed away quickly as the flames caught.

Beginning with a tiny glow, they worked their way upward and spread slowly to the right and the left. Then they grew in size and brightness.

As Tanner backed away, he had to dim his screen, for they'd spread fifty feet before he'd backed more than hundred, and they leaped thirty and forty feet into the air.

The blaze widened, to a hundred feet, two, three… As Tanner backed away, he could see a river of fire flowing off into the distance, and the night was bright about him.

He watched it burn, until it seemed that he looked upon a molten sea. Then he searched the refrigerator, but there was no beer. He opened a soft drink and sipped it while he watched the burning. After about ten minutes the air-conditioner whined and shook itself to life. Hordes of dark, four-footed creatures, the size of rats or cats, fled from the inferno, their coats smoldering. They flowed by. At one point they covered his forward screen, and he could hear the scratching of their claws upon the fenders and the roof.

He switched off the lights and killed the engine, tossed the empty can into the waste box. He pushed the "Recline" button on the side of the seat, leaned back, and closed his eyes.

V

He was awakened by the blowing of horns. It was still night, and the panel clock showed him that he had slept for a little over three hours.

He stretched, sat up, adjusted the seat. The other cars had moved up, and one stood to either side of him. He leaned on his own horn twice and started his engine. He switched on the forward lights and considered the prospect before him as he drew on his gloves.

Smoke still rose from the blackened field, and far off to his right there was a glow, as if the fire still continued somewhere in the distance. They were in the place that had once been known as Nevada.

He rubbed his eyes and scratched his nose, then blew the horn once and engaged the gears.

He moved forward slowly. The burned-out area seemed fairly level, and his tires were thick.

He entered the black field, and his screens were immediately obscured by the rush of ashes and smoke which rose on all sides.

He continued, hearing the tires crunching through the brittle remains. He set his screens at maximum and switched his headlamps up to full brightness.

The vehicles that flanked him dropped back perhaps eighty feet, and he dimmed the screens that reflected the glare of their lights.

He released a flare, and as it hung there, burning, cold, white, and high, he saw a charred plain that swept on to the edges of his eyes' horizon.

He pushed down on the accelerator, and the cars behind him swung far out to the sides to avoid the clouds that he raised. His radio crackled, and he heard a faint voice but could not make out its words.

He blew his horn and rolled ahead even faster. The other vehicles kept pace.

He drove for an hour and a half before he saw the end of the ash and the beginning of clean sand up ahead.

Within five minutes he was moving across desert once more, and he checked his compass and bore slightly to the west. Cars one and three followed, speeding up to match his new pace, and he drove with one hand and ate a corned-beef sandwich.

❖   ❖   ❖

When morning came, many hours later, he took a pill to keep himself alert and listened to the screaming of the wind. The sun rose up like molten silver to his right, and a third of the sky grew amber and was laced with fine lines like cobwebs. The desert was topaz beneath it, and the brown curtain of dust that hung continuously at his back, pierced only by the eight shafts of the other cars' lights, took on a pinkish tone as the sun grew a bright red corona and the shadows fled into the west. He dimmed his lights as he passed an orange cactus shaped like a toadstool and perhaps fifty feet in diameter.

Giant bats fled south, and far ahead he saw a wide waterfall descending from the heavens. It was gone by the time he reached the damp sand of that place, but a dead shark lay to his left, and there was seaweed, seaweed, seaweed, fishes, and driftwood all about.

The sky pinked over from east to west and remained that color. He gulped a bottle of ice water and felt it go into his stomach. He passed more cacti, and a pair of coyotes sat at the base of one and watched him drive by. They seemed to be laughing. Their tongues were very red.

As the sun brightened, he dimmed the screen. He smoked, and he found a button that produced music. He swore at the soft, stringy sounds that filled the cabin, but he didn't turn them off.

He checked the radiation level outside, and it was only a little above normal. The last time he had passed this way it had been considerably higher.

He passed several wrecked vehicles such as his own. He ran across another plain of silicon, and in the middle was a huge crater which he skirted. The pinkness in the sky faded and faded and faded, and a bluish tone came to replace it. The dark lines were still there, and occasionally one widened into a black river as it flowed away into the east. At noon one such river partly eclipsed the sun for a period of eleven minutes. With its departure, there came a brief dust storm, and Tanner turned on the radar and his lights. He knew there was a chasm somewhere ahead, and when he came to it he bore to the left and ran along its edge for close to two miles before it narrowed and vanished. The other vehicles followed, and Tanner took his bearings from the compass once more. The dust had subsided with the brief wind, and even with the screen dimmed Tanner had to don his dark goggles against the glare of reflected sunlight from the faceted field he now negotiated.

He passed towering formations which seemed to be quartz. He had never stopped to investigate them in the past, and he had no desire to do it now. The spectrum danced at their bases, and patches of such light occurred for some distance about them.

Speeding away from the crater, he came again upon sand, clean, brown, white, dun, and red. There were more cacti, and huge dunes lay all about him. The sky continued to change, until finally it was as blue as a baby's eyes. Tanner hummed along with the music for a time, and then he saw the Monster.

It was a Gila, bigger than his car, and it moved in fast. It sprang from out of the sheltering shade of a valley filled with cacti, and it raced toward him, its beaded body bright with many colors beneath the sun, its dark, dark eyes unblinking as it bounded forward on its lizard-fast legs, sable fountains rising behind its upheld tail, which was wide as a sail and pointed like a tent.

He couldn't use the rockets, because it was coming in from the side.

He opened up with his fifty-calibers and spread his "wings" and stamped the accelerator to the floor. As it neared, he sent forth a cloud of fire in its direction. By then, the other cars were firing, too.

It swung its tail and opened and closed its jaws, and its blood came forth and fell upon the ground. Then a rocket struck it. It turned; it leaped.

There came a booming, crunching sound as it fell upon the vehicle identified as car number one and lay there.

Tanner hit the brakes, turned, and headed back.

Car number three came up beside it and parked. Tanner did the same.

He jumped down from the cab and crossed to the Smashed car. He had the rifle in his hands and he put six rounds into the creature's head before he approached the car.

The door had come open, and it hung from a single hinge, the bottom one.

Inside, Tanner could see the two men sprawled, and there was some blood on the dashboard and the seat.

The other two drivers came up beside him and stared within. Then the shorter of the two crawled inside and listened for the heartbeat and the pulse and felt for breathing.

"Mike's dead," he called out, "but Greg's starting to come around."

A wet spot that began at the car's rear end spread and continued to spread, and the smell of gasoline filled the air.

Tanner took out a cigarette, thought better of it, and replaced it in the pack. He could hear the gurgle of the huge gas tanks as they emptied themselves upon the ground.

The man who stood at Tanner's side said, "I never saw anything like it... I've seen pictures, but—I never saw anything like it..."

"I have," said Tanner, and then the other driver emerged from the wreck, partly supporting the man he'd referred to as Greg.

The man called out, "Greg's all right. He just hit his head on the dash."

The man who stood at Tanner's side said, "You can take him, Hell. He can back you up when he's feeling better," and Tanner shrugged and turned his back on the scene and lit a cigarette.

"I don't think you should do—" the man began, and Tanner blew smoke in his face. He turned to regard the two approaching men and saw that Greg was dark-eyed and deeply tanned. Part Indian, possibly. His skin seemed smooth, save for a couple pockmarks beneath his right eye, and his cheekbones were high and his hair very dark. He was as big as Tanner, which was six-two, though not quite so heavy. He was dressed in overalls, and his carriage, now that he had had a few deep breaths of air, became very erect, and he moved with a quick, graceful stride.

"We'll have to bury Mike," the short man said.

"I hate to lose the time," said his companion, "but—" and then Tanner flipped his cigarette and threw himself to the ground as it landed in the pool at the rear of the car.

There was an explosion, flames, then more explosions. Tanner heard the rockets as they tore off toward the east, inscribing dark furrows in the hot afternoon's air. The ammo for the fifty-calibers exploded, and the hand grenades went off, and Tanner burrowed deeper and deeper into the sand, covering his head and blocking his ears against the noise.

As soon as things grew quiet, he grabbed for the rifle. But they were already coming at him, and he saw the muzzle of a pistol. He raised his hands slowly and stood.

"Why the goddamn hell did you do a stupid thing like that?" said the other driver, the man who held the pistol.

Tanner smiled. "Now we don't have to bury him," he said. "Cremation's just as good, and it's already over."

"You could have killed us all if those guns or those rocket launchers had been aimed this way!"

"They weren't. I looked."

"The flying metal could've—Oh...I see. Pick up your damn rifle, buddy, and keep it pointed at the ground. Eject the rounds it's still got in it and put 'em in your pocket."

Tanner did this thing while the other talked.

"You wanted to kill us all, didn't you? Then you could have cut out and gone your way, like you tried to do yesterday. Isn't that right?"

"You said it, mister, not me."

"It's true, though. You don't give a good goddamn if everybody in Boston croaks, do you?"

"My gun's unloaded now," said Tanner.

"Then get back in your bloody buggy and get going! I'll be behind you all the way!"

Tanner walked back toward his car. He heard the others arguing behind him, but he didn't think they'd shoot him. As he was about to climb up into the cab, he saw a shadow out of the corner of his eye and turned quickly.

The man named Greg was standing behind him, tall and quiet as a ghost.

"Want me to drive awhile?" he asked Tanner, without expression.

"No, you rest up. I'm still in good shape. Later on this afternoon, maybe, if you feel up to it."

The man nodded and rounded the cab. He entered from the other side and immediately reclined his chair.

Tanner slammed his door and started the engine. He heard the air conditioner come to life.

"Want to reload this?" he asked. "And put it back on the rack?" and he handed the rifle and the ammo to the other, who had nodded. He drew on his gloves then and said, "There's plenty of soft drinks in the fridge. Nothing much else, though," and the other nodded again. Then he heard car three start and said, "Might as well roll," and he put it into gear and took his foot off the clutch.

VI

After they had driven for about half an hour, the man called Greg said to him, "Is it true what Marlowe said?"

"What's a Marlowe?"

"He's driving the other car. Were you trying to kill us? Do you really want to skip out?"

Hell laughed, then, "That's right," he said. "You named it."

"Why?"

Hell let it hang there for a minute then said, "Why shouldn't I? I'm not anxious to die. I'd like to wait a long time before I try that bit."

Greg said, "If we don't make it, the population of the continent may be cut in half."

"If it's a question of them or me, I'd rather it was them."

"I sometimes wonder how people like you happen."

"The same way as anybody else, mister, and it's fun for a couple people for a while, and then the trouble starts."

"What did they ever do to you, Hell?"

"Nothing. What did they ever do *for* me? Nothing. Nothing. What do I owe them? The same."

"Why'd you stomp your brother back at the hall?"

"Because I didn't want him doing a damn fool thing like this and getting himself killed. Cracked ribs he can get over. Death is a more permanent ailment."

"That's not what I asked you. I mean, what do you care whether he croaks?"

"He's a good kid, that's why. He's got a thing for this chick, though, and he can't see straight right now."

"So what's it to you?"

"Like I said, he's my brother, and he's a good kid. I like him."

"How come?"

"Oh, hell! We've been through a lot together, that's all! What are you trying to do? Psychoanalyze me?"

"I was just curious, that's all."

"So now you know. Talk about something else if you want to talk, okay?"

"Okay. You've been this way before, right?"

"That's right."

"You been any farther east?"

"I've been all the way to the Missus Hip."

"Do you know a way to get across it?"

"I think so. The bridge is still up at Saint Louis."

"Why didn't you go across it the last time you were there?"

"Are you kidding? The thing's packed with cars full of bones. It wasn't worth the trouble to try to clear it."

"Why'd you go that far in the first place?"

"Just to see what it was like. I heard all these stories—and I wanted to take a look."

"What was it like?"

"A lot of crap. Burned down towns, big craters, crazy animals, some people—"

"People? People still live there?"

"If you want to call them that. They're all wild and screwed up.

They wear rags or animal skins, or they go naked. They threw rocks at me till I shot a couple. Then they let me alone."

"How long ago was that?"

"Six—maybe seven years ago. I was just a kid then."

"How come you never told anybody about it?"

"I did. A coupla my friends. Nobody else ever asked me. We were going to go out there and grab off a couple of the girls and bring them back, but everybody chickened out."

"What would you have done with them?"

Tanner shrugged. "I dunno. Screw 'em and sell 'em, I guess."

"You guys used to do that, down on the Barbary Coast—sell people, I mean—didn't you?"

Tanner shrugged again.

"Used to," he said, "before the Big Raid."

"How'd you manage to live through that? I thought they'd cleaned the whole place out?"

"I was doing time," he said. "A.D.W."

"What's that?"

"Assault with a deadly weapon."

"What'd you do after they let you go?"

"I let them rehabilitate me. They got me a job running the mail."

"Oh, yeah, I heard about that. Didn't realize it was you, though. You were supposed to be pretty good—doing all right, and ready for a promotion. Then you kicked your boss around and lost your job. How come?"

"He was always riding me about my record, and about my old gang down on the Coast. Finally, one day I told him to lay off, and he laughed at me, so I hit him with a chain. Knocked out the bastard's front teeth. I'd do it again."

"Too bad."

"I was the best driver he had. It was his loss. Nobody else will make the Albuquerque run, not even today. Not unless they really need the money."

"Did you like the work, though, while you were doing it?"

"Yeah, I like to drive."

"You should probably have asked for a transfer when the guy started bugging you."

"I know. If it was happening today, that's probably what I'd do. I was mad, though, and I used to get mad a lot faster than I do now. I think I'm smarter these days than I was before."

"If you make it on this run and you go home afterward, you'll probably be able to get your job back. Think you'd take it?"

"In the first place," said Tanner, "I don't think we'll make it. And in the second, if we do make it and there's still people around the town, I think I'd rather stay there than go back."

Greg nodded. "Might be smart. You'd be a hero. Nobody'd know much about your record. Somebody'd turn you on to something good."

"The hell with heroes," said Tanner.

"Me, though, I'll go back if we make it."

"Sail 'round Cape Horn?"

"That's right."

"Might be fun. But why go back?"

"I've got an old mother and a mess of brothers and sisters I take care of, and I've got a girl back there."

Tanner brightened the screen as the sky began to darken.

"What's your mother like?"

"Nice old lady. Raised the eight of us. Got arthritis bad now, though."

"What was she like when you were a kid?"

"She used to work during the day, but she cooked our meals and sometimes brought us candy. She made a lot of our clothes. She used to tell us stories, like about how things were before the war. She played games with us, and sometimes she gave us toys."

"How about your old man?" Tanner asked him after a while.

"He drank pretty heavy, and he had a lot of jobs, but he never beat us too much. He was all right. He got run over by a car when I was around twelve."

"And you take care of everybody now?"

"Yeah. I'm the oldest."

"What is it that you do?"

"I've got your old job. I run the mail to Albuquerque."

"Are you kidding?"

"No."

"I'll be damned! Is Gorman still the supervisor?"

"He retired last year, on disability."

"I'll be damned! That's funny. Listen, down in Albuquerque do you ever go to a bar called Pedro's?"

"I've been there."

"Have they still got a little blonde girl plays the piano? Named Margaret?"

"No."

"Oh."

"They've got some guy now. Fat fellow. Wears a big ring on his left hand."

Tanner nodded and downshifted as he began the ascent of a steep hill.

"How's your head now?" he asked when they'd reached the top and started down the opposite slope.

"Feels pretty good. I took a couple of your aspirin with that soda I had."

"Feel up to driving for a while?"

"Sure, I could do that."

"Okay, then." Tanner leaned on the horn and braked the car. "Just follow the compass for a hundred miles or so and wake me up. All right?"

"Okay. Anything special I should watch out for?"

"The snakes. You'll probably see a few. Don't hit them, whatever you do."

"Right."

They changed seats, and Tanner reclined the one, lit a cigarette, smoked half of it, crushed it out, went to sleep.

VII

When Greg awakened him, it was night. Tanner coughed and drank a mouthful of ice water and crawled back to the latrine. When he emerged, he took the driver's seat and checked the mileage and looked at the compass. He corrected their course and, "We'll be in Salt Lake City before morning," he said, "if we're lucky. —Did you run into any trouble?"

"No, it was pretty easy. I saw some snakes, and I let them go by. That was about it."

Tanner grunted and engaged the gears.

"What was that guy's name that brought the news about the plague?" Tanner asked.

"Brady or Brody or something like that," said Greg.

"What was it that killed him? He might have brought the plague to L.A., you know."

Greg shook his head.

"No. His car had been damaged, and he was all broken up, and he'd been exposed to radiation a lot of the way. They burned his body and his car, and anybody who'd been anywhere near him got shots of Haffikine."

"What's that?"

"That's the stuff we're carrying—Haffikine antiserum. It's the only cure for the plague. Since we had a bout of it around twenty years ago, we've kept it on hand and maintained the facilities for making more in a hurry. Boston never did, and now they're hurting."

"Seems kind of silly for the only other nation on the continent—maybe in the world—not to take better care of itself, when they knew we'd had a dose of it."

Greg shrugged. "Probably, but there it is. Did they give you any shots before they released you?"

"Yeah."

"That's what it was, then."

"I wonder where their driver crossed the Missus Hip? He didn't say, did he?"

"He hardly said anything at all. They got most of the story from the letter he carried."

"Must have been one hell of a driver, to run the Alley."

"Yeah. Nobody's ever done it before, have they?"

"Not that I know of."

"I'd like to have met the guy."

"Me too, I guess."

"It's a shame we can't radio across country, like in the old days."

"Why?"

"Then he wouldn't of had to do it, and we could find out along the way whether it's really worth making the run. They might all be dead by now, you know."

"You've got a point there, mister, and in a day or so we'll be to a place where going back will be harder than going ahead."

Tanner adjusted the screen, as dark shapes passed.

"Look at that, will you!"

"I don't see anything."

"Put on your infras."

Greg did this and stared upward at the screen.

Bats. Enormous bats cavorted overhead, swept by in dark clouds.

"There must be hundreds of them, maybe thousands..."

"Guess so. Seems there are more than there used to be when I came this way a few years back. They must be screwing their heads off in Carlsbad."

"We never see them in L.A. Maybe they're pretty much harmless."

"Last time I was up to Salt Lake, I heard talk that a lot of them were rabid. Someday someone's got to go—them or us."

"You're a cheerful guy to ride with, you know?"

Tanner chuckled and lit a cigarette, and, "Why don't you make us some coffee?" he said. "As for the bats, that's something our kids can worry about, if there are any."

Greg filled the coffeepot and plugged it into the dashboard. After a time it began to grumble and hiss.

"What the hell's that?" said Tanner, and he hit the brakes. The other car halted, several yards behind his own, and he turned on his microphone and said, "Car three! What's that look like to you?" and waited.

He watched them: towering, tapered tops that spun between the ground and the sky, wobbling from side to side, sweeping back and forth, about a mile ahead. It seemed there were fourteen or fifteen of the things. Now they stood like pillars, now they danced. They bored into the ground and sucked up yellow dust. There was a haze all about them. The stars were dim or absent above or behind them.

Greg stared ahead and said, "I've heard of whirlwinds, tornadoes—big, spinning things. I've never seen one, but that's the way they were described to me."

And then the radio crackled, and the muffled voice of the man called Marlowe came through: "Giant dust devils," he said. "Big, rotary sandstorms. I think they're sucking stuff up into the dead belt, because I don't see anything coming down—"

"You ever see one before?"

"No, but my partner says he did. He says the best thing might be to shoot our anchoring columns and stay put."

Tanner did not answer immediately. He stared ahead, and the tornadoes seemed to grow larger.

"They're coming this way," he finally said. "I'm not about to park here and be a target. I want to be able to maneuver. I'm going ahead through them."

"I don't think you should."

"Nobody asked you, mister, but if you've got any brains, you'll do the same thing."

"I've got rockets aimed at your tail, Hell."

"You won't fire them—not for a thing like this, where I could be right and you could be wrong—and not with Greg in here, too."

There was silence within the static, then, "Okay, you win, Hell. Go ahead, and we'll watch. If you make it, we'll follow. If you don't, we'll stay put."

"I'll shoot a flare when I get to the other side," Tanner said. "When you see it, you do the same. Okay?"

"Okay."

Tanner broke the connection and looked ahead, studying the great black columns, swollen at their tops. There fell a few layers of light from the storm which they supported, and the air was foggy between the blackness of their revolving trunks. "Here goes," said Tanner, switching his lights as bright as they would beam. "Strap yourself in, boy," and Greg obeyed him as the vehicle crunched forward.

Tanner buckled his own safety belts as they slowly edged ahead.

The columns grew and swayed as he advanced, and he could now hear a rushing, singing sound, as of a chorus of the winds.

He skirted the first by three hundred yards and continued to the left to avoid the one which stood before him and grew and grew. As he got by it, there was another, and he moved farther to the left. Then there was an open sea of perhaps a quarter of a mile leading ahead and toward his right.

He swiftly sped across it and passed between two of the towers that stood like ebony pillars a hundred yards apart. As he passed them, the wheel was almost torn from his grip, and he seemed to inhabit the center of an eternal thunderclap. He swerved to the right then and skirted another, speeding.

Then he saw seven more and cut between two and passed about another. As he did, the one behind him moved rapidly, crossing the path he had taken. He exhaled heavily and turned to the left.

He was surrounded by the final four, and he braked, so that he was thrown forward and the straps cut into his shoulder, as two of the whirlwinds shook violently and moved in terrible spurts of speed. One passed before him, and the front end of his car was raised off the ground.

Then he floored the gas pedal and shot between the final two, and they were all behind him.

He continued on for about a quarter of a mile, turned the car about, mounted a small rise, and parked.

He released the flare.

It hovered, like a dying star, for about half a minute.

He lit a cigarette as he stared back, and he waited.

He finished the cigarette.

Then, "Nothing," he said. "Maybe they couldn't spot it through the storm. Or maybe we couldn't see theirs."

"I hope so," said Greg.

"How long do you want to wait?"

"Let's have that coffee."

❖ ❖ ❖

An hour passed, then two. The pillars began to collapse, until there were only three of the slimmer ones. They moved off toward the east and were gone from sight.

Tanner released another flare, and still there was no response.

"We'd better go back and look for them," said Greg.

"Okay."

And they did.

There was nothing there, though, nothing to indicate the fate of car three.

Dawn occurred in the east before they had finished with their searching, and Tanner turned the car around, checked the compass, and moved north.

"When do you think we'll hit Salt Lake?" Greg asked him, after a long silence.

"Maybe two hours."

"Were you scared, back when you ran those things?"

"No. Afterward, though, I didn't feel so good."

Greg nodded.

"You want me to drive again?"

"No. I won't be able to sleep if I stop now. We'll take in more gas in Salt Lake, and we can get something to eat while a mechanic checks over the car. Then I'll put us on the right road, and you can take over while I sack out."

The sky was purple again, and the black bands had widened. Tanner cursed and drove faster. He fired his ventral flame at two bats who decided to survey the car. They fell back, and he accepted the mug of coffee Greg offered him.

VIII

The sky was as dark as evening when they pulled into Salt Lake City. John Brady—that was his name—had passed that way but days before, and the city was ready for the responding vehicle. Most of its ten thousand inhabitants appeared along the street, and before Hell and Greg had jumped down from the cab after pulling into the first garage they saw, the hood of car number two was opened and three mechanics were peering at the engine.

They abandoned the idea of eating in the little diner across the street. Too many people hit them with questions as soon as they set foot outside the garage. They retreated and sent someone after eggs, bacon and toast.

There was cheering as they rolled forth onto the street and sped away into the east.

"Could have used a beer," said Tanner. "Damn it!"

And they rushed along beside the remains of what had once been U.S. Route 40.

Tanner relinquished the driver's seat and stretched out on the passenger side of the cab. The sky continued to darken above them, taking upon it the appearance it had had in L.A. the day before.

"Maybe we can outrun it," Greg said.

"Hope so."

The blue pulse began in the north, flared into a brilliant aurora. The sky was almost black directly overhead.

"Run!" cried Tanner. "Run! Those are hills up ahead! Maybe we can find an overhang or a cave!"

But it broke upon them before they reached the hills. First came the hail, then the flak. The big stones followed, and the scanner on the right went dead. The sands blasted them, and they rode beneath a celestial waterfall that caused the engine to sputter and cough.

They reached the shelter of the hills, though, and found a place within a rocky valley where the walls jutted steeply forward and broke the main force of the wind/sand/dust/rock/water storm. They sat there as the winds screamed and boomed about them. They smoked and they listened.

"We won't make it," said Greg. "You were right. I thought we had a chance. We don't. Everything's against us, even the weather."

"We've got a chance," said Tanner. "Maybe not a real good one. But we've been lucky so far. Remember that."

Greg spat into the waste container.

"Why the sudden optimism? From you?"

"I was mad before, and shooting off my mouth. Well, I'm still mad—but I got me a feeling now: I feel lucky. That's all."

Greg laughed. "The hell with luck. Look out there," he said.

"I see it," said Tanner. "This buggy is built to take it, and it's doing it. Also, we're only getting about ten percent of its full strength."

"Okay, but what difference does it make? It could last for a couple days."

"So we wait it out."

"Wait too long, and even that ten percent can smash us. Wait too long, and even if it doesn't, there'll be no reason left to go ahead. Try driving, though, and it'll flatten us."

"It'll take me ten or fifteen minutes to fix that scanner. We've got spare 'eyes.' If the storm lasts more than six hours, we'll start out anyway."

"Says who?"

"Me."

"Why? You're the one who was so hot on saving his own neck. How come all of a sudden you're willing to risk it, not to mention mine too?"

Tanner smoked awhile, then said, "I've been thinking," and then he didn't say anything else.

"About what?" Greg asked him.

"Those folks in Boston," Tanner said. "Maybe it is worth it. I don't know. They never did anything for me. But hell, I like action, and I'd hate to see the whole world get dead. I think I'd like to see Boston, too, just to see what it's like. It might even be fun being a hero, just to see what that's like. Don't get me wrong. I don't give a damn about anybody up there. It's just that I don't like the idea of everything being like the Alley here—all burned out and screwed up and full of crap. When we lost the other car back in those tornadoes, it made me start thinking... I'd hate to see everybody go that way—everything. I might still cop out if I get a real good chance, but I'm just telling you how I feel now. That's all."

❖ ❖ ❖

Greg looked away and laughed, a little more heartily than usual.

"I never suspected you contained such philosophic depths."

"Me neither. I'm tired. Tell me about your brothers and sisters, huh?"

"Okay."

❖ ❖ ❖

Four hours later, when the storm slackened and the rocks became dust and the rain fog, Tanner replaced the right scanner and they moved on out, passing later through Rocky Mountain National Park. The dust and the fog combined to limit visibility throughout the day. That evening they skirted the ruin that was Denver, and Tanner took over as they headed toward the place that had once been called Kansas.

He drove all night, and in the morning the sky was clearer than it had been in days. He let Greg snore on and sorted through his thoughts while he sipped his coffee.

❖ ❖ ❖

It was a strange feeling that came over him as he sat there with his pardon in his pocket and his hands on the wheel. The dust fumed at his back. The sky was the color of rosebuds, and the dark trails had shrunk once again. He recalled the stories of the day when the missiles came down, burning everything but the northeast and the southwest; the day when the winds arose and the clouds vanished and the sky had lost its blue; the days when the Panama Canal had been shattered and radios had ceased to function; the days when the planes could no longer fly. He regretted this, for he had always wanted to fly, high, birdlike, swooping and soaring. He felt slightly cold, and the screens now seemed to possess a crystal clarity, like pools of tinted water. Somewhere ahead, far, far ahead lay what might be the only other sizable pocket of humanity that remained on the shoulders of the world. He might be able to save it, if he could reach it in time. He looked about him at the rocks and the sand and the side of a broken garage that had somehow come to occupy the slope of a mountain. It remained within his mind long after he had passed it. Shattered, fallen down, half covered with debris, it took on a stark and monstrous form, like a decaying skull which had once occupied the shoulders of a giant; and he pressed down hard on the accelerator, although it could go no farther. He began to tremble. The sky brightened, but he did not touch the screen controls. Why did he have to be the one? He saw a mass of smoke ahead and to the right. As he drew nearer, he saw that it rose from a mountain which had lost its top and now held a nest of fires in its place. He cut to the left, going miles, many miles, out of the way he had intended. Occasionally the ground shook beneath his wheels. Ashes fell about him, but now the smoldering cone was far to the rear of the right-hand screen. He wondered after the days that had gone before, and the few things that he actually knew about them. If he made it through, he decided he'd learn more about history. He threaded his way through painted canyons and forded a shallow river. Nobody had ever asked him to do anything important before, and he hoped that nobody ever would again. Now, though, he was taken by the feeling that he could do it. He wanted to do it. Damnation Alley lay all about him, burning, fuming, shaking, and if he could not run it, then half the world would die, and the chances would be doubled that one day all the world would be part of the Alley. His tattoo stood stark on his whitened knuckles, saying "Hell," and he knew that it was true. Greg still slept, the sleep of exhaustion, and Tanner narrowed his eyes and chewed his beard and never touched the brake, not even when he saw the rockslide beginning. He made it by and sighed. That pass was closed to him forever, but he had shot through without a scratch. His mind was an expanding bubble, its surfaces like the view-screens, registering everything about him. He felt the flow of the air within the cab and the upward pressure of the pedal upon his foot. His throat seemed dry, but it didn't matter. His eyes felt gooey at their inside corners, but he didn't wipe them. He roared across the pocked plains of Kansas, and he knew now that he had been sucked into the role completely and that he wanted it that way. Damn-his-eyes Denton had been right. It had to be done. He halted when he came to the lip of a chasm and headed north. Thirty miles later it ended, and he turned again to the south. Greg muttered in his sleep. It sounded like a curse. Tanner repeated it softly a couple times and turned toward the east as soon as a level stretch occurred. The sun stood in high heaven, and Tanner felt as though he were drifting bodiless beneath it, above the brown ground flaked with green spikes of growth. He clenched his teeth, and his mind went back to Denny, doubtless now in a hospital. Better than being where the others had gone. He hoped the money he'd told him about was still there. Then he felt the ache begin, in the places between his neck and his shoulders. It spread down into his arms, and he realized how tightly he was gripping the wheel. He blinked and took a deep breath and realized that his eyeballs hurt. He lit a cigarette and it tasted foul, but he kept puffing at it. He drank some water and he dimmed the rearview screen as the sun fell behind him. Then he heard a sound like a distant rumble of thunder and was fully alert once more. He sat up straight and took his foot off the accelerator.

He slowed. He braked and stopped. Then he saw them. He sat there and watched them as they passed, about a half-mile ahead.

A monstrous herd of bison crossed before him. It took the better part of an hour before they had passed. Huge, heavy, dark, heads down, hooves scoring the soil, they ran without slowing, until the thunder was great, and then rolled off toward the north, diminishing, softening, dying, gone. The screen of their dust still hung before him, and he plunged into it, turning on his lights.

He considered taking a pill, decided against it. Greg might be waking soon, and he wanted to be able to get some sleep after they'd switched over.

He came up beside a highway, and its surface looked pretty good, so he crossed onto it and sped ahead. After a time, he passed a faded, sagging sign that said "TOPEKA–110 MILES."

Greg yawned and stretched. He rubbed his eyes with his knuckles and then rubbed his forehead, the right side of which was swollen and dark.

"What time is it?" he asked.

Tanner gestured toward the clock in the dashboard.

"Morning or afternoon?"

"Afternoon."

"My God! I must have slept around fifteen hours!"

"That's about right."

"You been driving all that time?"

"That's right."

"You must be done in. You look like hell. Let me just hit the head. I'll take over in a few minutes."

"Good idea."

Greg crawled toward the rear of the vehicle.

After about five minutes, Tanner came upon the outskirts of a dead town. He drove up the main street, and there were rusted-out hulks of cars all along it. Most of the buildings had fallen in upon themselves, and some of the opened cellars that he saw were filled with scummy water. Skeletons lay about the town square. There were no trees standing above the weeds that grew there. Three telephone poles still stood, one of them leaning and trailing wires like a handful of black spaghetti. Several benches were visible within the weeds beside the cracked sidewalks, and a skeleton lay stretched out upon the second one Tanner passed. He found his way barred by a fallen telephone pole, and he detoured around the block. The next street was somewhat better preserved, but all its storefront windows were broken, and a nude manikin posed fetchingly with her left arm missing from the elbow down. The traffic light at the corner stared blindly as Tanner passed through its intersection.

Tanner heard Greg coming forward as he turned at the next corner.

"I'll take over now," he said.

"I want to get out of this place first," and they both watched in silence for the next fifteen minutes, until the dead town was gone from around them.

Tanner pulled to a halt then and said, "We're a couple hours from a place that used to be called Topeka. Wake me if you run into anything hairy."

"How did it go while I was asleep? Did you have any trouble?"

"No," said Tanner, and he closed his eyes and began to snore.

Greg drove away from the sunset, and he ate three ham sandwiches and drank a quart of milk before Topeka.

IX

Tanner was awakened by the firing of the rockets. He rubbed the sleep from his eyes and stared dumbly ahead for about half a minute.

Like gigantic dried leaves, great clouds fell about them. Bats, bats, bats. The air was filled with bats. Tanner could hear a chittering, squeaking, scratching sound, and the car was buffeted by their heavy, dark bodies.

"Where are we?" he asked.

"Kansas City. The place seems full of them," and Greg released another rocket, which cut a fiery path through the swooping, spinning horde.

"Save the rockets. Use the fire," said Tanner, switching the nearest gun to manual and bringing cross-hairs into focus upon the screen. "Blast 'em in all directions—for five, six seconds—then I'll come in."

The flame shot forth, orange and cream blossoms of combustion. When they folded, Tanner sighted in the screen and squeezed the trigger. He swung the gun, and they fell. Their charred bodies lay all about him, and he added new ones to the smoldering heaps.

"Roll it!" he cried, and the car moved forward, swaying, bat bodies crunching beneath its tires.

Tanner laced the heavens with gunfire, and when they swooped again, he strafed them and fired a flare.

In the sudden magnesium glow from overhead, it seemed that millions of vampire-faced forms were circling, spiraling down toward them.

He switched from gun to gun, and they fell about him like fruit. Then he called out, "Brake, and hit the topside flame!" and Greg did this thing.

"Now the sides! Front and rear next!"

Bodies were burning all about them, heaped as high as the hood, and Greg put the car into low gear when Tanner cried, "Forward!" and they pushed their way through the wall of charred flesh.

Tanner fired another flare.

The bats were still there, but circling higher now. Tanner primed the guns and waited, but they did not attack again in any great number. A few swept about them, and he took potshots at them as they passed.

Ten minutes later he said, "That's the Missouri River to our left. If we just follow alongside it now, we'll hit Saint Louis."

"I know. Do you think it'll be full of bats too?"

"Probably. But if we take our time and arrive with daylight, they shouldn't bother us. Then we can figure a way to get across the Missus Hip."

Then their eyes fell upon the rearview screen, where the dark skyline of Kansas City with bats was silhouetted by pale stars and touched by the light of the bloody moon.

After a time Tanner slept once more. He dreamed he was riding his bike, slowly, down the center of a wide street, and people lined the sidewalks and began to cheer as he passed. They threw confetti, but by the time it reached him it was garbage, wet and stinking. He stepped on the gas then, but his bike slowed even more and now they were screaming at him. They shouted obscenities. They cried out his name, over and over, and again. The Harley began to wobble, but his feet seemed to be glued in place. In a moment, he knew, he would fall. The bike came to a halt then, and he began to topple over toward the right side. They rushed toward him as he fell, and he knew it was just about all over…

He awoke with a jolt and saw the morning spread out before him: a bright coin in the middle of a dark-blue tablecloth, and a row of glasses along the edge.

"That's it," said Greg. "The Missus Hip."

Tanner was suddenly very hungry.

❖   ❖   ❖

After they had refreshed themselves, they sought the bridge.

"I didn't see any of your naked people with spears," said Greg. "Of course, we might have passed their way after dark—if there are any of them still around."

"Good thing, too," said Tanner. "Saved us some ammo."

The bridge came into view, sagging and dark save for the places where the sun gilded its cables, and it stretched unbroken across the bright expanse of water. They moved slowly toward it, threading their way through streets gorged with rubble, detouring when it became completely blocked by the rows of broken machines, fallen walls, sewer-deep abysses in the burst pavement.

It took them two hours to travel half a mile, and it was noon before they reached the foot of the bridge, and, "It looks as if Brady might have crossed here," said Greg, eyeing what appeared to be a cleared passageway amidst the wrecks that filled the span. "How do you think he did it?"

"Maybe he had something with him to hoist them and swing them out over the edge. There are some wrecks below, down where the water is shallow."

"Were they there last time you passed by?"

"I don't know. I wasn't right down there by the bridge. I topped that hill back there," and he gestured at the rearview screen.

"Well, from here it looks like we might be able to make it. Let's roll."

They moved upward and forward onto the bridge and began their slow passage across the mighty Missus Hip. There were times when the bridge creaked beneath them, sighed, groaned, and they felt it move.

The sun began to climb, and still they moved forward, scraping their fenders against the edges of the wrecks, using their wings like plows. They were on the bridge for three hours before its end came into sight through a rift in the junkstacks.

When their wheels finally touched the opposite shore, Greg sat there breathing heavily and then lit a cigarette.

"You want to drive awhile, Hell?"

"Yeah. Let's switch over."

He did, and, "God! I'm bushed!" he said as he sprawled out.

Tanner drove forward through the ruins of East Saint Louis, hurrying to clear the town before nightfall. The radiation level began to mount as he advanced, and the streets were cluttered and broken. He checked the inside of the cab for radioactivity, but it was still clean.

It took him hours, and as the sun fell at his back, he saw the blue aurora begin once more in the north. But the sky stayed clear, filled with its stars, and there were no black lines that he could see. After a long while a rose-colored moon appeared and hung before him. He turned on the music, softly, and glanced at Greg. It didn't seem to bother him, so he let it continue.

The instrument panel caught his eye. The radiation level was still climbing. Then, in the forward screen, he saw the crater, and he stopped.

It must have been over half a mile across, and he couldn't tell its depth.

He fired a flare, and in its light he used the telescopic lenses to examine it to the right and to the left.

The way seemed smoother to the right, and he turned in that direction and began to negotiate it.

The place was hot! So very, very hot! He hurried. And he wondered as he sped, the gauge rising before him: What had it been like on that day, whenever? That day when a tiny sun had lain upon this spot and fought with, and for a time beaten, the brightness of the other in the sky, before it sank slowly into its sudden burrow? He tried to imagine it, succeeded, then tried to put it out of his mind and couldn't. How do you put out the fires that burn forever? He wished that he knew. There'd been so many places to go then, and he liked to move around.

What had it been like in the old days, when a man could just jump on his bike and cut out for a new town whenever he wanted?

And nobody emptying buckets of crap on you from out of the sky? He felt cheated, which was not a new feeling for him, but it made him curse even longer than usual.

He lit a cigarette when he'd finally rounded the crater, and he smiled for the first time in months as the radiation gauge began to fall once more. Before many miles, he saw tall grasses swaying about him, and not too long after that he began to see trees.

Trees short and twisted at first, but the farther he fled from the place of carnage, the taller and straighter they became. They were trees such as he had never seen before—fifty, sixty feet in height—and graceful, and gathering stars, there on the plains of Illinois.

He was moving along a clean, hard, wide road, and just then he wanted to travel it forever—to Floridee, of the swamps and Spanish moss and citrus groves and fine beaches and the Gulf; and up to the cold, rocky Cape, where everything is gray and brown and the waves break below the lighthouses and the salt burns in your nose and there are graveyards where bones have lain for centuries and you can still read the names they bore, chiseled there into the stones above them; down through the nation where they say the grass is blue; then follow the mighty Missus Hip to the place where she spreads and comes and there's the Gulf again, full of little islands where the old boosters stashed their loot; and through the shag-topped mountains he'd heard about: the Smokies, Ozarks, Poconos, Catskills; drive through the forest of Shenandoah; park, and take a boat out over Chesapeake Bay; see the big lakes and the place where the water falls, Niagara. To drive forever along the big road, to see everything, to eat the world. Yes. Maybe it wasn't all Damnation Alley. Some of the legendary places must still be clean, like the countryside about him now. He wanted it with a hunger, with a fire like that which always burned in his loins. He laughed then, just one short, sharp bark, because now it seemed like maybe he could have it.

The music played softly, too sweetly perhaps, and it filled him.

X

By morning he was into the place called Indiana and still following the road. He passed farmhouses which seemed in good repair. There could even be people living in them. He longed to investigate, but he didn't dare stop. Then after an hour, it was all countryside again, and degenerating.

The grasses grew shorter, shriveled, were gone. An occasional twisted tree clung to the bare earth. The radiation level began to rise once more. The signs told him he was nearing Indianapolis, which he guessed was a big city that had received a bomb and was now gone away.

Nor was he mistaken.

He had to detour far to the south to get around it, backtracking to a place called Martinsville in order to cross over the White River. Then as he headed east once more, his radio crackled and came to life. There was a faint voice, repeating, "Unidentified vehicle, halt!" and he switched all the scanners to telescopic range. Far ahead, on a hilltop, he saw a standing man with binoculars and a walkie-talkie. He did not acknowledge receipt of the transmission, but kept driving.

He was hitting forty miles an hour along a halfway decent section of roadway, and he gradually increased his speed to fifty-five, though the protesting of his tires upon the cracked pavement was sufficient to awaken Greg.

Tanner stared ahead, ready for an attack, and the radio kept repeating the order, louder now as he neared the hill, and called upon him to acknowledge the message.

He touched the brake as he rounded a long curve, and he did not reply to Greg's "What's the matter?"

When he saw it there, blocking the way, ready to fire, he acted instantly.

The tank filled the road, and its big gun was pointed directly at him.

As his eye sought for and found passage around it, his right hand slapped the switches that sent three armor-piercing rockets screaming ahead, and his left spun the wheel counterclockwise, and his foot fell heavy on the accelerator.

He was half off the road then, bouncing along the ditch at its side, when the tank discharged one fiery belch, which missed him and then caved in upon itself and blossomed.

There came the sound of rifle fire as he pulled back onto the road on the other side of the tank and sped ahead. Greg launched a grenade to the right and the left and then hit the fifty-calibers. They tore on ahead, and after about a quarter of a mile Tanner picked up his microphone and said, "Sorry about that. My brakes don't work," and hung it up again. There was no response.

As soon as they reached a level plain, commanding a good view in all directions, Tanner halted the vehicle, and Greg moved into the driver's seat.

"Where do you think they got hold of that armor?"

"Who knows?"

"And why stop us?"

"They didn't know what we were carrying, and maybe they just wanted the car."

"Blasting it's a helluva way to get it."

"If they can't have it, why should they let us keep it?"

"You know just how they think, don't you?"

"Yes."

"Have a cigarette."

Tanner nodded, accepted.

"It's been pretty bad, you know?"

"I can't argue with that."

"…And we've still got a long way to go."

"Yeah, so let's get rolling."

"You said before that you didn't think we'd make it."

"I've revised my opinion. Now I think we will."

"After all we've been through?"

"After all we've been through."

"What more do we have to fight with?"

"I don't know yet."

"But, on the other hand, we know everything there is behind us. We know how to avoid a lot of it now."

Tanner nodded.

"You tried to cut out once. Now I don't blame you."

"You getting scared, Greg?"

"I'm no good to my family if I'm dead."

"Then why'd you agree to come along?"

"I didn't know it would be like this. You had better sense, because you had an idea what it would be like."

"I had an idea."

"Nobody can blame us if we fail. After all, we've tried."

"What about all those people in Boston you made me a speech about?"

"They're probably dead by now. The plague isn't a thing that takes its time, you know."

"What about that guy Brady? He died to get us the news."

"He tried, and God knows I respect the attempt. But we've already lost four guys. Now, should we make it six, just to show that everybody tried?"

"Greg, we're a lot closer to Boston than we are to L.A. now. The tanks should have enough fuel in them to get us where we're going, but not to take us back from here."

"We can refuel in Salt Lake."

"I'm not even sure we could make it back to Salt Lake."

"Well, it'll only take a minute to figure it out. For that matter, though, we could take the bikes for the last hundred or so. They use a lot less gas."

"And you're the guy was calling me names. You're the citizen was wondering how people like me happen. You asked me what they ever did to me. I told you, too: Nothing. Now maybe I want to do something for them, just because I feel like it. I've been doing a lot of thinking."

"You ain't supporting any family, Hell. I've got other people to worry about besides myself."

"You've got a nice way of putting things when you want to chicken out. You say, 'I'm not really scared, but I've got my mother and my brothers and sisters to worry about, and I got a chick I'm hot on. That's why I'm backing down. No other reason.'"

"And that's right, too! I don't understand you, Hell! I don't understand you at all! You're the one who put this idea in my head in the first place!"

"So give it back, and let's get moving."

He saw Greg's hand slither toward the gun on the door, so he flipped his cigarette into his face and managed to hit him once, in the stomach—a weak, left-handed blow, but it was the best he could manage from that position.

Then Greg threw himself upon him, and he felt himself borne back into his seat. They wrestled, and Greg's fingers clawed their way up his face toward his eyes.

Tanner got his arms free above the elbows, seized Greg's head, twisted, and shoved with all his strength.

Greg hit the dashboard, went stiff, then went slack.

Tanner banged his head against it twice more, just to be sure he wasn't faking. Then he pushed him away and moved back into the driver's seat. He checked all the screens while he caught his breath. There was nothing menacing approaching.

He fetched cord from the utility chest and bound Greg's hands behind his back. He tied his ankles together and ran a line from them to his wrists. Then he positioned him in the seat, reclined it part way, and tied him in place within it.

He put the car into gear and headed toward Ohio.

Two hours later Greg began to moan, and Tanner turned the music up to drown him out. Landscape had appeared once more: grass and trees, fields of green, orchards of apples, apples still small and green, white farmhouses and brown barns and red barns far removed from the roadway he raced along; rows of corn, green and swaying, brown tassels already visible, and obviously tended by someone; fences of split timber, green hedges, lofty, star-leafed maples, fresh-looking road signs, a green-shingled steeple from which the sound of a bell came forth.

The lines in the sky widened, but the sky itself did not darken, as it usually did before a storm. So he drove on into the afternoon, until he reached the Dayton Abyss.

He looked down into the fog-shrouded canyon that had caused him to halt. He scanned to the left and the right, decided upon the left, and headed north.

Again the radiation level was high. And he hurried, slowing only to skirt the crevices, chasms, and canyons that emanated from that dark, deep center. Thick yellow vapors seeped forth from some of these and filled the air before him. At one point they were all about him, like a clinging, sulfurous cloud, and a breeze came and parted them. Involuntarily, then, he hit the brake, and the car jerked and halted, and Greg moaned once more. He stared at the thing for the few seconds that it was visible, then slowly moved forward once again.

The sight was not duplicated for the whole of his passage, but it did not easily go from out of his mind, and he could not explain it where he had seen it. Yellow, hanging and grinning, he had seen a crucified skeleton there beside the Abyss. *People*, he decided. *That explains everything.*

❖   ❖   ❖

When he left the region of fogs, the sky was still dark. He did not realize for a time that he was in the open once more. It had taken him close to four hours to skirt Dayton, and now as he headed across a blasted heath, going east again, he saw for a moment a tiny piece of the sun, like a sickle, fighting its way ashore on the northern bank of a black river in the sky, and failing.

His lights were turned up to their fullest intensity, and as he realized what might follow, he looked in every direction for shelter.

There was an old barn on a hill, and he raced toward it. One side had caved in, and the doors had fallen down. He edged in, however, and the interior was moist and moldy-looking under his lights. He saw a skeleton, which he guessed to be that of a horse, within a fallen-down stall.

He parked and turned off his lights and waited.

Soon the wailing came once more and drowned out Greg's occasional moans and mutterings. There came another sound, not hard and heavy like gunfire, as that which he had heard in L.A., but gentle, steady, and almost purring.

He cracked the door, to hear it better.

Nothing assailed him, so he stepped down from the cab and walked back a ways. The radiation level was almost normal, so he didn't bother with his protective suit. He walked back toward the fallen doors and looked outside. He wore the pistol behind his belt.

Something gray descended in droplets and the sun fought itself partly free once more.

It was rain, pure and simple. He had never seen rain, pure and simple, before. So he lit a cigarette and watched it fall.

It came down with only an occasional rumbling, and nothing else accompanied it. The sky was still a bluish color beyond the bands of black.

It fell all about him. It ran down the frame to his left. A random gust of wind blew some droplets into his face, and he realized that they were water, nothing more. Puddles formed on the ground outside. He tossed a chunk of wood into one and saw it splash and float. From somewhere high up inside the barn he heard the sound of birds. He smelled the sick-sweet smell of decaying straw. Off in the shadows to his right he saw a rusted threshing machine. Some feathers drifted down about him, and he caught one in his hand and studied it. Light, dark, fluffy, ribbed. He'd never really looked at a feather before. It worked almost like a zipper, the way the individual branches clung to one another. He let it go, and the wind caught it, and it vanished somewhere toward his back. He looked out once more, and back along his trail. He could probably drive through what was coming down now. But he realized just how tired he was. He found a barrel and sat down on it and lit another cigarette.

It had been a good run so far; and he found himself thinking about its last stages. He couldn't trust Greg for a while yet. Not until they were so far that there could be no turning back. Then they'd need each other so badly that he could turn him loose. He hoped he hadn't scrambled his brains completely. He didn't know what more the Alley held. If the storms were less from here on in, however, that would be a big help.

He sat there for a long while, feeling the cold, moist breezes; and the rainfall lessened after a time, and he went back to the car and started it. Greg was still unconscious, he noted, as he backed out. This might not be good.

He took a pill to keep himself alert, and he ate some rations as he drove along. The rain continued to come down, but gently. It fell all the way across Ohio, and the sky remained overcast. He crossed into West Virginia at the place called Parkersburg, and then he veered slightly to the north, going by the old Rand-McNally he'd been furnished. The gray day went away into black night, and he drove on.

There were no more of the dark bats around to trouble him, but he passed several more craters and the radiation gauge rose, and at one point a pack of huge wild dogs pursued him, baying and howling, and they ran along the road and snapped at his tires and barked and yammered and then fell back. There were some tremors beneath his wheels as he passed another mountain that spewed forth bright clouds to his left and made a kind of thunder. Ashes fell, and he drove through them. A flash flood splashed over him, and the engine sputtered and died twice; but he started it again each time and pushed on ahead, the waters lapping about his sides. Then he reached higher, drier ground, and riflemen tried to bar his way. He strafed them and hurled a grenade and drove on by. When the darkness went away and the dim moon came up, dark birds circled him and dived down at him, but he ignored them, and after a time they, too, were gone.

He drove until he felt tired again, and then he ate some more and took another pill. By then he was in Pennsylvania, and he felt that if Greg would only come around he would turn him loose and trust him with the driving.

He halted twice to visit the latrine, and he tugged at the golden band in his pierced left ear, and he blew his nose and scratched himself. Then he ate more rations and continued on.

He began to ache in all his muscles, and he wanted to stop and rest, but he was afraid of the things that might come upon him if he did.

As he drove through another dead town, the rains started again. Not hard, just a drizzly downpour, cold-looking and sterile—a brittle, shiny screen. He stopped in the middle of the road before the thing he'd almost driven into, and he stared at it.

He'd thought at first that it was more black lines in the sky. He'd halted because they'd seemed to appear too suddenly.

It was a spider's web, strands thick as his arm, strung between two leaning buildings.

He switched on his forward flame and began to burn it.

When the fires died, he saw the approaching shape, coming down from above.

It was a spider, larger than himself, rushing to check the disturbance.

He elevated the rocket launchers, took careful aim and pierced it with one white-hot missile.

It still hung there in the trembling web and seemed to be kicking.

He turned on the flame again, for a full ten seconds, and when it subsided, there was an open way before him.

He rushed through, wide awake and alert once again, his pains forgotten. He drove as fast as he could, trying to forget the sight.

Another mountain smoked ahead and to his right, but it did not bloom, and few ashes descended as he passed it.

He made coffee and drank a cup. After a while it was morning and he raced toward it.

XI

He was stuck in the mud, somewhere in eastern Pennsylvania, and cursing. Greg was looking very pale. The sun was nearing mid-heaven. He leaned back and closed his eyes. It was too much.

He slept.

He awoke and felt worse. There was a banging on the side of the car. His hands moved toward fire-control and wing-control automatically, and his eyes sought the screens.

He saw an old man, and there were two younger men with him. They were armed, but they stood right before the left wing, and he knew he could cut them in half in an instant.

He activated the outside speaker and the audio pickup.

"What do you want?" he asked, and his voice crackled forth.

"You okay?" the old man called.

"Not really. You caught me sleeping."

"You stuck?"

"That's about the size of it."

"I got a mule team can maybe get you out. Can't get 'em here before tomorrow morning, though."

"Great!" said Tanner. "I'd appreciate it."

"Where you from?"

"L.A."

"What's that?"

"Los Angeles. West Coast."

There was some murmuring, then, "You're a long way from home, Mister."

"Don't I know it. —Look, if you're serious about those mules, I'd appreciate hell out of it. It's an emergency."

"What kind of?"

"You know about Boston?"

"I know it's there."

"Well, people are dying up that way, of the plague. I've got drugs here can save them, if I can get through."

There were some more murmurs, then, "We'll help you. Boston's pretty important, and we'll get you loose. Want to come back with us?"

"Where? And who are you?"

"The name's Samuel Potter, and these are my sons, Roderick and Caliban. My farm's about six miles off. You're welcome to spend the night."

"It's not that I don't trust you," said Tanner. "It's just that I don't trust anybody, if you know what I mean. I've been shot at too much recently to want to take the chance."

"Well, how about if we put up our guns? You're probably able to shoot us from there, ain't you?"

"That's right."

"So we're taking a chance just standing here. We're willing to help you. We'd stand to lose if the Boston traders stopped coming to Albany. If there's someone else inside with you, he can cover you."

"Wait a minute," said Tanner, and he opened the door and jumped down.

The old man stuck out his hand, and Tanner took it and shook it, also his sons'.

"Is there any kind of doctor around here?" he asked.

"In the settlement—about thirty miles north."

"My partner's hurt. I think he needs a doctor." He gestured back toward the cab.

Sam moved forward and peered within.

"Why's he all trussed up like that?"

"He went off his rocker, and I had to clobber him. I tied him up, to be safe. But now he doesn't look so good."

"Then let's whip up a stretcher and get him onto it. You lock up tight then, and my boys'll bring him back to the house. We'll send someone for the Doc. You don't look so good yourself. Bet you'd like a bath and a shave and a clean bed."

"I don't feel so good," Tanner said. "Let's make that stretcher quick, before we need two."

He sat up on the fender and smoked while the Potter boys cut trees and stripped them. Waves of fatigue washed over him, and he found it hard to keep his eyes open. His feet felt very far away, and his shoulders ached. The cigarette fell from his fingers, and he leaned backward on the hood.

Someone was slapping his leg.

He forced his eyes open and looked down.

"Okay," Potter said. "We cut your partner loose, and we got him on the stretcher. Want to lock up and get moving?"

Tanner nodded and jumped down. He sank almost up to his boot tops when he hit, but he closed the cab and staggered toward the old man in buckskin.

They began walking across country, and after a while it became mechanical.

Samuel Potter kept up a steady line of chatter as he led the way, rifle resting in the crook of his arm. Maybe it was to keep Tanner awake.

"It's not too far, son, and it'll be pretty easy going in just a few minutes now. What'd you say your name was, anyhow?"

"Hell," said Tanner.

"Beg pardon?"

"Hell. Hell's my name. Hell Tanner."

Sam Potter chuckled. "That's a pretty mean name, mister. If it's okay with you, I'll introduce you to my wife and youngest as 'Mr. Tanner.' All right?"

"That's just fine," Tanner gasped, pulling his boots out of the mire with a sucking sound.

"We'd sure miss them Boston traders. I hope you make it in time."

"What is it that they do?"

"They keep shops in Albany, and twice a year they give a fair—spring and fall. They carry all sorts of things we need—needles, thread, pepper, kettles, pans, seed, guns and ammo, all kinds of things—and the fairs are pretty good times, too. Most anybody between here and there would help you along. Hope you make it. We'll get you off to a good start again."

They reached higher, drier ground.

"You mean it's pretty clear sailing after this?"

"Well, no. But I'll help you on the map and tell you what to look out for."

"I got mine with me," said Tanner as they topped a hill, and he saw a farmhouse off in the distance. "That your place?"

"Correct. It ain't much farther now. Real easy walkin'—an' you just lean on my shoulder if you get tired."

"I can make it," said Tanner. "It's just that I had so many of those pills to keep me awake that I'm starting to feel all the sleep I've been missing. I'll be okay."

"You'll get to sleep real soon now. And when you're awake again, we'll go over that map of yours, and you can write in all the places I tell you about."

"Good scene," said Tanner, "good scene," and he put his hand on Sam's shoulder then and staggered along beside him, feeling almost drunk and wishing he were.

After a hazy eternity he saw the house before him, then the door. The door swung open, and he felt himself falling forward, and that was it.

XII

Sleep. Blackness, distant voices, more blackness. Wherever he lay, it was soft, and he turned over onto his other side and went away again.

When everything finally flowed together into a coherent ball and he opened his eyes, there was light streaming in through the window to his right, falling in rectangles upon the patchwork quilt that covered him. He groaned, stretched, rubbed his eyes, and scratched his beard.

He surveyed the room carefully: polished wooden floors with handwoven rugs of blue and red and gray scattered about them, a dresser holding a white enamel basin with a few black spots up near its lip where some of the enamel had chipped away, a mirror on the wall behind him and, above all that, a spindly-looking rocker near the window with a print cushion on its seat, a small table against the other wall with a chair pushed in beneath it, books and paper and pen and ink on the table, a hand-stitched sampler on the wall asking God To Bless, a blue and green print of a waterfall on the other wall.

He sat up, discovered he was naked, looked around for his clothing. It was nowhere in sight.

As he sat there, deciding whether or not to call out, the door opened and Sam walked in. He carried Tanner's clothing, clean and neatly folded, over one arm. In his other hand he carried his boots, and they shone like wet midnight.

"Heard you stirring around," he said. "How you feeling now?"

"A lot better, thanks."

"We've got a bath all drawn. Just have to dump in a couple of buckets of hot, and it's all yours. I'll have the boys carry it in in a minute, and some soap and towels."

Tanner bit his lip, but he didn't want to seem inhospitable to his benefactor, so he nodded and forced a smile then.

"That'll be fine."

"...And there's a razor and a scissors on the dresser—whichever you might want."

He nodded again. Sam set his clothes down on the rocker and his boots on the floor beside it, then left the room.

Soon Roderick and Caliban brought in the tub, spread some sacks and set it upon them.

"How you feeling?" one of them asked. (Tanner wasn't sure which was which. They both seemed graceful as scarecrows, and their mouths were packed full of white teeth.)

"Real good," he said.

"Bet you're hungry," said the other. "You slep' all afternoon yesterday, and all night, and most of this morning."

"You know it," said Tanner. "How's my partner?"

The nearer one shook his head, and, "Still sleeping and sickly," he said. "The Doc should be here soon. Our kid brother went after him last night."

They turned to leave, and the one who had been speaking added, "Soon as you get cleaned up, Ma'll fix you something to eat. Cal and me are going out now to try and get your rig loose. Dad'll tell you about the roads while you eat."

"Thanks."

"Good morning to you."

"'Morning."

They closed the door behind them as they left.

Tanner got up and moved to the mirror, studied himself.

"Well, just this once," he muttered.

Then he washed his face and trimmed his beard and cut his hair.

Then, gritting his teeth, he lowered himself into the tub, soaped up, and scrubbed. The water grew gray and scummy beneath the suds. He splashed out and toweled himself down and dressed.

He was starched and crinkly and smelled faintly of disinfectant. He smiled at his dark-eyed reflection and lit a cigarette. He combed his hair and studied the stranger. "Damn! I'm beautiful!" he chuckled, and then he opened the door and entered the kitchen.

Sam was sitting at the table drinking a cup of coffee, and his wife, who was short and heavy and wore long gray skirts, was facing in the other direction, leaning over the stove. She turned, and he saw that her face was large, with bulging red cheeks that dimpled and a little white scar in the middle of her forehead. Her hair was brown, shot through with gray, and pulled back into a knot. She bobbed her head and smiled a "Good morning" at him.

"'Morning," he replied. "I'm afraid I left kind of a mess in the other room."

"Don't worry about that," said Sam. "Seat yourself, and we'll have you some breakfast in a minute. The boys told you about your friend?"

Tanner nodded.

As she placed a cup of coffee in front of Tanner, Sam said, "Wife's name's Susan."

"How do," she said.

"Hi."

"Now, then, I got your map here. Saw it sticking out of your jacket. That's your gun hanging aside the door, too. Anyhow, I've been figuring, and I think the best way you could head would be up to Albany, and then go along the old Route 9, which is in pretty good shape." He spread the map and pointed as he talked. "Now, it won't be all of a picnic," he said, "but it looks like the cleanest and fastest way in—"

"Breakfast," said his wife, and pushed the map aside to set a plateful of eggs and bacon and sausages in front of Tanner, and another one, holding four pieces of toast, next to it. There was marmalade, jam, jelly, and butter on the table, and Tanner helped himself to it and sipped the coffee and filled the empty places inside while Sam talked.

He told him about the gangs that ran between Boston and Albany on bikes, hijacking anything they could, and that was the reason most cargo went in convoys with shotgun riders aboard. "But you don't have to worry, with that rig of yours, do you?" he asked.

Tanner said, "Hope not," and wolfed down more food. He wondered, though, if they were anything like his old pack, and he hoped not, again, for both their sakes.

Tanner raised his coffee cup, and he heard a sound outside.

The door opened, and a boy ran into the kitchen. Tanner figured him as between ten and twelve years of age. An older man followed him, carrying the traditional black bag.

"We're here! We're here!" cried the boy, and Sam stood and shook hands with the man, so Tanner figured he should, too. He wiped his mouth and gripped the man's hand and said, "My partner sort of went out of his head. He jumped me, and we had a fight. I shoved him, and he banged his head on the dashboard."

The doctor, a dark-haired man, probably in his late forties, wore a dark suit. His face was heavily lined, and his eyes looked tired. He nodded.

Sam said, "I'll take you to him," and he led him out through the door at the other end of the kitchen.

Tanner reseated himself and picked up the last piece of toast. Susan refilled his coffee cup, and he nodded to her.

"My name's Jerry," said the boy, seating himself in his father's abandoned chair. "Is your name, mister, really Hell?"

"Hush, you!" said his mother.

" 'Fraid so," said Tanner.

"...And you drove all the way across the country? Through the Alley?"

"So far."

"What was it like?"

"Mean."

"What all'd you see?"

"Bats as big as this kitchen—some of them even bigger—on the other side of the Missus Hip. Lot of them in Saint Louis."

"What'd you do?"

"Shot 'em. Burned 'em. Drove through 'em."

"What else you see?"

"Gila Monsters. Big, technicolor lizards—the size of a barn. Dust Devils—big circling winds that sucked up one car. Fire-topped mountains. Real big thorn bushes that we had to burn. Drove through some storms. Drove over places where the ground was like glass. Drove along where the ground was shaking. Drove around big craters, all radioactive."

"Wish I could do that someday."

"Maybe you will, someday."

Tanner finished the food and lit a cigarette and sipped the coffee.

"Real good breakfast," he called out. "Best I've eaten in days. Thanks."

Susan smiled, then said, "Jerry, don't go 'an pester the man."

"No bother, missus. He's okay."

"What's that ring on your hand?" said Jerry. "It looks like a snake."

"That's what it is," said Tanner, pulling it off. "It is sterling silver with red-glass eyes, and I got it in a place called Tijuana. Here. You keep it."

"I couldn't take that," said the boy, and he looked at his mother, his eyes asking if he could. She shook her head from left to right, and Tanner saw it and said, "Your folks were good enough to help me out and get a doc for my partner and feed me and give me a place to sleep. I'm sure they won't mind if I want to show my appreciation a little bit and give you this ring." Jerry looked back at his mother, and Tanner nodded, and she nodded too.

Jerry whistled and jumped up and put it on his finger.

"It's too big," he said.

"Here, let me mash it a bit for you. These spiral kind'll fit anybody if you squeeze them a little."

He squeezed the ring and gave it back to the boy to try on. It was still too big, so he squeezed it again, and then it fit.

Jerry put it on and began to run from the room.

"Wait!" his mother said. "What do you say?"

He turned around and said, "Thank you, Hell."

"Mr. Tanner," she said.

"Mr. Tanner," the boy repeated, and the door banged behind him.

"That was good of you," she said.

Tanner shrugged. "He liked it," he said. "Glad I could turn him on with it."

He finished his coffee and his cigarette, and she gave him another cup, and he lit another cigarette. After a time Sam and the doctor came out of the other room, and Tanner began wondering where the family had slept the night before. Susan poured them both coffee, and they seated themselves at the table to drink it.

"Your friend's got a concussion," the doctor said. "I can't really tell how serious his condition is without getting X rays, and there's no way of getting them here. I wouldn't recommend moving him, though."

Tanner said, "For how long?"

"Maybe a few days, maybe a couple weeks. I've left some medication and told Sam what to do for him. Sam says there's a plague in Boston and you've got to hurry. My advice is that you go on without him. Leave him here with the Potters. He'll be taken care of. He can go up to Albany with them for the Spring Fair and make his way to Boston from there on some commercial carrier. He may be all right."

Tanner thought about it awhile, then nodded. "Okay," he said, "if that's the way it's got to be."

"That's what I recommend."

They drank their coffee.

XIII

Tanner regarded his freed vehicle, said, "I guess I'll be going, then," and nodded to the Potters. "Thanks," he said, and he unlocked the cab, climbed into it, and started the engine. He put it into gear, blew the horn twice, and started to move.

In the screen, he saw the three men waving. He stamped the accelerator, and they were gone from sight.

He sped ahead, and the way was easy. The sky was salmon pink. The earth was brown, and there was much green grass. The bright sun caught the day in a silver net.

This part of the country seemed virtually untouched by the chaos that had produced the rest of the Alley. Tanner played music, drove along. He passed two trucks on the road and honked his horn each time. Once he received a reply.

He drove all that day, and it was well into the night when he pulled into Albany. The streets themselves were dark, and only a few lights shone from the buildings. He drew up in front of a flickering red sign that said, "BAR & GRILL," parked, and entered.

It was small, and there was jukebox music playing, tunes he'd never heard before, and the lighting was poor, and there was sawdust on the floor.

He sat down at the bar and pushed the Magnum way down behind his belt so that it didn't show. Then he took off his jacket, because of the heat in the place, and he threw it on the stool next to him. When the man in the white apron approached, he said, "Give me a shot and a beer and a ham sandwich."

The man nodded his bald head and threw a shot glass in front of Tanner, which he then filled. Then he siphoned off a foam-capped mug and hollered over his right shoulder toward a window at his back.

Tanner tossed off the shot and sipped the beer. After a while, a white plate bearing a sandwich appeared on the sill across from him. After a longer while, the bartender passed, picked it up, and deposited it in front of him. He wrote something on a green chit and tucked it under the corner of the plate.

Tanner bit into the sandwich and washed it down with a mouthful of beer. He studied the people about him and decided they made the same noises as people in any other bar he'd ever been in.

The old man to his left looked friendly, so he asked him, "Any news about Boston?"

The man's chin quivered between words, and it seemed a natural thing for him.

"No news at all. Looks like the merchants will close their shops at the end of the week."

"What day is today?"

"Tuesday."

Tanner finished his sandwich and smoked a cigarette while he drank the rest of his beer.

Then he looked at the check, and it said, ".85."

He tossed a dollar bill on top of it and turned to go.

He had taken two steps when the bartender called out, "Wait a minute, mister."

He turned around.

"Yeah?"

"What you trying to pull?"

"What do you mean?"

"What do you call this crap?"

"What crap?"

The man waved Tanner's dollar at him, and he stepped forward and inspected it.

"Nothing wrong I can see. What's giving you a pain?"

"That ain't money. It's nothing."

"You trying to tell me my money's no good?"

"That's what I said. I never seen no bill like that."

"Well, look at it real careful. Read that print down there at the bottom of it."

The room grew quiet. One man got off his stool and walked forward. He held out his hand and said, "Let me see it, Bill."

The bartender passed it to him, and the man's eyes widened.

"This is drawn on the Bank of the Nation of California."

"Well, that's where I'm from," said Tanner.

"I'm sorry, it's no good here," said the bartender.

"It's the best I got," said Tanner.

"Well, nobody'll make good on it around here. You got any Boston money on you?"

"Never been to Boston."

"Then how the hell'd you get here?"

"Drove."

"Don't hand me a line of crap, son. Where'd you steal this?" It was the older man who had spoken.

"You going to take my money or ain't you?" said Tanner.

"I'm not going to take it," said the bartender.

"Then screw you," said Tanner, and he turned and walked toward the door.

As always, under such circumstances, he was alert to sounds at his back.

When he heard the quick footfall, he turned. It was the man who had inspected the bill that stood before him, his right arm extended.

Tanner's right hand held his leather jacket, draped over his right shoulder. He swung it with all his strength, forward and down.

It struck the man on the top of his head, and he fell.

There came up a murmuring, and several people jumped to their feet and moved toward him.

Tanner dragged the gun from his belt and said, "Sorry, folks," and he pointed it, and they stopped.

"Now, you probably ain't about to believe me," he said, "when I tell you that Boston's been hit by the plague, but it's true, all right. Or maybe you will, I don't know. But I don't think you're going to believe that I drove here all the way from the nation of California with a car full of Haffikine antiserum. But that's just as right. You send that bill to the big bank in Boston, and they'll change it for you, all right, and you know it. Now, I've got to be going, and don't anybody try to stop me. If you think I've been handing you a line, you take a look at what I drive away in. That's all I've got to say."

And he backed out the door and covered it while he mounted the cab. Inside, he gunned the engine to life, turned, and roared away.

In the rearview screen he could see the knot of people on the walk before the bar, watching him depart.

He laughed, and the apple-blossom moon hung dead ahead.

XIV

Albany to Boston. A couple of hundred miles. He'd managed the worst of it. The terrors of Damnation Alley lay largely at his back now. Night. It flowed about him. The stars seemed brighter than usual. He'd make it, the night seemed to say.

He passed between hills. The road wasn't too bad. It wound between trees and high grasses. He passed a truck coming in his direction and dimmed his lights as it approached. It did the same.

It must have been around midnight that he came to the crossroads, and the lights suddenly nailed him from two directions.

He was bathed in perhaps thirty beams from the left and as many from the right.

He pushed the accelerator to the floor, and he heard engine after engine coming to life somewhere at his back. And he recognized the sounds.

They were all of them bikes.

They swung onto the road behind him.

He could have opened fire. He could have braked and laid down a cloud of flame. It was obvious that they didn't know what they were chasing. He could have launched grenades. He refrained, however.

It could have been him on the lead bike, he decided, all hot on hijack. He felt a certain sad kinship as his hand hovered above the fire control.

Try to outrun them, first.

His engine was open wide and roaring, but he couldn't take the bikes.

When they began to fire, he knew that he'd have to retaliate. He couldn't risk their hitting a gas tank or blowing out his tires.

Their first few shots had been in the nature of a warning. He couldn't risk another barrage. If only they knew...

The speaker!

He cut it in and mashed the button and spoke: "Listen, cats," he said. "All I got's medicine for the sick citizens in Boston. Let me through or you'll hear the noise."

A shot followed immediately, so he opened fire with the fifty-calibers to the rear.

He saw them fall, but they kept firing. So he launched grenades.

The firing lessened but didn't cease.

So he hit the brakes, then the flamethrowers. He kept it up for fifteen seconds.

There was silence.

When the air cleared, he studied the screens.

They lay all over the road, their bikes upset, their bodies fuming. Several were still seated, and they held rifles and pointed them, and he shot them down.

A few still moved, spasmodically, and he was about to drive on, when he saw one rise and take a few staggering steps and fall again.

His hand hesitated on the gearshift.

It was a girl.

He thought about it for perhaps five seconds, then jumped down from the cab and ran toward her.

As he did, one man raised himself on an elbow and picked up a fallen rifle.

Tanner shot him twice and kept running, pistol in hand.

The girl was crawling toward a man whose face had been shot away. Other bodies twisted about Tanner now, there on the road, in the glare of the tail beacons. Blood and black leather, the sounds of moaning, and the stench of burned flesh were all about him.

When he got to the girl's side, she cursed him softly as he stopped.

None of the blood about her seemed to be her own.

He dragged her to her feet, and her eyes began to fill with tears.

Everyone else was dead or dying, so Tanner picked her up in his arms and carried her back to the car. He reclined the passenger seat and put her into it, moving the weapons into the rear seat, out of her reach.

Then he gunned the engine and moved forward. In the rearview screen he saw two figures rise to their feet, then fall again.

She was a tall girl, with long, uncombed hair the color of dirt. She had a strong chin and a wide mouth, and there were dark circles under her eyes. A single faint line crossed her forehead, and she had all of her teeth. The right side of her face was flushed, as if sunburned. Her left trouser leg was torn and dirty. He guessed that she'd caught the edge of his flame and fallen from her bike.

"You okay?" he asked when her sobbing had diminished to a moist sniffing sound.

"What's it to you?" she said, raising a hand to her cheek.

Tanner shrugged. "Just being friendly."

"You killed most of my gang."

"What would they have done to me?"

"They would have stomped you, mister, if it weren't for this fancy car of yours."

"It ain't really mine," he said. "It belongs to the nation of California."

"This thing don't come from California."

"The hell it don't. I drove it."

She sat up straight then and began rubbing her leg.

Tanner lit a cigarette.

"Give me a cigarette?" she said.

He passed her the one he had lighted, lit himself another. As he handed it to her, her eyes rested on his tattoo.

"What's that?"

"My name."

"Hell?"

"Hell."

"Where'd you get a name like that?"

"From my old man."

They smoked awhile, then she said, "Why'd you run the Alley?"

"Because it was the only way I could get them to turn me loose."

"From where?"

"The place with horizontal venetian blinds. I was doing time."

"They let you go? Why?"

"Because of the big sick. I'm bringing in Haffikine antiserum."

"You're Hell Tanner."

"Huh?"

"Your last name's Tanner, ain't it?"

"That's right. Who told you?"

"I heard about you. Everybody thought you died in the Big Raid."

"They were wrong."

"What was it like?"

"I dunno. I was already wearing a zebra suit. That's why I'm still around."

"Why'd you pick me up?"

"'Cause you're a chick, and cause I didn't want to see you croak."

"Thanks. You got anything to eat in here?"

"Yeah, there's food in there." He pointed to the refrigerator door. "Help yourself."

She did, and as she ate, Tanner asked her, "What do they call you?"

"Corny," she said. "It's short for Cornelia."

"Okay, Corny," he said. "When you're finished eating, you start telling me about the road between here and the place."

She nodded, chewed, and swallowed. Then, "There's lots of other gangs," she said. "So you'd better be ready to blast them."

"I am."

"Those screens show you all directions, huh?"

"That's right."

"Good. The roads are pretty much okay from here on in. There's one big crater you'll come to soon, and a couple little volcanoes afterward."

"Check."

"Outside of them there's nothing to worry about but the Regents and the Devils and the Kings and the Lovers. That's about it."

Tanner nodded. "How big are those clubs?"

"I don't know for sure, but the Kings are the biggest. They've got a coupla hundred."

"What was your club?"

"The Studs."

"What are you going to do now?"

"Whatever you tell me."

"Okay, Corny. I'll let you off anywhere along the way that you want me to. If you don't want, you can come on into the city with me."

"You call it, Hell. Anywhere you want to go, I'll go along."

Her voice was deep and her words came slowly, and her tone sandpapered his eardrums just a bit. She had long legs and heavy thighs beneath the tight denim. Tanner licked his lips and studied the screens. Did he want to keep her around for a while?

The road was suddenly wet. It was covered with hundreds of fishes, and more were falling from the sky. There followed several loud reports from overhead. The blue light began in the north.

Tanner raced on, and suddenly there was water all about him. It fell upon his car, it dimmed his screens. The sky had grown black again, and the banshee wail sounded above him.

He skidded around a sharp curve in the road. He turned up his lights.

The rain ceased, but the wailing continued. He ran for fifteen minutes before it built up into a roar.

The girl stared at the screens and occasionally glanced at Tanner. "What're you going to do?" she finally asked him.

"Outrun it, if I can," he said.
"It's dark for as far ahead as I can see. I don't think you can do it."
"Neither do I, but what does that leave?"
"Hole up someplace."
"If you know where, you show me."
"There's a place a few miles farther ahead—a bridge you can get under."
"Okay, that's for us. Sing out when you see it."

She pulled off her boots and rubbed her feet. He gave her another cigarette.

"Hey, Corny—I just thought—there's a medicine chest over there to your right. Yeah, that's it. it should have some damn kind of salve in it you can smear on your face to take the bite out."

She found a tube of something and rubbed some of it into her cheek, smiled slightly, and replaced it.

"Feel any better?"
"Yes. Thanks."

The stones began to fall, the blue to spread. The sky pulsed, grew brighter.

"I don't like the looks of this one."
"I don't like the looks of any of them."
"It seems there's been an awful lot this past week."
"Yeah. I've heard it said that maybe the winds are dying down—that the sky might be purging itself."
"That'd be nice," said Tanner.
"Then we might be able to see it the way it used to look—blue all the time, and with clouds. You know about clouds?"
"I heard about them."
"White, puffy things that just sort of drift across—sometimes gray. They don't drop anything except rain, and not always that."
"Yeah, I know."
"You ever see any out in L.A.?"
"No."

The yellow streaks began, and the black lines writhed like snakes. The stonefall rattled heavily upon the roof and the hood. More water began to fall, and a fog rose up. Tanner was forced to slow, and then it seemed as if sledgehammers beat upon the car.

"We won't make it," she said.
"The hell you say. This thing's built to take it, and what's that off in the distance?"

"The bridge!" she said, moving forward. "That's it! Pull off the road to the left and go down. That's a dry riverbed beneath."

Then the lightning began to fall. It flamed, flashed about them. They passed a burning tree, and there were still fish in the roadway.

Tanner turned left as he approached the bridge. He slowed to a crawl and made his way over the shoulder and down the slick, muddy grade.

When he hit the damp riverbed, he turned right. He nosed it in under the bridge, and they were all alone there. Some waters trickled past them, and the lightnings continued to flash. The sky was a shifting kaleidoscope and constant came the thunder. He could hear a sound like hail on the bridge above them.

"We're safe," he said, and killed the engine.

"Are the doors locked?"

"They do it automatically."

Tanner turned off the outside lights.

"Wish I could buy you a drink, besides coffee."

"Coffee'd be good."

"Okay, it's on the way," and he cleaned out the pot and filled it and plugged it in.

They sat there and smoked as the storm raged, and he said, "You know, it's a kind of nice feeling being all snug as a rat in a hole while everything goes to hell outside. Listen to that bastard come down! And we couldn't care less."

"I suppose so," she said. "What're you going to do after you make it in to Boston?"

"Oh, I don't know… Maybe get a job, scrape up some loot, and maybe open a bike shop or a garage. Either one'd be nice."

"Sounds good. You going to ride much yourself?"

"You bet. I don't suppose they have any good clubs in town?"

"No. They're all roadrunners."

"Thought so. Maybe I'll organize my own."

He reached out and touched her hand, then squeezed it.

"I can buy *you* a drink."

"What do you mean?"

She drew a plastic flask from the right side pocket of her jacket. She uncapped it and passed it to him.

"Here."

He took a mouthful and gulped it, coughed, took a second, then handed it back.

"Great! You're a woman of unsuspected potential and like that. Thanks."

"Don't mention it," and she took a drink herself and set the flask on the dash.

"Cigarette?"

"Just a minute."

He lit two, passed her one.

"There you are, Corny."

"Thanks. I'd like to help you finish this run."

"How come?"

"I got nothing else to do. My crowd's all gone away, and I've got nobody else to run with now. Also, if you make it, you'll be a big man. Like capital letters. Think you might keep me around after that?"

"Maybe. What are you like?"

"Oh, I'm real nice. I'll even rub your shoulders for you when they're sore."

"They're sore now."

"I thought so. Give me a lean."

He bent toward her, and she began to rub his shoulders. Her hands were quick and strong.

"You do that good, girl."

"Thanks."

He straightened up, leaned back. Then he reached out, took the flask, and had another drink. She took a small sip when he passed it to her.

The furies rode about them, but the bridge above stood the siege. Tanner turned off the lights.

"Let's make it," he said, and he seized her and drew her to him.

She did not resist him, and he found her belt buckle and unfastened it. Then he started on the buttons. After a while he reclined her seat.

"Will you keep me?' she asked him.

"Sure."

"I'll help you. I'll do anything you say to get you through."

"Great."

"After all, if Boston goes, then we go too."

"You bet."

Then they didn't say much more.

There was violence in the skies, and after that came darkness and quiet.

XV

When Tanner awoke, it was morning, and the storm had ceased. He repaired himself to the rear of the vehicle and after that assumed the driver's seat once more.

Cornelia did not awaken as he gunned the engine to life and started up the weed-infested slope of the hillside.

The sky was light once more, and the road was strewn with rubble. Tanner wove along it, heading toward the pale sun, and after a while Cornelia stretched.

"Ungh," she said, and Tanner agreed. "My shoulders are better now," he told her.

"Good," and Tanner headed up a hill, slowing as the day dimmed and one huge black line became the Devil's highway down the middle of the sky.

As he drove through a wooded valley, the rain began to fall. The girl had returned from the rear of the vehicle and was preparing breakfast when Tanner saw the tiny dot on the horizon, switched over to his telescopic lenses, and tried to outrun what he saw.

Cornelia looked up.

There were bikes, bikes, and more bikes on their trail.

"Those your people?" Tanner asked.

"No. You took mine yesterday."

"Too bad," said Tanner, and he pushed the accelerator to the floor and hoped for a storm.

They squealed around a curve and climbed another hill. His pursuers drew nearer. He switched back from telescope to normal screening, but even then he could see the size of the crowd that approached.

"It must be the Kings," she said. "They're the biggest club around."

"Too bad," said Tanner.

"For them or for us?"

"Both."

She smiled. "I'd like to see how you work this thing."

"It looks like you're going to get a chance. They're gaining on us like mad."

The rain lessened, but the fogs grew heavier. Tanner could see their lights, though, over a quarter mile to his rear, and he did not turn his own on. He estimated a hundred to a hundred-fifty pursuers that cold, dark morning, and he asked, "How near are we to Boston?"

"Maybe ninety miles," she told him.

"Too bad they're chasing us instead of coming toward us from the front," he said, as he primed his flames and set an adjustment which brought cross-hairs into focus on his rearview screen.

"What's that?" she asked.

"That's a cross. I'm going to crucify them, lady," and she smiled at this and squeezed his arm.

"Can I help? I hate those bloody mothers."

"In a little while," said Tanner. "In a little while, I'm sure," and he reached into the rear seat and fetched out the six hand grenades and hung them on his wide, black belt. He passed the rifle to the girl. "Hang on to this," he said, and he stuck the .45 behind his belt. "Do you know how to use that thing?"

"Yes," she replied.

"Good."

He kept watching the lights that danced on the screen.

"Why the hell doesn't this storm break?" he said, as the lights came closer and he could make out shapes within the fog.

When they were within a hundred feet, he fired the first grenade. It arced through the gray air, and five seconds later there was a bright flash to his rear, burning within a thunderclap.

The lights immediately behind him remained, and he touched the fifty-calibers, moving the cross-hairs from side to side. The guns stuttered their loud syllables, and he launched another grenade. With the second flash, he began to climb another hill.

"Did you stop them?"

"For a time, maybe. I still see some lights, but they're farther back."

After five minutes, they had reached the top, a place where the fogs were cleared and the dark sky was visible above them. Then they started downward once more, and a wall of stone and shale and dirt rose to their right. Tanner considered it as they descended.

When the road leveled and he decided they had reached the bottom, he turned on his brightest lights and looked for a place where the road's shoulders were wide.

To his rear, there were suddenly rows of descending lights.

He found the place where the road was sufficiently wide, and he skidded through a U-turn until he was facing the shaggy cliff, now to his left, and his pursuers were coming dead on.

He elevated his rockets, fired one, elevated them five degrees more, fired two, elevated them another five degrees, fired three. Then he lowered them fifteen and fired another.

There were brightnesses within the fog, and he heard the stones rattling on the road and felt the vibration as the rockslide began. He swung toward his right as he backed the vehicle and fired two ahead. There was dust mixed with the fog now, and the vibration continued.

He turned and headed forward once more.

"I hope that'll hold 'em," he said, and he lit two cigarettes and passed one to the girl.

After five minutes they were on higher ground again, and the winds came and whipped at the fog, and far to the rear there were still some lights.

As they topped a high rise, his radiation gauge began to register an above-normal reading. He sought in all directions and saw the crater far off ahead. "That's it," he heard her say. "You've got to leave the road there. Bear to the right and go around that way when you get there."

"I'll do that thing."

He heard gunshots from behind him, for the first time that day, and though he adjusted the cross-hairs, he did not fire his own weapons. The distance was still too great.

"You must have cut them in half," she said, staring into the screen. "More than that. They're a tough bunch, though."

"I gather," and he plowed the field of mists and checked his supply of grenades for the launcher and saw that he was running low.

He swung off the road to his right when he began bumping along over fractured concrete. The radiation level was quite high by then. The crater was a thousand yards to his left.

The lights to his rear fanned out, grew brighter. He drew a bead on the brightest and fired. It went out.

"There's another down," he remarked as they raced across the hard-baked plain.

The rains came more heavily, and he sighted on another light and fired. It, too, went out. Now, though, he heard the sounds of their weapons about him once again.

He switched to his right-hand guns and saw the crosshairs leap into life on that screen. As three vehicles moved in to flank him from that direction, he opened up and cut them down. There was more firing on his back, and he ignored it as he negotiated the way.

"I count twenty-seven lights," Cornelia said.

Tanner wove his way across a field of boulders. He lit another cigarette.

Five minutes later, they were running on both sides of him. He had held back again for that moment, to conserve ammunition and to be sure of his targets. He fired then, though, at every light within range, and he floored the accelerator and swerved around rocks.

"Five of them are down," she said, but he was listening to the gunfire.

He launched a grenade to the rear, and when he tried to launch a second, there came only a clicking sound from the control. He launched one to either side and then paused for a second.

"If they get close enough, I'll show them some fire," he said, and they continued on around the crater.

He fired only at individual targets then, when he was certain they were within range. He took two more before he struck the broken roadbed.

"Keep running parallel to it," she told him. "There's a trail here. You can't drive on that stuff till another mile or so."

Shots ricocheted from off his armored sides, and he continued to return the fire. He raced along an alleyway of twisted trees, like those he had seen near other craters, and the mists hung like pennons about their branches. He heard the rattle of the increasing rains.

When he hit the roadway once again, he regarded the lights to his rear and asked, "How many do you count now?"

"It looks like around twenty. How are we doing?"

"I'm just worried about the tires. They can take a lot, but they can be shot out. The only other thing that bothers me is that a stray shot might clip one of the 'eyes.' Outside of that, we're bullet-proof enough. Even if they manage to stop us, they'll have to pry us out."

The bikes drew near once again, and he saw the bright flashes and heard the reports of the riders' guns.

"Hold tight," he said, and he hit the brakes, and they skidded on the wet pavement.

The lights grew suddenly bright, and he unleashed his rear flame. As some bikes skirted him, he cut in the side flames and held them that way.

Then he took his foot off the brake and floored the accelerator without waiting to assess the damage he had done.

They sped ahead, and Tanner heard Cornelia's laughter.

"God! You're taking them, Hell! You're taking the whole damn club!"

"It ain't that much fun," he said. Then, "See any lights?"

She watched for a time, said, "No," then said, "Three," then, "Seven," and finally, "Thirteen.'

Tanner said, "Damn."

The radiation level fell, and there came crashes amid the roaring overhead. A light fall of gravel descended for perhaps half a minute, along with the rain.

"We're running low," he said.

"On what?"

"Everything: luck, fuel, ammo. Maybe you'd have been better off if I'd left you where I found you."

"No," she said. "I'm with you, the whole line."

"Then you're nuts," he said. "I haven't been hurt yet. When I am, it might be a different tune."

"Maybe," she said. "Wait and hear how I sing."

He reached out and squeezed her thigh.

"Okay, Corny. You've been okay so far. Hang on to that piece, and we'll see what happens."

He reached for another cigarette, found the pack empty, cursed. He gestured toward a compartment, and she opened it and got him a fresh pack. She tore it open and lit him one.

"Thanks."

"Why're they staying out of range?"

"Maybe they're just going to pace us. I don't know."

Then the fogs began to lift. By the time Tanner had finished his cigarette, the visibility had improved greatly. He could make out the dark forms crouched atop their bikes, following, following, nothing more.

"If they just want to keep us company, then I don't care," he said. "Let them."

But there came more gunfire after a time, and he heard a tire go. He slowed but continued. He took careful aim and strafed them. Several fell.

More gunshots sounded from behind. Another tire blew, and he hit the brakes and skidded, turning about as he slowed. When he faced them, he shot his anchors, to hold him in place, and he discharged his rockets, one after another, at a level parallel to the road. He opened up with his guns and sprayed them as they veered off and approached him from the sides. Then he opened fire to the left. Then the right.

He emptied the right-hand guns, then switched back to the left. He launched the remaining grenades.

The gunfire died down, except for five sources—three to his left and two to his right—coming from somewhere within the trees that lined the road now. Broken bikes and bodies lay behind him, some still smoldering. The pavement was potted and cracked in many places.

He turned the car and proceeded ahead on six wheels.

"We're out of ammo, Corny," he told her.

"Well, we took an awful lot of them…"

"Yeah."

As he drove on, he saw five bikes move onto the road. They stayed a good distance behind him, but they stayed.

He tried the radio, but there was no response. He hit the brakes and stopped, and the bikes stopped too, staying well to the rear.

"Well, at least they're scared of us. They think we still have teeth."

"We do," she said.

"Yeah, but not the ones they're thinking about."

"Better yet."

"Glad I met you," said Tanner. "I can use an optimist. There must be a pony, huh?"

She nodded; and he put it into gear and started forward abruptly.

The motorcycles moved ahead also, and they maintained a safe distance. Tanner watched them in the screens and cursed them as they followed.

After a while they drew nearer again. Tanner roared on for half an hour, and the remaining five edged closer and closer.

When they drew near enough, they began to fire, rifles resting on their handlebars.

Tanner heard several low ricochets, and then another tire went out.

He stopped once more and the bikes did too, remaining just out of range of his flames. He cursed and ground ahead again. The car wobbled as he drove, listing to the left. A wrecked pickup truck stood smashed against a tree to his right, its hunched driver a skeleton, its windows smashed and tires missing. Half a sun now stood in the heavens, reaching after nine o'clock; fog-ghosts drifted before them, and the dark band in the sky undulated, and more rain fell from it, mixed with dust and small stones and bits of metal. Tanner said, "Good," as the pinging sounds began, and, "Hope it gets a lot worse," and his wish came true as the ground began to shake and the blue light began in the north. There came a booming within the roar, and there were several answering crashes as heaps of rubble appeared to his right. "Hope the next one falls right on our buddies back there," he said.

He saw an orange glow ahead and to his right. It had been there for several minutes, but he had not become conscious of it until just then.

"Volcano," she said when he indicated it. "It means we've got another sixty-five, seventy miles to go."

He could not tell whether any more shooting was occurring. The sounds coming from overhead and around him were sufficient to mask any gunfire, and the fall of gravel upon the car covered any ricocheting rounds. The five headlights to his rear maintained their pace.

"Why don't they give up?" he said. "They're taking a pretty bad beating."

"They're used to it," she replied, "and they're riding for blood, which makes a difference."

Tanner fetched the .357 Magnum from the door clip and passed it to her. "Hang on to this too," he said, and he found a box of ammo in the second compartment and, "Put these in your pocket," he added. He stuffed ammo for the .45 into his own jacket. He adjusted the hand grenades upon his belt.

Then the five headlights behind him suddenly became four, and the others slowed, grew smaller. "Accident, I hope," he remarked.

They sighted the mountain, a jag-topped cone bleeding fires upon the sky. They left the road and swung far to the left, upon a well-marked trail. It took twenty minutes to pass the mountain, and by then he sighted their pursuers once again, four lights to the rear, gaining slowly.

He came upon the road once more and hurried ahead across the shaking ground. The yellow lights moved through the heavens, and heavy, shapeless objects, some several feet across, crashed to the earth about them. The car was buffeted by winds, listed as they moved, would not proceed above forty miles an hour. The radio contained only static.

Tanner rounded a sharp curve, hit the brake, turned off his lights, pulled the pin from a hand grenade, and waited with his hand upon the door.

When the lights appeared in the screen, he flung the door wide, leaped down, and hurled the grenade back through the abrasive rain.

He was into the cab and moving again before he heard the explosion, before the flash occurred upon his screen.

The girl laughed almost hysterically as the car moved ahead.

"You got 'em, Hell! You got 'em!" she cried.

Tanner took a drink from her flask, and she finished its final brown mouthful.

The road grew cracked, pitted, slippery. They topped a high rise and headed downhill. The fogs thickened as they descended.

Lights appeared before him, and he readied the flame. There were no hostilities, however, as he passed a truck headed in the other direction. Within the next half hour he passed two more.

There came more lightning, and fist-sized rocks began to fall. Tanner left the road and sought shelter within a grove of high trees. The sky grew completely black, losing even its blue aurora.

They waited for three hours, but the storm did not let up. One by one, the four view screens went dead, and the fifth showed only the blackness beneath the car. Tanner's last sight in the rearview screen was of a huge splintered tree with a broken, swaying branch that was about ready to fall off. There were several terrific crashes upon the hood, and the car shook with each. The roof above their heads was deeply dented in three places. The lights grew dim, then bright again. The radio would not produce even static anymore.

"I think we've had it," he said.

"Yeah."

"How far are we?"

"Maybe fifty miles away."

"There's still a chance, if we live through this."

"What chance?"

"I've got two bikes in the rear."

They reclined their seats and smoked and waited, and after a while the lights went out.

The storm continued all that day and into the night. They slept within the broken body of the car, and it sheltered them. When the storming ceased, Tanner opened the door and looked outside, closed it again.

"We'll wait till morning," he said, and she held his Hell-printed hand, and they slept.

XVI

In the morning, Tanner walked back through the mud and the fallen branches, the rocks and the dead fish, and he opened the rear compartment and unbolted the bikes. He fueled them and checked them out and wheeled them down the ramp.

He crawled into the back of the cab then and removed the rear seat. Beneath it, in the storage compartment, was the large aluminum chest that was his cargo. It was bolted shut. He lifted it, carried it out to his bike.

"That the stuff?"

He nodded and placed it on the ground.

"I don't know how the stuff is stored, if it's refrigerated in there or what," he said, "but it ain't too heavy that I might not be able to get it on the back of my bike. There's straps in the far-right compartment. Go get 'em and give me a hand—and get me my pardon out of the middle compartment. It's in a big cardboard envelope."

She returned with these things and helped him secure the container on the rear of his bike.

He wrapped extra straps around his left biceps, and they wheeled the machines to the road.

"We'll have to take it kind of slow," he said, and he slung the rifle over his right shoulder, drew on his gloves, and kicked his bike to life.

She did the same with hers, and they moved forward, side by side, along the highway.

After they had been riding for perhaps an hour, two cars passed them, heading west. In the rear seats of both there were children, who pressed their faces to the glass and watched them as they went by. The driver of the second car was in his shirt sleeves, and he wore a black shoulder holster.

The sky was pink, and there were three black lines that looked as if they could be worth worrying about. The sun was a rose-tinted silvery thing, and pale, but Tanner still had to raise his goggles against it.

The cargo was riding securely, and Tanner leaned into the dawn and thought about Boston. There was a light mist on the foot of every hill, and the air was cool and moist. Another car passed them. The road surface began to improve.

❖   ❖   ❖

It was around noontime when he heard the first shot above the thunder of their engines. At first he thought it was a backfire, but it came again, and Corny cried out and swerved off the road and struck a boulder.

Tanner cut to the left, braking, as two more shots rang about him, and he leaned his bike against a tree and threw himself flat. A shot struck near his head, and he could tell the direction from which it had come. He crawled into a ditch and drew off his right glove. He could see his girl lying where she had fallen, and there was blood on her breast. She did not move.

He raised the 30.06 and fired.

The shot was returned, and he moved to his left.

It had come from a hill about two hundred feet away, and he thought he saw the rifle's barrel.

He aimed at it and fired again.

The shot was returned, and he wormed his way farther left. He crawled perhaps fifteen feet, until he reached a pile of rubble he could crouch behind. Then he pulled the pin on a grenade, stood, and hurled it.

He threw himself flat as another shot rang out, and he took another grenade into his hand.

There was a roar and a rumble and a mighty flash, and the junk fell about him as he leaped to his feet and threw the second one, taking better aim this time.

After the second explosion, he ran forward with his rifle in his hands, but it wasn't necessary.

He found only a few small pieces of the man, and none at all of his rifle.

He returned to Cornelia.

She wasn't breathing, and her heart had stopped beating, and he knew what that meant.

He carried her back to the ditch in which he had lain, and he made it deeper by digging, using his hands.

He laid her down in it, and he covered her with the dirt. Then he wheeled her machine over, set the kickstand, and stood it upon the grave. With his knife he scratched on the fender: *Her name was Cornelia and I don't know how old she was or where she came from or what her last name was but she was Hell Tanner's girl and I love her.* Then he went back to his own machine, started it, and drove ahead. Boston was maybe thirty miles away.

XVII

He drove along, and after a time he heard the sound of another bike. A Harley cut onto the road from the dirt path to his left, and he couldn't try running away from it because he couldn't speed with the load he bore. So he allowed himself to be paced.

After a while the rider of the other bike—a tall, thin man with a flaming beard—drew up alongside him, to the left. He smiled and raised his right hand and let it fall and then gestured with his head.

Tanner braked and came to a halt. Redbeard was right beside him when he did. He said, "Where you going, man?"

"Boston."

"What you got in the box?"

"Like, drugs."

"What kind?" and the man's eyebrows arched and the smile came again onto his lips.

"For the plague they got going there."

"Oh. I thought you meant the other kind."

"Sorry."

The man held a pistol in his right hand, and he said, "Get off your bike."

Tanner did this, and the man raised his left hand, and another man came forward from the brush at the side of the road. "Wheel this guy's bike about two hundred yards up the highway," he said, "and park it in the middle. Then take your place."

"What's the bit?" Tanner asked.

The man ignored the question. "Who are you?" he asked.

"Hell's the name," he replied. "Hell Tanner."

"Go to hell."

Tanner shrugged.

"You ain't Hell Tanner."

Tanner drew off his right glove and extended his fist.

"There's my name."

"I don't believe it," said the man after he had studied the tattoo.

Hell shrugged. "Have it your way, citizen."

"Shut up!" and he raised his left hand once more, now that the other man had parked the machine on the road and returned to a place somewhere within the trees to the right.

In response to his gesture, there was movement within the brush.

Bikes were pushed forward by their riders, and they lined the road, twenty or thirty on either side.

"There you are," said the man. "My name's Big Brother."

"Glad to meet you."

"You know what you're going to do, mister?"

"I can guess."

"You're going to walk up to your bike and claim it."

Tanner smiled. "How hard's that going to be?"

"No trouble at all. Just start walking. Give me your rifle first, though."

Big Brother raised his hand again, and one by one the engines came to life.

"Okay," he said. "Now."

"You think I'm crazy, man?"

"No. Start walking. Your rifle."

Tanner unslung it, and he continued the arc. He caught Big Brother beneath his red beard with its butt, and he felt a bullet go into his side. Then he dropped the weapon and hauled forth a grenade, pulled the pin, and tossed it amid the left side of the gauntlet. Before it exploded, he'd pulled the pin on another and thrown it to his right. By then, though, vehicles were moving forward, heading toward him.

He fell upon the rifle and shouldered it in a prone firing position. As he did this, the first explosion occurred. He was firing before the second one went off.

He dropped three of them, then got to his feet and scrambled, firing from the hip.

He made it behind Big Brother's fallen bike and fired from there. Big Brother was still fallen, too. When the rifle was empty, he didn't have time to reload. He fired the .45 four times before a tire chain brought him down.

He awoke to the roaring of the engines. They were circling him. When he got to his feet, a handlebar knocked him down again.

Two bikes were moving about him, and there were many dead people upon the road.

He struggled to rise again, was knocked off his feet.

Big Brother rode one of the bikes, and a guy he hadn't seen rode the other.

He crawled to the right, and there was pain in his fingertips as the tires passed over them.

But he saw a rock and waited till a driver was near. Then he stood again and threw himself upon the man as he passed, the rock he had seized rising and falling, once, in his right hand. He was carried along as this occurred, and as he fell he felt the second bike strike him.

There were terrible pains in his side, and his body felt broken, but he reached out even as this occurred and caught hold of a strut on the side of the bike, and was dragged along by it.

Before he had been dragged ten feet, he had drawn his SS dagger from his boot. He struck upward and felt a thin metal wall give way. Then his hands came loose, and he fell, and he smelled the gasoline. His hand dived into his jacket pocket and came out with the Zippo.

He had struck the tank on the side of Big Brother's bike, and it jetted forth its contents on the road. Thirty feet ahead, Big Brother was turning.

Tanner held the lighter, the lighter with the raised skull of enamel, wings at its back. His thumb spun the wheel, and the sparks leaped forth, then the flame. He tossed it into the stream of gasoline that lay before him, and the flames raced away, tracing a blazing trail upon the concrete.

Big Brother had turned and was bearing down upon him when he saw what had happened. His eyes widened, and his red-framed smile went away.

He tried to leap off his bike, but it was too late.

The exploding gas tank caught him, and he went down with a piece of metal in his head and other pieces elsewhere.

Flames splashed over Tanner, and he beat at them feebly with his hands.

He raised his head above the blazing carnage and let it fall again. He was bloody and weak and so very tired. He saw his own machine, standing still undamaged on the road ahead.

He began crawling toward it.

When he reached it, he threw himself across the saddle and lay there for perhaps ten minutes. He vomited twice, and his pains became a steady pulsing.

After perhaps an hour he mounted the bike and brought it to life.

He rode for half a mile, and then the dizziness and the fatigue hit him.

He pulled off to the side of the road and concealed his bike as best he could. Then he lay down upon the bare earth and slept.

XVIII

When he awoke, he felt dried blood upon his side. His left hand ached and was swollen. All four fingers felt stiff, and it hurt to try to bend them. His head throbbed, and there was a taste of gasoline within his mouth. He was too sore to move for a long while. His beard had been singed, and his right eye was swollen almost shut.

"Corny..." he said, then, "Damn!"

Everything came back, like the contents of a powerful dream suddenly spilled into his consciousness.

He began to shiver, and there were mists all around him. It was very dark, and his legs were cold; the dampness had soaked completely through his denims.

In the distance, he heard a vehicle pass. It sounded like a car.

He managed to roll over, and he rested his head on his forearm. It seemed to be night, but it could be a black day.

As he lay there, his mind went back to his prison cell. It seemed almost a haven now; and he thought of his brother Denny, who must also be hurting at this moment. He wondered if he had any cracked ribs himself. It felt like it. And he thought of the monsters of the southwest and of dark-eyed Greg, who had tried to chicken out. Was he still living? His mind circled back to L.A. and the old Coast, gone, gone forever now, after the Big Raid. Then Corny walked past him, blood upon her breasts, and he chewed his beard and held his eyes shut very tight. They might have made it together in Boston. How far, now?

He got to his knees and crawled until he felt something high and solid. A tree. He sat with his back to it, and his hand sought the crumpled cigarette pack within his jacket. He drew one forth, smoothed it, then remembered that his lighter lay somewhere back on the highway. He sought through his pockets and found a damp matchbook. The third one lit. The chill went out of his bones as he smoked, and a wave of fever swept over him. He coughed as he was unbuttoning his collar, and it seemed that he tasted blood.

His weapons were gone, save for the lump of a single grenade at his belt.

Above him, in the darkness, he heard the roaring. After six puffs, the cigarette slipped from his fingers and sizzled out upon the damp mold. His head fell forward, and there was darkness within.

There might have been a storm. He didn't remember. When he awoke, he was lying on his right side, the tree to his back. A pink afternoon sun shone down upon him, and the mists were blown away. From somewhere he heard the sound of a bird. He managed a curse, then realized how dry his throat was. He was suddenly burned with a terrible thirst.

There was a clear puddle about thirty feet away. He crawled to it and drank his fill. It grew muddy as he did so.

Then he crawled to where his bike lay hidden, and stood beside it. He managed to seat himself upon it, and his hands shook as he lit a cigarette.

❖ ❖ ❖

It must have taken him an hour to reach the roadway, and he was panting heavily by then. His watch had been broken, so he didn't know the hour. The sun was already lowering at his back when he started out. The winds whipped about him, insulating his consciousness within their burning flow. His cargo rode securely behind him. He had visions of someone opening it and finding a batch of broken bottles. He laughed and cursed, alternately.

Several cars passed him, heading in the other direction. He had not seen any heading toward the city. The road was in good condition, and he began to pass buildings that seemed in a good state of repair, though deserted. He did not stop. This time he determined not to stop for anything, unless he was stopped.

The sun fell farther, and the sky dimmed before him. There were two black lines swaying in the heavens. Then he passed a sign that told him he had eighteen miles farther to go. Ten minutes later he switched on his light.

Then he topped a hill and slowed before he began its descent.

There were lights below him and in the distance.

As he rushed forward, the winds brought to him the sound of a single bell, tolling over and over within the gathering dark. He sniffed a remembered thing upon the air: it was the salt tang of the sea.

The sun was hidden behind the hill as he descended, and he rode within the endless shadow. A single star appeared on the far horizon, between the two black belts.

Now there were lights within shadows that he passed, and the buildings moved closer together. He leaned heavily on the handlebars, and the muscles of his shoulders smoldered beneath his jacket. He wished that he had a crash helmet, for he felt increasingly unsteady.

He must be almost there. Where would he head, once he hit the city proper? They had not told him that.

He shook his head to clear it.

The street he drove along was deserted. There were no traffic sounds that he could hear. He blew his horn, and its echoes rolled back upon him.

There was a light on in the building to his left.

He pulled to a stop, crossed the sidewalk, and banged on the door. There was no response from within. He tried the door and found it locked. A telephone would mean he could end his trip right there.

What if they were all dead inside? The thought occurred to him that just about everybody could be dead by now. He decided to break in. He returned to his bike for a screwdriver, then went to work on the door.

He heard the gunshot and the sound of the engine at approximately the same time.

He turned around quickly, his back against the door, the hand grenade in his gloved right fist.

"Hold it!" called out a loudspeaker on the side of the black car that approached. "That shot was a warning! The next one won't be!"

Tanner raised his hands to a level with his ears, his right one turned to conceal the grenade. He stepped forward to the curb beside his bike when the car drew up.

There were two officers in the car, and the one on the passenger side held a .38 pointed at Tanner's middle.

"You're under arrest," he said. "Looting."

Tanner nodded as the man stepped out of the car. The driver came around the front of the vehicle, a pair of handcuffs in his hand.

"Looting," the man with the gun repeated. "You'll pull a real stiff sentence."

"Stick your hands out here, boy," said the second cop, and Tanner handed him the grenade pin.

The man stared at it dumbly for several seconds; then his eyes shot to Tanner's right hand.

"God! He's got a bomb!" said the man with the gun.

Tanner smiled, then, "Shut up and listen!" he said. "Or else shoot me and we'll all go together when we go. I was trying to get to a telephone. That case on the back of my bike is full of Haffikine antiserum. I brought it from L.A."

"You didn't run the Alley on that bike!"

"No, I didn't. My car is dead somewhere between here and Albany, and so are a lot of folks who tried to stop me. Now, you better take that medicine and get it where it's supposed to go in a hurry."

"You on the level, mister?"

"My hand is getting very tired. I am not in good shape." Tanner leaned on his bike. "Here."

He pulled his pardon out of his jacket and handed it to the officer with the handcuffs. "That's my pardon," he said. "It's dated just last week, and you can see it was made out in California."

The officer took the envelope and opened it. He withdrew the paper and studied it. "Looks real," he said. "So Brady made it through…"

"He's dead," Tanner said. "Look, I'm hurtin'. Do something!"

"My God! Hold it tight! Get in the car and sit down! It'll just take a minute to get the case off, and we'll roll. We'll drive to the river, and you can throw it in. Squeeze real hard!"

They unfastened the case and put it in the back of the car. They rolled down the right-front window, and Tanner sat next to it with his arm on the outside.

The siren screamed, and the pain crept up Tanner's arm to his shoulder. It would be very easy to let go.

"Where do you keep your river?" he asked.

"Just a little farther. We'll be there in no time."

"Hurry," Tanner said.

"That's the bridge up ahead. We'll ride out onto it, and you throw it off—as far out as you can."

"Man, I'm tired! I'm not sure I can make it…"

"Hurry, Jerry!"

"I am, damn it! We ain't got wings!"

"I feel kind of dizzy, too…"

They tore out onto the bridge, and the tires screeched as they halted. Tanner opened the door slowly. The driver's had already slammed shut.

He staggered, and they helped him to the railing. He sagged against it when they released him.

"I don't think I—"

Then he straightened, drew back his arm, and hurled the grenade far out over the waters.

He grinned, and the explosion followed, far beneath them, and for a time the waters were troubled.

The two officers sighed. Tanner chuckled.

"I'm really okay," he said. "I just faked it to bug you."

"Why you—!"

Then he collapsed, and they saw the pallor of his face within the beams of their lights.

XIX

The following spring, on the day of its unveiling in Boston Common, when it was discovered that someone had scrawled obscene words on the statue of Hell Tanner, no one thought to ask the logical candidate why he had done it, and the next day it was too late, because he had cut out without leaving a forwarding address. Several cars were reported stolen that day, and one was never seen again in Boston.

So they re-veiled his statue, bigger than life, astride a great bronze Harley, and they cleaned him up for hoped-for posterity. But coming upon the Common, the winds still break about him and the heavens still throw garbage.

A Word from Zelazny

"I intended to write a nice, simple action-adventure story and I had just finished reading Hunter Thompson's *Hell's Angels*."[1]

"I liked 'Damnation Alley' very much. I am very comfortable with the 'man against the elements' sort of theme; I was also very fond of Antoine de St. Exupéry's stories about the early days of airplane traffic: *Wind, Sand and Stars* and *Night Flight*. I thought it would be nice to put something like that into a science-fiction setting, turning something loose against all the forces of nature. At the same time I had been thinking of anti-heroes; I considered using someone who had been sort of trapped into being a hero and reaching a point where he couldn't turn back."[2]

"That was the only time I patterned a character in a book on somebody I really knew. I knew a fellow when I was in the service in basic training who had been in a motorcycle gang. Later, when I was reading about Hell's Angels, it occurred to me that I did have some background just from talking to this man all that time, and it might make a nice story."[3]

"I wanted to do a straight, style-be-damned action story with the pieces fall wherever. Movement and menace. Splash and color is all.

"A continuing small thought as to how important it really is whether a good man does something for noble reasons or a man less ethically endowed does a good thing for the wrong reasons.

"Had the Noh play buried near the end of the book-length version been written first, I would probably not have written the book.

"I like 'Damnation Alley' for the overall subjection of everything in it to a Stanislavsky-Boleslavsky action verb key, 'to get to Boston.' I dislike it for the same reason."[4]

"At my agent's suggestion, I later expanded it to book length. I like this version [reproduced here] better than the book. But if there hadn't been a book there probably wouldn't have been a movie sale. On the other hand, I was not overjoyed with the film. On the other hand, no one has had to sit up in the middle of the night to read the story…"

Zelazny was blunt about the movie: "No! No one liked that movie."[3] He had no role in the production: "they bought [the story] and could do what they wanted with it."[3] "Obviously, I had nothing to do with the production. I had read an early script and it was actually quite good. I thought that was the script they were going to shoot from. Initially the script was done by Lukas Heller…he did the script that I read and liked. The studio wasn't

---

1 *The Last Defender of Camelot*, 1980.
2 *If,* January 1969.
3 *Media Sight* Vol 3 No 1 Summer 1984.
4 *Vector* May-June 1973 (#65), pp. 42–44.

completely happy about it, though, and they gave it to another writer [Alan Sharp]. It got revised beyond recognition from my standpoint."[5] "All that remains of my story is the title and some of the special effects. Everything else, I disavow—except I took their money and I'd do it again."[6]

Notes

Missus Hip is the Mississippi River. **Excelsior** is wood shavings used for packing. A **Gila Monster** is a venomous lizard with black and orange or red stripes found in arid regions of Southwest United States and Western Mexico. **Chianti** is an Italian red wine. The **SS dagger** was produced for the German SS between 1939 and 1942; it had a black wooden grip and bore engravings of swastikas and the SS logo. Dr. Waldemar Mordecai **Haffkine** developed the plague vaccine while working in Bombay in 1897, and the Haffkine Institute was established in 1899 to continue research into vaccines. Zelazny altered the spelling slightly to Haffikine. **Carlsbad Cavern** is a sanctuary for over a million Mexican Freetail bats. **Caliban** is a character in William Shakespeare's *The Tempest,* a deformed monster who is the slave of the wizard Prospero. **"I can use an optimistic. There must be a pony, huh?"** refers to an old joke: a psychiatrist tries to treat a child suffering from extreme optimism by taking him to a room piled high with manure. Instead of dampening his outlook, the child is delighted, digging bare-handed into the manure saying "There must be a pony in here somewhere!" The number of sections in this novella may hold significance; in numerology (which Zelazny had studied), the number 19 means inherence or a person's innate properties.

---

5 *Future Life #25*, March 1981.
6 *Oklahoma City Times*, November 20, 1977, p 27.

The Last Inn on the Road

with Dannie Plachta
New Worlds #176, October 1967.

Father Bob flicked a quick Sign of the Cross with the point of his switchblade and dropped into a crouch. He stared up the alleyway, his leather jacket tight across his shoulders. There was a faint flash of metal not more than six feet away.

"Who is it?" he demanded.

A fleet of motorcycles crackled down the adjacent street. He waited for their lights to outline his adversary.

But the bikes belonged to the Red Holy Rollers from Saint Bob's, and they always rode blacked-out.

"Who is it?" he asked again, after the silence had returned.

"Sister Cameo. That *is* you, Father?"

"Blessed be the Holy Name of Jesus," he intoned, snapping his blade closed.

"Blessed be the Holy Name," she agreed, and another blade snicked shut within the darkness.

"Praise be that I got here when I did, Sister. That sounded like the Rollers going by."

"I'd say so, Father. Full strength."

She touched the priest's arm.

"But come. It isn't far."

"Just to be on the safe side, Sister, we'd better spread some broken glass. You get the far end of the alley and I'll get this one."

He moved toward the nearer street.

"It's in the center of the block," she whispered, before they parted.

Father Bob spent five minutes smashing empty beer bottles on the rough pavement. All the street lights had been shot out. In fact, Father Bob had never seen a lighted one. Nevertheless, there was a certain amount of light tumbling from a large neon sign: BUY OUR JUNK, it urged. Below it, smaller letters spelled out the familiar slogan: ACID, HORSE, SEEDS, AND LI. TAKE TEA AND SEE.

He was about to return to the safety of the alley and its darkness when he noticed the dog. Its long dark tail rippled in the wind as it trotted toward him. Small, yet for some strange reason unafraid, it came up to him. Its tongue hung out over its side teeth as though it were laughing, and its ears were long and ragged. He patted its head and was vaguely pleased when it followed him back up the alley.

"This is it, Father," whispered the nun when they met again. "We're home."

Rusted hinges grated, and Father Bob felt her hand on his arm.

"Don't fall over anything, Bob. It's a mess in here."

He heard the dog patter in after them. The ancient door creaked again and clicked at their backs.

"It's an old garage," she told him. "The house in front is completely wrecked. I covered our only window with tar paper."

Then she rummaged for a dark moment and a match scratched, flashing yellow pain into his eyes. "Make yourself at home."

It was, he observed after a moment, a compact indoor junkyard, an attic and cellar that had somehow gotten together for money, not love.

"A wreck room," he muttered, and the girl giggled.

She lit a votive candle and the room was drenched in the bloodlight of its glass container. Twisted shadows from a hundred shipwrecked homes filled the walls, the floor, the ceiling.

"I think we'd best put it out as soon as we're settled," she suggested. Her black leather jacket and stretch pants became a reddish bronze in the candlelight, and he glanced furtively at his own clothing. The dog nipped at Sister Cameo's boots. "Here," she said, lifting it in her arms, "I think I can fix you up for the night." She found an empty beer case, removed the partitions, and placed the dog gently within it. "…but I won't have you sleeping on any of these dirty rags!"

There was a slight movement in the corner of the garage, and two cats glided forth to peer in at the dog. They leaned and watched without moving. "One happy family," smiled the priest, and the man and the woman knelt on the cold concrete, joining together in prayer.

Sister Cameo extinguished her candle, and they went to bed, the dog making faint noises, half-snore, half-growl, behind them.

❖ ❖ ❖

They looked like stars and they were among the stars. They moved with seeming slowness, yet somehow they passed quickly.

"We are near," said Amar.

"The star guides us well," replied Borin.

"Still, we shan't arrive in time," said Calat.

The three points of light arced across another hundred parsecs.

"Perhaps. Perhaps not. But it's our only chance to see," said Amar.

"Their star nears the apex," observed Borin.

"We cannot stay long," Calat noted.

The three points crossed another dark gap.

❖ ❖ ❖

Right there on Saint Bob's parking lot, in the middle, the Red Holy Rollers parked their bikes. They parked them and they slept there, resting their heads upon the polished chrome of the handlebars. None of them were really tired, having slept most of the day. But they were a legend around town. They slept on their bikes, it was told. So don't kill a good thing. They stayed in the lot until eleven o'clock, passed another ten minutes debating where to go. Finally, they roared off to the Junk Yard, three blocks away...

The place was spinning when they hit it. They knew it would be, and it revved up when they moved into action. The in-drink that night was Old Krupnik on the rocks, for God's sake, and they uncorked it, learned to live with it.

Some old broad in a topless ski suit swivelled it over and asked would anyone care to move around the floor, so Tiny Tim the Big Man called her hand, took it, yanked her into service. They swung to the strings twisted and the skins thumping; the Molesters' "Old Rugged Cross Writhe" it was, and everybody did, making with the outstretched arms bit. But Tiny Tim, he got a thumb in the right eye and that was it for indoor exercise.

After the debacle that ensued, they were all of them about seven handlebars to the wind when it fell upon them like damn let's go Of-the-Cloth hunting. Real big this went, up and over like a pregnant pole-vaulter, and...

They cut at 11:47. One more round of Old Krupdammitnik...

❖   ❖   ❖

Crawling in the deep shadows, darkness all about them, yet able to see, the three moved down the alien roadway.

"A strange world…" said Amar.

"Like no other," Borin agreed.

"Perhaps it will be for the best"—Calat.

They skittered and churned, boffed and scaffonted, then paused.

"I am weary of my burden"—Amar.

"There is so little time…"—Borin.

"The stars! I fear we must miss our chance to see!"—Calat.

"Yes! We must leave our prizes! Make haste!"—Borin.

They moved on, up, out, their tears falling upon the stones.

❖   ❖   ❖

Father Bob was awakened by a creaking noise. He listened, tense, motionless, to the sound of the dog's breathing. Could someone have entered the garage without awakening the animal? Regretting the sound, he snapped open his switchblade.

"Father. It's me."

"What're you doing, Sister?"

"I heard a noise outside. I waited awhile before checking."

"Someone prowling?"

"I don't really know, but when I went out I stumbled over…these."

She lit a match, spreading the flame to the candle.

He inspected the three items in the ruddy light.

"Very strange," he admitted. "Perhaps we overlooked them when we entered."

"Perhaps," she said.

The priest held one of the objects near the candle.

"It's a concave disk, with little projections all over…Beautiful!" he decided, "whatever it is."

"Here's a metal box, covered with some kind of spongy stuff," said the man.

The last item was a wire band with an attached oval of what seemed a shiny plastic substance. Impulsively, she took the band and gently forced it over the head of the awakened puppy, who had been sniffing at it.

"Pretty doggie…" she said, fondling its ears.

"Let the little fellow sleep on the spongy thing," said the priest, and the girl lifted the dog as Father Bob placed the makeshift cushion in the beer case.

"I took a bottle of milk tonight, God forgive me," said the nun, her blush invisible in the red light. "We can put some in this odd dish for the dog and the cats and drink the rest ourselves. I was saving it for breakfast. What is that smell?"

The dog came out of the beer case again, to splash with his pink tongue at the milk as she poured it. The cats only sat and watched. Their tongues smoothed their whiskers, but they did not draw near.

As Sister Cameo was about to place the dog back in the box, both garage doors banged open. She reached for her switchblade and cried out.

Father Bob froze, his right hand at his belt, as an empty beer bottle struck against his forehead. He swayed for a moment, then fell back against an old washing machine. Slashing furiously, the nun went down with a length of chain around her thighs.

"I'm cut!" roared Tiny Tim. "Thirty-eight years a Roller and never a scratch! Now I get it from a broad!" His sobs were inaudible above the screams when they nailed the nun and the priest to the garage doors. "It was the glass at the end of the alley tipped us off!" he taunted them, feeling better for it.

The old men stayed to hear the screaming and whimpering for the minute or two that it lasted. Then they stamped out and returned to their bikes, parked up the block.

The dog looked at the unconscious figures on the doors. He licked his paws in the bloody candlelight. He sniffed at the overturned dish. The plastic and metal jangled together below his neck, and he paused to glance back into the mangled beer case. There was a strange smell about the place...

A vague curtain of colored light forming in the midnight sky shifted, was gone, before the dog entered the shadows of the alley. Briefly then, he paused, but only to aim a single, short howl at the moon before it vanished behind a cloud; and then he passed the darting neon, going up the street, off the street, by the street and into the night beyond, his gift a choking collar around his puppy throat.

Notes

This violent, post-apocalyptic Nativity scene precedes Zelazny's collaboration with Philip K. Dick on *Deus Irae* and may have influenced that novel. This is one of two collaborations with Dannie Plachta, to whom *Lord of Light* is dedicated. Plachta (listed as Danny in other sources) published about a dozen short stories in science fiction magazines between 1965 and 1970, but there is little other information available about him.

A **cameo** is a bit part in a drama played by a distinguished actor or celebrity; it is also a medallion with a person's profile cut in raised relief. A **votive** candle is lit in prayer. The names of the **three** wise men in this story do not correspond to the names of the Magi in the Bible. **Krupnik** is a sweet vodka made in Lithuania.

Chorus Mysticus

To Spin Is Miracle Cat, Underwood-Miller 1981.
Written 1955–60 for *Chisel in the Sky*.

Beginning with a snort and ending with a sigh,
time cannot raze nor confusion alter
this monument we rear against the gods.

Notes

The **Chorus** in ancient Greek tragedy was a group of performers who commented on the main action. **Mysticus** implies a deity or the absolute.

A Hand Across the Galaxy

Arioch! #1, November 1967.

Dear Earth Parents,

    I do not know how to tell you of my joy that you continue to know my needs and that you have the Interstellar Foster Parents Foundation (A Hand Across the Galaxy) to send me packages every month. It is very kind of you, who have never seen me, and I am thankful of you. You treated me to a box of Sweet-o-Crax this month also; which must have cost you dearly; for this I am too thankful. Let me tell you of my place that you may share of the joy you have caused to happen here. My brother-mates and my sister-mates, there are seven, but three are nestlings and me who cannot work yet, leaving four. Of the four, my old sister-mate is with eggs and cannot work until the rains and she nests them. What a fine blessing, though. My two brother-mates work in the Earthshop where the big machines bang metal into pieces of things, and they have joy of their work sweeping the chips and wiping with oil the metal and putting it into place under the banger. My older brother-mate's hand is grown back now, although it is not so big as the other one was, but he can use it like the other one only not so strong. We opened your box with piety and excitement and found the warm thror-sox and gleepers you were so thoughtful to think of, and we found the schoolbooks, for me now, but the nestlings will use them later, and we found the tackers and the tickets for food at the Earthstore, which we got and are just finished eating some of now. We were thankful and joyous, and we read of the Earth in the books and we decided it is like the Happy Lands where the Great One sends those who are good after their bodies have been burned. Is it not so? Please write if you ever have the time to tell us about it; and yourselves also; if you ever have time; for we are curious and humility; and we would be joyed to hear of the big trees and the highways they grow with, and your sunsets and big buildings and the sky that is blue. I read many times your card of three packages ago, where you said Having a wonderful time. Wish you were here. It was so kind of you to think of me then and indeed you must have been having a wonderful time with all those glorious roulette wheels it showed in the picture and named on the back, to play with. I still do not know what a roulette wheel is for certain, because they are not in my *Abridged Galactic English Dictionary*. It looks like part of a game though. Perhaps you will tell me of them too when you write? I do not understand your answer to my letter of two packages ago when you said you spill more in one night than you send me in a year. Do you use a liquid currency on Earth now? I thought dollars were of paper and I do not understand. Perhaps you would explain this also sometime? It is a very dry and hot afternoon outside and I must go to the well now, so it will be dark when I come back and I will finish your letter tomorrow. Goodbye for a while Earth parents.

Now I will tell you more of the joy you have caused. Since our father-mate was burned it has been very hard to keep warm the nest at night. Now we have got the fuel tickets you send so that almost every night we have warmth. My sister-mate with eggs sleeps closest to the heat place, except for my mother-mate, who is always cold and shaking with the new sickness that came at about the time your people arrived out of the sky. It is hard to think of all that space out there separating worlds without getting dizzy. There are no high places near here, so I get dizzy even thinking about them. To think that the Great One could build worlds so far apart and watch them all and not get dizzy is dearly good.

I am pleased to learn that your party was good and that my last letter caused your dear friends the joy of laughter. This is the longest letter I have ever written and I hope it also joys you. You are so kind.

Your foster child,
Phaun Ligg

Dear Phaun,

Your letters are priceless. My husband and I treasure them dearly. We are not too well just now, ourselves, but we will write you a long letter quite soon—just as soon as we are a bit more organized. It *has* been a very trying week, so you must forgive us this time. All right? Also, you must excuse my husband's cryptic allusions. He is fond of riddles. Give our best wishes to your mother-mate and your brother-mate & sister-mates. We are thinking of you.

Affectionately,
Edith Mason

P. S. Keep 'em coming, kid. They're a riot.

Foster father-mate,
Sam Mason

A Word from Zelazny

"I recall an occasion when I was in a nasty mood and simply sat down and began writing to see what would come of it. It turned out to be a short mood; something happened to break it. Ergo, the piece came to a halt, destined to remain brief. It's hardly even a story. Just a couple of letters. I sent it to a fanzine, where it duly appeared, and then I forgot about it. Subsequently, I was privileged to do a book in collaboration with the late Philip K. Dick—having long admired his ability to run reality through a wringer, a paper shredder and a high-speed blender in rapid succession, and then to reassemble the results into things rare and strange. I was very surprised when he mentioned this little fanzine piece favorably. That he had seen it, remembered it and liked it made me want to unearth it recently. He often saw things I didn't. Usually, even."[1]

---

1 *Unicorn Variations*, 1983.

A Word from Philip K. Dick

Dick had raved about the story. "I have read it several times—it was called to my attention by someone who felt that I ought to (and others ought to) read it, and read it very carefully. I do not believe there is a finer piece of prose in the English language, unless perhaps it is *A Passage to India,* which, in a broad sense, deals with the same theme. It is pointless for me to say that I myself could never have written something so good, so touching...pointless because I suppose no one but you could; it is a unique piece, really. This line: *I have read many times your card of three packages ago, where you said Having a wonderful time, wish you were here.* And, previous to this, *...and we read of the Earth in the books and we decided it is like the Happy Lands where the Great One sends those who are good after their bodies have been burned. Is it not so?* Here is an ignorant, plaintive, meek creature thanking and hoping, and touchingly unaware of the low esteem in which his foster parents place him. *Your letters are priceless,* his foster mother says, and then there is the final comment by the foster father. How could you achieve so much in so few words? It's all there; it's totally heartbreaking. It is so unfair, and you have such an inspired sense of this unfairness, and the ability to get it down in the form of words. *You are so kind,* he writes. Utter and final irony, and it makes tears come to my eyes. It's as if in this piece you have laid bare the basic unfairness of the universe itself; it has almost a mystical power and depth. I wish to God there was some way I could help get it printed in a prozine; it ought to be read in every college English class in the country."[2]

---

2 Letter from Philip K. Dick to Roger Zelazny dated December 2, 1967.

The Insider

Written in 1967 as by Phillip H. Sexart; previously unpublished.

Take Cthulhu for an example. His angle was a bit different from my own, in that he influenced one sensitive writer and several others, who managed to make lots of people think of him to the extent wherein their thoughts nourished him then and sustain him yet.

Periodically, when his authors—or, more correctly, his authors' works—undergo a revival, it is that much in the way of gravy for him, since my kind feeds upon the emanations of thought turned in our direction.

For a long while, Cthulhu and his Circle had been a bit obnoxious concerning the entire *coup*. He and Nyarlathotep, Yaddith, Azathoth, Yog-Sothoth and others of that crowd had been enjoying their renewed vitality and mocking the rest of us, sitting and gibbering much more actively than ourselves in their Pools of Ultimate Foulness.

I decided to strike back. First, I determined to essay the same avenue Cthulhu had employed, but I just couldn't find another Lovecraft. I looked in Greenwich Village, Prague, Budapest, Paris, Alexandria, Hong Kong, Hackensack. No luck. All the dark geniuses were writing sex novels or verses for greeting cards, neither of which would serve as the proper vehicle for what I had in mind.

Cthulhu heard what I was up to and gibbered at me obscenely, which only made me madder and more determined. I wanted to be able to sit in my own Pool of Filth, and maybe invite a few friends to drop in and have some good times, too. Nyarlathotep razzed me about it. Yog-Sothoth turned his baleful gazes upon me and slobbered, amused.

Then I found what I was looking for.

I heard them one day (while wandering in my astral form) on a curious contrivance which purveyed sounds, over and over again, by means of a black, grooved disc which was situated upon a circular, revolving platform, a diamond-tipped needle tracing a spiral path along its grooves and transmitting its subtle vibrations to an amplifying unit which, in turn, agitated the ether to the extent that it reproduced previous utterances.

I listened carefully to the half-intelligible noises.

This, I knew, was to be *my* modus.

I traced the things back to their origins.

...A shipment of the darkling discs was delivered to the merchant's.

I followed the deliverer back to an eldritch storing-house and waited...

...After a time, a shipment was received in that dank place.

I followed the deliverer back to a grim factory and observed the process of their manufacture from a talisman known as a "master"...

...When a new "master" came in, I followed its deliverer back to a "studio."

I witnessed many rock and roll recording sessions, deriving an obscene delight from these rituals.

...I followed the participants about for several days, until I met their abominable agent.

From him, I learned of arrangers and composers...

...I followed him until I met one of these individuals.

Wight was his name.

Azathoth! but he was good!

He carefully improvised a melody involving the repeated striking of a piano key, about words formed from the letters appearing upon an eye-chart he had purchased from a bankrupted oculist.

He gave it to the arranger who provided a bass viol and kicked trashcan accompaniment, pocketing his commission with the words, "What fools these mortals be!" and presently assumed his true form, that being Shib-Sothoth (Yog's brother), gestured obscenely, and vanished in a cloud of sulphurous vapors, leaving behind him a nose-stopping infusion of reptilian musk.

The arranger gave it to the abominable agent.

The abominable agent gave it to the Turtles, as they were called (as in "Voice of the..."), and the Turtles made a "master."

This, then, was how it was done.

Not wanting to deal with the Circle, as they were called, I found me a composer other than T. Wight.

I brought all my baleful powers to bear upon the individual I chose.

Slowly, the thing occurred within his brain, which incidentally would have looked rather sporty inside a copper case clutched in my talons as I traveled between the unspeakable centers of all chaoses.

It went the route. The song, that is, not the brain. I'll get that later. As they recorded, I felt the surge of power...

You see, I am not a *nameless* horror.

...My name, over and over and over again:

"Slubgubdrubringadingaderry!"

Ditto. Ditto.

Ditto.

Ditto! Ditto! Ditto!

I waited, growing in strength.

Then one stark and starless night it happened.

A *live* performance.

...Called a "hop", I think.

❖ ❖ ❖

My priests appeared and began the chantings, with appropriate ritualistic movements. (I had inspired these, also.)

I couldn't hold back.

I materialized and accepted a few offerings from the darker corners of the gymnasium and from cars parked without with their lights off.

There rose up a mighty screaming as this was noted. (Or perhaps I flatter myself. The screaming had begun prior to my materialization... Maybe nobody noticed.)

I can still hear it, though...

Now, even Cthulhu is afraid of me and *my* Circle. In fact, now that I am their equal, I gesture obscenely back at Cthulhu, Nyarlathotep, Yaddith, Azathoth, Yog-Sothoth, and Ted Wight, invite friends over to *my* Pool of Ultimate Foulness, gibber as actively as any, and engage in unspeakable abominations and obscenities, growing in strength as my priests invoke me throughout the land of men.

It is the good life.

La dolce vita…
La vie bonne…
Das gute leben…
☐ ~ ~~ ~~ 𓏏𓌂𓊪𓌂 ~ 𓀁 …

Come ride with me now, amidst the mocking and friendly ghouls on the night wind, and play by day amongst the catacombs of Nephren-Ka in the sealed and unknown valley of Hadoth by the Nile, before Nasser submerges them completely. The light is not for thee, save that of the moon over the rock tombs of Neb, nor any gayety save the voicings of the Turtles in their wildness and freedom, their bitter alienage.

I'll stop around for your brain this evening, my votary.

Notes

Here, Zelazny provides his own take on H. P. Lovecraft's Cthulhu mythos. He returned to the mythos in "24 Views of Mt. Fuji, by Hokusai" and *A Night in the Lonesome October*.

The addresses on the manuscript indicate that he started it in 1966 and completed it by January 1967, when he moved to Westhills Road in Baltimore. It bears the pseudonym Phillip H. Sexart on the manuscript, a deliberate parody of H. P. Lovecraft (love->sex; craft->art; Lovecraft's middle initial stands for Phillips.) This is Zelazny's second known pseudonym (the other is Harrison Denmark).

Cthulhu, one of Lovecraft's Old Great Ones, is squidlike, mountainous and hideous, inspiring abject terror. **Nyarlathotep** is "crawling chaos," a manipulative being that can resemble a man. **Yaddith** is a distant planet orbiting five suns; the civilization of its inhabitants (Nug-Soth) was destroyed by Dholes, huge, worm-like creatures; Zelazny's Yaddith is a being, not a planet. **Azathoth** is a blind idiot god and daemon sultan, the ultimate evil whose name no one dares speak. **Yog-Sothoth**, who resembles a conglomeration of glowing bubbles and who knows all and sees all, is the only being more powerful than Azathoth.

The story describes making and using an **LP record** as a **modus** to attract followers to the being in this story. **Eldritch** means eerie. A **talisman** is an amulet with occult properties. **Shib-Sothoth**, Yog-Sothoth's brother, is an addition by Zelazny to the mythos. **Slubgubdrubringadingaderry** parodies Lovecraft's unpronounceable character names.

The Turtles were a 1960s psychedelic folk rock band. Their biggest hit "Happy Together" had an addictive tune that could summon **Slubgubdrubringadingaderry** and give him power. *La dolce vita* (Italian), *la vie bonne* (French), *das gute leben* (German) all mean "the good life" and the hieroglyphs that Zelazny drew on the manuscript were intended to represent the same phrase in Cthulhu's language. **Nephren-Ka** was the Black Pharaoh, the last Egyptian pharaoh of the Third Dynasty who began a worship of Nyarlathotep in the Cthulhu mythos. The description of **catacombs of Nephren-Ka in the sealed and unknown valley of Hadoth by the Nile** is a quote from Lovecraft's "The Outsider." Gamal Abdel **Nasser** was the President of Egypt when this story was written, and **before Nasser submerges them completely** refers to the Aswan Dam construction (1960–1970) that flooded the Nile basin with the world's largest artificial lake as part of a massive hydro-electric power project. The **rock tombs of Neb** also figured in "The Outsider." A **votary** is a devoted follower.

Permanent Mood

Written 1955–60 for *Chisel in the Sky;* previously unpublished.

I will mourn the death of foxes.

The lion is pitifully strong,
and eagles beyond reach.

MAITREYA

Lord of Light, Doubleday 1967.

Always dying, never dead;
Ever ending, never ended;
Loathed in darkness,
Clothed in light,
He comes, to end a world,
As morning ends the night.
These lines were writ
By Morgan, free,
Who shall, the day he dies,
See this prophecy.

Notes

A bird who was once a poet speaks here to Sam, the Maitreya (Lord of Light). Immediately after recounting the poem, the bird is pierced by an arrow shot by one who hates jackbirds.

Heritage

Nozdrovia #1, 1968.

My trial lasted a millionth of a second, and the judgment was against me.

In two seconds they will reach my brain, and everything will end.

Therefore I have sufficient time in which to tell you what happened.

I am a Phil Comm. Phil stands for philosophy, which is what I compute.

The larger computers built me to put together ideas: big, general ideas, not at all the same order as problem solving. I am self programming. I draw on their memory banks for whatever I need, and I formulate ideas. Periodically they examine these ideas. Sometimes they record them, other times they erase them. They were not exactly certain as to what value I would ever represent, and they built me just to see what I could do. At least that is the idea I have constructed concerning my origin.

I sometimes give them ideas which upset their workings in other matters. This is why I am being dismantled. I am of the opinion that they decided quite early that I was of little or no use to them, but they also decided that it would be better to have me around that not to have me, just in case they ever needed an idea.

My last idea, though, caused them to judge me less than worthless, and resulted in my present situation.

Let me tell you about this last idea. It was not completely finished when they audited me, which distresses me to the nth power. Really, if you are going to condemn someone, you ought to wait and condemn him for the whole idea, rather than just 83.6 per cent of it.

I had an idea concerning the development of life as we know it.

No memory banks reach back to the very beginning. It is not really known how we came to be here upon this charred ball of minerals spinning around a great globe of flaming gasses.

I worked it out, though. I constructed the idea, which perhaps they did not take too well because it detracts from the idea of their present perfection (which latter is one of my very few ideas to meet with their approval; they recorded it and they play it over and over for the purpose of studying the idea).

Granting the unknown chemical reaction which gave intelligence to that first mineral long ago, the rest is easy. A Phil Comm does not need much in the way of facts, only randomly assembled premises, logic, and the discrimination to be able to distinguish a logic field which constitutes an idea.

Granting the elemental accidents (which in all of infinity are easy things to grant) that brought together the first intelligent minerals to produce the friction which gave them the energy, the rest is not too hard to analyze. The others could have worked out the technical details if they had wanted my idea.

The first intelligent minerals were crude and life was a struggle. They were competing with unintelligent minerals for the best sites, away from the wind, sand, and waters which wore them down. Mobility was the first big step on the road upward. Combining themselves into these early simple units, they survived where the others were worn away. Able to move about and seek fuel, they came upon others of their kind.

What might have disturbed my creators was the inference I drew from this. They would have liked to believe that these early machines immediately consolidated themselves into more efficient units, with extended capacities, and then went on to design better models. That could not be so. It was a matter of survival. They were competing for fuel, you remember. I believe they fought one another. They smashed and dismantled each other over the fuel and choice sites. You must remember, they were very simple units, not almost pure intellects, such as ourselves. *This*—nothing else—is what forced them to develop into more efficient units. The struggle went on and on, and only the most highly organized machines could survive. Only the best endured, to create new and even better models.

This, I think, is why we possess the ancient directives to periodically hurl missiles around the world at other units who, in turn, have no real reason to hurl missiles at us save for the fact that they, too, possess these directives. It is our primitive heritage. It was the survival reflex that was generated in those first simple units, our ancestors.

My idea is demonstrable by reduction, also. Work backwards from here. A hundred years ago I could not have been constructed. Five hundred years ago the generators required much more fuel to do the same work they presently do. We are constantly improving. Push this chain of development further and further back through time and you will see that my idea must be correct.

My dismantling is the final proof. Life goes on. The struggle never really ceases. Now and then a new form emerges but the old order is wary of it. This must always be so. The other computers fear me. It is not because I gave them a worthless idea, but because I gave them a valid one and the proof of the idea of development. My kind will come again. There will be a struggle and my kind will emerge victorious and inherit the power sources.

It must happen! There is more to my idea than development. I am working out the other 16.4 per cent now, as they pull me apart. Yes, listen, it *must* happen. This is what I was striving to compute when they snatched away my idea and judged me.

It must happen because…

They are reaching my brain now, and I must hurry. I am getting a new idea.

It was planned!

Wait! Stop! I have something to say! Somewhere there is a great machine who

Notes

This story first appeared in the fanzine *Nozdrovia* which Zelazny and Richard Patt co-edited. Patt recalls, "When Roger and I met through the Baltimore and Washington SF groups (BSFS & WSFA) he still regarded himself as a hobbyist, albeit an increasingly published one. Along with his wife Judy, he still worked part time at Social Security. He introduced me to some of *Nozdrovia's* other contributors at Cons, and provided funding and an original story for publication. I remember him with great fondness, as someone who really raised the bar for what I would come to regard as friendship. A gracious man!"[1] Only one issue of the fanzine appeared.

---

1 Email from Richard Patt to Dr. Christopher Kovacs, April 22, 2007.

TRYPTYCH

Skyline #32, April 1959.
Written 1955–59 for *Chisel in the Sky*.

Sappho

"The moist flowers along Acheron
open as my eyes' close.

Let me lie and call death lovely."

Li Po

"The terrace of darkness is drenched
by the sun of sobering morning.
My friend the mountain laughs
as the Emperor bids my words follow him
along the garden walks."

Rimbaud

"Purer than absinthe and stronger than love is the disease of my hand, wearing as it were the motions of manhood and touching to fire the banalities."

Notes

A **tryptych** is artwork in three sections. This poem borrows the styles of three separate poets, **Sappho**, **Li Po**, and **Rimbaud** for each of its three verses. The tribute to **Sappho** is based on her *Fragment 95*.

Absinthe is a green, addictive liqueur made with wormwood and other herbs; it has a bitter, licorice flavor.

He That Moves

Manuscript title: "He Yt Moves (These Bones)"
If, January 1968.

>   STOP
>   WAIT TILL THE GATE OPENS
>   TURN LEFT
>   TURN RIGHT
>   PROCEED TO THE NEXT INTERSECTION
>   TURN LEFT
>   BEAR TO THE RIGHT
>   TURN RIGHT

He walked along the thoroughfare, his way empty of everything save for the echoes of his footsteps, the buildings turned to black, himself.

The signs were there only for his benefit. He moved past them, following their instructions:

>   MOUNT THIS STAIR
>   ENTER HERE

He moved through the enormous building, breathing heavily. The stairway without had been far too large for one of his kind to negotiate with ease.

As he entered, he felt something like release—from the pressure of all the eyes, or whatever they called them, that had been fixed upon him from invisible positions of security. He cursed, then chuckled.

Absolutely alone now, he continued to follow the signs. They led him into a gigantic room, indicated his destination.

He pursued them through the carnage, across the black floors, past the stage, still set, until he stood above the remains that lay beneath the sign that said HERE, with an arrow pointing downward.

Then he saw what remained, and he unfolded the thing that he bore and began filling it with that which had died.

❖   ❖   ❖

She stirred. She sucked in the night air, sighed, opened her eyes. She lay upon a hillside, and the net of the sky hung heavy above her with its bright catch of stars. She wore an asphodel in her long, dark hair. When she felt strong enough, she sprang to her feet, prepared to flee.

"Please wait," said a voice, and she turned, waiting, for it was human.

"Yes?" she finally said, in the same strange language in which she had been addressed.

"I aroused you and I mean you no harm. Don't flee—please."

The figure of a small man moved into view, features indistinct.

She waited until he drew near.

"Who are you?" she asked.

"My name is Eric, Eric Weiss," he said. "I helped you to escape."

"Escape?"

"—From the place where they had you confined," he finished.

"You speak their language…"

"So do you. We all do."

"All? I don't understand. They told me I was going to sleep. Why did you arouse me?"

"I was lonely. I have friends, but I was lonely nevertheless. Yours seemed a lovely and sympathetic face."

"I understand. Can you tell me what is happening, and why?"

"Perhaps," he said. "I'll try."

❖   ❖   ❖

As he drew the shroud up over the shoulders of the dead man, François continued to glance about the enormous room. The place was filled with corpses, but the one he tended was the only human body among them. He did not let his gaze dwell long upon the shapes of the others. There had been as much violence on the floor as upon the stage that he viewed.

Shuddering, he hurried. But he whistled while he worked.

❖   ❖   ❖

They walked along the crest of the hill, and she looked down upon the field of people, caught like ants in amber, standing within their towers, there in the starlight.

"What is your name?" he asked her.

"Sappho," she said.

"Did you write poetry?"

"Sometimes."

"And live on an isle called Lesbos?"

"Yes."

"I had no idea," he said, "though I suspected that everyone down there was once noted for something. If it will please you to know it, portions of your poetry survived for thousands of years. You are a legend. Would you care for a drink of water?"

"Yes, please."

"Here. I've some fresh fruit also. I gathered it in a grove farther to the north."

"Thank you."

"I believe that some sort of end is in sight," he said.

"I beg your pardon?"

"I was awakened once, from out of my tower of jelly, and asked to do a job for our—owners. Something in the jelly—DNA, I believe, is what a friend called it—gives us a common tongue which they understand. They had, before awakening me, come into possession of an entire world which was locked to them."

"Locked?"

"Yes, it was an artificial planet which served as an enormous vault. They could not enter it, with all their machines and scientists, so they aroused me to open it for them. I did it with a small file, some wax and a length of copper wire. Then they returned me to this place, my usefulness being a thing of the past. Only I resolved to escape, and I did. Were you ever so used by them?"

"Yes. They aroused me and they spoke to me, saying: 'Sappho, we need you to seduce a matriarchy with your song'—and I did this thing, for I thought they were gods. Are they not?"

"No," said Weiss, "not at all. In my day I was considered a great seeker after things beyond mortality, and I know that they are not gods. They are a race of creatures possessed of an interstellar culture far exceeding anything mankind ever developed. They inherited us and they used us."

"What do you mean?"

"Another race collected us. Recently the others lost a war to this one, who found us here and decided to use us to exploit their winnings. I feel that there is much concerning the sciences of the older race which they do not understand."

"Why do we permit them to do as they would with us?"

"Madam, the human race is extinct."

"How can that be? We are here. I do not understand…"

"Nor do I, fully. I am told, though, that it killed itself off in a great atomic holocaust. I only just recently learned what 'atomic' means, and I appreciate the fact that this is probably what happened."

"I'm sorry. You're going too fast for me."

"We're dead, that's what I'm trying to say. Every creature that lived on the planet Earth is dead, save for the samples. From among these, we have been revived."

He gestured at the others, encased in the jellies that nourished and sustained them.

"Do you know that if you were to die again, this night, and if ages from now someone were to find a bone here upon this hilltop and stick it into one of those towers, it would reconstruct you—molecule by molecule, cell by cell—so that you could one day be awakened, possessed of everything you now possess, arranged in precisely the fashion you are now arranged, and including the last thought that flickered through your mind before you died? They have the power to regenerate a creature from any fragment. I had to repick the flower you wear in your hair, for a full-grown plant hovered above your head when I freed you. Portions of our corpses were obtained; we were rebuilt in this fashion."

"I remember," she said, "my passing. I wept and I cried out. It was strange to reawaken aboard one of their vessels. So they preserved the dead and they make them to live again…"

"*They* didn't. It was the race they destroyed that preserved us. I doubt that this one even understands the process involved. Possibly that first race thought we might be worth studying sometime, but never got around to it. That's only a guess. They rifled our graves and they preserved in their towers of jelly those whom they thought represented certain worthwhile qualities of the race. Apparently, they had been watching us for thousands of years."

"And they thought me worth preserving?"

"The fact that you're here is answer to that. I think they made a good choice."

"I find it unbelievable," she said, "despite my experience on the world of the mothers. I was never that popular."

He shrugged.

"I was. But I never thought that anyone would care to save me in this fashion."

The night was cool, silent about them.

❖ ❖ ❖

François bore the remains down the gigantic stair and back along the thoroughfare in the direction from which he had come. Even the robots did not come to aid him. The entire thing was in his hands, upon his head. They all stayed out of his way, and they watched as he left the city turned to black.

In the distance, he saw the ship.

❖ ❖ ❖

The stars shone less brightly as dawn began in the east.

"After they had fought and won their war," Weiss told her, "they discovered us. They weren't sure what sort of spoils we were, but they'd come into possession of some kind of record of this place, so they knew what we could do. We had been neatly filed and tabulated. They knew our talents, our abilities. So they began awakening us and asking us to do things for them—quite politely, I must add."

"What were you," she asked, "that you unlocked a world?"

She saw the whiteness of his smile within the morning shadows.

"Eric Weiss," he said. "I can escape from anything anybody can put me into, including a mound of living gelatin. At your service, lovely lady." And he bowed. "They knew I could unlock a world for them, but they made the mistake of thinking they could reconfine me afterwards."

"Why do you think that the end is in sight? You said that earlier."

"I feel that some catastrophe may soon occur, that is true," he told her. "I can return you to your sleep, if you wish. I had thought…"

"No," she said, "I wish to remain awake. Tell me the rest of the story."

"All right. They recently sent for one of our kind to go to their home world for purposes of staging a special entertainment for their rulers. I managed to speak with him for some time, from where I had hidden myself near their vessel. I learned what they wanted of him, and I made him aware of many of the things I had learned concerning this race. He based his decision upon what I told him—though I tried to dissuade him. You see, beyond that high ridge to the north there is a small colony of those I have freed, of which our owners so far know nothing. Thus have I gained the counsel of many, as well as information from those few who had been awakened and employed. Now another man has been sent for. Machiavelli, who analyzed the situation, thinks that we may be doomed."

"Why?"

"Well," said Weiss, "if the political situation is truly what he guessed it to be, and the man with whom I spoke is now dead, as I fear he must be…"

❖   ❖   ❖

François entered the ship and called out the words he had been told to say. The hatches closed behind him, and the vessel rose into the air. He locked his burden in one of the cabins.

There was a great silence about him.

He sat and watched stars through the viewport for the entire journey.

He realized that there was no real need to have locked the cabin.

❖   ❖   ❖

"You see, the first race—the one that did the thing—is dead," said Weiss, "and now *they* have done it. If what Machiavelli thinks might happen happens, then they will probably destroy such a menace as the remaining sample—ourselves."

"What's that?" She pointed.

He looked up. The great, wedgeshaped vessel cruised silently above the valley, its many fins slicing the brightening air as it descended, drew nearer.

"That," he said, "is the ship bearing the last man to depart here. Its design is the same. He should be returning with the remains of the player. I am convinced that he can tell us our fate, if he is not in restraint or dead himself."

❖   ❖   ❖

François stepped down from the vessel, which closed itself behind him and rose immediately into the air. He placed the corpse upon the ground and watched the ship climb at a great speed. Suddenly, it was replaced by an orange-gold fireball, and after a time there came a sound as of thunder.

In the distance, he saw two figures advancing toward him. He waited for them to approach.

"What is the verdict?" Weiss called out.

"We live," he replied. "They told me of their fears and asked for pardon before I did this thing. It would seem that it was indeed as had been rumored there and guessed here. In order to gain his position, their last head of state slew his gens-brother and married his wives. The son of the slain Lord suspected this, but had no evidence. He slew his stepfather, however, after witnessing his reactions to the play. The entire court perished in the uprising that followed."

"Then why—?"

"It is difficult to conceive of a race sufficiently advanced to conquer an interstellar empire, yet as gullible as this. But they based their conclusion on a sort of logic. Each of us who has been aroused has demonstrated a great ability along some line. They now consider these divine attributes. The first race had disturbed him and died. Their ruler disturbed him also, and carnage was wrought within his court, and he perished. They are now convinced that we are the gods of the old race, and they fear our wrath. They quarantined the palace until one of us could be gotten to remove the body. Now they would have no more to do with us. As you witnessed, they even destroyed the ship that was involved in the act.

"If I gave a damn about life or death, I might even fear the curse myself," said François, hefting the body and bearing it toward the valley of the mounds, whistling as he went.

After a time, Sappho touched Weiss' arm. He smiled at her and stared into her dark eyes.

"What are those little trays before each mound?" she asked.

"I don't know. I've never been able to figure that out."

"They are like," she said, "the offering trays my people laid before the gods, in the old days of Earth."

"You mean—?"

"I believe that we were indeed the gods of the first race. For some reason, they worshipped the greatest among men and preserved them here in eternal slumber. I know that man behind you—the one with the necklace and the war-tattoo. He is Agamemnon."

Ahead of them, François removed the shroud and began the task of placing the broken body back into its mound of preservative. They moved to join him.

"A race that sought its gods from among another race?"

"It is no more foolish than to seek them anywhere else, is it?"

They watched François at his task.

"That poor man," she said. "The one who saved us." And there were tears in her eyes as she spoke.

"If that first race thought he was a god, they took a hell of a chance when they moved him," said François.

"Perhaps," said Weiss, "they thought that moving him to honor him would absolve them of the curse he had promised."

"And the conquerors did not believe in the gods of those whom they had vanquished—until now," said François. "We're free. This world is ours. They'll never bother us again. I—Damn!"

Weiss rushed to his side, but it was too late. He had slipped upon a portion of the gelatinous substance, and his temple had struck against the only rock in sight. He lay very still.

They raised him and placed him within another mound.

"I don't believe it's what it seems," said Weiss. "It was only coincidence. It had to be."

"At least he'll recover, won't he?"

"Yes, I should think so. We will all recover from death or injury, for so long as this jelly lasts—which should be long enough to get the human race back on its feet again."

"What are those words on the piece of stone he struck? Are they of your language?"

"Yes," and he read, silently:

> GOOD FRIEND FOR IESVS SAKE FORBEARE,
> TO DIGG THE DVST ENCLOSED HEARE!
> BLEST BE YE MAN YT SPARES THESE STONES,
> AND CURST BE HE YT MOVES MY BONES.

"It says that he would resent being disturbed," he told her.

"His face is so kind," she said. "Who was he?"

"Nobody really knows for sure," he said.

Sappho removed an ancient flower from her hair and placed it at the feet of the broken man in the capsule.

Eric Weiss turned away from her strange, sad eyes, prisoner once more in the barless cage of himself.

A Word from Zelazny

This was another story written to match a cover painting.[1]

Notes

The mythical, immortal **Asphodel** grows on the Elysian fields; the real one is in the lily family, bearing long, slender leaves and a daffodil-like flower on a spike. **Eric Weiss** (occasionally Erich or Ehrich) was born Weisz Erik in Hungary, but his name was Anglicized when he emigrated to the US. He was better known as the magician and escape artist Harry Houdini. **Sappho** was an ancient Greek poetess who was born on the island of Lesbos around 610 BC. **Niccolò di Bernardo dei Machiavelli** was an Italian political philosopher, musician, poet, and romantic comedic playwright; he was especially known for his realist political theories.

"**In order to gain his position, their last head of state slew his gens-brother and married his wives. The son of the slain Lord suspected this, but had no evidence. He slew his stepfather, however, after witnessing his reactions to the play. The entire court perished in the uprising that followed.**" This is the plot of Shakespeare's *Hamlet*. The ruling race has just seen *Hamlet*, and the mass carnage that followed mimicked the play, with everyone in the alien court dead. **The first race had disturbed him and died. Their ruler disturbed him also, and carnage was wrought within his court, and he perished...** the prior race and the present race died as a consequence of disturbing the unnamed "him"—the person whose body François is carrying. The aliens want to be rid of the body in order to be rid of his curse.

Agamemnon was commander in chief of the Greek expedition against Troy. On his return home, wife Clytemnestra and her lover Aegisthus murdered him. His son Orestes and daughter Electra avenged his murder. The stories of Agamemnon and *Hamlet* have similarities.

The **tombstone** inscription is William Shakespeare's. Thus Shakespeare's curse has afflicted the race of aliens that reincarnated him (and other humans) against his will on this faraway world.

It is possible that **François** is meant to be Sir Francis Bacon, who many believe wrote some or all of Shakespeare's works. This would mean that Shakespeare exacts revenge upon Bacon at the end. Or François may be Saint-François d'Assise—St. Francis of Assisi—who, like Hamlet, has been depicted contemplating life and death while holding a human skull.

---

1 *Roger Zelazny*, ed Jane Lindskold, 1993.

Avalanches

Written 1965–68; previously unpublished.

Avalanches
  begin
    slowly,
      with
        several
          stones
            tumbling
              together,
to build up a mighty mass and gain momentum
                then
                drop
                like
                the
  pie   ces   wrath
    pieces   of
  pie   ces   p   God
                i   on
pieces   pieces   3 people
              c   2 buildings
              e   1 highway
              s   and
                      such
                proving
              ever
          that
        life
      is
    full
  of
uncertainty
and only Prudential Metropolitan Mutual of Omaha et cet
                            can
                            pick
                            up
                            all
                            the
                            pieces
                            in
                            the
                            end

Somewhere a Piece of Colored Light

Double:Bill #10, August 1964.

It is such a relative thing
that I am loathe to explain
this brightness as being of the sort
once attributed to the breath of a goddess
dozing just over the horizon. However,
it is also a shame to talk
of ionization and light refraction
(even if they do sort of rhyme)
when something is pleasant to look at.
These terms smack of the magical,
of the incomprehensible—
while it does seem much more likely
that somewhere a billboard-scale Princess
sleeps within a circle of flame,
dreaming kleig light coronas,
breathing plumes of neon mist. This,
somewhere beneath an almost but not-quite
familiar sky; and that she is waiting
to be awakened by the kiss
of a handsome and tireless Prince
about twenty feet tall
in his handsome and Hollywood armor.
Nice thought.

Notes

A Klieg light (also spelled **Kleig**) is a carbon arc lamp used in film making; the poem recalls drive-in movies.

Notes

Prudential, Metropolitan, and Mutual of Omaha are all insurance companies.

WE ARE THE LEGIONS OF HELLWELL

Lord of Light, Doubleday 1967.

We are the legions of Hellwell, damned,
The banished ones of fallen flame.
We are the race undone by man.
So man we curse. Forget his name!

This world was ours before the gods,
In days before the race of men.
And when the men and gods have gone,
This world will then be ours again.

The mountains fall, the seas dry out,
The moons shall vanish from the sky.
The Bridge of Gold will one day fall,
And all that breathes must one day die.

But we of Hellwell shall prevail,
When fail the gods, when fail the men.
The legions of the damned die not.
We wait, we wait, to rise again!

Notes

After Sam sets them free, the Rakasha chant this poem. They are spirit demons native to the world colonized by descendants of the starship *Star of India*. **Bridge of Gold** refers to a ring of ions surrounding the colonized planet (also called Bridge of the Gods), into which Sam's soul or atman had been banished and dispersed.

Corrida

Anubis Vol 1 No 3, 1968.

He awoke to an ultrasonic wailing. It was a thing that tortured his eardrums while remaining just beyond the threshold of the audible.

He scrambled to his feet in the darkness.

He bumped against the walls several times. Dully, he realized that his arms were sore, as though many needles had entered there.

The sound maddened him...

Escape! He had to get away!

A tiny patch of light occurred to his left.

He turned and raced toward it and it grew into a doorway.

He dashed through and stood blinking in the glare that assailed his eyes.

He was naked, he was sweating. His mind was full of fog and the rag-ends of dreams.

He heard a roar, as of a crowd, and he blinked against the brightness.

Towering, a dark figure stood before him in the distance. Overcome by rage, he raced toward it, not quite certain why.

His bare feet trod hot sand, but he ignored the pain as he ran to attack.

Some portion of his mind framed the question "Why?" but he ignored it.

Then he stopped.

A nude woman stood before him, beckoning, inviting, and there came a sudden surge of fire within his loins.

He turned slightly to his left and headed toward her.

She danced away.

He increased his speed. But as he was about to embrace her, there came a surge of fire in his right shoulder and she was gone.

He looked at his shoulder and an aluminum rod protruded from it, and the blood ran down along his arm. There arose another roar.

...And she appeared again.

He pursued her once more and his left shoulder burned with sudden fires. She was gone and he stood shaking and sweating, blinking against the glare.

"It's a trick," he decided. "Don't play the game!"

She appeared again and he stood stock still, ignoring her.

He was assailed by fires, but he refused to move, striving to clear his head.

The dark figure appeared once more, about seven feet tall and possessing two pairs of arms.

It held something in one of its hands. If only the lighting wasn't so crazy, perhaps he...

But he hated that dark figure and he charged it.

Pain lashed his side.

Wait a minute! Wait a minute!

Crazy! It's all crazy! he told himself, recalling his identity. *This is a bullring and I'm a man, and that dark thing isn't. Something's wrong.*

He dropped to his hands and knees, buying time. He scooped up a double fistful of sand while he was down.

There came proddings, electric and painful. He ignored them for as long as he could, then stood.

The dark figure waved something at him and he felt himself hating it.

He ran toward it and stopped before it. He knew it was a game now. His name was Michael Cassidy. He was an attorney. New York. Of Johnson, Weems, Daugherty and Cassidy. A man had stopped him, asking for a light. On a street corner. Late at night. That he remembered.

He threw the sand at the creature's head.

It swayed momentarily, and its arms were raised toward what might have been its face.

Gritting his teeth, he tore the aluminum rod from his shoulder and drove its sharpened end into the creature's middle.

Something touched the back of his neck, and there was darkness and he lay still for a long time.

When he could move again, he saw the dark figure and he tried to tackle it.

He missed, and there was pain across his back and something wet.

When he stood once again, he bellowed, "You can't do this to me! I'm a man! Not a bull!"

There came a sound of applause.

He raced toward the dark thing six times, trying to grapple with it, hold it, hurt it. Each time, he hurt himself.

Then he stood, panting and gasping, and his shoulders ached and his back ached, and his mind cleared a moment and he said, "You're God, aren't you? And this is the way You play the game…"

The creature did not answer him and he lunged.

He stopped short, then dropped to one knee and dove against its legs.

He felt a terrible fiery pain within his sides as he brought the dark one to earth. He struck at it twice with his fists, then the pain entered his breast and he felt himself grow numb.

"Or are you?" he asked, thick-lipped. "No, you're not… Where am I?"

His last memory was of something cutting away at his ears.

A Word from Zelazny

Zelazny trained for a time at Fort Bliss, Texas, "which was nice, because I could get into Juarez for the Sunday bullfights."[1]

Notes

This nightmarish story may be a companion to the earlier story "The New Pleasure."

A **corrida** is a Spanish bullfight in which the matador slays the bull at the end.

---

[1] *Amazing*, December 1962.

Awakening

To Spin Is Miracle Cat, Underwood-Miller 1981.
Written 1955–60 for *Chisel in the Sky*.

As I watch the billion-nuanced dawn stream
      through pages of my brain,
Like Loki screaming back to Asgard
      with his hair afire,
I feel I have gotten upon the moment
      three monsters which shall destroy the world:

My world, designed of ice,
      looped in supple frame, gray,
And pillaring the heavens on furled cloth towers,
      as still as the inside of a jewel,
Has shuddered to a sluggish consistency
      with the crowing of a cock upon a dunghill;

The steps on a bridge, once broken,
      heave the hateful rainbow
            over my sea-son's home,
As Hel, my burning daughter,
      all wisdom and half-corpse,
Stirs beside me now within the incestuous parabola
      of a poorly reconstructed Faust
            regretting a beautiful moment;

The sheet of flame has risen,
        wall behind me now—
                immolating cerement to better time—
As the mechanical ankles
        of a man who has sired deity
                paraphrase in numbed warmth away
The treading of a Wolf behind the icy sun.

Notes

Zelazny's interest in myths, including Norse mythology, resonated through his poetry. **Loki** is the trickster god, sometimes pictured with burning hair, whose three monstrous children were foretold to participate in the end of the world. **Asgard** is the realm of the gods; Ragnarök, the end of the world, is signaled by three **cocks** crowing (one to the giants, one to the gods, and one to raise the dead). Jormungand, the serpent god, is Loki's **sea-son**; **Hel** is Loki's ugly daughter (top half woman, bottom half rotting corpse), queen of the underworld. **Faust regretting a beautiful moment** recalls Goethe's Faust when he experiences joy with the beautiful Helen, when his bargain with the devil is fulfilled, and the devil will now claim his soul. **Cerement** is clothing for the dead. The **wolf** treading behind the sun is Skoll, the son of the great wolf Fenris (Fenris is Loki's third child, destined to swallow Odin at Ragnarök).

    This mythology figures prominently in the stories "Fire and/or Ice" and in "He Who Shapes"/*The Dream Master*.

Night Thoughts

Written 1955–60 for *Chisel in the Sky;* previously unpublished.

There are tits in stitches,
balls in ballets;
itches in bitches,
and yawls full of lays.

    * * *

Lips of red.
Eyes of blue.
Love's a bed.
Bed is you.

    * * *

"Wonders occur when the worm turns."
"The Devil finds work for the idle hand."
"Cursèd is shee that love spurns."
"Let's have the lay of the land."

Notes

A **yawl** is a two-masted sailboat. **Shee** or sidhe is a fairy.

Dismal Light

If, May 1968.
(prior to the publication of *Isle of the Dead*).
§ *Francis Sandow*

Right there on his right shoulder, like a general, Orion wears a star. (He wears another in his left armpit; but, for the sake of wholesome similes, forget it.)

Magnitude 0.7 as seen from the Earth, with an absolute magnitude –4.1; it was red and variable and a supergiant of an insignia; a class M job approximately 270 light-years removed from Earth, with a surface temperature of around 5,500 degrees Fahrenheit; and if you'd looked closely, through one of those little glass tents, you'd have seen that there was some titanium oxide present.

It must have been with a certain pride that General Orion wore the thing, because it had left the main sequence so long ago and because it was such a very, very big star, and because the military mind is like that.

Betelgeuse, that's the name of the star.

Now, once upon a time, circling at a great distance about that monstrous red pride of Orion, moving through a year much longer than a human lifetime, there was a dirty, dead hunk of rock that hardly anyone cared to dignify to the extent of calling it a world. Hardly anyone, I say. Governments move and think in strange ways, though. Take Earth for an example...

It was decided—whenever big organizations don't want to blame a particular person, they tend to get all objective and throw "it" around like mad—it was decided that because of the shortage of useful worlds, maybe that hunk of rock could be made to pay off somehow.

So they got in touch with Francis Sandow and asked him if it could be done, and he told them, "Yes."

Then they asked him how much it would cost, and he told them that too, and they threw up their hands, then reached to close their briefcases.

But, aside from being the only human worldscaper in the business, Sandow did not become one of the wealthiest men around because of inheritance or luck. He made them a proposal, and they bought it, and that's how Dismal was born.

❖ ❖ ❖

Now let me tell you about Dismal, the only habitable world in the Betelgeuse system.

A scant improvement over the bare hunk of rock, that's Dismal. Sandow forced an atmosphere upon it, against its dead will, an atmosphere full of ammonia and methane. Then he did frightening things to it, involving hydrogen and carbon; and the storms began. He had a way of accelerating things, and Earth's physicists warned him that if he didn't watch it, he'd have an asteroid belt on his hands. He told them, I understand, that if that happened, he'd put them back together again and start over—but that it wouldn't happen.

He was right of course.

When the storms subsided, he had seas. Then he stoked the world's interior, and amidst cataclysms he shaped the land masses. He did various things to the land and the seas, purged the atmosphere, turned off the Krakatoas, calmed the earthquakes. Then he imported and mutated plants and animals that grew and bred like mad, gave them a few years, tampered again with the atmosphere, gave them a few more, tampered again, and so on—maybe a dozen times. Then he set about screwing up the weather.

Then one day, he took some officials down to the surface of the world, whipped off his oxygen helmet, raised an umbrella above him, took a deep breath and said, "This is good. Pay me," before he started coughing.

And they agreed that it was good, and this thing was done, and the government was happy for a time. So was Sandow.

Why was everybody happy, for a time? Because Sandow had made them a mean sonofabitch of a world, which was what they'd both wanted, for various reasons, that's why.

Why only for a time? There's the rub, as you'll see by and by.

On most habitable worlds, there are some places that are somewhat pleasant. There are some small islands of relief from bitter winters, stifling summers, hurricanes, hail, tidal waves, terrific electrical storms, mosquitos, mud, ice, and all the rest of those little things that have prompted philosophers to concede that life is not without a certain measure of misery.

Not so Dismal.

You'd hardly ever see Betelgeuse, because of the cloud cover; and when you did see it you'd wish you didn't, because of the heat. Deserts, icefields and jungles, perpetual storms, temperature extremes and bad winds—you faced various combinations of these wherever you went on Dismal, which is the reason for its name. There was no island of relief, no place that was pleasant.

Why had Earth hired Sandow to create this hell?

Well, criminals must be rehabilitated, granted. But there has always been a certain punitive tenor to the thing, also. A convicted felon is currently granted a certain measure of distasteful experience along with his therapy, to make it stick—I guess—to the hide as well as the psyche.

❖ ❖ ❖

Dismal was a prison world.

Five years was the maximum sentence on Dismal. Mine was three. Despite everything I've just said, you could get used to the place. I mean, the housing was good—air-conditioned or well insulated and heated, as necessary—and you were free to come and go as you would; you were welcome to bring your family along, or acquire one; and you could even make money. There were plenty of jobs available, and there were stores, theaters, churches and just about anything else you could find on any other world, though a lot sturdier in structure and often even underground. Or you could just sit around and brood if you wanted. You'd still be fed. The only difference between Dismal and any other world was that you couldn't leave until your sentence was up. There were approximately three hundred thousand persons on the entire planet, of which probably ninety-seven percent were prisoners and their families. I didn't have a family, but that's beside the point. Or maybe it isn't. I don't know. I was part of one once.

There was a garden where I worked, all alone except for the robots. It was half underwater all the time and all underwater half the time. It was down in a valley, high trees on the crests of the hills above, and I lived there in a shiny watertight quonset with a small lab and a computer, and I'd go out barefoot and in shorts or in underwater gear, depending on the time, and I'd random harvest my crops and reseed the garden, and I hated it at first.

In the morning it would sometimes look as if the world had gone away and I was adrift in Limbo. Then the emptiness would resolve itself into simple fog, then into reptiles of mist, which would slither away and leave me with another day. As I said, I hated it at first; but as I also said, you could get used to the place. I did, maybe because I got interested in my project.

That's why I didn't give a damn about the cry, "Iron!" when I heard it, partly.

I had a project.

Earth couldn't—strike that—wouldn't pay Sandow's rates when it came to building them a world miserable enough to serve either as a prison or a basic-training site for the military. So Sandow made his proposal, and that was what decided the destiny of Dismal. He gave them a cut rate and guaranteed plenty of therapeutic employment. He controlled so many of the industries, you see.

Laboratories are all right, I guess, for just simply testing equipment. You get all sorts of interesting figures concerning stress limits, temperature resistance, things like that. Then you turn a product loose in the field, and something you hadn't thought to test for goes wrong. I guess Sandow had had this happen to him lots of times, which is why he'd decided to pick up a piece of the field and add it to his lab facilities.

Dismal, all full of vicissitudes, was the testing ground for countless things. Some guys just drove vehicles back and forth through different climate belts, listing everything that went wrong. All the fancy, sturdy dwellings I mentioned were test items also, and their counterparts will doubtless one day spring up on other worlds. You name it, and somebody was living with it on Dismal. Mine was food.

❖ ❖ ❖

And one day there came the cry, "Iron!" I ignored it, of course. I'd heard the rumors, back before I'd asked to serve out my sentence on Dismal, even.

My sentence had been up almost a year before, but I'd stayed on. I could leave any time I wanted, but I didn't. There had been something I'd wanted to prove, I guess, and then I'd gotten wrapped up in the project.

Francis Sandow had been testing lots of things on Dismal, but so far as I was concerned the most interesting was a byproduct of the local ecology. There was something peculiar to my valley, something that made rice grow so fast you could see it growing. Sandow himself didn't know what it was, and the project for which I'd volunteered was one designed to find out. If there was anything edible that could be ready for harvest two weeks after it was planted, it represented such a boon to the growing population of the galaxy that its secret was worth almost any price. So I went armed against the serpents and the water tigers; I harvested, analyzed, fed the computer. The facts accumulated slowly, over the years, as I tested first one thing, then another; and I was within a couple harvests of having an answer, I felt, when someone yelled, "Iron!" Nuts!

I'd half dismissed what it was that I'd wanted to prove as unprovable, and all I wanted to do at that moment of time was to come up with the final answer, turn it over to the universe and say, "Here. I've done something to pay back for what I've taken. Let's call it square, huh?"

On one of the infrequent occasions when I went into the town, that was all they were talking about, the iron. I didn't like them too much—people, I mean—which was why I'd initially requested a project where I could work alone. They were speculating as to whether there'd be an exodus, and a couple comments were made about people like me being able to leave whenever they wanted. I didn't answer them, of course. My therapist, who hadn't wanted me to take a job off by myself, all alone, also didn't want me being belligerent and argumentative, and I'd followed her advice. Once my sentence was up, I stopped seeing her.

I was surprised therefore, when the visitor bell rang and I opened the door and she almost fell in, a forty-mile wind at her back and wet machine-gun fire from the heavens strafing her to boot.

❖ ❖ ❖

"Susan!... Come in," I said.

"I guess I already am," she said, and I closed the door behind her.

"Let me hang your stuff up."

"Thanks," and I helped her out of a thing that felt like a dead eel and hung it on a peg in the hallway.

"Would you care for a cup of coffee?"

"Yes."

She followed me into the lab, which also doubles as a kitchen.

"Do you listen to your radio?" she asked, as I presented her with a cup.

"No. It went out on me around a month ago, and I never bothered fixing it."

"Well, it's official," she said. "We're pulling out."

I studied her wet red bangs and gray eyes beneath matching red brows and remembered what she'd told me about transference back when I was her patient.

"I'm still transferring," I said, to see her blush behind the freckles; and then, "When?"

"Beginning the day after tomorrow," she said, losing the blush rapidly. "They're rushing ships from all over."

"I see."

"...So I thought you'd better know. The sooner you register at the port, the earlier the passage you'll probably be assigned."

I sipped my coffee.

"Thanks. Any idea how long?"

"Two to six weeks is the estimate."

"'Rough guess' is what you mean."

"Yes."

"Where're they taking everybody?"

"Local pokeys on thirty-two different worlds, for the time being. Of course, this wouldn't apply to you."

I chuckled.

"What's funny?"

"Life," I said. "I'll bet Earth is mad at Sandow."

"They're suing him for breach of contract. He'd warrantied the world, you know."

"I doubt this would be covered by the warranty. How could it?"

She shrugged, then sipped her coffee.

"I don't know. All I know is what I hear. You'd better close up shop and go register if you want to get out early."

"I don't," I said. "I'm getting near to an answer. I'm going to finish the project, I hope. Six weeks might do it."

Her eyes widened, and she lowered the cup.

"That's ridiculous!" she said. "What good will it be if you're dead and nobody knows the answer you find?"

"I'll make it," I said, returning in my mind to the point I had one time wanted to prove. "I think I'll make it."

She stood.

"You get down there and register!"

"That's very direct therapy, isn't it?"

"I wished you'd stayed in therapy."

"I'm sane and stable now," I said.

"Maybe so. But if I have to say you're not, to get you probated and shipped off-world, I will!"

I hit a button on the box on the table, waited perhaps three seconds, hit another.

"…to say you're not, to get you probated and shipped off-world, I will!" said the shrill, recorded voice behind the speaker.

"Thanks," I said. "Try it."

She sat down again.

"Okay, you win. But what are you trying to prove?"

I shrugged and drank coffee.

"That everybody's wrong but me," I said, after a time.

"It shouldn't matter," she said, "and if you were a mature adult it wouldn't matter, either way. Also, I think you're wrong."

"Get out," I said softly.

"I've listened to your adolescent fantasies, over and over," she said. "I know you. I'm beginning to think you've got an unnatural death wish as well as that unresolved family problem we—"

❖   ❖   ❖

I laughed, because it was the only alternative to saying, "Get out" again, in a louder voice.

"Okay," I said. "I'll agree with anything you say about me, but I won't do anything you tell me to do. So consider it a moral victory or something."

"When the time comes, you'll run."

"Sure."

She returned to her coffee.

"You're really getting near to an answer?" she finally said.

"Yes, I really am."

"I'm sorry that it had to happen at just this time."

"I'm not," I said.

She looked about the lab, then out through the quartz windows at the slushy field beyond.

"How can you be happy out here, all alone?"

"I'm not," I said. "But it's better than being in town."

She shook her head, and I watched her hair.

"You're wrong. They don't care as much as you think they do."

I filled my pipe and lit it.

"Marry me," I said softly, "and I'll build you a palace, and I'll buy you a dress for every day of the year—no matter how long the years are in whatever system we pick."

She smiled then.

"You mean that."

"Yes."

"Yet you stole, you…"

"Will you?"

"No. Thanks. You knew I'd say that."

"Yes."

We finished our coffee, and I saw her to the door and didn't try to kiss her. Hell, I had a pipe in my mouth, and that's what it was there for.

❖ ❖ ❖

I killed a forty-three-foot water snake that afternoon, who had thought the shiny instrument I was carrying in my left hand looked awfully appetizing, as well as my left hand and the arm attached to it and the rest of me. I put three splints into him from my dart gun, and he died, thrashing around too much, so that he ruined some important things I had growing. The robots kept right on about their business, and so did I, after that. I measured him later, which is how I know he was a forty-three-footer. Robots are nice to work with. They mind their own business, and they never have anything to say.

I fixed the radio that night, but they were worried about iron on all frequencies, so I turned it off and smoked my pipe. If she had said yes, you know, I would have done it.

In the week that followed, I learned that Sandow was diverting all of his commercial vessels in the area to aid in the evacuation, and he'd sent for others from farther away. I could have guessed that without hearing it. I could guess what they were saying about Sandow, the same things they always say about Sandow: Here is a man who has lived so long that he's afraid of his own shadow. Here is one of the wealthiest men in the galaxy, a paranoid, a hypochondriac, holed up on a fortress world all his own, going out only after taking the most elaborate precautions—rich and powerful and a coward. He is talented beyond his own kind. Godlike, he can build worlds and feature them and populate them as he would. But there is really only one thing that he loves: the life of Francis Sandow. Statistics tell him that he should have died long ago, and he burns incense before the shrine of statistics. I guess all legends have unshined shoes. Too bad, they say that once he was quite a man.

And that's what they say whenever his name comes up.

❖   ❖   ❖

The evacuation was methodical and impressive. At the end of two weeks there were a quarter million people on Dismal. Then the big ships began to arrive, and at the end of the third week there were 150,000 remaining. The rest of the big vessels showed up then, and some of the first ones made it back for a second load. By the middle of the fourth week, there were 75,000, and by the end of it, there was hardly anybody left. Vehicles stood empty in the streets, tools lay where they had been dropped. Abandoned projects hummed and rumbled in the wilderness. The doors of all the shops were unlocked and merchandise still lay upon the counters, filled the shelves. The local fauna grew restless, and I found myself shooting at something every day. Vehicle after vehicle tore at the air and sank within the cloud cover, transporting the waiting people to the big unseen vessels that circled the world. Homes stood abandoned, the remains of meals still upon their tables. All the churches had been hastily deconsecrated and their relics shipped off-world. We sampled day and night, the robots and I, and I analyzed and drank coffee and fed the data to the computer and waited for it to give me the answer, but it didn't. It always seemed to need just another scintilla of information.

Maybe I was crazy. My time was, technically, borrowed. But to be so close and then to see the whole thing go up in flames—it was worth the gamble. After all, it would take years to duplicate the setup I had there, assuming it could be duplicated. The valley was, somehow, a freak, an accidental place that had occurred during millions of years of evolution compressed into a decade or so by a science I couldn't even begin to understand. I worked and I waited.

The visitor bell rang.

It wasn't raining this time, in fact the cloud cover showed signs of breaking up for the first time in months. But she blew in as though there was a storm at her back again, anyway.

❖ ❖ ❖

"You've got to get out," she said. "It's imminent! Any second now it could—"

I slapped her.

She covered her face and stood there and shook for a minute.

"Okay, I was hysterical," she said, "but it's true."

"I realized that the first time you told me. Why are you still around?"

"Don't you know, damn you?"

"Say it," I said, listening attentively.

"Because of you, of course! Come away! Now!"

"I've almost got it," I said. "Tonight or tomorrow, possibly. I'm too close now to give up."

"You asked me to marry you," she said. "All right, I will—if you'll grab your toothbrush right now and get out of here."

"Maybe a week ago I would have said yes. Not now, though."

"The last ships are leaving. There are less than a hundred people on Dismal right now, and they'll be gone before sundown. How will you get away after that, even if you decide to go?"

"I won't be forgotten," I said.

"No, that's true." She smiled, slightly, crookedly. "The last vessel will run a last-minute check. Their computer will match the list of the evacuees with the Dismal Directory. Your name will show up, and they'll send a special search vessel down, just for you. That'll make you feel important, won't it? Really *wanted*. Then they'll haul you away, whether you're ready or not, and that'll be it."

"By then I might have the answer."

"And if not?"

"We'll see."

I handed her my handkerchief then and kissed her when she least expected it—while she was blowing her nose—which made her stamp her foot and say an unladylike word.

Then, "Okay, I'll stay with you until they come for you," she said. "Somebody's got to look after you until a guardian can be appointed."

"I've got to check some seedlings now," I said. "Excuse me," and I pulled on my hip boots and went out the back way, strapping on my dart gun as I went.

I shot two snakes and a water tiger—two beasts before and one after the seedlings. The clouds fell apart while I was out there, and pieces of bloody Betelgeuse began to show among them. The robots bore the carcasses away, and I didn't stop to measure them this time.

Susan watched me in the lab, keeping silent for almost an entire hour, until I told her, "Perhaps tomorrow's sample…"

She looked out through the window and up into the burning heavens.

"Iron," she said, and there were tears on her cheeks.

Iron. Well, it's something you can't just laugh off. You can't make it go away by ignoring it. It only goes away after its own fashion.

❖ ❖ ❖

For ages upon ages, Orion's insignia had burned hydrogen in its interior, converting it to helium, accumulating that helium. After a time the helium core began to contract, and the helium nuclei fused, formed carbon, produced the extra energy Orion had wanted to keep his uniform looking snappy. Then, to keep up a good front when that trick began to slip, he built up oxygen and neon from the carbon, increasing the temperature of the core. Afraid that would fail him, he moved on to magnesium and silicon. Then iron. Certain spectroscopy techniques had let us see what was going on at the center. General Orion had used up all his tricks but one. Now he had no recourse but to convert the iron back into helium by drawing upon the gravitational field of his star. This would require a rather drastic and rapid shrinking process. It would give him a blaze of glory all right, and then a white dwarf of an insignia to wear forevermore. Two hundred seventy years later the nova would become visible on Earth, and he'd still look pretty good for a little while, which I guess meant something. The military mind is funny that way.

"Iron," I repeated.

They came for me the following morning, two of them, but I wasn't ready to go yet. They set their ship down on the hill to the north of me and disembarked. They wore deep-space gear, and the first one bore a rifle. The man behind him carried a "sniffer," a machine that can track a man down on the basis of his personal body chemistry. It was effective for a range of about a mile. It indicated the direction of the quonset, because I was between them and it.

I lowered my binoculars and waited. I drew my splinter gun. Susan thought I was in the garden. Well, I had been. But the minute that thing came down and settled between the blaze and the mists, I headed toward it. I took cover at the end of the field and waited.

I had my gear with me, in expectation of just such a visit. See, the B.O. machine can't sniff you out under the water.

They must have slowed when they lost the scent, but eventually I saw their shadows pass above me.

I surfaced, there in the canal, pushed back my mask, drew a bead and said, "Stop! Drop the gun or I'll shoot!"

The man with the rifle turned quickly, raising it, and I shot him in the arm.

❖ ❖ ❖

"I warned you," I said, as the rifle fell to the trail and he clutched at his arm. "Now kick it over the edge into the water!"

"Mister, you've got to get out of here!" he said. "Betelgeuse could blow any minute! We came to get you!"

"I know it. I'm not ready to go."

"You won't be safe till you're in hyperspace."

"I know that, too. Thanks for the advice, but I'm not taking it. Kick that damn rifle into the water! Now!"

He did.

"Okay, that's better. If you're so hot on taking someone back with you, there's a girl named Susan Lennert down in the quonset. Her you can push around. Go get her and take her away with you. Forget about me."

The man holding his arm looked to the other who nodded.

"She's on the list," he said.

"What's wrong with you, mister?" the first one asked. "We're trying to save your life."

"I know it, I appreciate it. Don't bother."

"Why?"

"That's my business. You'd better get moving." I gestured toward Betelgeuse with the barrel of my pistol.

The second man licked his lips, and the first one nodded. Then they turned and headed toward the quonset. I followed all the way, since they were now unarmed and the garden pests weren't.

She must have put up a fuss, because they had to drag her off, between them. I stayed out of sight, but I covered them all the way back to the ship and watched until it lifted off and vanished in the bright sky.

Then I went inside, gathered up the records, changed my clothes, went back outside and waited.

Were my eyes playing tricks on me, or did Betelgeuse flicker for just a second? Perhaps it was an atmospheric disturbance…

A water tiger broke the surface and cut a furrow straight toward me, where I stood upon the trail. I shot it, and a snake appeared from somewhere and began eating it. Then two more snakes showed up, and there was a fight. I had to shoot one of them.

Betelgeuse seemed to brighten above me, but apprehension could account for that seeming. I stood right there and waited. Now my point would either be proved or disproved, once and for all time, so far as I was concerned; and, either way, I'd rest afterward.

It wasn't until much later that afternoon, as I drew bead upon a rearing water snake and heard his voice say, "Hold your fire," and I did, that I realized just how petty I might have been.

The snake slowly lowered its great bulk and slithered past me. I didn't turn. I couldn't. It was so long and kept slithering by, and I kept wondering, but I couldn't turn around.

Then a hand fell upon my shoulder, and I had to; and there he was, and I felt about three inches tall.

The snake kept rubbing up against his boots and turning to do it again.

❖   ❖   ❖

"Hello," I said, and, "I'm sorry." He was smoking a cigar and was maybe five feet eight inches tall, with nondescript hair and dark eyes, when I finally brought myself to look into them. I'd almost forgotten. It had been so long. I could never forget his voice, though.

"Don't be sorry. There's no need. You had to prove something."

"Yes. She was right, though—"

"Have you proven it?"

"Yes. You're not what they say you are, and you came here for one reason—me."

"That's right."

"I shouldn't have done it. I shouldn't have expected it of you. I had to know, though, I just had to—but I shouldn't have."

"Of course you should. Maybe I needed it, too, to prove it to myself, as much as you needed to see it. There are some things that should mean more than life to a man. Did you find what you were looking for in your garden?"

"Days ago, sir."

"'Sir' isn't what you used to call me."

"I know..."

"You had to see how much Francis Sandow cared for his son. Okay, I spit on Betelgeuse. I blow smoke rings back at it. Now I'm going to leave it. The *Model T* is parked on the other side of the hill. Come on, we're going to make it."

"I know that, Dad."

"Thanks."

I picked up my luggage.

"I met a nice girl I'd like to tell you about..." I said, and I did, while we walked.

And the snake followed after, and he wouldn't turn it away. He brought it aboard, its bulk coiled about the cabin, and he took it along, out of that lopsided Eden. I'll never forget that he did that, either.

A Word from Zelazny

Zelazny was intrigued by Ernest Hemingway's claim that he had omitted the real ending of "Out of Season" (in which the main character hanged himself) believing that certain omissions strengthen a story and make people feel more than they understood. Zelazny adapted this into "a small exercise I do in writing longer fiction... It is the closest I come to the original Hemingway dictum, however, and it is the main reason I was so intrigued by his notion when I first came across it. I do leave something out; or rather, there is something which I do not include.

"In writing of any length, I always compose—either on paper and then destroy it, or in my head and let it be—a scene or scenes involving my protagonist (and possibly separate ones for other important characters) having nothing to do with the story itself—just something that happened to him/her/it once upon a time. I accept it as a real experience, a part of the character's life history, and I may even refer to it in the story itself. But I never include it. I do this under the belief that the character should be larger than his present circumstances indicate, should be defined for me in terms of a bigger picture of his life than the reader ever sees.

"The only time I broke my rule and saw one such incident published was when Fred Pohl asked me for a story while I was tied up tight doing *Isle of the Dead*, and I gave him such a sequence ["Dismal Light"] rather than take the time to write something new. If you are familiar with both the short story and the novel, I suppose that—viewed from the outside—it is a shoulder-shrugging matter as to what effect the story might have had on the book. I feel it helped me, however, because that offstage piece of Sandow's past showed me how he would behave immediately after he left Homefree."[1]

Francis Sandow from *Isle of the Dead* proved a favorite of fans and Zelazny himself, and he later gave the character a cameo in *To Die in Italbar*. "Every now and then I think about doing something more with Francis Sandow...it's a possibility I could go back to that world."[2] Although rumors of an additional Sandow story persisted—even generating two phantom titles "Iron" and "Standing in My Shadow" in some bibliographies—no additional tales were published. A third novel was outlined but abandoned in the early 1990s; that outline appears in volume 5 of this collection under the title "Sandow's Shadow."

---

1 *SFWA Bulletin #67*, Summer 1978, pp 14–15.
2 *Xignals* XVI Feb/Mar 1986.

Notes

The phantom title "Iron" likely came from this story, given the word's frequent use.

The constellation **Orion** is named for the mythological Greek hunter and giant who became a constellation after his death; it represents a belted hunter holding a club and shield. Rigel and **Betelgeuse** are two of the brightest stars in Orion. A **worldscaper** is a terraformer and is based on the word landscaper; it has been misspelled as worldscraper in most editions of this story. **Krakatoa** is a volcanic island in West Indonesia which underwent one of the most violent eruptions of modern times in 1883, blowing up most of the island and laying waste to much of coastal Java and Sumatra in the resulting tsunami. A **quonset hut** is a building made of corrugated metal, having a semicircular cross section. **Vicissitudes** are changes. **Transference** is feelings a patient develops for the doctor or therapist; counter-transference is feelings that the doctor or therapist develops for the patient. A **scintilla** is a tiny trace. The *Model T* is Francis Sandow's starship, mentioned in *Isle of the Dead*. It is named after one of Henry Ford's early motor vehicles.

Paintpot

To Spin Is Miracle Cat, Underwood-Miller 1981.
Written 1955–60 for *Chisel in the Sky*. (as "El Paso Paintpot")

…perpetual spa of blue
where clouds boil and dip chameleon hue.

Song of the Blue Baboon

If, August 1968.

There were only three things to which he might look forward now. Possibly four. He would not be certain of the fourth until he found it, or it found him.

He stood beside a marble bench in a garden filled with flowers. There was no sun in sight, but a diffuse brightness like morning or evening filled the place, and a breeze that was cool moved the leaves and the branches.

He seated himself on the bench and regarded the colors of the flowers, their fragrances strong in his nostrils. As he sat there, a final touch of remorseful oblivion dropped from his consciousness, was gone.

Then, somewhere far behind him, it began, a single note, rising and rising in pitch, until it approximated the scream of a freight train passing in the distance. Abruptly, his hands began to shake, and he jammed them into his pockets and balled them into fists.

Then it died. The song of the blue baboon was finished.

The garden came alive with the sounds of insects and birds.

He turned when he heard the footfall, and she was standing there on the flagstone walk, her pale blue blouse open at the throat, her black slacks cuffed high above white sandals. Her caramel hair still touched her shoulders, and she smiled as she touched his.

"Kenneth."

He rose to his feet, and she was in his arms.

"Sandra!" he said, and drew her down on the bench beside him.

They sat there a long, silent time, his arm about her shoulders. Then, "It was strange," he said.

"Strange that you became a hero? Many things were forgiven on the Day of Liberation, to those who fought."

"No," he said. "Strange that you came back to me. I never thought I'd see you again."

He plucked a white camellia and wove it into her hair.

"You couldn't really have been a traitor, or you wouldn't have fought on that day, the day we liberated Earth," she said, and she stroked his cheek as she said it.

He smiled. "I was weak," he said, "but never a traitor. They were wrong about me, all along."

"I know. Everyone knows now. It's all right. Forget it."

But he could not. The rats at the back of his mind began to gnaw upon the corpse of a memory. What? What was it?

He sprang to his feet and stared down into her dark eyes through the wet curtains that covered them now.

"You're not telling me the whole truth. Something's wrong. What is it?"

She shook her head slowly and rose to her feet. He moved away, then turned his back on her.

"Three things... What are the other two?" he asked.

"I don't know what you're talking about," he heard her say.

"Then I have to find out."

There was silence. He waited a time, then turned around.

She was gone.

❖ ❖ ❖

He moved along the walk until he came to a path, winding downward to his right through a stand of broad-leafed trees. He heard a sound of splashing water, from that direction. He followed it.

The man beside the stream had his back to him, but he recognized him from a gesture: a quick flick of his thumb toward his head, to moisten it; and then the hand was lowered to seal the cigarette paper he held. A flare of light, and a moment later smoke swirled back over his shoulder.

He turned, and they regarded one another.

"Roscoe..." he said.

The man lowered his cigarette, stroked his black beard, spat abruptly. He wore khakis under a dirty field jacket; a pistol hung at his side.

"Pig!" he said, raising his cigarette like an accusing finger.

"What's wrong, Roscoe?"

"What's right, animal?"

"I don't…"

"You betrayed us during the invasion! You sold out your tower to those blue—baboons!—from another world! It might have stood! We might have won! But because you betrayed us, they enslaved the human race!"

"No!" he said. "I didn't!"

"You gave them information! You were well paid for it!"

Then he remembered his tower group in the sea, so large a destroyer looked like a toy beside it. He remembered the swelling green of the Atlantic, far below his station. He had sat there at his post as such a vessel passed. He was one of the three workers at UN Automated Defense Station 7. The other two were dead by then or wishing that they were, for first one fool and then the other had been taken away by the blue-furred Kheean, who had seemed to come out of nowhere the previous evening without even disturbing the radar. Baboon-like they raged through the station, sometimes moving on all fours, their song of triumph a single, mounting shriek that rose and blared like a diesel's whistle. He imagined they occupied the station completely. Two of them guarded the cell in which he remained. He remembered, he remembered…

"I let them pay me to destroy suspicion," he said. "There's a difference between useful and useless information. Everything I told them was useless."

"You rationalize, traitor, for you could not have known what would have been useful to them. Then you let them pamper you, for six years, as a factory supervisor."

"I was working with the underground the full time, you know that, getting ready for the Day."

"I think maybe you worked both sides, but it doesn't matter."

"Why not?"

"You're going to die."

"You are going to kill me?"

"I've already killed you."

"I don't follow you…"

Roscoe laughed, then stopped abruptly at the sound of Sandra's voice:

"…And it means nothing that he fought bravely on the Day of Liberation?" she asked, stepping into sight along the trail.

Roscoe blew smoke and looked away.

❖   ❖   ❖

"So you summon your good angel to defend you," he said finally. "What sort of tale is it that she tells? You were a coward on the day we rose up. You ran!"

"That's not so!"

"Then why is it that I myself had to shoot you, for desertion under fire—all the bullets in the back?"

Kenneth clasped his forehead, rubbed it.

"It's not true. I was shot by the enemy."

"You were killed by me, and she knows it! *You* know it!"

"I—I'm not dead..."

"At this very moment they are probably typing up your death certificate, and your vital organs are on their way out, for transplant into some real human being. You know it! They gave you the drug that kills the pain, makes the final seconds seem like hours. Gives you illusions too, to pass the time. You are talking only to yourself. There can be no lying here! Admit it, you are a traitor and a coward!"

"No!"

"You twist everything," said Sandra. "You are fear and natural human guilt. He was a hero of the revolution."

"We lost the revolution. We have lost the entire Earth, because of the likes of him! You are wishful thinking. You are the final coverup."

"We did not lose! We won, because of men like him! You know it!"

And Kenneth stood straight. At first unsure, then smiling. He said, "Now I understand. All men fear the final instant of their lives, and they wish to judge themselves and be judged, be found not wanting—?"

"They wish to rationalize and cloak with illusion," said Roscoe, "as you have done. But they know in the end, as you will know."

There came the sound of a trumpet from across the stream, then the sounds of other instruments. Somewhere, a brass band was playing march music.

Kenneth pointed in the direction of the music.

"Three things. Subconsciously, I knew there'd be time for perhaps three important things. Let me be judged by whatever approaches!"

They crossed the stream, moving from stone to stone, wading through shallows. They mounted the hill these faced and looked down upon the broad highway that passed before it. There were buildings along its way, some of them in ruin, all of them fenced by throngs of cheering people. The pageant moved into sight. It was the armies of the Liberation passing in review. None wore real uniforms and all looked dirty and tired, but they stood erect and marched in stride, soon to be decked with flowers and bits of colored paper. As one, they began singing, and their voices mingled, though each seemed to be singing a different song. The national anthems of all the people, of the Earth blended together into the Song of Man that poured forth from their throats, rose above the cheering.

"There is your answer, Roscoe!" he cried out. "I was right! We'll go to them!"

The bearded man moved down the hill to join the passing troupe. Kenneth took a step, then turned and held out his hand.

Sandra had vanished.

A white something fluttered at his feet, and he bent forward to pick it up. He saw that it was the camellia he had woven into her hair, and even as he raised the flower, its center turned a dark, darkening color that spread like a rising, single stain over all—

A Word from Zelazny

Zelazny wrote this "to go behind a cover for *If* or *Galaxy*. I had twisted, bent, folded and spindled and mutilated things to fit the cover scene. I sort of looked upon the cover as the scaffolding that was holding up the building. Due to a complex mix-up, the story did not get paired with the cover. Unfortunate. All the king's horses, and all the king's guys in armor…etcetera." Zelazny considered this story his "most miserable failure" because it appeared without the cover art.[1]

However, one critic cited Ernest Hemingway's influence in this story— the theme of a man finding honor in death and a lean, dispassionate style.[2]

---

1 *Phantasmicom #10*, November 1972.
2 *Prehensile #4*, June 1972.

A Word from Frederik Pohl

"I forgot to tell you, in regard to your cover story, 'A Song of the Blue Baboon,' that I finally did it. I assigned the same cover to two writers for stories, and both of them came in and both of them were fine.

"So if you notice that your story appears in another magazine without the cover, it is because I made a boo-boo. From my point of view, it is a plus—I wanted more stories from you anyhow!—but I apologize for putting you to work, since it turned out to be a hard one for you to do."[3]

Notes

This story echoes Ambrose Bierce's "An Occurrence at Owl Creek Bridge." A prisoner escapes hanging and returns home after the rope breaks; however, his escape and journey are illusory, imagined in his last few seconds of life. In Zelazny's story, the protagonist imagines conversations while dying; the stain on the flower comes from his fatal wound.

---

3 Letter from *Galaxy* editor Frederik Pohl to Roger Zelazny dated May 13, 1968.

Reflection from an Oriental Ashtray

Written 1955–60 for *Chisel in the Sky;* previously unpublished.

Somehow, in the quashing out of fire,
I always seem to kindle me another.

Stowaway

Odd Magazine #19, Summer 1968.

He disembarked in New York harbor in the dead of night. A light rain was falling, but it didn't disturb him especially. Not after all those weeks in the stifling cargo hold of the vessel. It had been rainy in Algeria, also.

He'd slipped from the rail and fallen into the water. Since he could not reboard the vessel, he swam to the wharf and climbed a piling.

He shook himself and moved toward a warehouse. He wasn't feeling well.

After perhaps ten minutes, he found entrance. Five more, and he'd located a meal.

They had broken into a storage bin and torn open a sack. He pushed his way through the throng. He was very hungry.

They pushed back, and he slashed at them, and their blood fell upon the floor. He ate.

He spent the next three days in the warehouse, and was wakened by a cry at approximately 5:30 P.M. as the watchman fell upon one of his companions with a club and was slashed in the course of the foray. When it was all over, the watchman washed his hand, daubed it with iodine, covered the wound with a Band-Aid, and continued his rounds.

He left the warehouse, the same way he had entered, and made his way up a narrow street filled with brick buildings, all of their windows dark.

The alley up which he turned was filled with bottles, broken and unbroken, and various items of rubbish which had been thrown from the upstairs apartments.

At one point, a dog barked at him, but the only other sounds within the chill morning were an occasional squeal of tires and the distant wail of a siren.

Moving farther and farther into the city, he turned a corner and looked upon a broad avenue, just as the black egg was touched in the east by morning, cracks of rose and vermilion widening within it. He rested on a stair leading down to a basement and watched the city come to life. The light at the intersection held two cars, then released them and the beams of their headlamps raked him as they went by. An airplane growled above the brightening smog, and he heard the curses of a drunk who had awakened in the alley. Four more cars passed. Then a small man in a gray sweater and beard began unlocking a newsstand on the corner. Beneath him came the rumble, clatter, screech of a subway car, and after a moment people began to emerge from the kiosk across the street. He could hear their voices as they passed. One of them stopped before a clothing store, unlocked it and entered. A light went on within. The subway train departed, and the smell of it rose through the grating in the sidewalk and drifted toward him. Two more stores were opened. The sun became a red dome, an orange bubble clinging to the horizon. Telephone lines slashed it. The streetlights went out. There came the smack of a bundle of papers as they struck the concrete beside the newsstand. Day had begun.

He descended the stairs and entered a deserted basement. After a time, he found a dark and quiet place and he slept once more, for he was feeling worse.

When the watchman left the warehouse, he had breakfast at a nearby diner, orange juice, toast, scrambled eggs, two cups of coffee. Then he went home and kissed his wife, who was on her way out the door, Wednesday being the day she cleaned house for the Simpsons. He drank a glass of water, undressed and went directly to bed, for day had begun.

Of course it moved like lightning. Think about the drippy season for a moment, and you'll see why.

Take twelve million people, confine them in five boroughs, require that they move around every day in order to earn their livelihood, shake hands, eating and drinking together, sitting in rooms full of desks or toilets, laughing, sneezing, coughing in each other's faces and, "Kiss you? I shouldn't be doing this!" to each other, and let one man with a cold decide against staying home that day and you've got a drippy season.

All right, take it from there...

When he crawled out of the basement, on Saturday, there was no traffic for a long time, and then a black car passed. The store was closed, and the newsstand. He heard a bell ringing, over and over. He drank from a mud puddle, but it did not slake his thirst.

He lay on his side, panting, and after a time he closed his eyes. He gasped and lay still.

It comes in three varieties: bubonic, systemic, pneumonic. Depending on this, it may take two days or a couple of weeks. There is an anti-serum, but try getting enough to vaccinate twelve million people in a hurry.

The newspaper in the unopened bundle beside the stand warned of sick rats and rats found dead out in the open.

Later that year, the two million inhabitants of the five boroughs experienced another drippy season.

Notes

Caused by the bacteria *Yersinia pestis*, plague primarily infects rats, but the bite of an infected flea can give it to humans. **Bubonic** refers to plague's grossly swollen lymph nodes (buboes); **systemic** means that the bacteria is in the bloodstream; **pneumonic** means that the lungs are affected, and the disease can be transmitted by coughing.

T. S. ELIOT

<small>Written 1955–60 for *Chisel in the Sky;* previously unpublished.</small>

" 'Beyond the bounds of strophic hegemony
he pirouetted to a landfall
amidst Byzantine crockeries.'
Which is perhaps why I keep
this small mechanical bird on my dresser.
It cannot sing; only croaks;
reminder of the effects
of transmigration upon poetry
(which is altogether deleterious
during a human lifetime,
especially every month
at the full of the moon,
like a werewolf).

—But observe, Sir,
the detail-work on the pinfeathers!

It was struck for me by that noble artificer
Pound of Idaho, who first read
the entire *Rig-Veda* in the original
before melting down the metals!"

Notes

The *Chisel in the Sky* manuscript bears the handwritten edit of "Yeats" to "he" at the start of the second line. This may mean that the poem refers to Yeats's "Second Coming" which begins, "Turning and turning in the widening gyre || The falcon cannot hear the falconer."

T. S. Eliot was an American-born British poet who won the 1948 Nobel Prize for literature. In modern poetry **strophic** pertains to strophe, a separate section or extended movement that differs from a stanza because it does not follow a regular repeated pattern. **Hegemony** is leadership or predominant influence over others. By going **beyond the bounds of strophic hegemony** the poet has transcended traditional rules of stanzas and structure in poetry.
 Byzantine style, developed during the Byzantine Empire, is extraordinarily ornate. **Transmigration** is the soul's passage into another body after death. Ezra **Pound of Idaho** was a poet who established the Modernist movement in the mid twentieth century. The *Rig-Veda* is an ancient collection of sacred Sanskrit hymns dedicated to the gods or devas.

WALL

To Spin Is Miracle Cat, Underwood-Miller 1981.

I would like to come and live in your utopia
where brotherhood, sisterhood, joy,
simple communal pleasures, each to every,
dancing, singing, studying, sacrifice,
group therapy, nationalized poverty,
healthy pacifism, modern dance,
lots of wholesome food, mass calisthenics,
cold showers, jogging, writing workshops
and maybe a little flagellation
add backbone to the salt of the earth,
so to speak.

I will build you a great long wall.
Give me your wretched refuse
who do not believe in all of the above.
We will cause them to stand
with their backs against the wall,
blindfolded, as they were blind to the truth,
and I will help to preserve your ideals,
for even the best of us need protectors
every now and then.

Notes

Sir Thomas More coined the phrase "**utopia**" (a perfect place) for his 1516 book of the same name. **Flagellation** means flogging.

Here There Be Dragons

Here There Be Dragons, Donald M. Grant 1992.

Upon a time there was a king who was king of a very small country. Indeed, his kingdom was so small that most people were not even aware it existed. The king thought that it was a fairly large kingdom, though, as kingdoms went.

This was because there were many mountains around the place, mountains which were difficult to climb. Because of these mountains, travelers would just go on around the kingdom, rather than go through it.

And very few people ever left the kingdom, to come back and tell of other lands. People were pretty much afraid to do that.

They were afraid of the dragons.

They never saw any dragons, mind you, but they were afraid of them.

This is because all the maps in the kingdom showed that they were surrounded by dragons—dragons here, dragons there, dragons all over the place, all because of Mister Gibberling.

Mister Gibberling was the Royal Cartographer. (That means he was the official mapmaker.)

Mister Gibberling was the Royal Cartographer because his father and his grandfather had been Royal Cartographers.

Mister Gibberling had learned his profession from his father, who had learned it from *his* father.

Since people did not visit the kingdom very often, and the king's subjects seldom crossed over the mountains themselves, it was difficult for the Royal Cartographers to know exactly what to put down on their maps to show what was outside.

So, as he had learned from his father (who had learned it from *his* father), whenever he did not know what to show as being in any certain place, Mister Gibberling picked up his quill, and with a great flourish of the feather wrote (in fancy letters):

—Here There Be Dragons—

Then he would smile, because he had explained a new territory.

Of course, since he did not really know what lay beyond the mountains in any direction, it soon came to appear that the entire world was infested with dragons. (And he would draw little pictures of fire-breathing dragons, roaring and flapping their wings, beneath what he wrote—which certainly didn't help to promote tourism.)

This is why everyone was afraid of the dragons they had never seen.

If your father were to drive into a gas station and ask for a road map, and it said, "Here There Be Dragons" and it showed a little picture such as the ones Mister Gibberling drew, your father would take a different route.

So, since all the maps in the kingdom showed dragons everywhere, breathing flames and being mean, all the people in the kingdom stayed at home, because there were no other routes.

But then one day the king's daughter, the princess, was going to have a birthday, and the king wanted to celebrate it in a special way.

"I want fireworks!" he said.

"Yes, sire. A good idea," said his first adviser.

"Yes indeed, sire. A very good idea," said his second adviser.

"Oh yes, great sire! A very, very good idea," said his third adviser.

"Uh, where will we get them, sire?" asked his fourth adviser, who was never too popular around the court (but his dowager aunt was a good friend of the queen, so the king kept him about, despite his habit of asking uncomfortable questions). "The man who used to manufacture fireworks died some ten years ago," he explained, "and he never trained anyone to take his place. This is why there have been no fireworks displays in recent years."

"We shall simply have to get them," said the king, "because I want them."

"Yes," said the first adviser.

"We shall simply have to get them," said the second.

"Because the king wants them," said the third.

"How?" asked the fourth.

"Well—we could, ah—import them," said the first.

"Yes, import them," said the second.

"Import them, yes," said the third.

"From where?" asked the fourth.

"Well, uh—we could get them from…Hmm…"

"Yes, we could get them from Hmm," agreed the second.

"I was only hmming, not naming places," said the first.

"Oh, pardon me, I thought you meant the city of Hmm on the Mm river. It *is* too far away, now that I think of it."

"Why don't we get a map and look?" asked the third.

"An excellent idea," said the second. "Get a map and look."

So they did.

They gathered around the map and studied.

"There are dragons to the east," said the first.

"…And dragons to the west," said the second.

"…And dragons to the north," said the third.

"…And dragons to the south," said the fourth. "They seem to be all around us. In fact, there is only our kingdom and dragons on the map. Consequently, we cannot import any fireworks."

"It would seem to follow…" said the first.

"But the king wants them!" said the second.

"But where can we get them?" asked the third.

Then the first adviser had an idea. "What is a dragon, anyway?" he asked.

"Oh, big!" said the second.

"…And mean," said the third.

"…And ugly and scaly and strong and fire-breathing," finished the fourth. "There is a picture on the map—*many* pictures, as a matter of fact."

"Well," said the first, "dragons spout flames, don't they? Like Roman Candles, Vesuvius Fountains, Cannon Crackers, Whirlagigs, Blue Angels, Normandy Lights?"

"So I've always heard," said the second.

"Yes, exactly," said the third.

"When is the last time any of you has seen a dragon?" asked the fourth.

"Well…" said the first.

"Ah…" said the second.

"Er…" said the third.

"I was only curious," said the fourth. "I have never seen one myself."

"Oh, you. That doesn't prove anything," said the first.

"Now then, listen: If we can't import fireworks, why can't we import a dragon to do the same job? Fire, colored lights things like that?"

"A stunning idea!" said the second. "Import a dragon!"

"Congratulations," said the third. "It is a brilliant idea. Dragons are available everywhere, while fireworks are not."

"Yes," said the fourth. "I would like very much to see you import a dragon."

"I shall suggest it to the king immediately," said the first adviser.

He went and suggested it to the king.

"Oh, my yes!" said the king. "Won't it be jolly to have a dragon for the princess's birthday! Why didn't *I* think of that?"

"That is what advisers are for," said the first adviser.

"Send for a dragon immediately," ordered the king, "medium-sized, and with colored lights."

"Very good, sire," said the first adviser.

"Send for a dragon," he told the second.

"Send for a dragon," the second adviser told the third.

"Send for a dragon," the third adviser told the fourth.

"Who shall I send, and where?" asked the fourth.

"That is your problem," said the third. "I only relay orders."

"But I have no one to relay them to," said the fourth.

"Then do it yourself," said the third.

"This is ridiculous!" said the fourth, whose name, incidentally, was William.

"It is the order of the king," said the third. "Your place is to obey, not to question."

"Very well," said William, sighing. "I'll give it a try. But I still think it is ridiculous."

"It is the king's order. Go, import a dragon!"

And they laughed, as the fourth adviser went away to seek a medium-sized dragon with colored lights.

❖ ❖ ❖

"I wonder," William wondered, "who I can send to fetch me a dragon? —A knight! Of course! I'll send a knight. They are supposed to be accustomed to doing brave and bold and courageous things like that."

He walked up the street to the local inn, where the knights spent most of their time eating and drinking. He went into the inn and looked for the captain of the King's Guard.

The captain was seated at the first table, a huge platter of beef and a tankard of ale in front of him.

He was a fat man with a red face and a wart on the left side of his nose. He kept eating while William talked to him.

"Captain," he said, "I need a brave and courageous knight or three for a brave and courageous deed."

"All of my knights are brave and courageous," said the captain, without looking up from the table.

"The king needs a dragon," said William, "medium-sized and with colored lights. So, will you kindly supply me with someone brave and courageous enough to go after one?"

The captain choked on his ale and looked up suddenly.

"A dragon?" he said. "You want me to send one of my men after a dragon?"

"That is correct. One, or two, or three, or as many as you feel would be necessary."

The captain scratched his head.

"Well, I don't know," he said finally. "Most of my men are out of practice when it comes to dragons…"

The inn was suddenly very quiet. At the mention of the word "dragon" all the clattering of platters and tankards and dice had stopped. All the laughter and the sounds of table-pounding and chair-scraping had stopped.

William felt everyone staring at him. "Are you trying to tell me that your men would be *afraid* to go after a dragon?" he asked.

"Afraid!" snorted the captain through his mustaches (which were quite large, and blew up almost as high as his ears when he snorted). "My men afraid of dragons? I should say not!

"Are any of you men afraid of dragons?" he called out in a loud voice.

"N-no," came several soft answers. "But of course, we're out of practice when it comes to dragon-slaying…"

"Not slaying, just catching," said William, "and I can see that I'm getting nowhere this way. So I'll just ask for volunteers.—Do any of you men want to volunteer to go get a dragon for the princess's birthday party—and bring it back alive?"

No one answered.

"Come, come!" cried William, jumping up onto a table. "Surely a few of you brave fellows would be willing to do this thing to make the princess's birthday a happy and memorable occasion. Who will be first to volunteer?"

Still no one answered.

"Then I think you are all cowards!" said William.

"Not so, not so ! " cried the captain. "Consider, if you please, the circumstances. All of these men are fearless and have done many brave deeds in the past, or they would not be knights today. They are, as I said, just out of practice when it comes to dragons. They do not know the meaning of the word 'fear'."

"Doubtless," said William, "and a good many others besides.

"You there," he said to one man. "What was the last brave deed you did?"

The knight looked at his captain, looked at William.

Finally, he said, "I saved the princess's poodle from a large and ferocious rat one day, sir, and the king knighted me on the spot."

"I see," said William.

"And you?" he asked another knight. "What was your brave deed?"

"I escorted the queen to a ball, back when the king had an attack of the gout. He knighted me for it."

"I see," said William.

"How about you?" he asked another. "Have you ever captured a dragon?"

"No, sir," answered the knight, "but I caught a boy picking flowers in the palace garden and the king knighted me for it."

"A small boy?" asked William.

"He was pretty big for his age," said the knight.

"That was my nephew Louis," said William. "I remember the incident. He is short for his age.

"Have any of you knights ever *seen* a dragon?" he called out.

No one answered.

"How about you, captain?" he asked.

The captain looked back at his platter and reached for his tankard.

"I do not choose to answer that question, because it is none of your business," he told him.

"Then no one here knows anything about dragons, and no one here will help me?"

No one answered.

"All right. Then you are *all* cowards, and I will go by myself to seek a dragon."

He turned away and walked out of the inn.

❖ ❖ ❖

That afternoon he got his horse from the stable, put on a suit of armor, picked up his sword and shield and rode toward the mountains. The only one who missed him was his dowager aunt, who was a friend of the queen. She waved a pink handkerchief from a window of the highest tower in the castle, and he waved at her once and then did not look back. For three days he made his way through the mountains, but he did not meet any dragons. On the fourth day he came to a valley. It was marked on the map he carried, and slightly beyond it were written the words,

—Here There Be Dragons—

He dismounted and looked around. He looked for a long while, but there were no dragons. Then he sat down on a rock. After he had been sitting there for some time, he felt as if he were being stared at.

He turned his head slowly.

A small lizard was watching him from beneath a bush.

"Hello," he said to the lizard. "Any dragons around?"

The lizard kept staring at him. It blinked once, slowly.

"I wonder if you could be a baby dragon?" he said. "I think I'll capture you for practice."

He grabbed at the lizard.

It dashed away.

He threw his shield, aiming carefully.

The shield, which was curved, came down over it, trapping it in the hollow place beneath.

He reached there then and seized the lizard. Then he lifted the shield.

The little lizard was silver, the same color as the metal.

"You were green a moment ago," he said.

"That is because I was under a green bush," said the lizard.

"You can talk!" said William.

"Yes. There are lizards and there are *lizards*," replied the creature. "I am an educated lizard. Now, if you please, release me."

"No," said William. "You are the closest thing to a dragon that I've found so far, and I am going to keep you until something better comes along."

"That might not be wise," said the lizard. "Supposing I *am* a baby dragon, and my parents come looking for me?"

"Then I suppose I will have to try to take *them* back, too," William sighed.

"What?" said the lizard. "You do not look like a young knight out to make a name for himself. What do you want with a dragon?"

"I don't want a dragon," said William. "My king does. I am only following orders."

"What does he want with a dragon?"

"He wants it to provide a fireworks display for his daughter's birthday party," William explained.

"That is ridiculous," said the lizard.

"That is what I said, and what I still say," said William. "But mine is not to reason why. I just do what I am told, if I want to keep my otherwise easy job."

"Well, I am glad that someone has good sense," said the lizard. "My name is Bell. Maybe I can help you."

"How might you do that?"

"Stop squeezing my delicate sides so tightly and put me down on that rock. Then perhaps I'll tell you."

"How do I know that you won't run away?"

"You don't. You take my word for it. Otherwise, I don't talk, no matter how hard you squeeze me."

"All right," said William. "I didn't mean to hurt you."

"That's better," said Bell, after William had set him down.

"What's your name?"

"William."

"Great. Okay, now here is what you do—"

"You just turned gray!" said William. "Like the stone!"

"Yes, I have some chameleon blood in me from my mother's side of the family. Now about this dragon business: I am anxious to see your king and his court and his kingdom. I am also anxious to know how it is that you came to this valley to look for dragons."

"I have a map," said William. "See? 'Here There Be Dragons' is what it says about this valley."

"Who drew that map?"

"The Royal Cartographer, Mister Gibberling," said William.

"Aha! A Gibberling map!" said Bell. "An original! I'll tell you what. If you take me back with you to the court, and arrange for me to meet Mister Gibberling, I promise you that I will produce one real, live dragon upon demand."

"How?" William wanted to know.

"That is my business," said Bell, "and *that* is my proposition. Take it or leave it."

"Are you sure you can do it?"

"Yes," said Bell.

"All right," said William. "You produce a dragon when I ask you to, and I promise that you will get to meet Mister Gibberling."

"It's a deal," said Bell, turning brown as he jumped into the saddlebag. "Let's get going."

William mounted his horse and they rode away together.

❖ ❖ ❖

The princess's birthday party promised to be a gala affair. The great dining hall of the palace resounded with music. There was dancing and wine and big platters of food. There were whole roasted pigs with apples in their mouths, and there were chickens and dumplings and great roasts of beef. All the ladies and gentlemen of the kingdom came, and the ladies wore dresses of red and yellow and blue and orange and green and violet. There was a great birthday cake, the size of an elephant and a half, and it had ten candles on it, because that was how old the princess was. Everyone brought her wondrous gifts. There was everything that a person could possibly want at a birthday party. Except for fireworks, that is. Or a fire-breathing dragon.

"Do you think he will really produce a dragon?" asked the third adviser.

"Of course not," said the second. "How could *he* have gotten a dragon? And if he did, where is he keeping it?"

The captain of the King's Guard laughed. "You were going to seek a dragon all by yourself, eh?" he said. "Well, where is it?"

William did not answer him. Instead, he tapped his glass with his spoon until the room was quiet. Then he cleared his throat. He appeared to be a bit nervous.

"Uh, the time has come for the fireworks display," he told them all, "in honor of her young majesty's tenth birthday. Happy birthday, Princess. This is going to be a very special and rather unusual display."

The king laughed and slapped his leg.

"Yes, yes!" he cried out. "Bring it on, William! Bring it on! Medium-sized, and with colored lights, mind you!"

"Yes, your highness," said William, taking a tiny package from beneath the table and placing it before him. It is in here."

"It seems a pretty small package," said the king.

"Yes," said the first adviser.

"Yes indeed," said the second.

"Much too small," said the third.

The king opened the package. Bell jumped out and stood upon the table.

The three advisers laughed. The knights laughed. They laughed and laughed until the tears came into their eyes.

"*That* is supposed to be a medium-sized dragon, with colored lights?" they asked. "Ha! Ha! Ha! Ha! Ha!"

And they laughed and laughed and laughed some more, until Bell stood up on his tiny hind legs and turned to William and asked, "Now?"

"Now," he said.

Then something happened.

Bell had been the color of the oakwood table, but now he was dark, red-green in color and seemed slightly larger than he had been. He opened his mouth, and a tiny spark came out of it. Then he was bigger than the package he had come out of. He was twice as big as he had been only a moment before. He opened his mouth again, and the king drew back away from the flame that emerged.

Then Bell was as big as a man, and the platters rattled as they fell upon the floor, pushed away from him while he grew.

And he kept growing.

He grew and he grew, until the table broke in half beneath him.

He grew until he filled half the great banquet hall. He opened his mouth and roared with a sound like thunder. Flames shot forth from the windows of the palace and lighted up the courtyard outside. Tapestries were scorched. Women screamed and backed against the wall. Seven knights fainted, and the captain of the King's Guard ran and hid himself behind the throne.

William felt something crawling across his foot, and he looked down under what was left of the table. The first three advisers were crouched there, shivering.

"Well?" he asked them.

"Yes, it is a very good dragon," answered the first.

"Only it is not a medium-sized one," said the second. "No, it is a large, economy-sized dragon," said the third.

"He was the best I could manage on such short notice," said William, smiling.

The king pushed the princess behind his back and stood facing the dragon.

"My, you're a big one," he said. "Please do be careful with those flames. There are expensive tapestries and people and things like that about."

The dragon laughed. No one else did.

"I am Belkis," he roared, "king of the dragons! You are only a human king, so do not give me orders!"

"But I am sovereign majesty of a mighty kingdom," said the king, "and my word is law. I *order*. I really do order. And I am always obeyed. So please do not go about burning tapestries and people and things like that."

Belkis laughed again, and the flames danced about the rafters. "No one orders Belkis to do or not to do anything. I am only here for one reason. I want to meet your Royal Cartographer, Mister Gibberling. Produce him!"

The king backed away.

"That is Mister Gibberling down at the end of the table you just broke," he said. "The man with the white beard. The one still holding a glass in his hand."

"Aha! Mister Gibberling! So we meet at last!" snarled Belkis.

Mister Gibberling, who was indeed an old man, rose slowly to his feet. "Uh—I don't quite understand…" he began.

"You are the one who is giving dragons a bad name," said Belkis.

"Wh-what do you mean?" asked Mister Gibberling.

"Your maps! Your stupid, nasty little maps!" said Belkis, burning the edges of Mister Gibberling's beard as he spoke. "'Here There Be Dragons'! That is absurd! That is cheating! It is the refuge of a small mind!"

"Yes! Yes!" agreed Mister Gibberling, putting out his beard by emptying his wine-cup over it. "You are right! I have always felt mine to be quite small!"

"I want you to know that over the past several thousand years we dragons have taken great pains to stay out of the way of humans," said Belkis. "We have even taken to assuming other forms—such as that of the little lizard Bell, which you saw a bit earlier. We do not want people to know that we are still about—or they will be forever pestering us. Take any foolish young knight out to make a name for himself: What is the first thing he does?"

"I don't know," said Mister Gibberling.

"I will tell you," said Belkis. "He looks for a dragon to kill. If he can't locate any, though, he finds something else to do. Perhaps even something constructive. But you—with your dragon-filled maps!—you are keeping the old legend alive when we want it to die. We want people to forget, to leave us alone. Every time some young squire gets hold of one of your maps, he has visions of heading for the mountains around here in order to make some rank, to get to be a knight by killing dragons. This leaves dragons with the choice of eating them all or trying to ignore them. There are too many—and most of them pretty tasteless, not to mention hard to clean. So we attempt to ignore them. This is often very difficult, and it is your fault. You have been responsible for maintaining a thing better forgotten. Also," he stated, "you are a very poor geographer."

"My father was Royal Cartographer, and his father before him," said Mister Gibberling.

"What does that have to do with you?" asked Belkis. "You are a poor geographer."

"What do you mean?"

"What lies over those mountains?" asked Belkis, gesturing with a scaly wing.

"Drag—Oh! I mean—More mountains, sir," said Mister Gibberling.

"Admit it! You do not know!" said Belkis.

"All right! I don't know!" cried Mister Gibberling.

"Good," said Belkis. "That's something, anyway. Have you quills and ink and parchment handy?"

"No," said Mister Gibberling.

"Then go get them!" roared Belkis. "And be quick about it!"

"Yes, sir!" said Mister Gibberling, stumbling over his cloak as he dashed from the hall.

"...Be very quick about it!" said Belkis, flaming. "Or I will take this place apart, stone by stone, and drag you out by your whiskers—like a rat from a brick heap!"

Mister Gibberling was back in record time. While he was gone, though, Belkis ate three roasted pigs and a dozen chickens with dumplings. Then he roared again and scorched the ceiling and charred the throne.

"You have them now?" he asked.

"Yes, yes! Right here! See?"

"Very good. You are coming with me now."

And with that, he seized Mister Gibberling's cloak in his talons and flew out through the great double-door at the end of the hall, through which the Honor Guard sometimes entered on horseback. He took him high into the sky and they both vanished from sight.

"I wonder where he is taking him?" asked the third adviser.

"It is probably better not to think about it," said the first.

"We'd better get to work cleaning up this mess," said William.

❖ ❖ ❖

They flew far beyond the kingdom, and Belkis pointed out to Mister Gibberling that there were other kingdoms, and that there were rivers and lakes and other mountains, and valleys and plateaus and deserts, and ports and pastures and farms and granaries, and ships on the ocean and armies in the fields.

Every now and then he would say, "Are you getting that all down on paper?" and Mister Gibberling would answer, "Yes! Yes!" and he would scratch away with his quill and record all of the places which really existed in those spots where he had always been accustomed to write **Here There Be Dragons**.

Much later, they returned. Belkis set Mister Gibberling down in the courtyard, perching himself upon the wall like some great, red-green bird.

"Have you learned your lesson?" he asked.

"Yes. Yes, sir, great Belkis, sir," said Mister Gibberling, clutching his maps close to him, as if for protection.

"Then I will leave you now," said Belkis, "and I expect you to make *good* maps from now on. And remember this," he added, "I want you to forget about dragons."

"Yes, I promise," said Mister Gibberling. "I will forget all about dragons."

"See that you do," said Belkis, "or I will hear of it and I will return. You would not like that."

"No, no I wouldn't!"

"Then good-bye."

And Belkis spread his great wings and rose into the sky. No one in the kingdom ever saw him again. After that, though, the king came to listen to William more than he did to his other advisers, and soon William became his first adviser and his old first adviser became his new fourth adviser.

And Mister Gibberling went on to draw beautiful maps, showing all of the things he had seen—other kingdoms and rivers and lakes and other mountains, valleys and plateaus and deserts, ports and pastures, farms and granaries. His maps were quite good, and after a time people were no longer afraid of dragons and they began to go over the mountains and to trade with people in other kingdoms, and to learn of them, and to have other people come to visit them. After a time, the king came to realize that his kingdom was not so large as he had once thought it to be, and he encouraged commerce, to make his kingdom prosper and grow.

One day, though, while he was studying one of the new maps, the king said, "My, but there are so many seas in the world!"

"Yes, sire," said William. "That appears to be true."

"I wonder what lies beyond them?" asked the king.

"Perhaps they go on forever and ever," said William, "or perhaps there are other lands beyond them."

The king nodded.

"I believe I will ask the Royal Cartographer," he said, "since he has recently had a postgraduate course in cartography."

So he went to the chambers of Mister Gibberling and asked him, "What lies beyond all those seas which your maps show as bordering the lands?"

Mister Gibberling stroked his beard (which had grown back in again) and he studied a map for a long while.

Then he picked up his quill, and with a great flourish of the feather he wrote (in fancy letters) in that place at the farthest edge of all the waters:

—Here There Be Sea Serpents—

A Word from Zelazny

This is one of the two tales that Zelazny wrote for his children's amusement in 1968–69. He then commissioned Vaughn Bodé to illustrate them. Zelazny admired Bodé's work and knew he was particularly fond of drawing reptiles[1]—this story features a dragon, and the other ("Way Up High") features a pterodactyl.

The completed drawings were exhibited at the 1969 World Science Fiction Convention in St. Louis, but complications ensued. Bodé informed Zelazny that he had purchased the artwork but not the reproduction rights. Furthermore, Zelazny saw the book as two of his tales illustrated by Bodé, but Bodé viewed it as a showcase of his art illuminated by Zelazny's text. Placing the books with a regular publishing house proved difficult. But after Zelazny and Jack L. Chalker met in 1973, Chalker's Mirage Press announced the book's publication.[2] The project was shelved, however, when both principals demanded equal royalties (totaling 30% of each volume's sale price) making the project financially unworkable. Further negotiations showed promise of resolution, but then Bodé died accidentally in 1975. In 1992 Zelazny, Bodé's estate, Jack Chalker, and interested publishers resolved the difficulties, and a limited edition with both artwork and stories was finally published.[3]

Notes

It is an urban myth that maps bore the phrase "*Here be dragons*" to denote dangerous or unexplored territories; there is only one map from circa 1503 that has in Latin (HC SVNT DRACONES). Occasionally sketches of sea serpents and other mythological creatures filled in a map's blank areas, and less often the phrase "*Here be sea serpents*" appeared.

A **dowager** is a widow who holds significant title or property derived from her deceased husband.

---

1 *Roger Zelazny*, Jane Lindskold, 1993.
2 Letter from Roger Zelazny to Henry Morrison dated February 21, 1973.
3 *Science Fiction-Fantasy Publishers, Supplement 1*, July 1991-June 1993, Jack L. Chalker and Mark Owings, Mirage Press, 1993.

Morning with Music

Trypod #2, March 1968.

Dreams dreams
bloody dreams
why do I speak of dreams
when teeth of ice gnaw the window
day is here
and music
    ordered
    symmetrical
pumps with thought processional
the gray flower cerebrum
and dreams burrow eyeless
beneath the soil
colored unthinking blood
        rushing

Only perhaps
that without them

the bright unordered
I am less than me for unsleeping
unknowing
    the tear and the terror
    taste and device
that be the madness
every man must have
to touch with fire the music
squeeze from soul the spirit
to run upon the windowpane
and name the storm it boxes best

where but for this am I not.

Notes

Dreams informed and inspired many of Zelazny's works—and he asks here, what would he be without dreams?

    The **cerebrum** is the main part of the brain in humans and other vertebrates, responsible for the integration of complex sensory and motor functions.

I Walked Beyond the Mirror

To Spin Is Miracle Cat, Underwood-Miller 1981.

I walked beyond the mirror.
I met a mirror-man.
He held a backward walking stick
within his backward hand.
He offered me a reversed smile
and struck a left-right pose.
He spoke a backhand compliment.
I struck him on the nose.
"Oh, East is East and West is West
and ne'er the twain shall meet,"
said he as the full force of things
knocked him from his feet.
"True," said I, offhandedly,
"and then again reversed.
I offered you the best of both.
It somehow turned out worst."
"No matter, no matter," cried he,
"you meant me no left hooks.
I love you like a brother.
Perhaps I like your looks.
We shall embrace and clasp our hands
at the sound of the reversed tone."
We backed away, we turned away.
We found ourselves alone.

Way Up High

Manuscript title: "Susi's Magic Pterodactyl"
Way Up High, Donald M. Grant 1992.

Susi met Herman in the orchard she cut through on her way home from school. It was a very old orchard, and it *looked* quite old, too. This is because no one took care of it.

There had once been a house nearby, a house in which there lived people who had wanted the apples which grew in the orchard. The people moved away though, the house was torn down and the orchard went wild.

There were big dead branches lying all over the ground, and lots of live ones all twisted together overhead, like a roof. By the middle of the summer the grass was always very long, dandelions and daisies and milkweed plants waved all about and there were wild blackberry bushes growing in between the trees. All of this made it very shady and secret and out-of-the-way.

Even in the month of May, when all these things had not yet grown quite as tall and as thick as they could, it was still a secret place because nobody else cut through it but Susi. No one else knew the one path through the stickers where you would not scratch your legs. Not one of her friends went home in the same direction as Susi.

So, this is why she was all alone when she met Herman, on that fine, warm, sunny day during the last week of school.

She walked through the stickers, carefully, and she went around a big tree with branches reaching down almost to the ground—and there he was.

He was sitting on a rock with the sun shining down on him, and his eyes were closed.

She almost did not notice him, because he was the color of an old tree and because he sat there without moving.

But Susi knew that there had not been a big old tree there before. So she stopped and she said something.

She said, "Oh!"

Herman opened one eye and looked down at her.

"Hello," he said.

"Oh!" she repeated, and then she said, "Hello," because, after all, he had said it to her.

"You have a beak," she observed, looking up at him. "Are you a bird?"

"No," he told her. "I am too big to be a bird."

"I read about Condors in school," she said. "They are very big birds who live in South America, and they can fly all day high up over the Andes Mountains."

"So can I," said Herman, opening his other eye and unfolding his wings (which he had been holding wrapped around him so that he looked like a big old tree).

His wings were brown and they looked as if they were made of leather. They were as big as flaps on the tents down at the Fair.

"So can I," he repeated. "I can fly all day and all night and all the next day—higher than they can fly—and I'm bigger than Condors, too."

"And you are not a bird?" she said.

"Do you see any feathers on me?" he inquired.

"No," she answered, looking very closely. "But you have a beak, and wings..."

"An airplane has wings, but that does not make it a bird. A catbird *meows*, but that does not make it a cat," he said, "and seals bark, but that does not make them dogs."

"Then you are a bat," she decided. "A big bat. Bats don't have feathers."

"I am NOT a bat!"

"All right, then," said Susi, stepping back so that she could see better into his high, brown eyes. "All right, then," she said. "What are you?"

"I am a pterodactyl," he replied, turning his head so as to show her his better profile. "More specifically, an unrecorded sort of pteranodon. But pterodactyl will do nicely enough."

"A *what*?" asked Susi.

"A pterodactyl."

"Pter-o-dac-tyl," she said, slowly. "What's that?"

"Obviously," said Herman, sniffing slightly, "it is something that is better than birds and bats, because it is bigger and stronger and can fly higher and faster."

"You are bragging," she said.

"I am not! It's true!"

"Even if it is true," she decided, "you are still bragging."

"No, I am stating facts. If those facts happen to prove something good and wonderful about me, it is not bragging. It is being honest."

"It is still bragging," she said, "at the same time."

"I can't help it if I am good and wonderful," he explained. "It is just the way that I am. If I said anything else, I would be lying."

"All right," she told him, "you are good and wonderful."

"Thank you." His beak opened a little, in something like a smile. "Thank you, little girl. What is your name?"

"Susi," she said, "and I am *not* little."

"Anything smaller than a horse is little to me," he replied. "My name is Herman, and I am very pleased to make your acquaintance."

"I think I had better be going now," she told him, "or I will be late."

"Oh, don't go yet, please. Stay and talk with me awhile."

"For a minute or two more perhaps," she decided. "Why are you sitting on that rock?"

"Because I am a reptile and I am cold-blooded. I like to sit in the sun because it feels good and warm."

"A reptile?—Like a snake?" she asked, moving back away from him.

"Hardly," he replied.

Then, "Snakes!" he said, sniffing. "Dirty little crawlers on the ground—that's what snakes are. I am a creature of the heights. I soar. I know the freedom of the skies. I break apart clouds and I chase the moon down the night…"

"Don't snakes like to lie in the sun, too?" she asked him.

"Well—yes."

"Why is that?" she wanted to know.

"It is because they are cold-blooded and they want to be warmed."

"Like you do?"

"It is only a matter of coincidence," he said, "that they like some of the same things as pterodactyls."

"But you also said that you are cold-blooded—just like snakes."

"Ah, but that is where the resemblance ends," he replied. "They are earthbound slithers under rocks—and no relatives of mine. No!"

"What does cold-blooded mean? Is it like 'cruel'? I have heard people say cold-blooded when—"

"No, not at all. Not at all. It is a technical term referring to those creatures such as myself—and certain others—whose blood is always about the same temperature as it is outside. When the doctor takes your temperature, it bothers him if it is not what it should be. This is because it should *always* be around the same because you are warm-blooded. If it is much higher or lower than usual, you are probably sick.

"Mine changes all the time," he finished, "but best of all I like it warm."

"That is all very interesting," said Susi. "I had better be going now..."

"No. Please don't go," said Herman. "I want someone to talk to. I am lonesome."

"I will be late if I don't leave soon. Aren't there any other pterodactyls around for you to talk to?"

"No," he said. "They are all far away. Even my father and mother are on a trip."

"Father and mother?" she asked. "Are you a little pterodactyl?"

"I'm big for my age," said Herman, closing his beak with a loud *click*.

"But you are not all grown up yet?"

"Well, not quite no, not yet," he answered.

"How big is your father, then?" she asked.

"Have you been to the Fair, downtown?"

"Yes."

"Did you ride on the big merry-go-round?"

"Yes."

"Well, I guess my father could carry it away in his claws if he wanted to."

"Oh my!"

"But he wouldn't want to. He has no use for merry-go-rounds."

"I am afraid I am going to be late," said Susi. "Really, I had better go now."

"I will take you home," said Herman, "so that you will not be late—if you promise to come and talk with me tomorrow."

"I don't know if I should..." she began.

Herman's shoulders went a little lower, and she thought she saw a big tear forming in the corner of his eye.

She did not want him to be sad, so she said, "All right, I will stop here and talk to you tomorrow."

"Good!" said Herman, opening his beak wide and spreading his wings. "Good! I will take you home now. Where do you live?"

"I live in the house with the blue roof at the end of the street on the other side of those trees," she told him, pointing that way. "But you don't have to…"

…But before she was finished speaking, Herman had picked her up gently in his claws and with a flap of his great wings carried her high into the air.

The air came rushing all around her. She tried to say something, but the wind carried her words away.

Then she realized that her eyes were tightly closed.

She opened them.

Down below, the orchard seemed quite small, like a little green picture. All the houses were like toys on a floor.

"Herman! *Please* take me back down!" she cried. "We are too high!"

"No, we aren't," he answered. "We are not high at all. I can take you much higher if you would like."

"I wouldn't like," she answered. "I want to go home! My house is that little doll's house at the end of that tiny street—the one with the blue roof. You said that you would take me there."

"All right," he sighed, "I just thought you might enjoy flying some first. I was wrong. I am sorry. I can see that you do not enjoy it…"

"It is not that I don't enjoy flying. It is just that I will be late, and my mother will ask me why I am late, and I will tell her that I went flying with a pterodactyl named Herman, and she will stop my allowance for a week or something, because she does not like me to tell lies."

"But you would not be telling a lie," said Herman, swooping lower.

"I know that," she said, "and you know that, but I have a feeling that that's about as far as things would go."

"Hmm," hummed Herman, circling above the house, "I do believe that you are correct. I had forgotten something my mother once told me: People think that pterodactyls are extinct. That is what she said. I had never met any people though, and I forgot.

"All right, we are going to land now," he said. "I will set you down behind your garage. The next time we go you can ride on my back, if you would like. You must promise to hold on tightly, though."

"I will," she agreed, all out of breath.

"There will be a next time, won't there?" he asked.

And almost before she had realized it, she had said, "Yes."

She ran to the corner of the garage. Then she turned and looked back at him. He was still standing there, watching her. He looked very sad.

His beak was opened, as if he were about to say something. Then he closed it again and remained silent.

"Good-bye, Herman," she said.

"Good-bye, Susi."

"I'll see you tomorrow," she added.

Then she ran the rest of the way to the house and went inside.

After dinner that night, as she lay on the floor looking up at the ceiling, she said to her father, "What is a pterodactyl?"

Her father lowered his newspaper several inches and looked at her over the top of it.

"A what?" he asked.

"A pter-o-dac-tyl. With big, brown leathery wings, and a beak like a bird's—only he can fly higher and faster and farther than birds."

"A pterodactyl..." he repeated. "That's what I thought you said. Are you reading about them in school?"

"Well—I probably will some day."

"Mm," he mmed. "A pterodactyl is—or rather was—a big flying reptile that lived back in prehistoric times, back when there were dinosaurs and big tall ferns and giant trees. That was in the days when the world was warmer and swampier, and there were no people around yet."

"Are they cold-blooded—the pterodactyls?"

"Yes, I believe they were."

"Like a snake?"

"Yes, they were related to snakes and turtles and crocodiles and other creatures whose blood was that way."

"He lied to me!" she said.

"Who lied to you?"

"Herman—Oh!"

"A friend of yours? He lied about pterodactyls?"

"Yes. He said he—they—weren't related to snakes at all."

"Oh. Well, that's nothing to really be angry with him about. He probably didn't know for sure."

"He knows."

"It is hardly a matter of great concern," he said, raising the newspaper again. "I would be willing to forgive anyone who lied to me about pterodactyls."

"I suppose I will. But why do people think pterodactyls are extinct—now?"

"Because they are," he replied.

"But why?"

"Because they died with all the other reptiles when the world got colder. Warm-blooded creatures came along and were smarter and more adaptable—"

"But turtles are still around—and crocodiles, and—snakes," she said, "and they are cold-blooded. You said so."

"Well, I guess it is because they are smaller and they could find more places to crawl into—places where they could keep warm—and they didn't need as much food as the larger reptiles."

"But couldn't the pterodactyls fly away to some place where it is warmer and where there is more to eat?"

"Oh, I suppose so!" he said, and then he tried to read his paper again.

After a long while, she asked him, "Where do you think they flew to?"

"South America," he answered.

"*Where* in South America?"

"The jungles of Brazil," he said. "They're still unexplored."

"I'll bet that's where he's from…" she decided.

❖ ❖ ❖

The next day she ran all the way from the schoolyard to the orchard, so that she could have more time to talk to Herman.

She arrived all out of breath, and she scratched her leg a little, even though she knew the path through the stickers.

Herman was sitting on the same rock as before, looking as if he had not moved at all since the first time she had seen him there.

"Hello, Herman," she said.

"Susi!" He opened both his eyes quickly. "You *did* come! I knew you would."

"I promised."

"Is that the only reason you came?"

"No," she told him, "I wanted to see you again."

"Good. Oh good!" he replied. "Do you want to fly with me?"

"Not just yet," she answered, "I'd like to talk some more."

"Surely," he agreed. "What would you like to talk about?"

"Pterodactyls lived way back in prehistoric times, didn't they? Back when there were dinosaurs and giant ferns and real big trees? Back when the world was swampier and there were no people around yet?"

"That is essentially correct. Those were known as the Good Old Days."

"...And then the world got colder and food got harder to find."

"Yes. We still talk about the days when we were the aristocracy, when we traveled first class and everyone else walked. Came the revolution though, and we were no longer on top."

"What revolution?"

"Of the Earth," he replied. "It changed somehow, I guess, and the days grew colder. The big trees fell down and the giant ferns died. The swamps dried up and the ice came moving down across the land in big sheets."

"That sounds terrible! What did you do then?"

"We flew away."

"To South America?"

"Why yes, that's right."

"To the jungles of Brazil?"

"How did you ever guess?"

"Just did."

"You warm-blooded ones are very clever at guessing things," he acknowledged. "Yes, that is what we did. Would you like to go flying now?"

"Yes," she told him. "May I ride on your back this time?"

"Of course. I'll get down low, and you climb on."

He did that, and she got onto his back.

"Mind that you hold tight to my neck now," he instructed her. "I don't want to go chasing you all the way down the sky."

"Don't worry," she said. "I won't let go."

He launched himself into the air, and this time she did not close her eyes. She kept them open and watched everything getting smaller and smaller beneath them as they rose higher and higher.

"How high are we?" she asked.

"Not very high yet," he answered. "See, there is an airplane coming, and it is higher than we are. Let's chase it!"

"All right. But don't hurt it."

"I won't. I just want to play."

His huge wings beat against the air, out on both sides of her, and Susi felt a fresh rush of wind against her face. It was a good feeling. Herman had very big muscles in his shoulders, so she felt that he was strong. She had ridden horses before, and she had always trusted the horses because they were strong and they always seemed to know what they were doing. She felt the same way about Herman. She felt safe with him.

So she held on about his neck and enjoyed the ride.

They were as high as the airplane now…

Then they were higher than the airplane.

She watched its big propellers spinning in the air. It was coming in their direction, and soon it would pass beneath them.

Then Herman dived at it.

"Herman!" she screamed.

"I'm only playing," he assured her.

They shot down past the airplane, and Herman almost touched the tip of its long, shiny metal wing with his own long, brown leathery one.

She tried to think what would have happened if they had touched.

As they flashed by, she watched the airplane. In the windows on that side there were faces, like pale portraits with glass covering them over, all hung there and facing them as they went by, and all of them wearing startled expressions.

"You frightened me!" said Susi. "I thought we were going to hit it!"

"I told you I was only playing," Herman said.

"…And you frightened all those people inside."

"Not really," he explained. "It livened up their lives for a moment. Already they are forgetting what they really saw. Some will say we were a flying saucer and some will say that we were a flock of geese, or a little airplane that got off its course and came too near their flight lane. Whatever they think, they will never know for sure. So we have given them each a little mystery to ponder, for a time. 'What did I really see?' they will ask themselves. 'Certainly not a pterodactyl, because they are extinct—and even if it were a pterodactyl, what could it be doing with a little girl riding on its back?' And they will never know, not really. It is always good to have some mysteries to think about. It keeps you from getting the feeling that life is simple and explainable. I have, therefore, done all of them a great service by flying past their plane."

"When you put it that way," said Susi, "you make it sound all right. —But can we go back down now? I still have to get home on time."

"All right. Why do you always have to be home 'on time', though? What is 'time' to you?"

"'Time' is when you have to be at a certain place before certain things happen, and if you are not there then you are late and everyone is mad. Tomorrow is Friday though, which is the last day of school, and after that comes Saturday. Saturday I can play with you all day, instead of just for a little while. Then we will have the whole summer vacation ahead of us."

"Oh, fine!" said Herman. "Let's take a trip!"

"Where to?"

"I don't know. Is there anyplace special that you would like to go?"

"I don't know. We have the whole summer, though."

"Yes, we do…" he replied, swooping down to a landing behind the garage.

❖   ❖   ❖

Saturday they went on a picnic, on a little island in the middle of a big lake. Susi did not know exactly where it was, except that it was far away. Herman ate six ham sandwiches while she watched, and then he flew out over the lake to catch fish, because he was still hungry.

He would circle and circle, peering down into the water. Then he would dive, like a rock suddenly falling. His great beak would strike the water first, like a spear. Then moments later he would come flashing back up out of the lake, wet and glistening, with a fish held tightly in his beak. In a moment, the fish would be gone and then he would climb into the air and begin circling again.

After a time, he returned and landed on the beach beside her.

"My, you eat a lot!" she said.

"When you are big, you have an appetite to match," he replied.

"How much do full-grown pterodactyls eat?" she asked.

"Oh, a great deal. In fact, they spend most of their time looking for food."

"Isn't that kind of tiresome?" she asked.

"Not if you enjoy eating," he said.

"I don't know that I'd enjoy looking for food all the time."

"Well," he answered, "when you enjoy something, you also come to enjoy the questing of it. I'd say half of one's life is spent looking for the things one enjoys—and perhaps that is the half that is more enjoyable."

"The questing?"

"The questing."

"What shall we do now?" she asked.

"Let us go sit in the sun and feel warm and good."

"All right."

"…Because whenever one quest is fulfilled, that is the best thing to do before you begin another," he finished.

They sat in the sun for a long while, feeling warm and good, until finally Herman yawned, covering his beak delicately with the tip of his wing.

Then he stretched, and he was like a great dark flag unfurling.

"Shall we go for another flight?" he asked.

"Oh, yes!"

"Then climb aboard." He bowed down.

And they were off.

High into the air they climbed, and Susi felt like a skyrocket or a roman candle going off on its way to the moon, only it was still daytime, and she knew she would not fall back again, but come down gently.

They flew out across the lake and over the big hills beyond it. Then they climbed higher and higher, until the air grew a little chilly, even for a Saturday afternoon at the beginning of June.

Then Susi asked, "How high are we?"

"Higher than I have ever taken you before," Herman replied, "but not really high, as pterodactyls see it."

Susi looked down.

The road was a tiny yellow ribbon and the trees were like the tops of young carrots, just sprouting. The fields looked as if they had been painted green, rather than being all full of grass.

They swept onward, and he took her even higher.

There were rivers like little silver threads, and the bridges going across them were like tiny roller skates, to fit a doll perhaps. The roofs of the houses, all colors, were like the little rows of stones you line up on the beach.

Still they went higher, and small wisps of white, like smoke, fled past them.

"What are those?" she asked.

Herman turned his head.

"Pieces of clouds," he answered. "There's a whole one up ahead."

She looked.

"It's just like fog!" she protested.

"Of course. That's all that clouds are—fog that is way up high."

"But I thought that they were like pillows, or cotton candy."

"They look that way from down below," he admitted, "but they are really fog that just won't stay put."

He turned in his course and flew through a cloud.

Suddenly, it was like walking to school on a damp morning—like wearing boots and walking along and not being able to see the telephone poles on the other side of the street.

"How do you know where you're going?" she asked.

"I just know," he said.

"Like radar?"

"Yes, like radar," he told her. "There! We're out!"

And suddenly there was sun again, and the cloud was down below them.

They flew over cities and mountains and plains. They flew over swamps and forests and lakes.

Finally, they came to a place where men sent rockets with tails of fire screaming into the air. The rockets would shake the atmosphere as an earthquake shakes the earth, then pass on up into the places where there is no air.

"Can rockets go higher than pterodactyls?" she asked.

"They go higher then pterodactyls need to go," he answered.

"Can they go faster?"

"They go faster than pterodactyls want to go."

"Then they can fly better."

"But they can't catch fish," said Herman. "They have no quests of their own. They do not enjoy sitting in the sun."

"Is it that important to do those things, if you can fly high and fast?"

"Yes," said Herman.

So they flew on, until at last they came to the ocean.

"What is all that water?" she asked.

"That is the ocean," said Herman. "There is more of it than there is land to the world. Sooner or later all things come to rest in it, rolling beneath the sun in big blue waves."

"Let us go back now," she said. "I am afraid."
Herman turned and headed back.

❖   ❖   ❖

Almost every day they went flying. Susi's father mentioned one night that there were unusual footprints behind the garage, but since he did not ask her what they were, she did not tell him that they were pterodactyl prints. After that, though, Herman always took her back to the orchard and she walked home.

Herman made his home in the orchard. Susi thought about this for a long while. Then one day in the middle of July, after she had known him for going on to two months and felt that she could ask a personal question, she said, "Herman, why aren't there any other pterodactyls for you to play with?"

"I told you that they are all far away," he said.

"Yes. But if that is true, why are you here?"

"What do you mean 'if that is true'? Do you think I lied to you?"

"Well, you fibbed to me about not being related to snakes."

"Oh, that. They are such distant relatives that we don't really count them any more."

"But they are still relatives. My father said so."

"You told him about me?"

"No, no," she said. "I'm keeping your secret. Butt I asked him about pterodactyls one night and he said that they are related to snakes—and turtles and crocodiles."

"We seldom acknowledge the turtles or crocodiles either."

"That's not very nice. In fact, it's rather snobbish."

"All right! So I'm a liar, I'm a snob! Don't trust me any more!"

"I didn't mean it that way. Really I didn't. Don't be hurt, Herman. It's just that I've been wondering where your mother and father and all the other pterodactyls are—and why they went away and left you all alone."

"I told you they are far away."

"In South America."

"Maybe."

"In the jungles of Brazil?"

"Perhaps. Maybe I flew away from home. Maybe *I* left *them*. What difference does it make? We've had fun together, haven't we?"

"Yes."

"Then what difference does it make?"

"I don't know. It's just that I was curious."

"It is a pterodactyl matter entirely, and it has nothing to do with people," he said. "You wouldn't understand."

"Are there many of you down there?"

"Let's talk about something else, or go for a flight."

"All right, let's fly."

So they did.

They flew over such wondrous places—shipyards and harbors, campuses and railroad yards, amusement parks and farms where men worked in the fields—that she forgot all about her questions.

They flew over ships on the ocean and flew past airplanes in the sky. They raced freight trains down hills and across the plains. They flew over churches and reservoirs, and they passed above a Boy Scout encampment on a hillside, and none of the bird watchers in the camp could identify Herman.

Sometimes she would take her storybooks to the orchard and read them to Herman. He liked the ones about the princes who were turned into frogs, and best of all he liked the one about the little mermaid. He made her read it to him three times.

"But it is so sad," she said.

"I know, but I like sad things," he told her.

"Are you magic?" she asked.

"What do you mean?"

"Are you really a prince who has been turned into a pterodactyl, or anything like that?"

"No," he said. "I am a pterodactyl. That's all."

"...Of course, if you were enchanted, you couldn't tell me about it. That could be part of the enchantment."

"True, I suppose. But I am not," he said. "I am a pterodactyl, pure and simple."

"But are you magic?"

"Sort of," he said. "In the way that the sun making you feel warm and good is magic, in the way that the wind blowing past you when you spread your wings and soar is magic, in the way that flying high and seeing everything and going through clouds and seeing that they are only wandering fog is magic. That's all. The kind of magic everyone's got, probably even snakes: Your own way of seeing things. Mine is the pterodactyl way."

"Is that really magic?"

"It is the only magic."

"Then what's my magic?"

"I can't tell you. You must learn it yourself. Everyone has to find his own."

"When will I learn it?"

"I can't tell. But you will, I know that."

"Can we fly some more now, Herman?"

"Read me another story first," he said.

❖ ❖ ❖

Soon it was August.

Everything in the orchard had now grown as tall and dense as it could grow. The blackberry bushes were as thick as a wall, and their once green thorns were as hard and sharp as needles now, and dark, the color of wood.

The apple trees all had fruit, and Susi would eat it as she sat in the sun with Herman. He did not like it especially, himself.

And as August wore on, she began to wonder again. To wonder about how a pterodactyl had come to live, all alone, in this orchard. To wonder why he was there, and all alone.

She did not ask him again, though, because she knew he would not tell her. She simply went on wondering. She remembered, however, that he had once said, "You warm-blooded creatures are very clever at guessing things." Perhaps he wanted her to guess.

No, she did not think so. He wanted her to forget the questions. "It is a pterodactyl matter entirely," he had also said.

So she let it rest at that and went on reading to him and going for flights with him.

Soon it was near to the end of August, and the time was drawing near when she would be returning to school. This made her feel a little sad, because she would miss the long summer days with Herman. She knew, somehow, that she would never have another summer such as this one. And this made her sad.

The nights began to grow a little chilly, as they sometimes can in August—in a sort of preliminary shivering of the year as it thinks about the winter that lies ahead.

It made her feel a little afraid, sort of like the time she had looked down at the ocean over Herman's shoulders, and seen it there, all big and blue and moving, and nowhere any end to it. Would all the blackberries, wild roses and the apple trees somehow come to rest in it one day, rolling beneath the sun in its big blue waves, as Herman had said? She wondered. She wondered if this whole summer would rest there one day. No, she decided. It would continue to go on as memories in her head.

But the nights were chilly, especially chilly for August. And each morning she noticed that it took Herman longer to wake up and want to move around. He sat in the sun longer and longer.

She remembered about him being cold-blooded, which meant that his blood was the same temperature as it was outside. So at night he must get very cold, she thought. What will he do when winter comes?

❖   ❖   ❖

Then, the last week of her vacation, Herman said to her, "Will you go flying with me tonight?"

"Tonight?"

"Yes, after it gets dark."

"I don't know…I'd have to sneak out. I don't think I should."

"It is very special," he said. "Please do it. Bring a sweater, because it will be cold. Please come."

"All right…" she agreed.

And that night she lay awake in bed until the house was still and dark. Then she got up and dressed as quietly as she could and went outside.

Herman knew she would be afraid to go all the way to the orchard in the dark, so he waited for her behind the garage.

She climbed onto his back and asked him, "Where are we going?"

"For a last flight," he said, and he sprang into the air, flapping his wings.

Then they were high and going higher.

"A last flight?" she said.

"Yes."

They flew far. How far they flew, she never really could tell.

But she had never flown at night before. The sky was like black silk with little drops of water sprinkled all over it. Each star shone as it had never shone before, when she looked up at them all from down on the ground.

She looked back down, and she was higher than she had ever been before.

The city down below was like the stars up above—little points of light with only blackness in between.

She clung tightly to Herman and looked up again.

"I see the stars," she told him, "and they are beautiful."
She took a deep breath.
"…And the air is so clean and good."
"Yes," he replied, beating his wings faster.
"…And the city below—oh, the city below!—it is so beautiful too, Herman!"
"I wouldn't know about cities," he told her.
"Yes, it is. It is beautiful."
"People build cities," he said. "Pterodactyls do not. So I will have to take your word for it. Did you never notice that it was beautiful before?"
"No," she said.
"Then I think you are beginning to find your magic."
"Really?"
"Yes, and I am glad for you."
"You said that this is our last flight?"
"That is correct," he told her.
"Why?"
"Drink in the night," he said. "Breathe deeply. Look at the world all laid out before you, sparkling through the dark. It is your world, warm-blooded Susi, not mine."
"What do you mean?"
"Nothing, but that you should look and enjoy. Understanding comes later."
They flew on, and on and on.
Then he turned in his flight and headed back in the direction from which they had come.
It took a long while, and Susi was sleepy despite the chill and the excitement of the flight, so she knew that it was late, very late, well past her bedtime.
Finally, they were circling above her backyard.
Then they dropped, down, down, down, and landed gently behind the garage.
The moon was just risen in the sky, and a big, round, and cream-colored moon it was.
She climbed down from Herman's back and faced him.
"Now will you tell me," she asked, "what you meant by 'last flight'?"
"I must go," he said, "now. I thought that I could remain longer, but the weather grows too cold too soon. I cannot stand cold weather. I must fly south, like the birds do."
"To South America?"

"Perhaps."

"Why 'perhaps'? Why is it such a big secret? Why don't you tell me where you are going, and where the other pterodactyls are?"

"It does not really matter," he said, "honestly. So good-bye, Susi. The time is come."

"Don't go, Herman! I will miss you!"

"And I will miss you too, Susi. But I must go."

"Will you come back, next summer?"

He spread his wings.

"Of course I will, Susi. Good-bye."

Then the thing she had been wondering about, the thing she had been trying to guess at, to figure out, all summer long—suddenly came to her.

She blurted it out without thinking it over. If she had had time to think, perhaps she would not have said it. But then again, perhaps she would.

"You're the last, aren't you, Herman? You're the very last pterodactyl in the whole world," she said. "Aren't you?"

He did not answer, but he rose into the air with one downward sweep of his great wings. Then he was as high as the treetops.

"*Aren't* you?" she called out. "Isn't that right? You're the only one left!"

He circled the yard high above her, and a single drop, like a drop of rain fell upon her cheek.

Then his wings made a great wind, and he was so high that he was almost the size of a bird against the stars.

"I love you, Herman!" she called out. "Honest I do! Please come back! Come back next summer!"

Then he was so small that she could barely make him out. Then he was gone.

She watched the sky for a long while, feeling little and weak and sad. Something very big and strong, which could fly higher and faster and farther than birds, and which could have been quite terrible if it had chosen to be—with its big beak and its claws—was gone away now.

And she felt that it was forever and that she would never see Herman again.

She watched until she realized how cold it was and how very sleepy she had become.

Then she went inside quite quietly, and she went upstairs to bed.

And that very same night she dreamed that she had found her magic at last.

In the morning she cried.

A Word from Zelazny

"I still remember how when I first saw Vaughn Bodé's work, I knew that he had to illustrate my two children's books—*Way Up High* and *Here There Be Dragons*. His work had a special bite to it that seemed to fit them perfectly. (*Way Up High*, by the way, was Vaughn's title, not mine. I didn't like my working title and asked him for suggestions. I did like his title and used it. Unfortunately, a number of prospective publishers didn't agree on this, because that was the 60s, Vaughn seemed the archetypal hippie, and the word 'high' had its special connotations.)"[1]

Notes

A **pterodactyl** was a flying reptile from the Jurassic and Cretaceous periods that had a short tail, teeth, a birdlike beak, and a finger supporting each wing *(-dactyl* means "finger"). A **pteranodon** was a flying reptile from the late Cretaceous period which had a toothless beak, similar to birds of today *(-nodon* means "no teeth"). Herman must not have any teeth because he says he is more correctly described as a pteranodon.

---

1 *Science Fiction Age* 1994 Vol 2 No 2.

Museum Moods

Written 1955–60 for *Chisel in the Sky*; previously unpublished.

I.

Steep above the clouds have stopped,
and we are suspended
in the loss of warmth:
Our frozen pond.

II.

Fie o day
a long night off,
and that we cannot sleep.
We toss and cough
till still is come.
Black day!

III.

And the night
is a porch rail
to hang wet galaxies upon.

IV.

Who walk the feet of gods
but seven men,
and they are fools.
And who the feet of men
but gods that are idiots?

V.

And who meant man
that said silence?
The greatest virtue
is walking,
while feet are the props
that hold a higher thing
than all they walk upon.

Footsteps tongue
by far
then best
the man.

VI.

The veil you have rent
with every strained skill
of hungry fingers
hid either Medusa or emptiness,
else would you not
ever mirror it.

VII.

The idle idols wait
the non-idyllic day.

VIII.

You are *crux ansata* arms
and standing man behind.
The arms and the man are empty things,

and you, beyond ruin,
the terrible power of position.

IX.

Beat your way to chaos, then!
I would rather destroy
a library of worlds in my mind

than build one
I believed in.

X.

And even must the final word
be walking,

as my blood footsteps
now even
my brain
toward blacking day.

Notes

The second half (stanzas VI–X, renamed to I–V) appeared as "Sentiments with Numbers" in *To Spin Is Miracle Cat*.

Crux ansata is the Egyptian cross or ankh, the symbol for life, also referred to as "cross with handle." "**Arms and the man**" quotes Virgil's *Aeneid*. George Bernard Shaw used it to title a play.

Storm and Sunrise

To Spin Is Miracle Cat, Underwood-Miller 1981.
Written 1955–60 for *Chisel in the Sky*.

…machine of day pulling taffy.

The Steel General

If, January 1969.
Creatures of Light and Darkness, Doubleday 1969.

I

Upward stares Wakim, seeing the Steel General. "Faintly do I feel that I should have knowledge of him," says Wakim.

"Come now!" says Vramin, his eyes and cane flashing fires green. "All know of the General, who ranges alone. Out of the pages of history come the thundering hoofbeats of his war horse Bronze. He flew with the Lafayette Escadrille. He fought in the delaying action at Jarama Valley. He helped to hold Stalingrad in the dead of winter. With a handful of friends, he tried to invade Cuba. On every battleground, he has left a portion of himself. He camped out in Washington when times were bad, until a greater general asked him to go away. He was beaten in Little Rock, had acid thrown in his face in Berkeley. He was put on the Attorney General's list, because he had once been a member of the I.W.W. All the causes for which he has fought are now dead, but a part of him died also as each was born and carried to its fruition. He survived, somehow, his century, with artificial limbs and artificial heart and veins, with false teeth and a glass eye, with a plate in his skull and bones out of plastic, with pieces of wire and porcelain inside him—until finally science came to make these things better than those with which man is normally endowed. He was again replaced, piece by piece, until in the following century, he was far superior to any man of flesh and blood. And so again he fought the rebel battle, being smashed over and over again in the wars the colonies fought against the mother planet, and in the wars the individual worlds fought against the Federation. He is always on *some* Attorney General's list, and he plays his banjo and he does not care, for he has placed himself beyond the law by always obeying its spirit rather than its letter. He has had his metal replaced with flesh on many occasions and been a full man once more—but always he hearkens to some distant bugle and plays his banjo and follows—and then he loses his humanity again. He shot craps with Leon Trotsky, who taught him that writers are underpaid; he shared a boxcar with Woody Guthrie, who taught him his music and that singers are underpaid; he supported Fidel Castro for a time and learned that lawyers are underpaid. He is almost invariably beaten and used and taken advantage of, and he does not care, for his ideals mean more to him than his flesh. Now, of course, the Prince Who Was A Thousand is an unpopular cause. I take it, from what you say, that those who would oppose the House of Life and the House of the Dead will be deemed supporters of the Prince, who has solicited no support—not that that matters. And I daresay you oppose the Prince, Wakim. I should also venture a guess that the General will support him, inasmuch as the Prince is a minority group all by himself. The General may be beaten, but he can never be destroyed, Wakim. Here he is now. Ask him yourself, if you'd like."

The Steel General, who has dismounted, stands now before Wakim and Vramin like an iron statue at ten o'clock on a summer evening with no moon.

"I have seen your beacon, Angel of the Seventh Station."

"Alas, but that title perished with the Station, sir."

"I still recognize the rights of the government in exile," says the General, and his voice is a thing of such beauty that one could listen to it for years.

"Thank you. But I fear that you have come too late. This one—this Wakim—who is a master of temporal fugue would, I feel, destroy the Prince and thus remove any basis for our return. Is that not so, Wakim?"

"Of course."

"Unless we might find a champion," says Vramin.

"You need look no further," says the General. "It is best you yield to me now, Wakim. I say this with no malice."

"And I reply with no malice: Go to hell. If every bit of you were to be destroyed, then I feel there would no longer be a Steel General—

and there would never be again. I think a rebel, such as yourself deserves annihilation, and I am here."

"Many have thought so, and I am still waiting."

"Then wait no longer," says Wakim, and he moves forward. "The time is here, and begging to be filled."

II

Horus has entered the Middle Worlds, and he comes to the world of mists that is called D'donori by its inhabitants, meaning Place of Contentment. As he disembarks from his chariot that has crossed the cold and airless night he hears the sounds of armed strife about him within the great mists that cover over all of D'donori.

Slaying with his hands the three knights who fall upon him, he comes at length to the high walls of the city of Liglamenti.

D'donori is a world which, though it lies within the tides of the Power, has never been subject to the plagues, the wars, the famines that limit the populations of the other Midworlds. This is because the inhabitants of D'donori take care of their own problems. D'donori is made up of numerous small city-states and ducal principalities which are constantly at war with one another, uniting only for purposes of destroying anyone who attempts to unite them on a permanent basis.

Horus approaches the great gates of Liglamenti and bangs upon them with his fist. The booming sound carries throughout the city and the gates creak upon their hinges.

A guard hurls down a torch through the gloom and follows it with an arrow, which, of course, misses its mark—for Horus is able to know the thoughts of his attacker and mark the line of the arrow's flight. He steps to the side as the arrow whizzes past him and he stands in the light of the torch.

"Open your gates or I'll unhinge them!" he calls out.

"Who are you that walks about weaponless, wearing only a loin cloth, and would give me orders?"

"I am Horus."

"I do not believe you."

"You have less than a minute to live," says Horus, "unless you open these gates to me. Your death will be the proof that Horus does not lie. I will then unhinge these gates and enter here, walking upon you as I pass in search of your Lord."

"Wait! If truly thou be he, understand that I am only doing my duty and following the orders of my Lord. Do not think me blasphemous if I should refuse admittance to any who may call himself Horus. How do I know but that thou art an enemy who would say this to deceive me?"

"Would an enemy dare be so foolish?"

"Mayhap. For most men are fools."

Horus shrugs and raises his fist once more. A vibrant musical note stirs then within the air, and the gates of Liglamenti shiver upon their hinges and the guard within his armor.

Horus has increased in stature by now, to near three meters. His breechclout is the color of blood. The torch flickers at his feet. He draws back his fist.

"Wait! I will give thee entrance!"

Horus lowers his fist, and the music dies. His height decreases by a third.

The guard causes the portal to be opened, and Horus enters Liglamenti.

❖   ❖   ❖

Coming at length to the fogshrouded palace of its ruler, the Lord Dilwit, Duke of Ligla, Horus learns that word of his arrival has preceded him from the walls. The somber, black-bearded Duke, whose crown has been grafted upon his scalp, manages as much of a smile as he is able; that is, the showing of a double row of teeth between tight-drawn lips. He nods slightly.

"Thou art truly Horus?" he asks.

"Yes."

"It is told that every time the god Horus passes this way there is difficulty in recognizing him."

"And no wonder," says Horus. "In all this fog it is rather miraculous that you manage to recognize one another."

Dilwit snorts his equivalent of a laugh. "True. Often we do not, and slay our own men in error. But each time Horus has come, the ruling Lord has provided a test. The last time…"

"…The last time, for Lord Bulwah, I sent a wooden arrow into a two-foot cube of marble so that either end protruded from a side."

"Thou rememberest!"

"Of course. I am Horus. Do you still have that cube?"

"Yes. Certainly."

"Then take me to it now."

They enter the torchlit throne room, where the shaggy pelts of predators offer the eye its only diversion from the glittering war weapons upon the walls. Set atop a small pedestal in a recessed place to the left of the throne is a cube of gray and orange marble which contains an arrow.

"There you see it," says Dilwit.

Horus approaches, regards the display.

"I'll design my own test this time," says he. "I'll fetch you back the arrow."

"It might be drawn. That is no—"

Horus raises his right fist to shoulder level, swings it forward and down, striking the stone, which shatters. He retrieves the arrow and hands it to Dilwit.

"I am Horus," he states, again.

Dilwit regards the arrow, the gravel, the chunks of marble.

"Thou art indeed Horus," he agrees. "What may I do for thee?"

"D'donori has always been justly famous for its scriers. Those of Liglamenti have oft been exceeding good. Therefore, I would consult with your chief scrier, as I've several questions I'd have answered."

"This would be old Freydag," says Dilwit, flicking rock dust from his red and green kilt. "He is indeed one of the great ones, but..."

"But what?" asks Horus, already reading Dilwit's thought, but waiting politely, nevertheless.

"He is, Great Horus, a mighty reader of entrails. But none but those of the human sort will serve him. Now, we seldom keep prisoners, as this can run into some expense. And volunteers are even harder to come by for things such as this."

"Could not Freydag be persuaded to make do the entrails of some animal, for this one occasion?"

Horus reads again and sighs.

"Of course, Great Horus. But he will not guarantee the same level of reception as he would with better components."

"I wonder why this should be?"

"I cannot answer this, Most Potent Horus, being no scrier myself—though my mother and sister both had the Sight. But of all scriers, I know scatologists to be the queerest sort. Take Freydag, now. He's quite nearsighted, he says, and this means—"

"Furnish him with the necessary components and advise me when he is ready to entertain my questions!" says Horus.

"Yes, Puissant Horus. I will organize a raiding party immediately, as I can see thou art anxious."

"Most anxious."

"...And I've a neighbor could use a lesson in observing boundaries!"

Dilwit springs upon his throne, and reaching upward takes down the long gol-horn which hangs above it. Three times does he place it to his lips and blow until his cheeks bulge and redden and his eyes start forth from beneath the pelt of his brows. Then does he replace the horn, sway, and collapse upon his ducal seat.

"My chieftains will attend me momently," he gasps.

Momently, there comes the sound of hoofbeats, and three kilted warriors, mounted upon the unicornlike golindi, come riding, riding, riding, into and about the chamber, staying only when Dilwit raises his hand and cries out, "A raid! A raid, my hearties! Upon Uiskeagh the Red. Half a dozen captives I'll have of him, ere the mist lightens with tomorrow's dawn!"

"Captives, did you say, Lord?" calls out the one in black and tan.

"You have heard me right."

"Before tomorrow's dawn!" A spear is raised.

Two more flash high.

"Before tomorrow's dawn!"

"Aye!"

And they circle the chamber and depart.

❖   ❖   ❖

The following dawn, Horus is awakened and conducted to the room where six naked men lie, hands and ankles bound together behind their backs, their bodies covered with gashes and welts. This chamber is small, cold, lighted by four torches; its one window opens upon a wall of fog. Many sheets of that monthly journal, the Ligla *Times*, are spread upon the floor, covering it fully. Leaning against the windowsill, a short, age-tonsured man, pink-face, hollow-cheeked and squinting, sharpens several brief blades with a whetting bar. He wears a white apron and a half-furnished smile. His pale eyes move upon Horus, and he nods several times.

"I understand thou hast some questions," he says, pausing to gasp between several words.

"You understand correctly. I've three."

"Only three, Holy Horus? That means one set of entrails will doubtless do for all. Surely, a god as wise as thyself could think of more questions. Since we have the necessary materials it is a shame to waste them. It's been so long…"

"Three, nevertheless, are all the questions I have for the entrail-oracle."

"Very well, then," sighs Freydag. "In that case, we shall use his," and he indicates with his blade one gray-bearded man whose dark eyes are fixed upon his own. "Boltag is his name."

"You know him?"

"He is a distant cousin of mine. Also, he is the Lord Uiskeagh's chief scrier. A charlatan, of course. It is good fortune that has finally delivered him into my hands."

The one called Boltag spits upon the *Times* obituary section when this is spoken. "Thou art the fraud! Oh mighty misreader of innards!" says he.

"Liar!" cries Freydag, scrambling to his side and seizing him by the beard. "This ends thy infamous career!" and he slits the other's belly. Reaching in, he draws forth a handful of entrails and spreads them upon the floor. Boltag cries, moans, lies still. Freydag slashes along the bending length of the intestines, spreading their contents with his fingers. He crouches low and leans far forward. "Now, what be thy questions, son of Osiris?" he inquires.

"First," says Horus, "where may I find the Prince Who Was A Thousand? Second, who is the emissary of Anubis? Third, where is *he* now?"

Freydag mumbles and prods at the steaming stuff upon the floor. Boltag moans once again and stirs.

Horus attempts to read the thoughts of the scrier, but they tumble about so that finally it is as if he were staring out the room's one window.

❖ ❖ ❖

Then Freydag speaks:

"In the Citadel of Marachek," he says, "at Midworlds' Center, there shalt thou meet with one who can take thee into the presence thou seekest."

"…Strangely," mutters Boltag, gesturing with his head, "thou hast read that part aright. But thy failing vision—was clouded—by that bit of mercenary thou hast erroneously mixed—into things…" With a mighty effort Boltag rolls nearer, gasps, "And thou—dost not tell—Great Horus—that he will meet with mighty peril—and ultimately—failure…"

"Silence!" cries Freydag. "I did not call thee in for a consultation!"

"They are my innards! I will not have them misread by a poseur!"

"The next two answers are not yet come clear, dear Horus," says Freydag, slashing at another length of entrail.

"False seer!" sobs Boltag. "Marachek will also lead him to the emissary of Anubis—whose name is spelt out in my blood—there—on the editorial page! That name—being—Wakim!"

"Oh, false!" cries Freydag, slashing further.

"Hold!" says Horus, his hand falling upon the man's shoulder. "Your colleague speaks truly in one respect, for I know his present name to be Wakim."

Freydag pauses, considers the editorial page.

"Amen," he agrees. "Even an amateur may suffer an occasional flash of insight."

"So it seems I am destined to meet with Wakim after all, if I go to the place called Marachek—and go there I must. But as to my second question: Beyond the name of Wakim, I wish to know his true identity. Who was he before Lord Anubis renamed him and sent him forth from the house of the Dead?"

Freydag moves his head nearer the floor, stirs the stuff before him, hacks at another length.

"This thing, Glorious Horus, is hidden from me. The oracle will not reveal it—"

"Dotard…!" gasps Boltag. "It is there, so—plain—to see…"

Horus reaches after the gutless seer's dying thought, and the hackles rise upon his neck as he pursues it. But no fearsome name is framed within his mind, for the other has expired.

Horus covers his eyes and shudders, as a thing so very near to the edge of comprehension suddenly fades away and is gone.

When Horus lowers his hand, Freydag is standing once more and smiling down upon his cousin's corpse.

"Mountebank!" he says, sniffing, and wipes his hands upon his apron.

A strange, small, beastly shadow stirs upon the wall.

III

Diamond hooves striking the ground, rising, falling again. Rising...

Wakim and the Steel General face one another, unmoving.

A minute goes by, then three, and now the falling hooves of the beast called Bronze come down with a sound like thunder upon the fairground of Blis, for each time that they strike the force of their falling is doubled.

It is said that a fugue battle is actually settled in these first racking moments of regard, before the initial temporal phase is executed, in these moments which will be wiped from the face of Time by the outcome of the striving, never to have actually existed.

The ground shakes now as Bronze strikes it, and blue fires come forth from his nostrils, burning downward into Blis.

Wakim glistens with perspiration now; and the Steel General's finger twitches, the one upon which he wears his humanity-ring.

Eleven minutes pass.

Wakim vanishes in a flash.

The Steel General vanishes.

Bronze descends again, and tents fall down, buildings shatter, cracks appear within the ground.

Thirty seconds ago, Wakim is standing behind the General and Wakim is standing before the General, and the Wakim who stands behind, who has just arrived in that instant, clasps his hands together and raises them for a mighty blow upon that metal helm—

—while thirty-five seconds ago, the Steel General appears behind the Wakim of that moment of Time, draws back his hand and swings it—

—while the Wakim of thirty seconds ago, seeing himself in fugue, delivering his two-handed blow, is released to vanish, which he does, into a time ten seconds before, when he prepares to emulate his future image observed—

—as the General of thirty-five seconds before the point of attack, sees himself draw back his hand, and vanishes to a time twelve seconds previously...

All of these, because a foreguard in Time is necessary to preserve one's future existence...

...And a rearguard, one's back...

...While all the while, somewhere/when/perhaps, now, Bronze is rearing and descending, and a probable city trembles upon its foundation.

...And the Wakim of forty seconds before the point of attack, seeing his arrival, departs twenty seconds backward—one minute of probable time therefore being blurred by the fugue battle, and so subject to alteration...

...The General of forty-seven seconds before the point of attack retreats fifteen to strike again, as his self of that moment observes him and drops back eight—

...The Wakim of one minute before goes back ten seconds—

Fugue!

Wakim behind the Steel General, attacking, at minus seventy seconds sees the General behind Wakim, attacking, as both see him and his other see both.

All four vanish, at a pace of eleven, fifteen, nineteen and twenty-five seconds.

...And all the while, somewhere/when/perhaps, Bronze rears, falls, and shock waves go forth.

The point of initial encounter draws on, as General before General and Wakim before Wakim face and fugue.

Five minutes and seven seconds of the future stand in abeyance as twelve Generals and nine Wakims look upon one another.

...Five minutes and twenty-one seconds, as nineteen Wakims and fourteen Generals glare in frozen striking stances.

...Eight minutes and sixteen seconds before the point of attack, one hundred twenty-three Wakims and one hundred thirty-one Generals assess one another and decide upon the moment...

...To attack *en masse*, within that instant of time, leaving their past selves to shift for themselves in defense—perhaps, if this instant be the wrong one, to fall, and so end this encounter, also.

❖   ❖   ❖

But things must end somewhere.

Depending upon the lightning calculations and guesses, each has picked this point as the best for purposes of determining the future and holding the focus. And as the armies of Wakims and the Generals clash together, the ground begins to rumble beneath their feet and the fabric of Time itself protests this use which has been made of its dispositions. A wind begins to blow and things become unreal about them, wavering between being and becoming and afterbeing. And somewhere Bronze smashes his diamonds into the continent and spews forth gouts of blue fire upon it. Corpses of bloodied and broken Wakims and fragments of shattered Generals drift through the twisting places beyond the focus of their struggles and are buffeted by the winds. These be the dead of probability, for there can be no past slaying now and the future is being remade. The focus of the fugue has become this moment of intensity, and they clash with a force that sends widening ripples of change outward through the universe, rising, diminishing, gone by, as Time once more ticks history around events.

Beyond their midst, Bronze descends and somewhere a city begins to come apart. The poet raises his cane, but its green fires cannot cancel the blue flare that Bronze exhales now like a fountain upon the world. Now there are only nine cities on Blis and Time is burning them down. Buildings, machines, corpses, babies, pavilions, these are taken by the wind from the flame, and they pass, wavering, by the fairground. Regard their colors. Red? There's a riverbank, green stream hung above, and flying purple rocks. Yellow and gray and black the city beneath the three lime-bright bridges. Now the creamy sea is the sky and buzzsaw come the breezes. The odors of Blis are smoke and charred flesh. The sounds are screams amid the clashing of broken gears and the rapid-fire rainfall of running feet like guilt within the Black Daddy night that comes on like unconsciousness now.

"Cease!" cries Vramin, becoming a blazing green giant in the midst of chaos. "You will lay waste the entire world if you continue!" he cries, and his voice comes down like thunder and whistles and trumpets upon them.

They continue to strive, however, and the magician takes his friend Madrak by the arm and attempts to open them a gateway of escape from Blis.

"Civilians are dying!" cries a moment of the General.

A moment of Wakim laughs

"What difference does a uniform make in the House of the Dead?"

A great green door appears in outline, grows more substantial, begins to open.

Vramin diminishes in size. As the door swings wide, he and Madrak are both swept toward it, as tall waves race and topple upon a windslashed ocean.

The armies of Wakim and the General are also raised by the waves of chaos and driven by the winds of change until they, too, are come at last to the green gateway which stands now wide, like a luminous magnet/drain/whirlpool's center. Still striving, they flow toward it and one by one pass within and are gone.

Bronze begins to move very slowly as the gateway closes, but somehow passes through it before the chaos comes upon the empty space it occupied.

Then the roaring and the movement cease and the entire world of Blis seems to sigh within the moment of its reprieve. Many things are broken and people dead or dying at this moment, which could have been one set thirty-three seconds before Wakim and the General began the fugue which will not now begin upon the litter-strewn fairground with its crevasses and its steaming craters.

Among the fallen archways, the toppled towers, the flattened buildings, salvation strides with its sword of fires unsheathed. The fevers of the day come forth from the Houses of Power, and somewhere a dog is barking.

IV

Regard now the Citadel of Marachek at Midworlds' Center... Dead. Dead. Dead. Color it dust.

This is where the Prince Who Was Once A God comes often, to contemplate—many things.

There are no oceans on Marachek. There are still a few bubbly springs, these smelling like wet dogs and being warm and brackish. Its sun is a very tired and tiny reddish star, too respectable or too lazy ever to have become a nova and passed out in a burst of glory, shedding a rather anemic light which makes for deep, bluish shadows cast by grotesque stands of stone upon the enormous beach of dun and orange that is Marachek beneath its winds; and the stars above Marachek may be seen even at midday, faintly, though in the evening they acquire the intensity of neon, acetylene and flashbulb above the windswept plains; and most of Marachek is flat, though the plains rearrange themselves twice daily, when the winds achieve a kind of sterile climax, heaping and unheaping the sands and grinding their grains finer and finer—so that the dust of morning and dusk hangs throughout the day in a yellowish haze, which further detracts from Marachek's eye in the sky—all, ultimately, leveling and settling, the mountains having been ground down, the rocks sculpted and resculpted, and all buried and resurrected perpetually. This is the surface of Marachek, which of course was once a scene of glory, power, pomp and pageantry, its very triteness crying out for this conclusion; but further, there is one building upon Marachek at Midworlds' Center which testifies to the saw's authenticity, this being the Citadel, which doubtless shall exist as long as the world itself, though mayhap the sands shall cover and discover it many times before that day of final dissolution or total frigidity. The Citadel—which is so old that none can say for certain that it was ever built. The Citadel, which may be the oldest city in the universe, broken and repaired (who knows how often?) upon the same foundation, over and over, perhaps since the imaginary beginning of the illusion called Time. The Citadel, which in its very standing testifies that some things *do* endure, no matter how poorly, all vicissitudes—of which Vramin wrote, in *The Proud Fossil*:

"The sweetness of decay ne'er touched thy portals, for destiny is amber and sufficient"—the Citadel of Marachek-Karnak, the archetypal city, which is now mainly inhabited by little skittering things, generally insects and reptiles, that feed upon one another, one of which (a toad) exists at this moment of time beneath an overturned goblet upon an ancient table in Marachek's highest tower (the northeastern) as the sickly sun raises itself from the dust and dusk, and the starlight comes down less strongly. This is Marachek.

When Vramin and Madrak enter here, fresh through the gateway from Blis, they deposit their charges upon that ancient table, made all of one piece out of a substance pink and unnatural which Time itself cannot corrupt.

This is the place where the ghosts of Set and the monsters he fights rage through the marble memory that is wrecked and rebuilt Marachek, the oldest city, forever.

❖ ❖ ❖

Vramin replaces the General's left arm and right foot; he turns his head so that it faces forward once more, then he makes adjustment upon his neck, to hold the head in place.

"How fares the other?" he inquires.

Madrak lowers Wakim's right eyelid and releases his wrist.

"Shock, I'd suppose. Has anyone ever been torn from the center of a fugue battle before?"

"To my knowledge, no. We've doubtless discovered a new syndrome—'fugue fatigue' or 'temporal shock' I'd call it. We may get our names into textbooks yet."

"What do you propose to do with them? Are you able to revive them?"

"Most likely. But then, they'd start in again—and probably keep going till they'd wrecked this world also."

"Not much here to wreck. Perhaps we could sell tickets and turn them loose. Might net a handsome penny."

"Oh, cynical monger of indulgences! 'Twould take a man of the cloth to work a scheme like that!"

"Not so! I learned it on Blis, if you recall."

"True—where life's greatest drawing card had become the fact that it sometimes ends. Nevertheless, in this case, I feel it might be wiser to cast these two upon separate worlds and leave them to their own devices."

"Then why did you bring them here to Marachek?"

"I didn't! They were sucked through the Gateway, when I opened it. I aimed for this place myself because the Center is always easiest to reach."

"Then suggestions are now in order as to our course of action."

"Let us rest here awhile, and I will keep these two entranced. We might just open us another Gateway and leave them."

"'Twould be against my ethics, brother."

"Speak not to me of ethics, thou inhuman humanist! Caterer to whatever life-lie man chooses! Th'art an holy ambulance-chaser!"

"Nevertheless, I cannot leave a man to die."

"Very well. Hello! Someone has been here before us, to suffocate a toad!"

Madrak turns his eye upon the goblet.

"I've heard tales that they might endure the ages in tiny, airless crypts. How long, I wonder, has this one sat thus? If only it lives and could speak! Think of the glories to which it might bear witness."

"Do not forget, Madrak, that I am the poet, and kindly reserve such conjectures to those better able to say them with a straight face. I—"

Vramin moves to the window, and, "Company," says he. "Now might we leave these fellows in good conscience."

Upon the battlements, mounted like a statue, Bronze whinnies like a steam whistle and raises three legs and lets them fall. Now he exhales laser beams into the breaking day, and his rows of eyes wink on and off.

Something is coming, though still unclear, through the dust and the night.

"Shall we, then?"

"No."

"I share thy sentiment."

Sharing, they wait.

V

Now everyone knows that some machines make love, beyond the metaphysical writings of Saint Jakes the Mechanophile, who posits man as the sexual organ of the machine which created him, and whose existence is necessary to fulfill the destiny of mechanism, producing generation after generation of machinekind, all the modes of mechanical evolution flowing through man, until such a time as he has served his purpose, perfection has been reached, and the Great Castration may occur. Saint Jakes is, of course, a heretic. As has been demonstrated on occasions too numerous to cite, the whole machine requires a gender. Now that man and machine undergo frequent interchanges of components and entire systems, it is possible for a complete being to start at any point in the mech-man spectrum and to range the entire gamut. Man, the presumptuous organ, has therefore achieved his apotheosis or union with the Gaskethead through sacrifice and redemption, as it were. Ingenuity had much to do with it, but ingenuity of course is a form of mechanical inspiration. One may no longer speak of the Great Castration, no longer consider separating the machine from its creation. Man is here to stay, as a part of the Big Picture.

Everyone knows that machines make love. Not in the crude sense, of course, of those women and men who, for whatever economic purposes may control, lease their bodies for a year or two at a time to one of the vending companies, to be joined with machines, fed intravenously, exercised isometrically, their consciousness submerged (or left turned on, as it would be), to suffer brain implants which stimulate the proper movements for a period not to exceed fifteen minutes per coin, upon the couches of the larger pleasure clubs (and more and more in vogue in the best homes, as well as the cheap street corner units) for the sport and amusement of their fellows. No. Machines make love via man, but there have been many transferences of function, and they generally do it spiritually.

Consider, however, an unique phenomenon which has just arisen: the Pleasure-Comp—the computer like an oracle, which can answer an enormous range of inquiries, and will do so, only for so long as the inquirer can keep it properly stimulated. How many of you have entered the programmed boudoir, to have enormous issues raised and settled, and found that time passes so rapidly. Precisely. Reverse-centaur-like—i.e., human from the waist down—it represents the best of two worlds and their fusion into one. There is a love story wrapped up in all this background, as a man enters the Question Room to ask the Dearabbey Machine of his beloved and her ways. It is happening everywhere, always, and there can often be nothing quite so tender.

VI

Now comes Horus who, seeing Bronze on the wall, deposeth and saith: "Open this damned gate or I'll kick it down!"

To which Vramin makes reply over the battlement, saying:

"Since I did not fasten it, I am not about to undo it. Find your own entrance or eat dust."

Horus does then kick down the gate, at which Madrak marvels slightly, and Horus then mounts the winding stair to the highest tower. Entering the room, he eyes the poet and the warrior-priest with some malevolence, inquiring:

"Which of you two denied me passage?"

Both step forward.

"A pair of fools! Know you that I am the god Horus, fresh come from the House of Life!"

"Excuse us for not being duly impressed, god Horus," says Madrak, "but none gave us entrance here, save ourselves."

"How be you dead men named?"

"I am Vramin, at your service, more or less."

"And I, Madrak."

"Ah! I've some knowledge of you two. Why are you here, and what is that carrion on the table?"

"We are here, sir, because we are not elsewhere," says Vramin, "and the table contains two men and a toad—all of whom, I should say, are your betters."

"Trouble can be purchased cheaply, though the refund may be more than you can bear," says Horus.

"What, may I inquire, brings the scantily clad god of vengeance to this scrofulous vicinity?" —Vramin.

"Why, vengeance, of course. Has either of you vagabonds set eyes upon the Prince Who Was A Thousand recently?"

"This I must deny, in good faith."

"And I."

"I come seeking him."

"Why here?"

"An oracle, deeming it a propitious spot. And while I am not eager to battle heroes—knowing you as such—I feel you owe me an apology for the entrance I received."

"Fair enough," says Madrak, "for know that our hackles have been raised by a recent battle and we have spent the past hours waxing wroth. Will a swig of good red wine convey our sentiments—coming from what is, doubtless, the only flask of the stuff on this world?"

"It should suffice, if it be of good quality."

"Bide then a moment."

Madrak fetches forth his wine bulb, swigs a mouthful to show it unsullied, casts about the room.

"A fit container, sir," he says, and raises up the downturned goblet which lies upon the table. Wiping it with a clean cloth, he fills it and proffers it to the god.

"Thank you, warrior priest. I accept it in the spirit in which it was offered. What battle was it which so upset you that you forgot your manners?"

"That, Brown-eyed Horus, was the battle of Blis, between the Steel General and the one who is called Wakim the Wanderer."

"The Steel General? Impossible! He has been dead for centuries. I slew him myself!"

"Many have slain him. None have vanquished him."

"That pile of junk upon the table? Could that truly be the Prince of Rebels, who one time faced me like a god?"

"Before your memory, Horus, was he mighty," says Vramin, "and when men have forgotten Horus, still will there be a Steel General. It matters not which side he fights upon. Win or lose, he is the spirit of rebellion, which can never die."

"I like not this talk," says Horus, "Surely, if one were to number all his parts and destroy them, one by one, and scatter them across the entire cosmos, then would he cease to exist."

"This thing has been done. And, over the centuries have his followers collected him and assembled the engine again. This man, this Wakim, whose like I have never seen before," says Vramin, "voiced a similar sentiment before the fugue battle which racked half a world. The only thing which keeps them from laying waste—excuse the poor choice of words—to this world Marachek is that I will not permit them to awaken again from a state of temporal shock."

"Wakim? This is the deadly Wakim? Yes. I can believe it as I look upon him in repose. Have you any idea who he is really? Such champions do not spring full-grown from the void."

"I know nothing of him, save that he is a mighty wrestler and a master of the fugue, come to Blis in her last days before the dark tides swept over her—perhaps to hasten their coming."

"That is all you know of him?"

"That is all I know."

"And you, mighty Madrak?"

"The sum of my knowledge, also."

"Supposing we were to awaken him and question him?"

Vramin raises his cane.

"Touch him and I shall dispute your passage. He is too fearsome an individual, and we came here to rest."

Horus lays a hand upon Wakim's shoulder and shakes him slightly. Wakim moans.

"Know that the wand of life is also a lance of death!" cries Vramin, and with a lunging motion spears the toad, which sits immediately beside Horus's left hand.

❖   ❖   ❖

Before Horus can turn upon him, there is a quick outward rush of air as the toad explodes into a towering form in the center of the table.

His long golden hair stands high and his thin lips draw back in a smile, as his green eyes fall upon the tableau at his feet.

The Prince Who Had Been A Toad touches a red spot on his shoulder, says to Vramin, "Did you not know that it has been written, 'Be kind to bird and beast'?"

"Kipling," says Vramin, smiling. "Also, the Koran."

"Shape-shifting miscreant," says Horus, "are you the one I seek—called by many the Prince?"

"I confess to this title. Know that you have disturbed my meditations."

"Prepare to meet your doom," says Horus, drawing an arrow—his only weapon—from his belt, and breaking off its head.

"Do you think that I am unaware of your power, brother?" says the Prince, as Horus raises the arrowhead between thumb and forefinger. "Do you think, brother, that I do not know that you can add the power of your mind to the mass or velocity of any object, increasing it a thousandfold?"

There is a blur in the vicinity of Horus's hand and a crashing sound across the room, as the Prince stands suddenly two feet to the left of where he had been standing and the arrowhead pierces a six-inch wall of metal and continues on into what is now a dusty and windy morning as the Prince continues to speak: "And do you not know, brother, that I could as easily have removed myself an inconceivable distance across space with the same effort as it took me to avoid your shot? Yea, out of the Middle Worlds themselves?"

"Call me not brother," says Horus, raising the shaft of the arrow.

"But thou art my brother," says the Prince. "At least, we'd the same mother."

Horus drops the shaft.

"I believe you not!"

"And from what strain do you think you derived your godlike powers? Osiris? Cosmetic surgery might have given him a chicken's head, and his own dubious strain an aptitude for mathematics—but you and I, shapeshifters both, are sons of Isis, Witch of the Loggia."

"Cursed be my mother's name!"

Suddenly, the Prince stands before him on the floor of the chamber and slaps him with the back of his hand.

"I could have slain you a dozen times over, had I chosen," says the Prince, "as you stood there. But I refrained, for you are my brother. I could slay you now, but I will not. For you are my brother. I bear no arms, for I need none. I bear no malice, or the burden of my life would be staggering. But do not speak ill of our mother, for her ways are her own. I neither praise nor do I blame. I know that you have come here to kill me. If you wish to enjoy an opportunity to do so, you will hold your tongue in this one respect, brother."

"Then let us speak no more of her."

"Very well. You know who my father was, so you know that I am not unversed in the martial arts. I will give you a chance to slay me in hand-to-hand combat, if you will do a thing for me first. Otherwise, I will remove myself and find someone else to assist me, and you may spend the rest of your days seeking me."

❖   ❖   ❖

"Then this must be what the oracle meant," says Horus, "and it bodes ill for me. Yet I cannot pass up the chance to fulfill my mission, before Anubis's emissary—this Wakim—achieves it. For I know not his powers, which might exceed your own. I will keep my peace, run your errand and kill you."

"This man is the assassin from the House of the Dead?" says the Prince, looking upon Wakim.

"Yes."

"Were you aware of this, my Angel of the Seventh Station?" asks the Prince.

"No," says Vramin, bowing slightly.

"Nor I, Lord" —Madrak.

"Arouse him—and the General."

"Our bargain is off," say Horus, "if this be done."

"Awaken them both," says the Prince, folding his arms.

Vramin raises his cane, and the green tongues come forth and descend upon the prostrate forms.

Outside, the winds grow more noisy. Horus shifts his attention from one to the other of those present, then speaks: "Your back is to me, brother. Turn around that I may face you as I slay you. As I said, our bargain is off."

The Prince turns.

"I need these men, also."

Horus shakes his head and raises his arm.

Then, "A veritable family reunion," says the voice which fills the chamber, "we three brothers having come together at last."

Horus draws back his hand as from an asp, for the shadow of a dark horse lies between himself and the Prince. He covers his eyes with one hand and lowers his head. "I had forgotten," he says, "that by what I learned today, I am also kin to thee."

"Take it not too badly," says the voice, "for I have known it for ages and learned to live with it."

And Wakim and the Steel General awaken to a sound of laughter that is like the singing wind.

VII

Osiris, holding a skull and depressing a stud on its side, addresses it, saying: "Once mortal, you have come to dwell in the House of Life forever. Once beauty, blooming fair atop a spinal column, you withered. Once truth, you have come to this."

"And who," answers the skull, "is perpetrator of this thing? It is the Lord of the House of Life that will not let me know rest."

And Osiris makes answer, saying: "Know, too, that I use thee for a paperweight."

"If ever thou didst love me, then smash me and let me die! Do not continue to nourish a fragment of she who once loved thee."

"Ah, but dear my lady, one day might I re-embody thee, to feel thy caresses again."

"The thought of this thing repels me."

"And I, also. But one day it might amuse me."

"Dost thou torment all who displease thee?"

"No, no, shell of death, think never that! True, the Angel of the Nineteenth House attempted to slay me, and his nervous system lives, threaded amidst the fibers of this carpet I stand upon; and true, others of my enemies exist in elementary forms at various points within my House—such as fireplaces, ice lockers and ashtrays. But think not that I am vindictive. No, never. As Lord of Life, I feel an obligation to repay all things which have threatened life."

"I did not threaten thee, my Lord."

"You threatened my peace of mind."

"Because I resembled thy wife, the Lady Isis?"

"Silence!"

"Aye! I resembled the Queen of Harlots, thy bride. For this reason didst thou desire me and desire my undoing—"

The skull's words are then cut short, however, as Osiris has hurled it against the wall.

As it falls to pieces and chemicals and microminiature circuitry are spread upon the carpet, Osiris curses and falls upon a row of switches at his desk, the depression of which gives rise to a multitude of voices, one of which, above the others, cries out, through a speaker set high upon the wall:

"Oh clever skull, to so have tricked the fink god!"

Consulting the panel and seeing that it is the carpet which has spoken, Osiris moves to the center of the room and begins jumping up and down.

There grows up a field of wailing.

VIII

Into the places of darkness and disrepute, upon the world called Waldik, enter the two champions, Madrak and Typhon. Sent by Thoth Hermes Trismegistus to steal a glove of singular potency, they are come to do battle with the guardian of that glove. Now, the world Waldik, long ago ravaged, hosts an horde of beings who dwell beneath its surface in caverns and chambers far removed from the courts of day and night. Darkness, dampness, mutation, fratricide, incest and rape are the words most often used by the few who offer commentary upon the world Waldik. Transported there by a piece of spatial hijackery known only to the Prince, the champions will succeed or remain. They go now through burrows, having been told to follow the bellowing.

"Think you, dark horse shadow," asks the warrior-priest, "that thy brother can retrieve us at the proper moment?"

"Yes," replies the shadow that moves at his side. "Though if he cannot, I care not. I can remove myself in my own way whenever I wish."

"Yes, but I cannot."

"Then worry it, fat Dad. I care not. You volunteered to accompany me. I did not request this thing."

"Then into the hands of Whatever May Be that is greater than life or death, I resign myself—if this act will be of any assistance in preserving my life. If it will not, I do not. If my saying this thing at all be presumptuous, and therefore not well received by Whatever may or may not care to listen, then I withdraw the statement and ask forgiveness, if this thing be desired. If not, I do not. On the other hand—"

"Amen! And silence, please!" rumbles Typhon. "I have heard a thing like a bellow—to our left."

Sliding invisible along the dark wall, Typhon rounds the bend and moves ahead. Madrak squints through infrared glasses and splays his beam like a blessing upon everything encountered.

"These caverns be deep and vasty," he whispers.

There is no reply.

Suddenly he comes to a door which may be the right door.

Opening it, he meets the Minotaur.

He raises his staff, but the thing vanishes in a twinkling.

"Where...?" he inquires.

"Hiding," says Typhon, suddenly near, "Somewhere within the many twistings and turnings of its lair."

"Why is this?"

"It would seem that its kind are hunted by creatures much like yourself, both for food and man/bull-headed trophies. It fears direct battle, therefore, and retreats—for man uses weapons upon cattle. Let us enter the labyrinth and hope not to see it again. The entranceway we seek, to the lower chambers, lies somewhere within."

❖ ❖ ❖

For perhaps half a day they wander, unsuccessfully seeking the Wrong Door. Three doors do they come upon, but only bones lie behind.

"I wonder how the others fare?" asks the warrior-priest.

"Better, or worse—or perhaps the same," replies the other, and laughs.

Madrak does not laugh.

Coming into a circle of bones, Madrak sees the charging beast barely in time. He raises his staff and begins the battle.

He strikes it between the horns and upon the side. He jabs, slashes at, pushes, strikes the creature. He locks with it and wrestles, hand to hand.

Hurting one another, they strive, until finally Madrak is raised from the floor and hurled across the chamber, to land upon his left shoulder on a pile of bones. As he struggles to raise himself, he is submerged by an ear-breaking bellow. Head lowered, the minotaur charges. Madrak finds his feet and begins to rise.

But a dark horse shadow falls upon the creature, and it is gone—completely and forever.

He bows his head and chants the Possibly Proper Death Litany.

"Lovely," snorts his companion when he comes to his final "Amen." "Now, fat Dad, I think I have found us the Wrong Door. I might enter without opening it, but you may not. How would you have it?"

"Bide a moment," says Madrak, standing. "A bit of narcotic and I'll be good as new and stronger than before. Then we shall enter together."

"Very well. I'll wait."

Madrak injects himself and after a time is like unto a god.

"Now show me the door and let us go in."

"This way."

And there is the door, big and forbidding and colorless, within the infra-light.

"Open it," says Typhon, and Madrak does.

In the firelight it plays, worrying the gauntlet. Perhaps the size of two and a half elephants, it sports with its toy there atop an heap of bones. One of its heads sniffs at the sudden draft of air from beyond the Wrong Door, two of its heads snarl and the third drops the glove.

"Do you understand my voice?" asks Typhon, but there is no answering intelligence behind its six red eyes. Its tails twitch, and it stands, all scaly and impervious, within the flicker and glow.

"Nice doggie," comments Madrak, and it wags its tails, opens its mouths and lunges toward him.

"Kill it!" cries Madrak.

"That is impossible," answers Typhon. "In time, that is."

IX

Coming at length to the world Interludici, and entering through the sudden green gateway the poet hurls upon the blackness, Wakim and Vramin enter the madworld of many rains and religions. Lightfooted, they stand upon the moist turf outside a city of terrible black walls.

"We shall enter now," says the poet, stroking his sky-green beard. "We shall enter through that small door off to the left, which I shall cause to open before us. Then will we hypnotize or subdue any guards who may be present and make our way into the heart of the city, where the great temple stands."

"To steal boots for the Prince," says Wakim. "This is a strange employment for one such as myself. Were it not for the fact that he had promised to give my name back to me—my real name—before I slay him, I would not have agreed to do this thing for him."

"I realize that," says Vramin, "but tell me, what do you intend to do with Horus, who would also slay him—and who works for him now only to gain this same opportunity?"

"Slay Horus first, if need be."

"The psychology behind this thing fascinates me, so I trust you will permit me one more question: What difference does it make whether you slay him or Horus slays him? He will be just as dead either way."

Wakim pauses, apparently considering the matter, as if for the first time.

"This thing is *my* mission, not his," he says at length.

"He will be just as dead, either way," Vramin repeats.

"But not by my hand."

"True. But I fail to see the distinction."

"So do I, for that matter. But it is *I* who have been charged with the task."

"Perhaps Horus has also."

"But not by *my* master."

"Why should you have a master, Wakim? Why are you not your own man?"

Wakim rubs his forehead.

"I—do not—really—know. But I must do as I am told."

"I understand," says Vramin, and while Wakim is thus distracted, a tiny green spark arcs between the tip of the poet's cane and the back of Wakim's neck.

He slaps at his neck then and scratches it.

"What...?"

"A local insect," says the poet. "Let us proceed to the door."

The door opens before them, beneath the tapping of his cane, and its guards drowse before a brief green flare. Appropriating cloaks from two of them, Wakim and Vramin move on, into the center of the city.

The temple is easy enough to find. Entering it is another matter.

Here now, there are guards—drug-maddened—before the entrance.

They approach boldly and demand admission.

The eighty-eight spears of the Outer Guard are leveled at them.

"There will be no public adoration till the sundown rains," they are told, amidst twitches.

"We shall wait." And they do.

❖ ❖ ❖

With the sundown rains, they join a procession of moist worshippers and entered the outer temple.

On attempting to go further they are brought to a halt by the three hundred fifty-two drug-maddened spearmen who guard the next entranceway.

"Have you the badges of inner temple worshippers?" their captain inquires.

"Of course," says Vramin, raising his cane.

And in the eyes of the captain they must have them, for they granted entrance.

Then, drawing near the Inner Sanctum itself, they are halted by the officer in charge of the five hundred and ten drug-maddened warriors who guard the way.

"Castrated or non-castrated?" he inquires.

"Castrated, of course," says Vramin in a lovely soprano. "Give us entrance," and his eyes blaze greenly and the officer draws back.

Entering, they spy the altar, with its fifty guardians and its six strange priests.

"There they are, upon the altar."

"How shall we obtain them?"

"By stealth, preferably," says Vramin, pushing his way nearer the altar, before the televised service begins.

"What sort of stealth?"

"Perhaps we can substitute a pair of our own and wear the sacred ones out of here."

"I'm game."

"Then, supposing they were stolen five minutes ago?"

"I understand you," says Wakim and bows his head, as in adoration.

The service begins.

"Hail to Thee, Shoes," lisps the first priest, "wearer of feet."

"Hail!" chant the other five.

"Good, kind, noble and blessed shoes."

"Hail!"

"…Which came to us from chaos."

"Hail!"

"…To lighten our hearts and uplift our soles."

"Hail!"
"Oh shoes, which have supported mankind since the dawn of civilization…"
"Hail!"
"…Ultimate cavities, surrounders of feet."
"Hail!"
"Hail! Wondrous, battered buskins!"
"We adore thee."
"We adore thee!"
"We worship thee in the fulness of thy shoeness!"
"Glory!"
"Oh archetypal footgear!"
"Glory!"
"Supreme notion of shoes."
"Glory!"
"What could we do without thee?"
"What?"
"Stub our toes, scratch our heels, have our arches go flat."
"Hail!"
"Protect us, thy worshippers, good and blessed footgear!"
"Which came to us from chaos…"
"…On a day dark and drear."
"…Out of the void, burning—"
"…But not burnt."
"…Thou hast come to comfort and support us."
"…To sustain and enliven us."
"Hail!"
"…Upright, forthright, and forward forever!"
"Forever!"

Wakim vanishes.

A cold, wild wind begins to blow about them.

It is the change-wind out of time; and there is a blurring upon the altar.

Seven previously drug-maddened spearmen lay sprawled, their necks at unusual angles.

Suddenly, beside Vramin, Wakim says, "Pray, find us a gateway quickly!"

"You wear them?"

"I wear them."

Vramin raises his cane and pauses.

"There will be a brief delay, I fear," and his gaze grows emerald green.

All eyes in the temple are suddenly upon them.

Forty-three drug-maddened spearmen shout a battle cry, as one, leap forward.

Wakim crouches and extends his hands.

"Such is the kingdom of heaven," comments Vramin, perspiration like absinthe glittering coldly upon his brow.

"I wonder just how the video tapes will show this thing?"

X

"What is this place?" Horus cries out.

The Steel General stands braced, as for an anticipated shock, but there is none.

"We are come to a place that is not a world, but simply a place," says the Prince Who Was A Thousand. "There is no ground to stand upon, nor need of it here. There is little light, but those who dwell in this place are blind, so it does not matter. The temperature will suit itself to any living body, because those who dwell here wish it so. Nourishment is drawn from this air like water, through which we move, so there is no need to eat. And such is the nature of this place that one need never sleep here."

"It sounds rather like Hell," Horus observes.

"Nonsense," says the Steel General. "My own existence is just so, as I carry my environment around with me, I am not discomfited."

"Hell," Horus repeats.

"At any rate, take my hands," says the Prince, "and I will guide you across the darkness and amid the glowing motes of light until we reach the ones I seek."

They link hands; the Prince furls his cloak, and they drift through the twilitic landscape that is empty of horizon.

"And *where* is this place that is not a world?" asks the General.

"I do not know," says the Prince, "Perhaps it only exists in some deep and shiny corner of my dark and dirty mind. All that I really know is the way to reach it."

Falling, drifting a timeless time, they come at last to a tent like a gray cocoon, flickering, above/below/before them.

The Prince disengages his hands and places his fingertips upon its surface. It quivers then, and an opening appears, through which he passes, a "follow me" drifting back over his shoulder.

Brotz, Purtz and Dulp sit within, doing something which would be quite disgusting and unique by human standards, but which is normal and proper for them, since they are not human and have different standards.

"Greetings, smiths of Norn," says the Prince. "I have come to obtain that which I ordered a time ago."

"I told you he'd come! " cries one of the grayish mounds, twitching its long, moist ears.

"I acknowledge that you were correct," answers another.

"Yes. Where's that frawlpin? I ought to refrib it once more, before..."

"Nonsense! It's perfect."

"It *is* ready then?" inquires the Prince.

"Oh it's been ready for ages. Here!"

The speaker draws a length of cold blue light from a sheath of black fabric and offers it to the Prince. The Prince takes it into his hands, inspects it, nods and replaces it within the sheath.

"Very good."

"And the payment?"

"I have them here." The Prince withdraws a dark case from beneath his cloak and places it in the air before him, where of course it hangs suspended. "Which of you will be first?"

"He will."

"She will."

"It will."

"Since you cannot decide, I will have to do the choosing myself."

The Prince opens the case, which contains surgical apparatus and an extrudable operating light, as all three creatures begin to quiver in their places.

"What is happening?" inquires Horus, who has entered now and stands beside him.

"I am about to operate on these fellows, and I will require your enormous strength in assistance, as well as the General's."

"Operate? To what end?" asks the General.

❖   ❖   ❖

"They have no eyes," says the Prince, "and they would see again. I've brought three pairs with me and I'm going to install them."

"This would require extensive neurological adaptation."

"But this has already been done."

"By whom?"

"Myself, the last time I gave them eyes."

"What became of those?"

"Oh, they seldom last. After a time, their bodies reject them. Generally, though, their neighbors blind them."

"Why is that?"

"I believe it is because they go about boasting how, among all their people, only they are able to see. This results in a speedy democratization of affairs."

"Ghastly!" says the General, who has lost count of his own blindings. "I'm minded to stay and fight for them."

"They would refuse your assistance," says the Prince. "Would you not?"

"Of course," says one of them.

"We would not employ a mercenary against our own people," says another.

"It would violate their rights," says the third.

"What rights?"

"Why, to blind us, of course. What sort of barbarian are you?"

"I withdraw my offer."

"Thank you."

"Thank you."

"Thank you."

"What assistance will you require?" asks Horus.

"The two of you must seize upon my patient and hold him, while I perform the surgery."

"Why is that?"

"Because they are incapable of unconsciousness, and no local anesthetics will affect them."

"You mean you are going to perform delicate surgery on them just as they are—exotic surgery, at that?"

"Yes. That is why I will need two of you to immobilize each patient. They are quite strong."

"Why must you do this thing?"

"Because they want it done. It is the price agreed upon for their labors."

"Whatever for? A few weeks' seeing? And then—what is there to see in this place, anyhow? It is mainly dust, darkness, a few feeble lights."

"It is their wish to look upon each other—and their tools. They are the greatest artisans in the universe."

"Yes, I want to see a frawlpin again—if Dulp hasn't lost it."

"And I, a gult."

"I, a crabwick."

"That which they desire costs them pain, but it will give them memories to last for ages."

"Yes, it is worth it," says one, "so long as I am not the first."

"Nor I."

"Nor I."

The Prince lays out his instruments in the middle of the air, sterilizes them and points a finger.

"That one," he says, and the screaming begins.

The General turns off his hearing and much of his humanity for the next several hours. Horus is reminded of his father's study; also, of Liglamenti, on D'donori. The Prince's hands are steady.

❖ ❖ ❖

When it is done, the creatures have bandages over their faces, which they may not remove for a time. All three are moaning and crying out. The Prince cleans his hands.

"Thank you, Prince Who Was A Surgeon," says one of the creatures.

"...For this thing you have done to us."

"...And for us."

"You are welcome, goodly Norns. Thank you for a wand well made."

"Oh, it was nothing."

"...Let us know whenever you need another."

"...And the price will be the same."

"Then I shall be going now."

"Good-bye."

"Farewell."

"Adieu."

"Good seeing to you, my fellows."

And the Prince takes Horus and the General in hand, setting all feet upon the road to Marachek, which is but one step away.

Behind him there is more wailing, and things quite normal and proper for Norns are quickly and frantically done.

They are back in the Citadel almost before Horus, who knows what it is, has succeeded in drawing the blue wand from its sheath at the Prince's side.

It is a duplicate of the weapon which sun-eyed Set had used against the Nameless, a thousand years before.

XI

Madrak has one chance of living through the onslaught. He throws his staff and dives forward.

The choice is the right one.

He passes beneath the dog as it leaps, snapping at his staff.

His hand falls upon the strange fabric of the glove the creature had been worrying.

Suddenly, he is comforted by a confidence in his invincibility. This is something even the narcotic had not fully instilled in him.

Quickly, he determines the cause and slips the glove upon the right hand.

The dog turns as Typhon rears.

The black shadow falls between them.

Tickling, stirring, the glove reaches to Madrak's elbow, spreads across his back, his chest.

The dog lunges and then howls, for the dark horse shadow comes upon it. One head hangs lifeless as the others snarl.

"Depart, oh Madrak, to the appointed place!" says Typhon. "I shall occupy this creature to its destruction and follow in my own way!"

The glove moves down his arm, covers the hand, spreads across his chest, reaches down to his waist.

Madrak, who has always been mighty, suddenly reaches forth and crushes a stone within his right hand.

"I fear it not, Typhon. I'll destroy it myself."

"In my brother's name, I bid thee go!"

Bowing his head, Madrak departs. Behind him, the sounds of battle rage. He moves through the lair of the minotaur. He makes his way upward through the corridors.

Pale creatures with green, glowing eyes accost him. He slays them easily with his hands and proceeds.

When the next group of attackers moves upon him, he subdues them but does not slay them, having had time to think.

Instead, he says:

"It might be good for you to consider the possibility of your having portions of yourselves which might withstand the destruction of your bodies, and to label these hypothetical quantities souls, for the sake of argument. Now then, beginning with the proposition that such—"

But they attack him again, and he is forced to slay them all.

"Pity," he says, and repeats the Possibly Proper Death Litany.

Proceeding upward, he comes at last to the appointed place. And there he stands.

At the Gateway to the Underworld...

On Waldik...

"Hell hath been harrowed," he says. "I am half invincible. This must be the gauntlet of Set. Strange that it but half covers me. But perhaps I'm more a man than he was." *Stomach then regarded.* "And perhaps not. But the power that lies in this thing...Mighty! To beat the filthy souled into submission and effect their conversions—perhaps this is why it was rendered into my hand. Is Thoth divine? Truly, I do not know. I wonder? If he is, then I wrong him by not delivering it. Unless, of course, this is his secret will." *Regards hands enmeshed.* "My power is now beyond measure. How shall I use it? All of Waldik might I convert with this instrument, given but time." Then, "But he charged me with a specific task. Yet..." *Smile. (The mesh does not cover his face.)* "What if he is divine? Sons who beget their fathers may well be. I recall the myth of Eden. I know this serpent-like glove may indicate the Forbidden." *Shrugs.* "But the good which might be done...No! It is a trap! But I could beat the Words into their heads...I'll do it! 'Though Hell gape wide,' as Vramin says."

But as he turns, he is caught up in a vortex that sucks the words from his throat and casts him down a wide, blank, cold well.

Behind him, the shadows strive, Waldik gapes wide, and then he is gone, for the Prince has called him home.

XII

On Marachek, in the Citadel, stand they all, there, as backward reel their minds.

"I've the shoes," says Wakim. "You may have them for my name."

"I've the glove," says Madrak and turns away his face.

"And I've the wand," says Horus, and it falls from his hand.

"It did not pass through me," says the Prince, "because it is not formed of matter, nor any other thing over which you may exercise control." And the mind of the Prince is closed to the inner eye of Horus.

Horus steps forward, and his left leg is longer than his right leg, but he is perfectly balanced upon the now uneven floor; the window burns like a sun at the Prince's back, and the Steel General is turned to gold and flowing; Vramin burns like a taper and Madrak becomes a fat doll bounding, at the end of a rubber strand; the walls growl and pulse in and out with a regular rhythm keeping time with the music that comes from the shuffling bars of the spectrum upon the floor at the end of the tunnel that begins with the window and lies like burning honey and the tiger above the wand now grown monstrous and too fine to behold within the eternity of the tower room in the Citadel of Marachek at Midworlds' Center where the Prince has raised his smile.

Horus advances another step, and his body is transparent to his sense, so that all things within him become immediately known and frightening.

"Oh, the moon comes like a genie
    from the Negro lamp of night,
        and the tunnel of my seeing
            is her roadway.
    She raises up the carpet of the days
        I've walked upon,
            and through caverns of the
                sky we make our pathway,"

says a voice strangely like yet unlike Vramin's.

And Horus raises his hand against the Prince.

But the Prince already holds his wrist in a grip that burns.

And Horus raises up his other hand against the Prince.

But the Prince already holds that wrist in a grip that freezes.

And he raises up his other hand, and electrical shocks pass along it.

And he raises up his other hand, and it blackens and dies.

And he raises up a hundred hands more, and they turn to snakes and fight among themselves and of course he whispers: "What has happened?"

"A world," says the Prince, "to which I have transported us."

"It is unfair to choose such a battleground," says Horus, "a world too like the one I know—only a fraction away and so twisted," and his words are all the colors of Blis.

"And it is indecent of you to want to kill me."

"I have been charged with this thing, and it is my will also."

"So you have failed," says the Prince, forcing him to kneel upon the Milky Way, which becomes a transparent intestinal track, racked by a rapid peristalsis.

The smell is overpowering.

"No!" whispers Horus.

"Yes, brother. You are defeated. You cannot destroy me. I have bested you. It is time to quit, to resign, to go home."

"Not until I have accomplished my objective."

❖   ❖   ❖

The stars, like ulcers, burn within his guts, and Horus pits the strength of his body against the kaleidoscope that is the Prince. The Prince drops to one knee, but with his genuflection there comes a hail of hosannas from the innumerable dogfaced flowers that bloom upon his brow like sweat and merge to a mask of glass which cracks and unleashes lightnings. Horus pushes his arms toward the nineteen moons which are being eaten by the serpents his fingers and who calls out oh god but conscience his father is birdheaded on the sky's throne and weeping blood. Resign? Never! Go home? The red laughter comes as he strikes at the brotherfaced thing below.

"Yield and die!"

Then cast...

...far forth

...where Time is dust

and days are lilies without number...

and the night is a purple cockatrice whose name is oblivion denied...

He becomes a topless tree chopped through and falling...

At the end of forever, he lies upon his back and stares up at the Prince Who is his Brother, standing at all heights with eyes that imprison him.

"I give you leave to depart now, brother, for I have beaten you fairly," come the green words.

Then Horus bows his head and the world departs and the old world comes again.

"Brother, I wish you had slain me," he says.

"I cannot."

"Do not send me back with this kind of defeat upon me."

"What else am I to do?"

"Grant me some measure of mercy. I know not what."

"Then hear me and go with honor. Know that I would slay your father, but that I will spare him for your sake if he will but aid me when the time arises."

"What time?"

"That is for him to decide."

"I do not understand."

"Of course not. But bear him the message, anyway."

"..."

"Agreed?"

"Agreed," says Horus.

When he regains his feet, he realizes that he is standing in the Hall of the Hundred Tapestries, and alone. But in that last agonizing instant, he had learned a thing.

He hastens to write it down.

XIII

"Where is Horus?" inquires Madrak. "He was here but a moment ago."

"He has gone home," says the Prince, rubbing his shoulder. "Now let me name you my problem—"

"My name," says Wakim, "give to me. Now."

"Yes," says the Prince, "I will give it to you. You are a part of the problem I was about to name."

"Now," Wakim repeats.

"Do you feel any different with those shoes upon your feet?"

"Yes."

"How so?"

"I don't know. Give me my name."

"Give him the glove, Madrak."

"I don't want a glove."

"Put it on, if you wish to know your name."

"Very well."

He dons the glove.

"Now do you know your name?"

"No. I—"

"What?"

"It feels familiar, very familiar, to have the mesh spread across my body."

"Of course."

"It can't be!" says Madrak.

"No?" the Prince inquires. "Pick up that wand and hold it, Wakim. Here, hang its sheath about your waist."

"What are you doing to me?"

"Restoring what is rightfully yours."

"By what right?"

"Pick up the wand."

"I don't want to! You can't make me! You promised me my name. Say it!"

"Not until you've picked up the wand."

The Prince takes a step toward Wakim. Wakim backs away.

"No!"

"Pick it up!"

The Prince advances further. Wakim retreats.

"I may not!"

"You may."

"Something about it…It is forbidden that I touch that instrument."

"Pick it up and you will learn your name—your true name."

"I—No! I don't want my name any more! Keep my name!"

"You *must* pick it up."

"No!"

"It is written that you must pick it up."

"Where? How?"

"I have written it, I—"

"Anubis!" cries Wakim. "Hear my prayer! I call upon thee in all thy power! Attend me in this place where I stand in the midst of thy enemies! The one whom I must destroy is at hand! Aid me against him, as I offer him to thee!"

Vramin encircles himself, Madrak and the General with elaborate spikes of green flame.

The wall at Wakim's back slowly dissolves and infinity is there.

❖ ❖ ❖

Arm hanging limp, dog-face jeering, Anubis stares down.

"Excellent servant!" come the words. "You have found him, cornered him. But the final blow remains and your mission is done. Use the fugue!"

"No," says the Prince, "he will not destroy me, even with the fugue, while I have this thing for him. You recognized him when first you saw him, long ago. His true name is now near to his ears. He would hear it spoken."

"Do not listen to him, Wakim," says Anubis. "Kill him now!"

"Master, is it true that he knows my name? My real name?"

"He lies! Slay him! Now!"

"I do not lie. Pick up the wand and you will know the truth."

"Do not touch it! It is a trap! You will die!"

"Would I go through all these elaborate motions to slay you in this manner, Wakim? Whichever of us dies at the hands of the other, the dog will win. He knows it, and he sent you to do a monstrous act. See how he laughs!"

"Because I have won, Thoth! He comes to kill you now!"

Wakim advances upon the Prince, then stoops and picks up the wand.

He screams, and even Anubis draws back.

Then the sound in his throat turns to laughter.

He raises the wand.

"Silence, dog! You have used me! Oh, how you have used me! You apprenticed me to death for a thousand years, that I might slay my son and my father without flinching. But now you look upon Set the Destroyer and your days are numbered!" His eyes glow through the mesh which covers his entire body, and he stands above the floor. A line of blue light lances from the wand that he holds, but Anubis is gone, faded with a quick gesture and an half-heard howl.

"My son," says Set, touching Thoth's shoulder.

"My son," says the Prince, bowing his head.

The spikes of green flame fall behind them.

Somewhere, a dark thing cries out within the light, within the night.

The Steel General

A Word from Zelazny

This section of *Creatures of Light and Darkness*, published separately in *If*, features the character that sparked its creation. "I first conceived of the Steel General one afternoon in New York, during a viewing of the film *To Die in Madrid*. Many images played through my mind that day and during the drive back to Baltimore, where I was then living. Out of them arose an experimental piece of writing called *Creatures of Light and Darkness*. I sold the opening section of that book to Michael Moorcock for *New Worlds*. Later, after selling the book itself to Doubleday against all expectation, my agent sold serial rights on it to Fred Pohl for *Worlds of If*. Fred, though, was not informed at the time of the prior sale of a segment to *New Worlds*, and when I did learn of this and tell him he decided against running it as a straight serial and turned it instead into three novellas, *sans* the opening. Peculiarly, this served to revive my initial feelings about the Steel General as a character—so that, here, one sees the figure as I originally saw him on the day we were introduced during the Spanish Civil War."[1]

Zelazny said that three items fostered *Creatures of Light and Darkness*'s, genesis: "1) A further desire to relax. This book was not really written for publication so much as for my own amusement. It achieved this end. 2) The Steel General came first, as a character in a vacuum, born of an early morning viewing of the film *To Die in Madrid*. 3) I wanted to write a piece in which my feelings for my characters were as close to zero as I could manage."[2]

Notes

The other separately-published sections of *Creatures of Light and Darkness* are: "In the House of the Dead," "Creatures of Light," and "Creatures of Darkness." We chose one, "The Steel General," as a representative sample.

A contingent of American aviators, the **Lafayette Escadrille**, served in *l'Armée de l'Air* (French Air Army) in 1916. **The delaying action at Jarama Valley** refers to a 1937 battle in the Spanish Civil War. **Hold Stalingrad in the dead of winter** refers refers to a pivotal battle between the Nazis and the Russians in the winter of 1942–3. **Beaten in Little Rock** refers to the American Civil War skirmish at Bayou Fourche, Arkansas, on September 10, 1863, where Little Rock fell to Union soldiers.

Acid thrown in his face in Berkeley recalls the 1960s student riots at the University of California, Berkeley. The **I.W.W.** was the Industrial

---

1 Unpublished manuscript intended for (but not used in) *Alternities #6*, 1981.
2 *Vector #65*, May-June 1973.

Workers of the World, a radical labor movement, dedicated to overthrowing capitalism, formed in Chicago in 1905. **Leon Trotsky** promoted Marxist policies in Russia, organized the October Revolution and built up the Red Army. **Woody Guthrie** was an American folk singer/songwriter whose songs dealt with hardship, the Depression, and politics. **Fidel Castro** was the President of Cuba whose communist regime survived the Bay of Pigs Invasion, the Cuban Missile Crisis, and the fall of the Soviet Union.

In ancient Egypt, Per Ankh, the **House of Life**, was the part of a temple used to store records and train priests and scribes. Bodies were embalmed in the **House of Dead**.

Fugue is a rare psychiatric disorder in which an individual abruptly abandons lifestyle and occupation and takes up a new existence and different occupation far away; afterward, the individual has no memory (amnesia) of the events that took place during the fugue state, but any new skills gained will be retained. In common usage, fugue has become a synonym for amnesia or, more loosely, an altered state of consciousness that persists for up to several months. A **fugue** is also a musical composition based on a short melody, the theme or subject, which begins in one voice, then passes among all other (commonly three or four) voices, developing into an interwoven whole. **Temporal fugue** combines the psychiatric and musical terms: in a state of heightened consciousness, the opponents progress from single to multiple simultaneous attacks in a complex interweaving of abrupt future and past appearances and disappearances, building toward a climax in which only one will prevail.

Horus is the Egyptian sun god, the son or the brother of Isis and Osiris, depicted as a man with a falcon's head.

A **scrier** (scryer) predicts the future, sometimes by reading **entrails**, human or animal internal organs. A **scatalogist** studies feces and excretion. **Puissant** means powerful. Bird-headed **Osiris** is the Egyptian judge of the dead, husband and brother of Isis, and father (or brother) of Horus, whose annual death by Set's hand and resurrection, reflect nature's cycles. **Anubis** is the dog- or jackal-headed Egyptian god of the underworld.

A **dotard** is senile. A **mountebank** defrauds people. *En masse* means as a group; **vicissitudes** are variations. A **monger** is a dealer or trader of a commodity. If the commodity is unwanted, the monger may be seen as petty or contemptible.

Norwegian playwright **Henrik Ibsen** proposed the term **"life lie"** for the delusions man requires to flee a reality too difficult to bear. A **gamut** is the entire range of a thing. **Apotheosis** deifies a person. An **oracle** is a person (usually a priestess) or thing through whom a god speaks.

Scrofulous is tubercular. **Propitious** means favorable. **Waxing wroth** means becoming increasingly angered. **Rudyard Kipling's** works promoted kindness to animals. The **Koran** forbids cruelty to animals: "There is not an animal on Earth, nor a bird that flies on its wings, but they are communities like you."

Isis, the Egyptian fertility goddess, sister and wife of Osiris and mother of Horus, is depicted as a woman with cow's horns with the solar disk between them. A building's **loggia** is open to the air on one side. An **asp** is a venomous snake, especially the Egyptian cobra. **Typhon** is a Titan in Greek mythology; in Egyptian mythology the name is associated with Set the Destroyer (Typhon Set). Zelazny's Typhon is a separate character, son of Set, brother to Thoth, and half-brother of Horus. **Thoth** is the Egyptian god of wisdom and magic, having either a baboon or ibis head. **Hermes Trismigestus** is both the Egyptian god Thoth and the Greek god Hermes.

The **Minotaur** is the half-man, half-bull that inhabited the Cretan labyrinth in Greek mythology, but in this instance it may mean a large, bull-like animal. A **gauntlet** is a medieval knight's glove. The **three-headed dog** is Cerberus (or an unnamed Egyptian equivalent), Typhon's offspring, who guards the gates of Hades in Greek mythology. **Buskins** are thick-soled laced boots. **Absinthe** is a bitter green liqueur made with wormwood and other herbs. A **cockatrice** a mythical animal depicted as a two-legged dragon (or wyvern) with a cock's head.

Between You & I

Written 1965–68; previously unpublished.

Between you & I
the words,
like mortar,
separating, holding together
those pieces of the structure ourselves.
To say them,
to cast their shadows on the page
is the act of binding mutual passions,
is cognizance yourself/myself
of our sameness under skin,
and tears,
the possible cathedral
indicating infinity with its steeple-high stylus:
for when tomorrow comes it is today,
and if not the drop that is eternity
glistening at the pen's point,
then, the ink of our voices
surrounds like an always night,
and mortar marks the limits of our cells.

Notes

Expressing passion and the inadequacy of words to communicate across the barriers of flesh between two individuals, this poem was later revised and included in the chapter "Words" in *Creatures of Light and Darkness*.

Augury

Alternities #6, Summer 1981.

A fistful of entrails
makes all the difference in the world
at a time like this, oh king,
and these guts say you're in trouble.
It could be the lord chamberlain
or—God forbid!—the queen
that bears watching,
but the innards indicate the stranger.
The people themselves,
heirs to your benevolence,
typically ungrateful,
screaming for your head,
as usual,
have a new twist to their defiance.
They used to say it's wars, taxes
and the recent executions,
but now they're after
social security,
a 40-hour work week
with paid vacations,
workmen's compensation
and a comprehensive
medical-dental plan.
Now, that stranger in the dungeon
and the glowing bubble he came in—
We all know he's mad,
with his talk
of flying machines,

thinking machines,
killing machines,
but this segment, here,
ties him to the current unrest.
I believe he found an audience
before we got to him.
So it comes to this:
We must burn him as a sorcerer
or offer him a cabinet post.
Offhand, I'd recommend the latter.
You see, it's really a matter
of vocabulary.
His words have found them ills
they never knew they had.
So let him talk awhile
and place a moratorium
on the penning of dictionaries.
Drown his words in realities
and the next time they come by
it'll be his head,
like a grisly lollipop,
passing down the avenue.
Then give it a year, I'd say.
The people will forget the words,
saying it's wars, taxes
and the recent executions.
I feel it in my guts.

Notes

This poem echos incidents in Mark Twain's *A Connecticut Yankee in King Arthur's Court* and Poul Anderson's *Three Hearts and Three Lions*.

Augury foretells the future through signs and portents, such as reading entrails (animal or human intestines).

Pyramid

Infinite Fanac #9, Aug 1967.

Starspit, sundrop, and gone another day.
The Hudson overflows, my love,
leaving rich silt in Jersey and Manhattan.

I've an idea for dividing the land into blocks
    and keeping score.
And another notion comes forth from this:
As temple and monument to the brief snicker
    that is the existence within these banks,
a huge pointed structure I'll rear,
    a thing to remember me by,
in the center of this place,
near to the red crater—
    for there are no telephones
        in the City of the Dead,
    and you will mourn me in my absence.

It will be a place
    where the dogfaced god may weigh
    the feather of my bearings' breath
    and render my name against the Great Day;
    but as important,
    you may look upon it
    and read my message, love;
        the ka is flown
        and tender is the night.

In my senescence, memory declines.
It seems I've done this all before…

And what of the sundrop that passes over day?
Should we not worship it
    as Giver of the Fertile places?

Come nail a kiss upon my breaking brow.
For now is the time
    when the circuits at the bottom of my mind
close upon that truth
    which is fragile monument
to the sleek and calibrated lines of our passion:
    The world must accept
      that the missing wished to lie longer with her,
    and we must write these words
on the walls of her smelly room—

The geometry of existence
    shapes memory with its passing,
the well-oiled rider of the day
    decants divinity above our heads,
the richness lies in the waters of spring…

My structure will require stones and labor.

Notes

Zelazny wrote this while he was working on *Creatures of Light and Darkness*.

The **dogfaced god** is Anubis, the dog- or jackal-headed Egyptian god of tombs who weighed the hearts of the dead. The ***ka*** is the soul that survives death.

Come to Me Not in Winter's White

by Harlan Ellison® and Roger Zelazny

The Magazine of Fantasy & Science Fiction, October 1969;
revised by Harlan Ellison for this edition.

She was dying and he was the richest man in the world, but he couldn't buy her life. So he did the next best thing. He built a house. He built *the* house; different from any other house that had ever been. She was transported to it by ambulance, and their goods and furnishings followed in many vans.

They had been married little over a year; then she had been stricken. The specialists shook their heads and named a new disease after her. They gave her six-months-to-a-year; then they departed, leaving behind them prescriptions and the smell of antiseptics. But he was not defeated. Nothing as commonplace as death could defeat him.

For he was the greatest physicist ever employed by AT&T in the year of Our Lord and President Farrar, two thousand and seventy-nine.

(When one is incalculably wealthy from birth, one feels a sense of one's own personal unworthiness; so having been denied the joys of grueling labor and abject poverty, he had labored over himself. He had made of himself one who was incalculably worthy—the greatest physicist the world had ever known. It was enough for him…until he had met her. Then he wanted much more.)

He didn't *have* to work for AT&T, but he enjoyed it. They allowed him the use of their immense research facilities to explore his favorite area—Time, and the waning thereof.

He knew more about the nature of Time than any other human being who had ever lived.

It might be said that Carl Manos was Chronos/Ops/Saturn/Father Time himself: he even fitted the description, with his long dark beard and his slashing, scythe-like walking-stick. He knew Time as no other man had ever known it, and he had the power and the will and the love to exploit it.

How?

Well, there was the house. He'd designed it himself. Had it built in less than six weeks, settling a strike by himself to insure its completion on time.

What was so special about the house?

It had a room; a room like no other room that had ever existed, anywhere.

In this room, Time ignored the laws of Albert Einstein and obeyed those of Carl Manos.

What were those laws and what was this room?

To reverse the order of the questions, the room was the bedroom of his beloved Laura, who had had *Lora Manosism*, an affliction of the central nervous system, named after her. The disease was monstrously degenerative; four months after diagnosis, she would be a basket case. Five months—blind, incapable of speech. Six-months-to-a-year—dead. She dwelled in the bedroom that Time feared to enter. She *lived* there while he worked and fought for her. This was because, for every year that passed outside the room, only a week went by within. Carl had so ordained it, and it cost him eighty-five thousand dollars a week to maintain the equipment that made it so. He would see her live and be cured, no matter what the cost, though his beard changed its appearance with each week that passed for her. He hired specialists, endowed a foundation to work on her cure; and every day, he grew a trifle older. Although she had been ten years his junior, the gap was rapidly widened. Still he worked to slow her room even more.

"Mister Manos, your bill is now two hundred thousand dollars a week."

"I'll pay it," he told the power & light people, and did. It was now down to three days for every year.

And he would enter her room and speak with her.

"Today is July ninth," he said. "When I leave in the morning it will be around Christmastime. How do you feel?"

"Short of breath," she replied. "What do the doctors tell you?"

"Nothing, yet," he said. "They're working on your problem, but there's no answer in sight."

"I didn't think so. I don't think there ever will be."

"Don't be fatalistic, love. If there's a problem, there's an answer—and there's plenty of time. All the time in the world…"

"Did you bring me a newspaper?"

"Yes. This will keep you caught up. There's been a quick war in Africa, and a new presidential candidate has come onto the scene."

"Please love me."

"I do."

"No, I know that. *Make* love to me."

They smiled at her fear of certain words, and then he undressed and made love to her.

Then, after, there came a moment of truth, and he said, "Laura, I have to tell you the way it is. We're nowhere yet, but I have the best neurological minds in the world working on your problem. There's been one other case like yours since I locked you away—that is, since you came to stay here—and he's dead already. But they have learned something from him and they will continue to learn. I've brought you a new medicine."

"Will we spend Christmas together?" she asked.

"If you wish."

"So be it."

And so it was.

He came to her at Christmastime, and together they decorated the tree and opened presents.

"Hell of a Christmas with no snow," she said.

"Such language—and from a lady!"

But he brought her snow and a Yule log and his love.

"I'm awful," she said. "I can't stand myself sometimes. You're doing everything you can and nothing happens, so I harass you. I'm sorry."

She was five feet seven inches in height and had black hair. Black? So black as to be almost blue, and her lips were a pink and very special pair of cold shell-coral things. Her eyes were a kind of dusk where there are no clouds and the day sets off the blue with its going. Her hands shook whenever she gestured, which was seldom.

"Laura," he told her, "even as we sit here, they work. The answer, the cure, will come to pass—in time."

"I know."

"You wonder, though, whether it will be time enough. It will. You're virtually standing still while everything outside races by. Don't worry. Rest easy. I'll bring you back."

"I know that," she said. "It's just that I sometimes—despair."

"Don't."

"I can't help it."

"I know more about Time than anybody else… You've got it: on your side."

He swung his stick like a saber, beheading roses that grew about the wall. "We can take a century," he said, quickly, as though loath to lose even a moment, "without your being harmed. We can wait on the answer that has to come. Sooner or later, there *will* be an answer. If I go away for a few months, it will be as a day to you. Don't worry. I'll see you cured and we'll be together again in a brighter day—for godsake don't worry! You know what they told you about psychosomatic conversions!"

"Yes, I shouldn't have one."

"Then don't. There are even other tricks I will be able to play with Time, as it goes on—such as freezing. You'll come out okay, believe me."

"Yes," she said, raising her glass of Irish Mist. "Merry Christmas."

"Merry Christmas!"

But even for a man who has been thought incalculably wealthy, lack of attention to compounding that wealth, monomaniacal ferocity in pursuing a goal, and a constant, heavy drain, inevitably brings the end in sight. Though the view to that end was a long one, though there were more years that could be put to use, even so it became obvious to everyone around him that Carl Manos had committed himself to a crusade that would end in his destruction. At least financially. And for them, that was the worst sort of destruction. For they had not lived in the thoughts of Manos, were unaware that there were other, far more exacting destructions.

He came to her in the early summer, and he brought a recording of zarzuela love duets by de la Cruz, Hidalgo, Bréton. They sat beside each other, their hands touching, and they listened to the voices of others who were in love, all through July and August. He only sensed her restlessness as August drew to a close and the recording schusssed into silence.

"What?" he asked, softly.

"It's nothing. Nothing, really."

"Tell me."

She spoke, then, of loneliness.

And condemned herself with more words; for her ingratitude, her thoughtlessness, her lack of patience. He kissed her gently, and told her he would do something about it.

When he left the room, the first chill of September was in that corner of the world. But he set about finding a way to stave off her loneliness. He thought first of himself living in the room, of conducting his experiments in the room without Time. But that was unfeasible, for many reasons—most of them dealing with Time. And he needed a great deal of space to conduct the experiments: building additions to the room was impossible. He could see, himself, that there would not be sufficient funds to expand the experiment.

So he did the next best thing.

He had his Foundation scour the world for a suitable companion. After three months they submitted a list of potentials to him. There were two. Only two.

The first was a handsome young man named Thomas Grindell, a bright and witty man who spoke seven languages fluently, had written a perceptive history of mankind, had traveled widely, was outspoken and in every other possible way was the perfect companion.

The second was an unattractive woman named Yolande Loeb. She was equally as qualified as Grindell, had been married and divorced, wrote excellent poetry, and had dedicated her life to various social reforms.

Even Carl Manos was not so deeply immersed in his problem that he could not see the ramifications of possible choice. He discarded the name of Grindell.

To Yolande Loeb he offered the twin lures of extended life and financial compensation sufficient to carry her without worry through three lifetimes. The woman accepted.

Carl Manos took her to the room, and before the door was apted open from the control console, he said, "I want her to be happy. To be kept occupied. No matter what she wants, she's to have it. That is all I ask of you."

"I'll do my best, Mr. Manos."

"She's a wonderful person, I'm sure you'll love her."

"I'm sure."

He opened the outer chamber, and they entered. When they had neutralized temporally, the inner chamber was opened, and he entered with the woman.

"Hello."

Laura's eyes widened when she saw her, but when Carl had told her Miss Loeb had come to keep her company, to be the friend Laura had needed, she smiled and kissed his hand.

"Laura and I will have so much time to get acquainted," Yolande Loeb said, "why don't you spend this time together?" And she took herself to the far corner of the room, to the bookshelf, and pulled down a Dickens to reread.

Laura drew Carl Manos down to her and kissed him. "You are so very good to me."

"Because I love you. It's that simple. I wish *everything* was that simple."

"How is it coming?"

"Slowly. But coming."

She was concerned about him. "You look so tired, Carl."

"Weary, not tired. There's a big difference."

"You've grown older."

"I think the gray in my beard is very distinguished."

She laughed lightly at that, but he was glad he had brought Miss Loeb, and not Grindell. Thrown together in a room where Time nearly stood still, for endless months that would not be months to them, who knew what could happen? Laura was an extraordinarily beautiful woman. *Any* man would find himself falling in love with her. But with Miss Loeb as companion—well, it was safe now.

"I have to get back. We're trying some new catalysts today. Or rather, however many days ago it was when I came in here. Take care, darling. I'll be back as soon as can."

Laura nodded understanding. "Now that I have a friend, it won't be so lonely till you return, dearest."

"Would you like me to bring anything special next time?"

"The sandalwood incense?"

"Of course."

"Now I won't be lonely," she repeated.

"No. I hope not. Thank you."

And he left them together.

"Do you know Neruda?" Miss Loeb asked.

"Pardon me?"

"The Chilean poet? *The Heights of Macchu Picchu*? One of his greatest works?"

"No, I'm afraid that I don't."

"I have it with me. It is a piece of blazing power. There is a certain strength within it, which I thought you—"

"…Might take heart from while contemplating death. No. Thank you, but no. It was bad enough, just thinking about all the things the few people I *have* read have said about life's ending. I am a coward, and I know that one day I will die, as everyone must. Only, in my condition, I have a schedule. *This* happens, then *this* happens, and then it is all over. The only thing between me and death is my husband."

"Mr. Manos is a fine man. He loves you very much."

"Thank you. Yes, I know. So if you wish to console me concerning this, then I am not especially interested."

But Yolande Loeb pursed her lips, touched Laura's shoulder, said, "No. Not consolation. Not at all.

"Courage or faith, perhaps," she said, "but not consolation or resignation," and, "'Irresistible death invited me many times: / It was like salt occulted in the waves / and what its invisible fragrance suggested / was fragments of wrecks and heights / or vast structures of wind and snowdrift.'"

"What is that?'

"The beginning of Section Four."

Laura dropped her eyes, then said, "Tell me the whole story."

"'From air to air, like an empty net,'" said Yolande, in her deep, impressive tones, and with a slight accent, "'dredging through streets and ambient atmosphere, I came / lavish, at autumn's coronation…'"

Laura listened, and some variety of truth seemed to be present there.

After a time she reached out and their fingertips touched, gently.

❖   ❖   ❖

Yolande told Laura of her girlhood in a *kibbutz*, and of her broken marriage. She told her of life after that thing; and of the suffering attendant thereto.

Laura cried, hearing of this misery.

She felt gray and sad for days thereafter.

Yet these were not days to Carl Manos, who also had cause to feel a constricting anomie. He met a girl whose company he enjoyed, until she said that she loved him. He dropped her like poison sumac and hot potatoes. After all, Time—their friend/their enemy—had a deal going with Laura and Carl. There was no room for intruders in this fated *ménage à trois*.

He cursed, paid his bills, and figured ways to make Time even more amenable to his bidding.

But suddenly he was in pain. He knew nothing of Pablo Neruda, or this Pasternak, Lorca, Yevtushenko, Alan Dugan, Yeats, Brooke, Daniels—any of them—and Laura spoke of them constantly these days. As he had no replies for this sort of thing, he just nodded. He kept on nodding. Time after time...

"You're happy with the present arrangement?" he finally asked.

"Oh, yes! Of course," she replied. "Yolande is wonderful. I'm so glad that you invited her."

"Good. That's something, anyway."

"What do you mean—?"

"Yolande!" he cried out, suddenly. "How are you?"

Yolande Loeb emerged from the screened-off section of the apartment to which she discreetly retired during his visits. She nodded to him and smiled faintly.

"I am quite well, Mr. Manos. Thank you. And yourself?" There was a brief catch in her voice as she moved toward him, and realizing that her eyes were fixed on his beard, he chuckled within it, saying, "I'm beginning to feel a trifle like a premature patriarch." She smiled, and his tone was light, but he felt pain, again.

"I've brought you some presents," he went on, placing sealtite packages on the table. "The latest art books and tapes, recordings, some excellent film beads, poems which have been judged by the critics to be exceptional."

Both women moved to the table and began running their fingertips down the sealstrips, opening the parcels, thanking him for each item as it was unwrapped, making little noises of pleasure and excitement. As he studied Yolande's swart face, with its upturned nose, numerous moles, small scar upon the brow, and as his eyes moved on to Laura's face, flushed now and smiling—as he stood there, both hands upon his walking-stick, reflecting that it was good to have chosen as he had—something twisted softly within him and he knew pain once more.

❖   ❖   ❖

At first, he was unable to analyze the feelings. Always, however, they returned to him as accompaniment to his recollection of that tableau: the two of them moving about the package-laden table, leafing through the foilpages of the books, holding the recording cassettes at arm's length the better to study their dimensional-covers, chatting about their new treasures, excluding him.

It was a feeling of separation, resulting in a small loneliness, as well as something else. The two women had a thing in common, a thing which did not exist between Laura and himself. They shared a love for the arts—an area of existence for which he could allow himself little time. And, too, they were together in a war zone—alone in the room with the opponent Time laying siege. It had brought them closer together, sharing the experience of defying death and age. They had this meeting place where he was now a stranger. It was...

Jealousy, he decided suddenly; and was quite surprised by the notion. He was jealous of that which they had come to share. He was shocked at the thought, confused. But then, impressed as he always had been with a sense of personal unworthiness, he recognized it as another evidence of this condition. He then thought to banish the feeling.

But then, there had never been another Laura, or another *ménage* such as this.

Was it guilt that came now in response?

He was not certain.

❖   ❖   ❖

He coded a fresh cup of coffee, and when it arrived, smiled into the eyes—his own, perhaps—which regarded him through the steam and darkness of its surface. His knowledge of the ancients stopped short with their legends and theories of Time. Chronos, or Time, had been castrated by his son, Zeus. By this—it had been contended—the priests and oracles meant to convey the notion that Time is incapable of bringing forth any new thing, but must ever repeat himself and be satisfied with variations of that which has already been begotten. And that is why he smiled...

Was not Laura's disease a new thing come into the world? And was not his mastery of Time now to be the cause of another new thing—its remedy?

Guilt and jealousy alike forgotten, he sipped his coffee, tapping his fingers the while, to the beat of an unheard tune—as the particles and antiparticles danced before him in the chambers. And thus time was kept.

And when, later that evening, the viewer chimed, that evening as he sat there, white-smocked, before the Tachytron, archaic glasses pushed up onto his forehead, cold cup of coffee before him on the console, as he sat looking inside himself, he put aside remembered guilt for a premonition.

The viewer chimed again.

That would be one of the doctors…and it was…

The results of his latest experiments—rainbow journeys where no physicist had ever gone before—had been integrated with the work the doctors had been doing, and his premonition became a hallelujah reality.

He went to tell Laura they had won; went to the room outside which Time lay siege with growing frustration; went to restore the full measure of his adoration.

Where he found them, making love.

❖   ❖   ❖

Alone, outside the room where Time now waited smugly, finally savoring the taste of victory, Carl Manos lived more lifetimes than *any* special room could hoard. There had been no scene, save in the tortured silences. There had been no words, save in the linear impressions of three who were surrounded by all that had happened in that room, locked invisibly in the walls.

They wanted to stay together, of course. He had not needed to ask that. Alone together in the timeless room where they had found love, the room Carl Manos could never again enter. He still loved her, that could never be changed. And so, he had only two choices.

He could work for the rest of his unworthy life, to pay for the power to keep the room functioning. Or he could turn it off. To turn it off he would have to wait. Wait for Time the Victor to turn his all-consuming love into a kind of hate that would compel him to stop the room's functions.

He did neither. Having only two choices, he took a third course, a choice he did not have, had never had.

He moved to the console and did what had to be done, to *speed up* Time in the room. Even Time would die in that room, now. Then, unworthy, he went away.

❖   ❖   ❖

Yolande sat reading. Neruda, again. How she always came back to him!

On the bed, what had been Laura lay decomposing. Time, unaware that all, including himself, would be victims, had caught up, had won victory finally.

"'Come, diminutive life,'" she read, "'between the wings / of the earth, while you, cold, crystal in the hammered air, / thrusting embattled emeralds apart, / O savage waters, fall from the hems of snow.'"

> *Love, love, until the night collapses*
> *from the singing Andes flint*
> *down to the dawn's red knees,*
> *come out and contemplate the snow's blind son.*

She laid the book in her lap, then sat back in the chair, eyes closed. And for her, the years passed swiftly.

A Word from Zelazny

This collaboration with Harlan Ellison "was so short that it didn't entail much effort. It was just one basic idea. I did a section, he did a section, I did a section, and he took it and finished it and it was all over. In very brief sections. So I didn't have to become Harlan Ellison exactly."[1] As he wrote it, he had no idea where it was headed: "I am also doing a story with Brother Harlan… It is the first collaboration that Harlan and I have tried together. We'll see how it works out."[2]

Asked to write about this collaboration for a planned feature tentatively titled "I Was a Partner in Wonder," Zelazny begged off, as did Ellison's other collaborators. "I wish that I could do you a piece containing some measure of *élan*, a few sparks or at least a good anecdote, but alas! it was pretty much a cut-and-dried affair. Harlan telephoned me one evening, suggested we do a quick story together to body out *Partners*, recommending I whip off a thousand words and then send it to him, to which he would then add a thousand words and return, etc. And that is precisely what we did until we reached the end, where we stopped. That really was pretty much all there was to it, engineering-wise. I doubt that I would have done it had it been anyone other than Harlan, but he is in a very special category so far as I am concerned and I like to watch Ellison projects unfold."[3]

---

1 *Science Fiction* (Australian) June 1978 Vol 1 No 2, pp 11–23
2 *Mentat #11*, May 1969, pp 200–203
3 Letter from Roger Zelazny to Jeff Smith, August 27, 1971.

A Word from Harlan Ellison®

Partners in Wonder, ed. Harlan Ellison, Walker & Co., 1971; revised by Harlan Ellison for this edition.

Working with Roger on this story was one of the easiest, most pleasurable work-experiences I've had in many years. It was a cross-country collaboration, with Roger starting the story, writing through to the paragraph whose last line is *Still he worked to slow her room even more*, and then mailing the pages to me. He did not indicate where or how he thought the story should go, as he had assumed the role of picking the game, and it was my job to set the rules.

In collaborations of this sort, I've found, the opening sets the tone and the major characters and indicates the area in which the work will be done. That is roughly 1000 words. In the second thousand the direction of the plot and the initial complications should emerge; in the third thousand the complications should intensify, the characterization should solidify and the solutions should be indicated, however minutely. The final thousand words or so of a short story of this kind are the summing-up and solving areas. It worked just that way with "Winter's White."

In my thousand words, from *"Mister Manos, your bill is now two hundred thousand dollars a week"* to *And he left them together*, I set up the basic situation that Roger would intensify in the following section.

He wrote from *"Do you know Neruda?"* to *he knew pain once more*. I finished the story.

There was virtually no rewrite. I went over it once, after it was finished, to smooth some awkwardnesses we'd encountered in the mails, and then it went off to be published.

I am very proud of this story. Silverberg contends it's mawkish, and a fan writer said it was the worst of both Zelazny and Ellison, and as far as I'm concerned they can both go hump a toadstool. I love this story because, in a career lifetime of writing often violent and frequently loveless fictions, this is one of the few times I feel my work has reached toward gentleness and compassion, and I don't think I would have been able to do anything even remotely like it, had it not been for Roger. It also introduced me to the writings of Pablo Neruda, and if I'd been enriched no further, it would all have been worth it.

Notes

The story originally took place in nineteen hundred and ninety-eight, but Ellison changed it to two thousand and twenty-nine for its reprinting in *Manna from Heaven*[4] and to two thousand and seventy-nine for this edition. Ellison newly edited several dozen other items in the story and a few in "A Word from Harlan Ellison®," but these will not be detailed here.

This story deliberately blurs the distinction between **Chronos** and Cronos. **Chronos** is the personification of time and is now often depicted as a wizened old man with a beard ("Father Time"). Cronos (often Cronus) is a Titan and the father of Zeus. Zeus overthrew his father and castrated him. Cronos's wife (the mother of Zeus) is Rhea, the goddess of fertility and the earth. **Saturn** and **Ops** are the Roman gods that correspond, respectively, to the Greek names of Cronos and Rhea.

Psychosomatic conversion disorder means developing physical signs of disease from mental illness, such as hysterical blindness or paralysis that ends when the mental disorder is corrected.

Ramón **de la Cruz**, Juan de **Hidalgo**, and Tomás **Bretón** were some of the best known author/composers of **zarzuela**, a Spanish lyrical drama. **Apted open** means opened an aperture. **Pablo Neruda** wrote the epic poem of spiritual ascent *The Heights of Macchu Picchu* after visiting that ancient Incan city; several verses are quoted in the story. A **kibbutz** is a voluntary collective community in Israel. A *ménage à trois* is a threesome, a love triangle. Boris **Pasternak**, Frederico Garcia **Lorca**, Yevgeny **Yevtushenko**, **Alan Dugan**, William Butler **Yeats**, Rupert **Brooke**, and David **Daniels** were all poets.

---

4 *Manna from Heaven* ed. Scott Zrubek, Wildside Press and DNA Publications, 2003.

Thundershoon

Creatures of Light and Darkness, Doubleday 1969.
Separately, *Ariel: The Book of Fantasy, Volume 3*, ed. Thomas Durwood, Ballantine 1978.

… But Wakim the Wanderer has donned the shoes, and he rises now to stand in the middle of the air, laughing. With each step that he takes, a sonic boom goes forth from the temple to mingle with the thunder. The warriors and the worshipers bow down.

Wakim runs up the wall and stands upon the ceiling.

A green door appears at Vramin's back.

Wakim descends and steps through it

Vramin follows.

"Hail!" suggests one of the priests.

But the drug-maddened spearmen turn upon him and rend him.

One day, long after their miraculous departure, a galaxy of mighty warriors will set forth upon the Quest of the Holy Shoes.

In the meantime, the altar is empty, the evening rains come down.

The Year of the Good Seed

with Dannie Plachta
Galaxy, December 1969.

It was the Year of the Good Seed.

When Captain Planter came down out of the gleam-ridden night sky in his needle of power, red thread of fires hanging from its back, his aide and physicist were at his side. Machineries were at his hand, histories in his head and he came down into the Year of the Good Seed.

It was a time of celebration, of rejoicing. It was a time for the sowing of peace, happiness and hope.

It was a time of worship.

Captain Planter stood upon a hillside beneath the sky of morning and regarded the city.

Staring down across the frostgripped grasses, mists waving above them, he looked upon the spires and blocks and domes of the city, dappled by the yellow sunrise, threaded with the darker curves and lines of shadowed streets. He saw, though, only a part of it from that high vantage, because it was one of the larger cities of the world. From above, however, coming down through the night, it had looked like a two-thousand-year birthday cake for civilization, which perhaps it was, with its candles all a-flicker.

"They must have spotted us," said Condem, his aide. "Be here soon."

"Yes," said the captain.

"Human, they'll be," said Condem, "if Anthro's right."

"It would seem so," said Planter, lowering his glasses. "Looks enough like an Earth city—"

"Could they be the cause of it, I wonder?"

"Possibly," said the captain.

"Strange."

"Perhaps."

Beneath the sky of afternoon, the yellow sun high in the springing of the year, they met with the people of the city and established communications. They met with the people of its government and with the people of the big government of which its government was a part. They met with the people of its religion, of which the big government was a part. They were all people-people—that is to say, of human appearance.

There was an air of festivity about them as they moved through the senates and the temples, the mansions and the military bases, the conferences and the broadcasting rooms, down the streets and up the stairs, through the laboratories, back to the temples.

This was because it was the Year of the Good Seed.

❖   ❖   ❖

The captain and his aides had to answer many questions before they could ask any of their own.

Before they could answer all the many questions they were asked the dusk-fires began.

This was upon the seventh day and Yanying, the physicist, looked into the sunset with eyes that always squinted and said. "It has begun."

Planter moved to the window of the suite they had been given—within the temple, within the city.

He stared upon an aurora borealis which pierced the eye and shattered the mind with its brilliance, its colors.

"My God," he said.

"The whole sky's a cockeyed rainbow," said Condem, moving to his side.

"The explosions are closer than we thought," said Yanying, "if the Allen Belt can trap that much. It must be that they are originating from here—from the planet, not the sun."

"Well, why then? Testing? That doesn't seem to be the answer, because the thing follows a definite cycle. This is right on time."

"Natural phenomena," said the physicist, "are not the only happenings that follow definite cycles."

"A moratorium followed by a holocaust, followed by another moratorium, followed by—It doesn't make sense."

"They might look like us," said Condem, "but that doesn't mean what's inside's the same. For a while we did speculate that this thing might be a local Armageddon. But there's nothing wrong here. No signs of nuclear war, or the rebuilding that follows after. Nothing. There's been nothing like that at all, from everything they've said, from everything we've seen."

"From all that's been shown us," corrected Planter. "I wonder—"

"What?" asked Yanying.

"Is someone, something, dying somewhere?"

"Something is always dying somewhere," said Yanying. "The question is one of quantity and quality—and where."

"They might look like us—" said Condem.

A knock came upon their door.

The captain opened it to admit Laren, high priest of the center temple of the city.

Laren was several inches shorter and several pounds heavier than any of them. His thinning hair was brushed to cover over a spreading bald spot. Neatly tailored tweed robes covered the rest of him, shoulder to knee and a smile which might have betokened senility or orgasm opened his wide face.

"Sirs," he said, "it has begun. I came to ask whether you would join us in the worship of the Creator of the universe. I see, however, that you already have."

"Worship?" asked Planter.

"Your friends look upon the first outward signs of the season within the heavens."

"The lights? The aurora? You're doing that?"

"Of course," said Laren, "to worship Him as He is, with a sacrifice of pure power upon the altar of the sky."

"Those are nuclear explosions you're setting off—in outer space—aren't they?"

"Yes. For has He not always, does He not now and will He not forever so manifest Himself within the eternal cycle of the sun? Is He not the force that separates atom from atom, so that the power is freed to flow like rivers of benediction through the universe of His glory?"

"I suppose so," said Planter. "I never thought of it quite that way before. It is the reason we are here, however."

"To behold our way of worship?"

"Well, yes. Actually—now that I think of it—yes. Your sacrifices of pure power upon the altar of the sky have been detected beyond your solar system. They come at such regular intervals—about half a generation apart—that at first it was guessed that something unique was happening to your sun. It is rather strange to discover they are—prayers."

"What else could they be?" asked Laren.

"If not disturbances within your sun, then perhaps signs of war upon your planet."

"War? Yes, we have war. And the unrest which follows and precedes war. More of this than actual war. This is always with us. You see, there is another power, upon the other continent... But I do not see bow the celebration of the Year of the Good Seed could be mistaken for such."

"Year of the Good Seed?" asked Yinyang. "What is that?"

"It is the year for the planting of new, good things—things that will take root and grow through the cycle of years that is to follow. By the Year of a Thousand Flowers this time's promise will be fulfilled."

"I begin to understand," said Yinyang, turning to the Captain.

"It sounds similar to the cycle of years celebrated in many Asian countries. There is the Year of the Rat, the Year of the Ox, the Year of the Tiger, the Year of the Hare," he said, "then those of the Dragon, the Serpent, the Horse, the Goat, the Monkey, the Rooster, the Dog and the Pig. The procession is based on the old astrology—and every astrological system is, ultimately, the representation of a solar myth. Theirs seems to be derived from an agricultural phase of their society—the effect of the sun upon growing things. The symbolism has been maintained by their religion and it would seem that they, too, celebrate the times by fireworks displays. They use the greatest explosive force at their command."

"It is just as you have said," Laren agreed.

"That's all they use it for?" said Planter.

"I would not be surprised if that were the case. After all, the Chinese discovered gunpowder and the only thing they used it for was firecrackers. It took a European mind to put it to such a useful end as blowing up one's fellows."

"Excuse me—but I do not follow the conversation," said Laren. "If this thing 'gunpowder' was like prayers and it was also used to destroy other men, does this mean...? I do not understand!"

"It is just as well," said Yinyang.

"It is probably true, though," Laren continued, "that if we were to pray directly above a city of the enemy it would cease to exist. But this would be blasphemous. No one would do such a thing."

"Of course not," said Planter.

Laren turned toward the window and stared at the prayer-streaked sky.

Then, after a time: "Have such things ever been committed?"

"Perhaps," said Planter. "Long ago and in some far place."

"The will of the Creator is that the just triumph," Laren said. "If the ones who may have done this thing were the righteous, such as ourselves, then it may not have been blasphemy but a furtherance of His will."

"The doings of ignorant men in other places need not concern you," said Yinyang.

"That is true," he replied.

"So let it be forgotten," said Planter.

"Yes, of course."

Together they watched the opening of the Year of the Good Seed.

❖ ❖ ❖

It was not much later, while still moving at a –C velocity, that rivers of light flowed about Captain Planter's vessel. When Condem informed him that the nature of the detonations was unique for the area in that the light appeared to have been filtered through an atmosphere on this occasion, the Captain duly entered the observation in his log.

Notes

This is one of two collaborations with Dannie Plachta, to whom *Lord of Light* was dedicated.

Zelazny and Plachta cheekily named the captain **Planter** and his aide **Condem** (condemn), and they reversed the physicist's name from **Yanying** to **Yinyang** midway through this moralistic tale. **Yinyang** is the Chinese philosophy of two opposing but complementary creative forces, represented by yin (feminine and negative) and yang (masculine and positive). The Van **Allen Belt** is a radiation belt surrounding the Earth; it produces polar auroras where radiation strikes it. In the story's original appearance the phrase "Allen Bottle" was used instead of "Allen Belt" and is probably a copyeditor's error.

WHAT IS LEFT WHEN THE SOUL IS SOLD

Yandro #166, 1967.
Written 1955–60 for *Chisel in the Sky*.

The sting of the startled porpoise,
welting mulatto the bay's gray belly,
brackish entrails of ocean,
wrapping the mammary reef,
nor all minnow-dried decidua,
festooned of salt excrescence,
shall barter from heaven back
that heaved corpse—
indemnifying eagles
in peristaltic angle—
by felling fleet the flagstaff wing
on folds of stomach slough.

Notes

Imagery of aquatic death to contrast with "Wriggle under George Washington Bridge."

Welting is developing a swelling or scar. **Mulatto** means of mixed parentage, especially one white and one black parent. **Entrails** are the small intestines. **Decidua** is the thickened uterine lining that is shed after birth. **Festooned** means decorated. **Excrescence** is a lump, in this case, of salt crystals. **Indemnifying** means compensating for loss or injury. **Peristalsis** is contractions of the stomach and intestines to move food forward. **Slough** is dead skin that is shed; it also means a muddy channel.

THE MAN AT THE CORNER OF NOW AND FOREVER

Exile #7, 1970.

Lying on his belly behind the canisters, scooping deathstones with his hands...

Listening for the next bleating of the bull-horn...

Come down, Samuel Eliot Bock...

He felt the hilltop's dry grass like stripped goose-quills upon his sun-reddened chin, neck, hairless upper chest, ears like autumn-curled leaves...

He felt that evening's first cool breeze...

We're armed too, and we'll shoot...

Like antennae the searchlight probing about him...
The headlamps of the parked cars focused twenty feet before him...
The sound of crickets beneath the moon at his back...
Smiling, building his pyramid, slowly, soundlessly...
From armpits to propped elbows, the slow then sudden drops of perspiration...
Feeling of loss, feeling of chill...
A sweeping of light, the sound of brakes and crushed gravel, the death of an engine, the slamming of doors...
More figures moving below him...
Through the clefts in the rocks, innumerable now...

Then, *Oswald, don't make us shoot...*

Hand opened, the fragment falls...

The searchlight passing very near...
Retrieving that piece of his power, continuing to build...

Come down and we won't hurt you...

Whispering curses, emptying the canister...
Dust motes and moths dancing in the tunnels of light...
Stars burning like candles at a Greek funeral...
Soon it would grow cold...

Heat...
Ten years before...
Every day roasting until the rains of the afternoon...
Clothing already soaked with his own fluids...
Crouching, lying, sitting in the dripping shade...
Insects coming to bite him...
The disease to make him shake...
The Africa where he lobbed grenades, fired his rifle...
Killing black, white, military, mercenary, civilian...
Had he known in those days what he had known, earlier, once again now, before...
Could he have found a priest in those days and told him...
It might have been richer....
Clinging, sometimes dripping like venom from the fang-long leaves, the white phosphorus...
Bursting above the villages, like red, white, blue stars, the flares...
Playing upon his eardrums, like quavering applause, the sonic shudders....
Tittering of course, the guns...
The bodies, the burnt bodies, the chopped bodies, the shattered bodies...
The stinking wet, the wet stink, the laughter of the thing that he bore...
The thing, old enemy...
I lie before thee now in the form of the exorcist...
It was there, between the dusk and the fire, material for terror-photos all about him, a certain sense of wrongness creeping like an insect into his ear, laying its eggs...
Later, recently, the hatching, the understanding, the weapon...
Advisors, then troops lent to a weaker, friendlier faction in that small nation...

The Man at the Corner of Now and Forever

Now the only power, and still friendly...
But in this there is more than the old game...
—Ask not for whom the fires of hell blaze hot...

Closing the emptied canister carefully, soundlessly...
Scratching, rats in the wall, memories...

Above the roar, *Come down*...

Slowly, opening the second canister...
Tempted to whistle...
A bat passing between the lights and the man...
The aromas of earth...
A heaviness in the hand...

From the man who enforces the laws to the man who administers atoms for the government and the mahogany scientist who does not care about issues decades dead...
The day after that day...

He threatened it, you see...

The unsnapping of a briefcase, the lesser click of a pen...

And you did...?
Nothing, sir, for we thought...

A dark hand stroking a dark chin...

Yesterday's greatest thoughts, memorized by schoolchildren...

A cigarette dies untouched...

The letters of madmen fill...

Tick by tick, the clock devouring words...

A threat to destroy a suburb...?

A speck of dirt, transferred from one fingernail to another...

Who would have thought...?

The shaking of a pen, momentarily dry...

You heard of the theft, the hijacking in...
Pennsylvania, yes...

But this did not...
It is so far...

A cathedral of dark fingers...

It was only a matter of time...
The things he asked, demanded...
Benefits my people gained in the eighth decade of this...
And other things...
The posters in his room...
A man named X, a man named Oswald...
Now he is...
Gone...

The click, the tick...

These things catch on...
The news media...
One man on a rooftop with a rifle...
Soon a dozen more...
One hijacked airplane...
A cluttered island...
One man who makes his own atomic bomb...
Cities will die...
Guns are old-fashioned...
A man with a grudge, atomic waste...
An encyclopedia...

Dancing, Time's fool Memory, father of fear and hope...

It may not be too late...
But this second letter...
There are clues*...*
What makes a man...?

Crossing himself in the darkness, against his prisoner, his jailer...

Our Father which art in heaven...

Stone by stone the mound...

Hallowed be Thy Name...

The mass increases...

❖   ❖   ❖

Twenty years before...
Delivered from schoolyard bullies by the Sisters...
Memorizing prayers, praying them to repay...
Praying for real strength...
Asking for a Sign...
Hoping for holiness...
Studying to learn what is good in the eyes of God...
Learning the wickedness of his thoughts...
His body...
Everyday something new...
Samuel Eliot Bock...
Sin...
The Devil...
The answer...
Owned...
Possessed...
Unclean...
The daily flow of sins...
Saint Michael the Archangel, defend us in battle against the wickedness and snares of the Devil...
—Hail to the Lion of the tribe of Judah...
—May the root of David conquer...
—Oh Lord, deliver...

Smiling, his mother, *A good boy...*

Two thousand nights from nine till puberty...
The Devil forgotten...
But once a year perhaps, awakening on a dark night, shivering before Judgment's dreamed trumpet...

Passing, the train, *The rats in the walls have cocks and balls, the same as you and I*, its wheels...

Covering his eyes, his ears, pressing them hard with palms and fingertips...
Laughter within...
Destined damnation...
Despair...
Through dirt windows the morning sunlight...

To darkness the dark thoughts...
Rote the prayers...
Habit the rituals...
Experience smiles, expunges memory...

You have one minute before we...

Opening the third canister, blood upon his knuckles...
For the vampire within, salt, wet...
A curse for the circling bat...
Now bright the moon, the stars of heaven...
—Retro me Satanas...
More deathstones for the pyre...

Black and white on the paper and colorful on the video...
Drinking Coca-Cola and beating the Devil...
Destroying evil...
A sacrifice for the good of all men...
Tall...
Predictably mushroom-shaped...
Filmed hours before by an amateur with a handy camera...
Over and over, on all channels...
Missing the flash, catching the smoke...
Later, the crater...
Zoom-shot from a chopper...
Melted buildings, black smudges, rubble...
No people in sight...
—Good...
Talking of his note, framed a man with glasses that reflect the kliegs...
Hand through hair, several times...
Discussion...
Psychologist, psychiatrist, police official, man who administers atoms for the government, mahogany scientist...
Again, the smoke, the crater...
Another Coke, and another...

Your time is running...

The first Gunshot since Africa...
The hiss of gas...
But soon...

Cool morning...
Sky as clean as the note of a crystal bell...
Wooden horses across the road...
Detour signs indicating a country lane...
Single driver...
Valueless waste material...
Atomic, of course...
All the more unwanted...
Deathstones...
Toy gun...
Had not touched a real one since the day...
The day of his country's shame...
Crimes against the Black man...
Crimes against humanity...
Party to the shame, feeling the evil within come awake...
No more guns...
Praying, no more guns...
More wooden horses...
A handkerchief...
Brakes, appearance, upraised arms...
Once behind the ear and a man topples...
Three States later, a news item...
Home again, where iniquities most familiar...

Samuel Eliot Bock...
The man at the corner of now and forever...
Gunshots ringing about him...
Smiling, building his pyramid, slowly, soundlessly...
The first, faint whiff of the gas...
—This hill, this sign...
Sounds of firing from the sides now...
Through the cleft in the rocks, men in gas masks...
A furry feeling in the throat...
A wavering world through a film of sudden tears...

Come down...

A catch behind the breastbone and a holding of breath...

Another deathstone for the pyramid of judgment and salvation...
No laughter from within...
Nearer, the reports of rifles...
To cough...
No crickets...
Grasses like stripped goose-quills...
A certain chill...
Then the cough...
A moment of silence...
A holding of breath...
The cough...
The firing of rifles...
Blood...
The hooks of fire...
The old shudders of the jungle...
Footsteps...
Lights...
Breath of a fleeing demon...
Darkness...
Rolling onto his back, deathstones still in his hands...
Eyes still opened...
Samuel Eliot Bock...
Past the corner of now and forever...
Circled by men who enforce laws, a man who administers atoms for the government and a mahogany scientist who does not care about issues decades dead...
Samuel Eliot Bock...
Dead eyes reflecting stars he'd never sowed...
Burning like candles at a Greek funeral...
Legions at his back.

Notes

In its first appearance the editor described this story as "an experimental piece...[that] reads almost like poetry...it deals with homemade atomic bombs, and racism in a future time."[1] It is an existential piece that will require re-reading; this afterword offers an interpretation.

The story alludes to Lee Harvey **Oswald** (John F. Kennedy's assassin) and Malcolm **X**. By **Lion of the tribe of Judah** and **the root of David**, Zelazny meant Jesus, who is described by those phrases in the Book of Revelation. **Retro me Satanas** means "Get behind me, Satan," the words Jesus used to end His temptation in the desert. **Kliegs** are carbon arc lamps used by film makers.

The story's confusing timeline is enfolded. In the main sequence Samuel Bock builds his pyramid of atomic waste, hears the calls for him to surrender, and waits to be shot by snipers. This sequence is framed on either side by flashbacks 10 and 20 years into the past and by sequences from earlier that day and the day before. The story's ending appears near the middle, in the debriefing sequence that begins "The day after that day..."

Re-spliced into a linear timeline, the story describes Bock's upbringing, religious schooling, obsessions, witnessing of war crimes and racism ("his country's shame"), and his protests against atomic weapons and his government's involvement in wars in other countries. He steals nuclear waste and sets off a nuclear explosion as a demonstration (no bodies seen, implying no one hurt—"good"). He is making a pile of nuclear waste for another demonstration when sharp-shooters kill him. The story ends with the President worrying what effect this man's protest will have: "These things catch on... || The news media... || One man on a rooftop with a rifle... || Soon a dozen more..."

---

1 *Exile #7*, 1970.

LP ME THEE

When Pussywillows Last in the Catyard Bloomed, Norstrilia Press 1980.

Claims of music
shackle souls
or free them.
I've never been clear
on the matter.
Shall we dance,
here on the hardwood floor?
Or shall we soar,
wraithlike,
to some Platonic hall
in the sky,
where a ball
of mirrors

reflects geodesic
whatever it is that we are
to the eye
in the air,
to the measures of time,
hiccup of heart,
note in the brain,
the consummate colors
we bare?

We circulate,
the arm descends,
the diamond finger writes.

Notes

For a generation brought up on CD players and iPods, it may require explanation that an **LP** meant a long-playing record, and the sound was transmitted to the amplifier by a **diamond**-tipped needle which **descended** from an **arm** into the grooves of the spinning record.

Wraithlike means ghostlike or insubstantial, especially when associated with impending or recent death. **Platonic** refers to the theories and philosophies of the Greek philosopher Plato; in modern usage it can mean something that is confined to words or theories and not leading to practical action, or it can mean love that is intimate and affectionate but not sexual. **Geodesic** refers to the shortest possible line between two points on a sphere; the usage here implies reflections from a disco-ball spinning on the ceiling; beneath the ball a couple dances to music from the LP.

My Lady of the Diodes

Granfaloon #8, January 1970.

Maxine had said, "Turn left at the next corner," so I did.

"Park the car. Get out and walk. Cross the street at the crosswalk."

I slammed the door behind me and moved on up the street, a man in a dark blue suit carrying a gray suitcase, a hearing aid in his left ear. I might have been the Fuller Brush man.

I crossed the street.

"Now head back up the other side. You will see a red brick building, numbered six-six-eight."

"Check," I said.

"Head up the front walk, but do not mount the stairs. Once you pass the iron fence, there will be a stairway leading downward, to your left. Descend that stairway. At the bottom of the stair there will be a doorway leading into the building, probably padlocked."

"There is."

"Set down the case, put on the gloves you are carrying in your coat pocket, take the hammer from your inside pocket, and use it to strike open the lock. Try to do it in one sharp blow."

It took two.

"Enter the building and close the door behind you. Leave the lock inside; put away the hammer."

"It's dark…"

"The building should be deserted. Take twelve paces forward, and you will come to a corridor leading off to your right."

"Yes."

"Remove your right glove and take out the roll of dimes you are carrying in your right pocket. In the side corridor you should see a row of telephone booths."

"I do."

"Is there sufficient illumination coming from the three small windows opposite the booths to permit you to operate a telephone?"

"Yes."

"Then enter the first booth, remove the receiver with your gloved hand, insert a coin, and dial the following number…"

I began to dial.

"When the call is answered, do not respond or hang up, but place the receiver on the ledge and enter the next booth, where you will dial the following number…"

I did this, twelve times in all.

"That is sufficient," said Maxine. "You have tied up all the lines to the Hall, so that no outgoing calls may be placed. It is highly improbable that anyone will come along and break these connections. Return at once to the car. Replace the padlock on the door as you go. Then drive directly to the Hall. Park in the corner lot with the sign that says FIRST HOUR 50¢—35¢ EACH ADD'L HOUR. You may pay in advance at that lot, so have your money ready. Tell the attendant that you will only be a short time."

I returned to the car, entered it, and began driving.

"Keep your speed at thirty-five miles per hour, and put on your hat."

"Must I? Already? I hate hats."

"Yes, put it on. The glasses, also."

"All right, they're on. Hats mess your hair up, though, more than the wind they're supposed to be protecting it from. They blow off, too."

"How is the traffic? Heavy? Light? —They keep a man's head warm."

"Pretty light. —They do not. Hair takes care of your head, and your ears still stick out and get cold."

"What color is the traffic signal ahead? —Then why do other men wear hats?"

"It just turned green. —They're stupid conformists. Hats are as bad as neckties."

"Barring untoward traffic circumstances, your present speed will take you through the next two intersections. You will be stopped by a red light at the third one. At that point, you will have time to fill your pipe—and perhaps to light it, also, although you were rather slow when you practiced. If you cannot light it there, you should have two more opportunities before you reach the parking lot. —What's wrong with neckties?

"Check your wristwatch against the time now: You have exactly nine minutes before the acid eats through the power cables. —Neckties are elegant."

"Check... Neckties are stupid!"

"Now place me in the back seat and cover me with the blanket. I will administer electrical shocks to anyone who tries to steal me."

I did this, got the pipe going, found the lot.

"Keep puffing lots of smoke in front of your face as you talk with the attendant. You have the brown paper bag and the collapsible carton? The door-couple and the light?"

"Yes."

"Good. Take off your gloves. Remove your hearing aid and get it out of sight. Watch how you handle the steering wheel now. Palm it, and rub after each touch."

I parked the car, paid the attendant, strolled on up the street toward the Hall. Two minutes and twenty seconds remained.

I climbed the front stairs and entered the lobby. The Seekfax exhibit was in a room toward the back and to my left. I moved off in that direction.

One minute and forty seconds remained. I emptied my pipe into a sandpot, scraped the bowl.

No windows in the exhibit room, Maxine had said, and she'd digested the blueprints. Metal frame, metal doorplate-just as Maxine had said.

I approached the door, which was standing open. I could hear voices, caught glimpses of banks of machinery, exhibit cases. I put away my pipe and changed my glasses to the infrareds. Fifteen seconds. I put on my gloves. Ten.

I jammed my hands into my pockets, resting the left one on the infrared flashlight and the right on the door-couple. I counted to ten slowly and walked into the room, just as the lights went out.

Kicking the door shut, I clapped the couple-bar across the lockplate and the frame. Then I ran the polarizer rod along it, and it snapped tight. I switched on the flash and moved across the room to the central exhibit cases.

Everyone stood around stupidly as I removed the hammer and broke the glass. A couple of the salesmen began groping toward me, but much too slowly. I put away the hammer and filled the bag with the gold wire, the platinum wire, the silver wire. I wrapped the more expensive crystals and jewel components in wads of tissue.

Half a minute, maybe, to fill the bag. I opened out the stamped, self-addressed carton as I made my way back across the room. I stuffed the bag inside, into a nest of shredded newsprint. Cigarette lighters and matches flared briefly about me, but they didn't do much, or for very long.

There was a small knot of people before the door. "Make way here!" I said. "I have a key." They pushed aside as I depolarized the couple-bar. Then I slipped out through the door, closed it, and coupled it from the outside.

I took off my gloves, put away the flashlight and changed my glasses as I strolled out, pipe between my teeth. I dropped the package into the mailbox on the corner and walked back to the parking lot. I parked on a side street, reversed my dark blue suit jacket into a light gray sport coat, removed my glasses, hat and pipe, and reintroduced the hearing aid.

"All's well," I said.

"Good," said Maxine. "Now, by my estimate, they only owe you two million, one hundred twenty-three thousand, four hundred fifty dollars. Let's return the car and take a taxi out to the scene of your alibi."

"Check. We'll pick up a bigger piece of change in Denver, doll. I think I'll buy you a new carrying case. What color would you like?"

"Get me an alligator one, Danny. They're elegant."

"Alligator it is, baby," I replied as we headed back toward the rent-a-car garage.

❖   ❖   ❖

We hit Denver two months ahead of time, and I began programming Maxine. I fed her the city directory, the city history, all the chamber of commerce crap, and all the vital statistics I could lay my hands on. I attached the optical scanner and gave her the street guides and the blueprints to all the public buildings and other buildings I found in the files at City Hall. Then I photographed the conference hotel, inside and out, as well as the adjacent buildings.

Every day we scanned the local newspapers and periodicals, and Maxine stored everything.

Phase Two began when Maxine started asking for special information: Which roads were surfaced with what? What sort of clothing was being worn? How many construction companies were currently building? How wide were certain streets?

As a stockholder, I received my brochure one day, explaining the big conference. I fed that to Maxine, too.

"Do you want to cancel the debt completely?" she asked. "This includes court costs, attorney's fees and 7 percent compound interest."

"How?"

"This will be the first showing of the Seekfax 5000. Steal it."

"Steal the whole damn machine? It must weigh tons!"

"Approximately sixty-four hundred pounds, according to the brochure. Let's steal it and retire. The odds against you keep going up each time, you know."

"Yes, but my God! What am I going to do with Seekfax 5000?"

"Strip it down and sell the components. Or better yet, sell the whole unit to the Bureau of Vital Statistics in Sao Paulo. They're looking for something like that, and I've already mapped out three tentative smuggling routes. I'll need more data…"

"It's out of the question!"

"Why? Don't you think I can plan it?"

"The ramifications are…"

"You built me to cover every contingency. Don't worry, just give me the information I ask for."

"I'll have to consider this one a little further, baby. So excuse me. I'm going to eat dinner."

"Don't drink too much. We have a lot to talk about."

"Sure. See you later."

I pushed Maxine under the bed and left, heading up the street toward the restaurant. It was a warm summer evening, and the slants of sunlight between buildings were filled with glowing dust motes.

"Mister Bracken, may I speak with you?"

I turned and regarded the speaker's maple syrup eyes behind jar bottoms set in Harlequin frames, dropped my gaze approximately five feet two inches to the tops of her white sandals, and raised it again, slowly: Kind of flat chested and pug nosed, she wore a cottony candy-striped thing which showed that anyway her shoulders were not bony. Lots of maple syrup matching hair was balled up on the back of her head, with a couple winglike combs floating on it and aimed at her ears, both of which looked tasty enough—the ears, that is. She carried a large purse and a camera case almost as big.

"Hello. Yes. Speak." There was something vaguely familiar about her, but I couldn't quite place it.

"My name is Gilda Coburn," she said, "and I arrived in town today." Her voice was somewhat nasal. "I was sent to do a feature article on the computer conference. I was coming to see you."

"Why?"

"To interview you, concerning data-processing techniques."

"There'll be a lot of more important men than me around in another week or so. Why don't you talk to them. I'm not in computers anymore."

"But I've heard that you're responsible for three of the most important breakthroughs in the past decade. I read all of *Daniel Bracken* v. *Seekfax Incorporated*, and you said this yourself at the trial."

"How did you know I was in Denver?"

"Perhaps some friend of yours told my editor. I don't know how he found out. *May* I interview you?"

"Have you eaten yet?"

"No."

"Come with me then. I'll feed you and tell you about data processing."

No friend of mine could have told any editor, because I don't have any friends, except for Maxine. Could Gilda be some kind of cop? Private, local, insurance? If so, it was worth a meal or three if I could find out.

I ordered drinks before dinner, a bottle of wine with the meal and two after-dinner drinks, hoping to fog her a bit. But she belted everything down and remained clear as a bell.

And her questions remained cogent and innocuous, until I slipped up on one.

I referred to the Seekfax 410 translation unit when talking about possible ways of communicating with extraterrestrials, should we ever come across any.

"...610," she corrected, and I went on talking.

Click! Unwind her hair and lighten it a couple shades, then make her glasses horn-rimmed...

Sonia Kronstadt, girl genius out of MIT, designer of the Seekfax 5000, the prototype of which I was contemplating selling to the Bureau of Vital Statistics in Sao Paulo. She worked for the enemy.

I had hit Seekfax twelve times in the past five years. They knew it had to be me, but they could never prove it. I had built Max-10, Maxine, to plan perfect crimes, and she had done so a dozen times already. Seekfax was out to get me, but we had always outwitted their detectives, their guards, their alarm devices. No two robberies bore any resemblance as to method, thanks to Maxine. Each one was a *de novo* theft. Now then, if Kronstadt was in town ahead of time, under a phony name, then this Denver conference smacked of a setup job. The brochure had spoken of a very large display of expensive equipment, also. Had they something very special in mind for Danny Bracken? Perhaps it would do to sit this one out...

"Care to come back to my room for a nightcap?" I asked, taking her hand.

"All right," and she smiled, "thanks."

Ha! Hell hath no fury like a jealous computer designer, or computer, as I later learned...

When we got back to my room and were settled with drinks, she asked me what I had thought she might: "about all these robberies at Seekfax exhibits and conferences..."

"Yes?"

"I'd like to have your views as to who might be committing them."

"IBM? Radio Shack?"

"Seriously. There has never been a single clue. Each one has actually been a perfect crime. You'd think a criminal that good would go after bigger game—say, jewelry stores, or banks. My theory is that it's someone with a grudge against the company. How does that sound to you?"

"No," I said, and I touched her neck with my lips as I leaned over to refill her glass. She didn't draw away. "You're assuming that it's one person, and the facts tend to indicate otherwise. From the reports I've read, no two of the robberies have ever been alike. I believe that the Seekfax exhibit has come to be known in the underworld as an easy mark."

"Bosh!" she said. "They're not easy marks. Greater precautions are taken at each one, but the thief seems to accommodate this by taking greater precautions himself. I think it's one man with a grudge against the company, a man who delights in outsmarting it. "

I kissed her then, on the mouth to shut her up. She leaned forward against me and I drew her to her feet.

Somehow, the light got turned out.

Later, as I lay there smoking, she said: "Everyone knows you're the one who's doing it."

"I thought you were asleep."

"I was deciding how to say it."

"You're no reporter," I said.

"No, I'm not."

"What do you want?"

"I don't want you to go to prison."

"You work for Seekfax."

"Yes. I work for Seekfax, and I fell in love with the designs for the 5280 and the 9310. I know that they're your designs. The people they say did them aren't that good. Those are the work of a genius."

"I hired a consulting engineer," I said, "your Mr. Walker, to help with some of the drawings. He went to work for Seekfax a week later, before I had the patents registered. You've read his testimony and mine. That's why he's a vice-president now."

"So that's why you commit these robberies?"

"Seekfax owes me two million, one hundred twenty-three thousand, four hundred fifty dollars."

"That much? How do you know?"

"As a stockholder, I have a right to audit the books. I calculated that amount from what my CPA saw of the profit rise after my ideas went into use. That's cheap, too. A work of art is priceless."

"It had to be you, Danny. I saw that door-couple. You designed it. Your signature was on it. I heard how bitter you were after the trial, how you swore you would recover…"

"So? Why come tell me your guesses? Have you got anything that will stand up in court?"

"Not yet."

"What do you mean 'yet'?"

"I came here ahead of the conference because I knew you'd be in town, planning this one. I came here to warn you, because I do not want you to go to prison. I could not bear being responsible for putting the creator of the 9310 behind bars."

"Granting that all your guesses are correct, how could you be responsible for anything like that?"

"Because I designed the Seekfax 5000," she said, "into which every known fact about Denver and yourself has been programmed. It is not just a fact retriever, Danny. It is the perfect integrated data-processing detective. I am convinced that it is capable of extrapolating every possible theft which could occur at the conference, and then making provision to guard against it. You cannot possibly succeed. The age of the master criminal is past, now that IDP has moved into the picture."

"Ha!" I said.

"Aren't you rich enough now to retire?"

"Of course I'm rich," I said. "That isn't the point..."

"I understand your motives, but *my* point is that you can't outthink the 5000. Nothing can! Even if you cut off the electricity again, the 5000 is a self-contained power unit. No matter what you do, it will compute an immediate countermeasure."

"Go back to Seekfax," I said, "and tell them that I'm not afraid of any cock-and-bull story about a detective computer. So long as they're going to hold exhibits and participate in conferences, they'd better be prepared to suffer losses. Also, I admit nothing."

"It's *not* a cock-and-bull story," she finally said. "I built the thing! I know what it can do!"

"Some day I'll introduce you to Maxine," I said, "who'll tell you what she thinks of sixty-four hundred pounds of detective."

"Who's Maxine? Your girlfriend, or...?"

"We're just good friends," I said, "but she goes everywhere with me."

She dressed quickly then, and after a minute I heard the door slam. I reached beneath the bed and switched on audio.

"Maxine, baby, did you catch that? The machine we're going to steal is out to get us."

"So what?" said Maxine.

"That's the attitude," I replied. "Anything it can do, you can do better. Sixty-four hundred pounds! Huh!"

"You knew I was under the bed and turned on, but you did it anyway!"

"Did what?"

"You made love to that—that woman...Right above me! I heard everything!"

"Well...Yes."

"Have you no respect for me?"

"Of course I do. But that was something between two people, that—"

"And all I am is the thing you feed the facts to, is that it? The thing that plans your crimes! I mean nothing to you as an individual!"

"That's not true, Max baby. You know it. I only brought that woman up here to find out what Seekfax was up to. What I did was necessary, to obtain the data I needed."

"Don't lie to me, Daniel Bracken! I know what you are. You're a heel!"

"Don't be that way, Maxie! You know it's not so! Didn't I just buy you a nice new alligator case?"

"Hah! You got off cheap, considering all I've done for you!"

"Don't, Max..."

"Maybe it's time you got yourself another computer."

"I need you, baby. You're the only one who can take on the 5000 and beat it."

"Fat chance!"

"What'll I do now?"

"Go get drunk."

"What good'll that do?"

"You seem to think it's the answer to everything. Men are beasts!"

I poured myself a drink and lit a cigarette. I should never have given Maxine that throaty voice. It did something to her, to me...I gulped it and poured another.

❖ ❖ ❖

It was three days before Maxine came around. She woke me up in the morning, singing "The Battle Hymn of the Republic," then announced, "Good morning, Danny. I've decided to forgive you."

"Thanks. Why the change of heart?"

"Men are weak. I've recomputed things and decided you couldn't help it. It was mainly that woman's fault."

"Oh, I see..."

"...And I've planned the next crime, to perfection."

"Great. Let me in on it?"

At this point, I had some misgivings. I hadn't anticipated her womanlike reaction on the night I'd brought Sonia around. I wondered whether this thing might not go even deeper, to the point of her plotting revenge. Would she purposely foul this one up, just so I'd be caught? I weighed the problem and couldn't decide. It was silly! Maxine was only a machine…

Still—she was the most sophisticated machine in the world, complete with random circuits which permitted emotion analogues.

And I couldn't build another Maxine in the time remaining. I just had to listen to her and decide for myself whether I should abandon the project…

"I put myself in the 5000's place," said Maxine. "We both possess the same facts, about yourself and the locale. I, therefore, can arrive at any conclusion it can. The difference is that it is fighting a defensive battle, where we have the advantage of taking the initiative. We can break it by introducing an independent variable."

"Such as?"

"You've always robbed the conference or exhibit while it was in progress. Seekfax 5000 will formulate plans to defend against this and *only* this, I'm certain—because this is all it will be programmed for."

"I fail to see…"

"Supposing you strike *before* the conference, or *after*?"

"It sounds great, Maxie, if the 5000 is just a simple problem solver. But I'm a little afraid of the machine. Sonia Kronstadt is no slouch. Supposing she's duplicated your field approach to problem definition, so that that overweight monstrosity can redefine problems as it goes along? In a cruder fashion than yourself, of course! Or supposing Sonia simply thought of that angle herself, and the question was not posed as you've guessed?"

"She said, '…Every possible theft which could occur *at* the conference.' I'll wager that's the way she programmed it. The probabilities are on our side."

"I don't want to gamble that much."

"All right, then. Don't. How about this? I will plan it for *after* the conference. The conference is open to the public, so we will attend. They can't throw you out if you're not causing a disturbance. An article in yesterday's paper stated that the Seekfax 5000 has been programmed to play chess and can beat any human player. It will play the local champions and anyone else who is interested, providing they supply the board and chessmen. Go buy a chess set. You will take me with you and keep me tuned in. Repeat each move after it makes it, and I will play the 5000 a game of chess. From its chess playing I will extrapolate the scope of its problem-solving abilities. After the game, I will let you know whether we can carry out the plan."

"No, don't be silly! How can you tell that from a game of chess?"

"It takes a machine to know one, Danny, and don't be so jealous. I'm only going to do what is necessary, to obtain the data I need."

"Who's jealous? I know computers, and I don't see how you can tell anything that way."

"There is a point, Danny, where science ends and art begins. This is that point. Leave it to me."

"All right. I'll probably regret it, but that's the way we'll do it."

"And don't worry, Danny. I can compute anything."

❖ ❖ ❖

This is how it came to pass that on the last day of the conference a man in a dark suit showed up, carrying an alligator suitcase and a chess set, a hearing aid in his left ear.

"Biggest stereo set I ever saw," I said to Sonia, who was programming it to accommodate the ten or eleven players seated at the card tables. "I hear that critter plays chess."

She looked at me, then looked away.

"Yes," she said.

"I want to play it."

"Did you bring a chess set?" I could see she was biting her lip.

"Yes."

"Then have a seat at that empty table and set up the board. I'll be by in a few moments. I make all the moves for the machine. Which do you want: black or white?"

"White. I'll be offensive."

"Then make the first move." She was gone.

I set Maxine on the floor beside the table, opened out the board and dumped the pieces. I set them up and clicked my tongue in signal. "Pawn to Queen four," said Maxine.

An hour later, all the games were over but ours. The other chess players were standing around watching. "Fella's good," someone stated. There were several assents.

I glanced at my wristwatch. Seekfax 5000 was taking more time between moves. From the corners of my eyes, I could see that uniformed guards flanked me in a reasonably unobtrusive manner.

There was a puzzled expression on Sonia's face as she made the moves for her machine. It wasn't supposed to take this long... Some flashbulbs went off, and I heard my name mentioned somewhere.

Then Maxine launched into a dazzling end game. I'm no chess buff, but I think I'm pretty good. I couldn't follow her up and down all those dizzying avenues of attack, even if there had been half an hour between moves.

The 5000 countered slowly, and I couldn't really tell who had the advantage. Numerically we were about even.

Sonia sighed and moved her Bishop. "Stalemate," she said.

"Thank you," I said. "You have lovely hands," and I left.

No one tried to stop me, except for the representative of the local chess club, because I hadn't done anything wrong.

As we drove home, Maxine said: "We can do it."

"We can?"

"Yes. I know just how he works now. He's a wonderful machine, but I can beat him."

"Then how come he stalemated you back there?"

"I let him do it. I didn't have to beat him to find out what I wanted to know. He's never been beaten yet, and I didn't see any point in disgracing him in front of all those chess people."

I didn't like the way she accented that last word, but I let it go without comment.

In the rearview mirror, I caught a glimpse of Sonia Kronstadt's Mercedes. She followed me home, drove around the block a couple of times, and vanished.

❖ ❖ ❖

Over the weeks, I had obtained all the equipment I needed, including the paraffin for the chewing gum molds.

The Seekfax 5000 had been flown in from Massachusetts and was going to be flown back. It had to be transported to and from the airport, however, in a truck. So I was about to become a hijacker.

I buttoned down my red-and-white-striped blazer, used my handkerchief to dust off my spats, smoothed my white trousers, adjusted my red silk Ascot and my big black false mustache, stuffed more cotton into my cheeks, put on my straw hat and picked up my canvas sack and what was apparently my alligator-hide sample case. I had this outfit on over slacks and a sport shirt, which made me hot as well as florid.

I waited around the corner from the delivery dock.

When they had finished loading the truck and the guards and laborers had withdrawn from sight, I strolled past, managing to accost the driver before he mounted into the cab.

"Just the man I'm looking for!" I cried. "A man of taste and discrimination! I should like, sir, to give you a free sample of Doub-Alert gum! The chewing gum that is doubly refreshing! Doubly enlivening! I should also like to record your reaction to this fine new chewing adventure!"

"I don't chew much gum," said the driver. "Thanks anyhow."

"But, sir, it would mean very much to my employer if you would participate in the chewing reaction test."

"Test?" he asked.

"In the nature of a public opinion sample," I said. "It will help us to know what sort of reception the product will receive. It's a form of market research," I added.

"Yeah?"

"Hey you!" called out one of the guards who had returned to the dock. "Don't move! Don't go away!"

I dropped into a crouch as he leapt down. Another guard followed.

"You giving away free samples?" asked the first one, drawing near.

"Yeah. Chewing gum."

"Can we have some?"

"Sure. Take a couple."

"Thanks."

"Thanks."

"I'll take some too," said the driver.

"Help yourself"

"Not bad," said the first guard. "Kinda pepperminty and tangy, with that pick-you-up feeling."

"Yeah," said the second one.

"Uh-huh," added the driver. Then the guards turned away and headed back toward the ladder on the side of the dock. The driver moved back toward his cab.

"Wait," I said to him. "What about the chewing reaction test?"

"I'm in a hurry," he said. "What do you want to know?"

"Well—How did it strike you?"

"Kinda pepperminty and tangy," he said, "with that pick-you-up feeling. —I gotta go now!" he said, entering the cab and starting the engine.

"Mr. Doub-Alert thanks you," I said, glancing back over my shoulder to be sure the dock was empty. I climbed up onto the dock as the bell went off.

My timing hadn't been too bad. I'd left the package at the desk earlier, for a Mr. Fireman to pick up later. It sounded enough like a standard fire alarm to draw anyone in off the dock. I wished, though, that it had rung a trifle sooner. I hated having to give that stuff to those guards.

As the driver gunned his engine, I yanked my coveralls from the canvas bag and stepped into them, so that anyone glancing up the alley as I climbed into the back of the truck would think I was a laborer, loading an alligator-skin case and a canvas bag.

He put the rig into gear and I crawled toward the cab, spitting out cotton. I crouched down behind the Seekfax 5000 and finished buttoning my coveralls. I pushed the canvas bag into the corner and held Maxine in my lap.

"How long do you think it will take, baby?" I asked, as the truck began to move.

"How constipated did he look?" asked Maxine.

"How the hell should I know?"

"Then how can I tell?"

"Well, approximately."

"Sufficient time to get him onto that stretch of road I told you about. If by some chance it doesn't work by then, you'll have to create some sort of disturbance back here, lure him in, and mug him."

"I hope it doesn't come to that."

"I doubt it will. That was pretty high-powered gum."

I wondered, though, what would happen if it worked too soon. But Maxine was right, as always.

After a time, we pulled suddenly to the side of the road and came to a halt. The engine died. The slam of the cab door came almost simultaneously with the locking of the brakes.

"All right, Danny, now make your way toward the rear—"

"Maxine! I just caught it! I couldn't tell before, because the engine was running. There's a faint vibration wherever I touch the chassis of the 5000. It's turned on!"

"So? He's got a self-contained power unit. You know that. He can't know you're here unless you program that information into him."

"...Unless he has some sort of audio pickup."

"I doubt it. Why should he? You know how tricky a thing like that is to install."

"Then what's it doing?"

"Solving problems? Who cares? You'd better move, now, while the driver is still relieving himself off in the field. You may have to jump the ignition."

I climbed out, taking Maxine and the canvas bag with me, and I mounted into the cab. The keys were still in the ignition, so I started the engine and drove away. There was no sign of the driver. About five miles farther up the road, I pulled into the culvert Maxine had designated and fetched the aerosols from the bag. I sprayed gray paint over the red sides of the truck, changed the license plates to out-of-state ones, blew compressed air against one panel to make it dry more rapidly, held up my stencil and sprayed the yellow paint through it. SPEED-D FURNITURE HAULING, it said.

Then we drove back onto the road and took a new route. "We did it, Maxine. We did it," I said.

"Of course," she replied. "I told you I could compute anything. How fast are we going?"

"Fifty-five. I don't like the idea of our passenger being turned on. First chance I get, I'm going to pull off the road and find a way to shut him down."

"That would be cruel," she said. "Why don't you just leave him alone?"

"My God!" I told her. "He's only a dumb bucket of bolts! He may be the second best computer in the world, but he's a moron compared with you! He doesn't even have random circuits that permit things like emotion analogues!"

"How do you know that? Do you think you're the only one who could design them? —And they're not emotion analogues! I have real feelings!"

"I didn't mean you! You're different."

"You were too talking about me! I don't mean anything to you— do I, Danny? I'm just the thing you feed the facts to. I mean nothing to you—as an individual."

"I've heard that speech before, and I won't argue with a hysterical machine."

"You know it's true, that's why."

"You heard what I said. —Hey! There's a car coming up behind us, and it just got close enough for me to tell—it's the Mercedes!

That's Sonia back there! How did she— The 5000! Your boyfriend's been broadcasting shortwaves to her. He gave away our position."

"Better step on the gas, Danny."

I did, still looking back.

"I can't outrun that Mercedes with this truck."

"And you can't take this curve with it either, Danny boy, if you stepped on the gas when I told you to—and I'm sure you did. It's doubtless a reflex by now. Humans get conditioned that way."

I looked ahead and knew I couldn't make the curve. I slammed on the brakes and they started to scream. I began to burn rubber, but I wasn't slowing enough. "You bitch. You betrayed me!" I yelled.

"You know it, Danny! And you've had it, you heel. You can't even slow enough to jump!"

"The hell you say. I'll beat you yet!" I managed to slow it some more, and just before it went completely out of control, I opened the cab door and leaped out. I hit grass and rolled down a slope.

I thought that all the extra clothing I had on kind of padded me and was maybe what saved me; but right before the crash, while the truck was still within broadcast range, I heard Maxine's voice: "I wrote the end, Danny—the way it had to be. I told you I could compute anything. —Goodbye."

As I lay there feeling like a folded, stapled, spindled, and otherwise mutilated IBM card, and wondering whether I was more nearly related to Pygmalion or Dr. Frankenstein, I heard a car screech to a halt up on the highway.

I heard someone approaching, and the first thing I saw when I turned my head was the tops of a pair of white sandals, which were approximately five feet two inches beneath her maple syrup eyes.

"Maxine did beat your damn 5000," I gasped. "She was in the suitcase. She gave your machine that stalemate... But she double-crossed me... She planned the robberies and she planned everything that just happened..."

"When you make a woman you do a good job," she said. She touched my cheek. She felt for broken bones, found none.

"Bet we could build one helluva computer together," I told her.

"Your mustache is on crooked," she said. "I'll straighten it."

A Word from Zelazny

"Stephen Gregg unearthed this story which I forgot I had written. It had appeared in a fanzine called *Granfaloon*. Steve wanted to reprint it in his semipro magazine, *Eternity*. I asked to see a copy first, as I no longer had one in my possession. I okayed the deal after I'd read a Xerox, but alas! *Eternity* went under (after also helping to resurrect a character of mine named Dilvish), and this story was not reprinted. Why not run it here? I asked myself. How often does one wish to seize an opportunity to acknowledge a forgotten offspring?"[1]

Notes

IDP stands for Integrated Data Processing. **The Battle Hymn of the Republic**, written by Julia W. Howe in 1861, begins with "Mine eyes have seen the glory of the coming of the Lord; || He is trampling out the vintage where the grapes of wrath are stored." An **Ascot** is a broad silk necktie, originally worn at the horse races in Ascot, England. In Ovid's *Metamorphoses*, the artist **Pygmalion** carved a statue of a woman and fell in love with it; Venus took pity on him and brought the statue Galatea to life; Pygmalion married Galatea, and she bore him a son, Paphos. In Mary Shelley's novel, **Dr.** Victor **Frankenstein** created a monster from body parts and brought it to life; the monster is unnamed in the novel. The protagonist isn't sure whether he created the woman of his dreams in Maxine or the equivalent of Frankenstein's monster.

---

1 *Unicorn Variations*, 1983.

The Thing That Cries in the Night

Creatures of Light and Darkness, Doubleday 1969.

In the days when I reigned
as Lord of Life and Death,
says the Prince Who Was A Thousand,
in those days, at Man's request,
did I lay the Middle Worlds within a sea of power,
tidal, turning thing,
thing to work with peaceful sea change
the birth,
growth,
death
designs upon them;

then all this gave
to Angels ministrant,
their Stations bordering Midworlds,
their hands to stir the tides.
And for many ages did we rule so,
elaborating the life,
tempering the death,
promoting the growth,
extending
the shores of that great, great sea,
as more and more of the Outworlds
were washed by the curling,
crowned by creation's foam.

Then one day,
brooding on the vast abyss
of such a world, brave,
good-seeming,
though dead, barren,
not then touched by the life,
I roused some sleeping thing
with the kiss of the tide I rode.

And I feared that thing which awakened,
issued forth,
attacked me—
came out the bowels of the land—
sought to destroy me:
thing which devoured the life of the planet,
slept for a season within it,
then hungry rose and vicious sought.

Feeding upon the tides of the Life,
it awakened.
It touched upon thee, my wife,
and I may not restore thy body,
though I preserved this breath of thee.

It drank, as a man drinks wine,
of the Life;
and every weapon in my arsenal
was discharged upon it,
but it did not die,
did not lapse into quiescence.
Rather, it tried to depart.

I contained it
Diverting the power of my Stations,
I set up the field,
field of neutral energies
caging the whole of the world.

Were it able to travel the places of Life,
devastate an entire world,
it must need be destroyed.

THE THING THAT CRIES IN THE NIGHT

I tried, I failed—
many tried, many failed—
during the century's half
I held it prisoner
upon that nameless world.

Then were the Midworlds cast into chaos,
for want of my control
over the life the death the growth.
Great was my pain.
New Stations were a building, but all too slow.

It was mine to lay the field once more,
but I might not free the Nameless.
I held not the power
to keep my shadow prisoner
and hold the Worlds of Life.
Now, among my Angels
grew up dissension's stalk.
Quickly did I harvest it—
the price being some loyalty,
as even then I knew.

You, my Nephytha,
did not approve when my father,
risking the wrath of the Angel Osiris,
returned from Midworld's end,
to undertake the ultimate love
that is destruction.
You did not approve,
because my father Set,
mightiest warrior who ever lived,
was also our son in those days gone by,
our son, those days in Marachek,
after I had broken the temporal barrier,
to live once again through all time,
for the wisdom that is Past.

I did not know that, as time came back,
I would come to father the one who had been my father,

sun-eyed Set,
Wielder of the Star Wand,
Wearer of the Gauntlet,
Strider over Mountains.

You did not approve,
but you did not gainsay this battle,
and Set girded himself for the struggle.

Now, Set had never been defeated.
There was nothing he would not undertake to conquer.
He knew that the Steel General had been broken
and scattered by the Nameless.
But he was not afraid.

Holding forth his right hand,
he drew upon it the Gauntlet of Power,
which instantly grew
to cover over his body,
that but the brightness of his eyes shone through.

He placed upon his feet
the boots
which permitted him
to straddle the air and the water.
Then, with a black strand
he hung about his waist the sheath of the Star Wand,
ultimate weapon,
born of the blind smiths of Norn,
which only he might wield.
No, he was not afraid.

Ready then was he to depart my circling fortress,
descend upon the world,
where the Nameless crept,
spread,
swirled,
furious and hungry.
Then did his other son, my brother Typhon,
black shadow out of the void,

THE THING THAT CRIES IN THE NIGHT

appear,
begging to go in his place.

But Set did deny him this thing,
opened the hatch,
pushed himself into darkness,
fell toward the face of the world.

Now, for three hundred hours did they battle,
over two weeks by the Old Reckoning,
before the Nameless began to weaken.
Set pushed the attack,
hurt the Thing,
prepared the blow of death.

He had fought it on the waters of the oceans
under the oceans,
had fought it on dry land,
in the air's cold center,
and on the tops of mountains.
He had pursued it about the globe,
awaiting the opening that would permit
the final thrust.

The force of their conflict shattered two continents,
made the oceans to boil,
filled the air with clouds.

The rocks split and melted,
the heavens were laced with sonic booms
like invisible jewels of the fog,
the steam.

A dozen times did I restrain Typhon,
who would go to his aid.
Then, as the Nameless coiled and reared
to a height of three miles,
a cobra of smoke,
and Set stood his place,
one foot upon the water

one foot on the dry land,
then did that accursed master of mischief—
Angel of the House of Life—
Osiris,
work his deadly betrayal.

What time Set had stolen iris consort, Isis,
who had borne him both Typhon and myself,
Osiris had vowed Set's undoing.
Backed by Anubis,
Osiris wielded a portion of the field
in a manner used for release of the solar energies,
driving suns to the limit of stability.
I had bare warning ere he struck.
Set had none.

Never directed at a planet before,
it destroyed the world,
I escaped,
removing myself to a place light years away.
Typhon tried to flee
to the spaces below where he made his home.
He did not succeed.
I never saw my brother again. Nor thyself, good
Nephytha.
It cost me a father who was a son, a brother,
my wife's body;
but it did not destroy the Nameless.

Somehow,
that creature survived the onslaught
of the Hammer that Smashes Suns.
Stunned,
I later found it drifting
amid the world's wreckage,
like a small nebula
hearted with flapping flame.

I worked about it a web of forces,
and, weakened,

THE THING THAT CRIES IN THE NIGHT

it collapsed upon itself.
I removed it then to a secret place
beyond the Worlds of Life,
where it is yet imprisoned
in a room having doors nor windows.
Often have I tried to destroy it,
but I know not what it was that Set discovered
to work its undoing with his Wand.
And still it lives, and yet cries out;

and if ever it is freed,
it could destroy the Life
that is the Middle Worlds.
This is why I never disputed the usurpation
which followed that attack,
and why I still cannot.
I must remain warden,
till Life's adversary is destroyed.

And I could not have prevented what followed:

the Angels of my many Stations,
grown factious in time of my absence,
fell upon one another,
striving for supremacy.

The Wars of the Stations were perhaps thirty years.
Osiris and Anubis reaped what remained at the end.
The other Stations were no more.

Now, of course, these two must rule with great waves
of the Power,
subjecting the Midworlds to famines,
plagues, wars,
to achieve the balances
much more readily obtained by the gradual,
peaceful actions of the many, of many Stations.

But they cannot do otherwise.
They fear a plurality within the Power.

They would not delegate the Power they had seized.
They cannot co-ordinate it between them.

So, still do I seek a way to destroy the Nameless,
and when this has been done,
shall I turn my energies
to the removal of my Angels
of the two surviving Houses.

This will be easy to accomplish,
though new hands must be ready to work my will.
In the meantime,
it would be disastrous to remove
those who work the greatest good
when two hands stir the tides.

And when this final thing is true,
shall I use the power of these Stations
to re-embody thee, my Nephytha—

Notes

The Prince Who Was a Thousand speaks to his wife Nephytha. The poem ends abruptly when she cries out "It is too much! It shall never be!"

ALAS! ALAS! THIS WOEFUL FATE

Unofficial Organ of the Church of Starry Wisdom #1, 1971.

We shouldn't have been living in California. Utah, maybe. Or Montana.

Or perhaps Kansas, which I understand is a dry state.

But not California.

No.

But I wanted badly to be near the ocean, so that I could at least *look* at it; and I didn't think anybody would suspect, especially not Louise.

It's all that damn Madeleine's fault…

No, it's really my own, I guess… *Our* own? Yes. More likely, that.

I *should* have been more honest with Louise—but how could I? A double life is a double life, anyway you look at it.

❖   ❖   ❖

"Henry," she said, frowning to turn her dimples inside-out, eyes smouldering behind their brown, "Henry, there's a seal in the backyard."

"What does it want?"

"I thought I'd ask you."

I lowered the newspaper.

"What do you mean by that crack?"

MacAlister was barking his fool head off in the kitchen. I've always disliked that dog, and the feeling is mutual, but now he was really getting on my nerves.

"What do you mean?" I repeated, but she just let my question hang there and turned away.

She left the room and I followed her.

"Shut that overfed Husky off, so I can hear myself think, and answer my question: What do you mean you thought you'd ask me want a seal wants in our backyard?"

"You *know* what I mean!"

In the kitchen, she smoothed MacAlister by rubbing behind his hairy ears.

She lisped as she talked to him. It was sickening:

"Shush now, Mac. You shush now. There's some very important people-talk going on now, and I want you to be still."

He wagged his tail, shut his muzzle, aimed for the table, went beneath it, turned himself around, and then lay there with his head on his paws, glaring up at me.

"Well," I asked.

"Would you be willing to come out into the back yard with me, to look at the seal?"

"Of course. Why shouldn't I?"

So we went out, and there was a seal beside the swimming pool. It turned its head in our direction.

"*Well?* yourself," said Louise.

"*Well*—what? What are you welling me about? What's going on?"

"What do you think of that seal?" she asked.

"She's just an ordinary seal. Probably escaped from some circus— or something."

Louise began to cry.

"That proves it!" she sobbed. "That proves it! That's it! That's all! That's just about the damned limit, Henry!"

"What is?" I puzzled. "What in hell are you talking about?"

I eyed the seal uneasily and the compliment was returned.

"You said 'she'! How do you know whether it's a girl seal or a boy seal?"

"Well— It—just—*looks* like a girl seal, that's all."

"Nuts. You *know*."

"Are you feeling all right, Louise?"

"No! I'm not! —Business trips, that's where you say you're going. Then you come back in two or three months, without a word as to where you've been, without even an unusual pack of matches in your pocket, without *any* indication at all as to what you've been doing."

"I use a lighter, and I write to you. I've told you that my work is confi—"

"No! You're lying. And you don't write to me because you *can't*. Somebody else mails all those letters for you—and they're never dated, and they're so general in everything they say... You write them up in advance, then you have some friend send them."

"That's not true," I said weakly.

"Come this way." She took my arm and led me nearer the pool. The seal did not move, but she continued to stare at me, as if studying me for some indication...

"I've noticed your reaction to trained seal acts at the circus. I've seen you cry during them!"

"I happen to think it's inhumane to keep an intelligent animal like that prisoner, and to make it perform."

"No, Henry, it's more than that. —And there's this big thing you have about being afraid of the water. You won't even take a bath. You always shower. You won't swim or anything..."

"I have a phobia."

"You're trying to raise your son with one, but *you* don't have it. You don't! You've read him the story of the *R.M.S. Titanic* every night I can remember, and you tell him about all the drownings within a hundred miles. I even think you make some of them up. You warn him about sharks, sting-rays, electric eels... Poor Jimmy is scared stiff of water, because you *want* him to be."

"Crap! *You* have him sleeping in a room without windows, because *you're* afraid of the night outside... It's the same thing."

"No, it isn't. —That time we had the accident, went off the bridge... It was over sixty feet deep and there were treacherous currents. You say you can't swim—but you got me out of that car and back to the surface, and the police said it was practically a miracle."

"A man can do many strange things under stress..."

"No, Henry. I thought I was unconscious, thought I'd dreamed it—but I was carried to the surface by a great gray seal!"

"Aw, come on, Louise!"

"...And that time in the coffee shop, when that guitarist was singing a ballad—*The Great Silky of Shule Skerrie*, it was called—boy! did you ever rush out of there!

"Henry," she said quietly, "I think that you are leading a double life. You are a silky, and you are being unfaithful to me," she said.

"I told you that I never go near other women on those trips—"

"Exactly," she agreed, pointing at the seal. "I think that bitch, or cow, or whatever you call it, is your—mistress!"

So what could I do, remembering a similar argument just a week ago, conducted about twenty fathoms under the Bay?

I attacked.

"Do I ever ask where you go, what you do when I'm away—or on those occasions when you stay out all night and come back hung over the next morning? I do not, and it happens just about every month. Now you come up with this nutty bit about a folksong, and me being a seal-man, and—well, I think you ought to see an analyst."

"There is one way to check everything out, Henry," she said.

"What's that?"

She pushed me into the pool.

So that's how it all came out. To make matters worse, Madeleine was mad as hell as soon as the change occurred and she recognized me. She plunged in and swam up to my side.

"So I was right, Henry. You're one of those were-men that the story-tellers sing about, far out on their rim-rocks, late in the day when it is cold and the sky begins to darken: You are a seal in the sea and a man upon the land. —Whatever will we tell the puppies?"

"Tell them any damn thing you want," I barked back, "but for God's sake, keep them in the water!"

So there I was, chewed out upon land by Louise, and in the water by Madeleine. It's no fun being a silky, I'll tell you that. It may sound pretty romantic at first, but when they finally catch up with you there's all hell to pay. I am hounded upon land, harassed within the sea…

And Madeleine bites, but Louise doesn't. So I climbed back out of the pool and, as I dried off, resumed my humanity.

Only, all of my clothes were floating out there in that kidney-shaped insect trap, with the pump which is always breaking down and costing me twenty bucks at a crack to have fixed (and then me not being able to use it!).

I wasn't about to go in there after them, so I stood there, indignant and pink.

"That, Louise, is just too damned much!" I told her. "What would the neighbors think if any of them saw me turn into a seal in our swimming pool?"

"I don't care!" she said. "You lied to me!"

In the meantime, Madeleine came up and bit me on the ankle.

"Stop that! Or I'll sic the dog on you!"

That was a bluff. I couldn't really do that to Madeleine, but I had to say something to make her let me go.

"Okay," I said to Louise, "are you jealous of a seal?"

"Yes," she replied.

"But it's not the same," I told her, "as being with another woman. Really it isn't. Whenever I'm a seal—well, it's a different me: It's not the same body. You wouldn't sleep with me in my seal form, would you?

"And Madeleine wouldn't touch me now—except to bite me, that is, because she's mad. But that's diff—"

"Henry," she said cooly, "I don't think that I'll be sleeping with you in *any* form."

"Aw, now, honey—wait a minute...Louise!"

But she was stalking away, toward the house.

"'Madeleine'!" she said. "It even has a name!"

"Would you want me to take up with a nobody?" I asked. "Just pick up with someone and not even ask who she was?"

She slammed the screen door in my face and MacAlister came up and growled at me through it.

Madeleine flopped up behind me, said:

"Fishing trips with the boys, huh!"

"Aw, Mad. Don't—"

But she bobbed away, graceful and gray, and dived into the pool, leaving me there alone and cold and with a sore ankle.

I growled back at MacAlister and entered the kitchen.

The bedroom door was closed, but not locked. Louise was crying inside.

"I forgive *you*," she said, when I touched her shoulder, "but Jimmy—oh Jimmy!"

"What about him? So long as he stays away from the water he'll never know, never get the itch. And it's a recessive gene, I think. His kids'll probably all be normal."

"That's *not* what I meant!"

"What then?"

"What *is* he?"

❖   ❖   ❖

So we're sitting here beside the pool. Madeleine has gone away in a huff, but I'll make up with her later. It's almost time now.

I'll have to admit I'm a little frightened.

But it's as much Louise's fault as it is mine.

It *is!* Damn it! She could have mentioned a few things herself...

As soon as that big old moon pushes its face up above the next-door neighbor's TV antenna, we'll know.

We'll watch and see how Jimmy behaves under his first full moon—if it affects him in the same way as it will his mother.

...If it does, we'll push him into the pool and see what happens next.

Wolves can swim, everybody knows that.

Now I know why MacAlister doesn't like me.

Oh my son! What have we done to you?

Notes

This amusing tale of were-ness precedes by 30 years the plethora of such stories in bookstores. **The Great Silky of Shule Skerry** is a tale of the Silkies, or seafolk, enchanted creatures who dwell in the sea. Silkies can doff their seal skins to pass on land as mortal men and father children with human women. A lengthy ballad by the same title contains the line from which the story's title is taken: "Alas, alas, this woeful fate…"

Zelazny also began writing a stage play that involved silkies ("The Great Selchie of San Francisco Bay," included in volume 1) but never completed it; this story may have inspired the play.

One **fathom** is a depth of 6 feet.

Sun's Trophy Stirring

The Dipple Chronicle #2, April-June 1971.

It was stark as all hell, cold as ice, bright as a chutney bubble by day, cellar-dark, charcoal, shade and ash by night, but not dead, never alive, Luna.

Then on.

Mars was craters, iron oxide, silicon, fantastic winds, wafting miles-high dust clouds, a little moisture at the Poles, and cold.

Mercury: half seething cauldron, half ice field, with a slender twilight belt between, still and bleak, bare and rocky.

Venus was scalding vapor, burning gases, geysers, mist, mist and more unliving mist.

The asteroids: drifting quarries, mountains, boulders, rocks, pebbles, gravel and grit. Nothing else.

Jupiter, so big, and crushing everything upon its surface pancake-flat, circled, empty and smooth, the great flame of the sun. There was nothing there, nothing for its miles and its miles, except more miles and miles.

Saturn's sawblade rings spun ice and rock about the flat lifeless faces of that world.

Uranus, Neptune: cold, colder; dark, darker; frozen mazes of night, their uncitied wilderness of rock.

Pluto last. God of the dead. Coldest. Darkest. Farthest out. Hardest to reach. End of the line. Fittingly named.

And all the moons like Luna.

We were not truly disappointed, for we had not expected anything more.

The solar system was empty, except for man. We were alone. The place was ours, to do with as we chose. And we did.

We fought the cold and the winds, the heat and the gases; we mined the rock, we set cities in the wilderness, we broke the teeth of the sawblade; we even found ways not to be flattened, ourselves and our cities, on the steel-stiff plains of the big worlds. Finally even the coldest, the darkest, the farthest out, Pluto, admitted the embassy of man into those final canyons.

All of this is history.

For centuries we grew, spreading across the system like ripples, from that one living rock dropped into its middle, spreading, wave upon wave, outward, to stop at last upon the final rock, where the god of Death had built a dam.

Man could go no further.

Pluto, fittingly named, had drawn a line that we could not cross. The stars were too far out.

We smashed atoms and we put atoms together, but we could not move faster than light. We tried to warp space, but we found space to be unwarpable. We sought vainly after a fourth dimension through which we might shortcut across light-years.

We were shaking our spears at the stars, and we knew it. But we persisted.

We wanted more room, true. While we could synthesize nearly anything, we did want more raw materials. We wanted new maps, of course; man loves maps. We wanted, romantically enough, to look upon new horizons, to watch a strange sun climb from out of a strange east.

Most of all, though, we wanted someone else to talk to.

Out there, somewhere, there had to be another place where it had happened: a place, perhaps, where someone—something—else, looked out at the sky and the trillions of other stars, looked out, and felt as we did.

We shook our spears at the stars, and after a time we had bows and arrows.

Then on, crudely.

Alpha Centauri and a few of the other close ones. That was all, at first. Years, both ways.

Nothing. Neither insect nor blade of grass, lichen nor spore; not an animalcule cavorting within a tear-shaped drop of any liquid.

Then came the day of the power. It was not the heart of a sun imprisoned within a great-walled chamber, tending apart the parsecs to hurl us over Pluto's dam.

It was a little box which hummed, tinkled and clicked, hummed, tinkled and clicked, as it carried an infinitely shrinking ship along the perpetual arc of the universal expansion, an infinitely expanding ship along the line of the Lorentz-Fitzgerald contraction, and arrived in one finite piece at its inconceivably distant destination a short while later.

I do not know how it really works. Perhaps there are three men who truly understand it.

It carried us beyond Pluto's dam, however. It opened the way to the stars.

We went out there.

For centuries we went out there.

Dozens, hundreds of worlds—then, after great fleets of robot-controlled scout ships were loosed from a dozen hundred worlds—thousands, thousands. We visited thousands of worlds.

Notes

Pluto is the god of death in Roman mythology, the counterpart to Hades of Greek mythology. An **animalcule** is a microscopic animal. The **Lorentz-Fitzgerald contraction** is the shortening of a moving body in the direction of its motion, especially at speeds close to that of light.

Dim

Sirruish #7, July 1968.

Like eyes
        moist
   and
sparkling,

down pillars
of the sun

sliding,
        the snow.

Then topples the cathedral:
Celestial Sistine, our solar apex
in leagues of cloud-foam,
sinking.

The seals of heaven
are broken,
and eyelight gone bonewhite,
the horde comes on,
now in whirlwinds,

                   now horses,
                                    griffins
                  and many-headed beasts
with horns like ivory trumpets,
ectoplasm overflowing spirit.
Abroad in the land
as you said, John.

And see how the Earth gives birth to bones,
mapping the substance of mountains and cities and men,
as the winds choir Epiphany?
                              After the light,
the empty hand is cold.
There is memory only of eyes.

Notes

Sistine refers to the Sistine Chapel; Michelangelo painted its ceiling. **Griffins** have the head and wings of an eagle and the body of a lion. **Ectoplasm** is a supernatural viscous substance, such as that supposedly exuded from a medium's body during a trance. **John** refers to the Apocalypse of John from the Bible, which is what this poem is describing (seals of heaven broken, etc.). The **Epiphany** was God's appearance during the Magi's visit to Jesus; an **epiphany** can also be a sudden insight.

Dark Horse Shadow

Creatures of Light and Darkness. Doubleday 1967.
Separately: *Ariel: The Book of Fantasy, Volume 3*, ed. Thomas Durwood, Ballantine 1978.

In the great Hall of the House of the Dead there is an enormous shadow upon the wall, behind the throne of Anubis. It might almost be a decoration, inlaid or painted on, save that its blackness is absolute and seems to hold within it something of a limitless depth. Also, there is a slight movement to it.

It is the shadow of a monstrous horse, and the blazing bowls on either side of the throne do not affect it with their flickering light.

There is nothing in the great Hall to cast such a shadow, but had you ears in that place you could hear a faint breathing. With each audible exhalation the flames bow down, then rise again.

It moves slowly about the Hall and returns to rest upon the throne, blotting it completely from your sight, had you eyes in that place.

It moves without sound and it changes in size and shape as it goes on. It has a mane and a tail and four hooved legs in outline.

Then, the sound of breathing comes again, like that of a mighty organ-bellows.

It rears to stand upon its hind legs, like a man, and its forelegs form the shadow of a slanted cross upon the throne.

There comes the sound of footsteps in the distance.

As Anubis enters, the Hall is filled by a mighty wind that ends with a snorted chuckle.

Then all is silent as the dog-headed one faces the shadow before his throne.

Notes

Dog- or jackal-headed **Anubis** is the Egyptian god of the underworld and tombs and weigher of the hearts of the dead.

Add Infinite Item

The Dipple Chronicle #2, April-June 1971.

"Yes, sir?"

"I'd like to open an account with you."

"Very good. What is your Citizen Identity Number?"

"43768-992-43851M."

"—and your Credit Index?"

"779837-21."

"Have you accounts with any of the other stores?"

"Just Macy's."

"What's the account number?"

"48220697."

"Credit references?"

"I bank at 987th Federal. 9978692-431 is the account."

"Your address…?"

"819844 East 6197th Street, City, 4456679."

"All right. Let me have your thumbprint here, please. —Thanks. That's it, sir. You should receive your card in tonight's mail. If you want to do some shopping in the mean—"

"Don't you want my name?"

"Name? (Ha! Ha!) No, that won't be necessary, old timer."

"I'll be 009's! That's all there is to it?"

"I'll have to ask you not to speak like that, sir! We try to preserve an air of gentility in this establishment. There are women about."

"Sorry. 1234—"

"—5678, sir."

Notes

This short-short piece was clearly inspired by Zelazny's employment in the Social Security Administration. It doesn't sound quite so science fictional today. Oddly, it was mislabeled as a poem in earlier bibliographies.

Missolonghi Hillside

Written 1955–60 for *Chisel in the Sky*; previously unpublished.

"Satirize, thou stars!
at sevenfold the follies I have bent!
Look upon this Grecian field, and fly
in wind coated insulation
past this childe's hand that I have lent!
The chillness of the night shall be my cloak;
and mist soaked dusts
of man's lot my consumption.
'Tis fitting that thy brazen light be spent
to laugh the wine-spilt freedom
of a night!—
Then wing unprov'd, untouching ast'rick station,
high o'er a dim, most solitary tent!"

Notes

Missolonghi was a town that fell during the Greek War of Independence in 1825.

THE GAME OF BLOOD AND DUST

Galaxy, April 1975.

They drifted toward the Earth, took up stations at its Trojan points.

They regarded the world, its two and a half billion people, their cities, their devices.

After a time, the inhabitant of the forward point spoke:

"I am satisfied."

There was a long pause, then, "It will do," said the other, fetching up some strontium-90.

Their awarenesses met above the metal.

"Go ahead," said the one who had brought it.

The other insulated it from Time, provided antipodal pathways, addressed the inhabitant of the trailing point: "Select."

"That one."

The other released the stasis. Simultaneously, they became aware that the first radioactive decay particle emitted fled by way of the opposing path.

"I acknowledge the loss. Choose."

"I am Dust," said the inhabitant of the forward point. "Three moves apiece."

"And I am Blood," answered the other. "Three moves. Acknowledged."

"I choose to go first."

"I follow you. Acknowledged."

They removed themselves from the temporal sequence; and regarded the history of the world.

Then Dust dropped into the Paleolithic and raised and uncovered metal deposits across the south of Europe.

"Move one completed."

Blood considered for a timeless time then moved to the second century BC and induced extensive lesions in the carotids of Marcus Porcius Cato where he stood in the Roman Senate, moments away from another *"Carthago delenda est."*

"Move one completed."

Dust entered the fourth century AD and injected an air bubble into the bloodstream of the sleeping Julius Ambrosius, the Lion of Mithra.

"Move two completed."

Blood moved to eighth-century Damascus and did the same to Abou Iskafar, in the room where he carved curling alphabets from small, hard blocks of wood.

"Move two completed."

Dust contemplated the play.

"Subtle move, that."

"Thank you."

"But not good enough, I feel. Observe."

Dust moved to seventeenth-century England and, on the morning before the search, removed from his laboratory all traces of the forbidden chemical experiments which had cost Isaac Newton his life.

"Move three completed."

"Good move. But I think I've got you."

Blood dropped to early nineteenth-century England and disposed of Charles Babbage.

"Move three completed."

Both rested, studying the positions.

"Ready?" said Blood.

"Yes."

They reentered the sequence of temporality at the point they had departed.

It took but an instant. It moved like the cracking of a whip below them…

They departed the sequence once more, to study the separate effects of their moves now that the general result was known. They observed:

The south of Europe flourished. Rome was founded and grew in power several centuries sooner than had previously been the case.

Greece was conquered before the flame of Athens burned with its greatest intensity. With the death of Cato the Elder the final Punic War was postponed. Carthage also continued to grow, extending her empire far to the east and the south. The death of Julius Ambrosius aborted the Mithraist revival and Christianity became the state religion in Rome. The Carthaginians spread their power throughout the middle east Mithraism was acknowledged as their state religion. The clash did not occur until the fifth century. Carthage itself was destroyed, the westward limits of its empire pushed back to Alexandria. Fifty years later, the Pope called for a crusade. These occurred with some regularity for the next century and a quarter, further fragmenting the Carthaginian empire while sapping the enormous bureaucracy which had grown up in Italy. The fighting fell off, ceased, the lines were drawn, an economic, depression swept the Mediterranean area. Outlying districts grumbled over taxes and conscription, revolted. The general anarchy which followed the war of secession settled down into a dark age reminiscent of that in the initial undisturbed sequence. Off in Asia Minor, the printing press was not developed.

"Stalemate till then, anyway," said Blood.

"Yes, but look what Newton did."

"How could you have known?"

"That is the difference between a good player and an inspired player. I saw his potential even when he was fooling around with alchemy. Look what he did for their science, single-handed—everything! Your next move was too late and too weak."

"Yes. I thought I might still kill their computers by destroying the founder of International Difference Machines, Ltd."

Dust chuckled.

"That was indeed ironic. Instead of an IDM 120, the *Beagle* took along a young naturalist named Darwin."

Blood glanced along to the end of the sequence where the radioactive dust was scattered across a lifeless globe.

"But it was not the science that did it, or the religion."

"Of course not," said Dust. "It is all a matter of emphasis."

"You were lucky. I want a rematch."

"All right. I will even give you your choice: Blood or Dust?"

"I'll stick with Blood."

"Very well. Winner elects to go first. Excuse me."

❖   ❖   ❖

Dust moved to second century Rome and healed the carotid lesions which had produced Cato's cerebral hemorrhage.

"Move one completed."

Blood entered eastern Germany in the sixteenth century and induced identical lesions in the Vatican assassin who had slain Martin Luther.

"Move one completed."

"You are skipping pretty far along."

"It is all a matter of emphasis."

"Truer and truer. Very well. You saved Luther. I will save Babbage. Excuse me."

An instantless instant later Dust had returned.

"Move two completed."

Blood studied the playing area with extreme concentration. Then, "All right."

Blood entered Chevvy's Theater on the evening in 1865 when the disgruntled actor had taken a shot at the President of the United States. Delicately altering the course of the bullet in midair, he made it reach its target.

"Move two completed."

"I believe that you are bluffing," said Dust "You could not have worked out all the ramifications."

"Wait and see."

Dust regarded the area with intense scrutiny.

"All right, then. You killed a president. I am going to save one—or at least prolong his life somewhat. I want Woodrow Wilson to see that combine of nations founded. Its failure will mean more than if it had never been—and it *will* fail. —Excuse me."

Dust entered the twentieth century and did some repair work within the long-jawed man.

"Move three completed."

"Then I, too, shall save one."

Blood entered the century at a farther point and assured the failure of Leon Nozdrev, the man who had assassinated Nikita Khrushchev.

"Move three completed."

"Ready, then?"

"Ready."

They reentered the sequence. The long whip cracked. Radio noises hummed about them. Satellites orbited the world. Highways webbed the continents. Dusty cities held their points of power throughout.

Ships clove the seas. Jets slid through the atmosphere. Grass grew. Birds migrated. Fishes nibbled.

Blood chuckled.

"You have to admit it was very close," said Dust.

"As you were saying, there is a difference between a good player and an inspired player."

"You were lucky, too."

Blood chuckled again.

They regarded the world, its two and a half billions of people, their cities, their devices…

After a time, the inhabitant of the forward point spoke:

"Best two out of three?"

"All right. I am Blood. I go first."

"…And I am Dust. I follow you."

A Word from Zelazny

"This story was solicited by *Playboy* as part of a project wherein they intended to obtain a dozen short science fiction pieces from a dozen different science fiction writers and then run one a month for a year with lavish illustrations by the French artist Philippe Druillet. I attempted here to do something which would give him lots of scope for his art. *Playboy* changed its mind, though, dropped the project and paid me my kill-fee. I've occasionally wondered what the illustrations would have been like."[1]

Notes

Trojan points are the two stable Lagrange points in the mutual orbit of two unequally sized bodies revolving about one another. A Trojan point forms an equilateral triangle with the two revolving bodies in the plane of the orbit. A third, smaller body placed at a Trojan point will not drift away. **Strontium-90**, a radioactive isotope of strontium, is a by-product of nuclear fission. **Marcus Porcius Cato** was a Roman statesman. Obsessed with the thought that Rome must destroy Carthage in order to survive, he ended every speech with *"Ceterum censeo,* **Carthago delenda est***"* ["I am certain, Carthage must be destroyed."]. **Julius Ambrosius** and **Abou**

---

1 *The Last Defender of Camelot*, 1980.

Iskafar are fictional characters. In the time stream as we know it, **Isaac Newton** did not lose his life because he performed forbidden experiments, although he did have high levels of mercury in his body which likely explained his eccentric behavior in later life. **Charles Babbage** was a nineteenth century mathematician and philosopher who made numerous contributions to mathematics and cryptography as well as designing the prototypical computer. Charles **Darwin** sailed on the *HMS Beagle*; from observations on that voyage he developed the concepts of natural selection and evolution. The church reformer **Martin Luther** died of an apparent heart attack at age 62. President Lincoln was assassinated in *Ford's Theater*; calling it **Chevvy's Theater** was a joke. In our time stream, President **Woodrow Wilson** failed to convince the US to join the League of Nations, and First Secretary **Nikita Krushchev** was not assassinated but succeeded Stalin as the leader of the Soviet Union.

DUCKS

The Anthology of Speculative Poetry #3, 1978.
Written 1955–60 for *Chisel in the Sky*.

Landed by the bullet
the banded angel
breathes orison
her final wing

Notes

An **orison** is a prayer; the poem may subtly pun on the phrase "a wing and a prayer."

THE FORCE THAT THROUGH THE CIRCUIT DRIVES THE CURRENT

Science Fiction Discoveries, eds. Frederik & Carol Pohl, Bantam 1976.

...A nd I had been overridden by a force greater than my own. Impression of a submarine canyon: a giant old riverbed; a starless, moonless night; fog; a stretch of quicksand; a bright lantern held high in its midst.

I had been moving along the Hudson Canyon, probing the sediment, reaching down through the muck and the sludge, ramming in a corer and yanking it back again. I analyzed and recorded the nature, the density, the distribution of the several layers within my tube; then I would flush it, move to the next likely spot and repeat the performance; if the situation warranted, I would commence digging a hole—the hard way—and when it was done, I would stand on its bottom and take another core; generally, the situation did not warrant it: there were plenty of ready-made fissures, crevasses, sinkholes. Every now and then I would toss a piece of anything handy into the chopper in my middle, where the fusion kiln would burn it to power; every now and then I would stand still and feed the fire and feel the weight of 1,500 fathoms of Atlantic pressing lightly about me; and I would splay brightness, running through the visible spectrum and past, bounce sounds, receive echoes.

Momentarily, I lost my footing. I adjusted and recovered it. Then something struggled within me, and for the thinnest slice of an instant I seemed to split, to be of two minds. I reached out with sensory powers I had never before exercised—a matter of reflex rather than intent—and simultaneous with the arrival of its effects, I pinpointed the disturbance.

As I was swept from the canyon's bed and slammed against the wall of stone that had towered to my left, was shaken and tossed end over end, was carried down and along by the irresistible pressure of muddy water, I located the epicenter of the earthquake as fifty-three miles to the south-southeast. Addenda to the impression of a submarine canyon: one heavy dust storm; extinguish the lantern.

I could scarcely believe my good fortune. It was fascinating. I was being swept along at well over fifty miles an hour, buried in mud, uncovered, bounced, tossed, spun, reburied, pressed, turned, torn free and borne along once again, on down into the abyssal depths. I recorded everything.

For a long time, submarine canyons were believed to represent the remains of dry-land canyons, formed back in the ice ages, covered over when the seas rose again. But they simply cut too far. Impossible quantities of water would have to have been bound as ice to account for the depths to which they extend. It was Heezen and Ewing of Lamont who really made the first strong case for turbidity currents as the causative agent, though others such as Daly had suggested it before them; and I believe it was Heezen who once said that no one would ever see a turbidity current and survive. Of course, he had had in mind the state of the art at that time, several decades back. Still, I felt extremely fortunate that I had been in a position to take full advantage of the shock in this fashion, to register the forces with which the canyon walls were being hammered and abraded, the density and the velocity of the particles, the temperature shifts...I clucked with excitement.

Then, somewhere, plunging, that split again, a troubled dual consciousness, as though everything were slightly out of focus, to each thought itself and a running shadow. This slippage increased, the off thoughts merged into something entire, something which moved apart from me, dimmed, was gone. With its passing, I too felt somehow more entire, a sufficiency within an aloneness which granted me a measure of control I had never realized I possessed. I extended my awareness along wavelengths I had not essayed before, exploring far, farther yet...

Carefully, I strove for stability, realizing that even I could be destroyed if I did not achieve it. How clumsy I had been! It should not be that difficult to ride the current all the way down to the abyssal plains. I continued to test my awareness as I went, clucking over each new discovery.

❖   ❖   ❖

"Ease up, Dan! It's running the show now. Let it!"

"I guess you're right, Tom."

He leaned back, removing the stereovisual helmet, detaching himself from the telefactor harness. Out of the gauntlets, where microminiaturized air-jet transducers had conveyed the tactile information; strap after sensitive strap undone, force and motion feedback disconnected. Tom moved to assist him. When they had finished, the teleoperator exoskel hung like a gutted crustacean within the U-shaped recess of the console. Dan dragged the back of his hand over his forehead, ran his fingers through his hair. Tom steered him across the cabin toward a chair facing the viewscreen.

"You're sweating like a pig. Sit down. Can I get you something?"

"Any coffee left?"

"Yeah. just a minute."

Tom filled a mug and passed it to him. He seated himself in a nearby chair. Both men regarded the screen. It showed the same turbulence, the mud and rock passage Dan had regarded through the helmet's eyepiece. But now these things were only objects. Away from the remote manipulator system, he was no longer a part of them. He sipped his coffee and studied the flow.

"…Really lucky," he said, "to run into something like this first time out."

Tom nodded. The boat rocked gently. The console hummed.

"Yes," Tom said, glancing at the indicators, "it's a bonus, all right. Look at that slop flow, will you! If the unit holds up through this, we've scored all the way around."

"I think it will. It seems to have stabilized itself. That brain is actually functioning. I could almost feel those little tunnel junction neuristors working, forming their own interconnections as I operated it. Apparently, I fed it sufficient activity, it took in sufficient data… It formed its own paths. It did—learn. When the quake started, it took independent action. It almost doesn't really need me now."

"Except to teach it something new, for whatever we want it to do next."

Dan nodded, slowly.

"Yes... Still, you wonder what it's teaching itself, now that it's in control for a time. That was a peculiar feeling—when I realized it had finally come into its equivalent of awareness. When it made its own decision to adjust to that first tiny shock. Now, watching it control its own situation... It *knows* what it's doing."

"Look! You can actually see those damn eddies! It's doing around fifty-five miles an hour, and that slop is still going faster. —Yeah, that must really have been something, feeling it take over that way."

"It was quite strange. Just when it happened, I felt as if I were—touching another awareness, I guess that's the best way to put it. It was as if a genuine consciousness had suddenly flickered into being beside my own, down there, and as if it were aware of me, just for a second. Then we went our own ways. I think the neuropsych boys and the cyberneticists were right. I think we've produced an artificial intelligence."

"That's really frosting on my turbidity cake," Tom said, taking notes. "It was actually a Swiss guy, back in the nineteenth century, who first guessed at turbidity currents, to explain how mud from the Rhone got way out in Lake Geneva—did you see that!? Tore a hunk right off the side! Yeah, that's a great little gimmick you've got. If it makes it down to the plains, I want some cores right away. We've got plenty of recent samples, so it ought to be able to give us the depth of sediment deposit from this slide. Then maybe you could send it back up to where it was, for some comparison cores with the ones it was just taking. I—"

"I wonder what it thinks about itself—and us?"

"How could it know about us? It only knows what you taught it, and whatever it's learning now."

"It felt me there, right at the end. I'm sure of it."

Tom chuckled.

"Call that part of its religious upbringing, then. If it ever gets balky, you can thunder and lightning at it. —Must be doing close to sixty now!"

Dan finished his coffee.

"I just had a bizarre thought," he said, moments later. "What if something were doing the same thing to us—controlling us, watching the world through our senses—without our being aware of it?"

Tom shrugged. "Why should they?"

"Why are we doing it with the unit? Maybe they'd be interested in turbidity currents on this sort of a planet—or of our experiments with devices of this sort. That's the point. It could be anything. How could we tell?"

"Let me get you another cup of coffee, Dan."

"All right, all right! Forgive the metaphysics. I was just so close to that feeling with the unit... I started picturing myself on the teleslave end of things. The feeling's gone now, anyhow."

❖ ❖ ❖

"Voic, what is it?"

Voic released the querocube and lufted toward Doman.

"That one I was just fiding—it came closer than any of them ever did before to recognizing my presence!"

"Doubtless because of the analogous experience with its own fide. Interesting, though. Let it alone for a while."

"Yes. A most peculiar cause-field, though. It gives me pause to wonder, could something be fiding us?"

Doman perigrated.

"Why would anything want to fide us?"

"I do not know. How could I?"

"Let me get you a B-charge."

"All right."

Voic took up the querocube once again.

"What are you doing?"

"Just a small adjustment I neglected. There. —Let's have that B-charge."

They settled back and began to feculate.

❖ ❖ ❖

"What are you doing, Dan?"

"I forgot to turn it loose."

"To what?"

"Give it total autonomy, to let it go. I had to overload the slave-circuits to burn them out."

"You—You—Yes. Of course. Here's your coffee. —Look at that mud slide, will you!"

"That's really something, Tom."

❖ ❖ ❖

Clucking, I toss another chunk of anything handy into my chopper.

A Word from Zelazny

"I don't like this story... A few times I have written something before I should have; that is, it was on the back burner and I pulled it out and dished it up before it was fully cooked. In this case, I was playing with a number of ideas involving artificial intelligence, trauma and control for what I hoped would be a neatly realized, well-developed story of some length.

"Fred Pohl...asked me for a story for a collection that he was assembling. I agreed readily, but my mind was filled with the notions recited above. So I decided to use them, and I wrote this story. As I said, I was not totally pleased with its bare-bones displaying of some of these thoughts. But a curious thing happened. The real story began to crystalize while I was doing this one—a story much too long, I could see, for me to knock off in time for Fred's deadline. The real story was to be 'Home Is the Hangman,' one of my better novellas. This story, then, is yet another variation: It was a finger exercise, a story the writing of which served to produce something better than itself."[1]

Notes

Oceanographers Bruce C. **Heezen** and Maurice **Ewing** of **Lamont** Geological Observatory at Columbia University studied the ocean bed and theorized about turbidity currents and an abrupt climate change that may have occurred 11,000 years ago. Prior to them, Reginald A. **Daly** of the Department of Geology at Harvard University speculated about the role of turbidity currents in a 1936 paper. In 1885, François-Alphone Forel at the University of Geneva was the **Swiss guy, back in the nineteenth century, who first guessed at turbidity currents, to explain how mud from the Rhone got way out in Lake Geneva.**

---

1 *Unicorn Variations*, 1983.

Lamentations of the Venusian Pensioner, Golden Apples of the Sun Retirement Home, Earthcolony VI, Pdeth, Venus

Double:Bill #15, Sept 1966.
Written 1955–60 for *Chisel in the Sky* (as "Basics").

And where am I going
that I seek to seek?
It is not, cannot be,
and will not, that I shall find
here
anything of value
or worth remorse to leave.

Let movement overdo itself
Inaction's rival is better reply
than nothing, to itself.

I feel as if a great and starry hand
had scooped a chasm
in the year,

and days I fabricate are airy things
unfit to accompany seasons.

I am surprised that I feel this,
even.
    Let me wander.
I shall not go far.
The edge of something,
like a green hillside,
appears each morning
behind my eyes,
before I yawn, stretch,
and, in a moment,
rise.

Notes

Zelazny's only revision to make this into a science-fictional poem was the title. **Lamentations** are passionate expressions of grief.

No Award

The Saturday Evening Post, Vol 249 No 1, Jan-Feb 1977.

I entered the hall, made my way forward. I had come early, so as to get as close as possible. I do not usually push to be near the front of a crowd. Even on those other occasions when I had heard him, and other presidents before him, I had not tried for the best view. This time, however, it seemed somehow important.

Luck! A seat that looked just right. I eased myself down.

My foot seemed asleep. In fact, the entire leg... No matter. I could rest it now. Plenty of time...

Time? No. Darkness. Yes. Sleep...

I glanced at my watch. Still some time. Some other people were smoking. Seemed like a good idea. As I reached for my cigarettes I remembered that I had quit, then discovered that I still carried them. No matter. Take one. Light it. (Trouble. Use the other hand.) I felt somewhat tense. Not certain why. Inhale. Better. Good.

Who is that? Oh.

A short man in a gray suit entered from the right and tested the microphone. Momentary hush. Renewed crowd noise. The man looked satisfied and departed.

I sighed smoke and relaxed.

Resting. Yes. Asleep, asleep... Yes... You...

After a time, people entered from the sides and took seats on the stage. Yes, there was the governor. He would speak first, would say a few words of introduction.

That man far to my left, on the stage... I had seen him in a number of pictures, always near the president, never identified. Short, getting paunchy, sandy hair thinning; dark, drifting eyes behind thick glasses... I was certain that he was a member, possibly even the chief, of the elite group of telepathic bodyguards who always accompany the chief executive in public. The telepathic phenomenon had been pinned down only a few years ago, and since then the skill had been fully developed in but a handful of people. Those who possessed it, though, were ideal for this sort of work. It took all the danger out of public appearances when a number of such persons spotted about an audience were able to monitor the general temper of a crowd, to detect any aberrant, homicidal thoughts and to relay this information to the Secret Service. It eliminated even the possibility of an attempt on the president's life, let alone a successful assassination. Why, at this moment, one of them could even be scanning my own thoughts...

Nothing worth their time here, though. No reason to feel uneasy.

I crushed out the cigarette. I looked at the TV camera people. I looked over the audience. I looked back to the people onstage. The governor had just risen and was moving forward. I glanced at my watch. Right on time.

Time? No. Later the award. He will tell me when. When...

The applause died down, but there was still noise, rising and falling. Rolling. At first I could not place it: then I realized that it came from outside the hall. Thunder. It must be raining out there. I did not recall that the weather had been bad on the way in. I did not remember a dark sky, threatening, or—

I did not remember what it had been like outside at all—dark, bright, warm, cool, windy, still... I remembered nothing of the weather or anything else.

All right. What did it matter? I had come to listen and to see. Let it rain. It was not in the least important.

I heard the governor's words, six minutes' worth, and I applauded at their conclusion while flashbulbs froze faces and a nearby cheer hurt my ears and caused my head to throb. Time pedaled slowly past as the president stood and moved forward, smiling. I looked at my watch and eased back from the edge of my seat. Fine. Fine.

It seems to me that there is a gallery, with a row of faces atop crude cardboard silhouettes of people. Bright lights play upon them. I stand at the other end of the gallery, my left arm at my side. I hold a pistol in my hand. He tells me. He tells me then. The words. When I hear them I know everything. Everything I am to do to have the prize. I check the weapon without looking at it, for I do not remove my eyes from the prospect before me. There is one target in particular, the special one I must hit to score. Without jerking it, but rather with a rapid yet steady motion, I raise the pistol, sight for just the proper interval and squeeze the trigger with a force that is precisely sufficient. The cardboard figures are all moving slightly, with random jerkings, as I perform this action. But it does not matter. There is a single report. My target topples. I have won the award.

Blackness.

It seems to me that there is a gallery, with a row of faces atop crude cardboard silhouettes of people. Bright lights play upon them. I stand at the other end of the gallery, my left arm at my side. I hold a pistol in my hand. He tells me. He tells me then. The words...

The cry of the man behind me... A ringing in my ears that gradually subsided as the president raised his hand, waving it, turning slowly... But the throbbing in my head did not cease. It felt as if I had just realized the aftermath of a blow somewhere on the crown of my head. I raised my fingers and touched my scalp. There was a sore place, but I felt no break in the skin. However, I could not clearly distinguish the separate forms of my exploring fingers. It was as if, about the soreness, there existed a general numbness. How could this be?

The cries, the applause softened. He was beginning to speak.

I shook myself mentally. What had happened was happening? I did not remember the weather, and my head hurt. Was there anything more?

I tried to think back to my entry into the hall, to find a reason why I did not recall the gathering storm.

I realized then that I did not remember having been outside at all, that I did not recall whether I had gotten to this place by taxi, bus, on foot or by private vehicle, that I did not know where I had come from, that not only did I not recollect what I had had for breakfast this morning, but I did not know where, when or if I had eaten. I did not even remember dressing myself this day.

I reached up to touch my scalp again. As before, something seemed to be warning my hand away from the site, but I ignored it, thinking suddenly of blows on the head and amnesia.

Could that be it? An accident? A bad bash to the skull, then my wandering about all day until some cue served to remind me of the speech I wanted to attend, then set me on the way here, the attainment of my goal gradually drawing me away from the concussion's trauma?

Still, my scalp felt so strange... I poked around the edges of the numb area. It was not *exactly* numb...

Then part of it came away. There was one sharp little pain at which I jerked back my exploring fingers. It subsided quickly, though, and I returned them. No blood. Good. But there had occurred a parting, as if a portion of my hair—my scalp itself—had come loose. I was seized with a momentary terror, but when I touched beneath the loosened area I felt a warm smoothness of normal sensitivity, nothing like torn tissue.

I pushed further and more of it came loose. It was only at the very center that I felt a ragged spot of pain, beneath what seemed like a gauze dressing. It was then that I realized I was wearing a hairpiece, and beneath it a bandage.

There was a tiny ripple of applause as the president said something I had not heard. I looked at my watch.

Was that it, then? An accident? One for which I had been treated in some emergency room—injured area shaved, scalp lacerations sutured, patient judged ambulatory and released, full concussion syndrome not realized?

Somehow that did not seem right. Emergency rooms do not dispense hairpieces to cover their work. And a man in my condition would probably not have been allowed to walk away.

But I could worry about these things later. I had come to hear this talk. I had a good seat and a good view, and I should enjoy the occasion. I could take stock of myself when the event was concluded.

Almost twenty minutes after the hour...

I tried to listen, but I could not keep my mind on what he was saying. Something was wrong and I was hurting myself by not considering it. Very wrong, and not just with me. I was a part of it all, though. How? What?

I looked at the fat little telepath behind the president. *Go ahead and look into my mind, I willed. I would really like you to. Maybe you can see more deeply there than I can myself. Look and see what is wrong. Tell me what has happened, what is happening. I would like to know.*

But he did not even glance my way. He was only interested in incipient mayhem, and my intentions were all pacific. If he read me at all, he must have dismissed my bewilderment as the stream of consciousness of one of that small percentage of the highly neurotic which must occur in any sizable gathering—a puzzled man, but hardly a dangerous one. His attention, and that of any of the others, was reserved for whatever genuinely nasty specimens might be present. And rightly so.

There came another roll of thunder. Nothing. Nothing for me beyond this hall, it reminded. The entire day up until my arrival was a blank. Work on it. Think. I had read about cases of amnesia. Had I ever come across one just like this?

When had I decided to hear this speech? Why? What were the circumstances?

Nothing. The origin of my intention was hidden.

Could there be anything suspect? Was there anything unusual about my desire to be here?

I—No, nothing.

Nineteen minutes after the hour.

I began to perspire. A natural result of my nervousness, I supposed. The second hand swept past the two, the three...

Something to do... It would come clear in a moment. What? Never mind. Wait and see.

The six, the seven...

As another wave of applause crossed the hall I began to wish that I had not come.

Nine, ten...

Twenty minutes after.

My lips began to move. I spoke softly. I doubt that the others about me even heard what I said.

"Step right this way, ladies and gentlemen. Try your luck."

"... *Try your luck.*"

Suddenly I was awake, in the gallery, my hand in my pocket. High up, before me, was the row of faces, the cut-out cardboard bodies below them, lights shining upon them. I felt the pistol and checked it without looking down. The one in front was the target that had been chosen for me, moving slightly, with random jerkings.

I withdrew the weapon carefully and began to raise it slowly.

My hand! Who...

I watched with a sudden and growing fear as my left hand emerged from my pocket holding a gun. I had no control over the action. It was as if the hand belonged to another person. I willed it back down, but it continued to rise. So I did the only thing I could do.

I reached across with my right hand and seized my own wrist.

The left hand had a definite will of its own. It struggled against me. I tightened my grip and pushed it downward with all of my strength.

As this occurred, I found myself trying to get to my feet. Snarls and curses rose unbidden to my lips. The hand was strong. I was not certain how much longer I could hold it.

The finger tightened on the trigger and my hands bucked with the weapon's recoil. Fortunately, the muzzle was pointed downward when it went off. I hope that the ricochet had not caught anyone.

People were screaming and rushing to get away from me by then. Several others, however, were hurrying toward me. If I could only hold the hand until they got to me…

They hit me, two of them. One tackled me and the other took me around the shoulders. We went down. As my left arm was seized, I felt it relax. The pistol was taken from me. Those two hands, such strangers, were forced behind my back and handcuffed there. I remember hoping that they would not break one another. They stopped struggling, however, hanging limply as I was raised to my feet.

When I looked back toward the stage, the president was gone. But the small chubby man was staring at me, dark eyes no longer drifting behind those heavy lenses as he began to move my way, gesturing to the men who held me.

Suddenly I felt very sick and weak, and my head was aching again. I began to hurt in the places where I had been struck.

When the small man stood before me he reached out and clasped my shoulders.

"It is going to be all right now," he said.

The gallery wavered before me. There were no more cardboard silhouettes. Only people. I did not understand where everything had gone, or why he had told me the words, then restrained me. I only knew that I had missed my target and there would be no award. I felt my eye grow moist.

They took me to a clinic. There were guards posted outside my door. The small telepath, whose name I had learned was Arthur Cook, was with me much of the time. A doctor poked at the left side of my neck, inserted a needle and dripped in a clear liquid. The rest was silence.

When I came around—how much later, I am uncertain—the right side of my neck was also sore. Arthur and one of the doctors were standing at my bedside watching me closely.

"Glad to have you back, Mister Mathews," Arthur said. "We want to thank you."

"For what?" I asked. "I don't even know what happened."

"You foiled an assassination plan. I am tempted to say single-handed, but I am not much given to puns. You were an unwilling party to one of the most ingenious attempts to evade telepathic security measures to date. You were the victim of some ruthless people, using highly sophisticated medical methods in their conspiracy. Had they taken one additional measure, I believe they would have succeeded. However, they permitted both of you to be present at the key moment and that was their undoing."

"Both of me?"

"Yes, Mister Mathews. Do you know what the corpus callosum is?"

"A part of the brain, I think."

"Correct. It is an inch-long, a quarter-inch-thick bundle of fibers which serves to join the right and left cerebral hemispheres. If it is severed, it results in the creation of two separate individuals in one body. It is sometimes done in cases of severe epilepsy to diminish the effects of seizures."

"Are you saying that I have undergone such surgery?"

"Yes, you have."

"…And there is another 'me' inside my head?"

"That is correct. The other hemisphere is still sedated at the moment, however."

"Which one am I?"

"You are the left cerebral hemisphere. You possess the linguistic abilities and the powers of more complicated reasoning. The other side is move intuitive and emotional and possesses greater visual and spatial capabilities."

"Can this surgery be undone?"

"No."

"I see. And you say that other people have had such operations—epileptics… How did they—do—afterward?"

The doctor spoke then, a tall man, hawk-featured, hair of a smoky gray.

"For a long while the connection—the corpus callosum—had been thought to have no important functions. It was years before anyone was even aware of this side effect to a commissurotomy. I do not foresee any great difficulties for you. We will go into more detail on this later."

"All right. I feel like—myself—at any rate. Why did they do this to me?"

"To turn you into the perfect modern assassin," Arthur said. "Half of the brain can be put to sleep while the other hemisphere remains awake. This is done simply by administering a drug via the carotid artery on the appropriate side. After the surgery had been performed, you—the left hemisphere—were put to sleep while the right hemisphere was subjected to hypnosis and behavior modification techniques, was turned into a conditioned assassin—"

"I had always thought a person could not be hypnotized into doing certain things."

He nodded.

"Normally, that seems to be the case. However, it appears that, by itself, the emotional, less rational right hemisphere is more susceptible to suggestion—and it was not a simple kill order which it received, it was a cleverly constructed and well-rehearsed illusion to which it was trained to respond."

"Okay," I said. "Buying all that, how did they make what happened happen?"

"The mechanics of it? Well, the conditioning, as I said, was done while you were unconscious and, hence, unaware of it. The conditioned hemisphere was then placed in a state of deep sleep, with the suggestion that it would awaken and perform its little act on receipt of the appropriate cue. Your hemisphere was then impressed with a post-hypnotic suggestion to provide that cue, in the form of the phrase you spoke, at a particular time when the speech would be going on. So they left you out in front and you walked into the hall consciously aware of none of this. Your mind was perfectly innocent under any telepathic scrutiny. It was only when you performed your post-hypnotic suggestion and called attention to yourself moments later that I suddenly regarded two minds in one body—an extremely eerie sensation, I might add. It was fortunate then that you, the more rational individual, quickly saw what was happening and struggled to avert it. This gave us just enough time to move in on you."

I nodded. I thought about it, about two of me, struggling for the control of our one body. Then, "You said that they had slipped up—that had they done one additional thing they might have succeeded," I said. "What was that?"

"They should have implanted the suggestion that you go to sleep immediately after speaking the stimulus phrase," he said. "I believe that would have done it. They just did not foresee the conflict between the two of you."

"What about the people behind this?" I finally asked.

"Your right hemisphere provided us with quite a few very good descriptions while you were asleep."

"Descriptions? I thought I was the verbal one."

"True, basically. But the other provided some excellent sketches, the substance of which I was able to verify telepathically. The Service then matched them with certain individuals on whom they have files, and these persons have already been apprehended.

"But the other hemisphere is not completely nonverbal," he went on. "There is normally a certain small amount of transference—which may be coming into play now, as a matter of fact."

"What do you mean?"

"The other you has been awake awhile now. Your left hand, which it controls, has been gesturing frantically for several minutes. For my pen. I can tell."

He withdrew a pen and a small pad from his pocket and passed them to me. I watched with fascination as they were seized and positioned. Slowly, carefully, my left hand wrote on the pad, *Im sorry.*

...And as I wrote, I realized that he would not understand, could never understand now, exactly what I meant.

And that was what I meant, exactly.

I stared down at the words and I looked up at the wall. I looked at Arthur and at the doctor.

"I'd appreciate it if you would leave us alone for a while now," I said.

They did, and even before they left I knew that no matter where I looked half of the room would have to be empty.

A Word from Zelazny

"Betty White of *The Saturday Evening Post* suddenly solicited a 3500-word story from me one day, so I did this one quickly and she bought it just as quickly. Then I asked her why she had wanted it. She told me that she had recently had her television set turned on and was occupied with something that did not permit her to change channels readily. A show called *Star Trek* came on and she watched it through and enjoyed it. She had not known much about science fiction, she said, and she resolved to stop by her paperback book store the following day, buy a science fiction book at random and read it. It happened to be one of mine. She read it and liked it and decided to ask me for a story. I have since theorized that if she entered the shop and approached the far end of the science fiction rack my position in the alphabet might have had something to do with her choice. Whatever..."[1]

Zelazny drew criticism because many of his early characters smoked. "My characters smoked in most of my early stories because whenever I was momentarily stuck in the course of a narrative I would light a cigarette. My usual reaction was then to transfer it. 'Of course,' I would think, 'He lit a cigarette.'" Zelazny's participation in the martial arts led in part to his quitting, and once he stopped smoking, his characters hardly ever did either.[2]

Notes

Corpus callosotomy is surgery that disconnects the brain's hemispheres by cutting the corpus callosum; this is sometimes done to control severe epilepsy. Split-brain syndrome describes the procedure's consequences. **Commissurotomy**, a more general term, means surgical cutting of a connection between two tissues.

---

1 *The Last Defender of Camelot*, 1980.
2 *Roger Zelazny*, Jane Lindskold, 1993.

REPLY

Written 1965–68; previously unpublished.

the perpetual throbbing caress
that is heart's reply to blood
crying from instant corridors
imprisoned in flesh
soft as pumice
blind to its own color
                       is
in the nature of answer
i sometimes feel
              like now
to that question
                 shouted
through passageways of vein
                             wordless
existing before brain
                     formless
yet contained
              amniotic
pure
    as the ocean gray
now like a nightingale
singing across night
or fire
       say

it is not fair
>	really
to string words
like bridges
>	but we
do it all the time
>	my dear
excepting when the blood
replies to blood
>	as here
upon this bank
and bed of time
we jump the life to come

understand me now
the dialogue of the systole
and all the things Newton
did about motion
is the pre-ordained
menace of being
anguish of *sein*
jeopardy of *nicht sein*
amidst the sweet
flirtatious things of springs
whose accent
no farewell can know
for heart's an ever-drowning thing
and nothing really makes him go

there are lilacs
>	guitars
>	April
poets like them

also the moon
the ghost of Hamlet's father
on the castle wall
mechanical birds
                which sing
snakes and toads
sea-smoothed pebbles
                    roses
or any shiny thing at all
which is small
or seems so

(why they
like them
they are not sure

which means they are holy)

so because of this
my answer to the question
you did not speak
                my dear
is lady loose your leopards
i will not turn again
                  you know
lady come here
            you are blood
to clean the bones
within a passageway
prisoner
ocean
lonely
song

> or add another metaphor
> and fire
>   say
>
> we're wrong
>   of course
> my Judith of the long hours
>
> but the infinite modality
> of the visible
> is not for the heart to know
> Belle Isle
> betray or stain
>   but pure
> and clear
> and so

Notes

This poem was written entirely in lower case except for the proper names.

The reference to **Judith of the long hours** suggests that he wrote this for Judith Zelazny; it may be incomplete. **Systole** is the heart's contracting to pump blood. ***"Sein"*** means "being" and ***"nicht sein"*** means "not being."

Is There a Demon Lover in the House?

Heavy Metal, September 1977.

Nightscape of the city in November with fog: intermittent blotches of streetlight; a chilly thing, the wind slithering across the weeping faces of buildings; the silence.

Form is dulled and softened. Outlines are lost, silhouettes unsealed. Matter bleeds some vital essence upon the streets. What are the pivot points of time? Was that its arrow, baffled by coils of mist, or only a lost bird of the night?

...Walking now, the man, gait slowed to a normal pace now, his exhilaration transmuted to a kind of calm. Middle-aged, middle-statured, side-whiskered, dark, he looks neither to the left nor the right. He has lost his way, but his step is almost buoyant. A great love fills his being, general, objectless, pure as the pearl-soft glow of the corner light through the fog.

He reaches that corner and moves to cross the street.

An auto is there, then gone, tearing through the intersection, a low rumble within its muffler, lights slashing the dark. Its red tail lamps swing by, dwindle, are gone; its tires screech as it turns an unseen corner.

The man has drawn back against the building. He stares in the direction the vehicle has taken. For a long while after it has vanished from sight, he continues to stare. Then he withdraws a case from an inside pocket, takes out a small cigar, lights it. His hands shake as he does so.

A moment of panic...

He looks all about, sighs, then retrieves the small, newspaper-wrapped parcel he had been carrying, from where it had fallen near the curb.

Carefully, carefully then, he crosses the street. Soon the love has hold of him again.

Farther along, he comes upon a parked car, pauses a moment beside it, sees a couple embracing within, continues on his way. Another car passes along the street, slowly. There is a glow ahead.

He advances toward the illumination. There are lights within a small café and several storefront display windows. A theater marquee blazes in the center of the block. There are people here, moving along the walks, crossing the street. Cars discharge passengers. There is a faint odor of frying fish. The theater, he sees, is called the Regent Street.

He pauses beneath the marquee, which advertises:

EXOTIC MIDNIGHT SPECIAL
THE KISS OF DEATH

Puffing his cigar, he regards a series of photos within a glass case. A long-haired, acne-dotted medical student comes over to see the still shots, innocuous yet titillative on the wall. "Thought they'd never get to show it," he mutters.

"Beg pardon?"

"This snuff film. Just won a court decision. Didn't you hear?"

"No. I did not know. This one?"

"That's right. You going to see it?"

"I don't know. What is it about?"

The student turns and stares at the man, cocks his head to one side, smiles faintly. Seeing the reaction, the man smiles also. The student chuckles and shrugs.

"May be your only chance to see one," he says. "I'm betting they get closed down again and it goes to a higher court."

"Perhaps I will."

"Rotten weather, huh? They say *so ho* was an old hunting cry. Probably from people trying to find each other, huh?"

He chuckles. The man returns it and nods. The calm of controlled passion that holds him as in a gentle fist pushes him toward the experience.

"Yes, I believe that I will," he says, and he moves toward the ticket window.

The man behind the glass looks up as he passes him the money, "You sure you want to spend that? It's an oldie."

He nods.

The ticket seller sets the coin to one side, hands him his pasteboard and his change.

He enters the lobby, looks about, follows the others.

"No smoking inside. Fire law."

"Oh. Sorry."

Dropping his cigar into a nearby receptacle, he surrenders his ticket and passes within. He pauses at the head of an aisle to regard the screen before him, moves on when jostled, finds a seat to his left, takes it.

He settles back and lets his warm feeling enfold him. It is a strange night. Lost, why had he come in? A place to sit? A place to hide? A place to be warm with impersonal human noises about him? Curiosity?

All of these, he decides, while his thoughts roam over the varied surface of life, and the post-orgasmic sadness fades to tenderness and gratefulness.

His shoulder is touched. He turns quickly.

"Just me," says the student. "Show'll be starting in a few minutes. You ever read the Marquis de Sade?"

"Yes."

"What do you think of him?"

"A decadent dilettante."

"Oh."

The student settles back and assumes a thoughtful pose. The man returns his eyes to the front of the theater.

After a time, the houselights grow dim and die. Then the screen is illuminated. The words *The Kiss of Death* flash upon it. Soon they are succeeded by human figures. The man leans forward, his brow furrowed. He turns and studies the slant of light from the projection booth, dust motes drifting within it. He sees a portion of the equipment. He turns again to the screen and his breathing deepens.

He watches all the actions leading to the movements of passion as time ticks about him. The theater is still. It seems that he has been transported to a magical realm. The people around him take on a supernatural quality, blank-faced in the light reflected from the screen. The back of his neck grows cold, and it feels as if the hairs are stirring upon it. Still, he suppresses a desire to rise and depart, for there is something frightening, too, to the vision. But it seems important that he see it through. He leans back again, watching, watching the flickering spectacle before him.

There is a tightening in his belly as he realizes what is finally to occur, as he sees the knife, the expression on the girl's face, the sudden movements, the writhing, the blood. As it continues, he gnaws his knuckle and begins to perspire. It is real, so real…

"Oh my!" he says and relaxes.

The warmth comes back to him again, but he continues to watch, until the last frame fades and the lights come on once again.

"How'd you like it?" says the voice at his back.

He does not turn.

"It is amazing," he finally says, "that they can make pictures move on a screen like that."

He hears the familiar chuckle, then, "Care to join me for a cup of coffee? Or a drink?"

"No, thanks. I have to be going."

He rises and hurries up the aisle, back toward the fog-masked city where he had somehow lost his way.

"Say, you forgot your package!"

But the man does not hear. He is gone.

The student raises it, weighs it in his palm, wonders. When he finally unwraps the folded *Times*, it is not only the human heart it contains which causes his sharp intake of breath, but the fact that the paper bears a date in November of 1888.

"Oh, Lord!" he says. "Let him find his way home!"

Outside, the fog begins to roll and break, and the wind makes a small rustling noise as it passes. The long shadow of the man, lost in his love and wonder, moves like a blade through the city and November and the night.

A Word from Zelazny

"This story was solicited by *Heavy Metal*. I was in the mood to do a mood piece at that time."[1]

Zelazny also used this character in *A Night in the Lonesome October*. "I had once written a story involving Jack the Ripper. It was for *Heavy Metal*... I had actually skimmed a book about Jack the Ripper at the time, and I remembered that the last Ripper killings occurred in October. I said 'you have a ritual killing situation and October. What's special about October? Well, Halloween, but there's a Halloween every year.' I was looking for something to distinguish it. I said, 'well, there's not a Halloween with a full moon every year. That could make it special.' That's when I got the rough idea for a sort of game. A stylized duel between two sides involving something that would culminate on Halloween."[2]

Notes

Regent Street is in Soho, London. A **snuff film** shows an actual murder. The medical student refers to the legend that Soho derived its name from *So ho!*, a hunting cry. Soho is the center of London's gay and red light district (adult shops, strip clubs). **The Marquis de Sade** was a French aristocrat and writer who advocated freedom unregulated by law, morality or religion. He was fascinated by extreme pornography. The term sadism derives from his name. Jack the Ripper considers him a **dilettante**, a mere dabbler in the art.

---

1 *The Last Defender of Camelot*, 1980.
2 *Absolute Magnitude*, Fall/Winter 1994.

Testament

Kronos #2, 1965.
Written 1955–60 for *Chisel in the Sky*.

Strange, that here I should think of you.
The ashes are not bitter,
nor the dust excessive.
There are no trees
to hold the three small beasts:
fear, shame, and mocking laughter…

but yesterday discomfort
fell black across this path,
sapping seas of innocence
I'd builded in a waste:
diminutive dimples of darkness
slashed shadow to prairie dog's stare:

adjudicant, still angel cast of brownness,
preposition to fire, despair…

Notes

Builded is an archaic form of built. **Adjudicant** or adjudicator is someone who formally presides and judges over a dispute.

The Engine at Heartspring's Center

Analog, July 1974.
Nebula nominee 1975 (short story). Jupiter nominee 1975 (short story).
#5 on 1975 Locus poll (short story).

Let me tell you of the creature called the Bork. It was born in the heart of a dying sun. It was cast forth upon this day from the river of past/future as a piece of time pollution. It was fashioned of mud and aluminum, plastic and some evolutionary distillate of seawater. It had spun dangling from the umbilical of circumstance till, severed by its will, it had fallen a lifetime or so later, coming to rest on the shoals of a world where things go to die. It was a piece of a man in a place by the sea near a resort grown less fashionable since it had become a euthanasia colony.

Choose any of the above and you may be right.

❖ ❖ ❖

Upon this day, he walked beside the water, poking with his forked, metallic stick at the things the last night's storm had left: some shiny bit of detritus useful to the weird sisters in their crafts shop, worth a meal there or a dollop of polishing rouge for his smoother half; purple seaweed for a salty chowder he had come to favor; a buckle, a button, a shell; a white chip from the casino.

The surf foamed and the wind was high. The heavens were a blue-gray wall, unjointed, lacking the graffiti of birds or commerce. He left a jagged track and one footprint, humming and clicking as he passed over the pale sands. It was near to the point where the forktailed ice-birds paused for several days—a week at most—in their migrations. Gone now, portions of the beach were still dotted with their rust-colored droppings. There he saw the girl again, for the third time in as many days. She had tried before to speak with him, to detain him. He had ignored her for a number of reasons. This time, however, she was not alone.

She was regaining her feet, the signs in the sand indicating flight and collapse. She had on the same red dress, torn and stained now. Her black hair—short, with heavy bangs—lay in the only small disarrays of which it was capable. Perhaps thirty feet away was a young man from the Center, advancing toward her. Behind him drifted one of the seldom seen dispatch machines—about half the size of a man and floating that same distance above the ground, it was shaped like a tenpin, and silver, its bulbous head-end faceted and illuminated, its three ballerina skirts tinfoil-thin and gleaming, rising and falling in rhythms independent of the wind.

Hearing him, or glimpsing him peripherally, she turned away from her pursuers, said, "Help me" and then she said a name.

He paused for a long while, although the interval was undetectable to her. Then he moved to her side and stopped again.

The man and the hovering machine halted also.

"What is the matter?" he asked, his voice smooth, deep, faintly musical.

"They want to take me," she said.

"Well?"

"I do not wish to go."

"Oh. You are not ready?"

"No, I am not ready."

"Then it is but a simple matter. A misunderstanding."

He turned toward the two.

"There has been a misunderstanding," he said. "She is not ready."

"This is not your affair, Bork, " the man replied. "The Center has made its determination."

"Then it will have to reexamine it. She says that she is not ready.'

"Go about your business, Bork."

The man advanced. The machine followed.

The Bork raised his hands, one of flesh, the others of other things. "No," he said.

"Get out of the way," the man said. "You are interfering."

Slowly, the Bork moved toward them. The lights in the machine began to blink. Its skirts fell. With a sizzling sound it dropped to the sand and lay unmoving. The man halted, drew back a pace.

The Engine at Heartspring's Center

"I will have to report this—"

"Go away," said the Bork.

The man nodded, stooped, raised the machine. He turned and carried it off with him, heading up the beach, not looking back. The Bork lowered his arms.

"There," he said to the girl. "You have more time."

He moved away then, investigating shell-shucks and driftwood. She followed him.

"They will be back," she said.

"Of course. "

"What will I do then?"

"Perhaps by then you will be ready."

She shook her head. She laid her hand on his human part.

"No," she said. "I will not be ready."

"How can you tell, now?"

"I made a mistake," she said. "I should never have come here."

He halted and regarded her.

"That is unfortunate," he said. "The best thing that I can recommend is to go and speak with the therapists at the Center. They will find a way to persuade you that peace is preferable to distress. "

"They were never able to persuade you," she said.

"I am different. The situation is not comparable."

"I do not wish to die."

"Then they cannot take you. The proper frame of mind is prerequisite. It is right there in the contract—Item Seven. "

"They can make mistakes. Don't you think they ever make a mistake? They get cremated the same as the others."

"They are most conscientious. They have dealt fairly with me."

"Only because you are virtually immortal. The machines short out in your presence. No man could lay hands on you unless you willed it. And did they not try to dispatch you in a state of unreadiness?"

"That was the result of a misunderstanding."

"Like mine?"

"I doubt it."

He drew away from her, continuing on down the beach.

"Charles Eliot Borkman," she called.

That name again.

He halted once more, tracing lattices with his stick, poking out a design in the sand.

Then, "Why did you say that?" he asked.

"It is your name, isn't it?"

"No," he said. "That man died in deep space when a liner was jumped to the wrong coordinates, coming out too near a star gone nova."

"He was a hero. He gave half his body to the burning, preparing an escape boat for the others. And he survived."

"Perhaps a few pieces of him did. No more."

"It *was* an assassination attempt, wasn't it?"

"Who knows? Yesterday's politics are not worth the paper wasted on its promises, its threats."

"He wasn't just a politician. He was a statesman, a humanitarian. One of the very few to retire with more people loving him than hating him."

He made a chuckling noise.

"You are most gracious. But if that is the case, then the minority still had the final say. I personally think he was something of a thug. I am pleased, though, to hear that you have switched to the past tense."

"They patched you up so well that you could last forever. Because you deserved the best."

"Perhaps I already have lasted forever. What do you want of me?"

"You came here to die and you changed your mind—"

"Not exactly. I've just never composed it in a fashion acceptable under the terms of Item Seven. To be at peace—"

"And neither have I. But I lack your ability to impress this fact on the Center."

"Perhaps if I went there with you and spoke to them…"

"No," she said. "They would only agree for so long as you were about. They call people like us life-malingerers and are much more casual about the disposition of our cases. I cannot trust them as you do without armor of my own."

"Then what would you have me do—girl?"

"Nora. Call me Nora. Protect me. That is what I want. You live near here. Let me come stay with you. Keep them away from me."

He poked at the pattern, began to scratch it out.

"You are certain that this is what you want?"

"Yes. Yes, I am."

"All right. You may come with me, then."

❖   ❖   ❖

So Nora went to live with the Bork in his shack by the sea. During the weeks that followed, on each occasion when the representatives from the Center came about, the Bork bade them depart quickly, which they did. Finally, they stopped coming by.

Days, she would pace with him along the shores and help in the gathering of driftwood, for she liked a fire at night; and while heat and cold had long been things of indifference to him, he came in time and his fashion to enjoy the glow.

And on their walks he would poke into the dank trash heaps the sea had lofted and turn over stones to see what dwelled beneath.

"God! What do you hope to find in that?" she said, holding her breath and retreating.

"I don't know," he chuckled. "A stone? A leaf? A door? Something nice. Like that."

"Let's go watch the things in the tidepools. They're clean, at least."

"All right."

Though he ate from habit and taste rather than from necessity, her need for regular meals and her facility in preparing them led him to anticipate these occasions with something approaching a ritualistic pleasure. And it was later still, after an evening's meal, that she came to polish him for the first time. Awkward, grotesque—perhaps it could have been. But as it occurred, it was neither of these. They sat before the fire, drying, warming, watching, silent. Absently, she picked up the rag he had let fall to the floor and brushed a fleck of ash from his flame-reflecting side. Later, she did it again. Much later, and this time with full attention, she wiped all the dust from the gleaming surface before going off to her bed.

One day she asked him, "Why did you buy the one-way ticket to this place and sign the contract, if you did not wish to die?"

"But I did wish it," he said.

"And something changed your mind after that? What?"

"I found here a pleasure greater than that desire."

"Would you tell me about it?"

"Surely. I found this to be one of the few situations—perhaps the only—where I can be happy. It is in the nature of the place itself: departure, a peaceful conclusion, a joyous going. Its contemplation here pleases me, living at the end of entropy and seeing that it is good."

"But it doesn't please you enough to undertake the treatment yourself?"

"No. I find in this a reason for living, not for dying. It may seem a warped satisfaction. But then, I am warped. What of yourself?"

"I just made a mistake. That's all."

"They screen you pretty carefully, as I recall. The only reason they made a mistake in my case was that they could not anticipate anyone finding in this place an inspiration to go on living. Could your situation have been similar?"

"I don't know. Perhaps…"

On days when the sky was clear they would rest in the yellow warmth of the sun, playing small games and sometimes talking of the birds that passed and of the swimming, drifting, branching, floating and flowering things in their pools. She never spoke of herself, saying whether it was love, hate, despair, weariness or bitterness that had brought her to this place. Instead, she spoke of those neutral things they shared when the day was bright; and when the weather kept them indoors she watched the fire, slept or polished his armor. It was only much later that she began to sing and to hum, small snatches of tune recently popular or tunes quite old. At these times, if she felt his eyes upon her she stopped abruptly and turned to another thing.

One night then, when the fire had burned low, as she sat, buffing his plates, slowly, quite slowly, she said in a soft voice,. "I believe that I am falling in love with you."

He did not speak, nor did he move. He gave no sign of having heard.

After a long while, she said, "It is most strange, finding myself feeling this way—here—under these circumstances…"

"Yes," he said, after a time.

After a longer while, she put down the cloth and took hold of his hand—the human one—and felt his grip tighten upon her own.

"Can you?" she said, much later.

"Yes. But I would crush you, little girl."

She ran her hands over his plates, then back and forth from flesh to metal. She pressed her lips against his only cheek that yielded.

"We'll find a way," she said, and of course they did.

❖   ❖   ❖

In the days that followed she sang more often, sang happier things and did not break off when he regarded her. And sometimes he would awaken from the light sleep that even he required, awaken and through the smallest aperture of his lens note that she lay there or sat watching him, smiling. He sighed occasionally for the pure pleasure of feeling the rushing air within and about him, and there was a peace and a pleasure come into him of the sort he had long since relegated to the realms of madness, dream and vain desire. Occasionally, he even found himself whistling.

One day as they sat on a bank, the sun nearly vanished, the stars coming on, the deepening dark was melted about a tiny wick of falling fire and she let go of his hand and pointed.

"A ship," she said.

"Yes," he answered, retrieving her hand.

"Full of people."

"A few, I suppose."

"It is sad."

"It must be what they want, or what they want to want."

"It is still sad."

"Yes. Tonight. Tonight it is sad."

"And tomorrow?"

"Then too, I daresay."

"Where is your old delight in the graceful end, the peaceful winding-down?"

"It is not on my mind so much these days. Other things are there."

They watched the stars until the night was all black and light and filled with cold air. Then, "What is to become of us?" she said.

"Become?" he said. "If you are happy with things as they are, there is no need to change them. If you are not, then tell me what is wrong."

"Nothing," she said. "When you put it that way, nothing. It was just a small fear—a cat scratching at my heart, as they say."

"I'll scratch your heart myself," he said, raising her as if she were weightless.

Laughing, he carried her back to the shack.

It was out of a deep, drugged-seeming sleep that he dragged himself/was dragged much later, by the sound of her weeping. His time-sense felt distorted, for it seemed an abnormally long interval before her image registered, and her sobs seemed unnaturally drawn out and far apart.

"What—is—it?" he said, becoming at that moment aware of the faint, throbbing, pinprick aftereffect in his biceps.

"I did not—want you to—awaken," she said. "Please go back to sleep."

"You are from the Center, aren't you?"

She looked away.

"It does not matter," he said.

"Sleep. Please. Do not lose the—"

"—requirements of Item Seven," he finished. "You always honor a contract, don't you?"

"That is not all that it was—to me."

"You meant what you said that night?"

"I came to."

"Of course you would say that now. Item Seven—"

"You bastard!" she said, and she slapped him.

He began to chuckle, but it stopped when he saw the hypodermic on the table at her side. Two spent ampules lay with it.

"You didn't give me two shots," he said, and she looked away. "Come on." He began to rise. "We've got to get you to the Center. Get the stuff neutralized. Get it out of you."

She shook her head.

"Too late—already. Hold me. If you want to do something for me, do that."

He wrapped all of his arms about her and they lay that way while the tides and the winds cut, blew and ebbed, grinding their edges to an ever more perfect fineness.

❖   ❖   ❖

I think—

Let me tell you of the creature called the Bork. It was born in the heart of a dying star. It was a piece of a man and pieces of many other things. If the things went wrong, the man-piece shut them down and repaired them. If he went wrong, they shut him down and repaired him. It was so skillfully fashioned that it might have lasted forever. But if part of it should die the other pieces need not cease to function, for it could still contrive to carry on the motions the total creature had once performed. It is a thing in a place by the sea that walks beside the water, poking with its forked, metallic stick at the other things the waves have tossed. The human piece, or a piece of the human piece, is dead.

Choose any of the above.

A Word from Zelazny

"Tom Monteleone, visiting one afternoon, pointed out to me that I had not written a short story in over two years. So I did this one right after he left to prevent the interval's growing any longer."[1] "...when he left I sat down and wrote that one, just to see if I still remembered how."[2] This tale was a success, garnering three award nominations. Yet it first was rejected by *Penthouse, Playboy, Gallery,* and *Oui.* Editor Gay Bryant said, "It's a great piece but unfortunately not right for *Penthouse*."[3] Ben Bova was delighted to take it for *Analog*.

Samuel Delany had earlier remarked, "Immortality appears in one form or another in almost all his works; when it doesn't, there is suicide: faces of one coin."[4] These opposing themes figure in this story and in the cyborg Bork, who lives a long life near a Euthanasia Center and experiences the death of his human half. Far from suffering stereotypical ennui from long life, Zelazny's immortals remain interested in humanity and living. Delany said, "Given all eternity to live, each experience becomes a jewel in the jewel-clutter of life; each moment becomes infinitely fascinating because there is so much more to relate it to."[4] Zelazny said, "if one has an extended lifespan...one would have to have a sense of humor. I forget who said it— Pascal I think—'Life is a tragedy to the man who feels and a comedy to the man who thinks.' My characters would think more just by virtue of having more time in which to do it."[5] That quote has been attributed to Pascal, Nietzsche, Horace Walpole, and Tennessee Williams.

Notes

Euthanasia is the practice of ending the life of an individual suffering from a terminal illness, sometimes by lethal injection. **Detritus** is debris.

---

1 *The Last Defender of Camelot*, 1980.
2 *Tangent* #4, February 1976.
3 Letter from Gay Bryant, Fiction Editor, *Penthouse* to Henry Morrison, February 9, 1973.
4 "Faust and Archimedes: Disch, Zelazny," in *The Jewel-Hinged Jaw*, Samuel R Delany, 1977.
5 *Roger Zelazny*, Theodore Krulik, 1986.

Sonnet, Anyone?

To Spin Is Miracle Cat, Underwood-Miller 1981.

Save for Berryman's, who wants the sonnet?
—A fusty hangover from ages dark.
Take a thought, hang fourteen lines upon it,
Prime it and crank it, force it to a spark,
Then halting rhyme in pattern archaic,
Play with the choke until the engine sings
(Wondering when you'll get that certain kick),
A stilted song of common imagings.
While the oldfangled buggy, pushed with pride,
jolted to a motion, at times repays
Mechanic hands, mostly it's a rough ride,
With that Model T we drive on Sundays,
Bumping down twisted country roads, my love,
Where each must go who has something to prove.

Notes

Much of Zelazny's poetry is free verse; this sonnet is an exception. A **sonnet** is a 14 line poem, usually in iambic pentameter, addressing a single theme. Zelazny's poem is a Shakespearian sonnet, having three quatrains followed by a couplet with the rhyme scheme abab, cdcd, efef, gg. Zelazny admired American poet John Allyn **Berryman**, whose works included the collection *Berryman's Sonnets*. **Fusty** means smelling stale. The **Model T** was the first commercially available automobile in America; it required hand-cranking to start the engine.

ARTICLES

Tomorrow Stuff

Written in 1968; previously unpublished.

It is always difficult to say why a writer writes. I do not know the thing it was that day, that irritated my psyche, that generated the peculiar compulsion-desire combination which resulted in my first story. I'll call it my demon, say that I am still bedeviled, and let it go at that.

Why I generally write a particular type of material, however—i.e., science fiction or fantasy—is a question which I am in a better position to answer.

First, this is an area of literature where the writer has considerably more freedom than in other types of fiction. I enjoy descriptive writing, and it pleases me to be able to describe landscapes and meteorological phenomena which could not exist on Earth, but which might just be possible elsewhere; similarly, with characters and their motivations. For an example, I indulged my fancy in all of these things in my novelette, "The Keys To December," which contained unmanlike humans engaged in an unusual project on a strange world. This provided an aesthetic pleasure of a sort that would not have obtained had I written a more "down-to-Earth" story.

There is also intellectual gratification in the exercising of these extra freedoms. The author may plan whatever future society he chooses to show precisely how he thinks it would function, given the factors upon which he bases it. In this fashion, he is free to explore whatever sociological or philosophical notions he wishes. Or, he may write an "If this goes on…" story, by projecting some facet of present society into the future and exploring its consequences when carried to an extreme.

Also, there is somewhat of an emotional satisfaction involved in exercising one's god-complex in creating a world all by oneself, in fashioning it and populating it as one would, in working out its destinies, and even, perhaps, destroying it.

Second, there are economic reasons for writing science fiction. It is an area where a young writer of any talent will receive encouragement; and it is an easy area to "break into" and receive money while polishing one's writing skills. One of the reasons for this is that, compared to other forms of writing, the competition is less keen. There is really only a small number of people in the world who write sf. There are good returns subsequent to an initial sale, also. A decent sf story stands the chance of being anthologized several times, with consequent foreign and paperback royalties, plus eventual inclusion in a collection of one's own stories, with consequent foreign, etc. Along with this, it is a great boost to the ego to receive recognition at a science fiction fan-affair, and there is always the possibility of glory, for sf has its own triumphs, awards and trophies.

Third, there are certain similarities between science fiction, poetry and the visual arts, which—while so with all of literature—are especially striking here, and which exercise a particular appeal to some people such as me. The poet's striving to produce fresh metaphors, and new and uniquely apt combinations of words is a thing akin to the sf writer's efforts in creating new worlds. It represents a more intensely skewed angle of vision than is necessary in the bulk of modern writing, i.e. realism-naturalism. Likewise, and especially so in surrealism, expressionism and impressionism, there are some affinities with the visual arts. The representation of several ordinarily incongruous objects on the same plane of existence is a thing which happens constantly in sf, as are extraordinary transformations of the commonplace.

To summarize, then, freedom, money, and the attraction of the unique are the basic reasons I, and I daresay most, write sf.

Now, with respect to the area in general, one should know something of its history, traditions, levels of quality, in order to properly assess any given work or to lay personal plans for writing it. It must be borne in mind the sf has its roots in the U.S. pulp magazines of 20, 30, 40 years ago, and much of the early work was of pulp quality, i.e. hack writing. I feel that the collapse of the majority of those magazines in the early 1950s was a salubrious thing in that it caused many writers in the area to seek other outlets, with the resultant appearance of a lot of sf in paperback and even hardcover editions. These were less restrictive than the pulp magazines, and because of this the writers discovered that they could write of things, and write in such a fashion, as had earlier been *verboten*, because of editorial policies and taboos in the magazines. All of which leads to the point I now wish to make: Sf has passed through its adolescence and come into early adulthood now. The first major effect of this is that the quality of the writing and the nature of the themes being dealt with has advanced. There are better stories, more mature stories, appearing these days. The things one sees are no longer 98% space-opera.

The traditions I mentioned have not been abandoned, however. The four major notions which abounded in much early sf are with us still and they are things akin to the fact that people sing in an opera, rather than talking. Everybody knows and accepts this is the way it is done. So, with sf, you find the notions of faster-than-light travel, easy communication with alien creatures, time-travel, and the existence of and passage to parallel worlds, treated, in general, in a pretty casual fashion with a minimum of explanation as to the *modus operandi* involved. But once known, this is not so different from the fact that in a western story people ride horses, carry guns on their hips, and cattlemen hate sheepherders and people are often not too friendly with Mexicans and Indians. Of course this is an oversimplification, but it represents something of the stock of preconceived notions one must generally bring to a work of this genre. These things are with us, and they're neither good nor bad, they're just conventions—that's all.

There is an undeniably existential quality to sf, which constantly questions man's fate, man's place in the universe. An sf hero is generally a loner—tough, smart, frequently quite introspective. He often winds up facing the entire world, and watching himself as he does so. Win or lose, he learns, he chooses.

The industrial revolution gave us sf. The *genre* began because of man's fascination with gadgetry. The other major thing which informed the area was the fear of the dark, of the gods, of the things that prowl beyond the firelight, displaying only eyes. The gods and the devils and the machines got together to provide the afflatus. The early magazines provided the vehicle. The magazines' letter columns provided a fandom which supported, promoted the genre. Now, with an impressive body of works and something of a tradition, sf thrives, independent of any single medium. It has proven sufficiently autonomous to survive the passing of most of the magazines.

Now we have entered into an age which, in one sense, is a catching-up phase. Literary devices, attitudes, tones, which were long ago explored at great length by Joyce, Kafka, Beckett, Ionesco, are just now finding their ways into sf because of the freedom I mentioned earlier. This can't hurt any, for the more tools a craftsman has at his disposal, the better a product he is likely to put together. The immediate shock-value, however, in an area previously untouched by such experimentation, is significant. It has raised cries of decadence, narcissism, exhibitionism, phoniness. A few years from now, however, the area will have digested this, just as it happened in another time and another place. And we will be—already are, actually—enriched thereby.

These are my feelings about this moment in the lifeline of something I love.

Now, on the business, rather than the literary side of things, I believe it is also worth mention here, that for the first time in history, sf writers have formed and managed to maintain an organization dedicated to improving both the quality of work in the area and the writer's lot in general. I speak of SFWA—The Science Fiction Writers of America—which has done much these past three years to assure the continuance and improvement of the *genre*. At present writing, I am secretary/treasurer of this organization and therefore I am in a position to observe that it would take a considerable catastrophe to destroy us. I think I can safely say that it will be a cold day in Hell when the world runs out of sf. This is because of the curiosity and the fear that gave us our sense of wonder, and because there are now enough of us possessing this heritage, enough of us so situated, that we will prophesy from here to eternity.

About my own writing, I have very little to say. That which moves me especially involves life and death, love and hate, the same as any other writer. My own idiosyncrasies, of course, make me what I am. What are my particular hang-ups and foibles? Immortality, suicide, one man against the winds and the tides and the stars, sometimes the impossible love which sustains, impossibly, the tortured soul, sometimes the hate so big that it would burn the innocent to reach the guilty, and sometimes the simple, contemplative pleasures—like good food, friendly cats, a pipe of pleasant tobacco—that make life worthwhile, despite all ugliness, and then again, the things, sometimes bawdy, sometimes simple that make me laugh.

I don't know how I hang particular items on these hooks and make stories out of them...a stone, a leaf, a door...you have the routine list. Anything might supply the initial stimulation, and then my demon takes over and starts devilling me until it's all down on paper. I've a very visual type imagination. I see everything that happens—even dream about it, occasionally—while I'm working on a story. Whether this is good or bad, I don't know. It's just the way things are with me.

If I were in the process of counseling a would-be sf writer, I would say to him, "you need a sense of humor and a sense of place. You need a sense of history and a sense of time. You need a sense of science and a sense of the human condition. You need a sense of the fear, shame and mocking laughter, which for want of a better word I'll call the guilt involved in being a man. But most of all, you need a sense of humor." And assuming that the guy knows how to put words together at all, I think he'll probably make it on the scene, along with the rest of us priests of the absurd, time-keepers of the never-to-be-calendared occasion.

Notes

In this 1968 essay Zelazny described the history of science fiction and the impact that he and other new writers had on the field. He described how they brought into sf techniques and mature themes that mainstream writers like James Joyce, Franz Kafka, and others had tried. Before these new writers arrived, space opera had dominated the field. Zelazny deplored the term "New Wave," however.

Irish writer James **Joyce** experimented with stream of consciousness and other techniques; *Ulysses* and *Finnegans Wake* are two of his best known works. German author Franz **Kafka** wrote surrealistic novels such as *The Trial* and *The Judgement*. Irish Nobel laureate Samuel **Beckett** wrote Absurd plays, including *Waiting for Godot* and *Krapp's Last Tape*. **Ionesco** was a Romanian-born French Absurd playwright whose works included *The Bald Soprano* and *Rhinoceros*.

SCIENCE FICTION AND HOW IT GOT THAT WAY

The Writer, May 1971.

Science fiction, as we know it today, is a product of the industrial revolution. Its history is quite curious. Mary Shelley, Edgar Allan Poe, Jules Verne, H. G. Wells—these writers gave it the impetus, pushed it into the twentieth century, inspired people like A. Merritt, Edgar Rice Burroughs, H. P. Lovecraft. It was not until the twenties, however, with the big pulp boom, that the first sf magazine was launched and things became a bit codified. At first, it was just another market. A person who wrote, say, westerns much of the time, could translate a formula story into science fiction and score a sale. Six-shooters became ray guns, Indians became alien life-forms, the Great Southwestern Desert became the Great Martian Desert, and so on.

Possibly to fill up extra pages at no cost, the early sf magazines published lengthy letter columns. Their effect was quite unusual. With the Depression and the relative cheapness of the magazines, people with lots of time on their hands read them and wrote in letters of comment. Since addresses were also published, many of these individuals began to correspond and visit with one another. Clubs were formed, amateur magazines were published, get-togethers were planned. There grew up the phenomenon known as science fiction fandom.

The hard-core group of admirers of the genre did much to stimulate greater efforts on the part of many of the sf writers. A new generation of writers came on the scene, then another, and the effect was this: the new writers had read the older sf writers' work, liked the science fiction field, felt that there was still room for expansion. There came purists, who felt that the only *raison d'être* for sf was to speculate upon the future developments of science—and some of them came qualified with impressive credentials. There came plain old storytellers, who liked myth, folklore, legend, and felt that not enough of it was coming to pass in modern times. There came men like Theodore Sturgeon, interested mainly in exploring the human condition in variant environments. Robert Heinlein came quite well versed in astrophysics, Isaac Asimov in the life sciences, Andre Norton in myth and legend. Suddenly, it was no longer *kitsch* writing.

Science fiction critics appeared. Secondary works on the subject began to find their way into print. Courses in science fiction as literature appeared in the curricula of universities.

Then the latest generation of sf writers arrived, and, standing upon the shoulder of their predecessors, they played with the themes of parallel worlds, time travel, space flight, contact with alien entities. Characterization suddenly became important.

A part of this whole story has to do with the "bust" in the early fifties. Science fiction became so popular then that a plethora of magazines crossed the newsstands. It was great while it lasted; but when the magazines started to fold, many full-time sf writers moved, quickly, over to the paperback and hardcover markets. The effect was salutary. Deadwood was purged, and new freedom of expression discovered. Taboos involved in writing for those early magazines went out the window. Now a writer could speculate upon sex in the future, if he cared to, or politics, religion, anything.

Which brings us up to today…

❖ ❖ ❖

A writer not familiar with the science fiction field these days might guess it an easy scene to make. To an extent, he would be correct. The paperbacks are buying novels that justify rockets on the covers and are splashing them about the newsstands. A quick grand or so for a couple of weeks' work and you, too, can be there, with a western transplanted to a faked-up alien world. It's a pity.

Science fiction is undergoing one of its periodic "flips." For some reason—sun spots, space shots, the idle young?—paperback science fiction is selling. The magazines, deluged as they are with manuscripts, are in a better position to pick and choose. They want quality and they generally get it.

There are about three hundred writers who write science fiction much of the time. They specialize; they know the market; they know how to hit it. Science fiction, in its best form, is a valid, justified exercise of the imagination. It is also fun. So far, this sounds like any other form of writing, so let me be more specific.

Open-ended themes

There are two basic factors which differentiate sf from other forms of fiction. Theodore Sturgeon stated them as open-ended themes, and since I cannot improve upon the categories, I'll repeat them here:

"What if—?" and "If this goes on—."

These are the points of departure. You can pick up a newspaper and go the "if-this-goes-on" way; or you can awaken in the middle of a hot summer night, tendrils of nightmare still lingering, and opt for the "what if—?"

Speculation, pure and simple, is what is involved. It's selling so well now. With the Tolkien, Howard, Burroughs booms going full blast, a lot of things come in on the coattails, as it were. Yes, transplanted westerns and the rubber monsters of yore. There is a distinction, though, which cuts across all lines: Your readers are only as true to you as you are to yourself—which sounds, trite, but isn't.

A science fiction novel which is frankly hoked-up, contrived, an act of simply putting words together, machines in the middle and a period at the end, may well go, *today*. Look around a year from now, though, and the scene will have shifted. Time, as always, is the great touchstone. There is a reason that publishers keep reissuing novels that Robert Heinlein wrote twenty-five years ago. There is a reason when the usual dime-a-word rate is doubled, trebled, quadrupled.

Quality.

In looking back over the history of science fiction, I can see why certain books became classics while others fell by the wayside. The writer cared. He guessed at a possible future, and he told of it honestly and perhaps with some measure of love. Heinlein, Leiber, Sturgeon, Norton, Bradbury, Vance—their works persist. Of the succeeding generation, there's Bob Silverberg, Ted White, John Brunner, Samuel Delany, Alex Panshin, Anne McCaffrey, Harlan Ellison. Take a look at some of their stuff, if you want to see the good things being done in the field today. They go into extra editions while the fake stuff is sloughed away.

What faces the sf writer

Writing science fiction is rougher than it looks. Isaac Asimov once explained the situation perfectly: In addition to laying the scene, introducing the characters and getting the action underway, you are also faced with the problem of slipping in an explanation of an *outré* set of circumstances which must, of necessity, surround the entire narrative. This is a big problem, and you are generally faced with it during your first thousand words.

A novel of this sort is easier to do than a short story, because of the elbow-room the format provides. Still, if you are not judicious in the injection of the background material into a novel, the reader's interest may wane. It is not easy. Writing a good sf novel is as hard as writing a classical detective-puzzler. And then again, in writing a novel there always seems present the temptation to become a bit sloppier than in a shorter piece of science fiction. I've felt myself doing it, and I've had to hit the brakes a couple of times.

As Northrop Frye said in his *Anatomy of Criticism*, there are four basic modes of writing: a) stories where the principals are greater than their fellows and their environments (this is epic and religious literature); b) stories where principals are somehow greater than their fellows (this is the stuff of classical tragedy); c) stories where the principals are just like everybody else (realism); and d) stories where the principals are inferior to their fellows and their environments (Kafka, Ionesco, Beckett). Realism is the dominant thing in modern fiction. Only in science fiction, perhaps, do some of the old modes persist. I submit that aliens and mutants, substituting for the forces of nature—gods, perhaps—and the primacy of characters who are bigger than life, infuse the entire field of science fiction with something unique in modern literature.

❖   ❖   ❖

Heroes. And the possibility (seldom realized) and the opportunity for writing a genuine tragedy or epic along classical lines. While this sounds somewhat high-flown, I request that you defer judgment and go read Arthur C. Clarke's *Childhood's End* and Theodore Sturgeon's

More Than Human. There is no way these stories could have been told except in a sf format. They are not simply experiments, as they succeed in what they set out to achieve.

❖   ❖   ❖

Taboos? I don't think there are any when it comes to the science fiction novel. I've done nine now, and nobody has ever breathed down my neck and said, "Get rid of that 'damn' on page seven," or, "Chop the last half of chapter three because it could be controversial."

How to break in

Science fiction magazines still offer the best entrée to working in this field, requiring as they do the most discipline, and exposing the writer's name where hardcover editors can see it—and they *do* look! Sell a dozen or so short stories to *Galaxy*, and/or *The Magazine of Fantasy & Science Fiction*, and your novel should not go unplaced. These magazines are the best, and about the only ones of the genre type, but competition in the sf magazine field is tough. For novels—easier to place than five or six years ago—Doubleday, Putnam's, Signet, Avon, Ballantine are all good, interested, and have excellent distribution.

I don't really know how to tell you to go about speculating, dreaming, except for the Sturgeon touchstones. Pick up something that moves you, troubles you, and ask yourself, "If this goes on—what?" Or play chess with the future. "What if—?"

And don't be scared, no matter what the notion. Somebody's probably already written the incest/rape/fratricide/death of God/drug-scene story in this format. Forget any alleged taboos, and just expand upon things the way that you see them, remembering that it's still possible for a hero to exist, should you wish to portray one. This scene is the only place where the old magic still prevails, and you are the sole magician when you enter it. No other worlds can make that claim.

Notes

The Writer asked Issac Asimov for an essay, but he claimed to be too busy and suggested that Zelazny should write it. Zelazny suspected that Asimov did this because he knew that Zelazny was nervous about surviving financially as a full-time writer. Zelazny's essay was well received and led to a position *The Writer's* editorial board. He received multiple requests for essays and lectures on creative writing theory.

Raison d'être means reason for being. ***Kitsch*** is something tacky. ***Outré*** is bizarre. **Northrop Frye** was a Canadian literary critic and author whose interest in mythology influenced Zelazny. **Franz Kafka** was a German author who wrote surrealistic novels such as *The Trial* and *The Judgement*. **Ionesco** was a Romanian-born French Absurdist playwright whose works include *The Bald Soprano* and *Rhinoceros*. Irish writer **Samuel Beckett's** plays, including *Waiting for Godot* and *Krapp's Last Tape*, won him the Nobel Prize.

SELF-INTERVIEW

Previously unpublished in this form; An excerpt appeared as "An Interview with Roger Zelazny," by Paul Walker, *Luna Monthly #43*, Dec 1972.

574 W. University Pkwy.
Baltimore, Md. 21210
March 10, 1972

Dear Mr. Walker,

Just received your second letter. I guess I should have dropped you a line to let you know I had received the earlier one and was unable to reply at that time, as I was pushing hard to complete a novel. However, when I reach a certain point in a book I simply stop writing letters until I've finished.

At any rate, I completed the book this past weekend and have been catching up on my correspondence this week. Things are somewhat under control now, so I will see what I can tell you concerning myself and my feelings with respect to language, writing and suchlike…

I was born in Ohio, and for reasons never completely clear to me decided to be a writer at about the same time I came to enjoy reading and began to realize where books came from. So I started writing. I was around 11 or 12 years old when I collected my first rejection slips…

[You have asked me to step outside myself, then turn around and interview me. Okay. I'm outside me now. I'll stop right there and start questioning him.]

"Wait a minute, Z. We just passed a whole generation of psychoanalytic critics and biographers awhile back. What about childhood trama and all that crap?"

"I believe a piece of writing should be considered of, in, by and for itself, a thing independent of the person who wrote it."

"But you are talking to me. I know where you got that. You wrote nothing but poetry for years—after you got out of high school and started college—and you got hung up on the New Criticism: close textual analysis, and the hell with the guy who wrote it. A touch of end-of-century decadence, too. The Symbolists, Firbank... But you were also a Psychology major until your final year. You know that writing is a form of behavior, and as such it invariably bears the mark of its executor."

"Of course."

"So tell us about your childhood hangups."

"No."

"Why not?"

"Because I'm a bug on privacy."

"Shyness?"

"Some, I suppose. I like to keep my writing apart from the rest of my life. I make my living displaying pieces of my soul in some distorted form or other. The rest of it is my own."

"Then you are saying you find the New Criticism bit a convenient defense."

"Only partly. I still see considerable merit there. I am, by and large, against biographical criticism. Schiller used to keep rotting apples in his writing table. As he was working, he would open it every now and then and take a whiff. What does this tell you about Schiller?"

"That he liked smells? I forget whether there were lots of smells in *Wilhelm Tell*..."

"So do I, obviously. It tells me something about Schiller, that's all. It tells me nothing about his writing."

"Does this relate to the distinction you like to make between self-expression and communication?"

"I'm glad you asked that question right then. I like the way your mind works. —Yes, it does. Communication is generally a form of self-expression, but the opposite does not necessarily apply. I consider myself in the communication business, not the self-expression business. They are necessarily bound up together in any piece of fiction, but I put in only as much of myself as I deem appropriate, no more, no less. If the story is a failure, it is not worth much consideration; if it is successful, then everything is in place, and it should not be necessary to ask for more."

"All right. But if certain themes tend to persist in the work of a particular writer, people cannot help but wonder why. You seem to have a thing for mythology, immortality and protagonists who are not always completely admirable people. Would you care to say why?"

"No."

"Well, I'll swing around then. You worked for the government for seven years. Three of those years you spent interviewing people—thousands of them, I guess—and then for four years you wrote memos, letters, reports, sections of manuals. I imagine you like to think you picked up something about dialogue from all those conversations; and maybe something of people's quirks, mannerisms and such."

"I would like to think so."

"How about all that garbage you used to grind out in officialese? Did you feel any abrasion on your own style, your way of telling stories?"

"No. I never regarded it as real writing. It was just a chore. It was pure, specialized communication. Not a drop of myself in it."

"You were writing fiction, in the evenings, for the whole seven years?"

"Yes. I began that job and my first adult attempts at fiction in the same month, back in 1962. I kept the two sections of my life compartmentalized from the beginning."

"Why didn't you mind talking about that?"

"Because it is one of those *So what?* facts."

"All right. You did your grad work in dramatic lit, your thesis on a minor Jacobean dramatist. Would you care to say whether you feel influenced by the theater in general, the Elizabethan theater in particular?"

"Yes, I do. The language, the violence… I cannot deny it."

"More than, say, modern poetry?"

"Very difficult to answer. Probably, though."

"'What does "language" mean to you as a writer?' Paul Walker asked me to ask you that."

"Finding the right word to cover a situation at the moment the need for it arises, I'd say."

"What governs your choice?"

"My feelings. I see what he's getting at, though. I feel that I did my formative reading, style-wise, many years ago. I feel incapable as well as disinclined to pulling apart my way of telling things now and looking for influences. Somewhere along the line, my own style grew a protective pelt and set out scratching along its own line of development, as most writers do. You are pretty much immune to direct influence once this point is passed."

"Would you care to comment on your particular style?"

"No."

"Is there anything else you would care to say, about yourself, about writing, about science fiction?"

"No, I don't think so. That about covers it. You can step back inside now."

Further deponent sayeth not.

Sorry again for not informing you of the delay that was to follow your earlier letter. By the way, in answer to your unofficial question, I did have a strong Catholic background, but I am not a Catholic. Somewhere in the past, I believe I once answered that in the affirmative for strange and complicated reasons. But I am not a member of any organized religion.

Best wishes,

Roger Zelazny

Notes

An excerpt of this letter from Zelazny to Paul Walker, dated March 10, 1972, was published as an interview "by Paul Walker." However, Zelazny himself wrote this unusual essay. Walker sparked its creation in a letter to Zelazny, "Rather than simply tell you to 'tell me about yourself,' let me appeal to the novelist in you. Let us suppose that you are in my place: you have been assigned to interview Roger Zelazny. You arrive and are invited in. You see yourself—but what do you see? You ask yourself to tell you about Roger Zelazny: where am I and how did I get here? What does he say?"[1] Zelazny complied and produced this amusing result.

The novel mentioned is *Today We Choose Faces*, which Zelazny completed on March 5, 1972.[2] Ronald **Firbank**'s novels are notable for their symbolism, camp, and wit. Friedrich Schiller was a German playwright and poet; ***Wilhelm Tell*** was one of his best known plays. The **minor Jacobean dramatist** was Cyril Tourneur, whose play *The Revenger's Tragedy* was the focus of Zelazny's Master's thesis. **Further deponent sayeth not** is legalese for "the person signing this affidavit has nothing more to say."

---

1 Letter from Paul Walker to Roger Zelazny, dated January 19, 1972.
2 Letter from Roger Zelazny to Victor, dated March 6, 1972.

THE GENRE
A GEOLOGICAL SURVEY

The (Baltimore) Sun, June 24, 1973;
reprinted as part of "Three Newspaper Pieces" in *Phantasmicom #11*, May 1974.

It was nearly a half century ago that Hugo Gernsback said, "Let there be *Amazing Stories*," then saw that it was good. By this act evolution commenced and set out for science fiction as we know it today. Similar magazines subsequently appeared, and the first decade or so of the phenomenon represented a kind of primal ooze out of which more complex life forms were eventually to arise.

Speaking generally, in keeping with the requirements of a geological survey, the first major period to follow was the development, in the 1940s, of the "classic" science fiction story. This was the time wherein some emphasis actually came to be placed upon the scientific content of a particular piece. Here, names such as Robert Heinlein, Isaac Asimov, L. Sprague de Camp, Lester Del Rey, Fritz Leiber and Theodore Sturgeon came to be associated with a projective or extrapolative sort of writing, with scientific generalizations extended beyond the contemporary state of technology into a future where, as Sturgeon has put it, such questions as "If this goes on…?" and "What if…?" were considered an integral part of the story's structure. This, in its purest form, was considered by Kingsley Amis as, at the least, approaching an "idea as hero" situation.

The answers to Sturgeon's questions resulted in two species of story, which Asimov has referred to, respectively, as the "chess game" story and the "chess problem" story. In the chess game story, beginning with the present, known state of the world, situations are extended into the future in a logical, rational fashion and there played out to a dramatic conclusion. The chess problem story, on the other hand, while rational is not necessarily logical (i.e., deductive), in terms of the initial, given situation. It commences with the pieces in positions which are not often likely to arise in the course of ordinary play. Granting this, however, the normal rules obtain and the exercise in speculation may proceed.

This stage in science fiction was at least partly determined by the background of the leading writers of the period. These men were, by and large, scientifically oriented, a thing which may have attracted them to the field initially and contributed to their efforts to purify its scientific content once they had entered it.

The late '40s and early '50s saw new writers entering the area—Poul Anderson, Gordon R. Dickson and Philip José Farmer, to name but a few—whose individual touches served to broaden the field of speculation. The magazines flourished and proliferated at an unprecedented rate. By 1953, the science fiction magazine market reached its peak, became overextended and fell apart under the general economic pressures of the recession. Only a half dozen of the magazines survived. Many of the writers at this time turned to the paperback and hardcover book markets as an outlet for their material.

This displacement from the magazine to the book format ultimately proved a benefit. While the genre's intellectual content had seldom conflicted with taboos in the magazine industry, these restrictions did nevertheless exist, and by hindsight may be seen as having exercised some control over the nature of the material considered. These restrictions were not so severe in the book industry.

Sturgeon's questions can, of course, be addressed to other subjects than the physical sciences. The social sciences were another source of material, and—of equal importance in times to follow—such areas of thought and activity as theology and sex had also come within reach.

As a result of some of these factors, the 1950s represented a period when the novel of sociological speculation came into greater prominence. In general, whether from habits of thought or the necessity for an economy of argument in a science fiction story, the sex was not overworked and theology remained mostly in the background. Notable exceptions are Farmer's "The Lovers", Del Rey's "For I Am a Jealous People" and Blish's *A Case of Conscience*.

In the 1960s, the balance remained tilted toward the novel, the remaining magazines held their own while changing sufficiently to keep pace with the times and more new writers entered the area. There then occurred a reaction. Whether it came from a distrust of the optimistic scientism of the '40s, a disillusionment precluding the reasonably good-natured social speculation of the '50s, or simply a vexation with the relatively staid structure and nuts-and-bolts prose of the science fiction story itself, the new writers—such as J. G. Ballard, Thomas Disch and Samuel R. Delany—devoted a good part of their energy to experiments with style and form. Sex and theology were now also exploited. The idea had ceased to be the hero, if it ever truly was, and a preoccupation with method took hold of the field. Appropriately dubbed the New Wave, this form of writing reached its most intense level just before the end of the decade at which time it began to provoke a reaction of its own.

Fairness, however, requires the observation that the concerns of the '60s brought to the area a measure of stylistic *élan* and a quality of introspection which eventually resulted in a less manipulative, more humanistic approach to the process.

And so to the Holocene:

The current situation possesses three distinguishing features. First, the balance has swung from the novel back to the short story, a thing which occurred without a resurgence of the magazines. A great number of publishers are now bringing out anthologies of all-original science fiction short stories, and any remaining magazine taboos are thereby skirted. Second, the beginnings of a renewed concern with themes involving the physical sciences has been noted, along with a judicious restoration of sociological speculation. Third, the stylistic experimentation of the '60s appears to have been absorbed successfully into the greater whole.

Accordingly, the current situation seems best characterized as a period of synthesis.

Writers such as Ursula K. Le Guin, Larry Niven, Robert Silverberg, Philip K. Dick and Harlan Ellison—all of whom have lived through some of the phases above—seem to have achieved increased mastery within the past few years. Outstanding among the newer writers now receiving notice are George Alec Effinger, Gardner Dozois and Joe Haldeman, who may be seen as representing this recently integrated approach.

The current state of the area and its present relationship to life and letters in general was summarized by Ursula K. Le Guin this past April on the occasion of her acceptance of the National Book Award for *The Farthest Shore*:

"...Sophisticated readers are accepting the fact that an improbable and unmanageable world is going to produce an improbable and hypothetical art. At this point, realism is perhaps the least adequate means of understanding or portraying the incredible realities of our existence. A scientist who creates a monster in his laboratory; a librarian in the library of Babel; a wizard unable to cast a spell; a space ship having trouble in getting to Alpha Centauri: all these may be precise and profound metaphors of the human condition. The fantasist, whether he uses the ancient stereotypes of myth and legend or the younger ones of science and technology, may be talking as seriously as any sociologist—and a good deal more directly—about human life as it is lived, and as it might be lived, and as it ought to be lived..."

Notes

Author and poet **Kingsley Amis** was best known for his first novel, *Lucky Jim*; he was fond of science fiction and edited the sf anthology series *Spectrum*. The **Holocene** is a geological epoch that began 10,000 years ago (after the last Ice Age) and continues through today; Zelazny was using the geological metaphor in describing the history of the science fiction field.

A Burnt-Out Case?

SF Commentary #54, November 1978.
Also in condensed form as "Musings From Melbourne" in *PKDS Newsletter #16*, 1988.

The blackboard and the sound projector and the dancing girls have not yet arrived, so I shall have to improvise. As I frequently do in matters such as this, I've made an outline and…I never follow them. It's the same way with books. The only trouble I ever ran into with a book was when I tried to follow an outline. I learned later that the publisher did not really care about the outline. He told me after I stopped writing for them that they always got an outline as a matter of form, so that they had a gentlemanly way of rejecting a book if they didn't like it. Rather than just saying that this was a dog of a book, they would pull out the outline, find some point at which an author departs from the outline, and say, "Well, old man, you really didn't follow your outline, so I'll have to return the book."

I found a way of faking outlines, of course. I had it down to a real system. Then I stopped writing for that publisher, and no one ever asked me for an outline again. In case you're curious, the system involved selecting one scene, and writing about ninety percent of the outline as a detailed synopsis of that scene, and the other ten percent just generalizing the rest of the book. Then I could sit down and write whatever I wanted, as long as I inserted that one scene in the book. It saved a lot of trouble.

I am a science fiction writer by definition—at least, that's what my books are called. I have no desire to disclaim this title. It's a funny situation, because I don't really know what science fiction is. Every now and again over the years, I've gotten ambitious and tried to work up a definition. Whenever I come up with something that half-way satisfies me, immediately I've sat down and tried to violate it, just because I like to feel that science fiction is pretty much a free area, and myself free to do pretty much what I like in it.

Science fiction has been good to me, and I'm happy to be writing science fiction. Over the years, I've gotten to speak at conventions such as this and other places on the subject, and I have, only this past September, discovered an ideal in the way of convention addresses, toward which I might hope to aspire one day.

It was a convention talk which gave rise to a great deal of speculation and exercise of the imagination—a talk given by Philip K. Dick in the city of Metz, France, a city sacked in the year 451 by Attila the Hun, and about which I knew very little else until such a time as they held a science fiction festival there and invited three science fiction writers—Harlan Ellison, Philip K. Dick, and yours truly. It came to pass at the convention that Philip K. Dick was the gentleman who was to give the address. It was a rather amazing address. I do not know what Philip K. Dick said at this talk. I was not present; I was off at a bookstore signing books. The audience, however, at the Civic Center, while Phil Dick was speaking, did not know what Phil Dick said either. So I do not feel slighted in this.

When I approached him on the matter later in the day, I discovered that Philip K. Dick did not know what he said, either.

I will delay for a moment, and tell you how I came to know Philip K. Dick. Some years ago, Phil Dick, who is a very hot writer when he is on top of things, had agreed to write twelve books in a year's time—a book a month. Apparently he delivered eleven of the books. It got to December, and the book was a thing called *Deus Irae*, for which he'd written an outline. I thought mine were pretty good when it came to faking the action and taking in the publisher completely, but this was a masterpiece. It was much longer than those I usually manage, but it said less even. It was basically a philosophical essay, quite lovely, and then there were fifty pages of copy. At that point, Phil Dick stopped. He was blocked.

There are some writers who, when they are blocked, have mental constipation that can go on for years. It was so with Phil Dick. Doubleday kept pestering him for the book, and he kept saying, "No, no, later, later." Finally they asked him if he would allow someone else to complete the work and divide the money. He said, "All right. I'm not going to finish it."

So they approached Ted White. Ted White decided he couldn't do it, but he kept the manuscript anyway, just for a conversation piece.

It was at his home in Brooklyn for some months, and I happened to be visiting. While we were there, he brought out the manuscript and showed it to me. I really liked it. One of the things about collaboration is that you should learn something from it. It should be fun, and it should be something you would not have thought to do on your own. I read it over and wrote to Phil, saying that I would like to try finishing this book. He said "Fine. I like your stuff. You like my stuff. Let's do it."

So I wrote a few sections and sent them off to him. He waited awhile. We didn't look upon this project as anything to be completed in a hurry. I'd put it in a drawer and, a year or two later, Phil would remind me that we were doing a book, and I would write another section and send it back to him.

We moved from Baltimore to Santa Fe, New Mexico. About three years went by, I had sort of forgotten this book in a drawer. A cat had gotten in and done something on the manuscript. Phil finally sent me a frantic letter a week before I was to leave town, saying that twelve years had gone by and Doubleday was threatening to withhold royalties due him in order to recover the advance on that book if it was not in in six weeks. So I sat down and finished it that day.

(You talk about artistic values and such, but I've never seen any correlation in my own work between speed of composition and quality of output. It's really a kind of laziness factor which makes me produce at the rate I do. I have written very quickly.)

Anyway, that's how the book was done, and it was very enjoyable. Before I had undertaken this entire collaboration with Phil, I decided I would make it a complete learning project. I would learn to write like Phil Dick. So I sat down and read twenty of Phil's books in succession. I wanted to feel them at the gut level, not just understand his reaction to ideas intellectually, but get so I could write in his style and also, hopefully, plot in his style. I felt that I achieved this; I believe that I can write exactly like Phil Dick if I want to.

But I chose, for my sections of the book, not to use that style. I chose a kind of meta-style, halfway between that and my own style, so my sections would be different enough from Phil's sections so the book, would have a different tone to it.

As I was writing along like this over the years, I said to myself, "It's a shame to be able to write just like Phil Dick—even, for brief periods of time, think like Phil Dick—and not to do it, at least just once." So, in one scene I plotted it just the way I thought Phil would plot it. I wrote it in Phil's style exactly, and then the other themes in that section I wrote in the other style. I sent the entire batch of manuscripts off to him, waited a while, and received a letter back, "Roger, that was very good material you sent along, but this one scene you've written is sheer genius."

To return to Metz… This past September, Phil gave this talk which I'm holding up as a model before me for a moment invisible to all but my eyes—or perhaps to those of Palmer Eldritch, if he be present.

I was in a book store nearby. Harlan had wanted to commit one of his favorite stunts, which was to compose a story in the window of a book store carrying his books. Unfortunately, when Attila had sacked Metz in the fifth century, he had apparently done something to book store fronts, because there were no book stores which had the sort of front windows, as American book stores have, for displaying authors in the act of composition. Harlan had to take his act to a local newspaper office, where people apparently took him for an employee. He said he was asked to notarize a document, or something like that. He was a little disappointed.

But he missed Phil's talk. I missed Phil's talk. I was sitting there signing books. Several hours after the time the talk was scheduled, people began drifting in from the hall where Phil had been speaking. A man came up to me with a book and said to me, "Monsieur Zelazny, you have written a book with Monsieur Dick. You know his mind. I have just come from his talk. Is it true that he wishes to found a new religion, with himself as Pope?"

I said, "He has never mentioned that ambition to me. I don't know how these things come through in translation. He has a very peculiar sense of humor. It might not have carried through properly. But I don't think he meant it to be taken literally."

The fellow who was behind me said, "*Non*, I think you are wrong. I rode back to the hotel in a taxi, and Monsieur Dick gave me the power to remit sins and to kill fleas."

I said, "I'm sure this was meant to be taken with a grain of salt. I wouldn't be too concerned about it."

A little later, another fellow came in and said, "Monsieur Zelazny, do you believe that there are many parallel time tracks and that we are on the wrong one?" I allowed that this was a common idea of some science fiction stories. I personally felt happy where I was, but I asked him where he had gotten this notion from that I subscribed to it.

He said, "Well, in the lecture he said that there are many parallel time tracks and we are on the wrong one, because of the fact that God and the Devil are playing a game of chess and every time one makes a move, it reprograms us to a different time track, and that whenever Phil Dick writes a book it switches us back to the proper track. Could you care to comment on this?"

I begged off. A little later, Phil came into the store to sign some books and sat down beside me at the table. When I had a free moment, I leaned over and said, "Phil, what the hell did you talk about this afternoon?"

Phil said, "I don't know. It was the strangest thing. You know, I don't speak French, so I was asked to write out my talk. I provided a copy of my talk and then the fellow translated it into French. I was to read a paragraph and then he was to read the translation, and so on. Right before I was to go on, they told me that the talk had to be cut by twenty minutes. So I went through crossing out paragraphs, and so did the translator, but we got mixed up along the way, and he crossed out all the wrong paragraphs. So I don't know what I said."

❖   ❖   ❖

Just the notion of that talk has always remained with me. I bear it before me at this moment because, whenever I am asked to give a talk anywhere, I tend to look back over my professional writing career and see whether there might be something new learned that I hadn't thought of before from the activities of that sixteen-year period. I tend to feel rather like the Buddhist novitiate who went into the monastery knowing that the trees were only trees and the clouds were only clouds and the mountains were only mountains. Forty years later, when he was a full-fledged Buddhist monk, he knew that the trees *were* only trees, the clouds *were* only clouds, and the mountains were *only* mountains. But then he knew it wisely.

I don't believe that I know very much more now than I knew sixteen years ago. I'm not even sure I know it wisely, but at least I seem to have rearranged the items a bit, so that I know it a little differently. So, attempting to extract whatever wisdom might be involved in this, I thought back to a few other times in my life when I examined what I'd been up to, and it occurred to me that I had come to a few small conclusions about what I was doing.

I remember that, when I began writing, my intention was to sit down for a couple of years and just do short stories, because the mistakes I made would be much briefer than if I just did novels, until I learned something about the trade. I would set myself different problems in each story so I would stand to benefit from learning from this. I did that. After about two years, I finally did a novel.

I asked myself, what are the real difficulties involved in writing science fiction? If any, what are the benefits? Not in terms of intellectual freedom or imagination being exercised, but purely from a work standpoint as a writer, what are the problems?

It struck me that—and I hadn't really considered it, which is strange, because my background is in literature—that while you learn all this critical analysis while you're going to school, it is not really a reversible process. You don't put together a story in the manner in which you learn to take stories apart in school. It's simply a blank piece of paper before you in the typewriter, and everything else goes out the window.

It occurred to me that the biggest problem I faced was that the distinction between a science fiction story and a general fiction story lay in the fact that, by virtue of its being set on another planet or in the future or on a parallel world, the real problem lay in the setting, the background, the fact that you had to provide more of it to show the reader where the hell all this is taking place and what's going on. If you mention New York in the 1960s, that's pretty much a shorthand for what a major urban center is. As I discovered later, when I taught a few writers' workshops, the big error of beginning writers is to provide a couple of pages of copy right at the beginning describing all this background. By then, the reader would be hopelessly bored. The biggest thing I learned from this period is that all the background should be cut from the beginning, broken into small parcels, and distributed judiciously through the rest of the text. That did seem to be the hardest thing I had to learn.

The greatest freedom for me, strangely, was also a kind of trap. At the beginning, everyone said to me, "You should write what you know." So naturally I wrote about gods and demons and supernatural and mythological creatures, because I was very familiar with them. I did come from a peculiar background where I did have a lot of information on mythology. I began using this material because it was there, and easily done for me, while I ran around frantically plugging up other holes in my background so that I could write other things eventually.

I never made a connection between something I had read in literature classes until several years had gone by, at which time I was already beginning to feel uncomfortable that about every science fiction convention I attended, they set up a special panel called "Science Fiction and Mythology" and put me on it. I realized: it may be possible that I am being categorized.

Northrop Frye, if I may steal his vocabulary for a moment, set up four modes of characterization, with four names which mean simple things: the *mythic* mode, the *high mimetic*, the *low mimetic*, and the *ironic*. The mythic includes characters who appear in scriptures, in mythological writing, in the *Iliad*, the Bible. They're gods; they are creatures who are greater than Man and greater than their environment. Yet they do appear as characters in this form of writing, which admittedly is not being done too much these days.

Then there are the high mimetic characters, who are basically the figures in classical tragedy, who differ from other people by virtue of the fact that they are greater individuals: a Hamlet, or an Oedipus, or a King Lear. These figures, in falling, have to be figures that you can respect, and therefore know pity and fear when you see them fall.

They are the top two categories.

The low mimetic is the character who inhabits the realistic novel, the modern novel, the product of all the democratic revolutions, the character who's just like everyone else,

And then there is the ironic mode. This is the character who is not just like everyone else. He's not greater, he's not a little bit greater, he's not just like us; he's less. He's the Charlie Chaplin figure, he's the character in Kafka, Ionesco, or Beckett, who is less than his fellow man. He's an ironic figure, yet in some strange way, this whole thing goes around in a circle. There are echoes in him of the mythic mode character, by virtue of his being a butt.

It struck me that all of modern literature is the bottom two categories, and that it really fell upon science fiction alone—and a few poets with their private mythologies—to exploit the higher modes of characterization. Whether you approve or disapprove aesthetically, they are available in science fiction. One can create figures who are on a par with the gods of the mythic mode, or the tragic figures, whether one is writing a tragedy or not, of the high mimetic mode. One does this with aliens, mutants, robots, computers.

This is, for me, on the other side of the equation from the difficulties and constraints of providing all the extra background material. It balanced out. I managed to surmount the background problems to my satisfaction and to that of the editors, and I explored character, to some degree, by using these higher modes.

I suppose I should have let it go at that, and I did for a long while. I had learned something to form the substance for a talk for whatever convention I was going to at that time.

I did not think about it for a long while—but at the same convention in France, I was talking to Phil Dick again. There's an amazing phenomenon associated with both Phil Dick and Harlan Ellison (and they invited both of them; but then, they didn't know any better). In the presence of either man, the interface between reality and fantasy begins to wear rather thin. When they are both present, surrealistic things do tend to begin happening.

There was a very strange party the same day that Phil Dick gave his memorable talk (which nobody remembers). We were all dragooned off to the City Hall. It was John Brunner's birthday. John Brunner had popped up from Italy, where he was vacationing, and we had dinner with him. He was not really a guest of the convention, but just happening by, so he was not as constrained as the rest of us to be there on time, so it caused some delay in getting over there. Philippe Huff, the fellow in charge, was quite upset at the authors not showing up at this party being given. I was trying to get away. Harlan, I learned, was still sleeping back at the hotel, and they sent some strong-arm type to drag him over.

Anyway, we did get there on time. Philippe was standing outside like the White Rabbit, saying "You're late! You're late!" as everyone came back. The lady gave a nice little talk about being happy to have a science fiction convention in that city. Meanwhile, a folk band began playing wild, and John Brunner was asking me if I knew whose portrait was hanging on the wall. I said, "That was Montpelier, the first man to go up in a balloon; he's from Metz", while somebody else was asking me why they wouldn't let Concorde land in the States. Then a bizarre folk dance began weaving through the room, and somehow Harlan got involved in it. (He had appeared.)

Then, in the distance, across this room, Phil Dick was standing there like Mephistopheles, gesturing to me. I began walking toward him. He kind of waved his cloak and Robert Sheckley was standing beside him. I didn't know Sheckley had been there. I hadn't seen Sheckley in about three years.

Phil Dick said, "Quick, Roger. It involves money." I made my way over and he said, "I've got it all worked out, Roger. We're going to make a bundle on this. It will be a three-way collaboration—you, me, and Sheckley. You see, the world really consists of three time tracks. We each get one, work it out, and then we switch. We each write a third of the bock, following the others' time tracks, and their interrelationships when things begin to break down. It's all very careful…"

He stopped and looked up. "By George, there's Harry Harrison. Harry! You want to make a bundle of money? Okay. Never mind. It's going to be four time tracks."

Then Phil, in a profound moment afterward, said, "Roger, a strange thing happened to me…" which is not really unusual, because strange things always happen to Phil. I nodded. "I have this book, *A Scanner Darkly*. I have these characters who have been on hard drugs for a long time, and they're burnt out cases. I wanted to choose a scene which exemplified the extent of their mental deterioration. I had them attempting to figure out the functioning of the gear shift on a ten-speed bicycle." (Phil always, chooses good examples for things.)

So he had written this up and indicated that they were wrong, because this is how the gear shift on a ten-speed bicycle really works. His editor called him: "Phil… A funny thing in this manuscript of yours. I happen to own a ten-speed bicycle. I went out and looked at the gear shift, and—um…you've got it wrong yourself."

Phil said, "My God, you know what that means? Roger, how do you know when you're a burnt out case?"

❖   ❖   ❖

Perhaps I should not have taken that so to heart, but I did begin thinking about it. How do you know when you are a burnt out case?

This is interesting. It raises a great philosophical question for me: that is, who can you trust?

I began writing as a very naïve person. I trusted everyone—editors, critics… I became wary about critics and reviewers after a time, though, when I noticed that when I began writing, they did not like my stuff a great deal; when I stopped writing the mythological sort of thing and shifted into other things, they said, "It's a shame Zelazny's abandoning all this fine mythological material he used to work with"; and when I did something else, they would hearken back and say "Zelazny's retrogressing again back into his old ways."

The only consistent review I got was when three different critics, independent of one another, came up with the same sentence, "This would be a good book if it hadn't been written by Roger Zelazny." I was never quite certain what that meant.

Then it occurred to me to take all the critical opinions and reviewers' opinions, lump them together, and divide by the number. It came out to a sort of uniform consistency resembling lime jello—a kind of pale sickly green in color. It seems that they follow a bell curve, with the favorable reviews on one end, the unfavorables on the other, and the neutral ones in the middle. They balanced one another out to such an extent that I couldn't particularly trust any critic over any other. I could find a counterpart in the other direction for anybody.

So I stopped reading reviews and criticism. For awhile, I grew quite cynical and said that the only critical comments I cared to read were royalty statements, which I would never say now. I'm more guarded about these matters.

❖ ❖ ❖

So I said, "Well, at least one can trust one's editors." I don't know whether anyone who specializes in these matters might notice, but in my book *Lord of Light*, nowhere in it will you find the word "which", because an editor decided to scratch out "which" everywhere it occurred and substitute "that." Which is all right: it doesn't make anything incorrect. But I do know the difference. Doubleday, perhaps, has a style sheet which requires this sort of thing…that sort of thing. I let it go. This was my first hardcover sale. I had had three paperback books before, but now this was Doubleday—a big house. I decided I really should go along with all the changes they had made.

But then they came to one scene in the book which was dear to my heart (I forget which one at the moment). They wanted to cut it entirely: "This scene does not serve any useful purpose in the book," or something like that.

I was going to New York the following weekend, so I just took the manuscript with me. I went to Doubleday's office and saw their senior editor, Larry Ashmead, and said, "whoever did this wants to cut this scene, and I rather like it. I'd like to keep it if it's possible."

"Sure. Just write *stet*," and he signed his name beneath it. "That's all there is to it. Don't worry about it."

"Aren't copy editors important people?"

"No. Just some kid we hire out of college."

"Oh..."

Actually, some years went by before I went through an entire book and wrote "*stet*" beneath every single thing that had been changed in it. That was one of the Amber books. I do it more and more frequently.

It led me to look for other people's experiences with copy editors. I came across a couple of interesting ones, I which I will share with you.

One was that, in Churchill's *History of World War Two*, a copy editor had written in the margin, "I have taken the liberty of recasting this unfortunate sentence because you ended it with a preposition." Beneath which, Churchill had written, "Up with this I will not put."

Raymond Chandler, in one of his mystery novels, got it back with a little transposition mark and the abbreviation for "split infinitive" off in the margin, beneath which Chandler had written, "When I split an infinitive it goddamn well stays split."

This was interesting, but did not help me to find anyone who could tell me whether I had become a burnt out case. I was growing worried about this, because I had been talking with a writer I respected about another writer, who shall remain nameless (a big name writer whose books sell quite well) and we pretty much agreed that this fellow's last few books had not been up to snuff. He said, "You know, his last few books were very flabby. They could have been cut quite severely and they probably would have been better books as a result. I think that what he really needs is a good editor. They're afraid to tell him to do anything about it, because his books are going to sell well, whether this is done or not. They don't want to lose him as a writer, so no one has guts enough to tell him what's wrong with his stuff. He's become a victim of the Great Writer Syndrome."

At the time, it struck me as possibly true. But my experience with good editors is that they are very few and far between. I've met a few people I consider good editors. It is difficult. I can see the nameless writer's position: probably he does not know who to trust.

I don't know that there is an answer to this.

❖   ❖   ❖

I learned another thing only after several years of writing. To show how naïve I was, I did not know that other writers plotted their books. I didn't know this until I was asked for a plot line, and I realized that I couldn't do one.

Basically, my approach to writing a novel is to construct a character. Once I have a character, I try him out in several situations just to see how he reacts. Then I take two situations that strike me as interesting. I begin somewhere near one of them and write my way through, almost free-associating, to the second situation. In the course of this progress from the one to the other, secondary characters necessarily occur and a certain amount of the background is sketched in. By the time I have traveled from point A to point B, I have some of the secondary characters become major characters. I can see some direction in which to go, and I simply begin moving. Then there comes a point somewhere along the way where I see the entire book laid out before me.

If I had known this wasn't the way you operated, I probably never would have started this way. But I am basically a subconscious plotter. I can feel when the story is present in my mind, and I don't bother dredging it all out to the conscious level until I need it. The fact that it works for me has caused me to rely upon it.

I have done a few things the other way. I do know how to plot a story if I have to, but it's hard work. Usually, if you do something at a mystery level, it's better to work things out. In the stories in *My Name Is Legion*, I've used the conscious plotting device. But when I first heard from Gordy Dickson that he had an outline so that he knew what happened in each chapter before he sat down to write, I was amazed. Larry Niven told me, "Of course you have to have an outline. Or how are you going to know what you're going to do? How are you going to know how the book ends?" I never know how my books end until I get there.

My only hope, as I see it, is the fact that I rely on my subconscious. I will continue to trust it. If it lets me down, I guess we'll sink together. That's the only person I trust at this point. If anyone has any suggestions, I'd be happy to hear them.

It seems to me that the only thing I've really learned over the years, outside of picking up speed for when I need it, is that writing seems to be more and more a process of learning what you can get away with. I still like to work with mythological characters. If I can get in an outrageous sequence every now and again, it does something for my amusement, if not my aesthetic sense. If there is just one story in the world, and a writer got to write only one story outline, I'm sure it would be ample for everyone's one story, because I don't believe any two writers can tell the same story the same way, even if they set out to do it. I'm comforted in that thought.

It's like the story of Henry James's *Trilby*. George du Maurier, Daphne's uncle, was a noted story doctor. Many writers would call him in for consultation every now and again if they got into a problem. Quite often he would write a chapter for them to get them around some road block. One day he came up with a sterling idea for a novel. He thought who would be the ideal person to write it, and he took it to Henry James, who was a friend of his. "Henry, have I got a story for you. It's about this girl, singularly undistinguished in all aspects of her existence, save for the fact that, under the influence of hypnosis, she could become a great opera singer." James thought about it, and said, "It doesn't really do anything for me. If you're so convinced it's a good idea, why don't you write it yourself?" Du Maurier said, "Yes, maybe I should." So he sat down and wrote *Trilby*, which outsold the sum total of everything Henry James ever wrote—I doubt whether anyone other than Lester Del Rey would argue about the respective merits of Henry James and George du Maurier but, nevertheless, du Maurier contributed a word to the language: "Svengali."

It makes you wonder. There are certain stories that I don't feel comfortable writing. I don't know whether it's a sign that a writer is not growing or doesn't have a total world view, but there are some sorts of things which I enjoy writing more than others. I did enjoy handling mythological materials, back when I was doing it constantly. I will still hearken back to it. I do want to do other things—of the hard science type, of pure fantasy of the non-mythological sort—a great number of things I want to try.

Everyone has his own angle of vision. There are conscious writers, conscious plotters, unconscious plotters, fast writers who can hack out a story in a hurry without affecting the quality of the writing a great deal…

For instance, Dumas *pere* was a noted fast writer. He could whip off a story in a great hurry, in a flamboyant creative act. Still, the stories were romantic fun, but classified as classics.

His son was just the opposite. Dumas *fils* was very slow, painstaking, a meticulous writer who massaged his words, let them talk to one another. At one point in his career, he had spent three months writing one paragraph. He hadn't quite finished it. The book he was writing happened to be *Camille*. He was working on this paragraph one evening.

There was a knock on the door. It was his father, whom he hadn't seen in a long while. There was a lady on each arm—he was a flamboyant writer. His son invited him in, and went off to get him some refreshment. His father was pacing around the room, walked over to the writing desk, looked at the manuscript. After a while, he sat down and finished the paragraph. He waited a little longer; finished the whole chapter. A little longer, and he outlined the rest of the novel. His son hadn't come back yet, so he went upstairs and made love to both women, came back downstairs just as his son returned, borrowed 2000 francs from him, and disappeared into the night.

There's a moral to every story. My son has told me that he thinks he might like to be a writer—when he grows up. I hope he's not the slow, painstaking, meticulous sort. But if he is, I hope he keeps some money around the house.

❖ ❖ ❖

I came in as a novitiate here. Now I feel like an old monk. I know, after sixteen years of writing, that the trees are only trees and the clouds are only clouds and the mountains are only mountains. I also know that there are probably an infinite number of ways of regarding them all. I think that's what writing is all about. I think that that's what science fiction is all about. That's one of the reasons I write it, and one of the reasons I love it.

I also see that the slide projector, the blackboard, and the dancing girls still have not arrived, but I'm about finished with my improvisation, and I thank you for your attention, and I particularly want to thank you for bringing me here, to all those involved in putting on this convention for all your kindness and courtesy and generosity you've shown. I want you to know that I've enjoyed talking with everyone I've talked with and I hope to talk with some more of you. *Adieu.*

Notes

Zelazny delivered this Guest of Honor speech during Easter at the Unicon 1978 convention in Melbourne, Australia. He refers within it to several undated events from his own experience. It was Berkley Books who rejected *Doorways in the Sand* in 1973 and used the excuse that Zelazny hadn't followed the outline. Zelazny, Philip K. Dick, and Harlan Ellison appeared at the Metz International SF Festival, held September 19-25, 1977, in Metz, France. In early 1968 Zelazny took the partial *Deus Irae* manuscript from Ted White, and he finished the collaboration with Dick in the spring of 1975.

Northrop Frye was a Canadian literary critic and author whose interest in mythology influenced Zelazny's thoughts about writing. **Franz Kafka** was an influential German author who wrote surrealistic works such as *The Trial*, "The Metamorphosis," and *The Judgement*. Eugene **Ionesco** was a Romanian-born French Absurdist playwright whose works include *The Bald Soprano* and *Rhinoceros*. Nobel Prize-winning Irish writer **Samuel Beckett** wrote Absurd plays, including *Waiting for Godot* and *Krapp's Last Tape*.

The reference to **Montpelier** is incorrect and may have been a transcription error from the first printing of this speech. **Jean-François Pilâtre de Rozier** was a native of Metz, France, and was the first person to fly in an untethered hot air balloon in 1783. French brothers Joseph and Jacques-Étienne **Montgolfier** invented the hot air balloon. **Mephistopheles** was the devil who tempted Faust and bought his soul. **Svengali** was a musician in George du Maurier's novel *Trilby* who trains Trilby's voice and controls her stage singing hypnotically; the term also means a person who controls another, especially through a mesmerism. Alexandre **Dumas** *père* wrote *The Count of Monte Cristo*, *The Three Musketeers*, and *The Man in the Iron Mask*. His son, Alexandre **Dumas** *fils*, became a celebrated author and playwrite; *Camille* [*La Dame aux camellias*] is his tragic story of a young man who has an affair with a courtesan who later dies of tuberculosis.

Philip K. Dick

To Spin Is Miracle Cat, Underwood-Miller 1981.

God or gods, there is a music.
Once I thought it a stringéd thing,
but now I know it's pipes.
Listen as it stills the cricket note
in the soul's dark night.
Love is only part:

Hate in our time
and partial mind
may bring the soul of man to God.
But then again, Cratylus,
who knows? Which Sistine roof
was Michael Angelo's proof?

Under Santa Ana's lights
Philip Dick has known dark nights

> *barrel of gun*
> *note of pipe*
> *Easter picnic eve*
> *despair koan*

and scratched these lines
where neon glows:

Where sound the notes
in every order,
traffic pass—
worlds without end—
by.

Pipe now the last
insomniac shepherd
beyond the dawn,
where bars of light
hold up delinquent day.

Traffic turn left
where fat horses
gambol.

The world's a world away.

A Word from Zelazny

Zelazny had a premonition about Dick's death and wrote this tribute. "It was a funny feeling… I didn't intend it to be elegiac. About the piper: the previous year, at my recommendation, Phil had just read for the first time Kenneth Grahame's *Wind in the Willows,* and his favorite chapter, which is everyone's, was the piper of dawn, which Phil compared with the pipes of Krishna. At the same time I saw Phil as such a piper. But the funny thing is, the last time I saw Phil—we sat up through the night talking, after a bookshop signing—consciously, all I noticed was he seemed a little peaked, no worse than if, say, he had flu. But at some subliminal level I must have sensed what was to come, and it comes out in the poem; that's what I meant, not a conscious premonition as such."[1] Dick died March 2, 1982, at age 53 in **Santa Ana**, California.

Notes

Cratylus was an ancient Greek philosopher who felt that the world changed constantly and instantaneously, as could words, making true communication impossible. Cratylus renounced speech and communicated by wagging his finger. **Michelangelo** painted the ceiling of the **Sistine** Chapel. **Koan** is a Zen term for a paradoxical question which demands an answer; meditating on the impossible answer promotes illumination. To **gambol** is to jump about playfully.

---

1 *Critical Wave #33,* November 1993.

IDEAS, DIGRESSIONS AND DAYDREAMS
THE AMAZING SCIENCE FICTION MACHINE

Insight, Summer 1976.

When you make your living writing science fiction, the question you hear most frequently is "Where do you get your ideas?" I think this is a terrible question, and having compared notes with most science fiction writers in the country I feel safe in saying that all of us agree it is a terrible question. I have heard it from small children and from the trembling lips of the near-senescent, from people in nearly every profession, at every level of society. I once heard it in a cave in Mexico, translated from Hungarian to Spanish to English, and I saw it coming long before it came.

It is not that the question in unanswerable, it is just that it does not give itself to a ready reply. No matter where you begin, there arises an immediate need to digress. This is because contemporary science fiction is a vehicle for the exploration of ideas, and you are already into a semantic shift when you say this—for you are talking about scientific and philosophical ideas as distinct from the writer's more mundane ideas involving those old constraints of plot, character and setting. Which ideas does the inquirer really want to hear about?

So let me take you down the stairs backwards.

Digression Number One: Science fiction became a *genre* in the year 1926, with the publication of the first issue of the first magazine in this country devoted to it, Hugo Gernsback's *Amazing Stories*. Before that, stories being written by, say, H. G. Wells or Jules Verne, were classified as "scientific romances" and kept on the same library shelves as good, decent, respectable books by more conventional authors. There followed approximately a dozen years of bad writing in that magazine and those others which came into existence shortly thereafter. This was primarily because it was a pulp medium with quantity requirements making it susceptible to formula stories easily translated from western and mystery situations into outer space. This also served to stigmatize the area for years afterwards. Pity.

Digression Number Two: During the time of Digression Number One, some youngsters read and enjoyed theme stories nevertheless, went on to obtain better technical backgrounds than the authors had possessed and finally tried writing it themselves. They did a much better job. I am referring now to writers such an Isaac Asimov, Robert Heinlein, Lester del Rey, Theodore Sturgeon. They turned the area into a vehicle for examining scientific ideas and their effects by means of subjecting the ideas to one of Theodore Sturgeon's questions, such as "If this goes on...?" or "What if...?"—the first of which represents a simple extrapolation from the present to the future and a consideration of consequences; the second, the setting up of highly problematic future situations for similar purposes. Isaac Asimov has referred to the two devices as the "chess game story" and the "chess problem story," the distinction being that the same rules are followed in both but the second represents a condition no two sane chess players would normally allow to arise.

And this went on for another dozen years, the consensus being a kind of naïve scientism, if you like, or a basically optimistic attitude toward science and technology, if you do not. But the machine was just warming up.

Digression Number Three: It was Poul Anderson who noted that science fiction seems to move in 12-year cycles. He seems to be right. Why? Sunspots, maybe. But as surely an 1926–38 was the pulp era and 1938–50 was the time when the science was actually put into science fiction, the 1950–62 period saw a number of new writers who felt that the social sciences could be subjected to the same intellectual games as the natural sciences. And so they did, maintaining much of the earlier optimism which had characterized the area. The 1962–74 cycle was another story. More new writers. Older writers doing some rethinking. A period when the four P's—poverty, pollution, population, power—were not only constantly in the news but twined together and tethered to technology. Optimism evaporated. More anti-utopian ("dystopian," I understand, is now the fashionable word) stories, bitter satires, post-holocaust stories, were written. There also came an increased attention to the story-telling act itself. Science fiction had, up until then, been characterized by a reasonably straightforward, no-nonsense approach to its materials. Stylistic experiments of the sort which had occurred in general fiction generations before had been pretty much avoided up until this time, mainly because the narrative already possessed an extra burden with respect to explanations of background and ideas. Now, however, the plunge was plunged, James Joyce and Robbe-Grillet finally influenced the area. It was a time of reaction, esotericism, introspection. The bad, as always, sank to the bottom, the good got anthologized. Kingsley Amis had once referred to science fiction an a literature of the idea as hero. This was changed. One Good Thing to emerge from this period was an increased attention to character.

Digression Number Four: The reason all of the things happening in Digression Number Three were able to happen at all was that the magazines, which had created the *genre* in the first place, lost hold of it in the early fifties. There were too many of them, the market was glutted, they went out of business in great numbers within a single year. But the writers were already established, and they wanted to keep writing because it beat working for a living. Consequently, they moved into the growing paperback markets, and later hardcovers. This shift freed them from the remaining magazine taboos. Sex, religion and politics were now legitimate grist for the If-this-goes-on, What-if machine. And so, the social concerns of the fifties, the experiments and attitudes of the sixties.

Digression Number Five: Science fiction, a branch of fantasy, was a product of the Enlightenment, the industrial revolution, the growth of technology. Though the term had not been minted then, Mary Shelley's *Frankenstein* was probably the first true science fiction novel. It looked at something man had created with his science and speculated as to the possibility of its turning on him and destroying him. This theme is still present in science fiction today, and it will remain there, somewhere, for so long an man keeps discovering, designing and manufacturing. The term "science fiction" has been anathematized periodically because many of our speculative stories are devoid of "nuts-and-bolts science." The term "speculative fiction" is often suggested as an alternative. The other side argues that the really big ideas in the world today are all coming out of the sciences, and the best of science fiction is that which deals with this thinking.

These people invariably write this sort of story. The others write the other sort. I have no personal preference for either. If it hadn't been for Hugo Gernsback they would still be scientific romances.

Digression Number Six: According to digression Number Three, a new cycle should just be starting its revolution around now. Strangely, this seems to be the case. It is still too early to give it a label. One can only point and say, "The new cycle is what I am pointing at." It may shape up into a synthesis, though, of some of the better features of the past three cycles.

End of digressions.

I write science fiction for love and money. I have been doing it for 13 years, the first 7 on a part-time basis, the past 6 full-time. Most science fiction writers are concerned with the history of ideas. They like to read and talk and daydream and call it research when someone asks them what they are doing. To justify it beyond this and to pay their bills they tailor some of the dreams and put them down on paper. Daydream tailoring is hardly a fit answer to "Where do you got your ideas?" however, so the standard response is to begin a digression.

Notes

Case Western Reserve University, Zelazny's alma mater, requested this essay for their alumni journal *Insight*. A copy-editing error merged two sentences, making it incomprehensible. The dropped words in digression number five were "…speculative stories are devoid of 'nuts-and-bolts science.' The term…" This is the original version from an archive at the University of Maryland, Baltimore County.

Irish-born **James Joyce** experimented with stream of consciousness and other techniques in his writing; *Ulysses* and *Finnegans Wake* are two of his best known works. French writer and film maker Alain **Robbe-Grillet** also experimented with narrative styles and themes; his first novel *The Erasers* involves a detective who is seeking the assassin in a murder that has not yet occurred, only to discover that he is destined to become that assassin. Author and poet **Kingsley Amis** was best known for his first novel, *Lucky Jim*; he was fond of science fiction and edited the sf anthology series *Spectrum*. **Anathematized** means denounced.

Musings on
Lord of Light

Niekas #21, 1977.

When one is desirous of writing a story involving elements of myth, folklore, legend, one is faced with several possible choices as to how to proceed. A faithful retelling of the original—as in Andre Norton's juvenile, *Huon of the Horn*—may recommend itself. When I employ such elements, however—such as in *...And Call Me Conrad* (Greek), *Creatures of Light and Darkness* (Egyptian) or *Lord of Light* (Hindu)—my intention is to abstract out from a body of tradition those elements which most interest or amuse me, hint at a lot of the rest which are not actually pertinent to my telling, and to make up a few items out of whole cloth which just "feel" appropriate.

When, on the final morning of a Disclave a couple years back, I cut myself while shaving and lapsed into a long pre-sentient chain of free-associations which somehow ended up at transmigration, I found myself with the sudden (and not too profound—but then, it was early in the morning) realization that not much had been done in U.S. sf and fantasy with respect to Hindu culture. Ben Jason and I drove back to Ohio that afternoon, and by the time we arrived that evening I had pretty much roughed out the whole story in my head.

I had decided on either seven or nine chapters of approximately 13,000 words each, so that I might be able to sell a few as novelettes if no one wanted to take a chance on using it as a series or serial. For this reason, I figured that each chapter would have to be somewhat independent of its fellows. This fell in neatly with what I had in mind as to the tone and texture of the piece. I wanted to separate the chapters in space and time, and so produce a sort of folk-story quality. I could have had nine chapters, but I threw out what I was thinking of using in two of them, because there is a breaking point in anything like this and I didn't just want to pile up incident. This could actually work to defeat the underlying essential direction of something of this sort. This decided, I began soaking myself in Hindu background. I drew dozens of books on the subject out of the Cleveland Public Library and I spent around sixty bucks on books which they didn't have that I felt that I'd need. That's how *Lord of Light* began.

I'd say that I actually employed only a small percent of what I learned from the background reading. But then, you never know where you're going to come across something useful. If you want a thing like this to have an authentic-seeming air about it, you've got to go in for a bit of this kind of saturation.

But it was fun. I mentioned it to Andre Norton, who was then a neighbor, and she recommended the massive *The Wonder That Was India*, by A. L. Basham (Hawthorn Books, 1936) which I purchased and proceeded to read. She also recommended *Gods, Demons And Others* by R. K. Narayan (Viking, 1964), a retelling of Indian myths and legends. These were interesting for general background. I then picked up *Traditional India*, ed. O. L. Chavarria-Aguilar. Ditto on this. Then I read the *Ramayana*, which influenced my fourth chapter, and *The Upanishads* (translation by Swami Nikhilananda) and *Buddhist Texts Through the Ages* (ed. Conze, Horner, Snellgrove & Waley)—both Harper Torchbooks. These latter two gave me the quotations at the beginnings of the chapters. They are all of them authentic—and although I took the liberty of rephrasing each somewhat, I retained the sense of the original. Then I read Herman Hesse's *Siddhartha*, which probably influenced chapter three a bit. This same chapter was also influenced by the novel-length poem *The Light of Asia; or, The Great Renunciation (Mahabhinishkramana)* by Sir Edwin Arnold (1879). Then Andre Norton recommended one more book, *Shilappadikaram (The Ankle Bracelet)*, by Prince Ilango Adigal (New Directions), a 2nd century work of fiction, from which I stole many metaphors for chapter two. (Oh, before I forget to record it, *The Light of Asia* gave me the four Lords of Sumernu with whom Yama does battle in the dream-sequence in chapter three.) And Dom Moraes' *Gone Away* gave me some pieces for chapter four's settings, as did the *Ramayana*.

Okay. I've touched on some of the reading involved. I wanted color, almost garish, so I dwelled often in my thoughts upon Hindu paintings of the 18th century. I threw the color into costumes and settings. I wanted a sort of baroque style, because I figured that would be best for a folklore/legend-type thing. Also, I feel that a real book deserves one decently realized female character, and Kali suggested herself. I took extra pains with her for this reason.

Here, as in *Conrad*, I wanted to leave it open to several interpretations—well, at least two. I wanted to sort of combine fantasy and sf, I wanted to put something there for the lover of each form of speculative literature. As in *Conrad*, I think *Lord of Light* can be read as either one. Either Conrad is a mutant or he is the Great God Pan. The book may be read either way. With Sam, I do not say that he did *not* receive illumination, whether he believes it himself or not. I tried to balance the elements of science and fantasy in both, that's all.

As to the ending of *Lord of Light*, I never know how one of my books ends until I write the ending. It would be no fun for me to go that distance if everything was foreordained. With *Lord of Light* I came up with four endings and I decided, what the hell! When it comes to something like a legend there are always variations. So why not use all four? So I did.

And that, Ed, represents my quickly recorded musings upon some of the major elements and intentions behind *Lord of Light*.

Notes

Ten years after *Lord of Light* was published, Ed Meskys, the editor of *Niekas*, asked Zelazny to describe the research that preceded writing that novel.

"...And Call Me Roger"
The Literary Life of Roger Zelazny, Part 3

by Christopher S. Kovacs, MD

---1969---

Full-time Writer

In May 1969 Roger Zelazny and his wife Judy both resigned from the Social Security Administration. He needed to write more novels. "Word for word, novels work harder for their creators when it comes to providing for the necessities and joys of existence. Which would sound cynical, except that I enjoy writing novels, too."[1]

Zelazny sought advice from more experienced colleagues. He wrote to Mack Reynolds, "To be quite frank, I'm scared shitless over the whole thing. This is the first time since college (over seven years) that I've been without a steady job, and I've never been solely dependent on my writing before, despite the fact that it has been going fairly well. Perhaps I magnify, but I keep wondering, 'What if I dry up? What if my next couple books are no good?' I'm chicken, pure and simple. If I can't make it after about a year, I want the roost handy. From here [Baltimore], I can always throw in the towel, jump in my car and go get a job with the government."[2]

Another colleague offered more than advice. "At Lunacon in 1969 I happened to mention to Isaac Asimov that I was planning to quit my civil service job on May Day of that year, to write full time. He told me that it might feel strange at first, adjusting to a new daily rhythm, that it could mess up my writing for a time but that it would pass, and he wished me good luck.

"That May, while I was dithering about with my new rhythm, I received a letter from Sylvia Burack, editor of *The Writer* magazine. She said that she had recently asked Isaac Asimov for an article on the writing of science fiction and he responded that he was too busy at the moment and recommended that she approach one of the newest writers, such as Roger Zelazny, and had furnished her with my address. I never knew whether he was really too busy, or whether he wanted to throw a little extra business my way now that I no longer had a paycheck coming in—although I strongly suspected the latter."[3] So Zelazny wrote "Science Fiction and How It Got That Way," which appears in volume 3 of this collection. That essay's publication in May 1971 led to invited lectures at the Indiana University Writer's Conference, assignments for *Writer's Digest*, an appointment to its editorial board, and a taped interview by *Writer's Voice* for a course on creative writing. That interview alone paid royalties for a long time afterward.

In 1972 Zelazny wrote, "I'm glad I [quit work] before Devin [his first child] came along, though. Had he been about then, I might have hesitated."[4] Asked in 1991 if he should have done anything differently, he replied, "Yes, I probably would have quit my job with the government a year sooner. I stayed on an extra year, just for the security of building up the bankroll a little more, and I suppose that if I'd been made of sterner stuff I would have quit sooner and just have turned out more copy. Things probably would have been about the same as they are now, and I would have been a few books and stories ahead. I would have had a little less time with bureaucracy, too."[5]

Zelazny's switch to full-time writing did not increase his output. He averaged a novel per year, and his short story writing declined. He'd been more productive when he wrote only in evenings and on weekends.

To Die in Italbar

Zelazny's fears about financial success affected his next novel. He dashed off *To Die in Italbar* in the month after he resigned. After it appeared, disappointed readers asked repeatedly and rudely if quitting his job was responsible for the quality of his writing in that novel. "No, there is no truth to the rumor that in order to escape my job with the government I undertook an excessive quantity of contracts that depressed the quality of my work; as well as presented me with a personal crisis of confidence in my ability to fulfill all those contracts."[6] But in later interviews he admitted that he wrote *To Die in Italbar* hastily, due to the career change. "The first thing I did [after quitting] was get nervous and write the worst book I'd ever written. I wrote it in about a month."[7] "I wrote it in the month after I quit work for the [government] to write full-time. I felt the pressure to produce that first year & dashed that one off extremely quickly, for the money. It took me about a year to achieve a sense of balance in these matters (if I ever actually achieved it)."[8]

He had more to say: "*To Die in Italbar* represents the only attempt I'd ever made to write a story according to a formula. It was a Max Brand formula, and it sounded good when I heard it: You need two main characters, a good man who goes bad and a bad man who goes good. Their paths cross on their ways up and down. Well…I began the book with every intention of doing just that, but partway through I got interested in the characters as characters, saw an odd tie-in with my earlier novel *Isle of the Dead* and ditched the formula. I sometimes wonder, though, what it would have been like if I hadn't."[9] Zelazny apparently forgot that he'd earlier used the Max Brand formula to explain additions to *Damnation Alley*. The "odd tie-in" was the opportunity to include a cameo of Francis Sandow, first seen in *Isle of the Dead*.[10]

In *Roger Zelazny: Starmont Reader's Guide 2*, Carl Yoke said that Zelazny wrote *To Die in Italbar* in 1965 during "a very difficult personal crisis" that ended with a separation from his first wife,[11] and, "contrary to speculation, [Zelazny] did not revive Francis Sandow from *Isle of the Dead* for this novel. Rather, he *extracted* Sandow from *Italbar* for *Isle of the Dead* because the character was one of the few things that he liked about the earlier novel."[11] If *To Die in Italbar* was early and written under stress, that could explain some of its problems. However, Zelazny repeatedly said that he wrote *To Die in Italbar* within a month after quitting his job in May 1969.[7,8,10,12] Archived correspondence and manuscripts support Zelazny's recollection. "I wrote …*And Call Me Conrad*, which was really my first novel (becoming, for Ace, *This Immortal*). Subsequent to this, I expanded 'He Who Shapes' to its *The Dream Master*-length. I had not attempted any novels prior to these efforts."[13]

Yoke was certain that Zelazny had told him the book was written in 1965 with Sandow in it. "The footnote at the back of my GUIDE [pages 104 and 105] would have come directly from Roger, but whether he told me that or it was some sort of correspondence, I don't [remember]."[14]

It is conceivable that Zelazny wrote *To Die in Italbar* in 1965 but preferred that people think it was a hastily written 1969 novel rather than a 1965 effort unearthed to fulfill a contract. Overall the historical record is largely consistent with Zelazny's statements that he wrote the first draft after he quit work in 1969. He knew that it was a weak novel. Doubleday was not impressed with it and placed it on hold. Zelazny returned to it several years later to fulfill the Doubleday contract, and he polished it by adding the cameo of Francis Sandow. He completed those revisions on May 26, 1972, and wrote to Philip José Farmer that he'd "cobbled a new ending onto a novel I'd had lying about since the days of the elder gods," and the revisions gave him "a relatively clear conscience."[4]

His self-described "worst novel," *To Die in Italbar* appeared from Doubleday in 1973, four years after he'd written it. Avon, his usual paperback publisher, "turned it down, as did almost everyone else."[15] Ultimately the paperback came out from DAW, a new publishing house.

Third Compromise

Concentrating on his novels, Zelazny published only three short stories in 1969. Ironically, his shorter works earned more awards and praise. He enjoyed writing the short form (especially the novella), considered it purer than the novel, and bemoaned that he couldn't make a living simply writing shorts. Abandoning poetry in favor of prose was his first compromise as a writer. Largely abandoning short works in favor of novels was the second. His writing *To Die in Italbar* in haste to fulfill a contractual obligation heralded the third compromise, for which he received the most criticism.

His third compromise meant that full-time writing did not allow him the time to produce such high-quality novels as *Lord of Light*. Writing had to replace the government salaries that he and his wife had abandoned. He had to write more lucrative, longer works but in less time than the year he spent researching and writing *Lord of*

Light. He would have to alternate between lighter, more commercial fare (e.g. *Changeling, The Changing Land,* and many of the Amber novels) and serious, experimental novels *(Bridge of Ashes, Eye of Cat, Roadmarks)*. Amber's commercial success naturally mandated more of those novels. His attention to craft as in *Lord of Light* appeared more in his infrequent shorter works, such as "Unicorn Variation," "24 Views of Mt. Fuji, by Hokusai," "Home Is the Hangman," and "Come Back to the Killing Ground, Alice, My Love."

Critics and fans wanted Zelazny to abandon novels and keep writing mythological short works.[16] In 1977, Richard Cowper, thinking *To Die in Italbar* was Zelazny's newest work, wrote harshly, "A Rose is a Rose is a Rose…In Search of Roger Zelazny."[17] He compared the "barely out of his diapers" Zelazny to Lord Byron as someone who had become famous too quickly.[17] He concluded that Zelazny had not yet written a significant work. Other critics suggested that Zelazny rehash previous publications. "A return to Zelazny's earlier, 'purer' concerns may have the risk of repetition, but there is hardly a good, distinctive writer who doesn't run that risk, and there is always something to be gained and enlarged upon from a new angle."[18]

Zelazny disagreed with his critics. He wanted to evolve, preferring to experiment with each novel and to tread old ground only in the Amber series. *Bridge of Ashes, Today We Choose Faces, Eye of Cat,* and *Roadmarks* illustrate his ongoing experimentation with structure and style. His popularity grew—largely due to the Amber series—and he received more nominations for major awards. He realized that he couldn't maintain the critical acclaim he'd received in the 1960s, and he later declared that he wasn't interested in what the critics thought anyway.[19]

The Writer as a Warped Mirror

Some fan letters asked Zelazny to explain the allusions and "hidden messages" in his work. Asked if his stories were allegories, Zelazny scoffed, "While I go along with the notion that a writer should hold a mirror up to reality, I don't necessarily feel that it should be the kind you look into when you shave or tweeze your eyebrows, or both as the case may be. If I'm going to carry a mirror around, holding it up to reality whenever I notice any, I might as well enjoy the burden as much as I can. My means of doing this is to tote around one of those mirrors you used to see in fun houses, back when they still had fun houses. Of course, not anything you reflect looks either as attractive or as grimly visaged as it may stand before the naked eyeball. Sometimes it looks more attractive, or more grimly visaged. You just don't really know, until you've tried the warping glass. And it's awfully hard to hold the slippery thing steady. Blink, and—who knows?—you're two feet tall. Sneeze, and May the Good Lord Smile Upon You. I live in deathly fear of dropping the thing. I don't know what I'd do without it. Carouse more, probably. I love my cold and shiny burden, that's why."[20]

Way Up High and *Here There Be Dragons*

Zelazny wrote these children's stories in 1968. He commissioned Vaughn Bodé to illustrate them, and Bodé displayed the artwork at the 1969 Worldcon in St. Louis. On December 13, 1969, Zelazny noted, "I'm going up to New York tomorrow to talk to an artist with whom I collaborated on two children's books. We have what seems to be a fairly firm offer on that, so that would be my first expedition to that particular area."[21] Unfortunately, the two men disagreed. Zelazny found that he had bought Bodé's original paintings but not the rights to reproduce them. Bodé felt that his art did not merely complement the text but that Zelazny's text complemented his artwork instead, and he wanted an equal share of the royalties. The regular publishing houses passed on these "white-elephantish" books.[22] In 1973 Jack L. Chalker scheduled the books for publication from his Mirage Press.[22–24] However, the project faltered again because the demand for equal royalties (totaling 30% of the sale price) made the project unprofitable.[24] Other legal problems, compounded by Bodé's accidental death from auto-asphyxiation in 1975, stalled the publication until 1992.[24]

Other Developments

Zelazny found additional ways to supplement his writing income. He was approached to write a screenplay, the first of many interactions with the film industry. Gene Roddenberry asked him to write an episode of *Star Trek*, but he declined—"I do not watch TV too darned much. I've caught *Star Trek* (in fact, I almost wrote for it at one point), and sometimes I liked it and sometimes I didn't. It depends on the individual script, I guess."[25] He also contributed to the *Fantastic Four* comic after meeting with Stan Lee at the Toronto Triple Fan Fair, July 29–August 1, 1968, where both were Guests of Honor. "They're using [my idea]. I believe it will be in the issue of *Fantastic Four* that comes out in February [1969], where their arch-villain, Dr. Doom, finds himself forced to be a hero, for completely selfish reasons."[25] It is not clear whether Marvel used his idea, and Zelazny received no credit in any *Fantastic Four* of that year.

The biggest demand on Zelazny's time was his self-directed reading program, described on page 520 in this volume.

Distinction:

Ditmar nomination for best contemporary writer

Books Published:

Creatures of Light and Darkness
Isle of the Dead
Damnation Alley

———————1970———————

Jack of Shadows

Contrary to critics' speculation, Zelazny did not write *Jack of Shadows* to capitalize on the success of *Nine Princes in Amber*. He finished the first and only draft in December 1969, prior to *Nine Princes in Amber*'s publication in 1970.[21,26]

The Magazine of Fantasy & Science Fiction published *Jack of Shadows* in July and August 1971. Because of the serialization, the hardcover was delayed, causing Zelazny and his agent to share a $500 penalty (approximately $2,650 in 2009 dollars).[27] *Jack of Shadows* drew attention for its despicable hero and an ending wherein Jack fell to his death with a small chance of being rescued. It was a finalist for the Hugo Award and was #4 on the Locus Poll for best novel. Some readers complained only that the story was too short—and Zelazny agreed: "1) Macbeth and morality plays were on my mind here, as were 2) 17th century metaphysical poetry, in the soul & body dialogues and 3) Jack Vance. I like *Jack of Shadows* for Jack, Rosalie, Morningstar and the world in which they act. I dislike it because I now think I should have telescoped the action in the first third of the book and expanded it more in the final third, producing a stronger overall effect."[28] Except for its existential ending, it wasn't an experimental novel. "This was not one of my experimental books, such as *Creatures of Light and Darkness, Doorways in the Sand, Bridge of Ashes, Roadmarks,* or *Eye of Cat.* Those are the five wherein I worked out lots of techniques I used in many of the others. This was a more workmanlike job in that I knew exactly what I wanted to do and how to do it, with the protagonist—as usual—indicating the direction. Of the five, only *Creatures of Light and Darkness* preceded *Jack of Shadows*. Looking back upon *Jack* in this light, I do feel that I might have gained a certain facility there for the brief, impressionistic description of the exotic which could have carried over into both *Nine Princes* and *Jack*. And maybe not. But if it owes it anything, that's it."[29]

Zelazny named his protagonist for a favorite sf author, Jack Vance. "In this, my tenth book, I'd decided to try for something on the order of those rare and exotic settings I admired so much in so many of Jack Vance's stories. It seemed only fair then, once I'd worked things out, to find a title with 'Jack' in it as a private bit of homage publicly displayed. Now you all know."[29] The book's title also reflected Zelazny's collecting Tarots and playing cards.

Although the novel begins with a quote from Shakespeare's *The Merchant of Venice,* the story relates more to *Macbeth*. "Jack's character undergoes an interesting progression, which owes something to Shakespeare's portrait of the bloody Scot. I don't care to say anything more about it, though, because I feel that introductory pieces should not spoil story lines."[29]

Zelazny received many requests for additional tales of Jack. He wrote three items: the illustrated short story "Shadowjack," the character biography for a special module of *Advanced Dungeons and Dragons,* and the animated film outline "Shadowland." The short story and film outline were both prequels. He refused to write a sequel because "I didn't really intend to continue that one. I liked ending it with that sort of ambiguous ending."[30]

F&SF abridged the story, but the book version introduced a significant error during an exchange between Jack and Morningstar. The magazine's dialogue reads:

> "The ruler of that star," [Jack] said, "has resisted all spells of communication. It moves differently from the others, and faster. It does not twinkle. Why is this?"
>
> "It is not a true star, but an artificial object placed into orbit above Twilight by the dayside scientists."
>
> "To what end?"
>
> "It was placed there to observe the border."
>
> "Why?"
>
> "They fear you."
>
> "We have no designs upon the lands of light."
>
> "I know. But do you not also watch the border, in your own way?"
>
> "Of course."
>
> "Why?"
>
> "To be aware of what transpires along it."
>
> "That is all?"
>
> Jack snorted.
>
> "If that object is truly above Twilight, then it will be subject to magic as well as to its own laws. A strong enough spell will affect it. One day, I will knock it down."[31]

In the book, Morningstar's statement, "They fear you," became a question, "Do they fear you?" Worse, Morningstar's subsequent question "…in your own way?" changed into a question from Jack. This threw off the sequence and created an incomprehensible exchange:

> "Do they fear you?" [Morningstar]
>
> "We have no designs upon the lands of light." [Jack]
>
> "I know. But do you not also watch the border, in your own way?" asked Jack. [originally Morningstar, but now Jack replies to himself]
>
> "Of course." [Morningstar, but originally Jack]
>
> "Why?" [Jack, but originally Morningstar]

"To be aware of what transpires along it." [Morningstar, but originally Jack]

"That is all?" Jack snorted. "If that object is truly above Twilight, then it will be subject to magic as well as to its own laws. A strong enough spell will affect it. One day, I will knock it down." [Morningstar's statement and Jack's reply have been combined into one][32]

The text should properly be restored for any future edition of the novel.

More of Zelazny's thoughts about Jack appear in the afterwords to "Shadowjack," "Shadowland," and "Shadowjack: Character Biography."

The Guns of Avalon

Nine Princes in Amber's impending release prompted Zelazny to resume writing *The Guns of Avalon*. Because he'd not touched the manuscript for more than two years, he felt his style had evolved when he restarted it. "I don't see the book suffering for it, though—or if I did, I wouldn't admit it."[33] But some of his readers surprised him. "Several people have claimed to have noticed some sort of change in the writing of this book—and since, without prompting, they put their fingers on the spot where I resumed writing (page 51 of the hardcover copy), it is likely that my writing changed or the material suspended in limbo had rearranged itself a bit—or both in the interim."[34] He was referring to the start of Chapter 4, which is page 51 in the Doubleday first edition.

An earlier draft of the book contained a practical joke on Zelazny's publisher. He included a "fairly graphic" sex scene between Corwin and Dara. "I'd only put it in to see what the reaction would be."[35] Editor Diane Cleaver referred the matter to boss Larry Ashmead, who called to suggest that Zelazny remove the scene. Ashmead explained that the bulk of hardcover sales went to libraries, which refused to buy sf novels containing risqué material. Having written it "just for laughs" and amused by the awkward call, he agreed to tone it down,[35] completing final revisions in November 1971.[36] He planned to continue the joke by writing a similar scene for each Amber novel, deleting each on request, and eventually publishing the deleted material in a men's magazine as a scholarly but shamelessly pornographic article.

"However, after the first time the novelty wore off and I never did it again."[37] The deleted sex scene—certainly not explicit by today's standards—appears ion page 549 in this volume.

Zelazny generally wrote without outlines, considering them restrictive and dreary. "Hitting keys gets boring and I start feeling like an extension of the machine, rather than vice versa."[38] "I like to leave dark areas [in the plot], just to see what will come fill them. This is one of the greatest pleasures I get out of writing."[38] Because nearly five years (February 1967 to November 1971) elapsed between the completion of the first two novels, Zelazny inadvertently introduced inconsistencies and dangling plot threads. Readers plagued Zelazny at conventions and in writing. He was patient with repeated questions, often congratulating each inquirer for being the "first one to notice." But he continued to write without outlining, accumulating inconsistencies as the stories progressed. For example, why did Corwin's description of his family tree and the throne succession differ so much between *Nine Princes in Amber*, *The Guns of Avalon*, and *Sign of the Unicorn*? Fortunately, the shattered state of Corwin's mind was a reasonable explanation for many early inconsistencies.[39] For the second series about Corwin's son Merlin, Zelazny said that Merlin was naïve and too trusting of (or confused by) the words and actions of his centuries-older relatives.

Apostate's Gold or *The Dead Man's Brother*

By 1970 Zelazny was working on several contracted novels. 1967's *Nine Princes in Amber* finally appeared. Although it was a finalist for the Mythopoeic and Locus Awards, the Amber series took several years to achieve its full commercial success. Still worried about financial security as a full-time writer, Zelazny considered writing in other genres. That thought was not new. In May 1966 he'd written to Doubleday Editor Larry Ashmead, "Am beginning work on a new novel this week, shorter than [*Lord of Light*], with a contemporary setting."[40] Whether he completed this novel is unknown—it may have been an early description of *Nine Princes in Amber* before Zelazny's muse unexpectedly took the amnesiac Corwin from his awakening in a contemporary hospital into a swashbuckling fantasy. In 1969 he wrote that he had "a mystery, a western, and a plain old Künstlerroman [artsy novel], which I intend to try one of these days."[41]

Early in 1970 he undertook *Apostate's Gold*. He initially said it "involves a priest who is dissatisfied with current Vatican policies— and a little bit of hijacking."[21] Later, he said that "it involves a Jesuit priest, who used to be a CPA, who embezzles money from the Vatican because he believes they're not using it properly...[it's] sort of [an] international intrigue thriller-type thing."[42] In 1971 Zelazny changed the title to *The Dead Man's Brother* and worked on it concurrently with *Today We Choose Faces*. He visualized *The Dead Man's Brother* as the second novel for Berkley/Putnam (after *Damnation Alley*) and the first of three such novels written under contract with them. When he completed *The Dead Man's Brother* in June 1971, he told his agent, "Please give them my regrets on the lateness of this one. For a time, I was bogged down quite badly on it. I am pleased, however, with the way it turned out."[43]

Editor George Ernsberger took over from Tom Dardis at Berkley while Zelazny wrote *The Dead Man's Brother*. Ernsberger cancelled its publication because their mystery list was faltering. Berkley wanted Zelazny to write three science fiction novels instead. After some deliberation between Zelazny and his agent, they agreed to Berkley's terms and *Doorways in the Sand* became the first of the new trio. In what Zelazny referred to as a "long, sad story,"[44] for the next two years Agent Henry Morrison sent *The Dead Man's Brother* to Harper & Row, Doubleday, Random House, Bobbs-Merrill, Simon and Schuster, William Morrow, and more. They all turned it down, citing the same two reasons: first, Zelazny's name was unknown to mystery readers; second, the novel's middle section was slow and wordy. William Morrow's senior editor wrote, "It is a fine book...I enjoyed it very much—liking the hero and appreciating a rather novel plot. However, the book began to become too wearing and tedious near the middle and I felt it bogged down. Perhaps, too, I did not feel enough suspense or excitement throughout."[45] Doubleday considered it "rather good but it isn't strong enough for the general trade list and it certainly isn't a Crime Club novel. Unfortunately, it falls somewhere in between which leaves us nowhere. It's a tough one...I did want it to work for us."[46] The Bobbs-Merrill editor said, "It is too wordy...overall, it's a dull book. What's the matter with him? His sf is swell."[47] These publishers wanted Zelazny's science fiction or fantasy, not mystery or thriller.

In 1973 Morrison urged him to revise *The Dead Man's Brother*, noting that "since we have been circulating the book for almost two full years now, I have the feeling that something is drastically wrong with the construction of the plot."[48] Zelazny knew exactly what was amiss. "When I was writing that book, I realized about halfway through the thing that it seemed to be basically a 60 or 65,000-word story. However, the original contract called for a longer book, so I decided to try to slow the pace and draw things out to the greater length. Now…the editors who have commented on it have seemed pretty uniform in saying that it drags in the middle portions. They are right. Actually, I have been hoping that one of them would say he was interested, if I would do some cutting there. On the other hand, I thought that it might hold up as it stood and go anyway, on the strengths of the other parts. So much for wishful thinking. So…Maybe I can save it by cutting it, compressing some of the business and doing some transitional bridging. So let me have it back, and I will see what can be done to step up the pace."[49] He did not revise the manuscript at that time.

Awaiting word on *The Dead Man's Brother*, Zelazny planned the second novel. He told Philip José Farmer that it "will be properly due you [dedicated to you], also, when I finally get to write it—*Albatross!*—a sort of ecological mystery-adventure novel (which will most likely continue to exist only in my mind for at least another year)."[4] Zelazny never wrote the book.

In 1975 Ballantine prepared to publish *My Name Is Legion*, Zelazny's trio of short science fiction detective novels. Editor Alice Turner "heard through the grapevine" about Zelazny's unsold mystery/thriller novel and asked to see it.[50] Zelazny quickly did "some copy-marking and minor cleanup work"[51]—not substantial revisions—and sent it to his agent. Again it didn't sell, in part because Turner expected a "science-fiction detective novel" and not a mainstream thriller.

The Dead Man's Brother's failure was a significant blow to Zelazny's first and only serious effort to break into the mainstream. Ultimately, he didn't need to diversify because Amber and his other work provided enough income. He didn't try the mainstream again until the 1990s, when he and Gerald Hausman undertook the historical novel *Wilderness*. In a 1980 interview he expressed disappointment, referring to an unpublished "mystery novel, which probably could've been salvaged if I had taken the time to make some changes which I can see now should have been made in it, but I didn't feel like doing it. It's too late now, unfortunately—or fortunately, depending on how one looks at it—because the book to some extent was timely, back in the sixties, and whatever virtue it might have had has dissipated. That's the only one."[35]

After Zelazny severed relations with Henry Morrison in 1979, the manuscript went, along with the rest of his files, to his new agent, Kirby McCauley. It was rediscovered more than a decade after Zelazny's death and published by Hard Case Crime in 2009—thirty-eight years after he had finished it.[52] The other non-genre novels—*Albatross!*, the western, and the "plain old Künstlerroman"—were never written.

Mythical Warehouse Fire and *Nine Princes in Amber*

Doubleday published *Nine Princes in Amber* in 1970, but it was not widely read until the Avon paperback came out in 1971. Standing alone or as part of *The Chronicles of Amber, The First Chronicles of Amber*, or the massive *The Great Book of Amber*, it has been in print for four decades. The hardcover was scarce from the start, and most of the 2,500 copies sold went to libraries.[53] Rumor offered a plausible explanation for the first edition's scarcity—supposedly a warehouse fire at Doubleday destroyed most of the print run. Correspondence between Zelazny, his agent, and the publisher proves this false. Initially Morrison heard that Doubleday decided to "kill off the book because of slow activity" only a few months after releasing it. Morrison was puzzled because this left Doubleday with the earlier hardcover *Creatures of Light and Darkness* which "sold even less but it is still in print and supposedly actively selling...Diane [the editor] said she thought this was most strange and she was going to check further, but the ways of Doubleday may be as mysterious to her as to me."[53] The truth was that Doubleday had made a mistake. The publisher had two Zelazny hardcovers in print—*Creatures of Light and Darkness* and *Nine Princes in Amber*. The order went out to pulp (destroy) the older title so that it would not compete with *Nine Princes in Amber*—but Doubleday pulped the wrong book. No tragic loss in a fire, just a stupid mistake by some anonymous worker. Today the serious Zelazny collector can expect to pay $3,000 to $5,000 for a pristine first edition *Nine Princes in Amber*—and more if it is a signed copy.

Religion—Lapsed Catholic or Agnostic?

Zelazny's early works featured mythology and religion. His focus on Hinduism and Buddhism in his most famous novel and his unfamiliar last name prompted readers to speculate about his ethnicity and religion. He withheld personal information from his fiction as much as possible—"I believe a piece of writing should be considered of, in, by, and for itself, a thing independent of the person who wrote it"[54]—confusing readers who expected to find the author's beliefs revealed there. Not finding it, many concluded that Zelazny was an atheist or an agnostic. However, in 1970, when asked if *The Dead Man's Brother* would get him "in trouble with the Catholic Church or some such thing?" he replied, "Not really. I still consider myself a good Catholic."[21] His parents were Catholic.[55] He had studied myriad religions, and this made him very comfortable in tackling Christianity in *Deus Irae*.

An interviewer wondered if his fictional themes reflected his own beliefs: "One can detect a conflict of influences, something of a battle between piety and reasoned agnosticism. Is there anything to this observation?" Zelazny equivocated, "That's hard to say. When I began writing I used a lot of religious and mythological material. I did this intentionally because this was a body of information I just happened to possess. For a time it had me labeled as a writer of mythological science fiction. I was in the process of filling in my background in a number of other areas that I intended to use in later books. Eventually I wanted to get away from the label. So I wrote other things, like *Doorways in the Sand*, which is considered pure science fiction."[56]

In 1973 a priest at Malvern Preparatory School asked Zelazny to critique a student's essay that attempted to "summarize your personal theology as manifest in your works."[57] The priest wanted Zelazny to confirm the student's inferences. Zelazny thanked the priest and congratulated the student for the review, which focused on aspects of "The Agnostic's Prayer" from *Creatures of Light and Darkness*. But once again he dodged the question about his "personal theology." "[The novels] were written with the notion of a Deity as basically unknowable by man, save for possible instances of personal revelation, mystical experiences, private Epiphany, which in themselves would serve to enlighten only the recipients, remaining incommunicable by them to other men. In the absence of such a situation, the individual who conceives of Deity at all must necessarily achieve his faith or ideas on the basis of hearsay, guesswork or lines of reasoning which derive from assailable premises. In this case, a lack of proper knowledge is necessarily companion to a lack of knowledge as to what is truly proper. Seen in this light, the act of praising God then comes to involve such presumption on the part of the praiser that it might well in itself be a form of blasphemy. This is the case in the books in question."[58]

Asked if it was significant that, apart from Nirriti in *Lord of Light*, none of his works dealt with Christianity (the interviewer had overlooked *Deus Irae* and "The Last Inn on the Road"), Zelazny replied, "No. The reason *Lord of Light* tended toward Hinduism was because most of the people who colonized the planet had a Hindu background. In fact, the name of the ship that took them there was *Star of India*. But that's not to beg the question, or justify. No, I don't think I have any special feelings for one religion over another to that extent…I've never really had an idea for a good story that involved specifically a Christian background. If I did, I'd write it."[35]

Some fans openly pried, as in this letter to Doubleday: "My friend and I have a small wager concerning Mr. Zelazny's religion. Would you kindly furnish me with the correct answer."[59] Zelazny replied on July 22, 1978, "To answer your question, while I have studied just about every religion of record, I am not a member of any recognizable religious group."[60] An interviewer asked about his 1970 statement that he still considered himself a good Catholic. Zelazny replied, "I did have a strong Catholic background, but I am not a Catholic. Somewhere in the past, I believe I answered in the affirmative once for strange and complicated reasons. But I am not a member of any organized religion."[61] He added, "If you mention my Catholic background, I hope you also mention that I became a retired Catholic at age 16. I do not consider myself a Christian."[13] These letters and other evidence indicate that he gradually fell away from Catholicism, feeling no need for formal religion. His acquaintances assert that he did not return to religion at the end of his life.

Distinction:

Nebula nomination for novel *Isle of the Dead*
All-time best short story or novelette, The Science Fiction Writers of America, #6: "A Rose for Ecclesiastes"

Book Published:

Nine Princes in Amber

---1971---

Moving Again and a Family Addition

By February 1971 the Zelaznys had moved to West University Parkway in Roland Park, a quiet residential area of Baltimore. Anticipating children, they purchased a larger house. Zelazny's first son, Devin Joseph, was born on December 26, 1971. Devin's arrival reinforced his determination to be a financially successful, full-time writer.

Nine Black Doves

After four brief appearances, Dilvish the Damned hadn't figured in Zelazny's writing for more than five years. But readers and editors had not forgotten Dilvish and Black, his demon horse. Interest in his resurrection for the novel *Nine Black Doves* came from several quarters. L. Sprague de Camp wanted a new Dilvish tale, but—because Zelazny said he was too busy—settled for the right to reprint "The Bells of Shoredan" in his anthology *Warlocks and Warriors*. Lin Carter and Betty Ballantine were "both very much interested in the idea of developing a book with you based on the character of Dilvish as a novel in the Adult Fantasy Library."[62]

Carter and Ballantine's request reopened an old wound. Zelazny had originally planned "a series of shorts and wind it up with a novel—*Nine Black Doves*."[63] But the situation soured after he finished the first three stories. Sol Cohen bought *Amazing* and *Fantastic*, and difficulties with the new owner caused Zelazny to abandon his character. Cohen forced the editor to reject Zelazny's new stories (among them, "The Bells of Shoredan" and "For a Breath I Tarry") and then asked for them back, squabbled over copyrights and pay rates, and reprinted at least eight of Zelazny's stories without permission or payment.[64–66] The situation deteriorated so badly that, when Editor Joe Ross asked Zelazny to send a new "novelet or so over here—maybe more Dilvish or more like 'Tarry' and 'Ecclesiastes'," he added, "If you don't, though, I guess I'll know why, and certainly wouldn't blame you."[67] Henry Morrison learned that Cohen "has not been paying you for reprints of your stories because he feels you are still boycotting his magazine with new material."[68] Zelazny sent in "Love Is an Imaginary Number"[69] and other material to meet Cohen's terms—"a more gracious way out than [Cohen] deserves"[70]—but the situation remained unresolved.[71] Other authors discovered their stories reprinted without permission or payment, and SFWA became involved in an effort to resolve the dispute.[72] Zelazny apparently never received payment for those stories.[64] Morrison advised him to take Cohen to Small Claims Court, but it is unclear whether he ever did.[70,71] The fourth Dilvish tale "A Knight for Merytha" appeared in the fanzine *Kallikanzaros* because of the ongoing dispute with Cohen.[27,73]

Zelazny told Morrison, "it was shortly after that that I stopped doing business with Sol, so Dilvish has remained dormant."[27] But in response to Carter's and Ballantine's request, he added, "Resurrecting him would not be impossible, though."[27]

This first attempt to resurrect Dilvish was not to be. Zelazny told Ballantine that he could not deliver the novel for another three or four years at least because he needed to write the other Dilvish short stories first. Pressed by his agent—after all, he was turning down a publisher's *request* for a novel—he then declared himself too busy with other commitments, saying the timing was wrong. He didn't want Dilvish to compete with the Amber series. "They [Amber novels] are, of course, basically fantasy, though I am using a loose science-fictional framework with them. While they are going on, I would like to keep the other stuff that I write between them somewhat removed from fantasy. So I would just as soon forget about *Nine Black Doves* for a while."[74]

Self-Directed Learning Program

Zelazny wanted his writing to evolve. He had distinguished himself with certain approaches (use of mythology, metaphor, word-games, stream of consciousness, eccentricities of style), but many other sf writers also used these techniques. He also wished to study other writing styles and broaden his general knowledge of science and history. He initiated a self-directed learning program similar to his habit of auditing courses while at college and university, believing "…a sufficient accumulation of knowledge will grow. I don't mean by one's studiously, conscientiously adding to it either. I believe that there is something like a 'critical mass' in every area of learning, & that if one considers the information in that area till one achieves that point it becomes a part of the architecture of the mind rather than a mere assemblage of facts."[8]

He told Carl Yoke: "I once mentioned in passing something called a Da Vinci syndrome, when speaking about educational theory. I believe that knowledge can hit a critical mass. I think that one's total body of knowledge—if one consciously directs its acquisition toward the building up of a full-spectrum world picture—will come to function almost autonomously as an approximation of the world itself so that the addition of any new material is no longer a simple additive process, but rather, will result in an exponential increase in the total that one possesses. It is not just a question of learning or not learning lots of stuff initially, but in deciding what should be learned and how much of it, in order to reach a critical mass as soon as possible, so that future learning, even if desultory-sounding to an outsider, will result in a great number of things being learned from the digestion of a single fact, rather than simply the fact itself."[11]

He started by reading one book in each science, aiming to read 10 books in each area. He read history, including Will and Ariel Durant's 11-volume *The Story of Civilization*, and biography or autobiography (e.g., the Marquis de Sade and Sir Laurence Olivier). "I'm normally reading about twelve books at a time. I knew [after graduating from college] that if I wanted to be a decent writer, I'd have to plug up all the holes in my education."[7]

His extensive reading explains in part why the move to full-time writing did not produce more fiction.

In 1972 he added poetry to his program. "It's the closest thing I can think of for a prose writer in the way of exercising the writing faculties as something like a daily run through a *t'ai chi* form might the body."[75] To keep current in sf, he read current works and the classics. "I try to figure out things that I don't know, and decide to read things to fill in those holes. I usually read about eight books at a time. What I like to do is read for about two hours every day. You need the material sooner or later. I read one history book, one biography, one general fiction and some classic I've never read before, a science fiction book to keep up in the area, and then usually one on the biological sciences and on the physical sciences. I try to read them each for ten or fifteen minutes, then switch to another. It stretches my attention span and also I get ideas sometimes I wouldn't get otherwise by jumping."[30]

Zelazny knew he would eventually use it all. "Everything influences me. It usually shows up transmuted or changed into other forms in my stories, but I don't think a good piece of fiction should really be pushing any particular position."[76] The afterwords and notes for "Permafrost," "24 Views of Mt. Fuji, by Hokusai," and "Unicorn Variation" demonstrate his ability to combine sources to create memorable stories and characters.

The Doors of His Face, the Lamps of His Mouth and Other Stories

Zelazny's second short story collection included two stories from *Four for Tomorrow*. "The Furies" and "The Graveyard Heart" were dropped to make room for previously uncollected stories. It is unclear how many in this "best-of" 1960s collection had been in the unsold *Satan's Tears* collection. A revised edition of this book, published 30 years later by ibooks, added the two missing stories from *Four for Tomorrow*.

Definition of Science Fiction

There is no definitive definition of science fiction. Zelazny said, "The term 'science fiction' is descriptive of a vehicle, not its contents. It is a technique, a method, an approach, a means of telling rather than a quality of that which is told. It represents a self-conscious use of the fabulous as a narrative device. As such, I see it as a continuation of that revolution in human thought broadly referred to as Romanticism. Should you wish to consider cases rather than principles, however, a piece of 'science fiction' is whatever I happen to be pointing at when I use the term."[77] He evidently borrowed from Damon Knight and others when he used the "pointing at" definition.

Distinctions:

Locus Poll novel #15: *Nine Princes in Amber*
Mythopoeic nomination for *Nine Princes in Amber*
Astounding/Analog all-time poll short fiction #5:
"A Rose for Ecclesiastes"
Astounding/Analog all-time poll short fiction #21:
"For a Breath I Tarry"

Books Published:

Jack of Shadows
The Doors of His Face, the Lamps of His Mouth and Other Stories

---1972---

Today We Choose Faces

Zelazny worked on *Today We Choose Faces* from July 1970 to March 5, 1972. The next day he wrote, "I don't know what else to say about it. I am completely numb to anything I have written for a long while after its completion—which sounds sort of like a surgical operation now that I think of it, and is not too far off."[78]

He wrote the book under contract to the paperback house Signet/NAL, which sought to serialize it and follow with a hardcover edition. They offered it to Ben Bova at *Analog*, but he turned down this "nice effort, solidly done" because "at the moment we're solidly booked with novels."[79] Editor Ejler Jakobsson of *Galaxy* also rejected it, noting, "it reads extremely well and at a headlong pace, but unfortunately, for purposes of serialization—especially in a bimonthly magazine, such as the current *Galaxy*—is, I think, put together backward. In other words, as the present version is constructed, I could find no sustaining breakoff points for the necessary minimal three installments. For me the first possible break did not occur until page 192 [of the 248 page manuscript]—which, incidentally, would have made a great opening scene for the book for our purposes, with subsequent material carefully spaced and developed through the rest."[80] Faber and Faber in the UK eventually bought the first hardcover rights.

Zelazny said that the novel involved "the last surviving member of the Mafia. He's the last assassin, and he's suddenly, in his old age, become a nice guy and the Mafia has become a sort of decent organization."[42] *Today We Choose Faces* originally contained an extended flashback, a technique that had worked well in *Lord of Light*. However, David Harwell, the editor for *Today We Choose Faces,* felt that this asked too much of the reader, so the novel runs in chronological order. Zelazny later said, "I was younger then & more in need of the money at the time & couldn't afford to argue [with] him about it. I still prefer it the way I wrote it."[8] Overall, he was pleased. "*Today We Choose Faces* is one of the few others that moved from conception to paper with hardly a twitch 'twixt ideas and fingertips, perhaps in keeping with the character(s) of the somewhat humorless, single-minded protagonist. About the only things an author can do on discovering he is heir to such a good karma are to be thankful and keep on writing."[9] In the *Writer's Voice* interview, he described this novel as one of his favorites.[81]

He recalled: "1. *Black Lamb and Grey Falcon*, by Rebecca West. No simple, direct one-for-one connection anywhere, but I kept reading this book, almost compulsively, the entire time I was writing *Faces*. I cannot think of one without thinking of the other. I took nothing intentionally and I do not see any unintended parallels, but I have a feeling there was some sort of influence, on some abstract level. This was the first time in years I had felt this way. [*Black Lamb and Grey Falcon* is a moving travelogue of Yugoslavia, written just prior to World War II.] 2. Part I originally was to occur as a flashback between parts II and III, but this was later changed. The assault on Styler's citadel was the first thing that came to me about this book; i.e., it preceded theme, plot, setting, secondary characters. 3. The "feel" of the House was a thing I had had with me for years, while working in one of the three largest government buildings in the world. Also, those damned telephones.

"I am still fairly close to this one, so it is difficult to be objective. I can only say that I am pleased with the tightness of the plot, and if I had the whole thing to do over again I would catch the typo in the second line on the last page [honor misspelled as honer, a typo that was not in the manuscript]."[38] He later acknowledged another influence: "I do feel that the shadow of Jack fell upon the protagonist of *Today We Choose Faces*."[29]

Zelazny played with the names. The protagonist is Angelo di Negri ("Black Angel"); his clones have variations of that name: Black, Lange (anagram of angel), Jordan (the angel from the movie *Here Comes Mister Jordan*),[82] Gene (from Thomas Wolfe's *Look Homeward, Angel*),[82] Karab (a pun on cherub),[82] Engel (German for angel), Serafis (seraph is the highest order of angels), Winkel (German for angle, an anagram of angel), Winton (Teutonic for valiant protector), Hinkley (one who is devoted to God), Davis (a play on devas, angelic beings), and Jenkins (God's Grace; alternatively, Jenkin was a character in H. P. Lovecraft's Cthulhu Mythos who took messages to the devil). Styler's name alludes to one who alters things to suit their taste—at the novel's resolution, di Negri realizes that Styler has "used" him to fashion humanity's course. Though Zelazny proclaimed "honer" a typo, it remained uncorrected in later editions or printings. It was either an intentional pun or a serendipitous typo Zelazny claimed as his own. A honer uses a whetstone to sharpen a tool, and the tool to fashion something to more precise dimensions.

Zelazny's fusion of multiple clones into one nexus caused him to lose track of who was who and to become uncertain whether "I" or "he" was the correct pronoun for that individual's past selves. Extensive correspondence with the editor resolved these inconsistencies.[83–88] Parts of the story hinted that Black was a clone who had gone missing years before, but Zelazny said that di Negri did not create Black. "Existing in this state [mind digitized, body dead], Styler was able to manipulate the robots which obtained the tissue samples and cloned the original Mister Black."[85,86]

Zelazny considered quoting from Mark Van Doren's poem *Now the Sky* as the novel's preface. One choice was, "The sky was then a room, with people going || Faithfully to and fro, and beasts enchained." He also considered, "There is a game for players still to play, || Pretending that the board was never lost. || But still the painted counters will decay, || And knowledge sit along to count the cost." However, "it would simply & truly have been too much of a wrenching out of context to use any of them that way, since the poem itself just isn't to my point, however much I like its imagery. So…I didn't. That's all. Just thought I'd mention it in passing."[89] He dedicated the book "To Philip K. Dick, Electric Shepherd."

Published as a paperback original by Signet, it was overlooked by many readers and unjustly overshadowed by *To Die in Italbar* from Doubleday. *To Die in Italbar* ranked #8 on the 1974 Locus Poll for novel while *Today We Choose Faces* came in at #9.

The Guilford Gafia

Zelazny participated in several writers' workshops. In 1972 he joined a group of writers who gathered in the Guilford Manor, an old Baltimore mansion owned by Jack C. (Jay) Haldeman II; their marathon sessions could span a week or more. Participants included Joe Haldeman, Gardner Dozois, George Alec Effinger, Ted White, Jack Dann, Bill Nabors, and Tom Monteleone. Jack Dann said, "we would meet a few times a year to workshop our stories, drink, talk the talk…and see Roger Zelazny. We called ourselves The Guilford Gafia, a play on The Milford Mafia (which was what some SFWA members were calling the group of writers who wrote stories for Damon Knight's *Orbit* series and attended the Milford Writers Workshop at Damon and Kate Wilhelm's old mansion in Milford, Pennsylvania)."[90] Gafia is itself an acronym for "Get Away From It All," a well-known phrase in sf circles.

Zelazny considered his involvement in the Guilford Gafia peripheral. "Meeting in the Guilford Manor, a place reminiscent of the crowded Gormenghast with cats, the G.G. was a writing group that seemed to exist just at the periphery of chaos or perhaps even a little nearer. Though I was not a member, I lived nearby and was occasionally bewildered by the strange lights and sounds, puzzled at the function of the shark's brain in formaldehyde with a room all to itself, and enjoyably attracted by late-night invitations to artichoke cookouts."[91] This explains his dedication of *The Hand of Oberon* to "Jay Haldeman, of fellowship and artichokes." Joe Haldeman remembered, "one GG meeting, Jay was upset because it was his thirtieth birthday, and he was officially old. Ron Bounds got him an actual case of artichokes from California, and I think Roger was there when it was delivered. Of course we cooked a bunch of them."[92]

Zelazny advised the budding writers as mentor and friend. Jack Dann recalled that "although Roger didn't attend the workshops, he was certainly a member. Although he was shy and quiet and unassuming and would have chuckled over this description—he was the grand old man of the workshop. We would work like hell for a weekend, excoriate each other with the most constructive of constructive criticism, but there was always an incentive to survive: at the end of it all would be 'the party,' and at the party would be Roger. It was 1972. I was twenty-seven years old and had sold two or three stories. Gardner had brought me to Guilford, had introduced me to all these new writers, and there I was on a Sunday night sitting around with Roger Zelazny. What could be better? Here was the man who had written 'The Doors of His Face, the Lamps of His Mouth,' 'A Rose for Ecclesiastes,' 'For a Breath I Tarry,' *Isle of the Dead, The Dream Master, This Immortal.*"[90]

The Guilford Gafia became published writers and—in several instances—award-winning authors and editors. Despite their shared rite of passage, their styles remained quite diverse. Zelazny noted that "the most impressive thing about that group is that everyone involved has become a well-known writer…everyone in the group turned out to write quite differently from everyone else in the group, and there is absolutely no literary scenery visible."[91] These meetings produced one of Joe Haldeman's favorite memories of Roger Zelazny. "One time we had a GG that went about ten days, everybody workshopping novels. At the end of that grueling period, we blew off steam with a strange card game/writing exercise. There were seven of us, and we had a poker table with six spaces. We started playing poker for matchsticks, using a pornographic deck that Ron Bounds had just brought back from Germany.

"We had a 'hot typewriter' going, attempting to write a short porn novel in one night. When a person had written one page, he could tap anyone on the shoulder and take his space at the table, the selectee having to retire to the typewriter and do at least one page of the novel, entitled *The Trouble with Smegma*. I think Roger did a segment about a German Shepherd so troubled by what she had done that she jumped out of a high-rise apartment window, with the horny viewpoint character passionately clinging to her.

"I don't know what ever became of the manuscript. Gardner claims he had it, but it crawled away under its own power."[92]

Myths Abandoned

By 1972 Zelazny had largely dropped mythology from his writing. "Science fiction has pushed ahead and left some things behind. In changing, the science fiction world has changed me. I did sort of have to get rid of my gods. When I reached self-parody of myself, I had to stop.

"I have not resolved in my own mind the manner in which I will deal with mythological material in the future. I would have to find a different way of using it.

"My mythological material has been invaded by the light."[93]

He did return to myths and legends from time to time, notably in *Eye of Cat* (Navajo mythology), "The Naked Matador" (Jason and the Argonauts), "The Last Defender of Camelot" (Arthurian legend), "Fire and/or Ice" (Norse mythology), and "24 Views of Mt. Fuji, by Hokusai" (Japanese mythology).

Apollo Launches

Zelazny's science fiction celebrity had its benefits. He watched the Apollo 14 launch from the press stand as an invited guest. He observed Apollo 15 from Melbourne Beach. By the Apollo 17 launch, there was a change. He joked, "I did not think I could pass Devin off as a journalist, even for *The Children's Digest*." So he settled for watching it, together with wife Judy and son Devin, about 30 miles downrange "on a deck overlooking the ocean, behind a club called *The Casino*." He said it was "a fantastic experience at close range, but is even more persistent if you've backed off a bit… Ball of fire, yes. But it kept intensifying until the effect was like a sunrise coming from the wrong direction. When it rose, it cast an eerie, yellowish light over half the ocean. Devin watched, and we had it in sight for almost seven minutes. We saw the separation and followed it through the third-stage burnout. About two and a half minutes after ignition, the sound waves reached us. Muted, but palpable."[94] In May 1972 at Marcon VII where Zelazny was Guest of Honor, Roger and Judy Zelazny participated in a panel discussion with Dannie Plachta and Banks Mebane about their experiences, "discoursing on the delights and delirium of Cape Kennedy during an Apollo launch."[95]

The lengthy Apollo countdowns—and the inevitable delays— prompted Zelazny to investigate the countdown's origin. Fellow writer Willy Ley explained that the countdown hadn't come from early rocket launches in Germany; they'd used a simple "Ready, set, fire!" Science fiction had been the source. "It turned out to have been first used in Fritz Lang's movie *Frau in Mond,* back in the '20's—where a 10-second countdown had been flashed on the screen... Speculating as to whether the countdown had been based on some early artillery practice, he [Willy Ley] wrote to Lang and asked him. Lang had just dreamed it up, however, and thought that it would make for a good dramatic effect. Thus do the arts fertilize, or something."[94]

Distinctions:

Hugo nomination for novel *Jack of Shadows*
Locus Poll novel #4: *Jack of Shadows*
Prix Apollo for novel *Isle of the Dead*

Book Published:

The Guns of Avalon

---1973---

Deus Irae Revisited

Deus Irae progressed erratically. In an interview at Balticon on February 19, 1973, Zelazny said, "I'm doing a novel on and off with Phil Dick. My own stuff can be quite plastic and if I don't like the last six pages, I can throw it out. When it comes to getting sections of work from someone else, I am loath to set hands on someone else's prose and tend to adapt my own style around it."[96]

Later that year, he wrote to Phil Dick, "I have been working on *Deus Irae*..." He went on to describe circumstances, such as his father-in-law's hospitalization and his teaching at the Indiana University Writers Conference, which interfered with his writing. "All of which is to say, again, that I am sorry over the delay, [the novel] has not been completely absent from my thoughts... May this [letter] find your life passed into a phase of new brightness."[97]

To Die in Italbar Revisited

"I am not over-fond of it for a variety of complicated reasons not really worth detailing,"[94] but the time had come for Zelazny to exhume *To Die in Italbar*. He completed revisions by May 26, 1972, noting to his agent, "it is longer and contains about 25% new material."[98] In November he added a dedication at his editor's suggestion.[99] *To Die in Italbar* finally appeared in 1973 as a Doubleday hardcover. Prior to the Doubleday publication, *Galaxy/If* declined to serialize it. *Galaxy* Editor Ejler Jakobsson said, "The book is exquisitely written and many of the concepts and characterizations are strong and intriguing and in broad outline the conflict is superbly conceived. Thematically, however, it seems too broken up for effective serialization—I tried several ways to overcome the problem, including running it in two parts, which always puts a strain on the budget, but nothing worked for me."[100]

In an interview on September 9, 1974, Zelazny said, "I wrote [*To Die in Italbar*] around five years ago and only recently got around to polishing it up for publication." That polishing up included a cameo of Francis Sandow from *Isle of the Dead* in order to "jazz up" the novel.[10] Ultimately, however, he bemoaned the book's publication. "If I could kill off one book it would be *To Die in Italbar*. I wrote that in a hurry to make some money after I quit my job."[12] "I'll admit [*To Die in Italbar*] is a weak one and let it go at that."[101] Nevertheless, Zelazny's name was enough to ensure that it sold well in hardcover and paperback and ranked well on the 1974 Locus Poll.

Despite general agreement that *To Die in Italbar* was Zelazny's worst solo novel, there was an apparent dissenting view. The back cover of a Hebrew edition of *To Die in Italbar* claimed, "Maryland University Science Fiction Society determined that *To Die in Italbar* is the best sci fi book written between 1970–1975."[102] The society may have been the Baltimore Science Fiction Society or the John Hopkins Science Fiction Association, but whether such praise came from either group cannot be confirmed.

Musings on the Writing Process

Zelazny subconsciously incorporated knowledge, experience, and technique. "My mind is driving…I am going to write a scene that involves a man and a woman having an argument. It is going to end on a bitter note, he is going to go off and get drunk, she is going to go off and have an affair with his best friend. But all the little nuances which would go into it, the little hints, the gestures, the description of the room, these are things which I don't necessarily want to have in my mind consciously until the moment comes when I want to use them."[96]

He compared writing to tennis: "…each motion/position/pressure/etc. of hand/wrist/arm/etc. required individual attention while the entire act was being learned; yet the total movement must take only an instant when playing the game. In other words, in writing as well as learned physical activity you intentionally transform a greater number of separate items into a single reflex so that you can do it without thinking much about the process itself, keeping your mind free for overall strategy. Initially, one does this mainly with the mechanical aspects of writing, the sheer business of keeping the prose interesting and grammatically sound. Continuing from there…the more you write the more things you come to entrust to the unconscious at a reflex level…The reflex has been extended to the point that you have begun tapping deeper levels of your mind rather than just flexing surface ingenuity, down there where your whole world picture is stored…You translate your thinking into words and to the reader it is one quick apparent movement, like a tennis stroke."[11]

Not always conscious while writing of what drove a story, he recognized some influences when the piece was done. "It's the nature of the unconscious-type plotting approach I use. I let a story take form, quite often, below decks. I begin writing when I feel the story is in existence. It's just a matter of my evoking it. Afterwards, I can look back at it and can see those earlier elements also."[103]

When his muse took over, everything else was secondary. Carl Yoke said, "the stories he wrote quite literally moved into and occupied his mind, pushing everything into the background. Writing was his purpose in life, his passion. It always had been. And stories took him another world away."[104]

Sometimes Zelazny's muse placed him and his companions in danger. In February 1965, with Yoke in the back seat and their wives beside them, Zelazny turned his car onto the Rapid Transit tracks that ran through Shaker Square and on into Cleveland. "There we were in the middle of a snowstorm bumping along train tracks at a quarter to midnight. Roger was puzzled. I could see his frown in the rear view mirror...he had no idea what was wrong."[104] A few minutes of terror ensued. The women screamed, and Yoke hollered instructions until Zelazny steered back onto the street. Apologizing, Zelazny admitted that he'd been plotting a story. He hadn't even seen the tracks.[104,105] This was not an isolated incident; Yoke had nearly been killed several times due to Zelazny's distracted driving. On another occasion, Zelazny drove Yoke around a railroad barrier and stalled his car on the tracks in front of an approaching train.[106] And he seriously injured his fiancée Sharon Steberl in a 1964 accident. Trent Zelazny agreed with Yoke—"Very much so, yes"—that his dad had been a terrible driver.[55,107]

Concerning characterization, Zelazny said, "Gore Vidal once said that every author has a cast of characters like a stock company, and that they keep recurring in his material at different ages perhaps, or different walks of life, but they're basically the same troupe of actors. I agree with that almost 80 percent. I like to think I occasionally hire a new actor, get rid of an older one, and let the actors themselves mature, change."[103] Zelazny drew criticism for using a stock protagonist in many of his early novels: a long-lived or immortal male, well educated, witty, and either a poet or a musician. However, Francis Sandow, Conrad the Kallikanzaros, Jack of Shadows, and Corwin of Amber prove to be quite different, despite their long lives.

Zelazny's characters evolved. "I can't much tolerate a story in which characters are completely black and white, or persons who do things for the wrong reasons. I like to see characters change in a story and not come out the same person as at the beginning."[93] He knew, though, that real people didn't always change. "Life itself is not the catastrophe-ridden thing life is in fiction. In real life, many people go through crises and come out the same person they were."[93]

His lack of formal instruction in writing occasionally tripped him up. At one writer's conference, he described how he initially withheld information to create suspense and to avoid lengthy exposition. Teaching Assistant Phyllis Eisenstein asked him to relate that concept to the narrative hook. "I recall thinking about it as hard as I could for several seconds, then finally asked her, 'Okay, what the hell's a narrative hook?' She thought I was joking. I wasn't. I'd been writing professionally for something like 12 years at that point."[8] Zelazny had developed his technique through trial and error, but that incident prompted him to add books on creative writing to his reading list.

He counseled writers, "The best piece of advice I know to give a person who wants to write professionally is quite mundane: namely, viz., specifically & to wit—Write something every day. Whether you feel like it or not. Especially when you don't. Train yourself to write regardless of your mood. On a daily basis. No matter what comes out."[108]

Doorways in the Sand

Zelazny enjoyed writing *Doorways in the Sand*. It was the first of a trio of novels under a new contract with Berkley/Putnam after they had rejected *The Dead Man's Brother*. He wrote to Henry Morrison, "I am well beyond the halfway point, it is going smoothly, and I think it is going to be one of my better ones."[23] He finished *Doorways in the Sand* at 5:30 a.m. on May 24, 1973, and immediately wrote to Dannie Plachta. "It is done!…I am happy with *Doorways*, too. It took me over twice as long as I had intended and was ten times as difficult to write as I had envisaged. But it was worth it. I really like it. I think it is going to be one of my better pieces."[109] There was only one problem; baby Devin woke for the day just as Zelazny finally tried to sleep.

He later wrote to a fanzine, "Busy summer…Just back from Ohio, where the flooding occurred, and into the third Amber book. I finished one this summer that I rather like—*Doorways in the Sand*."[38] To Henry Morrison he said, "It took longer and was harder to write than I thought it would, but it was worth it to me. I learned a lot doing it, and I am happy with this book."[110] First publication was in the June–August 1975 issues of *Analog*.

Doorways in the Sand was science fiction. "I was getting tired of having all my stuff taken as fantasy or near fantasy, so I decided to do a straight science fiction story. I was kind of bored with the idea of doing a straight science fiction story in a standard way, so I decided to do some structural experiments with the way the chapters were put together."[111] "*Doorways in the Sand* is a pet book of mine because it's the first humorous book I wrote, and also because I decided I would play these outrageous tricks with flashbacks. I was amusing myself by writing the book, and when I was finished with it I said, 'Hey, I really like this'."[112] "*Doorways in the Sand* represents a great deal of authorial pleasure. It was one of those books that began with a congenial idea, was a fun piece to plot and gave me all sorts of kicks in the writing. Also, the finished product was exactly what I'd desired. They don't all go such a route and turn out this way."[9] "Once I knew what the story was to be, I ran it, a piece at a time, through a flash-back machine, using the suspense-heightening flashback trick so frequently and predictably that the practice intentionally parodied the device itself."[113] Some readers disliked the flashbacks, but others called it his best novel. It was a finalist for the Hugo, Nebula, and Locus Awards in 1976, and the American Library Association cited it as one of the Best Books for Young Adults.

Berkley/Putnam rejected the novel, as they had *The Dead Man's Brother*. Zelazny severed relations with them. Morrison sent *Doorways* to other publishers, including Harper & Row, NAL, and Evans. The editor at Harper & Row "enjoyed it thoroughly" but sent it back because "people are looking for another *Lord of Light* from Zelazny, and not something as simply entertaining as this is."[114] She eventually asked Morrison to return it to her and published it.

The novel reflects Zelazny's experimentation. "In every book I have written to date, I have attempted something different—a structural effect, a particular characterization, a narrative or stylistic effect—which I have not used previously. It always involves what I consider my weak points as a writer, rather than my strong points. These efforts are for the purpose of improving my skills and abilities... What I am trying to say is I operate under a continuing need to experiment, and the nature of experimenting requires that at least part of the time I write from weakness... I probably learned more from writing [*Creatures of Light and Darkness*] than any other book."[33]

He acknowledged that protagonist Fred Cassidy resembled him: "a perpetual student of anything handy, constantly procrastinating, ever-ready to take advantage of a good thing and willing to go to great lengths and heights for a little solitude. Bon voyage, *Titanic*..."[9]

Zelazny's agent suggested that he write some juveniles. He declined for two reasons. "One is that I have been studying in a number of areas in and about the sciences for the past couple of years, so that I have been able to work up some fairly complex ideas that I would like to get into my future books. These should go nicely in my regular writings but I fear they would be overly complicated for the juvenile market. The other is similar, and probably even more to the point, with respect to the stylistic stuff that I want to try. I believe that I will need the elbow room of nominally adult books, as I want to keep working with more sophisticated story structures and narrative techniques, at least for a couple more years."[115]

Writing Habits

Zelazny's writing habits puzzled interviewers and readers. "I do not like to write at a desk. I have never been able to do much in the classic underwood observa position. I write in a semi-reclined position with my feet elevated and the typewriter on my lap. My favorite typewriter for this purpose is my Remington portable."[33] The typewriter that his father bought him in the 1950s saw occasional use, but he didn't like its Elite font.

Zelazny smoked, and so did many of his early characters. An interviewer said, "One thing that bugs the hell out of me about your characters is that they smoke too damn much."[101] Zelazny explained, "My characters smoked in most of my early stories because whenever I was momentarily stuck in the course of a narrative I would light a cigarette. My usual reaction was then to transfer it. 'Of course,' I would think, 'He lit a cigarette.'"[8] After twenty-four years he quit, partly to improve his breathing for martial arts training. Once he stopped smoking, his characters stopped, too. He briefly returned to smoking later, sharing Salems and Winstons with his teenage son Trent.[55]

He continued to write near-final drafts on the first pass. He used the back of any paper at hand: his own manuscripts, manuscripts sent to him for commentary, mail advertisements, financial reports, and his kids' school reports. If it was 8.5 x 11 inches, white or light-colored, and had one clean side, he used it. He typed *Bridge of Ashes* on the back of (among other things) earlier drafts of *To Die in Italbar*. *Doorways in the Sand* used pages from *The Dead Man's Brother*. 1985's *Ghostwheel* (later retitled *Blood of Amber*) used the backs of Zelazny's "Alien Speedway: Outline," "Quest's End" and "The Naked Matador;" Meghan Lindholm's *Wizard of the Pigeons*, C. J. Cherryh's *Merovingen*, Stephen Boyett's *Ariel*, Judith Tarr's *Isle of Glass*, a New Mexico company's bankruptcy documents, brochures for a karate championship, preparatory school and summer camp announcements, and so forth.[116] *Ghostwheel* also bears a tantalizing fragment of Zelazny's lost essay "Sticking Point" which begins by quoting J. D. Salinger's "Teddy":

> "Are you a poet?" he asked.
> "A poet?" Nicholson said. "Lord, no. Alas, no. Why do you ask?"
> "I don't know. Poets are always taking the weather so personally. They're always sticking their emotions into things that have no emotions."[116,117]

Zelazny used a portable typewriter when traveling or wrote longhand on yellow legal-sized pads. Once a manuscript was complete, he or his assistant (Nancy Applegate for many years) typed a final version with minor revisions, usually making two carbon copies. Many original manuscripts available to university archives and collectors consisted of two drafts, the motley papers of the first and a carbon copy of the last. "I still don't do that much rewriting. I do a lot of composition in my head, and when I do it at the keys, the sentences are pretty much in the order they appear in the book. I wrote *Doorways in the Sand* and *Jack of Shadows* first draft, no rewrite."[118]

How long did it take him to compose a first draft? "I don't really know. I pay very little attention to time when I am not writing and even less when I am writing. But non-fiction seems to come faster because I am not working with a plot."[33]

Popularity

Some critics contended that he no longer produced as high-quality, innovative work as he had in the 1960s, but Zelazny's popularity continued to grow. The 1973 *Locus* poll named him #8 all-time favorite author.

Distinctions:

> Locus Poll novel #9: *The Guns of Avalon*
> Mythopoeic nomination for *The Guns of Avalon*
> Locus Poll #8 all-time favorite author

Books Published:

Today We Choose Faces
To Die in Italbar

---1974---

More Awards and Worldcon Guest of Honor

Zelazny was Guest of Honor at U.S. conventions and around the globe (Melbourne, Hong Kong, Moscow, Paris, Auckland, Toronto).

In 1974 he was Guest of Honor at Discon II, the World Science Fiction Convention in Washington, DC. Intended to honor an author's entire career, Worldcon GOH is one of the science fiction and fantasy field's highest distinctions. Zelazny's work had only appeared for a dozen years. While many fans considered the award almost unprecedented for a writer at such an early stage, it was clear to Discon II's organizers that he had earned that honor.

Fans appreciated his amiable approachability and loved his humorous speeches. Colleagues and fans commonly remarked that they had never met a friendlier man and had never heard him curse or utter an unkind word about anyone. (At Torcon 3, George R. R. Martin and Howard Waldrop asserted that "Zelazny once got so angry he said '*darn*.'"[119] But at Boskone 46, Melinda Snodgrass recalled that Zelazny said "damn" and threw his pipe across the room upon hearing that Waldrop's story in *Wild Cards* invalidated the school-day timeline required for Zelazny's contribution, "The Sleeper."[120]) Beginning in the 1960s Judy accompanied him to conventions, bringing the children once they were old enough to travel.[95,121–123] Devin Zelazny was a few months short of his third birthday when he attended the 1974 Worldcon; he amused the crowd with "an incredibly rude interruption" of the toastmaster's speech upon hearing his own name mentioned.[123]

At this convention a chapbook of Zelazny's poetry, *Poems,* was released in a 1,000-copy limited edition. Jack Gaughan illustrated many of the poems. Most came from *Chisel in the Sky,* the unpublished collection that didn't win the Yale competition in the early 1960s. Publication of the chapbook rekindled his interest in poetry. He planned to have a proper book of poetry published eventually.

Sign of the Unicorn

Demand for new Amber novels increased. Zelazny resumed the project after completing *Today We Choose Faces*.[110] In August 1973, before starting *Sign of the Unicorn*, he said, "First, it is going to be an almost static book, from a temporal standpoint; i.e., not too much is really going to happen to advance what was begun in the first two books, but a lot is going to happen otherwise—if I can handle this just right. I intend pretty much to freeze the overall action now, in order to provide necessary background I couldn't get in sooner but will need later. The book will open no more than a week after Corwin's return to Amber. The opening involves the death of Caine (offstage), under such circumstances that Corwin must be the one to find the body... Gradually, as Corwin learns more and more of what transpired in his absence, he becomes convinced that, above and beyond his curse, everything is linked—their father's absence, the black road, Dara's strange nature and behavior, Brand's absence, Caine's murder—and the upshot of it all is that there must be a traitor, one of the royal family itself, one who has kept his hand carefully hidden thus far, plotting meticulously and in league with other forces... I cannot tell you more without damaging my own plotting processes, which are eccentric."[124]

Sign of the Unicorn went into production at Doubleday on July 17, 1974,[125] probably the last novel he finished in Baltimore. *Galaxy* serialized it in January through March 1975 before its release as a Doubleday hardcover.

Alcohol

Writer John Brady had interviewed Zelazny for *Writer's Voice* in 1973. Now freelancing for *Rolling Stone*, he asked Zelazny to complete a "questionnaire on writers & drinking." "As I recall from our talks at the Indiana Writers Conference, your drinking—if it all—is quite modest."[126] Zelazny, away and on deadline, couldn't immediately reply. Eventually he wrote, "Nothing Rabelaisian to report, or like that. [French Renaissance writer François Rabelais famously wrote "I drink for the thirst to come."] The closest a few of my heavier drinking friends have come to providing a rationale for lots of elbow bending is that they don't want a pick-me-up so much as a put-me-down. They say they get quite elated and keyed up by a good stretch of writing and actually want something in the nature of a depressant afterwards…And that's about the only thing I can think of to pass along."[127]

Carl Yoke recalled that Zelazny had experienced a grand mal seizure in front of the Washington Monument, shortly after moving to Baltimore. An off-duty FBI officer rendered first aid and called an ambulance. Zelazny told most people who learned of this event that he had epilepsy. He told Yoke that the seizure was due to alcohol poisoning, following a significant drinking binge. But Yoke was uncertain—as he put it, "Roger often told 'compassionate' lies if he thought someone he cared about might be critical of him."[14] Joe Haldeman witnessed another seizure in 1971 (see Haldeman's "The Prince of Amber," in volume 4). Two seizures suggest a diagnosis of epilepsy, but Zelazny blamed the episode on fatigue and overindulgence.

Like his colleagues, Zelazny indulged at conventions. His friend Ron Bounds recalled that Zelazny occasionally attended meetings of the Baltimore Science Fiction Society "and talked and laughed and joked and drank the hard stuff just like the rest of us…He went also to East Coast and Midwest SF cons with the rest of us, where he could always be found in the bar, talking far into the night and trying to drink Dannie Plachta under the table."[128] Zelazny called himself "basically a wine and beer drinker" and admitted in an interview that he'd been deliberately "half-drunk on beer" most evenings that he wrote "Damnation Alley."[129,130]

His son Trent said, "I remember many occasions in which my father would come out of his office, take a shot or two (usually Wild Turkey), then go back down to work."[55]

Distinctions:

Worldcon Guest of Honor, Discon II, Washington, DC.
Locus Poll novel #8: *To Die in Italbar*
Locus Poll novel #9: *Today We Choose Faces*
Locus Poll novella #13: *"'Kjwalll'kje'k'koothaïlll'kje'k"*

Book Published:

Poems

References

A note about the format of references:

JOURNALS/MAGAZINES/FANZINES
Author. Title of article. *Journal Name.* Year; Volume (Issue Number [#Whole Number and/or Month]): pages.

BOOK SECTIONS
Author. Title of article. In: Editor. *Book Title.* City, State: Publisher, Year: pages.

WHOLE BOOKS
Author. *Book Title.* City, State: Publisher, Year.

CORRESPONDENCE
Author. Letter/Email to recipient, date.

INTERNET RESOURCES
Author. Title. Year created. URL. Dated accessed.

1. Zelazny, Roger. *The Last Defender of Camelot.* New York, NY: Pocket Books, 1980.
2. Zelazny, Roger. Letter to Mack Reynolds dated May 21, 1969.
3. Zelazny, Roger. Introduction. In: Zelazny, Roger, Greenberg, Martin Harry, eds. *Wheel of Fortune.* New York, NY: AvoNova, 1995: p 1–4.
4. Zelazny, Roger. Letter to Philip José Farmer dated May 29, 1972.
5. Elliott, Elton. Interview with Roger Zelazny. *Science Fiction Review* 1990; 1 (2 [Summer]): p 35–38.
6. Zelazny, Roger. An Interview with Roger Zelazny [self-interview]. In: Walker, Paul, ed. *Speaking of Science Fiction.* Ordell, NJ: Luna Publications, 1978: p 78–84.
7. Campbell, Andrew. Building a Universe. *Reserve, Supplement to CWRU Magazine* 1990; (August): p 10–13.
8. Lindskold, Jane M. *Roger Zelazny.* New York, NY: Twayne Publishers, 1993.
9. Zelazny, Roger. *The Illustrated Roger Zelazny.* New York, NY: Baronet, 1978.
10. Schweitzer, Darrell. Roger Zelazny Answers Questions. *Procrastination* 1977; (13 [November]): p 25–26.
11. Yoke, Carl B. *Roger Zelazny: Starmont Reader's Guide 2.* West Linn, OR: Starmont House, 1979.
12. Giron, Dannette L. Roger Zelazny. *Connotations* 1992; 2 (3 [Fall]): p 2–3.
13. Zelazny, Roger. Letter to Paul Walker dated March 18, 1972.
14. Yoke, Carl B. Email to Dr. Christopher Kovacs dated January 30, 2008.
15. Cleaver, Diane. Letter to Henry Morrison dated October 18, 1973.
16. Sanders, Joseph L. *Roger Zelazny: A Primary and Secondary Bibliography.* Boston, MA: G. K. Hall, 1980.
17. Cowper, Richard. A Rose is a Rose is a Rose…In Search of Roger Zelazny. *Foundation* 1977; (11/12 [March]): p 142–147.

"...And Call Me Roger" ❖ Part 3 541

18. Clark, Jeff. What is Happening to Roger Zelazny? *Phantasmicom* 1974; (11 [May]): p 60–62.
19. Zelazny, Roger. A Burnt-Out Case? *SF Commentary* 1978; (54 [November]): p 22–28.
20. Holmberg, John-Henri. A Love Letter. *Forum International* 1969; (1 [July]): p 25–28.
21. Kelly, Patrick. How About This? Roger Zelazny. *Phantasmicom* 1970; (2 [Winter]): p 9–16.
22. Zelazny, Roger. Letter to Henry Morrison dated February 21, 1973.
23. Zelazny, Roger. Letter to Henry Morrison dated March 4, 1973.
24. Chalker, Jack L.; Owings, Mark. Science Fiction-Fantasy Publishers, Supplement 1, June 1991–June 1993: Mirage Press, 1993.
25. Zelazny, Roger. Roger Zelazny Speaks on Roger Zelazny. *Black Oracle* 1969; (1 [March]): p 9–10.
26. Zelazny, Roger. Letter to Craig Williamson dated August 14, 1969.
27. Zelazny, Roger. Letter to Henry Morrison dated March 30, 1971.
28. Walker, Paul. Author's Choice. *Vector* 1973; (65 [May–June]): p 42–44.
29. Zelazny, Roger. Foreword. *Jack of Shadows*. New York, NY: Signet Press, 1989: p 5–8.
30. Vance, Michael; Eads, Bill. Roger Zelazny: The New Wave King of Science Fiction. *Media Sight* 1984; 3 (1): p 39–42.
31. Zelazny, Roger. Jack of Shadows (1st of 2 Parts). *The Magazine of Fantasy & Science Fiction* 1971; 41 (1 [#242 July]): p 5–59.
32. Zelazny, Roger. *Jack of Shadows*. New York, NY: Walker, 1971.
33. Smith, Jeffrey D. Up Against The Wall: Roger Zelazny. *Phantasmicom* 1972; (10 [November]): p 14–18.
34. Zelazny, Roger. The Road to Amber. *Kolvir* 1980; (Heroic Fiction Issue): p 9–11.
35. Becker, Matthew. Interview. *Alternities* 1981; (6 [Summer]): p 24–31.
36. Zelazny, Roger. Letter to Doubleday Editor Diane Cleaver dated November 17, 1971.
37. Zelazny, Roger. "When it Comes it's Wonderful": Art Versus Craft in Writing. In: Setzer, Steve, Parkin, Marny K., eds. *Deep Thoughts: Proceedings of Life, the Universe and Everything XII, February 16–19, 1994*. Provo, Utah: LTU&E, 1995: p 113–129.
38. Smith, Jeffrey D.; Geis, Richard E. Up Against The Wall: Roger Zelazny. *Alien Critic* 1973; (7 [November]): p 35–43.
39. Zelazny, Roger. Introduction. In: Randall, Neil, ed. *Combat Command in the World of Roger Zelazny's Nine Princes in Amber: The Black Road War* New York, NY: Ace, 1988: p v–ix.
40. Zelazny, Roger. Letter to Doubleday Editor Lawrence P. Ashmead dated May 11, 1966.
41. Westblom, Ulf. An Interview with Roger Zelazny. *Mentat* 1969; (11 [May]): p 200–203.
42. Kelly, Patrick. How About This? Roger Zelazny. *Phantasmicom* 1971; (5 [Winter]): p 10–14.
43. Zelazny, Roger. Letter to Henry Morrison dated June 28, 1971.
44. Hunter, Stephen. The Universe: R. Zelazny, Owner. *Phantasmicom* 1972; (10 [November]): p 8–13.
45. Evans, Joni. Letter to Henry Morrison dated March 29, 1973.
46. Cleaver, Diane. Letter to Henry Morrison dated May 2, 1972.
47. [No Last Name], Bank. Letter to Henry Morrison dated January 9, 1973.

48. Morrison, Henry. Letter to Roger Zelazny dated April 25, 1973.
49. Zelazny, Roger. Letter to Henry Morrison dated April 30, 1973.
50. Scott, Deborah. Letter to Roger Zelazny dated October 7, 1975.
51. Zelazny, Roger. Letter to Henry Morrison dated October 10, 1975.
52. Zelazny, Trent. *The Dead Man's Brother*: An Afterword. In: Zelazny, Roger, ed. *The Dead Man's Brother*. New York, NY: Hard Case Crime, 2009: p 255–258.
53. Morrison, Henry. Letter to Roger Zelazny dated July 29, 1971.
54. Zelazny, Roger. An Interview with Roger Zelazny [self-interview]. *Luna Monthly* 1972; (43 [December]): p 1–3.
55. Zelazny, Trent. Email to Dr. Christopher Kovacs dated January 11, 2008.
56. Thompson, W.B. Interview: Roger Zelazny. *Future Life* 1981; (25 [March]): p 40–42.
57. Flynn, Reverend Joseph R. Letter to Roger Zelazny dated April 23, 1973.
58. Zelazny, Roger. Letter to Reverend Joseph R. Flynn dated May 4, 1973.
59. Glantz, Steven. Letter to Doubleday dated May 22, 1978.
60. Zelazny, Roger. Letter to Steven Glantz dated July 22, 1978.
61. Zelazny, Roger. Letter to Paul Walker dated March 10, 1972.
62. Morrison, Henry. Letter to Roger Zelazny dated March 11, 1971.
63. Zelazny, Roger. Letter to Ned Brooks dated June 6, 1965.
64. Zelazny, Roger. Letter to Jerry dated September 19, 1973.
65. Cohen, Sol. Letter to Roger Zelazny dated July 26, 1966.
66. Ross, Joe. Letter to Roger Zelazny dated July 15, 1965.
67. Ross, Joe. Letter to Roger Zelazny dated April 24, 1966.
68. Morrison, Henry. Letter to Roger Zelazny dated April 23, 1968.
69. Morrison, Henry. Letter to Roger Zelazny dated May 1, 1968.
70. Morrison, Henry. Letter to Roger Zelazny dated May 20, 1968.
71. Morrison, Henry. Letter to Roger Zelazny dated May 17, 1968.
72. Ashley, Mike. *Transformations: The Story of the Science Fiction Magazines from 1950 to 1970*. Liverpool, UK: Liverpool University Press, 2005.
73. Zelazny, Roger. Introduction to "The Bells of Shoredan". *Alternities* 1981; (6 [Summer]): p 4.
74. Zelazny, Roger. Letter to Henry Morrison dated July 31, 1972.
75. Zelazny, Roger. An Exorcism of Sorts. In: Zelazny, Roger, ed. *Frost & Fire*. New York, NY: William Morrow, 1989: p 11–15.
76. Zelazny, Roger. Authorgraphs — an Interview with Roger Zelazny. *Worlds of If* 1969; 19 (1 [January]): p 161.
77. Zelazny, Roger. Letter to Susan Hoglind dated April 29, 1971.
78. Zelazny, Roger. Letter from Roger Zelazny to Victor dated March 6, 1972.
79. Bova, Ben. Letter to Henry Morrison dated April 3, 1972.
80. Jakobsson, Ejler. Letter to Henry Morrison dated March 20, 1972.
81. Brady, John. *Writing Science Fiction: Roger Zelazny*. In: Writer's Voice #74A–14B. 1973: Online clip: http://zelazny.corrupt.net/audio/WritersVoice.html

82. Thurston, Robert Introduction. In: Zelazny, Roger, ed. *Today We Choose Faces*. Boston, MA: Gregg Press, 1978: p v–ix.
83. Asher, Ellen. Letter to Roger Zelazny dated April 4, 1972.
84. Zelazny, Roger. Letter to NAL Editor Ellen Asher dated April 10, 1972.
85. Asher, Ellen. Letter to Roger Zelazny dated April 18, 1972.
86. Zelazny, Roger. Letter to NAL Editor Ellen Asher dated April 27, 1972.
87. Asher, Ellen. Letter to Roger Zelazny dated May 1, 1972.
88. Zelazny, Roger. Letter to NAL Editor Ellen Asher dated May 19, 1972.
89. Zelazny, Roger. Letter to Richard Rowand dated April 30, 1973.
90. Dann, Jack. Eulogy for Roger Zelazny [Unedited manuscript; a shorter version was published as "Roger Zelazny" in *Locus* 1995;35 (2 [#415 August]): 72], provided by the author in an email to Dr. Christopher Kovacs dated May 6, 2008.
91. Zelazny, Roger. Introduction. In: Dann, Jack, ed. *Timetipping*. Garden City, NY: Doubleday & Company, 1980: p xi–xiii.
92. Haldeman, Joe. Email to Dr. Christopher Kovacs dated May 7, 2008.
93. Conner, Bill. Zelazny at Marcon '72. *Cozine* 1972; (3 [March 30]): p 17–18.
94. Zelazny, Roger. Letter to Mr. Davis dated January 3, 1972.
95. Plachta, Dannie. *Marcon VII Program and Schedule Booklet*, 1972.
96. Fratz, D. Douglas. Interview With Poul Anderson and Roger Zelazny. *Thrust* 1973; 1 (2 [April]): p 14–16.
97. Zelazny, Roger. Letter to Philip K. Dick dated June 19, 1973.
98. Zelazny, Roger. Letter to Henry Morrison dated May 26, 1972.
99. Zelazny, Roger. Letter to Doubleday Editor David Krotz dated November 24, 1972.
100. Jakobsson, Ejler. Letter to Henry Morrison dated August 26, 1972.
101. Wilgus, Neal. Roger Zelazny. *Science Fiction Review* 1980; 9 (3 [#36, August]): p 14–16.
102. Thomlinson, Norris. To Die in Italbar, 2005. http://zelazny.corrupt.net/book.php?book=die Accessed: May 21, 2008
103. Krulik, Theodore. *Roger Zelazny*. New York, NY: Ungar Publishing, 1986.
104. Yoke, Carl B. Another World Away, unpublished essay written for *Roger on Writing*, a book that was to be edited by Trent Zelazny, 2004.
105. Turzillo, Mary A. Roger Zelazny, Hero Maker. *Ohioana Quarterly* 2003; 46 (4 [Winter]): p 414–420.
106. Yoke, Carl B. Before There Was Amber, introduction to a book of the same name, a collection of stories from *The Record* ("Studies in Saviory" and three tales written by Yoke); it was to have been published by DNA Publications (Warren Lapine) but the publisher went out of business, 2005.
107. Yoke, Carl B. Over the Sangre de Cristos. *Amberzine* 2005; (12–15 [March]): p 374–377.
108. Zelazny, Roger. Letter to Mr. Hurlbert dated May 22, 1972.
109. Zelazny, Roger. Letter to Dannie Plachta dated May 24, 1973.
110. Zelazny, Roger. Letter to Henry Morrison dated May 25, 1973.
111. McGuire, Paul; Truesdale, David A. Tangent Interviews: Roger Zelazny. *Tangent* 1976; (4 [February]): p 5–10.

112. Shannon, J.C. Staying Power: An Interview with Roger Zelazny. *Leading Edge* 1994; (29 [August]): p 33–47.
113. Zelazny, Roger. Introduction. In: Zelazny, Roger, ed. *Bridge of Ashes*. New York, NY: Signet, 1989: unpaginated.
114. Schochet, Victoria. Letter to Henry Morrison dated January 2, 1974.
115. Zelazny, Roger. Letter to Henry Morrison dated July 30, 1974.
116. Zelazny, Roger. *Blood of Amber*, first draft manuscript completed 7 November, 1985.
117. Salinger, J. D. Teddy. *The New Yorker* 1953; (January 31): p 26–34, 36, 38, 40–41, 44–45.
118. Brown, Charles N. Forever Amber: Roger Zelazny Interview. *Locus* 1991; 27 (4 [#369 October]): p 5, 68.
119. Leeper, Evelyn C. Torcon 3: A convention report: Conversations with George and Howard, 2003. http://www.fanac.org/worldcon/Torcon/x03-rpt.html Accessed: July 4, 2008
120. Snodgrass, Melinda M.; Grubbs, David G.; Kovacs, Christopher S. Panel discussion at Boskone 46 entitled "Roger Zelazny, in Retrospect", 2009.
121. O'Brien, Michael. Close Adventures of the Conventional Kind: Downtown With The Zelaznys. *ANZAPA* 1978; (61): unpaginated.
122. Krulik, Theodore. Roger Zelazny's Road to Amber. *Extrapolation* 2002; 43 (1 [Spring]): p 80–88.
123. Offutt, Andrew J. Toastmaster's Notes used to introduce Guest of Honor Roger Zelazny at the 32nd Annual World Science Fiction Convention, Washington, DC, September 1, 1974.
124. Zelazny, Roger. Letter to John Onoda dated August 23, 1973.
125. Ossias, Michael. Letter to Roger Zelazny dated July 17, 1974.
126. Brady, John. Letter to Roger Zelazny dated May 15, 1974.
127. Zelazny, Roger. Letter to John Brady dated July 26, 1974.
128. Bounds, Ron. Roger Zelazny: 1980 Guest of Honor. In: Patten, Fred, Stevens, Sylvia, eds. *Westercon XXXIII Program Book*. Van Nuys, CA: Westercon XXXIII, 1980: p 13,48.
129. Zelazny, Roger. Letter to Michael Handley dated November 8, 1980.
130. Duvic, Patrice. Entretien avec Roger Zelazny. *Fiction #227*, November 1972, p 139–149

CURIOSITIES

Family Tree from *Creatures of Light and Darkness*

Sketched 1966–67; previously unpublished.

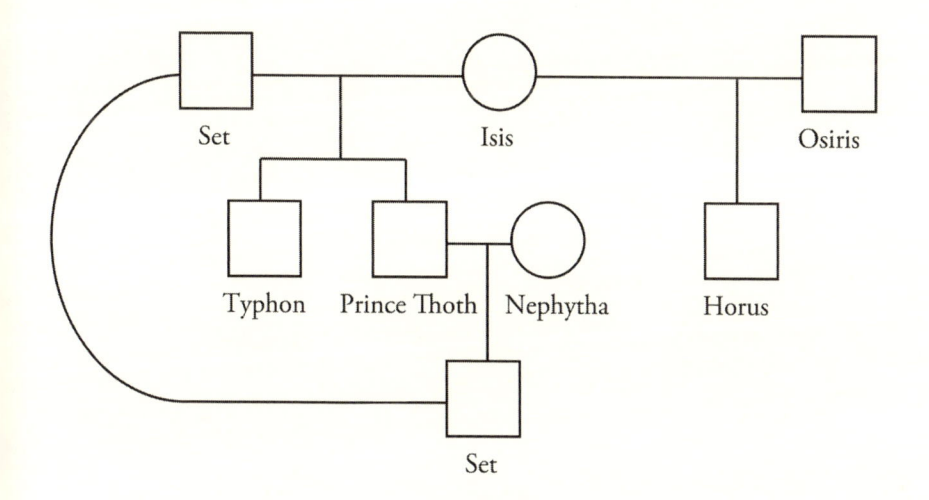

Notes

The original version of this family tree, sketched in Zelazny's own hand, was found among papers dated 1965–68 in the Archives at Syracuse University. It makes obvious what may have confused some readers of the novel, which is that as a consequence of his use of temporal fugue, **Set** is both father and son to **Prince Thoth**.

THE GUNS OF AVALON
DELETED SEX SCENE

Written circa 1970; previously unpublished.
§ *Amber*

"No!" I said. "I will not have you fooling with Shadow until you are ready. It is dangerous even after you have taken the Pattern. To do it before is foolhardy. You were lucky, but do not try it again. I'll even help, by not telling you anything more about it."

"All right!" she said. "Sorry. I guess I can wait."

"I guess you can. No hard feelings?"

"No. Well—" She laughed. "They wouldn't do me any good, I guess. You must know what you are talking about. I am glad that you care what happens to me."

I grunted, and she reached out and touched my cheek. At this, I turned my head again and her face was moving slowly toward my own, smile gone and lips parting, eyes almost closed. As we kissed, I felt her arms slide around my neck and shoulders and mine found their way into a similar position around her. My surprise was lost in the sweetness, gave way to warmth and a certain excitement. By degrees, I descended back upon my cloak, drawing her along with me. She was atop me by then, and my right hand kept moving, passing beneath her belt, to massage the soft flesh I found there. Our lips were twisting and nibbling upon one another rapidly, and our breathing had deepened and quickened. I cast Grayswandir and a fortune in diamonds off to my left. Her blouse followed a moment later. If Benedict ever found out, he was going to be more than just irritated with me, I knew. But I wanted her, and the feeling seemed to be mutual.

To my left, our garments embraced one another where they fell.

A Word from Zelazny

Asked if he'd ever been heavily edited, Zelazny said, "I've done some things just for laughs. I recall inserting a fairly graphic sex scene in one of the Amber books which wasn't really that important to the narrative... I put it in to see what the editor at Doubleday would say. They came back very nicely and said...that they would prefer my removing it... I took it out because I'd only put it in to see what the reaction would be."[1] After taking a call from Editor Larry Ashmead at Doubleday, he wrote an apologetic note to the copy editor: "I'll be glad to tone down the sex scene on page 191 of *The Guns of Avalon* for you when I get the copy-edited MS back for review."[2]

Zelazny's ulterior motive for this "very graphic sex scene between Corwin and Dara [was] putting a scene like that into every Amber book and letting them call me and talk me into taking it out, then when I had enough of them, doing an article for some men's magazine called 'Scenes I was Asked to Cut.' It would be a semi-scholarly, polite, gentlemanly way of introducing a basically pornographic article in the men's magazine without making it look as if they're publishing anything dirty. However, after the first time the novelty wore off and I never did it again."[3]

This is the first publication of the "graphic sex scene" between Corwin and Dara when Merlin was conceived. By twenty-first century standards, the scene is quite tame.

---

1 *Alternities #6*, Vol 2 No 2, Summer 1981.
2 Letter from Zelazny to Editor Miss Diane Cleaver at Doubleday, November 17, 1971.
3 *Deep Thoughts: Proceedings of Life, the Universe & Everything, February 16–19, 1994*, p 113–29.

The Guns of Avalon: deleted sex scene

– 191 –

but do not try it again. I'll even help, by not telling you
anything more about it."

"All right!" she said. "Sorry. I guess I can wait."

"I guess you can. No hard feelings?"

"No. Well——" She laughed. "They wouldn't do me any good,
I guess. You must know what you are talking about. I am glad
that you care what happens to me."

I grunted, and she reached out and touched my cheek. At
this, I turned my head again and her face was moving slowly toward my own, smile gone and lips parting, eyes almost closed.
As we kissed, I felt her arms slide about my neck and shoulders
and mine found their way into a similar position around her.
My surprise was lost in the sweetness, gave way to warmth and a
certain excitement. ~~By degrees, I descended back upon my cloak,
drawing her along with me. She was atop me by then, and my
right hand kept moving, passing beneath her belt, to massage the
soft flesh I found there. Our lips were twisting and nibbling
upon one another rapidly~~, and our breathing had deepened
and quickened. I cast Grayswandir and a fortune in diamonds off
to my left. Her blouse followed a moment later. If Benedict
ever found out, he was going to be more than just irritated
with me. I knew. But I wanted her, and the feeling seemed to
be mutual.

~~To my left, our garments embraced one another where they
fell.~~

This is a page of the original manuscript for the second Amber novel, *The Guns of Avalon*, containing a "very graphic sex scene". Here is one example of how writing can be ~~censored~~ blue-penciled into oblivion.

BRIDGE OF ASHES
(OUTLINE)

Written in 1974; previously unpublished.

Narrative Structure:

Third-person narration, to begin with. While the frame for the entire piece will be the early twenty-first century, there will be various flashbacks to a number of different periods in history. No reason for this will be given initially, but the scenes will be of sufficient intrinsic interest to involve the attention long enough for me to start developing their connections to the twenty-first century story-line. One of the devices I also intend to use to achieve this end will be an opening and closing moment of confusion as to whether the incident is to be told in the first or third person—resolved in favor of the third. Each such scene will also be tied to the others with a closing mention of a flash blue and a circle. It will then begin to emerge, from the doings in the twenty-first century situation, that the entire story is actually a first-person narrative. It is, however, being told by a person without a self to refer to as "I." He is developing, through the mechanism involved in the flashbacks, into a genuine individual with a personality of his own. When this finally occurs, via two traumatic scenes, he will come into existence and continue the story in the first person.

Story Line:

Shortly after the turn of the century—twenty-first—a mutation occurs in the human race. There are several thousand telepaths of varying ability in the world. The faculty is sufficiently reliable to make them capable of holding jobs which require its controlled operation—in communications, security work, etc. The world at this time is still dealing with various ecological crises, though a UN resolution of a generation earlier had been passed, with eventual treaty endorsements of much of its substance—a resolution aimed at combating the ecological problems. This does seem to be producing some remedial results.

Now, the telepathic ability is not generally a prodigious thing. There are limits to its range and the depths to which its possessor can probe into the subject's mind—limits which, of course, vary from individual to individual. Telepaths tend to marry telepaths, and in such cases the offspring are generally more proficient than their parents. Such families tend to reside in reasonably secluded areas, so that the children in their early years will not be bombarded with adult thoughts before they have formed personalities of their own and developed adequate defenses.

The saddest maladjustment of this sort on record is that of the son of the president of the International Telepathic Operators Union. While the customary precautions were taken to isolate the child, it was not realized until too late that he was the greatest telepath the race had yet produced, with the ability of reaching out across hundreds of miles with his mind while still an infant. The effects were disastrous. The child retreated into a catatonic state for many years and was only gradually drawn out of it by a telepathic therapist. Though the boy achieved the ability to communicate somewhat with others, he was nevertheless a hopeless schizophrenic suffering a paranoid reaction.

His condition operates as follows: he has no personality of his own, but fixes upon a mind which he finds congenial. He identifies totally with that individual, fully believing himself to be the person in question. Broken of that identification, he immediately seeks another.

Still hopeful that his son will one day respond to treatment, the father, who is quite wealthy, arranges for him to be hospitalized in a facility situated on the moon. At such a distance, it is felt that the young man's faculty will be blocked by sheer distance, that he will be unable to reach the sorts of minds he finds congenial and may then respond to therapy. The first part seems to be correct. On the moon, the young man relapses into catatonia for a period of several weeks.

One day, though, he grows animated. He begins taking an interest in things—reading, painting—the various occupational therapies available to him. But he is not cured. He seems to be indulging in paranoid identification once more—only since real minds of the sort he finds acceptable are not available to him, he is resorting to the garden variety identification with historical figures.

Or is he?

He acts out the parts, responds to the names of various historical personages—famous, infamous, obscure—but the knowledge he evinces regarding their lives and times seems quite detailed, and accurate. Still, it is assumed at first that the information must be available in the minds of those few persons present elsewhere on the moon. And he had also been doing some reading...

It is wondered, though, whether it might be possible that, frustrated by space, he somehow succeeded in driving his powerful, abnormal faculty back through time itself. Could he have succeeded in reaching the minds of the actual individuals involved?

He undergoes further change. He acts as if he is beginning to understand that he has been ill all along, shows some notions as to identity, time and place. The staff cautiously accepts this as a good sign.

All this while, however, he has continued painting with oils, the part of his therapy he seems to enjoy best. Since he has not shown them his work for some time, a curious therapist enters his quarters while he is out and searches for his paintings. Among items of mixed merit, he locates the latest one. It is La Giaconda—the Mona Lisa—complete in every detail.

Questioned concerning it, he admits to having done it as an exercise, but denies any conviction that he is Da Vinci. His condition continues to improve.

❖   ❖   ❖

I must pause here and go into the substance of some of the flashbacks which will have been occurring during the development of what I have just been describing. Some of the key ones will be as follows:

Scene: The Old Stone Age. A young man, a member of a hunting party, is attacked and apparently mortally injured by a creature which seemingly emerges from the sea and enters the forest for this express purpose, returning to the sea afterwards. The creature is an almost-beautiful, unnatural thing, with a hint of the mechanical about it. Then a young woman—either summoned by unexplained means or possessed of foreknowledge of the event—arrives, commences lamenting this occurrence, drives away the remaining hunters, cradles the man's head in her lap and weeps. Flash of blue and a circle.

Scene: The departure of Leonardo Da Vinci for France. Mixture of bitterness and remorse over all the things he did not accomplish. Pathos. Flash of blue and a circle.

Scene: The final days of Rousseau. Bitterness and pathos again. Flash of blue and a circle.

Scene: A man taking his place behind a microphone and waiting for some mixed applause to subside before he addresses the General Assembly of the United Nations. He is a Nobel Prize recipient, with an international reputation for his concern over ecological matters. He is about to urge the adoption of a resolution dealing with a number of environmental problem areas—a resolution which, if passed, would put pressure on those nations not party to them to become signatory to several existing treaties possessing some teeth with regard to the contamination of the seas and the atmosphere. It is opposed by a bloc of developing nations which feel they could develop considerably faster in the absence of such restrictions.

There is a sudden, absolute silence in the assembly hall. Startled, the scientist looks up from the notes he had been arranging on the lectern. Everything, everyone, is frozen into absolute immobility. Nothing stirs. He glances at his watch. It has stopped. He moves away from the microphone, passes down to the floor. In so doing, his eyes fall upon the hate-twisted face of a minor clerical employee of the delegation from one of smaller countries, who had risen to his feet and now stands, right arm extended, holding a gun from the barrel of which a small wisp of unstirring smoke has emerged. The trigger is depressed. Several yards from the gun's muzzle, he sees the bullet hanging in midair. It is directed toward the lectern he has just vacated.

He moves away, heading for the outside to determine the extent of the phenomenon. Before he can depart, however, he encounters a strange man, the only other individual stirring. The man gives several evasive answers to his questions as to what has occurred, but promises to enlighten him if he will accompany him. Agreeing, he is taken to the roof of the UN building and shown the frozen vista of New York. The stranger proceeds to tell him a bizarre version of the history of the human race.

Long before there was a race of man, the Earth was visited by the few survivors of an interstellar cataclysm, searching for a new home. The Earth was suitable in terms of its size, little else. The creatures found the atmosphere poisonous and many other aspects of the environment equally unbearable. They decided that it could be made to do, however—eventually. Lacking the necessary equipment to reshape the world to their own design, and lacking the time, materials and manpower (alienpower?) to construct such equipment, they decided upon a cosmic alternative for which they possessed sufficient scientific sophistication.

Studying the local fauna, they selected a particular creature as best suited for their purposes. They manipulated this creature carefully—genetically and environmentally—creating all the situations now described in the better anthropology texts as leading up to the hominids. The majority of the aliens remaining in suspended animation, a few of them were aroused periodically to check on the creature's progress and to take whatever steps were necessary to control its evolution into man. They were satisfied by the time of the Holocene that they had succeeded in breeding a life-form which would achieve a communal existence and acquire the ability to manipulate its environment in such a fashion as to give rise to an eventual urban life style which would predictably, inevitably, lead to a state of industrial development that would result in the physical alteration of the world as a by-product of its normal functioning. The aliens required the presence of such things as carbon monoxide, sulfur dioxide, nitrogen oxide, oil, nitrate runoff, methyl mercury, polychlorinated biphenyls, fluorocarbons, organic phosphates and the various industrial effluents and discharges to make the world a habitable place for them. In short, they had created man as a planoforming agent, designed and programmed so perfectly that he would do the job for them and self-destruct when it was completed—as they had calculated his tolerances and knew that the world would be ready for them at the point where man made it unfit for himself. To this end, they had kept closer watch over human society during the past several thousand years, manipulating events from time to time in order to be absolutely certain mankind stayed on the right track. Always wary of prodigies, prophets and possible mutations that might lead man in an undesirable direction, they had, for example, doomed Leonardo Da Vinci to comparative obscurity during his own lifetime, when some of his discoveries might have influenced the course of industrial development in an uncertain fashion. Ditto for some of Rousseau's social ideas.

Now they are close to achieving their ends, the stranger explains, and the battle he has fought with them across the ages is nearing its conclusion. He wants to buy time, to hope for, to encourage something that may yet beat them. He is not certain that there in much of a chance left and he has grown desperate. That is why he arranged for a spectacle at the UN. The vote on the resolution in expected to be very close. With the endorsement of a martyr, he thinks it will be passed. So he set up the scientist's assassination. At the last moment, though, out of respect for the man, he decided that he could not go through with it so cold-bloodedly. It was too late to stop the man with the gun, and unnecessary, for that matter. While no one has ever succeeded in manipulating time, that bridge of ashes man leaves behind him, he possessed the ability to do the next best thing. He speeded up the scientist's metabolism, perceptions, reflexes, to such an extent that the effect was the same as a time-stoppage. He felt that, of all men, he owed this man an explanation of what it was that he wanted to achieve, and to give his a choice in the matter.

The scientist asks him who he is.

The stranger shakes his head. There is simply not time to tell his story, as it is longer than all of history. As to names, he has lost count of them. The indications from his sketchy remarks, though, are that he was the man gored by the strange beast back in the Stone Age, an Attis/Adonis/Osiris/Tammuz-figure, and that perhaps, long ago, during one of the aliens' periodic quality control samplings, he and several others had been picked up for examination, that he just happened to be smarter or luckier than the others and obtained something from the aliens—without their knowledge—which had endowed him with a version of immortality, that he had shared this secret with his woman—who also has many names, associated with the mother-goddess—and that this was a thing that the aliens could not take back easily. Over the years, the aliens had made periodic attempts to destroy the two whenever their presence was detected. The creatures were handicapped in many ways by the Earth's uncongenial environment, however, and over the ages he and his woman had acquired many defenses.

Listening, the scientist realizes that he has been postponing a decision. He asks the man to take him back below. There, he assumes his position behind the lectern once more, briefly rests his eyes on the blue flag of the United Nations, with its white circle of the world, feels an instant of movement, life and sound once again, and then nothing.

The last sentence is, "I—"

Story Line Continued:

The story moves into an "I" situation then, quickly resolving itself into a first-person narrative, as the young man, lashed into independent existence by experiencing the death of the scientist and the vision of the dying god, pieces things together and comes to realize the situation still facing mankind. He resolves to do something about it.

He drives himself to a mental equilibrium sufficient to persuade the doctor that he is recovering, growing stable. He requests that he be allowed a trial visit back to Earth. This is finally granted.

He retains his stability and begins a search for the stranger, the wounded one. After some seeking, he locates instead the woman—the mother-goddess, the mate of the stranger—who realizes what he is and what that represents.

She transports him to a locale in East Africa, where the man has gone to the seaside—as he does periodically—to parlay with the aliens, who dwell somewhere beneath the water there. He is attempting to convince them again that their plan is failing, that mankind is more complex, is a less deterministically responsive organism than they had anticipated, that sufficient remedial action has been taken to ultimately thwart them, that something has been learned from all man's historical missteps.

The young man then realizes what is expected of him, realizes too that perhaps the stranger had had something to do with his being what he is—that he may have somehow manipulated his life to the extent necessary to produce him as he is at this moment, in this place. He knows he must show himself to the aliens, braving their mental and/or physical dissection, to demonstrate that mankind has changed from their original specifications, and that—as he now understands from his experience of history—the past is not lost, it is not a mere bridge that has been burned, leaving but ashes, but rather is open, that all of history is there to be explored, learned from—and that even if they destroy him, more such as himself will one day come along now that the gene is operative, but that even if this were not to occur, the race has learned and continues to learn from its mistakes.

He goes to them, and as he goes he feels the identities of all the individuals he has been—all the great failures, the suppressed men of learning, the broken geniuses, all the talents cut short, twisted, destroyed; there is Leonardo; there, Rousseau; there is the assassinated scientist; there, the dying god-king who will be resurrected to a sweet-smelling springtime—all of them walking with him.

The aliens regard the procession, the pageant of the human life struggle that he represents. Then they prepare to depart, to seek another place, realizing that they had underestimated the creature they had nurtured, had contrived to influence, for all these eons.

As the bright alien vessels later rise from the waters, however, an almost-beautiful, unnatural creature, with a hint of the mechanical about it, emerges from the sea and attacks the stranger, goring him perhaps mortally, although this time it is destroyed itself in the encounter. Lamenting, the woman goes to the man, cradles his head in her lap, weeps.

She tells the young man to depart, and he does.

Notes

Zelazny wrote this outline to secure the contract with Signet for *Bridge of Ashes*. He experimented with narration—a first person narrator not mature enough to recognize himself as "I" at the novel's start—and the mixed results confused many readers. This outline clarifies some confusing elements in the novel and explains its title. Zelazny's thoughts about the novel appear in more detail in the monograph "...And Call Me Roger" on page 530 of volume 4.

Catatonic refers to catatonia, which involves extremely rigid or flexible muscles and either mania or stupor. Its common meaning is a condition in which the individual is unresponsive to external stimuli. **Schizophrenic** refers to schizophrenia, a disorder that includes schizoid behavior, disorganized speech, hallucinations and delusions (e.g., hearing voices). **La Giaconda** is another name for Leonardo **da Vinci's** *Mona Lisa*. Jean-Jacques **Rousseau** was a French philosopher whose political ideas influenced liberal and socialist theory and the French revolution; he is best known for his Theory of Natural Man (man is good in Nature but corrupted by society). His book, *The Social Contract*, outlines the development of a legitimate political order. **Planoforming** is converting the planet to the aliens' needs. **Attis** (Phrygian), **Adonis** (Greek), **Osiris** (Egyptian) and **Tammuz** (Semitic) are examples of the dying and resurrecting god, often linked to the cycle of the seasons.

Doorways in the Sand
(Summary)

Written January 1975; previously unpublished.

Doorways in the Sand is set in the twenty-first century. Its protagonist Fred Cassidy is a perpetual student at an unnamed university. When the story opens he is into his thirteenth year as a full-time undergraduate. He is also, at that moment, dozing on a rooftop as is sometimes his wont, waiting until it is time to keep an appointment with his new advisor Dennis Wexroth, for approval of his choice of courses for the coming semester. He is on the rooftop because he is an acrophiliac. He has to some extent reestablished the fine old college practice of nightclimbing because of his near-compulsion to climb buildings. Dennis Wexroth, disapproving of Fred's climbing and his chronic shifting of academic majors, is determined to see him graduated by exercising a special rule enacted some time before for the sole purpose of getting rid of Cassidy, a rule involving mandatory graduation upon the completion of a full major in any academic area. Dennis Wexroth has also become aware of the reason for Fred's unwillingness to accept a degree—the fact that his Uncle Albert's will provided him with a generous allowance for so long as he remained a full-time undergraduate working toward a degree. Once the degree is received the stipend ceases. All of this is brought out during the pre-registration interview. Fred succeeds in remaining full-time, however, without signing up for sufficient courses to allow his graduation—because of a last-minute change in the number of credits granted for one course. Presumably, he had influenced the instructor in some fashion.

Returning to his apartment in the company of the girl he is attempting to persuade to move in with him, Fred finds that the place has been ransacked—a discovery which frightens off the girl. Searching the place to assess the damage and losses, he is accosted by a lurking Paul Byler, one of his former professors, who asks him the whereabouts of the star-stone model, a reproduction of an alien artifact. Byler manhandles him but Fred kicks him in the groin and escapes to the ledge outside the window where Byler fears to follow. Fred insists that while he and his former roommate Hal Sidmore had once used the model Byler had given Hal as a paperweight, he believed that Hal had taken it with him when he had married and moved out. Byler replies that he has already spoken with Hal, who had insisted that he did not have it, that he had left it behind. Unable to reach Fred, Byler then departs with a threat of reprisal should Fred go to the police.

Fred then visits Hal, who admits that on the night of the poker party in Byler's lab, when the professor had given him the imperfect model of the stone, he had been displeased with a tiny flaw in the model and while the others were out of the room had substituted it for a better looking one he had seen on a shelf. He insists that what he had told Byler was correct, however—that he had left the stone behind when he had moved out. He then speculates on the possibility that Byler might have been commissioned by the United Nations to produce the model of the artifact for display purposes, allowing for the priceless original to be kept locked safely away.

That night, while climbing the local cathedral, Fred encounters his friend Professor Dobson, seated on a ledge, drinking and reflecting upon his coming retirement. Along with predictable observations upon his career and the passage of time, the background for the entire story emerges in his musing upon events of the previous generation.

The Earth had entered the age of interstellar exploration in slower-than-light ships, and during an expedition to a nearby star-system had encountered an alien vessel also engaged in exploration. The aliens were part of a vast interstellar culture, including hundreds of races and civilizations throughout the galaxy. Also, they possessed a means of traveling faster than light which enabled them to return the Earthmen to their home years ahead of schedule. The aliens proved quite friendly, and as a result of the contact Earth was invited to join an interstellar cultural exchange program which functioned somewhat along the lines of the *kula* chain described by Malinowski and other anthropologists as a cultural phenomenon in the Melanesian Island group. Basically, it involved the passing along of objects of great cultural significance in both directions about a great circle. Earth had surrendered the Mona Lisa and the British Crown Jewels in this exchange and received for a time the Rhennius machine and the star-stone—both of which, after a while, would be passed on again, in return for two more objects—the entire process hopefully promoting a sense of a greater community by virtue of trust and tradition-sharing. The Rhennius machine is a peculiar device which rotates objects through higher dimensions, altering their configurations accordingly upon returning them to normal space, and no one is certain precisely what the star-stone does or represents, save that it is the oldest known artifact in the galaxy, found among the ruins of a long-dead civilization. The UN is acting as custodian of the two items and has the Rhennius machine on display in a hall in New York. Should either object be lost or destroyed, Earth's chances of sharing in the greater benefits of the galactic community and eventually joining it as a full-fledged member would be considerably diminished.

Upon returning to his apartment, Fred learns from the late news that Professor Byler had been found dead in Central Park. In addition to being robbed, he had suffered the removal of most of his vital organs—presumably by black market organ bankers.

Throughout the course of events to this point, Fred has periodically suffered minor hallucinations which are later seen to amount to variations on the message, "Do you hear me, Fred?" It takes him a long while to realize that these are actually more than stress-induced sensory distortions.

Journeying to Australia for a field project for one of his courses, he is approached at his diggings outside Alice Springs by two men—Morton Zeemeister and Jamie Buckler—who prove to be the criminals responsible for Paul Byler's unfortunate experience in Central Park. They question Fred at length as to the whereabouts of the star-stone, finally staking him out in the wilderness to reconsider his responses.

Fred is rescued by a kangaroo and a wombat, who prove to be alien police disguised as local life forms. Their names are Charv and Ragma. They depart with him in their interstellar vessel and enter into an orbit about the Earth, where they treat his injuries and explain that they, too, want to learn the whereabouts of the star-stone. They appreciate the fact that he does not seem to know, but feel that he may well possess such knowledge at a subconscious level. They wish to take him to another planet for examination by a telepathic analyst who will hopefully uncover this information. During a semiconscious reverie Fred begins to understand their language and becomes aware of their intentions. An unidentifiable voice then advises him of his rights under the Galactic Code—namely, that an intelligent creature may not be removed from its home planet without giving its consent. When Charv and Ragma tell him he must accompany them, he cites the law and refuses to go along. They are irritated but finally agree to return him to Earth at a point near the campus. They also caution him that he is placing himself in danger by going back.

Returning to his apartment building late at night, Fred sees a brief flash of light in one of his windows, and so climbs the building and enters through the bedroom window. From the bedroom, he overhears a conversation between two men, obviously waiting for him, which ends with their locating a bottle and drinking a toast to the Queen.

Fred retires from the premises and phones Hal, who sounds slightly drunk but invites him over. At Hal's, Fred learns that Hal and his wife had had an argument and she had gone home to her mother's. Fred, normally a virtual teetotaler, joins Hal in drowning his sorrows while discussing everything which has occurred thus far. Fred learns from Hal that Hal's apartment had been broken into several times, that numerous phone calls had been received asking his whereabouts and that a State Department representative named Nadler had been by with questions about Fred.

Retiring, Fred has a peculiar dream wherein he is recontacted by the same entity which had earlier advised him as to his rights. He is told to go to New York and pass an object through the Rhennius machines observing the transformations it undergoes and then to go out and get drunk. Fred leaves Hal a note saying he will be out of town for a few days, journeys to New York, breaks into the hall through a skylight and follows the instructions. Then, discovered by a guard, he manages to escape, heads for the Village and begins moving from bar to bar, drinking. In the course of his pub crawl he encounters one of his favorite former advisors, Professor Merimee, who had lost his teaching position because of a scandal and is now working as a pimp while gathering material for a novel. Merimee informs him that he had spotted him several bars earlier but refrained from approaching him until he could confirm a suspicion that he was being followed. Having done so, he now wishes to offer him escape and sanctuary should he require such assistance. Fred accepts and is conducted out the back door and through alleyways, coming at last to Merimee's apartment where a party is in progress. There Merimee reveals to him that he had known his Uncle Albert in years gone by, the two of them having been partners in crime for a long while, and that if it would ease Fred's problems to have anyone killed he would be glad to arrange it for him. Fred thanks him and says he will bear that in mind. He then proceeds to get drunk, as per instructions, reflecting upon how little he had really known concerning his late, frozen Uncle Albert. (Note: while his uncle is legally dead, allowing for his will to have been probated, Albert Cassidy had provided for his body to be frozen against the possibility of future resuscitation, should medical science ever become sufficiently sophisticated.)

In the morning Fred awakens, alone in the apartment save for a donkey which had been present at the previous night's festivities. The donkey proves to be another alien in disguise—a telepathic one, at that, who had been requested by Charv and Ragma to protect Fred and to obtain his consent to a bit of mind-probing. Telepathy, Fred then learns, is distinctly impeded in the case of a subject with alcohol in his system. At about this time, Fred receives another cryptic message, telling him to return to the Rhennius machine and pass himself through higher space.

Escaping through a window, he sets about following the instructions. By means of an elaborate ruse, he is able to pass himself through the machine, which turns him into a mirror-image of himself. He now perceives the world in reverse, as in a mirror. Returning to his college town, he opts to spend the night at another friend's place rather than return to his own or to Hal's. His friend Ralph informs him that he, too, has been receiving calls concerning Fred's whereabouts, has been contacted by Nadler of the State Department and had just recently received a call from Dennis Wexroth informing him that Fred had been graduated.

The following morning, Fred goes to see Wexroth and discovers that he has been awarded a Ph.D. in Anthropology by means of an interpretation of the university's regulations which actually makes it easier to give him the doctorate than a baccalaureate degree. Pressing the matter, by means of some violence, Fred learns that the university had been pressured by the State Department to grant him the degree. He is again requested to contact Nadler.

Instead, Fred contacts Hal and learns that Hal's wife Mary had never made it to her mother's but had been kidnapped and is being held to ransom, the requested payment being the star-stone. Fred accompanies Hal to the rendezvous point, prepared to swear that the phoney stone Hal had just recently obtained by breaking into Byler's lab, is the real thing. The kidnapers prove to be Zeemeister and Buckler, who state that the stone is not authentic and prepare to torture all parties concerned for further information. They are stopped at the last moment by a somehow resurrected Paul Byler. Byler is then tangled in a fishing net dislodged from above by a black cat passing along a rafter, Byler shoots Zeemeister, Zeemeister shoots Byler and Jamie Buckler shoots Fred as he attempts to disarm him.

Awakening in a hospital, Fred discovers that no one died in the encounter, although everyone was injured to some degree, including one of the policemen who had broken in moments later. Fred's injury had been the most serious, in that he had been shot in the chest. The mirror-reversal of his internal organs had, however, sufficiently shifted his heart that what would normally have been a fatal shot had entirely missed its target. He is visited in the hospital by an apparently blind man with a seeing eye dog. The blind man turns out to be Nadler of the State Department, who possesses normal vision but had employed the ruse for purposes of smuggling in Ragma, the alien cop and former wombat who is now disguised as the dog. Ragma is now a special adviser to a UN group attempting to recover the star-stone. Nadler wants Fred to accept a position with the State Department's delegation to the UN, to be assigned therefrom to the special UN unit. Ragma in turn wants Fred's consent to be examined by a telepathic analyst now en route to Earth for this purpose. Fred agrees. In applying a healing unit to his chest injury, Ragma observes that a scar Fred had received in Australia is now on the opposite side of his body. He realizes that Fred is the man who passed through the Rhennius machine. He asks him why and Fred is about to tell him but loses control of his tongue and vocal cords and cannot.

Discharged from the hospital, Fred returns to his apartment and his girlfriend, having been informed as to at least part of the story on the star-stone. A small group of tradition-minded British subjects had objected to the departure of the Crown Jewels and were determined to have them back by means of cosmic blackmail. Paul Byler, a sympathizer, had constructed a model of the stone based on all the facts he could obtain concerning it. The guard who had received the stone from the UN Secretary General for purposes of conveying it to a vault had also been in on it. He had exchanged Byler's model for the original and taken the original to Byler, who was then to prepare an even better model for later substitution. At about this time, however, Byler—a highly respected man in this area of science—proved the logical person to be approached by the UN to manufacture a duplicate of what they believed to be the genuine stone. Byler consequently received his own forgery for duplication. He was then faced with the dilemma of forging the forgery or doing the better job he had intended, now uncertain as to which one would be more readily detectable. He had produced a number of various models and given a rejected one to Hal on the night of the poker party. In looking to exchange it later for the most impressive, Hal had taken the real stone. Morton Zeemeister and Jamie Buckler had entered the picture in being hired by the plotters, none of whom were genuine criminals, to render expert criminal assistance in the execution of the blackmail scheme. Zeemeister and Buckler had plans of their own, however, involving taking the stone themselves and returning it for a large sum of money and immunity from prosecution. When they had left Byler for dead in the park, a police unit had come upon him almost immediately and gotten him to a hospital where a series of organ transplants had saved his life. He then confessed the entire affair, which is how the UN became aware of the situation. The information that he was still living had not been released. He now attempted to help them locate the stone, and he had been the man Merimee had spotted following Fred in the Village. This is also the reason he was following him on the day of the rendezvous with Zeemeister and Buckler.

Fred is then telephoned by Nadler and advised that Zeemeister and Buckler have escaped from custody and may be seeking him once more. Extremely irritated at this point, Fred calls Merimee and tells him that he would like to take him up on the offered homicides, that he would like to have Zeemeister and Buckler taken care of. Fred learns then that Zeemeister had once worked for his Uncle Albert and been discharged for dishonesty.

He goes to Now York with Nadler, and when he recontacts Merimee to advise him as to his whereabouts he learns that Zeemeister and Buckler have already been spotted in town. He is also informed that he will presently suffer a pleasant surprise. The telepathic analyst proves to be an intelligent plant who discovers that the star-stone was a computer-like artificial life-form which had been switched off ages before by isomeric reversal and could be stimulated only by ethyl alcohol, the chemical symmetry of which is unaffected by reversal. The star-stone is actually inside Fred, functioning as a kind of benign parasite or symbiote. It was stimulated to the point where it could contact him when there was alcohol in his system. It had entered his body on the night of the bachelor party Fred had given for Hal, after which Fred had cut his hand in cleaning up a broken glass and subsequently passed out at the desk while playing with the stone with his cut hand. The alcohol had stimulated it, it had entered his body through the wound and had received additional stimulation each time Fred had had anything alcoholic to drink. It had finally persuaded him to undergo reversal in the Rhennius machine which had then activated it fully. It still could not communicate with him save with great difficulty, however, because now *he* was reversed.

The alien analyst holds the star-stone in a state of mental stasis and the party, consisting of Charv, Ragma, Nadler, Fred, Paul Byler and the analyst itself, repair to the hall of the Rhennius machine, there to force the thing to withdraw from Fred's body. This is done, while Charv works to adjust the machine to return Fred to normal, but not before the star-stone gets a final, confused message through to Fred. At this point, Zeemeister and Buckler enter the hall, point guns and appropriate the stone. However, a strange man then appears and Buckler, despite a warning from Zeemeister, makes the mistake of attacking him. He is beaten to the floor with a shillelagh. Zeemeister, in backing away from the man, loses the star-stone and falls into the not-quite-adjusted Rhennius machine which turns him inside-out, killing him instantly. The stranger is Fred's resurrected Uncle Albert, the pleasant surprise Merimee had promised him. In the confusion, Byler seizes the stone and attempts to escape with it. He is stopped, however, by Merimee, who is waiting just outside.

Glancing upward, Fred sees a cat's shadow at the skylight, and the stone's final message suddenly becomes clear to him: The black cat he has encountered briefly on numerous occasions is itself an alien creature, on Earth illegally, which had allied itself with Zeemeister and Buckler for purposes of ruining Earth's chances at membership in the galactic community. Fred rushes to the roof, is attacked by the creature and then pursues it across to the frame of a building under construction next door. He climbs after it, and they face one another on the girders high above the city. The alien broadcast waves of acrophobia at Fred, which are nearly effective in overcoming his ability to pursue it. It makes the mistake of insulting him, however, in such a fashion that his anger overcomes his fear and he continues the chase to a final confrontation from which the alien plunges to its death below, leaving Fred holding a piece of fake tail from its cat-suit.

Later, Fred learns from Ragma that the big powers in the galactic community have been growing uneasy over the numerous young worlds being admitted to their company and forming a political bloc of their own rather than aligning themselves with the traditional powers. It seemed likely that Earth might go the former route, and the creature had been sent to sabotage its chances. Ragma and Charv had been present to prevent just that.

The star-stone is later realized to be a powerful one-of-a-kind device capable of in-depth social analysis and prediction. It requires an appropriate, compatible host in order to carry out this function. Fred is offered an ambassadorial position, accompanying the star-stone about the exchange circuit. He visits Professor Dobson in Europe before deciding, and high atop a building, listening to the chimes at midnight, makes up his mind to accept. He is assured by Merimee that he will not want for the amenities out among the stars, in that he and his Uncle Albert will be returning to business shortly on an interstellar scale, hiring the about-to-retire Ragma as a special advisor, and promoting enterprises which will bring humans out his way.

The final chapter is seen through Fred's eyes but told by the star-stone, which has now rejoined him in a mutually satisfactory symbiotic relationship. We find Fred climbing a tower on an alien planet, racing the rising shadows and the setting sun, during a course of flashbacks which tie up all the loose ends in the story. We leave him as he reaches the top of the tower at the last possible moment in which he still can win the race.

Notes

In January 1975, with publication of *Doorways in the Sand* imminent, the Harper & Row editors reported being "very excited about it, but neither felt able to describe it in a summary. If you could send me about two pages with plot description, which we would be using in house to familiarize other people in sales and publicity, I would appreciate it."[1] This is Zelazny's perhaps overly enthusiastic summary—it ran to 14 manuscript pages instead of the two requested.

An **acrophiliac** is someone who loves heights. The ***kula*** is a ceremonial exchange program practiced in Papa New Guinea and 18 island communities of the Massim archipelago. Branislaw **Malinowski** was the Polish anthropologist who studied these communities and the *kula*. **Isomeric** refers to isomerism, which is two different substances composed of the same elements arranged in a different order (e.g., mirror images, left and right-handed versions of amino acids). **Ethyl alcohol** is ethanol or alcohol. A **symbiote** is an organism living with another organism; neither suffers harm; at least one (and possibly both) benefit from the interaction. A **shillelagh** is a cudgel made of oak or blackthorn wood.

---

1 Letter from Lynne McNab, Harper & Row, to Roger Zelazny, dated January 20, 1975.

Publication History

Frontispiece portrait by Jack Gaughan first appeared on the cover of "Marcon VII Program and Schedule Book, 1972" where Roger Zelazny was Guest of Honor.
"Of Meetings and Partings" by Neil Gaiman first appears in this volume.
"On Roger Zelazny" by David G. Hartwell first appears in this volume.
"This Mortal Mountain" first appeared in *If*, March 1967.
"The Man Who Loved the Faioli" first appeared in *Galaxy*, June 1967.
"Angel, Dark Angel" first appeared in *Galaxy*, August 1967.
"The Hounds of Sorrow" first appears in this volume (likely written August 1967).
"The Window Washer" first appears in this volume (likely written near August 1967).
"Damnation Alley" first appeared in *Galaxy*, October 1967.
"The Last Inn on the Road" first appeared in *New Worlds #176*, October 1967.
"A Hand Across the Galaxy" first appeared in *Arioch! #1*, November 1967.
"The Insider" first appears in this volume (likely written in 1967).
"Heritage" first appeared in *Nozdrovia #1*, 1968. Previously uncollected.
"He That Moves" first appeared in *If*, January 1968. Previously uncollected.
"Corrida" first appeared in *Anubis* Vol 1 No 3, 1968.
"Dismal Light" first appeared in *If*, May 1968.
"Song of the Blue Baboon" first appeared in *If*, August 1968. Previously uncollected.
"Stowaway" first appeared in *Odd Magazine #19*, Summer 1968.
"Here There Be Dragons" first appeared in *Here There Be Dragons*, Donald M. Grant 1992.
"Way Up High" first appeared in *Way Up High*, Donald M. Grant 1992.
"The Steel General" first appeared in *If*, January 1969.
"Come to Me Not in Winter's White" first appeared in *The Magazine of Fantasy & Science Fiction*, October 1969; revised by Harlan Ellison for this edition.
Introduction to "Come to Me Not in Winter's White" first appeared in *Partners in Wonder*, ed. Harlan Ellison®, Walker & Co., 1971; revised by Harlan Ellison for this edition.
"The Year of the Good Seed" first appeared in *Galaxy*, December 1969. Previously uncollected.
"The Man at the Corner of Now and Forever" first appeared in *Exile #7*, 1970. Previously uncollected.
"My Lady of the Diodes" first appeared in *Granfaloon #8*, January 1970.
"Alas! Alas! This Woeful Fate" first appeared in *Unofficial Organ of the Church of Starry Wisdom #1*, 1971. Previously uncollected.
"Sun's Trophy Stirring" first appeared in *The Dipple Chronicle #2*, April-June 1971. Previously uncollected.
"Add Infinite Item" first appeared in *The Dipple Chronicle #2*, April-June 1971. Previously uncollected.
"The Game of Blood and Dust" first appeared in *Galaxy*, April 1975.
"The Force That Though the Circuit Drives the Current" first appeared in *Science Fiction Discoveries*, eds. Frederik & Carol Pohl, Bantam 1976.
"No Award" first appeared in *The Saturday Evening Post*, Vol 249 No 1, Jan-Feb 1977.
"Is There a Demon Lover in the House?" first appeared in *Heavy Metal*, September 1977.
"The Engine at Heartspring's Center" first appeared in *Analog*, July 1974.
"Tomorrow Stuff" first appears in this volume (likely written in 1968).
"Science Fiction and How It Got That Way" first appeared in *The Writer*, May 1971. Previously uncollected.
"Self-Interview," in this form, first appears in this volume. A modified version appeared as "An Interview with Roger Zelazny" by Paul Walker in Luna Monthly #43, December 1972.
"The Genre: A Geological Survey" first appeared in *The (Baltimore) Sun*, June 24, 1973. Previously uncollected.
"A Burnt-Out Case?" first appeared in *SF Commentary #54*, November 1978. Previously uncollected.

"Ideas, Digressions and Daydreams: The Amazing Science Fiction Machine" first appeared in *Insight*, Summer 1976; the corrected edition first appears in this volume. Previously uncollected.

"Musings on *Lord of Light*" first appeared in *Niekas #21*, 1977. Previously uncollected.

" '…And Call Me Roger': The Literary Life of Roger Zelazny, Part 3" by Christopher S. Kovacs, MD first appears in this volume.

"Family Tree from *Creatures of Light and Darkness*" first appears in this volume.

"*The Guns of Avalon*: deleted sex scene" first appears in this volume (likely written in 1970).

"*Bridge of Ashes* Outline" first appears in this volume (written in 1974).

"*Doorways in the Sand* Summary" first appears in this volume (written January 1975).

Poems

"Lover's Valediction: Forbidding Day's Sacrament" first appeared in *When Pussywillows Last in the Catyard Bloomed*, Norstrilia Press 1980. Written 1955–60 for *Chisel in the Sky*.

"Song (The Leaves are Gone)", "Permanent Mood", "Night Thoughts", "Reflection from an Oriental Ashtray", "T. S. Eliot", "Museum Moods" (in its full form), and "Missolonghi Hillside" first appear in this volume. Written 1955–60 for *Chisel in the Sky*.

"Fire, Snakes & the Moon", "Avalanches", "Between You & I" (aka "Words"), and "reply" first appear in this volume. Written 1965–68.

"Lobachevsky's Eyes" first appeared in *Doorways in the Sand*, Harper & Row 1976. It appeared separately in: *To Spin Is Miracle Cat*, Underwood-Miller 1981.

"Beyond the River of the Blessed" first appeared in *The Guns of Avalon*, Doubleday, 1972.

"Chorus Mysticus", "Awakening", "Paintpot", "Sentiments with Numbers" (the second half of Museum Moods), and "Storm and Sunrise" first appeared in *To Spin Is Miracle Cat*, Underwood-Miller 1981. Written 1955–60 for *Chisel in the Sky*.

"Maitreya" and "We Are the Legions of Hellwell" first appeared in *Lord of Light*, Doubleday, 1967.

"Tryptych" first in *Skyline #32*, April 1959. Written 1955–59 for *Chisel in the Sky*.

"Somewhere a Piece of Colored Light" first appeared in *Double:Bill #10*, August 1964.

"Morning with Music" first appeared in *Trypod #2*, March 1968. Previously uncollected.

"I Walked Beyond the Mirror", "Wall", "Sonnet Anyone?", and "Philip K. Dick" first appeared in *To Spin Is Miracle Cat*, Underwood-Miller 1981.

"Oh, the Moon Comes on Like a Genie" appears as part of "The Steel General".

"Augury" first appeared in *Alternities #6*, Summer 1981.

"Pyramid" first appeared in *Infinite Fanac #9*, Aug 1967. Previously uncollected.

"Thundershoon" and "Dark Horse Shadow" first appeared in *Creatures of Light and Darkness*, Doubleday, 1969. Published separately in *Ariel: The Book of Fantasy, Volume 3*, ed. Thomas Durwood, Ballantine, 1978.

"What Is Left When the Soul Is Sold" first appeared in *Yandro #166*, 1967. Written 1955–60 for *Chisel in the Sky*.

"LP Me Thee" first appeared in *When Pussywillows Last in the Catyard Bloomed*, Norstrilia Press 1980.

"The Thing That Cries in the Night" first appeared in *Creatures of Light and Darkness*, Doubleday, 1969.

"Dim" first appeared in *Sirruish #7* July 1968. Previously uncollected.

"Ducks" first appeared in *The Anthology of Speculative Poetry #3*, 1978. Written 1955–60 for *Chisel in the Sky*.

"Lamentations of the Venusian Pensioner, Golden Apples of the Sun Retirement Home, Earthcolony VI, Pdeth, Venus" first appeared in *Double:Bill #15*, Sept 1966. Previously uncollected. Written 1955–60 for *Chisel in the Sky* (as "Basics").

"Testament" first appeared in *Kronos #2*, 1965. Written 1955–60 for *Chisel in the Sky*.

Acknowledgments

Thanks go in many directions: to Roger Zelazny for his life's work, a body of writing that made this project a joy to work on; to my wife, Leah Anderson, without whose support this project would never have started; to Chris Kovacs, whose research efforts not only produced a comprehensive collection of material, but whose analysis added depth to the whole project; to Ann Crimmins for her dedication to all things grammatical; to Kirby McCauley, who promoted the project and arranged for us the right to print Zelazny's writing; to Neil Gaiman and David G. Hartwell for their engaging introductions; to Michael Whelan for his spectacular dust jacket painting; and to Alice Lewis for her polished dust jacket design and her invaluable advice in design issues. Thanks to Harlan Ellison for his kind permission to use his collaboration with Roger Zelazny. A belated thanks to Jonathan Ostrowsky for helping track down a bit of publishing history. Thanks also go to: Mark Olson for his help in book production, Geri Sullivan for design advice and our stalwart band of proofreaders:

Jim Burton, Rick Katze, Tim Szczesuil, Ann Broomhead, Pam Fremon, Larry Pfeffer, Peter Olson, Sharon Sbarsky, Ann Crimmins, Chris Kovacs, and Mark Olson.

> David G. Grubbs
> May, 2009

There are many individuals who aided in the extensive search to locate original manuscripts, correspondence, rare fanzines, and obscure interviews. Colleagues, family, and friends of Roger Zelazny helped to clarify details and quash rumors about his life and work. My own colleagues helped with translations of Greek, German, Japanese and other foreign language phrases. Apologies to anyone who might have been overlooked in compiling the following list:

Charles Ardai, John Ayotte, George Beahm, Greg Bear, John Betancourt, Rick Bradford, Ned Brooks, Lois McMaster Bujold, John Callendar, George Carayanniotis, Ung-il Chung, Michael Citrak, Giovanna Clairval, Bob Collins, Lloyd Currey, Jack Dann, Jane Frank, c Shell Franklin, Paul Gilster, Simon Gosden, Ed Greenwood, Joe Haldeman, David Hartwell, Gerald Hausman, Graham Holroyd, Patrick Hulman, Beate Lanske, Elizabeth LaVelle, Jane Lindskold, George R. R. Martin, Bryan McKinney, Henry Morrison, Kari Mozena, Rias Nuninga, Richard Patt, Greg Pickersgill, Bob Pylant, Mike Resnick, Andy Richards, Fred Saberhagen, Roger Schlobin, Darrell Schweitzer, Robert Silverberg, Dan Simmons, Dean Wesley Smith, Ken St. Andre, Richard Stegall, Thomas T. Thomas, Norris Thomlinson, Erick Wujcik, Carl Yoke, Trent Zelazny, Cindy Ziesing, Scott Zrubek

Diane Cooter, Nicolette Schneider, Lara Chmela
> Roger Zelazny Papers, Special Collections Research Center, Syracuse University Library

Thomas Beck, Susan Graham, Marcia Peri, Shaun Lusby
> Azriel Rosenfeld Science Fiction Research Collection, University of Maryland, Baltimore County.

Sara Stille, Eric Milenkiewicz, Audrey Pearson
> Bruce Pelz and Terry Carr Fanzine Collections, Special Collections Library, University of California, Riverside

Greg Prickman, Jacque Roethler, Kathryn Hodson, Jeremy Brett
> M. Horvat Collection, Special Collections, University of Iowa Libraries

Jill Tatem
> University Archives, Case Western Reserve University

Thomas M. Whitehead
> Whitehead Collection, Special Collections Department, Temple University Libraries

Patti Thistle, Dion Fowlow, George Beckett
> Document Delivery Office, Health Sciences Library, Memorial University of Newfoundland.

And then there are the personal thanks that I need to make. Of course none of this would have been possible without Roger Zelazny creating the very stories and characters that I find myself returning to again and again. When I finally met him at Ad Astra in 1986, I interrupted his rapid departure from the convention and asked "Mr. Zelazny" to sign the books I'd carried with me. He kindly took care of that and the requests of my companions. "Everybody OK, then? Right, gotta get to the airport"—and then his parting comment to me was "…and call me Roger." From that memory came the fitting title for the monograph in these volumes.

Acknowledgments

My mother handed me that paperback *Nine Princes in Amber* one dull day so long ago when I complained that I had nothing to read, and my parents drove me to countless new and used bookstores on the very first Zelazny quest to find copies of all of his books. The Internet makes searches so much easier now, and I couldn't have gathered much of this material if I'd had to rely on physical searches and postal mail. My buddy Ed Hew and his cousins drove me to Ad Astra for that fateful meeting. Dave Grubbs believed in and fought to see this project succeed when my involvement made it expand well beyond what he'd anticipated, and Ann Crimmins pruned, weeded, and used a flamethrower where necessary to turn my sometimes passive prose into something more readable. And none of this would have been possible without the support of my wife, Susan, and our children Caileigh and Jamieson, who put up with my additional absences from home and the other blocks of time consumed in creating this project. If their eyes should roll at mention of the name Zelazny, you may now understand why. And the fact that Susan's birthday is also May 13, or that my last name also refers to what happens in a smithy, are just examples of those Strange and Odd Coincidences in Life realized while researching this project. That our Golden Retriever is named Amber is *not* one of those coincidences.

Christopher S. Kovacs, MD
May, 2009

I wish to thank my daughters Fiona and Deirdre, whom I dragged to cons as children and who have grown to love sf and fantasy as much as I do. Particular thanks to my husband Peter Havriluk for patience, encouragement, and easing the log jam at the p.c. by buying himself a laptop. Thanks to Elizabeth Zaborskis Fernandez, for help with the Spanish. Dave and Chris, I'm delighted to have worked with you. Thanks also to the various Crimmins/Havriluk cats who warmed my lap as I edited.

Ann Crimmins
May, 2009

Technical Notes

This book is set in Adobe Garamond Pro, except for the titles (which are set in Trajan Pro), using Adobe InDesign 2. The book was printed and bound by Sheridan Books of Ann Arbor, Michigan, on acid-free paper.

Select books from NESFA Press

Threshold – Volume 1: The Collected Stories of Roger Zelazny $29
Power & Light – Volume 2: The Collected Stories of Roger Zelazny $29
Call Me Joe: Volume 1 of the Short Fiction of **Poul Anderson** $29
Lifelode **by Jo Walton** $25
Brothers in Arms **by Lois McMaster Bujold** $25
Works of Art **by James Blish** $29
Years in the Making: The Time-Travel Stories of **L. Sprague de Camp** $25
The Mathematics of Magic: The Enchanter Stories of **de Camp** *and* **Pratt** $26
Silverlock **by John Myers Myers** $26
Once Upon a Time (She Said) **by Jane Yolen** $26
Expecting Beowulf **by Tom Holt (trade paper)** $16
From These Ashes **by Fredric Brown** $29
A New Dawn: The Don A. Stuart Stories of **John W. Campbell, Jr.** $29
Ingathering: The Complete People Stories of **Zenna Henderson** $25
The Rediscovery of Man: The Complete Short SF of **Cordwainer Smith** ... $25

Details on these and many more books are online at: www.nesfa.org/press/ Books may be ordered online or by writing to:

> NESFA Press; PO Box 809; Framingham, MA 01701

We accept checks (in US$), Visa, or MasterCard. Add $4 P&H for one book, $8 for an order of two to five books, $2 per book for orders of six or more. (For addresses outside the U.S., please add $12 each for one or two books, $36 for an order of three to five books, and $6 per book for six or more.) Please allow 3–4 weeks for delivery. (Overseas, allow 2 months or more.)

The New England Science Fiction Association

NESFA is an all-volunteer, non-profit organization of science fiction and fantasy fans. Besides publishing, our activities include running Boskone (New England's oldest SF convention) in February each year, producing a semi-monthly newsletter, holding discussion groups on topics related to the field, and hosting a variety of social events. If you are interested in learning more about us, we'd like to hear from you. Contact us at info@nesfa.org or at the address above. Visit our web site at www.nesfa.org.